D0455220

The
Love
OF
Elspeth
Baker

Also by
MYRON S. KAUFMANN

Remember Me To God
Thy Daughter's Nakedness

The Love OF Elspeth Baker

by

Myron S. Kaufmann

ARBOR HOUSE
New York

Library of Congress Catalogue Card Number: 81-71681

ISBN: 0-87795-390-2

Manufactured in the United States of America

10 9 8 7 6 5 4 3 2

This book is printed on acid free paper. The paper in this book
meets the guidelines for permanence and durability of the Committee
on Production Guidelines for Book Longevity of the Council on
Library Resources.

The letter on page 90 is condensed from a real one that appeared in a Boston newspaper, written by a person unknown. With that exception, this story is imaginary, fictitious, a pack of lies, and any resemblance to actual persons is accidental and unintended.

The author thanks the many friends, including Howard M. Shaw, who sustained him in the course of this work.

in memory
of JOHN KAUFMANN *and*
ZELDA GORDON KAUFMANN

1

SHE tried to nestle against him, to lean her head on his shoulder, but his hand moved just then to start the windshield wipers and blocked her. The wipers swung in the drizzle.

"This has got to be it," he said. "There's the red barn." He shut off the engine. The barn and an old house were up a slope in the grayness. The house looked uninhabited, with boarded windows, and broken balusters in the railing of the porch. A scraggly fruit tree had white blossoms. On the windshield a fine mist formed anew.

"There's nobody here." The shivering was in her voice. "Do you think he'll show?"

"He better."

"Does he do it in the barn?"

"He said he'll meet us with a van. Maybe he'll take us somewhere."

Again she leaned her cheek and her flowing brown-red hair on the unyielding sleeve of his jacket.

Then she straightened, and found the pack of cigarettes in her shoulder bag. "Never mind those—why don't you smoke a joint like he said? It'll help relax you."

She found the little plastic bag.

She put the lumpy thin cigarette between his lips. She lighted it and dropped the match to the floor. His arm responded at last and extended around her woolly sweater when she leaned. She transferred the joint from his lips to hers, and drew. She exhaled.

"If I die," she said, "tell my parents it was a car accident."

"Elspeth, for Christ sake. Pull yourself together."

"I mean it, Jared. Promise. It's better for my parents and it's better for you. Put me in the car and release the handbrake on that hill on Quarry Road. The car's insured. You can say I was driving."

9

"You're not gonna die."

Her body was shaking under his arm, so that she could scarcely put the cigarette to her lips. "I didn't like that guy's looks," she said.

"Why? Just because of the beard? And the motorbike? What did you expect? A white coat? And a stethoscope? He lives on a commune. He seemed pretty intelligent to me, the way he talked. Didn't he to you? And I know somebody he did a good job for—a perfect job. The girl walked away like nothing happened. The whole thing only took about ten minutes. He's even had a couple of years of medical school."

She took a slow puff. She looked up at Jared, but he was staring at the blurry windshield. He bit a hangnail from his thumb. Who's he thinking of, Elspeth wondered. Me? Or her?

His young face, with thick black locks cut just below his ears, was not exactly handsome, but the overhanging brow, short nose, and well-defined bones had an intensity that had intrigued her from the first. She loved to look at him. She loved the clarity of his voice even when she hated what he said.

Maybe it had been wrong to think she could hold the attention of anyone so high-strung and talented. Everybody at Amherst and at Mount Holyoke agreed he was destined to take Broadway by storm. Shakespeare himself could not have seen Falstaff more vividly. To hear Jared play a scene clarified more than a professor's whole lecture. By the subtlest inflection in his voice, or a pause, he conveyed insights you had never noticed on the printed page. Someone who ought to know had said that even in England it was not done better.

"I read about a girl that died," Elspeth said, "and her boy friend and the abortionist cut her body up in little pieces, because they were scared about having a corpse on their hands, and the boyfriend disposed of the parts of her body in garbage bags in different litter barrels around the streets. He'd come down from the apartment with her head in a bag, and put it in the barrel on the corner, and then come down again with her right hand or something in another bag, and put it in a barrel on another corner—"

"Jesus! Where do you read this crap?"

"It's true, Jared. It was in an article."

"Some crazy scandal sheet, probably."

"No. In a good magazine. In the library. And everything from all the barrels went to this city disposal plant where it was ground up and pulverized with all the garbage, and she disappeared without a trace. She was missing for two years. But her father kept bugging the police, so finally they questioned the boyfriend again, and this time he contradicted himself, and they kept at him until he told the whole story, or they'd never have found out."

"Where did this happen?"

"New York. New York City. Ten, fifteen years ago."

"Fifteen years ago is practically prehistoric. Things like that don't happen now. It's not even like taking an appendix out. Or a tooth out. It's not even part of you.

They do something and the body expels it. You walk away. Haven't you talked to your friends? Don't you know any girls that have been through it?"

"No."

"Then they're not leveling with you."

Her sweater could not keep out the chill. Even the cigarette in her fingers kept up a slight steady shiver. "Pot never does anything for me," she said.

"You don't let it. You fight it."

"I don't know if it was worse for her or for him," she said. "After he'd loved her, to take hunks of her—how can he ever forget a thing like that. As long as he lives."

"Are you gonna have that damn story on your mind? You're morbid."

"I'm not morbid. Things happen. I had two brothers, you know. And one day one was gone, and one day the other was gone. Just like that. Eric didn't even reach the age I am now. The doctor said he had a cold, and in the morning he was dead."

Jared's hand kept moving upon her arm, as if he wanted to calm the shivering of her sweater. She was grateful for the caress.

"What do they do with the baby?" she mused. "The fetus. Throw it in the garbage?"

"What do you do with a tooth that falls out?" Jared answered. Then his eyes fixed suddenly on the mirror. "Hey! The van!"

He opened the door, leaned out in the wet and looked back. Elspeth turned to the foggy rear window. She could make out the square greenish vehicle. It seemed parked a hundred feet behind.

"At least he didn't just skip with the money," Jared said, getting out.

"Did you think he did?" She slid under the steering wheel and followed him.

"No."

It was a light rain, a fine spray that settled in a cold film on her face and in tiny droplets on the hairs of her sweater. Jared ran toward the van and she followed, her sneakers splattering on the cracked tar. The wipers of the van still oscillated, and behind one of them she saw the blond, bearded, spectacled face of the man she knew only as David. There seemed to be two other persons with him, girls maybe.

"Jared." She caught his arm. "You have to stay with me," she said, panting. "Stay with me, the whole time. Just to be another pair of eyes. To call an ambulance in case I hemorrhage or something."

He looked away.

"Please, Jared. If it's all that simple like you say, then you shouldn't be chicken about watching."

They walked together toward the parked van more slowly. She saw the three people watching them through the windshield. Otherwise the narrow road was as deserted as David had said. She had seen no other vehicles since entering upon it. The wilderness of dripping trees and low shrubs had new leaves in a variety of tints, some pale and still undersized.

They stopped below the window. "Hi," said Jared. David gave a slow nod. His hair and beard were shaggy. One of the young women had long hair, like Elspeth's, but straighter and stringier, and huge pink eyeglasses. The other was more plump, with braids and a headband and loops of glassy beads. Both were looking at Elspeth, and David's eyes fixed on her too, the way guys' eyes always did.

"How old are you?" he said. "You look like a kid."

"Eighteen."

"Well, go round to the back. We'll let you in."

"Can Jared stay with me?" Elspeth asked.

David shrugged.

"Where do you do it?"

"Right here," he told her. "In the van. In the back."

Jared walked around toward the rear and she followed him.

The tail pipe was still chugging out to the side. The double rear doors swung open. David and the two women had come to the back and the confines of the van seemed narrow over them. There was also a massive dog with a ferocious gray and brown face. She saw a narrow mattress with a black rubber sheet and bags of woven straw. She could smell the dog. Jared clasped David's hand and climbed in. David's denim jacket was open, and the hairs around his navel were as blond as his beard. Jared offered a hand to Elspeth but she drew back.

"I just need some air for a minute," she said. "Turn off the engine, okay?"

David moved forward.

"Your first time, honey?" the plump young woman with braids asked. She had a pleasant face, but with no upper front teeth. Her tentlike skirt had swirls of color.

Elspeth nodded, still standing on the road.

"You're very beautiful," the woman with braids said.

"Thank you."

"Well, don't be afraid, honey. There's nothing to it. I checked your horoscope and it's a perfect day for you. Couldn't be better. That's why we picked the day. That's why we postponed from Tuesday. You won't know you've had it. If you get some cramps tomorrow take a couple of aspirin, that's all. And if you have some bleeding don't worry. It's normal. You might even have a little fever. Low fever. Don't even call a doctor unless it's more like a hundred and three, hundred and four. And if your breasts hurt put on a tight bra a couple of days." She put her hands on her breasts as she said it. "Some girls like to hold a Christopher medal. I always bring one. And a rabbit's foot, and a prayer wheel, and a mezuzah, whatever you want. What religion are you?"

"I'm a nonbeliever. What religion are you?"

"I take the best of everything."

"What's the dog for?"

"Protection," the woman told her.

David had come back. "Don't you know enough to come in out of the rain?" he asked Elspeth, crouching on the wood and metal strapping of the van floor. "Let's move it. Get in and shut the doors, and strip below the waist."

She didn't move. She could feel the wetness of the hair against her face and the damp of the jeans on her thighs. "How do you do it?" she asked. "What method?"

"Don't worry about it."

"You leave it to me, honey," the plump woman said. "You got no problem. You're two months, right?"

"Do you do it?"

"I do it," the woman said. "Are you afraid? I've had seven. I have about one a year. I do it for Mary, and Mary does it for me." She gestured gracefully at the long-haired woman. "And now we do it for others, out of the goodness of our hearts." She plastered her hands on her breasts again. "And I've got two kids, and Mary has a kid. See? You can still have a kid whenever you want. It don't hurt anything."

Elspeth looked at Jared. He was sitting inside, against a wall of the van, arms limp on his knees, and looking at her, but when she caught his eye he looked away. The dog snorted. "Jared, I want to talk to you a minute."

He got down slowly from the van.

"I can give you a needle if you're nervous," David offered. "Have you ever had anything?"

"I thought you were supposed to be a doctor," she said to David.

"I never said I was a doctor. Look, baby, make up your mind. We can't hold your hand all day. You want to go ahead, we'll take care of you and you won't know it happened. You want to chicken out, chicken out, and let's split."

"I want a hospital," said Elspeth. She felt herself quaking in the cold.

"Okay," said David. "Go down to New York then, and check into a hospital. You want to go for that bullshit? They'll hit you for anywhere up to a thousand bucks. Doctors make a big deal out of everything. It's a racket."

"If she chickens out do I get my three hundred back?"

"You silly, man? It ain't on me. I put it in the mail, for safekeeping."

"Well, part of it, then? Could you mail it to me?"

David extended his palms. "Son, I came here in good faith. You called me. I didn't call you. Your friend recommended me. Your good friend. What did he tell you? Was he satisfied? Was his girl satisfied? Did David take care of them?"

"Yes," said Jared.

Elspeth resented David's calling him son. He must have been scarcely ten years older than Jared.

David looked at her. "If you're a flighty chick that don't know what you want, then you get yourself a little old shrink, and get your head on straight. But you wasted three people's time. You owe other people a little courtesy and consideration, don't you think? I'm a master carpenter. I gave up an afternoon's work. And two mothers left their children to accommodate you. We took risks to help you out. It's still illegal in this state."

"The legislature's gonna legalize it," said Elspeth. "Maybe in the next session."

"Okay, baby. You just wait till they take care of that then. We haven't got time to come out on a wild-goose chase like this. And it's not fair of you to

13

play games if you're not serious."

"She's not chickening out," said Jared. "Are you, Elspeth? Come on, get it over with. You'll feel better." He took her arm but she pulled back. "Come on, will ya?" he said. "What did we come here for? Get it over with, and we'll go get a good dinner, and I'll give you a loving."

He pulled her two steps forward with both arms. Elspeth screamed. Jared tugged again but could not budge her. She screeched. David glanced at the thinner woman, who moved behind him toward the driver's seat. He pulled the double doors shut.

Smoke burst from the tailpipe and the tires squealed in the wet. Elspeth knew there were tears on her face. She saw Jared run a step or two after the van. Then he stood limply, and watched it swerve past the black fender of his own car.

2

"WELL, you really blew that," Jared said.

"I got their license number," Elspeth said tearfully. "Or most of it, I think."

"A lot of good that will do." He turned to her angrily. She saw the dark bangs plastered to his forehead and the rain sliding down his face. "I know your angle. It's getting pretty transparent. And it's not gonna work."

"What do you mean by that? You think I got pregnant on purpose?"

"I don't say it was conscious completely. But it's a known fact that a woman doesn't become pregnant without subconsciously wanting to."

"Bull! Where'd you read that? Was it my fault the diaphragm slipped?"

"Why weren't you on the pill?"

"I hate pills!"

"You and your diaphragm. I've only got your word that you even used it."

"Oh!" she gasped breathlessly, her hands below her throat. "You bastard!"
She turned from him and ran.

"Hey!" he shouted. "Where are you going?"

She didn't look around or answer. She slowed to a brisk walk but continued back up the road.

She heard the car start, but she still didn't look around.

In a moment the car was beside her but she neither looked at it nor slowed. She was breathing deeply through her mouth and squinting, fighting an urge to sob.

"Get in," he said from the open window.

She kept on, without answering, the sneakers slopping on the road.

The car crept, keeping pace beside her.

"What do you think you're gonna do? Walk all the way home? It's about thirty miles."

"Get away from me! Leave me alone!" She continued her steady march, not glancing at him. The rain was still fine but more than a drizzle now.

"I've got your stuff here. Your bag."

"Drop it at my dorm."

"What are you trying to do? You're soaked to the skin. You want to die of pneumonia or something? You had a brother die of pneumonia."

"That would solve your problem very nicely, wouldn't it."

"It would solve *your* problem. I haven't got a problem. Come on. Get in, stupid."
The car stopped and he got out.

She quickened her pace. She wept and struggled when he caught her. She succeeded in whacking his face with her forearm, but he had her by the seat of her jeans and an arm and forced her toward the car. The engine was running and the wipers thumping and both doors hung open.

She was shoved in sobbing, upon her shoulder bag, banging her ankle. When her foot was out of the way he slammed the door, and entered at the other side. They sped off. She searched in the shoulder bag for tissues.

The car rattled underneath on every bump.

"I did not get pregnant on purpose. I didn't. And you could be decent enough to believe it."

"I said I didn't mean consciously. Okay?"

"But I didn't! Consciously or unconsciously."

"All right! All right! All right!"

"It just happened," she insisted. "I don't know how it happened. So don't get so high and mighty, and don't psychoanalyze me."

"Okay, okay."

"Big deal. You wouldn't let me drown out there in the rain. I'd rather walk, honest."

She found a mirror in the bag, and a small baby-blue comb. She began to straighten her long reddish hair, which hung nearly to the top of her bosom, gleaming wetly and clinging. There were some tangles. She combed a white petal or two from it, that must have loosened from a tree in the rain, and some seedlings.

She could smell her rain-soaked sweater.

"I can't afford to be pregnant. I don't have the kind of parents that would understand. My father's got ulcers as it is."

"Well, I did what I could. I sold my share in the car. I fixed you up with somebody."

15

"You sold your share in the car? This car?"

"Yeah. What other car? I've just got it on loan for today."

It surprised her that he would do that for her.

"How much did you get?"

"Three hundred dollars. The same three hundred you just blew. And that cleans me out. I haven't got any more. Even if I borrowed it from my father, and he hasn't got it, and took you to some doctor—how do I know you wouldn't chicken out again?"

"Maybe they'll send you back part of it. Call them up tomorrow."

"They will not."

"You can try."

"Why didn't you chicken out before the money was handed over?"

The car plunged through a deep puddle that showered on the windows and slowed it momentarily. If the exhaust system held through that, she thought, it'll hold till we get home.

"I'm sorry, Jared. Maybe I should've gone through with it."

"Damn right you should've."

"But those people seemed so crummy."

"What's that got to do with it? If she's done it to herself seven times she knows her stuff. They were well recommended. I even know somebody they took care of."

"But in a truck. On a country road, in the middle of nowhere. So—yuck. And that big dog standing over me."

"They'd have walked the dog, if the dog bothered you. I suggested a doctor, remember? But you were scared he might notify your parents. That was your main requirement. Someone you could count on not to notify anybody."

"Okay. I guess I panicked. But I couldn't take a chance on dying. My parents have buried two kids. I'm all they've got."

"Why would you die? If you're always scared of dying how can you live? You'd never get in a car. Or a boat, or anything. You'd never go to bed with anybody."

"You're right," she admitted.

They passed through the town where they had first made rendezvous with David on his motorcycle and given him the money. The rain came harder, battering on the windshield and turning the day to darkness. He had to slow. He switched on the headlights.

Soon the rain diminished. The sky brightened. They entered upon a broader road and the wet hum of the tires became steady. They passed from Connecticut back into Massachusetts.

There was a sudden clatter, followed by a harsh metallic dragging and scraping. He slowed. "What the hell is that?" he said.

"Sounds like your exhaust system," said Elspeth.

He steered onto the parking apron of a string of shops and halted. She got out even before he did.

The tip of the tail pipe was in the gravel. She knelt on the wet asphalt and peered

16

under the rear bumper, her hair hanging. She knew from its angle that the tail pipe was still firmly joined to the muffler and exhaust pipe.

"Can I get back with it?" Jared asked. He reached down to the rusted metal.

"Don't touch it yet, dummy!" she said. "You'll burn yourself."

She poked a stick into it and lifted it gently. She saw the muffler and the pipe beyond rise with it stiffly.

"How big a job is it?" said Jared.

She let the pipe return to the ground. She rose, wiping bits of gravel and sand from her jeans.

"Can I drive it?" he asked. "Slow?"

"Like that? The whole thing would come off. I'll pin it up or something. Don't worry."

She raised the lid of the trunk. There was nothing there but a worn spare tire, the jack frozen into its corroded clamps, bits of old newspaper, and a layer of fine dust. She closed it. She went around and leaned in toward the rear seat, and lifted its cushion.

"What are you looking for?" Jared asked her.

"Just to see what's around." She looked at the row of shops that lined the broad road ahead of them, ending at a Howard Johnson's at the traffic signal, and then at the row across the road.

"How big a job is involved?" he said.

"Not much. Just a couple of brackets. But you sold your share at the right time though. I have a feeling the whole exhaust system isn't long for this world. You see that dry cleaner's over there? Go over and ask them for a coat hanger. A wire coat hanger."

"A coat hanger?"

"Just a plain coat hanger, like they give out with stuff. A wire one."

He looked up and down the roadway and waited for cars to pass. She saw him start across.

She entered the car again and sat to wait. Maybe she should have told him the car was absolutely undrivable. He wouldn't know the difference. Or she could raise the hood while he's over there at the cleaner's, open the distributor and just spit into it. The moisture would short it, and Jared would have no idea why the car wouldn't start. He would flood the carburetor and wear the battery. And the jerks at the gas stations would probably never think of wiping the distributor cap. She and Jared would be stuck for hours, waiting for the nearest mechanic to have time to putter with the engine.

They could wander hand in hand through a shopping center meanwhile. Or find a movie. Or even a motel.

No, it wouldn't work. If he were told to leave the car he would suggest they hitchhike back. It wasn't that far.

Anyway, he was coming back across the street with the coat hanger.

He held it at her window. "Is this what you want?" He still looked puzzled.

"That's it." She got out, and took it. While he watched her hands untwisted the

17

neck of the hook, until the whole hanger became an open curlicue of wire, and finally a long crooked rod.

She lay down with it under a corner of the car. Jared squatted to watch. She bent a loop of wire around the tail pipe, and up through an opening in the frame and around any protrusion she could find. Orange rust sifted upon her face and she squinted.

"Will that hold?" Jared asked.

"It'll get you home without the exhaust system falling on the road. But tell him to get his brackets fixed."

There was some wire left, so she looped it under the tail pipe again.

She got to her feet, and shook the dirt from her hair and beat it from her jeans. Her shoulder was muddy when she twisted. "Wipe the grit off the back of my sweater, okay?"

He obliged with some strokes.

"It's good to keep a hanger in a car in case that happens," she said while his hand beat on her shoulder blades.

When he started the engine the exhaust system gave a tinny shudder.

"It'll be okay," she said.

It purred more smoothly.

"How about some coffee?" she suggested, hugging her arms in the soiled sweater. "Okay."

He drove slowly up the line to the Howard Johnson's. It was drizzling again.

"I could teach you a lot about cars," she said as they walked from the parking lot. "It's good for even an artist like you to know a few practical things."

He pulled the glass door and she walked in to the warmth. The wall behind the soda fountain was a mirror. Even wet and dirty she looked great. She wished Jared would notice the stare of the soda-fountain boy and even of the old guy seated around the bend of the counter. How could he forget that she had picked him when a couple of hundred guys had milled around her? He was climbing a stool at the counter, staring up at the list of flavors.

"Let's take a booth," said Elspeth.

He sat with her in a booth.

He drummed his fingers. He did not meet her eyes. It was as though neither of them could think of anything further to say. His hair barely covered his ears, with an exquisitely composed casualness. On his soft suede jacket there were tiny rain spots. His shirt was open at the neck, and black hairs curled above it.

The waitress came, her light hair in braids. Jared ordered two black coffees.

While they waited he occupied himself bricklaying a little wall of sugar lumps.

"How are you doing with Richard the Second?" Elspeth asked.

"Okay."

"Have you learned the lines yet? Or are you still studying the character mostly?"

"The latter." He didn't look at her. He was busy with his construction of sugar lumps. Outside the sky turned dark again. From the wall of glass beside them she felt the chill.

18

To fill the emptiness she fumbled in the shoulder bag for her pack of menthol cigarettes. She lighted one.

"They ought to make a law," she said, "that if a girl dies in an abortion, the guy gets his cock chopped off."

"Why? What for? That's stupid. What good would that do?"

"So they'd feel involved. If it's really as simple as you say, you'd have nothing to worry about."

"Elspeth, I tried to get you out of it. Now I'm broke. Don't bother me anymore. Please. Most girls wouldn't even bother a guy. They'd take care of it themselves. The guy wouldn't even know."

The girl brought the coffees. Elspeth warmed her hands on the mug. The rain intensified. Nearby, beyond the glass, a few people huddled under the canopy.

Elspeth sipped her coffee slowly. She watched his fingers repair the bricks of sugar, which had tumbled. He finished his coffee first.

"Do I look like I've been lying in the muck?" she said. "Under a car?"

"You look all right."

"Jared, what's she like?" Even as she said the words she regretted them.

"How do you mean?"

"I'm just curious. I mean, you said she isn't even good-looking. Can't I be curious?"

His annoyance made her redden.

"Elspeth, grow up. Let it go. Look, it's nothing against you. I doubt if she's the one I'm gonna spend my life with either. I'm young. And so are you. Don't eat your heart out."

Jared's fingers drummed on the formica impatiently. Her whole stomach tingled with anguish.

3

CLIMBING the dormitory stairs Elspeth tried to catch no one's eye.

But when she passed the showers Betty Anne Prescott came out, big and chubby-faced, wrapped in a towel, her hair flying. "Ellie!" Betty Anne cried out, her blue eyes widening. "Did you get rid of it?"

Elspeth shook her head, biting her lip.

"No? Are you okay? Hey, Ellie's back!"

Girls seemed to gather about her from every door as she made her way to her room. They were chattering. "She didn't go through with it," she heard Fletch say. "Why?" said Sally Bell. "Let her through," said Roxie. "Please. Let her get by."

Elspeth sat on her bed, dropping her shoulder bag to the floor. The sheltering arm of her roommate Roxie came around the bedraggled sweater. Elspeth buried her face in her hands and sobbed.

"Does everybody have to crowd in?" said Roxie. "Can't you leave her alone?" No one moved. Roxie patted her. She was a wisp of a girl with a short haircut, wearing shorts and a striped shirt.

Elspeth tried to stop crying. She looked up blurry-eyed. Whitey Hathaway was sitting on the opposite bed next to Fletch and Betty Anne, who still had nothing on but the towel about her hips, her large breasts glistening from the shower. Belinda von Schmertzing sat on Roxie's desk in riding breeches, sad-eyed and startlingly beautiful, her one massive braid slung around to the front. Claire Hu, with oriental eyes behind black-rimmed glasses, was in Elspeth's chair and Sally Bell was in Roxie's. There were others at the door and in the room too, including some like Robin Shapiro and Hester Holbrook who didn't even belong to this floor.

"I don't know what to do," Elspeth appealed, her eyes swimming. "My parents will go crazy. I just couldn't do it. They were these awful creeps, and they were gonna do it in a truck, and I got scared. And they took the money anyway and Jared's just wild."

They all murmured. "In a truck," said Fletch. "God."

"We'll take up a collection," said Whitey Hathaway, a frail bony towhead with a hoarse faint voice, "and you'll go down to New York and do it right."

"That costs a thousand dollars," said Elspeth, sobbing again.

"It does not," said Whitey in the faint raspy voice. "My cousin had it, in a clinic. It only cost a hundred and fifty."

Roxie gave Elspeth a handkerchief. Elspeth blew her nose. "How'm I gonna go to New York? In exam week? And I've got a term paper I haven't even started."

"Go after," said Fletch. "You've got time. You have up to twenty weeks I think."

"Twenty-four," said Claire Hu. "You've got ages. What are you, about eight weeks or something?"

"How about everybody clearing out and let her get some rest," said Roxie. She's had an upsetting day." No one stirred. "How about it," said Roxie. "Come on, split. Show some consideration."

Some got up to go, and Robin moved aside from the door. Betty Anne rose with her towel. "There's a man on the floor," Belinda told her.

"Arlene has her guy with her," Claire added. "He's supposed to be helping her with math."

Betty Anne fixed the towel about her more fully.

Elspeth lay down, clutching the handkerchief. "Take off my shoes, like a good kid," she asked. Roxie untied the wet sneakers. "My hair's a mess," said Elspeth. "So's my clothes."

Belinda had risen, statuesque in her riding pants and flannel shirt. "Maybe you'll get lucky and have a mis," she said.

"Ya," said Whitey Hathaway. "It's supposed to be awful easy to have a mis in the first three months. Just do all the things they tell expectant mothers not to do."

"Right, like strenuous exercise, and get sloshed, and stay up all night," said Fletch. "And Belinda and I'll take you horseback riding."

Most of the girls had paused on their way out. Some were drifting back. "I don't know anything about horseback riding," said Elspeth.

"So much the better."

"And there's things you can take to encourage it," said Roxie.

"Like sulphur and molasses," said Belinda.

"It's castor oil and baking soda, dopey," Fletch told her. "Not sulphur and molasses."

"Quinine's the one I heard of," said Roxie. "Quinine sulfate or something. It's the same thing they used to give soldiers for malaria."

"Or a mustard douche," said Claire.

"I've heard of a cola douche," said Robin. "I never heard of a mustard douche."

"I've heard of cola," said Hester.

"I think I'm about eleven weeks," said Elspeth gloomily. "The way I figure it."

"Oh, you'll have a snap," said Fletch.

"You want to try it, Ellie?" said Roxie.

"Which one?"

"Any one," said Fletch. "If one doesn't shake it loose another will. Try something every day."

"It can't hurt," said Claire.

"And if nothing works," said Whitey, "we'll take a collection and send you to New York like I said. We're your friends. We won't let you down."

"Somebody should go to Cannon's and get some quinine sulfate," said Roxie.

"You mean like now?" said Whitey. "I'll go."

"Good," said Roxie. "Go ahead, Whitey. We'll pay you back. Tell him somebody's got chronic malaria."

"Do you need a prescription?" Whitey rasped.

"I don't know. Try it though."

"And get some castor oil while you're at it," said Fletch. "And baking soda."

"And mustard," Claire called after Whitey.

"I've got some mustard downstairs," said Robin. "Want me to get it?"

"Get it," said Claire.

"Now how about letting her have some quiet," said Roxie.

"That's okay," Elspeth said weakly. "I'd just as soon have company. Or moral support."

"Quiet is the opposite of what she needs," said Fletch.

"Did you have any supper, Ellie?" asked Belinda.

"No."

"Yell down to Whitey," Roxie told somebody. "Quick, catch her. You want a hamburger, Ellie? Or a sub?"

"No. Don't call her. I don't want anything."

"I could use a hamburger," said Fletch.

"Me too," said Belinda. She had sat on the desk again, next to Sally Bell.

"It's not a party, you kids," Roxie told them.

"Want to try some exercises?" said Fletch. "Sit-ups ought to be good."

"In a while," said Elspeth. "Not yet."

Roxie massaged Elspeth's feet.

"That feels good," said Elspeth. "Sorry they're so dirty."

Robin Shapiro appeared at the door, slightly potbellied in her blue T-shirt, and held up a little half-full jar of mustard.

"Good!" said Claire. "Let's adjourn to the john. Bring a douche bag."

Elspeth began to raise herself, and Roxie and Fletch helped her to her feet. Fletch was tall and plain, with tight curls, and long thin legs. Betty Anne Prescott, in sweatshirt and shorts now, arrived at the door as they came out. Everyone trooped together down the hall to the toilets.

"How much do you put in?" Fletch asked at the sinks. Claire was pouring the mustard.

"Might as well use it all," said Claire. "There isn't that much." She turned the water tap on to a trickle.

"Do you know the proportions?" said Fletch. "Or are you just guessing?"

"I don't know," said Claire. "I'd think as strong as possible. That's logical, isn't it? And just enough water so it'll flow through. The idea is just to have an irritant." She shook the bag and looked into it. Then she screwed the cap on and handed it to Elspeth, tube and all. "Here. Let's see if that does anything."

Elspeth looked at it unhappily. She opened a stall and hung the bag on the hook, the tube draped over it.

"I don't think it'll work if you sit on the toilet, Ellie," Claire said. "It'll run out as fast as it goes in. You better lie down or something."

"Where can I lie down? On the floor?"

"Well, I'd think you'd have to give it a chance to soak in, Ellie. The mustard has to penetrate high. Up into the uterus. That's the whole idea."

"We can spread towels," Fletch said. "Roxie, get her towels."

"And spread toilet paper around," said Belinda. "It's gonna wreck the towels."

Fletch and Belinda began pulling toilet paper. Claire and Betty Anne and Sally Bell and Robin squatted and spread streamers of tissue on the tiles near the back wall, toward the corner by the sinks, getting in one another's way. Elspeth unfastened her jeans. "If there's really a guy in Arlene's room" she said, "don't let him in here."

Elspeth stepped out of the jeans and underpants. Fletch held the bag high and handed her the nozzle. The tiles felt hard through the toweling and the toilet paper. "Don't look," said Elspeth. "Somebody stand guard at the door, okay?"

"If it's this easy why do people spend hundreds of dollars for abortions?" said Betty Anne.

"Why do people go to beauty parlors when you can give yourself a home permanent?" Claire answered.

"It's running out all over the place," said Roxie.

"Slow down the flow," said Claire.

Elspeth grimaced, moving her heels and knees. One arm was under her head. The towels beneath her were wet. Robin's feet hung over her, dangling from a sink.

"You okay, Ellie?" Roxie asked.

"I guess."

"Her hair is such a magnificent color," said Sally Bell.

"Her hair where?" said Robin.

"It's the same," said Fletch.

Elspeth heard the door squeak open and shut again. "What the hell is going on?" said a new voice.

"A mustard douche," said Fletch.

"A mustard douche? What the hell is a mustard douche? On the floor?"

"Who's that?" Elspeth asked.

"Sis Fiske," a couple of the girls told her.

She saw Sis peer over shoulders and look down.

"Looks like an enema," said Sis.

"No, that's mustard, really," said Roxie. "It sort of spilled at the beginning."

"Sis, will you go about your business, please?" said Fletch. "There's enough people here."

"What's it for?" said Sis. "An abortion?"

"A mis," Claire corrected.

Elspeth heard Sis go to a booth and latch herself in.

"Can't you keep people out?" Elspeth asked.

"We're doing the best we can," said Betty Anne. "What do you think we're all around you for?"

23

"We can't keep people from using the hoppers," Fletch said.

"You New Englanders," said Belinda. "I hate that word hopper. It's a john."

"You feel anything yet, Ellie?" said Roxie.

"What's the difference between a mis and an abortion?" Sis Fiske's voice said from the booth.

"A mis is more like organic gardening, or like natural childbirth," Claire told her.

"Oh, come off it." There was a sound of flushing.

Elspeth fidgeted her knees and feet, and even shifted her behind an inch. "It stings," she said. "It stings like crazy."

"That's what you want, Ellie," said Claire. "You don't want it weak. The irritation is what's gonna start things happening. The mis is like a response to it."

"Why don't you idiots wipe up around her at least," Sis Fiske said.

"Good idea," said Roxie. She and Sally Bell pulled more streamers of toilet paper.

Sis edged Belinda aside and washed at the sink next to Robin. "Don't sit on the sink," she said to Robin, wiping her hands. "You'll break it."

Elspeth withdrew the nozzle while Sally Bell and Roxie dried the floor around her. It dribbled. She pinched the tube.

"What are you doing, Ellie?" said Claire.

"How much can I hold?" Her face was flushed. "It's only going on the floor. If it's supposed to irritate it's irritating. It's like burning."

"Maybe it's not getting to the right place though," said Claire. "If we could sort of prop your behind up or something. So it can seep back."

"We could sort of pick her up and tilt her back," Fletch suggested. Fletch's straight legs bent and she grasped Elspeth by a thigh. Belinda took the other thigh, jostling Robin's dangling feet at the sink. Elspeth cooperated as they lifted her, spreading her arms as a brace against the floor, and breathing hard.

"That's stupid," said Sis Fiske. "If you really want to get rid of it you poke something up there."

"And blood all over the place?" Elspeth gasped weakly. "No thank you."

"You either abort or you don't abort," said Sis. "There's no such thing as inducing a mis."

"Poor kid," said Roxie.

Sis left.

The hard floor pressed the bones of Elspeth's upper spine. Her head pressed the wall.

She heard the door squeak open again. "How's it going?" she heard Hester Holbrook's voice. "I've got every kind of cola if you want the cola douche."

"Put me down," Elspeth gasped. "It's killing my back."

They lowered her. "Valerie wants to know if she can have the fetus," Hester said. "Ouch!" Robin cried out sliding into the sink bowl, her feet flying up. A drinking glass struck the floor and smashed. "Jesus! Will you watch it!" she told Belinda angrily.

"It wasn't my fault. You shouldn't have been on there."

24

Sally Bell and Roxie and Betty Anne were scrambling about collecting broken glass. Robin lowered her feet to the floor, careful not to step on them or on Elspeth or on glass. "What happened?" said Hester.

"I just wrecked the base of my spine on the faucet is all," Robin said.

"Could somebody stand guard," Elspeth asked from the floor, "and not let anybody else in unless they really have to go to the john or something?" Hester had brought her roommate Valerie.

"Do you want to try the cola?" Hester asked. She was taking six-packs from a paper sack.

"We're trying the mustard," said Claire.

"And it hurts," Elspeth said, looking up at them tearfully. "I don't want to be a sissy but it hurts."

"But it's better than a knife, isn't it?" said Claire. "It's a much more natural way." Roxie and Sally Bell were still finding bits of glass and putting them with toilet paper into the barrel.

"Here, take a joint," said Hester. She took it from her lips and bent to place it in Elspeth's lips, but Fletch snatched it and threw it out the narrow window. "What'd you do that for?" said Hester.

"A joint would relax her," said Fletch. "I want her unrelaxed. You don't have a mis when you're relaxed."

"You didn't have to throw it out," said Hester. "I'd have smoked it."

"Go down and get it then," said Fletch.

"Can I have the fetus, Ellie?" said Valerie. She was long-necked, with big tinted eyeglasses and her hair in a bun. "You wouldn't do anything with it. Except chuck it in the crapper."

"Leave her alone," said Roxie.

"What would you do with it?" Fletch asked Valerie.

"Take it to the lab."

"And cut it up?" said Betty Anne. "Like a frog? Yuck!"

"It's just like anything else," Valerie said, coloring. "It's hard to get anything like that."

"It's not coming out anyway," Elspeth said miserably. She had propped herself and sat leaning against the wall in the soiled sweater, her hands on her crotch.

"Don't give up, Ellie," said Claire. "You only just started."

"What does it look like at this stage?" Belinda asked. "Does it still have a tail and everything?"

"Yes," said Fletch.

"I think so," Valerie said.

"Would we we able to see if it's a boy or a girl yet?" said Betty Anne.

"I'm gonna wash that mustard out, I don't care," Elspeth said. "If it were where it should be I wouldn't feel it where I feel it."

"It could be there too, Ellie," said Claire. "It could be getting where you can't feel it."

"Nothing's happening," said Elspeth. She didn't move, but remained on the

25

floor, slumped against the wall, her face depressed, her knees apart, and covering herself with her hands. Roxie sat down beside her.

"Here, try the cola," Hester suggested. "It's thinner. It might seep up there better."

"Okay," Elspeth said gloomily.

Hester uncapped a bottle in a slot of a metal soap dish affixed to the wall. The cap fell into the sink. She handed down the bottle. Whitey Hathaway pushed in, somewhat breathless, and lifted a paper sack. "I couldn't get quinine," the weak raspy voice said, "but I've got castor oil and baking soda."

"Is that another douche?" Elspeth asked.

"I don't know—I thought you were supposed to drink it."

"We're trying the cola," said Hester.

"Rinse the douche bag and put the cola in it," said Fletch.

"No, get another douche bag," said Claire. "Save the mustard, in case she wants to try it again."

"You could put the cola in straight from the bottle," Belinda said.

"You want to rest your head on my lap?" Roxie offered.

Valerie uncapped a bottle and drank from it. Elspeth lay with her head against Roxie's shorts, her reddish hair flowing in every direction. She tried to apply the bottle, her hands cupped to hide the point of contact. "I'm embarrassed," she said.

"Don't watch, everybody," said Fletch. "How would you like everybody staring at you?"

"Somebody get a sheet or something to cover her," said Belinda. She was sitting on a sink now, beside Robin's, and both of them were drinking from bottles.

"Here," said Roxie, and unbuttoned her shirt. Her bra was speckled with a pattern of forget-me-nots. She slipped out of the shirt and spread it over Elspeth's belly and thighs without taking Elspeth's head from her lap.

"You're a good kid, Roxie," Elspeth murmured.

"Quinine's just not to be had," said Whitey. "I even drove into town. Just impossible. Except the kind you drink, like a gin and tonic."

"Why didn't you get it?" asked Belinda.

"Why? Would that work?"

"Who knows?"

"Careful about putting the bottle in," Fletch said. "It can make a suction. It's dangerous."

"I know it," said Elspeth.

"Just try to spill it at the edge."

"I am. Most of it's just going under me."

"Stick a couple of fingers in."

From under the shirt Elspeth's legs were spread wide.

Betty Anne uncapped a bottle on a soap dish and Sally Bell uncapped another. "Don't drink them all," Fletch said. "She might need more than one."

"Yeah," said Roxie. "It's not a party."

"Is any going in?" Fletch asked Elspeth.

26

"Some."

"If I were a fetus," said Whitey, "and somebody stuck a bottle in at me, I'd piss in it."

A couple of the girls snickered.

"I would too," said Betty Anne.

"Cut it out, you kids," Fletch told them. "It's not a laughing matter."

"It's not even a fetus yet," said Claire. "It's only an embryo."

Elspeth flung the bottle out from under the shirt. It slid against Fletch's foot and rolled in another direction. Elspeth turned her head sideways on Roxie's lap and her eyes filled. "It just doesn't want to come out," she said. "I'm doing everything to get her out, and she's fighting." She climbed to her feet, tears on her face, looking at no one. Everyone's eyes were on her.

"How do you know it's a she?" Claire asked quietly.

"I just think of it as a she. I dreamed about her. Where's my pants?"

Someone handed her her underpants.

"Don't feel bad about it," Robin said on the sink, holding a half-emptied bottle. "There are too many people in the world anyway."

"Nothing's gonna work," Elspeth wept, putting on the pants. She was still wet where she had lain against the floor. "I know nothing's gonna work." Roxie embraced her, patting her back. Elspeth was smallish, but taller than Roxie, and she buried her face in Roxie's hair.

"Ellie, don't get discouraged," Claire said behind her. "If nothing works you can go to a clinic as a last resort."

"In a clinic they don't fool around," said Valerie. "A d. and c. They cut it right out. Or a saline."

"I just hate the thought of it."

"There's still lots of things you can try first, Ellie," said Claire. "Like exercise, and getting sloshed, and horseback riding. Not everything works for everybody."

"Mix up the castor oil and stuff," said Fletch. "Maybe she'll try that."

"Sex sometimes works," said Valerie. "A lot of sex in the first few months."

"Oh sure," Elspeth said into Roxie's hair, her voice breaking. "Just what I'm in the mood for. Send out the call for a gang bang."

"I meant, like if you were going with somebody," Valerie said lamely.

"Why don't you open your mouth a little wider, Valerie?" Belinda said. "Maybe you can get your foot in it."

Elspeth held onto Roxie, her eyes shut, trying to calm herself. "Whitey!" she heard Betty Anne say. "That's the bottle Ellie had inside her!"

"It is not," said the raspy voice. "Is it? I wiped it, anyway. It's the one Valerie had."

"No, it's Ellie's," said Betty Anne. "I saw it."

"How'd it taste, Whitey?" said Robin. "Sweet?"

"Could you taste the mustard?" said Betty Anne. There was some giggling.

"Maybe the mustard makes it sterile," said Robin.

"They're teasing," said Sally Bell. "Ellie's is over there."

"I know it," said Whitey.

"Ellie," said Claire, "you want to talk to a counselor in the health department?"

"A psych counselor won't make her unpregnant," said Fletch.

"I want to go lie down," Elspeth said, turning her stained face.

"Yes," said Belinda, slipping off the sink. "You've had a rotten day. Things'll look better tomorrow. You can't think it through when you're all upset."

Elspeth walked slowly toward the door, Roxie's arm around her. They all followed.

"What if you decided to just have the baby, Ellie?" Sally Bell asked. "Are your parents the kind that would understand?"

"Are you kidding?" Elspeth said. "I want to get rid of it before they even know."

IN her room Elspeth apologized for being such a crybaby, and said she had always cried easily. The crowd thinned, but some stayed with her. She said the kids could not really raise enough money to send her to a clinic, even though they meant well. She ought to have gotten Jared to take her to New York when he still had the three hundred dollars, instead of to those underground freaks. It had been a terrible misunderstanding.

Some of the girls were going to a movie and insisted she come along. "I have to study," she said.

"So do we all," said Fletch. "We've all got exams. But nobody can cram cram cram without a break, or you start forgetting. You couldn't study in the mood you're in anyhow."

She changed her clothes and combed her hair quickly and piled into Whitey's convertible with Fletch and Roxie and Betty Anne and Claire. The movie was a comedy, and while it did not push her problems from her mind entirely her mood improved. They rested their feet on the backs of the seats in front, and shared popcorn and wisecracked. The place was a Cinema I and II, and when the crowds poured out into the lobby at the film's end they managed to sneak without paying into the other side and saw the other film.

Afterward in the pizza joint Roxie said Elspeth should talk with girls who had had abortions, and lick her fear of it. But they didn't know anyone. Claire had heard about a friend's sister in Albany, and Whitey had a cousin, and Roxie had a friend in Harrisburg whose mother had had one, but there was no one in their own circle on campus.

"Keep trying for a mis for a few days," said Roxie. "And if nothing happens we'll start working on something. We'll ask around in the other dorms, and the older kids. Maybe somebody's related to a doctor who'll give you a break, and you can pay in installments. You never know till you try. My father always says to only worry about one day at a time."

"Good advice," said Fletch.

"And if it ends that you have to go down to New York or someplace," said Roxie, "I'll go with you. And hold your hand. That's a promise."

"When could I go? After exams my folks expect me home."

"We'll say we went to New York for a day or two to celebrate the end of exams. Why worry about that now? You might not even go. You want to try staying up all night tonight, Ellie? I'll stay up with you. And keep you awake with coffee and speed. And again tomorrow night. Keep awake for forty-eight hours. Or seventy-two hours. That ought to do something."

"And you can come riding with me tomorrow," Fletch offered. "Belinda and I go every Saturday. So why don't you come with us. Give it a chance."

"I don't know a thing about horses," said Elspeth.

"Haven't you ever had riding lessons?"

"No."

"Perfect," said Fletch. "If you don't know how to ride it'll really shake everything up in there."

"My father almost bought me a horse when I was nine," Elspeth said. "Maybe I should have let him."

"Will she have to wear a wide skirt or something and ride sidesaddle?" Betty Anne asked. "In case it starts coming out?"

"No, it can't be sidesaddle," said Fletch. "You want the saddle to keep bouncing you in the crotch. That's the whole idea."

"There'd be a warning anyway," Elspeth said. "I think when you have a mis you bleed first. So if I had jeans on I'd have time to get them off."

"I think so," said Fletch.

They climbed the dormitory stairs after midnight. Roxie borrowed Betty Anne's hot plate to boil water for coffee, and Whitey Hathaway's little bottle of speed. Whitey said she knew where she could borrow half a bottle of vodka.

Elspeth sat on the floor in her underwear and touched her toes twenty times. She did knee bends, until her thighs became numb and wobbly. She did sit-ups, with Sally Bell holding her feet. "Hey, there's no sense getting charley horses," Roxie told her. "Lay off, so you can do more tomorrow."

Elspeth sat resting on the floor, her arms on her knees.

"I don't think exercises are gonna do it for her anyway," Roxie said. "She's too limbered up to it. She does calisthenics bare-ass every day practically."

Claire Hu mixed the castor oil and baking soda meanwhile. Elspeth took it slowly, grimacing, and forcing herself to swallow. "Worst stuff I ever tasted," she said.

They sang, saying it was to keep up Elspeth's morale, and she joined them on a phrase occasionally between swallows. They chorused a ballad. Someone in the room above pounded for quiet, and girls in another dorm yelled across the spring night to keep it down. The castor oil and baking soda gave Elspeth a bellyache and sent her to the john. Even on the john she heard them still singing back in her room.

When she returned Whitey was there with a vodka bottle about a quarter full and a big can of grapefruit juice.

"I can't take much alcohol," said Elspeth.

"With the grapefruit juice you won't even taste it," Whitey said. "Take all you can. Don't be afraid to get good and sloshed."

Whitey was right. Elspeth could taste nothing but the grapefruit. The others were chatting quietly now instead of singing.

"What if Mary had aborted Jesus," Alison said. "It would have changed the whole history of the world."

"No it wouldn't," said Fletch. "They'd have thought up something else. The time was ripe."

"Mary says, 'Saint Joe dear, I'm pregnant by the Holy Ghost,' " Whitey said, putting a special strain in the raspy voice, "and Saint Joe says, 'well, stupid, don't you know what girls do when they're pregnant by the Holy Ghost? Get rid of it!' "

There was some laughter.

"I wish you wouldn't say things like that," Sally Bell said.

"Why?" said Whitey. "Are you a Christer or something? A Jesus freak?"

"She goes to chapel," Roxie told Whitey. "She belongs to the Fellowship."

"Oh," said Whitey. "I'm sorry."

"I'm not a Jesus freak," said Sally Bell. "But I respect some things."

As the night grew quieter the group thinned. After two-thirty only Roxie and Fletch remained with Elspeth. Their conversation drifted by the open window. Somebody shouted from another window for them to shut up over there. Roxie closed the window. They swallowed speed tablets and drank coffee. Elspeth refilled her vodka and grapefruit and held the glass in one hand and her coffee cup in the other.

"Your roommate is the most beautiful woman I ever saw," she told Fletch.

"Belinda?" said Fletch. "She says the same thing about you."

"Me? She couldn't have."

"You're real cute, Ellie," said Roxie.

"You are," said Fletch. "You've got the neatest body on the floor. In the whole building, maybe."

"I'm not in Belinda's league."

"You're a different type, Ellie," said Roxie. "I'd rather look like you than like

30

Belinda, if I had my druthers. Really. I can picture you in Playboy. 'Elspeth Ann Baker, five-foot-two, green eyes, pointy tits.'"

"They're not really pointy," said Fletch. "They look like that because her areolas swell out."

"I know," said Elspeth. "My breasts have breasts."

"Mine haven't been like that since I was fourteen," said Fletch.

"And my eyes aren't green, they're gray actually," said Elspeth. "It's my hair that makes you think they're green. And you'll never see me in Playboy."

"I hear they pay five thousand bucks," Roxie said.

"I'm not for sale," said Elspeth. "Anyway I have freckles."

"How many have you got? Eight? Ten?" Roxie said. "Around the bridge of your nose there? They make you cuter. And they've had freckles in the centerfold before."

"Your whole front is supposed to get bigger when you're pregnant," said Fletch.

"Well, I haven't noticed any change yet," said Elspeth. "My bras feel the same."

She began to hear a slurriness in her speech. She was halfway down the second glass of vodka and grapefruit. She took another cup of coffee. Then she sat silently, and listened to Roxie and Fletch talk to one another. She watched the pot steam on the hot plate. Her thoughts would drift until she was not sure whether she dreamed, or how long she had dozed, and then she would hear Roxie and Fletch again. She stared at the glow of their cigarettes, until she saw them double.

"If you were deciding whether to have an abortion," Roxie was saying, "would you feel better about aborting a boy than a girl?"

"I don't know," said Fletch. "I'd have to think about that."

Elspeth rose to take the speed bottle from Roxie. She slumped back into her chair and downed another tablet. Her head ached. Roxie was in the other chair and Fletch sat on the end of Roxie's bed. There was no sound in the night but the two voices. Except for the murmuring of Roxie and Fletch, and an occasional whispering breeze in new foliage beyond the reopened window, all was still. In the building there was not a footstep. From the streets there was no sound of traffic. She even heard the ticking of the little watch on her wrist.

"Why do people have to grow inside each other?" she heard Roxie say. "Why couldn't they just grow on trees or something?"

"It's to teach us compassion," said Fletch. "That we depend on one another."

Elspeth studied her yellow juice, sipping it. She rested her eyes against her fingers, her elbow on the curved arm of the chair.

"Ellie!" Roxie said, startling her. "Are you awake?"

"Yes." But she knew she must have dozed, in spite of the coffee and the tablets, because she had dreamed that Roxie's desk was against the other wall. Now she saw it in its regular place. She went to it, and put a spoonful of coffee powder in her cup, and filled it with hot water.

"That's how you can prove God isn't a woman," Fletch was saying to Roxie. "If God was a woman, She'd have fixed it so it's the boys who get pregnant."

Elspeth went back to her chair. About four o'clock Fletch yawned and said she had to catch forty winks. She rose, saying she'd be back with Belinda at seven to

31

take Elspeth to breakfast and the stables. She said the stables opened at eight on Saturday.

Soon afterward Elspeth felt nauseated. She did not make it to the toilets but vomited in the hall. She sank to the floor. Roxie wiped up the mess. "It's the pizza and the popcorn," Roxie said. She helped Elspeth to stumble back to the room and her chair. She took off Elspeth's shirt and buttoned her into a fresh one. She wiped Elspeth's chin.

Already birds were twittering, and by five o'clock there was a soft daylight. Elspeth felt brighter. She saw Roxie's head droop lower and lower, the short dirty-blond hair hanging forward about her face. Then Roxie would snap briefly awake, and begin to sag again.

"I think you better get some sleep," Elspeth said.

"No. I'll stay up till they come for you. I said I would." Without rising from her chair Roxie leaned to the desk and mixed more coffee.

"You think it would be okay if I tried more of the vodka now?" Elspeth asked.

"I'd think so," said Roxie. "You puked out what you had before."

Elspeth took another tablet and washed it down with juice. Again she returned to her chair in the gentle light from the window, coffee in one hand and vodka and juice in the other. She talked about Jared. "He's gonna do Richard the Second, you know. That's an extremely tough part. Most of the great actors never even dared tackle it. It's much tougher than Hamlet. Because of the changes in the guy's character. And the way you begin finally to create sympathy for this crumb, just when he's falling apart."

"If Richard the Second is a crumb," said Roxie, "Jared's the perfect guy to play him."

"Don't say that. He sold his car."

"Oh, tough. He'll have to walk. I don't see how he could ditch a face like yours for a beast like that Janice. He's got to be blind."

"Looks aren't everything," said Elspeth.

"But you're such a good kid besides."

"He needed an actress. I'm out of it in his world."

"Well, if I ever see that stinker," said Roxie, "I'll spit in his face."

Elspeth had favored the vodka and juice, waiting for the coffee to cool in her other hand, but now she switched.

Roxie and Elspeth made a trip together to the toilets. Roxie watched Elspeth brush her hair. They returned to their room and refilled their coffees.

Elspeth sat talking about her brothers, and how close she had felt to them. She told Roxie how Mark had been killed in Vietnam, and how an Army officer had brought the telegram to the house. She had been in the bathtub, and heard her mother scream.

And she told the crazy way Eric had died. He began gasping in the night, unable to breathe, and her parents rushed him over to the Lapham Hospital in Bradbury. The doctor on duty gave him some aspirin and a nasal decongestant, but said it was only a bad cold, and told them to take him home. In the morning he was

32

dead in his bed of epiglottitis. A wonderful kid, barely seventeen. Never sick before.

"No wonder your father has ulcers," Roxie said.

"I'm the only one left," said Elspeth. "Sometimes I get this feeling something awful's gonna happen to me too."

Fletch came to their door at a few minutes past seven when the sounds of feet in the hallways were only just beginning. She was tall, haggard and red-eyed, and wore canvas slacks and a plaid shirt. Belinda von Schmertzing was not with her. "Belinda's not coming," Fletch said. "She's gonna hole up in the library all day."

"Well, I'm turning in," said Roxie. "Good luck, Ellie." She gave Elspeth a pat on the behind.

Elspeth gave Roxie a little hug. "Thanks," she said. "Thanks for being so good to me."

In the stairwell the light from the window at a landing seemed blinding. Everything else turned green and dark. Elspeth answered the greeting of a girl who appeared to her as a green shadow against the light, without being able to see who it was. Then she stumbled on the stairs and snatched at Fletch.

"You okay?" Fletch asked her.

Her legs steadied and her vision returned. "I'm okay." She continued, leaning on Fletch, who was more than half a head taller, arms about one another's waists.

The dining room was about a quarter full. There was a clatter of trays. It seemed to reverberate in her aching head. "You think I should eat?" Elspeth asked.

"You're gonna need a little strength, if you're gonna ride a horse."

"Let me have a cigarette first. To calm the shakes."

"You don't look like you have the shakes."

"I feel it, though."

The headache subsided when she sat.

They had some scrambled eggs, toast, juice and coffee. "Your eyes are bloodshot," said Elspeth.

"So are yours. You look awful. But that's the whole idea. That thing is gonna say 'the hell with it, I'm moving out.'"

"I've got coffee coming out of my ears."

"Take more juice," said Fletch. "Coffee is alkaline and juice is acid. They neutralize."

When they walked on the grass and the gravel the headache throbbed anew. Overhead the branches whiffled and breathed. Fletch had the keys to Whitey Hathaway's convertible. The points of sun reflecting on paint and chromium bothered Elspeth's eyes. Fletch opened the door for her. The vinyl was baking hot through the faded jeans. But it was good to sit again.

"It's a gorgeous day," said Fletch.

The car rode smoothly in the breeze, but with a subtle motion as though on the sea. Elspeth knew her eyes were slits. But keeping them a bit open seemed to take all her effort.

"You haven't ever had any riding lessons at all?" Fletch asked. "Nothing?"

"Just a couple of times at camp. I was always involved with cars."

"Well, this guy's got a real gentle horse. I hope it's not taken. It'll just follow my horse. And we'll walk the horses through town to a country road I use a lot, where there's no traffic at all. And then I'll remind you what you need to know about posting, and if I see you're doing all right we can trot a little. If you don't post so good you'll just go bumpity bump more. Which could be just what you need. And if you're tired and unsteady hold tight onto the saddle. I can even ride beside you. We found this terrific road where there's never a bit of traffic."

At the stable there were flies. As soon as Elspeth rose from the car the headache resumed. The contrasts of sunshine and shade were such that she could scarcely make out the broad face of the stablemaster. "You want Tex?" he asked Fletch.

"Tex for me, and could you put my friend on Susannah? She's sort of a beginner, and I'm giving her instruction."

The horses looked enormous.

"Put on the saddle with the brass knob, could you please?" she heard Fletch say. "On Susannah."

She watched them ready the horses. Susannah was whitish with gray speckling. Elspeth was eager to be mounted, if only to be off her legs. To stand was agony. Her skull seemed to be cracking.

Fletch and the stablemaster boosted her by the behind and thigh and she got her leg across.

Presently she saw Fletch look back at her from the brown horse. "Okay, we're gonna take it real slow, so it'll take about an hour to get there, but it's worth it. You're gonna love that road."

A branch of a low sapling brushed Elspeth's leg. They emerged from the rutted drive onto the street. Elspeth clasped the knob and the loose reins together. She had no need to direct the horse. It followed the tail and the massive buttocks of the brown one.

She listened to the hoofs. They stayed close to the sidewalk. Children looked up at them. Cars passed slowly. Elspeth stiffened her arms to check the rhythmic bobbing of her bosom. But she could not keep her head from rocking back and forth with each step of the horse. Whenever she let her eyes close she began to dream, so she forced them to stay open. She began to hiccup, but the hiccups were in slower rhythm than the rocking of her head.

Fletch turned in her saddle. "You all right, Ellie?"

"All right." She hiccuped in the middle of saying it.

"You got the hiccups or something?"

"A little. It's okay."

They continued. A headache returned, smaller than before, in a low spot between her eyes. A silent belch came up between hiccups. She wished her head wouldn't swing back and forth so much. Her feet had lost the stirrups and could not find them. It would not matter if they continued this slow. Her stomach had grown queasy and she did not feel like speaking.

"We'll take a right at the traffic light," Fletch said without looking around.

It was a familiar block. Elspeth recognized the shops they passed.

The traffic light was red and the horses stopped, still in single file. Cars drifted to a halt beside them. Her whole insides grew unbearably nauseated and heaved. The vomit splashed on her hands and the brass knob and the broad back and mane. She saw the skin give a quiver under it. All her muscles gave way in a drowning weakness. She slid down to the right, unable to stop, grasping at the saddle and the stirrup. Her back and her head hit the pavement with a thud. Her vision was nothing but lights swimming in blackish green.

Then she saw the horse's leg, and a policeman, and heard commotion. Her tortured insides retched again, bringing up droolings of stinging sour stuff, and still retched. She saw the legs of the crowd, not their faces. The pain in her back and her head was nothing compared to the internal heaving that racked her. It seemed the worst sickness she had ever felt. "God, Ellie, you're white!" she heard Fletch cry.

The policeman was behind her, trying to help her up by the armpits. She tried to organize her legs beneath her but they kept buckling in all directions like a rag doll.

She heard Fletch talking to the policeman. "Elspeth Baker. She's a freshman at Mount Holyoke. My name's Alexandra Fletcher."

"WELL!" the nurse said. "You had quite a sleep! Do you feel better?" The Venetian blind rattled up.

"I don't know. I still have a headache."

"You're just lucky it's not a concussion. Or a fracture. Dr. Kemble said God protects drunks. Do you know your parents were here?"

"No!" Elspeth raised herself on an elbow.

"Do you think you can eat some supper? I couldn't even wake you for lunch. Dr. Kemble said let you sleep it off."

"Where are my parents?" Elspeth asked. She sat up.

"I think they went to your dormitory to pick up your things. I'll put you down

for the soup and crackers. We'll see if you hold that down. Dr. Kemble said ice cream's good for a hangover, but we haven't got any. It'll have to be the jello."
She waddled out, her flat feet noisy on the linoleum.

Elspeth sat on the edge of the bed, her bare legs dangling. She remembered lying on the stretcher and begging them not to notify her parents.

Orange sunshine came from the window horizontally and made shadows on the wall. The other bed was unoccupied, its sheet crisply fresh and tight.

She got down, felt behind herself to make sure the short gown was tied, and went barefoot to look for the toilets. She had seen the inside of the infirmary a few times the past winter, when Claire had had mono.

On the way back to her room she heard the footsteps and voices of her parents. Then they appeared around the corridor's bend, side by side, the rusty wavelets and the shiny baldness. "Elspeth!" her mother cried, arms extended, and ran to her, the heels clattering.

She embraced the chunky little form of her mother, their cheeks together. She watched her father approach sullenly. He averted his eyes. Her mother was sobbing.

"How's your ulcer?" Elspeth asked her father.

"Never mind my ulcer. You're certainly not doing it any good."

"The nurse gave him something," her mother said.

In her room Elspeth sat on her bed and her mother sat on the caning of the chair, the powder near the blue eyes tear-stained. Her father sat on the other bed.

"I knew there was something wrong," her mother said. "Because you didn't write for two weeks."

"I did!" said Elspeth. "I sent you a card last week."

"It was almost two weeks. I wanted to phone Thursday night, and I wanted to phone last night, and your father said no, and I said if there's no letter tomorrow I'm phoning. So I waited for the mailman and then I phoned. And they told me you were in the infirmary. I just knew it."

"Yeah, she knew it. She had to be right for a change. On the busiest day of the week. So what could I do? I left Homer alone in the store. Elspeth, what is it, did you have to get into this mess? For all we knew you were a virgin. I hoped. I was afraid to ask. But if they told me every girl in this college was screwing around, and only one got caught, one was pregnant, I'd know whose daughter it was. You guessed it. It'd have to be. Somebody up there hates me. It's always my kid. I'm a born shlemazel. The whole family was born unlucky. Every kid gets out of the draft. My kid they take. It was always like that. Three years he rode a motorcycle and never a scratch. But he takes a ride in another kid's car, he wasn't even driving, and he's in traction all summer. The other kids walked away from it. And the next summer, Vietnam. And Eric—I can't even think about it. The dumbest doctor that ever got through a medical school has to pick my kid to make mistakes on."

His sigh was like a shudder. Elspeth bit her lip, her eyes wet. Her mother wept silently, moving a crushed handkerchief from one nostril to the other. He looked at Elspeth in the little white cotton gown.

36

"Okay," he began again, "it's not the end of the world. I know I spoiled you rotten. You're eighteen years old and I can't tell you anything. You'll probably tell me they're all doing it. But haven't you got any sense? Couldn't you be a little more kind to yourself? Don't you know it's a boatload of headaches to be pregnant before you're ready? Before circumstances are right for it? You read about girls having to have abortions. Or giving up babies for adoption. Or working to raise a child out of wedlock, or having to get married before they're ready. And whichever they do, it's aggravation they needed like a hole in the head. Stupid. Everything's so stupid. They study so hard to get in here, and then they get in and it's playing around. You know what it costs me a year to send you here?"

"Yes."

"A fine return on my investment."

"I know." Her eyes were brimming. "Everything's a mess. I wish you didn't have to find out. I'd have given anything not to hurt you."

"Big deal. Don't you know what hurts you hurts me? When you hurt yourself you hurt me? What do I work for, sixty hours a week plus overtime? For me? What good is *my* life? You know what return I want on my investment? To see you happy, that's all. For your one life to be happy, and satisfying. Not all messed up. To see just one kid get a decent break. What did I do wrong?"

"You didn't do anything wrong, Daddy. I did it wrong. I goofed."

His backbone seemed to sag. His eyes drifted to vacancy. He exhaled a big sigh that dragged into a groan. It was the kind of sigh her mother called a krechts. Her mother was sobbing audibly now. Elspeth sniffled and looked to the one-legged bed table for a box of tissues, but there was none.

Her father's eyes fixed on her again, tiredly. "So what's the story, Elspeth? Who's the boy? Is he a student? Or a smart-aleck instructor with a wife and kids, or what." Her mother looked at her too, with blue eyes, the handkerchief at her nose, and paused in the sobbing.

"A student. He's a senior at Amherst."

"What's his name?"

"Jared Blumenthal."

"Blumenthal?" said her mother. "Jewish?"

"Thank God for small favors," her father said irritably. "Are you sure he's the father?"

"Positive."

"How many boys have you slept with?" he asked.

"One."

"Is that the truth?"

"What's the difference," she answered without spirit, averting her eyes.

"Don't aggravate me! Or I'll still take you over my knee. Like I should have. It's not too late."

Her mother wept anew. "It's the truth," Elspeth told him.

"I know it's the truth," her mother sobbed. "She always tells the truth."

Her father gave a more ordinary sigh. Then his hand struck his knee. "All right," he said. "Come on. We're taking you home." He rose, taking a cigar from his inside pocket.

"For how long?"

"Get your clothes on. I don't know. Till we figure this out. They tell me classes are finishing anyway. And I know you're not studying like you used to anyhow. You're probably flunking."

"Not necessarily."

"Go out, Joe," her mother said, "so she can get dressed."

"Right, right." He walked toward the door, biting the tip from the cigar. "With a stranger that doesn't care if she lives or dies anything goes. She can jump into bed and make babies. But a father's not supposed to see her underwear. Too modest."

Her mother shut the door behind him, and opened drawers looking for clothing. There were only the crumpled jeans and shirt and underwear and socks that had been put there in the morning. She picked them up to give to Elspeth, but then sniffed the jeans. "There's an odor. Like vomit or something."

"I threw up. I thought it missed my clothes." The odor was faint.

"I don't see anything," her mother said, examining the jeans. "Maybe a spot got on somewhere. All right, get it on quickly like a good girl. You can change in the car. Daddy's in a hurry. We should have brought one of the valises in with your clothes."

Elspeth slipped into the underpants and jeans before she untied the gown.

"Didn't you even use anything?" her mother asked.

"Of course we did."

"Well, whatever you used, either it didn't work or you didn't use it right."

"You can say that again."

"Your hair's a mess."

"I know it. What about my books and stuff?"

"Well, we packed everything that seemed to be yours. Your roommate was there. She gave us all your books. Your room's a mess. Don't you clean it, the two of you? Actual balls of dust."

"Usually. But we're heading into exam time."

"We were here before, you know. You were sound asleep."

They opened the door.

"Joe! They told you not to smoke."

"Where's he from?" he asked Elspeth.

"Boston. They live in Auburndale."

They set out down the corridor, Joe puffing the cigar. "Auburndale. Well, I'll have to drop over there some evening. And meet his parents. What does his father do?"

"He plays for the Symphony."

Joe walked nervously fast and got ahead of them. He was exactly Elspeth's height, and her mother was an inch or so less. Mark and Eric somehow had managed to grow more. Mark had been five-nine. The cigar smoke drifted back.

"I've got a good mind to sue this college," he said. "I wouldn't get any place, but even so. Let them explain a few things. I bet parents all over the place would back me up."

"Don't aggravate yourself," his wife said.

"Don't aggravate myself, she tells me. Everything's fine."

"I'm only thinking of your ulcer."

"Harriet, please! Get off my back. The ulcer's the least of my problems."

As they neared the entrance the nurse emerged flatfootedly from somewhere. "Are you leaving?" she asked Elspeth. "I was sending up your supper."

"I guess I'm going home."

"Mr. Baker!" the nurse said. "I told you—no smoking in this building."

"Shut up," he said. He pushed his way with Harriet out the door.

He forgot to hold it and it shut in Elspeth's face. She followed them out to the powder-blue Dart.

She let herself into the back and sat next to the valises, behind the bald head and the even waves of the rust-colored one. Her father drove with lurches and sudden starts, the way he did when he was upset. His blue smoke curled through the car.

"Could we just check my desk?" Elspeth asked.

"I went through your desk. I want to get home. My stomach's bothering me. If we missed anything they can send it."

Classes were over, and there were only exams to take, plus a term paper and an overdue lab report. Still, she would rather have stayed put till after exams. Except she could not have studied with her parents knowing. In a way it was easier just for now to have them telling her what to do, at least till she could get her mind clear and the baby resolved.

The car slowed behind a farmer's tractor on a curve. Her father exercised the horn with the hand that held the cigar. Then they zoomed out, swerving left and right, throwing Elspeth against the valises.

"Didn't you use contraceptives?" he asked without glancing back.

"Yes."

"The pill?"

"A diaphragm."

"Why not the pill?"

"Well, I tried pills. I didn't like it. And I didn't like the idea of tampering with myself chemically, sort of."

"When did you get the diaphragm?"

"Oh, pretty early on. When I saw it was gonna be steady."

"When did you meet him?"

"Well, really last October, except would you believe I actually met him five years ago but then I didn't see him again? They brought all the kids from his temple to our temple, and he was there, and I was thirteen and he was fifteen almost sixteen, and he kept dancing with me and Cindy Schaeffer and Abbie Millman. He was a real neat dancer. And we talked a while. He was smart. And the week after that we played them in basketball and I went with Mark, but he wasn't there.

And then all of sudden, last October, this bunch of guys came over from Amherst and there he was. He didn't remember me at all, but I remembered him."

"And jumped right into bed."

"I did not!"

"I know the type," her father said, still without turning. He gestured, and a length of ash fell from the cigar. "A gift of gab, I bet."

Elspeth reddened. How had he know that?

"Have you discussed marriage at all with this guy?" her father asked.

"It's not practical. He wants to go to the Yale School of Drama. He's in no position to—"

"So what!" Her father struck the steering wheel. "Let him grow up! If he can father children it's time to grow up!"

"Daddy could help him," her mother said, turning. "He could take him into the business."

"Jared wouldn't work in a hardware. He's gonna be an actor."

"He sounds kind of childish," said her father. "What is he, in a dream world?"

"No, he's really good. He can make you love Shakespeare. Like Shakespeare was now. You understand it."

"Then let him be an actor when he's making a living! He can be in all kinds of amateur things! Do you know how many starry-eyed kids aspire to be actors? What's he gonna do between plays? When he's out of work?"

"Daddy, maybe someday he'll love me. I hope. But until he does there's just no way I can force him. He doesn't love me. I've got to face it. He's in love with somebody else right now. Or he thinks he is."

"Oh, yeah? Who does he think he is? The playboy of the westen world? This kid has a responsibility! He's the one that's got to face it! I'm gonna bring pressure to bear. His responsibility is to you!"

"Daddy, that's old-fashioned—"

"What! And what are you? An imbecile?" He whacked the wheel. "He's had his fun! Had a great time for himself! And you're prepared to let him get away with that? You pay the price! A woman can be so God damn dumb! What the hell was the use of teaching you all about the birds and the bees? What was the use of it? Didn't any of it stick? You have to learn the hard way? Don't they teach in those sex ed courses that boys are full of shit when they start talking?"

Elspeth was coloring once more. Her mother was sniffling into a handkerchief. They circled the ramp onto the turnpike. He paused at the toll booth and snatched the ticket.

Elspeth saw the speedometer inch to seventy-five miles an hour, and then to eighty-five. She sat back. They rode in silence, except for Harriet's soft weeping and the wind blasting by the open deflector.

Daddy could not judge, Elspeth said to herself. No one could know how it was between two others. She had in fact gone to bed with Jared the first time they went out. But it was after many hours, actually toward daybreak. She almost refused. She had kept answering that she was not quite ready.

Though when she would be ready, maybe in another half year or so, she would want him to be the first. He explained to her that she was ready now. The proof of his rightness, as he himself remarked afterward, lay not in the logic of what he said, but in her own willingness to be persuaded by it. And anyway, in a thing like that, how could she have an isolated, disjunctive readiness? It was not her readiness, but their readiness. Who can know, at the start, what will be an enduring relationship, and what will be a chance encounter? You hope. You believe. But if you want the one, you risk the other.

The second night they went to bed rather earlier. It was always so good to lie with him by the hour, talking, or touching. Any seeming shortcomings in their coupling she attributed to her own awkwardness. Sometimes he would entertain her endlessly with his patter. He could mimic the styles of six different actresses in rapid succession, using the same line for each.

He loved her name. She had always thought it a bit of a tongue twister, and her grandparents had been unable to pronounce it. Jared said Elspeth was the most beautiful name in the language. And it was, when he mouthed it. His diction and modulation lent grandeur to the whole English language, and authority to whatever he uttered, and determined the mood of any occasion.

Once, while she sat combing and brushing, he read aloud an erotic passage from the Bible, that she had not known was there, in the most amazing voice, the words seeming to lap her skin. Love with him had many moods. Lifting her skirt could seem a cute prank, and stealing her underpants could seem hilarious.

If Roxie was ever wakened by their murmurings and snickerings, she gave no sign. Jared too was good about everything, and kept his eyes to Elspeth while Roxie dressed.

Her father banged the steering wheel again, startling her. The cigar between his fingers was shorter, the chewed end of it soggy. "What's wrong with the kids today? Do they just not give a damn or what? Don't they know their parents want them to be happy?"

"I'm sure he took advantage of her," her mother whispered.

"How can he take advantage? I don't care what he said to her! What is she, a five-year-old, that a little boy can come along and say let's play doctor and she doesn't know what's happening? A boy sniffing around her, and she stands there like a dog in heat, like she doesn't know what's coming?"

Her mother turned to her, wiping her eyes. "Is he a nice-looking boy?"

"What difference does that make?" said Joe.

"Not what you call handsome," Elspeth told her mother, "but a really terrific face. And dark hair. Sort of medium height. He wears elevators when he's on stage."

"What did you say his name is?" said her mother. "Jeffrey?"

"Jared."

"Do you love him?" asked her father. She still saw only the back of his head, shiny above the black fringe.

"Yes."

41

"Well, that settles it. I'm gonna talk to his parents. Find out what kind of people they are. Maybe they've got some influence on him."

And make everything even worse, Elspeth thought. Or was it actually possible that so crude and quaint an approach could accomplish something? She didn't dare hope.

"Thank God he's Jewish," Harriet said.

"Thank God he's white," Joe muttered.

6

ELSPETH spread some books and opened a loose-leaf notebook on the big varnished table, which she had used as a desk in her last two years of high school, and which Mark had used before. He had told her to take this bedroom for her own when he shipped out to Vietnam. Together he and she had carried out Eric's old table to the tiny front bedroom that had been Elspeth's, and carried in her white triple-mirrored vanity to take its place.

When she stood in the breeze at the back window she could look down upon the tire still hanging by a rope from a maple branch for a swing, and upon her mother in the big straw hat, preparing the vegetable plot in the sunny place in the middle of the yard, and upon the wooden ramp the boys had built for getting under cars, partly shaded by the oak near the back fence.

Except for the rustling of the big maple almost the only sound was the hourly bonging of the tall grandfather clock, and its slow tick, just around the corner at the opening to the stairs.

She had listened to its soothing familiar tick through much of the night, unable to sleep. She had recalled the day they acquired it. She had been allowed to carry all the booklets of Green Stamps and hand them to the man in the Green Stamp store, though she was only five. The upstairs hall was narrow, and the stairway was wider, so they had stood the clock right at the head of the stairs, against the bit of wall between the top of the stairs and the hallway. Then she and Mark and Eric had watched Daddy correct its tilt on the runner of carpeting with shims, until its tick was exactly even.

She tried to work on her term paper.

Daddy had this notion he could bring some kind of pressure upon Jared, and Jared's family. She couldn't believe it would accomplish much. But at least it would force Jared to remember a bit longer that she existed.

Ultimately her parents would fix her up with a proper doctor for a proper abortion. And then she would have to work at living this down. Help Dad in the store all summer, go back to school in the fall, and try someday to give them a little happiness. They hadn't had much.

She kept away from her parents and studied into the evening. Her father had phoned Jared's father and was supposed to phone him again in a day or so. She knew that the possibility of court action had been mentioned, and that Daddy was now allowing Mr. Blumenthal time to talk to his son. Daddy had phoned from the master bedroom but his voice sometimes carried through the closed door.

He brought her no details afterward, and she asked for none. She simply didn't leave her room much, and he did not come to it.

Tuesday morning she took her notebooks and papers to the town library. Her father always went to the store in the van, so Elspeth had the use of the Dart. From the gray-shingled house on Cabot Road it took scarcely seven or eight minutes up Peacemaker Avenue to Winslow Center. The public library had a massive historical atlas that served her purpose as well as anything she could have found on campus.

She traced the maps the term paper required, her mind on Jared. Maybe she was giving up too soon. His thing with Janice was too shaky to endure. Janice was too much like him, and would seek to upstage him and become the center of attention herself. Jared needed an audience, not a competitor, and Elspeth had been a perfect audience. Sooner or later he would remember that.

He would remember their good times too. She knew how to make him love himself, and that's what he wanted more than anything.

He was going to miss that. It was the baby that had turned her into a nuisance, but with the baby gone she would not be a nuisance.

Or suppose she had the baby, and Daddy took Jared to court and made him pay child support for years, forever, till the child was grown. That would force him not to forget her. Maybe someday he'd want to see the kid he was paying child support for.

Except she couldn't keep the kid. She couldn't do that to her parents. Either an abortion, or at least sign the baby away for adoption.

She left the Dart parked in front of the library, with her notebooks inside, and walked down the block to Sawyer's Hardware. When she was little she had urged her father to change the name to Baker's. But she understood now that you did not change the name of an old store that everybody knew and trusted.

The door jingled a bell when she opened it.

The high crowded racks made narrow corridors throughout the store. Her father was at the back counter, cutting a pane of glass for someone, and a couple of customers waited nearby. Homer Lathrop, gaunt and white-haired, was up near the ceiling, where the wheels atop the high ladder rolled on its track. He came down the ladder with two big round cans. "Elspeth! School over already? Or just back for a few days?" A customer followed him to the register.

"A little of both," she answered, while he wrapped the cans. "I'll have to go back for exams."

"Well, we could use you."

She made her way back between racks toward her father. In the house they had been coolly avoiding each other these couple of days, but it was time to stop that, lest the chill solidify. "Hi, Daddy," she said. He did not look up at her, but turned instead to a customer and began to explain how to use the putty and the pushpins and the putty knife. He was good with customers. Still, it was rare that he did not interrupt himself when she entered, to look up and smile and call her beautiful, or his favorite face.

She waited. When he looked up it was a passing glance of utter coldness, as though he did not know who she was. Then he beamed cordially at a new customer. Elspeth swallowed, her heart half stopping. She waited a bit longer, and then walked from the store. The bell jingled again as she left.

She had many times seen that icy anger, directed toward her mother, or the boys, or his parents, or relatives, or even toward Homer Lathrop, and sometimes he was involved in feuds at the temple or in his lodge. But never, never had he turned his anger toward herself. She got into the Dart, and headed back toward the house.

Daddy was a man who could be very warm or very cold. Demonstrative and affectionate toward those about him most of the time, but periodically turning summer to winter at a moment's notice if offended. Except that she had been exempt, privileged, immune. The whole world knew that Joe Baker was never harsh to a customer or to his little girl.

When she was four years old her mother used to say he was in love with her. She could climb upon his lap, hug his neck, and keep him smiling by the hour. He liked to call her Sugarcookie. If she and her brothers got into mischief together the boys could be spanked with a leather belt or shut in their room without supper, but nothing happened to Elspeth. I blame you! he would shout, pointing at Eric or Mark. She wouldn't do it if you didn't show her the way!

She had made it up to them—she could prevent Daddy from spanking Mark or Eric by crying and screaming and pulling his arm. That kid runs the house, her uncle had said.

And the boys too had loved her. At the age of thirteen she had taken Mark's car alone, without permission, and lost control of it and struck the curbstone of a rotary at the bottom of a hill, blowing out both front tires. She had phoned Mark from a booth. He was only glad she was unhurt. He didn't even tell on her.

She spread the notebooks once more on the big varnished table by her back window. It was hard to grasp that the magic power she had wielded over her father was gone.

At supper she kept trying to catch Daddy's eye, but couldn't. The hurt she knew he felt seemed to cut back at her. She tried to make conversation about the store. But he answered in grunts.

In the evening his voice came from the master bedroom, which was where the hall stopped just past the head of the stairs. He was talking to Jared's father again on the telephone. Elspeth lay in the lower bunk, her door nearly shut. Daddy was pleading for an appointment, and getting the runaround.

She shut her eyes against tears. To her parents she was grief, and to Jared a millstone. She and Eric and Mark had been so happy together—and it was such a short time ago—she was the only kid at Mount Holyoke who had had a happy childhood.

She wasn't dead, but her brilliant light had gone dim.

She heard Harriet on the telephone. Aunt Frieda was inviting her to a shower for Diana. And asking to borrow the tea wagon for it. Harriet sounded jittery, as though she could not decide whether to mention to Frieda that Elspeth had come home.

At breakfast her father looked at her across the table, but with distant, steely eyes.

"Daddy, please don't look at me like that," she said. "Didn't you ever go to bed with a girl before you were married?"

"That's none of your business," he said.

"I never did, no," said Harriet.

"I never got a girl pregnant," said Joe. "Never. I knew better. I thought kids today are supposed to be sophisticated—what the hell's the matter with them? They don't care?"

"I slept with one boy. I bet you slept with more girls than that."

"You want a slap across the mouth? You're begging for it. I never hit you when you were little. That was my big mistake."

She lowered her eyes, and cut the egg and toast with her fork.

"It's different for a man anyway," he added.

"Why?"

"Because a man doesn't get pregnant. He doesn't take the same risk."

That evening she heard him arguing and pleading again on the telephone. Finally he knocked and opened her door.

"All right," he said. "This guy's gonna meet us tomorrow afternoon at Symphony Hall, before the rehearsal. It's the only way. Says he's running around teaching all the time, hasn't got a free hour. So I'll take time off from the store. And you're coming with me. I want him to meet the girl his kid knocked up."

"Okay."

She held no hope for it. She was only glad she and Daddy had an errand together.

Early the next afternoon he came home in the van, while she sat combing and brushing. "Ready?" he said. "Come on. Snap to it. A skirt, not jeans. Look like a lady."

She rode beside him toward Boston in the Dart. They said little.

"Do you know if this kid's father is a Mason?" he asked after a while.

"I don't know."

"If he was, I could appeal to him as a brother." He banged the horn at somebody, holding the cigar. He sighed. "I don't know what's into kids today. A girl can give herself a moment of joy, or pleasure, that's worth about four dollars and ninety-eight cents, and pay for it for a lifetime with a billion dollars of misery." He gestured with the cigar. He glanced toward Elspeth. "Tell me, what did they tell you, a sexual orgasm is so beautiful, wonderful? The nectar of heaven? When I was a kid we could go to Scollay Square and buy it for two dollars. Two bucks." He shook his head.

In the parking lot he locked the car. They walked alongside the brick and the billboards toward the canopy. In the little side lobby a bearded young man was asking questions of the lady at the ticket window. Elspeth pulled open the white door. Joe pressed out the stub of cigar into the ash stand.

The Symphony season was over, and bare tables were in place for the Pops. The stage was littered with chairs and music stands, but no one was there except a woman tuning the harp. "I guess we're early," Elspeth said.

She looked up. She had always admired this hall and its faraway recessed ceiling of dusty whites and gilt. Above the highest galleries plaster statuary struck poses in niches. Straight-nosed gods with little-boy genitals, robed philosophers, smooth goddesses graceful-kneed and sphere-breasted. Elspeth waited with her father on chairs partway back.

On the stage far before them, under an array of towering gilded organ pipes, more and more musicians seated themselves, and tuned their instruments in a cacophony.

Elspeth knew at once which of the bass fiddle men was Hyman Blumenthal. There were the widespread knees, the shoulder and head dipping with each push of the bow, the slack-mouthed questioning upward glance when he adjusted the strings—everything exactly as Jared had mimicked him.

"That's him," she said, taking her father's hand.

They went forward, alongside the wall.

"Mr. Blumenthal," she said, below the stage. She beckoned and smiled.

He looked toward her, open-mouthed, his glasses a little crooked, pausing in the midst of a stroke of the bow. Then he got up slowly, laid down the bow and rested the big fiddle carefully against the wall. He left the stage by the back.

But presently he appeared near them in a side doorway. "All right," he said. "Let's talk." His heavy brow was like Jared's. But he was taller, although somewhat bent, and the eyes behind the glasses looked bewildered and tired. His hair was slung black and straggly across his head. They joined him out in the corridor. He motioned, and they walked slowly together toward the big front lobby.

"Look," he said as they walked. He put his hands to the vest that hung limp on his hollow chest. "Mr. Baker. It's up to the kids, you know. It's their business. We can't interfere. They're of age. We can't tell them anything." Joe opened his mouth, but Mr. Blumenthal, who despite his stoop towered over him, kept talking in his slow way, sometimes tossing a wrist in a gesture of fatigue or resignation. "I talked to him already. I went all the way out there. I didn't even tell my wife. He really

46

took this thing to heart, you know. He got rid of his car to get her fixed. And then she changed her mind and they ran away with the money anyway."

"I heard about that! He fixed her up with butchers."

"I don't know if it was butchers. I know the price was highway robbery. You know how long it took the kid to scrape together a few dollars for half the price of a car, to share with another kid? He waits on table. He's a singing waiter. He's gonna work in the Catskills this summer."

"Mr. Blumenthal, I buried two children already." Joe put his thumb to his chest. "If my daughter has to have it cut out of her it's gonna be the best doctor in the country, and the best hospital. The finest. And your son's gonna pay the bill. You tell him it's gonna cost him plenty."

"Mr. Baker. Can you get blood out of a stone? The kid hasn't got a dime. And I'll be honest with you, I haven't got a dime either. The maestro rides around in Cadillacs. He stands up there and waves a baton and they pay him like a movie star. And us guys that make the music, we're shleppers, they pay us like coolies. It's a scandal. I can't live on it. The trustees couldn't care less, as long as they've got a glamour boy for a conductor. I have to give lessons. To kids. They drive me batty. I couldn't afford a ticket to hear myself play. Can you believe that? My wife works in Filene's, on her feet all day. Does your wife work?"

"No."

"All right. You're richer than I am. You own a hardware store. You can afford it better than I can."

They had arrived in a spacious empty lobby of soiled marble. There was no one around, not even a ticket window. They turned to one another.

"How do you know she didn't get herself pregnant on purpose to hold onto him?"

"That's a lie!" Elspeth told him fiercely.

"Can you prove it?" he said easily.

"It just isn't true! It's absolutely not true! And if you ever say that again I hope your tongue falls out!"

Mr. Blumenthal shrugged sideways. "Look, I can't prove it, and you can't prove it." He looked at Joe. "But the boy always gets the blame. Right? A girl gets herself pregnant, so right away the boy's a cad, he's a bum. It's not fair. A lot of it's the fault of the girls these days. The way they go around, the boys can't help it. The skirts they wear, Jesus. They could go to the bathroom and not even have to hike them up."

"So is my daughter wearing a skirt like that? Look at her! What are you talking about! It's practically down to her knees!"

"I've never worn a mini," said Elspeth. "I think they're dumb."

"Even some of these Radcliffe hotshots," Mr. Blumenthal continued. "They come in here to hear the Symphony, and they sit down and cross their legs, and you can practically see what they had for supper. Girls have a responsibility too. And if a boy knocks off a piece, what do you expect? It's the normal natural thing, isn't it? The girls make themselves available. Jared's twenty-one years old. The girls love him. Mount Holyoke. Smith. U of Mass. That's the Garden of Eden out

47

there. My son's a nice, decent kid, Mr. Baker. But the girls won't let him alone. He's not out to get them in trouble. He told me with your daughter he even used rubbers the first couple of times, and then he understood she was taking care of it. He'd have kept on using it. I don't know, it's not like when we were kids. Girls don't want rubbers today. Even some older woman he had, she told him she had the tubes tied. I told him, I said, sonny boy, don't listen to that shit. You can't take any stock in what a woman says. You use the old raincoat. That way you don't have to worry that a girl's gonna come back with a story."

Joe again opened his mouth as though to reply, raising his hands. Then he dropped his hands and shook his head.

"What do you want from me?" Mr. Blumenthal asked quietly. "I should tell him to saddle himself with a family? Tell him yourself. He's old enough to know his mind."

"Don't you have any influence on him? You pay his college bills. Appeal to him! On his conscience! Doesn't he care that he fathered a child? Don't you care? It's your flesh and blood too!"

"Do kids listen to anybody today? He wants to be an actor. Maybe he'll get the breaks, maybe he won't. Meantime, how's he gonna support a family?"

"If he wants to be an actor he's an idiot."

"Mr. Baker, you can say that and I can say that. But he feels he has talent."

"He does have talent," said Elspeth.

"See?" Mr. Blumenthal smiled. "She knows. And my other kid's a math wizard. A brain like a computer. They're both good kids."

"They could do a lot worse than my daughter! Look at her! Look at that face! And brains! At Mount Holyoke, a top college! In high school they voted her Prettiest in the class!"

"Cutest," she corrected.

"It's the same thing. Did you ever see hair that color? And she can do anything! She tunes up my truck! She's almost a licensed plumber! She could have been an electrician at fourteen if they gave licenses to kids! A locksmith! She's my right arm! This girl was waiting on customers when she was nine years old! Unbelievable!"

"Mr. Baker," he said tiredly, "if he doesn't love her, what good is it? It wouldn't work. They'd have an unhappy marriage."

"So what!" said Joe. "Who says a marriage has to be happy? Nothing else is happy! There's no such thing as happiness. Are you happy?"

"No."

"Okay. There you are. Nobody's happy."

"All right, you have a point. But it's his life. He tells me he's going with a new chick already. A shikse yet. But that's how it is these days. What can ya do?"

"I'll make you a proposition," Joe said. "He marries Elspeth, all right? And gives the baby a name. And then they can get divorced right away, no questions asked, and we'll never ask a penny in support."

"No!" Elspeth cried, clapping her hands to the sides of her head. "Daddy! No! If I marry him it'll be to marry him! Not some phony crap like that!"

48

"You keep out of it!" Joe told her. "It's better than nothing, isn't it?"

"It is not! It's the same as nothing! Who'd we be kidding? It'd be a joke! A farce! Pointless!"

Joe stared at her, his face flushed. She stared back.

"She's right," Mr. Blumenthal said tiredly. "It's pointless."

For a moment no one spoke. Her face felt hot. There were three sets of doors, all closed, and the music came through them loudly.

"Shouldn't you be back in there?" she asked Mr. Blumenthal.

He almost smiled at her, looking down coyly over the top of his glasses. "The conductor doesn't know if I'm in there or not. He wouldn't miss me for six months. You think the great maestro thinks about me? The maestro thinks about the maestro. But you're right. He'll miss the fiddle. He'll look up, and he'll see that big fiddle and nobody playing it." He gave Joe a handclasp. "Mr. Baker, you went into business. You were smart. That's what I should have done. It's been a pleasure talking to you."

He turned and walked from them across the marble floor. The music drew itself up to a frenzied halt, the tympani pounding. Mr. Blumenthal opened one of the pairs of doors and went into the big hall. Joe followed half-confusedly, but then collapsed into a chair near the back. He leaned an elbow on the table and buried his face in his hand. The other hand pressed his stomach. He was perspiring. Elspeth sat beside him.

"What was the matter with you," he said weakly, not uncovering his face. "Arguing with me."

She said nothing.

"He doesn't have daughters," said Joe, "or he wouldn't be so smug."

Far away at the stage the conductor rapped the podium. "Feel it," they could hear him say. "Come on now."

The new piece began with a cheerless lowing of bassoons, as vibrant as a headache. The baton almost billowed, and the conductor's other hand moved as though pulling music from the air. Elspeth crossed her ankles under her chair and sat listening, her hands together on her lap.

"I'm not finished with him," said Joe. "Or his son either. They're gonna get a lawyer letter. I'll have Barney Rosenbaum send a lawyer letter. They're not getting away with this."

The violin bows came rocking up in unison. The composers had had rotten, messed-up lives, most of them, she remembered. As painful as hers could ever be, even if she devoted herself to raising an illegitimate child who grew up to kick her in the teeth. And yet they had composed music, to try to make sense of it.

Again and again the winds and brass came spreading over the strings like oil. Her father looked at her. "Shall we go home?" he asked.

"Let's listen, Daddy. Maybe it'll make the baby have a taste for music."

"What? Are you out of your mind?"

49

7

HER father let her take the Dart to South Hadley for her finals. It was possible to take all three exams the same day. She took the two for which she felt best prepared, and considered whether to take the third. But at the last moment she decided she'd better study at home another couple of days, and come back one more time.

The campus was quiet. Some girls had had all their exams and departed. It had turned hot, and a few sunbathed on the grass in shorts and halters.

She turned in her term paper. Then she went up to the room and found Roxie, who embraced her joyfully. "Let's you and me go over and have a big hot mushroom peetz," she said, "and a big cold lemonade, and cry on each other's shoulder."

"Sounds good to me."

"I don't suppose he called, or looked for me or anything."

"I'm afraid not."

"My father and my brothers spoiled me," Elspeth said as they went down the stairs. "I'm not used to the idea of somebody I love not loving me."

They had their pizza slowly, at a corner table. She told Roxie about her father's meeting with Mr. Blumenthal.

"The poor guy," she said. "He was fighting for me, and of course there was nothing he could do. It just made him feel helpless. I felt so sorry for him. It's like I'm his whole world, you know. I wish I weren't."

"How's your mother taking it?"

"Well, she adjusts better because she doesn't fight so hard. But it's lousy. I'm all she's got too."

"What are you gonna do?"

"It's gonna have to be the old dilatation and curettage, I guess. Someday soon. When the last exam's behind me. My father wants it to be at someplace like the Mass General or the BI. Or the Peter Bent. It's all so depressing. You know, I don't feel anything yet, no symptoms, except no period, but sometimes I get these dreams. I dreamed about this fetus, like it was bigger than me, with an enormous forehead you know, and its spindly limbs all scrunched together, and its eyes closed, but it was looking at me with big eyes right through the eyelids, like it had all the wisdom of the ages, like some superman of the future or something, and you could see all the veins inside it, and its brain was a whole bunch of these flat printed circuits like from an automatic appliance. I mean, nothing scary, but it was such a relief to wake up."

50

"I was thinking, Ellie, some of us were talking, if you wanted to have the baby, everybody in the dorm would help take care of it. We'd all take turns changing it, and getting up for the bottle, and if the dean's office hollered about a baby in the dorm we'd have a big rally and get it in the papers and they'd have to back down."

"That's not possible."

"Why not? Sally Bell said she'd help. I bet everybody would."

"Who'd pay my bills? My father's talking already about pulling me out of here and making me go someplace nearer home. I think I can talk him out of that. But let me keep the baby? No way."

They walked slowly to the Dart. The thought that Roxie would be in Pennsylvania all summer and they would not see each other till September made her eyes brim over.

"What's the matter, Ellie?"

"Oh, everything makes me cry. I'm a sentimental idiot. Maybe I'm having a breakdown or something."

They embraced, standing beside the car.

"Write to me," they both said at once, and laughed.

She headed for the turnpike. She arrived at the gray-shingled house as her parents were finishing supper. She said she'd had a huge pizza and wanted nothing more. She helped clear the table and load the dishwasher. She retrieved the cans and bottles from the trash, and reminded her mother to save glass and metals for recycling.

"I'm sorry," said Harriet. "I don't always remember."

Afterward Elspeth took Harriet in the Dart to the new shopping center where Winslow bordered on Bradbury, to pick up some monogrammed towels ordered as a shower gift for Diana. Harriet never drove, having failed the license test repeatedly many years before.

Elspeth walked with her in the inside mall. There was soft piped music and a tinkling fountain. "I told Frieda to tell everybody not to spend for an electric perk, or a blender, or anything Dad can get them a discount on until they call Dad first," Harriet said. "But nobody listens."

The towels were ready. They bought some glass mugs too as a shower gift from Elspeth.

On the way home Harriet said she had told Frieda they had brought Elspeth home from college early because they work the girls very hard at Mount Holyoke and Elspeth had become overtired. But it hadn't sounded right, and she suspected Frieda now supposed Elspeth had flunked.

"Why on earth did you say that?"

"What else could I say? I certainly couldn't tell her you're pregnant."

"Mama, you didn't have to say anything at all. I'm not really home early. All colleges end about now."

"Well, that's true. I messed it up. I guess I was nervous."

Elspeth did not study that evening. She still felt tense from the two exams taken during the day. She went to the paneled basement, and tried to pick out tunes on the upright piano. But when her parents turned on the television she came up to the living room and watched. No one spoke and no one laughed. The cigar smoke drifted. On top of the television stood the triple frames connected by hinges, with portraits of Mark, Eric and herself. On the mantelpiece the gold clock gave its lingering chime. Muffled in the distance behind her, from the top of the stairs in the entry hall, the grandfather clock bonged its echo. Harriet kept sighing.

"Maybe we should call Rabbi Quint," Harriet said.

"What for?" said Joe.

"Well, like a counseling session."

"Rabbi Quint?" said Joe. "That shmegeggy? What's he gonna do? Wave a magic wand and make the baby go away?"

Elspeth went to bed.

She buried herself in the lower bunk and in darkness. She was living in her little house, with her ten-year-old daughter. The child had never seen her father. She had told the girl about Uncle Mark, who'd been killed in Vietnam long ago, and how she and Mark had once promised each other they would build their own houses when they grew up, with their own hands, pouring the foundations and everything. But Mark was dead, so she had built her house alone, hammering amid the rafters, and her little daughter had helped, dragging boards. Then one day all the newspapers and television reported that the great actor had sent out a call for a child to play his daughter in a certain movie. Kids from all over America auditioned. But one little girl in a bargain-basement dress was outstanding. And the startling thing, the actor said, is that she looks like me. My eyes. My nose. My chin. What is your name, child? My name is Jennifer, said the child, and do you know who I am? He stared upon the red-brown hair. The realization dawned on him. Hi, Daddy. He enfolded his daughter into his arms. He could not contain his tears. Nor could the director, nor any of the actors and actresses in the room. They saw the master playing only his inmost self, more shattering than any of his roles. And where is your mother? he choked. How is she? Elspeth stepped forth from the crowd, some gray hairs amid the red, her bosom lower and less pointy now, some lines about her eyes, yet not much changed. Hi, Jared.

Her face was soaking the pillow. Thank God for fantasies, she said silently. She lay waiting for sleep. But another fantasy took shape. She had never seen the child. She did not even know who had adopted her. Then one day she saw her! A handsome young woman of twenty, intelligent, poised, drawing on her gloves, laughing with a tall companion. There was no mistaking her, the deep red hair, the gray-green of the eyes, the brow and nose exactly Jared's. My precious! she wanted to cry out. My darling! My baby! Tell me your name! Do you live in this city? But what if she did not even know her foster parents were not her own. The handsome young woman had turned without seeing her and was already lost to her hopelessly in the crowd. Oh God, she sobbed, oh God. Elspeth, what is the matter, asked her poor dumb husband who didn't know her past. What is the matter, asked her young children.

In the morning, after she had relaxed with a cigarette over the Ann Landers column and the advice that readers sent one another on the Chit Chat page, she returned upstairs and seated herself at the varnished table to review for the remaining exam.

She studied, but not always efficiently. Recollections would crowd upon her. She rose and wandered to the vanity to look at the one snapshot she had of him, placed in a corner of the central mirror. He was in a knit cap, squinting in the sun before the snow house they had built together in a snowy field half cloistered by dorms. Their mittened hands had rolled and lifted great balls of snow, and the igloo had turned out high and conical, not round and smooth, but with a tunnel entrance and a smoke hole like an Eskimo's. They had been able to sit together beneath its blue iciness while new flakes fell outside.

All her friends had admired that snow house. She also had a snap of Betty Anne Prescott's large rump in black ski pants as she took her turn crawling inside.

At eleven she put her books aside and dressed to take Harriet to Diana's shower. It was to take place at the apartment of a skinny beak-nosed lady named Beatrice, who was an aunt of Diana's though not of Elspeth's, and who had remained close to Frieda despite the divorce.

"Have you met Diana's fiance yet?" Elspeth asked Harriet as they drove together in the heat.

"No. I haven't met him. But Frieda says he's a lovely boy. Frieda's just crazy about him. She's really taking it awfully well. I don't know if I'd have taken it that well, if you or one of the boys grew up and came home with a gentile. But it's more accepted now, I guess. You see it every day. And I guess if I just got you safely married I wouldn't ask any questions. But anyway Frieda's adjusted beautifully, to the in-laws and everything. I give her credit. She was always very adaptable. And she's met his family, and they're fine people, and they love Diana."

"If Aunt Frieda's so adaptable," said Elspeth, "why's she so upset about Uncle Harry's new wife being invited?"

"Well, she's upset, and I don't blame her," said Harriet. "Do you think it's right for a girl to invite her father's new wife to a wedding? It's a family affair. She's got no business there. What are Frieda and Sylvia supposed to say to each other?"

"They don't have to say anything," said Elspeth.

There were flights of white concrete stairs, at right angles to one another between retaining walls, that climbed to the building entrance. But once inside a slow elevator took them up. Elspeth was in her blouse and skirt and she saw Harriet perspiring.

"Is this gonna be a hen party?" she asked in the elevator.

"Well, it's a shower," said her mother. "Just women are invited."

Beatrice let them in cheerily. The little apartment was crowded with a dozen or so chattering women of Harriet's and Aunt Frieda's generation. Frieda embraced Elspeth, who still held the gift-wrapped parcel. "Hi, Aunt Frieda." Frieda was Harriet's sister, somewhat younger and slimmer and taller.

Then Elspeth saw her cousin Diana, willowy and blond, the only other young person there. She handed her the package. "Oh, that's sweet," said Diana. "You didn't have to. I haven't seen you for ages! You look wonderful!"

Elspeth recognized Harriet's folding chairs, which had been loaned a few days before, and Harriet's tea wagon. She found an unoccupied folding chair by a window. The breeze was a relief. Down a steep hill the bases of apartment towers emerged above treetops. "How old are you?" one of the ladies asked her. "Let me guess. Fifteen? A sweet sixteen, I bet." Elspeth colored.

"She's six years younger than me, so she's got to be eighteen," Diana smiled.

"Eighteen," said Elspeth.

"The perfect age," said another lady. "That's the age little girls want to grow up to be, and old ladies like me wish they could get back to."

"I'd love to be a kid today," said Aunt Frieda. "I was born in the wrong generation. The kids today have it made."

"You think kids today are so happy?" Elspeth asked her.

"Aren't they?" said Aunt Frieda. "They don't know how lucky they are. There's a freedom and openness today that we didn't have."

"It's still a rotten world," said Elspeth.

"Well, there are wars, that's true," Aunt Frieda admitted. "And unfortunate things happen. Your family has certainly had its share."

Beatrice clapped hands and said Diana was going to open the presents. The decorated papers rattled. The ladies said ooh and aah, and Diana gushed and squealed and kissed each lady. Beatrice wheeled Harriet's tea wagon to the center of the room, laden with triangular sandwiches and a cake that had Best Wishes Diana in frosted script. Beatrice brought a wide tray with a clinking pitcher and styrofoam cups. "I made iced coffee," said Beatrice. "I didn't think anybody could stand hot coffee in this weather. Does anyone want hot coffee? I could still make it."

"There hasn't been any spring," one of the ladies said. "Right from winter to summer."

Elspeth took a plate of the thin sandwiches and a cup of iced coffee and returned to her place by the open window. She sipped the coffee. She disapproved of styrofoam cups, but there was no sense in making a point of it here. Styrofoam seemed only a step removed from throwaway bottles. In March she had been part of a campus group supporting an article in the South Hadley town warrant that would have forbidden the sale of beverages in cans or no-return bottles. They had been allowed to attend the town meeting as nonvoting observers, and the moderator had permitted one of their group, a black-haired sophomore from Watertown named Jacqueline Garabedian, to read a statement. There was so much waste. Plastic cups, big glass bottles, even gallon size, made to be used one and discarded. The war in Vietnam. All waste. Even the baby growing inside her was waste. Of course its fragments after the abortion would be biodegradable and would return to nature, but meanwhile the energy it took to form the baby was waste.

Diana came near her and smiled. There was not another chair there so she sat on the cold radiator by the sill. The window's breeze stirred the short blond hair.

"Hi," said Elspeth.

"Hi," said Diana. "You look just wonderful, you little bugger. You get more gorgeous every year. That figure!"

"There's nothing wrong with your figure."

"I'm okay, but I'm just ordinary. You're out of this world, Ellie. You've got the bozoom, and that waist, my God! That teensy waist. How do you do it?"

"The waist won't last."

"Sure it will. Just take care of yourself. I think it's in your genes. You've always had that incredible teensy waist. Every time I see you I can't believe it."

"I'm looking forward to meeing Donald," said Elspeth.

"Thanks. He's a great guy. And you're at Mount Holyoke now, right? What will you do this summer?"

"Well, I'll work for Daddy in the store again. How's Bob doing?"

"Bob? Little brother Bobby is doing just fine, bless him. He always does. He's just off his trolley, that's all."

"Bob?" said Elspeth. She saw from everyone's eyes and from the way her mother and Aunt Frieda looked away that they knew something she didn't.

"Bob's disowned me," Diana told her. "Haven't you heard? You don't think he can tolerate his sister marrying a goy?"

"Bob?" Elspeth was confused. "What would he care? If his parents don't even care?"

"You mean you didn't know? Bob's got religion."

"No, I didn't know," said Elspeth. "How often do I see Bob? Last I heard he was doing great at BU."

"Oh, sure. Actually he's at MIT now. He graduated from BU at midyears and he's got a fellowship to MIT. What's that got to do with it? One thing's got nothing to do with the other. He's just lucky that MIT doesn't have a rule excluding lunatics."

"When did he get religion?"

"Well, we saw it coming on for a long time. But this past year he's gotten more and more whacked out. He gets up every morning and wraps himself up in a great big prayer shawl down to the floor, with big black stripes and tassels, his security blanket my mother calls it, and he stands there mumbling prayers to the wall, and cooks in his own pots, and wears a potholder on his head all day—and oh, his holy underwear!" Diana reached to Elspeth, laughing. "Wait till you hear about the holy underwear! He wears this holy undershirt, it sort of hangs down front and back and open at the sides, and with strings and long tassels hanging down off the bottom of it, and then he goes to the john and forgets he has the holy undershirt on, and he sits to take a crap and the strings and the holy tassels hang in the toilet and get wet, and you hear him yell 'oh shit!' through the door." Diana screeched a laugh.

The ladies seemed nervously amused. Elspeth looked at Aunt Frieda's lined face and baggy eyes. Diana was still laughing.

"He's fanatic," said Aunt Frieda. "Worse by the day. It's gotten to where I can't take it anymore. If the phone rings on his holy sabbath, and I happen to be down in the basement with the wash, my God. He'd let it ring till doomsday. It's gotten ridiculous. But he's moving out, thank God. I can't put up with it. And naturally none of my food is acceptable. Except a boiled egg, or a piece of fruit."

"Is he coming to the wedding?" said Elspeth.

"Coming to the wedding!" Diana put one hand to her bosom and the other to Elspeth's arm. "Are you kidding? He thinks I'm a lost soul! Who wants him anyway? And so what. If a man can divorce his wife I guess a brother can divorce his sister. You think I want that creep at my wedding? He's embarrassing."

"I can't believe it," said Elspeth. "I just can't picture it."

"You'd believe it if you saw him standing there saying his prayers all wrapped up in his security blanket," said Aunt Frieda.

"But Bob was always so intelligent," Elspeth said.

"That's just it," said Diana. "It's always the smarties. Something gives. Something snaps."

"But where did he get this?"

"He met some kids that are the same way," Aunt Frieda told her.

"He's got a bunch of freaks," said Diana. "He's even got a girl friend like that."

"Have you met her?" asked Elspeth.

"Who wants to?" said Diana. "I can imagine what she's like. They probably never touch each other. She went to yeshivas all the way up from kindergarten."

"But what does Bob know about yeshivas?"

"Nothing," said Diana. "He's been going to some kooky study group."

"I don't understand the far-out kids today," said the hook-nosed Beatrice. "We were radicals, but we wanted to change society. These kids today just seem to want to put on blinders. Drugs. Even the religion thing is a kind of drug." There were some concurring murmurs. "And even when they're political, they're like complete anarchists," Beatrice continued. "What ever happed to responsible radicalism? There's not even a sense of Marxist discipline any more."

" 'Gimme dat ol' time religion,' " Diana sang, clapping her hands and tapping a foot, " 'Dat ol' time religion—' "

"Some people get a security from having a set of routines and rules to follow, the daily repetition," said a round-cheeked lady named Etta. "I think that's what it is with these kids that go in for religious cults."

"I suppose," sighed Aunt Frieda.

"It's a sign of immaturity," said Beatrice. "He'll get over it as he gets more mature."

Elspeth and Harriet were almost the last to leave. Diana put her hands about Elspeth's arms and smiled. "Thanks for coming, cousin. Let's not wait so long next time."

"Well, I'll see you at the wedding."

"How'll I get your chairs back to you?" Beatrice asked Harriet. "And the tea wagon."

"We could take them off your hands now if you want," Elspeth offered. "We've got the car."

"No, I'll send Joe for them," said Harriet.

"Why bother Daddy?"

"I'll have Bob take them," Aunt Frieda said. "He has a car. He can pick them up here and bring them over. Let Bob do it. He can bring them tomorrow morning. Before he goes to Woods Hole."

Elspeth and Harriet descended in the elevator. "Why didn't you tell me about Bob?" Elspeth said. "I was shocked."

"I was going to tell you," said Harriet. "There were so many other things."

The sun was directly on the long flights of cement stairs now. The heat and the whiteness radiated up.

"And what got into you, wanting to shlep chairs and a tea wagon down these steps?" said Harriet. "In your condition."

"What could happen to me? A miscarriage? Look at the money we'd save."

"Are you serious? A miscarriage out in the street? Without even a doctor around?"

"Mama, carrying a few things wouldn't have given me a mis. I'm not an invalid."

TOWARD midnight there was a savage thunderstorm. Elspeth closed windows on two sides of the house. Then she returned to the varnished table, lighted a cigarette, and continued studying till two in the morning, in a last review for her remaining examination.

"A sink full of garbage!" her father shouted when she came down to breakfast, raising the sopping, overstuffed brown bag upon his left hand. "Is this your job when you're home, or isn't it? Do you expect your mother to do everything? It doesn't look like you took it out once yesterday! Your day off, huh?"

"I'm sorry, Daddy. I forgot."

Joe opened the screen door and his left arm cast the bag out from his shoulder like a shot put. It burst in the air and scattered across the flagstones. "She forgot! I think she forgot that diaphragm she thought she used."

Harriet burst into tears to see him in such bad temper. Elspeth took a fresh sack from the cabinet beneath the sink.

The grass was still wet from the night's rain. She knelt in her jeans, and collected eggshells, skins of squeezed oranges, vegetable scrapings, slippery strands of fat. Coffee grounds clung to her fingers.

She paid no attention to the sound of a car and the shutting of its door. But presently her cousin Bob Shoemaker stepped around the corner of the house.

"Hi, Bob!" she exclaimed looking up.

"Hi, cousin." He was in jeans too and a sweatshirt, and two folded chairs hung from each hand. "What happened? Looks like you had an accident." He leaned the chairs against the gray shingles. He crouched and helped Elspeth gather up garbage. He had grown a little mustache. It was becoming to him, Elspeth thought.

"Who's that?" Harriet said from inside the screen. "Oh, Bob."

"Hi, Aunt Harriet. I've got your chairs, and there's a tea wagon."

"Oh. You didn't have to come around to the back door."

"Well, I didn't know where you wanted the stuff."

"Oh. The chairs belong down in the paneled room, and the tea wagon comes in to the dining room. Uncle Joe'll come out and help you."

"That's okay," he said.

"I'll help him," said Elspeth. She stepped on the pedal of the underground garbage barrel and dropped the bag inside. Bob was on his way back to the front to fetch more chairs. She saw the little crocheted skullcap that Diana had called a potholder on the back of his head. Its circular design was wine-red and white, and a bobbypin held it in place.

She carried the folded chairs to the basement as Bob brought them.

Bob carried the tea wagon over the flagstones.

"You busted the yolks again," Joe said to Harriet.

"Shall I make you new eggs?" Harriet asked him.

"Oh, sure, sure, new eggs. I'm a millionaire. Come in, Bob, come in. Sit down." Bob was fair-skinned, but with dark brown hair like his father's family. The front of the gray sweatshirt said BOSTON UNIVERSITY DEPARTMENT OF ATHLETICS. Elspeth wheeled the tea wagon to its place by the dining-room windows. Through the front window she glimpsed the parked car. "Have some breakfast," she heard her father say to Bob. "Pull up a chair."

"No thanks."

"The bacon bother you? Harriet, whip him up some eggs without the bacon."

"No, please. Nothing, Aunt Harriet."

"Cereal?" said Joe. "Or what's the matter, you don't want to eat off our dishes? Have a cup of coffee at least. A glass of juice."

"I've had breakfast. Honest, Uncle Joe. I had a big breakfast."

"Okay," Joe relented. Elspeth had returned to the kitchen. Bob still stood by the door. Like all the Shoemakers he was taller than anyone in the Baker family. Joe continued eating. "Who you staying with now?" he asked Bob. "Your mother or your father?"

58

"Oh, back and forth. I'm getting an apartment with some guys. For the fall. I'll be at Woods Hole for the summer."

"How long have you had the car?" Elspeth asked Bob.

"Oh, half a year."

"Can I look at it?"

"Sure. Come on. It's not much but it runs."

She went out the back way with him. "I don't think I've seen you since Grammy's funeral," she said.

"I know. We see each other's parents but we don't see each other. That's how it is, when you grow up and get involved in things, I guess."

They walked over the front lawn, which came to a sudden slope near the street. His car's further fender had no paint, only a partly-sprayed coat of primer in shades of gray and brown. She saw that the lower edge of the body was jagged and rusting.

As she came near she felt a sudden nausea. She could not keep some vomit from erupting into her mouth. She pitched foward and spat it upon the sidewalk, bracing her arm against the car. Some got on the door of the car anyway. She stood, holding to the car, one hand against her forehead, panting, her eyes half shut. Spots of red and green seemed to float before her.

"What the hell," said Bob, supporting her arm. "Want me to help you back to the house? Can you make it?"

"No. I'll be okay in a second," she breathed.

"Well, sit down then." He opened the door of the car. She sat. She put her feet inside.

He found a rag and squatted to wipe the vomit from the door.

"You okay?" he asked.

She was still breathing hard. "Better. Thanks. Gee, I'm sorry. I didn't mean to puke on your car."

"Forget it. It's all cleaned off. You've got a stomach upset or something."

"No. I think I know what it is."

He found a box of tissues on a shelf under the dash.

"You want to sit? Or shall I help you back."

"I'll just sit. I'm not gonna throw up anymore."

She felt stronger. They sat a while in silence, side by side in the car. On both sides the windows were down.

"In case you heard I flunked out of Mount Holyoke," she said, "it isn't true."

"I didn't hear anything."

"Actually I'll probably finish the year with something like a 3 average. Or a little over. I'm taking my last final today. I'll be heading out there in a little while."

"Well, take it easy if you don't feel good. You've probably got a virus."

"No, it's passed already. It was just a sudden thing. Tell me about you, Bob. I hear you got a fellowship to MIT. Congratulations."

"Thanks. Ya, I was lucky."

"What field?"

"Marine biology."

"You mean like whales and porpoises?"

"That's part of it. I may even end up in the botanical side. I'm not sure. I want to study the ocean floor."

"And what's at Woods Hole?"

"A research institute. Harvard and MIT and the Coast Guard run it together."

"Oh. If you don't mind a personal question, are you gonna be wearing the potholder around Harvard and the Coast Guard and MIT?"

"Why not? They couldn't care less. It's my family that can't stand it."

"Bob." Elspeth paused. "You shouldn't stay away from the wedding."

"Diana doesn't need me at her wedding," he said. "She doesn't need me and she doesn't want me."

"Bob, she's your sister. Your only sister. I'd give anything for Eric and Mark to be alive. And if they were, nothing in the world could keep me from Mark's wedding, or Eric's. Don't you love your sister?"

He fingered the lowered window, not looking at Elspeth. "It's not enmity. When out paths cross we'll speak, or kiss. But our life-styles clash, from top to bottom."

"Don't you want to be an uncle to her children?"

"The whole script they'd write for me is wrong. My sister's family and I would be lonelier together than apart. And that's the truth. I'd be hurting and in little pieces. Better to be hurt and whole. There's a time when you have to be true to yourself, and go live with people who understand when you do your thing."

"How did you get into this thing?" she asked sadly.

"Well, I guess the germ of it was always in me. When I was a kid my parents used to say, 'Bob, it's better if you fall in love with a Jewish girl of course, but you do as your heart dictates, and if it happens that you fall in love with a Christian girl, we'll understand.' And I used to want to say, what kind of crap are you giving me, don't you know what that would do to Gramps? Ellie, you know what Gramps was like? He was completely lacking in the capacity to hate anybody. He didn't know what it was to disrespect another person. And he had universal curiosity. And I think the two things were related. Not learned, but blessed with curiosity about everything. I'd bring him my turtle, or show him my shells, and the way his eyes would light up when he'd learn a new fact. He'd notice everything. When I was feeding that baby bird he'd ask about it every day, the first thing. He was the only one. And that week when he was dying, in that little house in Winthrop, and I'd go see him every day practically. He was too weak to pray anymore. And I knew his whole life, all his dumb mistakes, and stories about when he was a kid. And half a block away, girls in bathing suits on the back seats of motorcycles were scooting up and down the Shore Drive with their legs in the air, so full of life and everything. And I knew that Gramps had forgotten more than these kids would ever know. And I knew there I was gonna be someday. No matter how long it took, I was gonna be dying, with all kinds of dumb booboos behind me, and no second chance, just like him. I was living my own death, in preview. But he had something to make sense of life, and I didn't. And when he died, and they shoveled the dirt on him, it was like I felt his spirit enter into me. I felt rotten that none of us knew how to say kaddish. I made up my mind I was gonna learn to say kaddish. Ellie, you remember all those old books Gramps had? That he'd sit with?"

"I never paid much attention. I know he had stuff. Those real old ones?"

"Well," said Bob, "I never knew just what they were either. But he kept trying to get my mother to send them to some certain place before he died, and I don't know what happened, she said the place didn't want them, or they never picked them up, but after he died she just put them out with the rubbish. He didn't just die, it was like they erased him. Nothing of his was around anymore. Not even the tablecloth."

"But, Bob, there's one more thing you should have learned from Gramps. He was never a fanatic. He was such a sharp-eyed little old man, and so cute. And we'd all come piling in the house in our bathing suits to change, and he could be in his tallis saying his prayers over by the wall there, and we'd be tracking in sand and making a racket, and it could even be Saturday, and he'd never reprimand us or get mad. He didn't impose his ways on us."

"Would he have gone to my sister's wedding?"

"Well, I don't know. No, I suppose he wouldn't have. But he was raised in a different age. Diana has her own life to lead."

"And I have mine. Ellie, it's like my steps were guided. I was partners with this froomie in the physics lab, and I asked him how long it would take me to learn to say kaddish. And he asked me, 'what do you want to say it for, if you don't even know what it means?' He said, 'you know how saying kaddish for your grandfather helps your grandfather? If it changes *your* life, then it makes sense of *his* life. That's all.' So I dropped it. But a week later I asked him again. And when I discovered a whole community, that really did it. I thought, my God, it's alive! I thought it all died before I was born. But it's alive! And I started learning. I asked them what should I learn first? And they said, the alphabet. So I learned the alphabet. And I kept going."

The broad garage door under the gray shingles was flung up in its track noisily from the inside.

"I don't know, Bob," Elspeth said. "I loved Gramps too. I didn't talk deep stuff with him, and I didn't have anything like shells to show him. But even when I was real little, I could be playing with my dolls there on the floor, and I'd say something, and he wouldn't act like a little kid said it. He'd take it seriously like a grown-up said it."

"Right. That was Gramps."

The van had backed out between the retaining walls. It rolled past the car in which they sat. SAWYER'S HARDWARE was lettered on the side and across the pair of rear doors.

"But his death affected me differently," said Elspeth. "Eric was barely seventeen, and Gramps was past ninety. And one died like the other. A guy of ninety you think escaped all the pitfalls, but it doesn't matter. Even if I have a baby, someday that baby's got to die and go into the same black hole. Whether you're good or whether you're bad, there's no light at the end of the tunnel. You get stepped on like an ant."

"Ellie, I don't know why we weren't made immortal. But it's not like that's the only thing I don't know. I don't know anything hardly. I don't know why you do things, or why my father and mother do things, or why Diana does things, or why I do things. So how am I supposed to know why the Creator of the universe does things? I know a little more than a horse or an elephant, that's all. But not that much more."

"Do you believe in a Creator? Seriously, Bob? Did you ever try praying? You might as well pray to the wind. Gramps prayed. Every day. And in the end he was too weak to pray."

"Did you ever write a letter to the President?" Bob asked.

"What? Yes. I did."

"And did you conclude that the President doesn't exist, because he didn't answer your prayer? I know you wrote him. You wrote him after Mark died, and begged him to get us the hell out of Vietnam. I did too. And went to Washington. There were busloads of us. Okay. Are we out of Vietnam?"

"No."

"Damn right, no. We're still up to our bloody necks in it. So if a shmuck like the President doesn't have to do what I ask, why should I think God has to do what I ask?"

He changed his position, slumping somewhat in the sweatshirt and resting his hands on the bottom of the steering wheel. Elspeth fingered the box of tissues upon her jeans.

"I go to these shiurim," he began again. "Study groups. But we don't study theology. We study how to live. How to be nice. It's not easy. And I took a course with a guy by the name of Ed Gordon, this rabbi from Wilmerding Crosswalk that came down to run this study group once a week, and he put it in focus for me. I love that guy. He made it possible for me intellectually. He said a man trying to think about God is like a horse trying to think about trigonometry. We don't have the capacity. We can philosophize forever, and we'll no more come up with a conception of God than a lobster will come up with the theory of relativity. So we don't know what we're talking about. All we can do is assume, rightly or wrongly, that there is such a thing as moral truth, how we ought to behave, and that it's discoverable. If we do, maybe the world will come to make sense. If we don't, it surely never will. He said Torah isn't like the religion of the Greeks, where they told you all about the private life of the gods, and what the gods did for kicks and who they slept with. And it's not like Christianity, where they can tell you here's the street corner where God took a left turn, and who His mother and His brother were. The Torah has no description of God. It tells you nothing about God. Except what God expects of us. That's all we know and all we need to know."

"Well," said Elspeth, "if there are Jesus freaks, I guess it's okay for there to be Yid freaks. But if you've really got this need to get into religion, and mysticism, the eastern religions are where it's at now."

"They're not my bag. The eastern religions make you not care. But this one chucks you right into the maelstrom."

"Any organized religion turns me off, actually," she said.

"I can understand that. But this is a disorganized one. I can get together with any nine of my buddies, without any charter or authority from anybody, and if we know how to put on the show with reasonable accuracy we're for real. And even if the greatest ninety-nine-year-old rabbi in the world happened to find himself in the neighborhood he'd have to admit we're fit to pray with, and it would be up to us whether to give him a special thing in the service or not. Nobody could ask for our credentials. The fact that we're doing it is our credentials."

"Bob, it divides you from people. Which is a hell of a thing when the world's getting smaller."

"No, it gives me a culture. And that makes it easier for me to relate to anybody who has a culture. Even if it's a very different culture. Everybody's looking for peoplehood. Blacks, French-Canadians, everybody. What else is there? This consumer society? My parents' idea of kicks was always to get a bunch of their mindless friends over and scream at each others' dumb dirty jokes. And I'm tired of fashionable noncommitment. I've known committed people. And at some point in your life you've got to decide who you want to be like. Whose style is gonna be yours. Or else you just unconsciously adopt the changing and drifting fashions of the mob, without even knowing it and without ever examining or reflecting."

Elspeth leaned to restore the box of tissues to the shelf under the dash. "How can you rationalize a thing like kosher food?" she asked him.

"Could you justify vegetarianism?" he answered.

"Yes."

"Well, if I'm not ready to be a vegetarian, at least I only eat animals that I know were slaughtered instantly and without pain, and not with the young in sight of their mother."

"Why don't you eat pig?"

"It's not just pig, Ellie. Kosher means that as far as ninety-nine-point-ninety-nine percent of the all the species are concerned, I'm already a vegetarian. Rabbits don't have to worry that I'm going to eat them. And neither do horses. And neither do the whales, that the whale-eaters are about to make extinct."

She turned to him. He looked at her. "Well, enough of that," she said. "I hear you've got a new girl."

"Yes." he smiled.

"What's her name?"

"Karen. Karen Slater. She's the most sensational thing that ever walked. I met Karen, and life began to make sense."

"Are you gonna get married?"

"Yup."

"When?"

"As soon as we can."

"I'm happy for you, Bob. I'd love to meet her."

"You will."

"What became of Emily?"

He glanced away. "I just couldn't make myself love Emily. I tried. I liked her okay, but not like that."

"If you'd made Emily pregnant, would you have married her?"

"Yeah. I would've. That's how I am, I guess. Unfortunately. Of course you don't really know how you'd react till you're actually in the situation. But if I started a life forming, I don't think I could then turn around and say no to it. That's why I stopped screwing her, actually. I was scared to death of getting stuck like that. We did have a scare. A false alarm. And she'd had an abortion once, before she knew me, and she said she didn't want to have another one. And I didn't say anything, but inside me I didn't want a kid of mine to be aborted either. And wow, was I glad when her period finally came. We went out and bought steak and champagne. And then I went to bed with her just a few more times to be polite, and then I said let's lay off and not take a chance. And of course she thought it was because I was beginning to get into the religion thing. And then she thought I was losing interest because we weren't going to bed anymore. I'd tell her no, it's not that, I was just unsure and I wanted to protect her, but I couldn't make her understand. I don't know, Ellie. Sex, to stay fresh over a period of time, it needs increasing amounts of love with it. And love needs values in common."

"Bob, I'm pregnant."

He turned to her again, but she kept her eyes from him, staring vacantly toward the dash.

"By a guy that doesn't want me," she added. "He hates me. He can't stand me." Her eyes watered, but she controlled herself.

Bob said nothing.

Elspeth reached under the dash for a tissue. She dried her eyes and blew her nose. "It wasn't like he lied to me or anything. He was honest about it. I asked him if he loved me, and he said no. And I asked him if he ever could love me someday, and he said you never know, it's possible but he couldn't guarantee it. But I was sort of ready, and I loved him and I wanted him, so I just made up my mind I was gonna make him love me. I don't know, Bob. Some days it doesn't pay to get up in the morning. You're crazy, and I'm stupid."

"What are you gonna do?"

"What can I do? Daddy's gonna talk to Mama's gynecologist about an abortion."

He took her hand to show that he was sorry. She still didn't look at him.

"I used a diaphragm," she said. "I don't know if the doctor didn't fit it right, or if I got careless and got in a hurry with it or what. I didn't think I did." Her hand rested limply in his. "Bob, don't tell your parents or Diana or anybody."

"I won't say anything."

"And don't let my parents know I told you. They've been great, but they're awfully hurt. It's getting to Daddy especially."

9

WHEN she arrived back at the house after the last of the exams the appointment had already been made for her with her mother's gynecologist. She sensed it before she was told. She had parked the Dart before the wide garage door, beside the van, flung a knee onto the retaining wall, raised herself up, and crossed the front lawn in her faded denim shorts. Harriet had opened the screen door and stood at the iron rail waiting for her, which she did not usually do, her face red and puffed as though from weeping.

"It's all set with Dr. Edelstein," Harriet's low and somewhat broken voice said to her as she entered. "You have to be at his office tomorrow morning at eight. I'll go with you. And he says you'll be fine, and you'll be able to walk out of his office and drive the car home."

Elspeth had known she would have to come to this point, that it would have to be done, but the dismal finality gave her a cold chill.

"In his office? Not in a hospital?"

"He does them in his office."

Joe said nothing. It was he who had phoned Dr. Edelstein and arranged it. But he sat over his supper, opposite Elspeth, without looking at anyone or speaking. He did not eat either. He slumped heavily in his chair, a hand to his stomach, staring fixedly at his plate of chicken salad as though it nauseated him. The evening sun slanted in above the sinks and shone on the maple-colored tabletop.

"Is it your ulcer?" Harriet asked him timidly.

"No!" he said angrily, without looking at her, as though the question were an irritation.

Harriet picked at her salad wet-eyed, sighing, looking at no one. After a moment she rose, took Joe's untouched salad away, and set a glass of milk before him. He didn't move.

Elspeth had no appetite either. She had studied very late the night before and even after she had gone to bed she kept dreaming the formulas she had studied and waking.

She had driven home from South Hadley overtired.

Now the gloom around the table reminded her of how it had been after the deaths of Eric and Mark.

Joe pushed away from the table without a word or a glance.

Harriet slowly loaded the dishwasher, seeming to have no strength to look at

Elspeth or speak to her. Harriet pressed the button, her back to her. The noise of the dishwasher seemed to grate.

"Mama, I'm gonna go to bed too. I'm so tired. I stayed up and crammed for that exam half the night, and I'm a wreck."

"All right."

She buttoned her pajamas and fell gratefully into the lower bunk. The room was dim and outdoors it was twilight. She felt her exhaustion submerging her into sleep.

When she woke it was dark. In a moment the tired strain was there again behind her eyes and the jumpy anxiousness was all through her. She knew she had slept only a few hours.

She lay, hoping sleep would drift back.

What a seedy end to those beautiful first encounters with Jared, of which she had remembered and cherished every word.

And what a seedy beginning to her adult life.

At midnight she climbed from the lower bunk to the upper. It didn't help. She still heard every hour and every half hour, first the faint chime downstairs, lingering till you could not tell exactly when it died away, and then the deep bong a few feet from her door.

Reality was a horrible thing. Hopes and dreams were better. But they shielded you only for a time. She remembered Bob talking in his car yesterday about Gramps's death. Gramps lying in the earth, and Aunt Frieda dumping his treasured books in the trash. Everything comes eventually to an ugly end.

Even those poor fantasies about Jared coming back, that had sustained her these past few days—with word that she would go to Dr. Edelstein tomorrow they had come to a sudden end.

In the darkness a mosquito hummed. She lay still. The mosquito hummed again, close at her ear. She held her breath, waiting as though in ambush. The hum quieted suddenly. She felt the tiny sting, and gave it a split second more to become stuck, engrossed. With precise timing she slapped it dead.

She heard the rustling of the maple tree. Far off in Winslow Center the horn on the fire station mooed a call, several evenly spaced sounds, a pause, and some more. From long habit she counted them. A single alarm in Bobolink Acres. Nothing much. Eric had known the signal and location of every call box in the town of Winslow, so she had learned them too. She heard the distant wail of a lone fire engine.

At three o'clock she smoked a cigarette on the toilet. Then she tried the lower bunk again.

Sometime after four the night began to fade. She heard twitterings. She began to cry, voicelessly. She let the tears come. Maybe crying it out would ease the jumpiness. She lay in the dawning light, wetting the pillow, her breath broken by heaves and sobs.

When she thought it was finished she tried again to sleep. She turned the pillow over and lay holding a crushed handkerchief near her mouth. Quivering sobs shook her again.

66

After five o'clock she gave up trying to sleep. She clicked off the little alarm clock she had set for six.

She washed her face, running the tap in a slow thin stream so as not to wake her parents. She took a suppository that Harriet had told her Dr. Edelstein had ordered.

She wandered downstairs again, and out the back, closing the screen gently. It was light as day, but without harshness. The mowed grass was ticklish beneath her feet and moistened the bottom edges of pajama leg. The houses to either side, and up the hill to the back, were completely silent, as though the earth were no longer inhabited.

Her mother's squash vines were spreading over their part of the garden. They were in flower. Drops of dew lay on their leaves. Her mother meant to put in tomato plants again this year, but they were still small, in boxes of earth by the back doorstep. Their stakes had been brought up from the cellar and leaned in a bundle by the back fence.

All at once pink sunlight flooded sharply amid shadows on the gray of the house.

Elspeth wiped her bare soles on the bristly mat and returned upstairs. She combed the long reddish hair, seated before the three reflections of herself at the vanity. The tears welled again, occasionally jarring her with a silent hiccupy spasm. She kept combing. It was time to tear away that snap of Jared and the snow house from its place at the corner of the mirror and crumple it. But she couldn't yet. She didn't look at it.

She combed the other side. She had to face this day, come through this day. Put it behind her. But she had a foreboding that she would never forget. Even when she married, and had children, she feared she would remember this time, this circumstance, this first time she conceived.

She found a fresh pair of faded denim shorts. She checked the back of them in the triple mirror. She pulled the raggedy edges.

She sat on the front steps, between the iron railings, to wait for the newspaper. The denim shorts were tight like underwear.

The kid came coasting on his bike, his face a mass of freckles. He flung the folded newspaper in a high curve. Elspeth leaped up, ran on the sloping lawn, and caught it above her head with one hand.

"I could use you at second base," the boy said. He leaned with his bike and swerved down the hill.

Elspeth sat on the steps and read the headlines. Then she folded it back and read the funnies, and the ongoing colloquy among the anonymous readers who shared their troubles in the Chit Chat, and Ann Landers.

She had started the coffee perking in the kitchen when Harriet appeared, somewhat red-eyed. "Hi," Elspeth said.

"Dr. Edelstein doesn't want you to have breakfast," said Harriet. "You're supposed to be empty."

"I know. I don't think he'll mind my having coffee though."

"I know you didn't sleep much," Harriet said. "I kept hearing you. Did you sleep at all?"

"Not much, I guess. I should have. I didn't sleep much the night before."

"Are you all right?"

"I'm a little light-headed," Elspeth answered. "But I guess I'll be okay when I've had some coffee. I better have two cups though. Or maybe three. I'll see how I am."

Harriet sat heavily in her robe.

"You can eat, Mama. You don't have to starve on my account."

"No. I can't eat a thing at this hour."

"Did you sleep?"

"Oh, off and on," said Harriet. "I kept having dreams." She watched Elspeth sip the coffee.

"I don't want anesthesia," Elspeth said. "Does he use anesthesia?"

"I don't know. I suppose you can ask him for a local."

They left early.

The Dart backed out from its place beside the van. "Was Daddy awake yet when you came down?"

"No," said Harriet.

"He was, probably. Pretending. He'll probably get up as soon as he's sure I've left."

Elspeth turned the radio to the traffic report.

"Dr. Edelstein is coming in early specially to take care of you," said Harriet. "It's the only way he could fit you in. He's very good, you know. He's right in the neighborhood with all the hospitals. His whole building is all doctors."

For a long time they spoke little. As they neared Boston their progress slowed, cars and trucks crowding on either side. Harriet tried to adjust the radio and the knob fell off. She bent to feel for it on the floor.

"Let it go," said Elspeth. "We'll find it later."

"I thought we should tell the doctor to put it down as appendicitis," Harriet said, "for the medical insurance. But Daddy said no. Because if God forbid you ever really did get appendicitis, then we'd be in trouble." She sighed. Elspeth saw that her eyes had watered.

They arrived while there were still places to park along the curb.

"At nine," Elspeth said in the elevator, "you go down and put a dime in the meter, okay?"

"Okay."

"Will we still be here at nine? How long are these things supposed to take?"

"I have no idea," said Harriet. "He said you'll be able to drive home, but maybe he'll want you to rest a while. Especially if you've had a local anesthetic."

In the waiting room they were met by a tall middle-aged nurse, unsmiling and skinny, but with loose pale skin at the jowls and neck, and dark hollows under her eyes. She wore a black cardigan sweater over the starched white. Harriet knew her. "The doctor's here," the woman said. "He's just getting ready. Why don't I take down the history meanwhile. Have a seat."

Harriet sat. Elspeth took the chair next to her. There was a low table of magazines. Elspeth gave an involuntary shiver.

68

The skinny sour-faced woman had seated herself sideways behind the desk. She rolled a form into the typewriter. Elspeth gave another shudder. She massaged her arms. She was still in the faded denim shorts. Her thighs were all goose pimples. She told the woman how to spell Elspeth.

"Middle initial?"

"A. Is the air conditioning on?"

"Do you want the air conditioning on?"

"No. I want it off. I'm freezing."

"It's centrally controlled. I don't think they turn it on this early. Address?"

Elspeth told the address, though she supposed they must already have it somewhere for Harriet. Then date of birth. Occupation. Medical insurance. Person responsible for payment of bills.

The woman read a list of diseases and conditions, one by one, not looking away from the form, and manipulating the typewriter carriage this way and that for yes or no.

Harriet had opened a magazine upon her lap but wasn't reading it. She watched the interview watery-eyed. She helped answer about measles, chicken pox, whooping cough, inoculations.

"Ringing or buzzing in the ears?"

"I think maybe once. I was like about three years old."

"You never told me that," said Harriet.

"I didn't care. It sounded nice."

The doctor opened a door and looked in, wearing a smock. He seemed a slight, bony little man, younger than Harriet, bushy-haired, a little pop-eyed behind metal-rimmed glasses, with thin red blood vessels on a big pointed nose, and a bushy little mustache and a small chin. He darted quick smiles to Harriet and to Elspeth.

Harriet rose, the open magazine sliding to the floor, and unsnapped her purse. "Oh. Doctor. I have your check." She took it out folded, but Elspeth recognized it as a big pink one from the Sawyer's Hardware checkbook.

"Oh, that's all right," he said, waving her away.

"No, my husband gave me the check. He said he wanted to take care of it right away."

He accepted it sheepishly and put it into a pocket of the smock without looking at it. He threw Elspeth another of his nervous little smiles and wheeled about, his smock knocking some papers from a corner of the desk. He disappeared through the same door, his smock billowing behind.

The tall frowning woman stopped and retrieved the papers from the carpet. When she had straightened them on the desk she turned to Elspeth. "You can come with me now."

Elspeth followed her through the inner door, leaving Harriet in her chair.

They entered a corridor with several doors, but the woman ushered her into the first one. It was a spacious examining room. There was a leathery examining table with a fresh sheet of tissue paper lying the length of it, and raised stirrups.

69

The woman put down a thick folded square of linen. "Undress completely, and put on the gown. And we'll want a urine sample."

Then the woman left.

There was an adjoining water closet for the urine sample.

Elspeth left her clothes upon a chair, and her sneakers and socks beneath it. The linen gown was over-large. She found the tie at her shoulder blades and managed a bow. But the lower tie seemed to have one string missing.

The woman returned and had Elspeth stand on a scale. She moved the weights, and wrote on a card. She lowered the rod to measure Elspeth's height, saying nothing. She picked up the container from the water closet and disappeared once more. Elspeth climbed on the footstool and sat on the edge of the leathery table, her legs dangling. She massaged the goose pimples on her arms. The room had a variety of cabinets and equipment, including some tall iron tanks of gas with meters on top. There were long fluorescent lights overhead, and no windows at all. On the wall were framed photocopies of the same diplomas she had seen hanging in the waiting room. She let her teeth chatter noisily a moment. She let her feet swing.

The woman returned and Elspeth opened her mouth to receive the thermometer. The woman pricked her ear for a blood sample. Elspeth, with the thermometer still in her mouth, saw her seal a little tube of bright red blood. The woman wrapped a blood-pressure gauge on Elspeth's arm and pumped it tight. She wrote things on the card. She took the thermometer from Elspeth's lips and read it.

"When are we gonna get on with it?" Elspeth said. The shivering betrayed itself in her voice. "I mean, what's all this business for? Like what's my height got to do with it?"

"You've never seen Dr. Edelstein before. In a first visit he always does a complete examination." She took Elspeth's wrist as though to count her pulse. She changed her hold a few times as though having trouble.

The doctor came in. He looked down at Elspeth, the fluffy brown mustache making the same little smile about his big nose. A stethoscope hung from his neck. He turned a chair backwards and straddled it. The woman let go the wrist and stood by. "How do you know you're pregnant?" Dr. Edelstein said.

"We had a drugstore test," said Elspeth. "They sent it to a lab. That's after I missed the first period. And then I missed two more."

"You're shivering. Are you cold? Or just nervous?"

"Maybe both."

"A little of both?" he smiled.

"A lot of both. Listen, don't give me anesthesia, okay? Just a local if you have to. But don't put me to sleep."

"You don't like anesthesia?"

"Well, it's unnatural."

"Unnatural?" He looked at her quizzically.

"Listen, it scares me. Okay? Don't put me to sleep. I've heard some awful things. A girl in my dorm had a cyst removed and they goofed with the anesthesia and she almost died. She was in the hospital for months. All last fall and winter. The anesthesia was worse than the disease. I heard about a guy that had a spinal and he came out paralyzed."

"You knew someone that was paralyzed by a spinal tap? Or an injection?"

"Not somebody I knew. Somebody that knew somebody."

"Nothing like that will happen to you. Don't worry. How many periods did you say you've missed?"

"Three." One leg was swinging rapidly and the other a little, not in phase with it.

"Hm." He frowned. "Your father gave me the impression you weren't that far along."

"It's three, actually. Because the third would be now. Normally. Why? Does it make a difference?"

"Any other symptoms? Morning sickness? Nausea? Vomiting?"

"I puked yesterday. All over my cousin's car."

"On rising in the morning?"

"Well, I'd been up like an hour or so."

"Was that the only time?"

"Well, I puked one other time. But I was sloshed, and I was riding a horse. Does that count?" She was hugging her arms.

The woman handed him a large card on which she had noted data. He studied it.

"What about it being three?" Elspeth asked him. "Would you have arranged to do it in a hospital if you'd known it was three?"

He looked up over the card as though distracted. "What? No. No difference." He gave the woman the card and slipped the stethoscope to his ears, getting off the backwards chair and turning it about properly. He put the disc of the stethoscope to Elspeth on the gown, just beneath a breast.

"Then why'd you get worried when I told you three?"

He moved the stethoscope higher, here and there along the edges of a breast, without answering. She waited for his answer, and then realized he did not intend to answer. The stethoscope moved lower.

"Does it depress you?" she said. "I mean, what I'm here for. Doing these things?"

"Depress me?" he said, somewhat curtly, busy with the stethoscope, not looking up. "Should it?"

"I'd think it would give you the willies," she told him. "It sure would depress me. I think I'd get nightmares."

He put the stethoscope lower still.

"Can you hear the baby?" she asked. "Can you hear its heart beating?"

He shifted the stethoscope a couple of inches, and then again.

"I want to hear it," she said. "Let me listen."

"Turn around."

She bent her knees sideways on the leathery table and turned herself part way around.

He put the stethoscope to her back. "The fetal heartbeat wouldn't be audible this early. Cough."

She coughed.

He moved the stethoscope. "Cough."

She coughed. "You mean it's beating even though you can't hear it?"

He moved it again. "Cough." She coughed once more. He lay the stethoscope on the black shiny surface that topped the lower cabinets behind him. He put a hand to her shoulder and the other to her knee and turned her toward him. Again her legs dangled. He turned her head and shone a little light into her ear.

"Does the fetus come out whole, or in pieces?" she asked. He kept peering. "I mean, like in one piece," she said, "or all mashed up?"

He turned her head the other way and she felt the metal point of his light poking in her other ear.

"How do you dispose of it? Just chuck it in the garbage, like with stuff from your lunch and everything?"

"Why do you ask these things? What do you want to do, put it in a bottle and take it home like gallstones? Put it on the mantelpiece? Now keep your eyes on Miss Spencer, whichever way I turn your head." He was shining the light now closely into her left eye. He had cupped a thumb and finger lightly about her chin.

She kept her gaze on a button of Miss Spencer's black sweater as he moved her head from side to side. She was massaging her goose pimples slowly. The tiny bright light at her eyeball made Miss Spencer and everything else dim, but she did not lose sight of the button. He switched the light to her other eye. "I wouldn't flush it down the toilet if I were you," she managed to tell him, though he held her chin. "The fetus, I mean. A thing like that could clog."

He put aside the light. Her shivering became more uncontrollable. He turned to the black surface behind him and took up a hammer with a triangular rubber head. Her body gave a great shudder. She was glad he hadn't seen it. She glanced to see if Miss Spencer had noticed. The woman stood watching, arms folded.

The hammer struck Elspeth under the kneecap. It hit her again. Her foot swung up.

"What if the police find it? The fetus?"

"Don't worry about it." He hit the other knee.

"But it's not really legal yet. Not till they pass the bill."

"That's not your worry. There's no risk, or I wouldn't do it."

"Why is there no risk, if it's not really legal?" Her voice shook with her. "What if the week before the bill passes they pull a surprise raid and go through your garbage pail?"

"Listen, sister," he said irritably, looking at her. "What's the matter with you? I'm doing you a favor, you're not doing me a favor. I don't need this. In the first place, we all do it. And everybody knows they're gonna pass that bill. And finally, if you want to get technical, all I have have to do is ask another doctor to say we consulted, it's for your health, and that makes it all legal and shmegal. All right? Believe me, I know my business or I wouldn't be in business. So don't tell me about legal and shmegal. Lie down. Put your feet up in the stirrups. I think we better give you something to quiet you. Calm you."

Except for the shaking she didn't move. "Are you giving me a local? Who gives it to me? You? Or her?"

"Miss Spencer will give you a little injection. You'll hardly feel it."

"Is she a licensed anesthesiologist? That's the most dangerous part. In any operation. Anesthesia's a special specialty—"

His eyes had moved to the woman. "We're gonna have to knock her out," he muttered from the side of his mouth. "There's no other way. We've got to get this over with." He turned as if to go.

"Shall I set up the IV?"

"Set it up. I'll be back in a minute. Give her the needle first though."

Elspeth stared at the back of his smock as he left. Something made her turn suddenly and she saw Miss Spencer holding a glass syringe with a long slender needle. She drew back with a start. "No! No!"

"It's just something to relax your nerves."

"No! I told him not to! You're gonna knock me out! I heard him! No!"

"Now see here, young lady—" With one hand Miss Spencer seized an arm and with the other she seemed to poise the needle.

Elspeth screamed with all the power of her lungs. She batted Miss Spencer's hand. The syringe flew from it as the doctor burst in. It shattered against the baseboard. Elspeth screamed again. She leaped to the floor and threw him aside, running to the corridor and the waiting room, doors banging open to their doorstops. He came after her.

"Get out!" he shouted in the waiting room. "Get out! I don't need this! Do I need this? Get out!"

There was another patient there, a stout lady a few chairs from Harriet. She dropped her magazine and stared. Harriet rose, her mouth open. Elspeth wheeled about in the middle of the carpet gaping, to see if he had cornered her with nothing on but the flimsy open-backed linen. He had disappeared.

But he at once reappeared in the doorway holding her clothes. He threw the denim shorts at her. "Get out!" He flung the bra. Elspeth backed into Harriet. He looked wild-eyed, the glasses askew. He threw the shirt. "Get out of here! Get out!" He threw the underpants but they billowed with air and fell limply before him. He was gone for an instant, but then rushed back, framed in the doorway, throwing socks and sneakers. "I need this? I need this? Jesus! I've seen it all!" Elspeth raised a hand and a sneaker bounced from it. "She's crazy! She doesn't want a gynecologist, she wants a psychiatrist! Get out! I'll call the police! Here! Take your check!" He snatched it from the pocket of his smock and tore it again and again and again. He threw it. The pieces fluttered aimlessly in the air.

10

IN the elevator Harriet pressed the button and the door slid shut. "What got into you?" she asked.

"I don't know," Elspeth said, not looking at her.

The drive from Boston to Winslow took forty minutes, and they said nothing the whole way. Harriet rode slumped, her face flushed, eyes closed. She looked drained, exhausted.

Elspeth raised the wide garage door. They entered the house by the basement stairs. "I'm gonna have to call Daddy and tell him," Harriet sighed. "I don't know what he'll say."

In the kitchen Elspeth munched a doughnut and drank milk. The tension of driving and the odor and vibration of the highway seemed to have remained in her head. "Mama, I'm just gonna go upstairs and sleep," she said. "So don't even wake me for lunch. Okay? I'm ready to drop. I haven't had a wink in two nights. That's probably what the trouble was."

Harriet said nothing.

Elspeth closed the door of her room, pulled off her sneakers, and stretched out on the lower bunk. She unsnapped the frayed denim shorts. Her half-closed eyes gazed passively at Mark's high-school diploma, on the wall above the chest of drawers by the closed door. Then they fixed drowsily on a line of soft flickering sunbeams, made by the crack alongside the drawn windowshade and the leaves outside, and reflected from the vanity.

When she wakened the sunbeams were gone, the quality of light was quite different, and the air was stiller and stuffier. Outdoors there was a clink of garden tools. Elspeth raised the windowshade. Down in the yard she saw Harriet upon her knees, under the big straw hat, digging holes for the tomato plants. The weeds she had pulled lay in bunches. The afternoon sun was on the wide linen shorts and the veiny legs.

Elspeth put on her sneakers and went downstairs.

"I'll do that, Mama," she said, coming out at the back step. "Why don't you go in and rest."

Harriet looked up, panting, red-faced with the warmth. "All right. If you want to."

Elspeth squatted. She worked with the little spade. The reddish hair hung straight down on both sides of her face and tickled her thighs. The sun was hot on her

74

forearms. She heard the screen door spring shut behind Harriet.

She glanced at the boxes to count the plants. She dug. The soil here was good. Rich with dead roots, crawling with pink angleworms. Moist. Black. Like the walls of a grave.

She had died in childbirth. Jared came to the funeral. She saw her body lowered into the ground. There goes the last of the three, Jared heard her father say.

Elspeth moved forward in the garden and continued digging. Her parents of course did not know Jared. He remained inconspicuously on the outer fringe of the little crowd at the cemetery, with the collar of his raincoat turned up, his face averted, fearful that someone might see the tears running down his face. If they saw his grief they would guess who he was, and Joe might pick up a shovel and break his skull.

She set a tomato plant into its hole. Tears were wetting her cheeks too, and fell on her warm hands while she patted the soil around the root.

The grandparents grew white-haired and feeble. Jennifer was their sole support. Jennifer ran Sawyer's Hardware all by herself now. Proud, soft-spoken, erect of posture, seventeen years old. She never tired of asking her aged grandparents or Cousin Robert to tell her about her mother, how good her mother had been, how she had lacked the capacity to hate another person. And after store hours Jennifer studied hard, intending to go to law school at night, and run for Congress, and help do something about this messy world. She wanted to pass a law to protect the whales. Cousin Robert had told her how they were almost extinct.

Elspeth rose and surveyed the plants. She was massaging the stiffness behind her knees when she heard the van pull up in front. She heard her father lift the garage door while she raced into the house and up the stairs. She shut her door and lay on the lower bunk again.

When Harriet came to call her for supper she said she wasn't hungry. And too tired.

"Really? You didn't have any lunch. You're afraid to face Dad is what you mean."

"Mama, I had two sleepless nights. I'm bushed. Okay? I'll eat when I'm hungry."

Harriet left her, closing the door. Elspeth turned once more to the wall. She heard all the noises of supper. She was a little hungry actually, but she didn't move.

After a while she heard the churning of the dishwasher, and the slam of the screen and the clunk of the iron cover over the underground garbage pail. And at last her father's tread on the stairs.

He knocked and looked in. She rolled on the bunk and looked at him, her eyes slightly moist. He put the unlit, half-smoked cigar in his mouth, took the chair slowly from her varnished table, and turned it toward her. He sat. He lowered the dead cigar to his crossed knees.

"I don't know if you're crazy or what," he said. "What's the matter with you? Are you crazy?"

"I don't know."

"What am I gonna do with you?"

She made no answer.

"If you didn't want to go through with it, you could have told me." He put the cigar in his mouth, looking at her, and took it out again. "I could arrange it with another doctor. In a hospital. Edelstein doesn't want any part of you—he wouldn't touch you with a ten-foot pole. But if I arrange it with anyone else now, I've got to know definitely that you're going through with it this time. You're not gonna run out again. Because I don't want to set it up if you're just gonna make an idiot out of eveybody again. You're gonna have to promise and you're gonna have to mean it. Otherwise forget it. I've had it."

She lay there looking at him. He took the cigar and pointed with it.

"I'll tell you one thing, Elspeth, if you're gonna have this baby, I'm gonna hit that Blumenthal kid so hard with a paternity suit he won't know what hit him. Maybe that's what you want. Maybe Blumenthal was right—you're out to blackmail the kid. Maybe you think if you have the baby he'll start to feel for you and come back to you. Because let me tell you something—" Joe shook his head. "—if that's what's in your mind, it's a hell of a long-shot gamble, that's my opinion. You're taking an awful chance. It rarely works. That boy's had plenty of opportunity and he hasn't shown the least bit of interest. Not even a God damn phone call. My guess is he won't marry you. I'll slap him with a summons, but my instinct is he'd rather pay you off. Maybe you think otherwise, but I doubt it. And then what do you do? You're stuck. You can't keep the baby. What're you gonna do, saddle me and Mama with a child to bring up all over again in our old age? I'm in the store six full days. And your mother's no spring chicken anymore. She's not a well woman, to go chasing a little tot around. Don't you think we've earned a little rest? You're gonna have to give it out for adoption. You can't bring it up yourself. You've got three more years of college. What do you want, a life of poverty, supporting a fatherless kid in day-care centers? For God's sake, Elspeth. So you carry it to term, and give it away to an agency, if that's what you want. So what's the use of six more months of pregnancy and a big belly? Wouldn't it have made more sense to get rid of it this morning, when the doctor was ready? You can't go back to classes next fall with a big belly. You'll be huge by then. And by the time you have the baby it'll be too late to go back to school till the following year. A whole year lost. For what. For nothing."

He put the cigar in his mouth, took it out, and spat a bit of tobacco.

"So what do you want?" he said. "What do you want?"

"I don't know." Her eyes had filled.

"Don't know. Well, you better know. It's not a pretty bunch of choices, is it. All I ever asked of you is that you not mess your life up. That you use your head, grow up. Give yourself a chance. I can't be with you forever, protecting you forever. Well, you've made your bed now. You figure it out. Figure out which kind of heartache you want. Come to work in the store, and make up your mind what you want to do. So I'll know whether to look for another doctor, or call the agencies, or what." He sighed, and rose to go. "But make it up fast. The longer you wait the bigger the medical problem if you want to get rid of it."

At the door, with his hand on the knob, he turned toward her once more. She was still looking at him.

"Give me a kiss," he said, "okay?"

She sprang from the bunk and ran to him. She hugged him tight, pressing her wet cheek to his. The hand that held the cigar embraced her about the shoulders. His other hand gave the rounded tight back of the denim a spank.

"That's a nice toshy," he said. "My favorite toshy. Too bad you couldn't have saved it for a boy who'd appreciate it." He gave it another pat.

"You're a good daddy," she said, her face buried in his neck. "I don't know how you put up with me."

"How can I not put up with you? If you dish it out I have to take it. Who else am I living for? All right. Come down now. Have some supper."

In the morning, when she had combed her hair, she remained at the vanity and braided it. Braids were convenient when she worked at the store. The snap of Jared, grinning in his parka and his tilted knit cap in front of the snow house, was in the corner of the center mirror. She stuck her tongue out at him. She thumbed her nose at him. She stuck out her tongue again, long and undulating, with the ugliest grimace she could manage, and thrust up a middle finger.

She went down to breakfast. Joe glanced up from his cereal. "You coming to the store?"

"Yes. I guess so."

"Haven't you got a more presentable pair of slacks?"

"Well, the striped ones are short in the leg the last couple of years, and I got grape juice on the white ones."

"So put on a skirt then. Or a dress. Look decent. You can't wait on trade in jeans. It's a place of business."

Elspeth went back up. She found the pale green shirt dress her father liked.

She rode beside him in the van. "I'm glad to have you back," he told her. "You just can't get good help. Mama came in and helped out a little during the winter, when Homer was laid up."

"I know."

"She was more trouble than she was worth. She had to ask me everything."

At the bottom of the S-curve he paused at the stop sign and turned right onto Peacemaker Avenue. The van slowed, and would not accelerate. Then its strength returned.

"It seems to fade sometimes," Joe said. "Check it out for me when you get a chance, will ya?"

"I noticed that," said Elspeth. "I think it's the coil."

"Will you take care of it for me?"

"Sure."

He parked in one of the diagonal spaces before the store. He disconnected the burglar alarm with a key, and unlocked the door. The bell jingled when he opened it. "Line up the mowers outside, will you?"

Elspeth wheeled the power lawnmowers out to the sidewalk, and arranged them before the window in order of their price tags. Meanwhile the awning unfolded above her head.

Sawyer's Hardware was both wide and deep, with long narrow aisles hemmed in by drawers, shelving trays, pegboards, cubbyholes and bins. She was crouching at a drawer near the floor, matching galvanized bolts for a customer and fitting them to nuts and lock washers, when Homer Lathrop arrived, and did not have a chance to greet him, but she noticed that he did not hold himself as erect as formerly.

"Good to see you in braids again," Homer smiled when she finished with the customer. But a sixtyish round-shouldered man in a seersucker suit had wandered to her, carrying a rolled windowshade taller than himself.

"Can I help you?" she asked the new customer.

"Well, I don't know. This is the shade from our picture window. It won't go up anymore—I guess the spring's gone—it came from the Awning and Blind place over in Crowe, where I live, and they say it don't pay to replace the spring. So I thought first I'd come over here and ask you people if you can just put in a spring. Because it's gonna cost me thirteen-fifty if they have to make up a whole new one."

"Let's see it," said Elspeth. "You came all the way from Crowe?"

"North Crowe. I don't have occasion to get to Winslow much. But I remember you people fixed a toaster for me once, that nobody else could fix."

With thumb and forefinger Elspeth was twisting the little flat projection at the long roller's end. When she let it go it spun quickly. She wound it again.

"These big ones have to be made to order," the man said. "They cost an arm and a leg."

"The spring's fine," said Elspeth. "But the doohickies aren't falling into place to catch the ratchet. See?" She showed him, pushing them with a finger, and he stared as though bewildered. "Wait a minute," she said.

She carried the pole wrapped in its shade to the workbench where Joe was measuring and cutting glass. She squatted by his legs and rummaged in the low shelves.

"What are you looking for there?" Joe asked.

"Have you got any carbon tet open?"

"There should be. A yellow can there. Maybe behind something."

She rose with it, and rinsed the end of the roller with a few drops of the reeking liquid, until the sticky parts moved easily and fell when turned over. She wound the spring again and it held. She released it, and tested it again, until she was sure that either pawl would hold the ratchet. She brought the wound shade back to the man in the seersucker.

"It's just fine," she said. "You stick it back in your window rolled up and it should work now. And don't ever lubricate it. It looked to me like somebody gummed it with household oil."

"Well, I did, after it stopped working."

"Then it must have just gotten a little sticky from dust, or moisture, or bug juice. Who knows? You had a sticky doohicky."

"Well, fine. What do I owe you?"

"Nothing. There was nothing the matter with it. All I did was clean that end of it."

"Well, you people are really wonderful!"

"We try to be," Joe said, looking around from the workbench with a smile.

"I couldn't let you throw away a mechanism that's so precisely formed and functioning so beautifully," said Elspeth. "See how it works? Centrifugal force keeps the doohickies open at the right time and gravity locks them at the right time. It's ingenious. It's like a living organism. Okay? Have a nice day."

She began to turn her attention to another customer, but the man with the big windowshade spoke again.

"Tell me," he said, "are you the little girl with braids I saw here years ago, that used to stand on a box to reach the cash register?"

"Yes. That was me."

"Well! My goodness. A lot of water has gone under the bridge since then."

"That's right, sir. A lot of crap has gone down the trap."

"My, my."

Customers always seemed to come in bunches. For a while the store would be empty, though even then Elspeth would have sorting to do and Joe would do a little of the bookkeeping while Homer worked on inventory. Then there would be many people with Joe and Homer and Elspeth all waiting on trade and the bell that hung on the door jangling every moment. Elspeth admired her father's knack of paying attention to several persons at once, telling one where to look for what he wished while he fetched something for another and promised to explain some technique to a third. At lunchtime Elspeth twice had to put down her sandwich unfinished.

Late in the day Homer asked her to climb one of the sliding wall ladders that rode on rails. He needed certain sizes of lead plugs that were used to shield screws in mortar. He said the doctor had told him not to go that high on the ladders because he had attacks of vertigo.

When she had ascended into the warm air near the ceiling she glimpsed Homer's snowy head below, maneuvering for a view of her underpants.

He knew more or less where the lead shields were, and stood directly under her looking up, pretending to concentrate on the little wooden drawers she pulled from the wall, telling her to try this one and now that one. She thought of leaning her body to the ladder, so that the dress would fall shut against her back and be pressed to her by the steps in front. But when she tried it it was awkward. There was nothing she could do. From the height she surveyed the store to see where Joe was. She saw his bald head far away, busy on the telephone, beyond the cash register and the revolving rack of key blanks, where the short counter angled near the cellar stairs. There was no way Joe could notice. She tried to press a thigh to the ladder to keep the fabric close. But the dress was cut quite full at the bottom and as she searched the wooden drawers it widened.

Homer checked the length and thickness of each shield she handed down against a variety of screws he held, and passed it up to her again. She shut one drawer and opened another. She knew that as soon as she turned her attention to them he looked up. She knew also that he thought he was being quite circumspect, that he thought she was unaware.

There was no way to reprimand him. She couldn't embarrass him. He was old. He had worked for Daddy for longer than she could remember. His great-grandfather had been the Unitarian minister or an Abolitionist or something, and he had some ancestral connection to the Uzziah Lathrop House that the Winslow Historical Society was restoring.

The customer moved closer to Homer for a better view also. She knew which panties she had on. They were clinging and rose-tinted, with the slightest edging of beige-colored lace. She wondered how much they had ridden up.

As soon as Joe had locked the door and turned the key that connected the burglar alarm he lighted a cigar.

While she rode home beside him she undid her braids. "Daddy, I'm gonna have to wear pants in the store. When I go up the ladder customers can see right up my skirt."

"Oh. Well, wear pants then. You'll have to wear the jeans, I guess, meanwhile. Till you get yourself some decent slacks."

"I should have remembered."

"Don't wear the oldest ones. Try to wear some that aren't all faded and worn out."

The day's work had tired her, as though she had grown unused to it. In the evening she lay in her underwear on the lower bunk, with her feet raised on the crossbar. She dozed off, though she hadn't meant to. When she woke it was nearly ten. She rose, and did her accumulated laundering. It was past eleven when she went to bed. The house was dark and quiet.

She heard the pendulum miss a tick. It missed another, and then stopped altogether.

"Daddy, are you awake? You forgot to wind the clock."

"I guess I did," his voice said from the master bedroom.

"I'll do it."

In the hallway she clicked on the light. She found the key on top of the tall clock. While she was winding Joe came sleepily in his pinstriped pajamas from the master bedroom.

"It's because your favorite wayward daughter's on your mind," she said. "It's my fault. I give you problems."

"Sweetheart, I *wish* you could give me the problems. What gets me is that you give your*self* problems. Sometimes you're impulsive or something. You don't think things through. Though I don't know. I always thought things through and it didn't help much."

She restored the key and closed the glass over the face. "Come on down to the kitchen and I'll make us some warm milk," she said. "It'll help you sleep. And it's good for ulcers."

She flavored the milk with honey. She sat opposite him at the maple-colored table.

"I've got some things that need mending," he said. "If you'll do them it'll save Mama's eyes."

"Sure."

"Shall I just leave them in the sewing room?"

"No, give them to me tomorrow night. If you leave them there Mama will do them."

He was looking at her in her nightie. "How can that boy not love you? He's got to be crazy."

"There's no accounting for tastes."

She returned to the lower bunk. If I'm not asleep in half an hour I'll switch to the upper, she thought.

She listened to the tick tock. When they had brought that clock from the Green Stamp store Daddy and Mark and Eric had had a big argument about where to put it. Mark and Eric said the right place for a grandfather clock was the entrance foyer downstairs, where everyone would see it.

She thought of how Mark and Eric would build a throne of sand for her at Winthrop Beach when she was little, and play that she was the queen, and they were her generals.

It was as though, instead of resenting Daddy's favoring of their little sister, they identified thoroughly with his conviction that a little girl was the most wonderful thing in the world.

When all the neighborhood boys had built a tree house with a no-girls rule, Elspeth had been the sole exception. Mark and Eric had made the others accept her. So the tree-house gang had been a tribe of cannibals, and Elspeth had been their mysterious white goddess. She could scramble up the rope faster than most of the boys, though she was younger than any, or hang upside down from a branch by her knees, her hair dangling like flames, or hang by a hand like a monkey.

When Mark had died, so soon after Eric, and the coffin had been flown from Vietnam, and she had walked from the cemetery, she and Daddy supporting Mama, she had been certain she would never be happy again. Yet within a year there were happy times.

Maybe there would still be happy times, in spite of everything. She would have to start phoning all her old friends, tomorrow, the kids who had gone off to different colleges this past year, and who now must be home for the summer.

She climbed to the upper bunk. She tried to think of nothing but the tick tock.

The entrance foyer at the bottom of the stairs had a semicircular table against the only stretch of wall, and there had been no other spot in the foyer to stand the clock that would not crowd the closet, or block the tall tiny-paned windows on either side of the front door. Besides, the bong would have drowned out the delicate, resonant chime of the gold clock in the living room. She had told Mark and Eric that Daddy was right, and that had quieted them.

At Mount Holyoke there was so much talk about sibling rivalry. It had never seemed real to her. It was outside her experience, as though the psychologists and the other kids had made it up, to have something fashionable to talk about.

Except that Diana and Bob had always been in each other's hair.

She had known Bob better than Diana. He was only six months or so older than Eric and sometimes was brought to play with them. Between herself and Diana the age spread was too great. Even as a child, Diana had always been anxious to appear grown-up. She had been concerned about getting her dress dirty. And playing together with boys had been beneath Diana's dignity. She remembered Diana standing in her dress below the tree house and ordering Bob to come right down out of there this instant.

The bonging at midnight pulled Elspeth partway out of a doze. She slept again.

In the morning she wore jeans. She drove the truck with Joe beside her. "I'm sure it's the coil," she said. "Suppose I drop you off, and I'll go over to Healey's and get one."

In the evening, after the dishwasher and the garbage, she told her father to put his mending on her varnished table. Then she lay across her parents' bed and dialed her friends on the upstairs extension.

Meredith was going to tour the West with her mother and little sister and brother in a camper. Angela Capucci was going to be a counselor-in-training. Shelley Schwartz was going to visit her father. Of all her girl friends, only Cindy would be around.

She dialed a boy she used to date on Saturday nights, and that she had used to take for rides on the motorcycle she had owned for a short time. He was out. She asked his mother how he liked Harvard. "Oh, he loves it," his mother said. "And he's got a job on Martha's Vineyard for the summer."

"Oh, that's nice," said Elspeth. "Well, thank you, Mrs. Elkin. Tell Sonny I called."

If she went out with Sonny, should she tell him she was pregnant? No. Better to wait till it showed. She took her father's mending to the little front room that used to be hers when the boys were alive, and which they called the sewing room now. She threaded a needle. She searched in the button basket.

Sonny Elkin returned her call.

"It's for me, Mama," she said, and heard the kitchen phone click shut.

Sonny would hitchhike down to the ferry in two weeks. His job was only for room and board and tips. But he'd have time for lolling on the beach.

"Well," said Elspeth, "if you get time for a movie or bowling in the next couple of weeks, before you go, give a buzz. If my parents are out in the Dart I can get the truck. Okay?"

He seemed slow to respond. "Okay," he said.

He didn't suggest when. There was a moment's silence. A year ago the mere sound of her voice would have brought him running.

"And if we don't manage to get together," she added, "send me a card from the Vineyard, okay?"

"I'll do that."

11

"WE'LL send someone right over," Joe said. He hung up the black telephone, which sat beside the cash register where the short counter angled near the cellar stairs. "Elspeth, take the truck and go fix Mrs. Spector's toilet. You remember where she lives?"

"I remember. I'd like to fix Mrs. Spector's ass."

"Didn't I ask you not to make comments like that? You never know who's in the store."

The door jingled shut behind Elspeth. Truck meant van. She backed it from its diagonal space into Main Street.

She knew every part of the town, from Pumpkin Hill at one end to Firefly Hill at the other. She headed out toward the area known as Winslow-in-the-Meadow and the Crestwood section beyond.

The Spectors' house had only one bathroom, but the faucet handles were cutesy fishes with thick lips and wavy tails, plated in gold. Last summer Elspeth had found the threading inside the stems all corroded away, but they were a nonstandard item by an obscure manufacturer, and she could not find new stems to fit. She had even tried Mr. Crocker at Metcalf & Crocker, the other hardware store diagonally across from Sawyer's, which she hated to do. There was enough trade, including customers from surrounding towns, to support the two stores, but the competition had never been entirely friendly. Sawyer's was actually the older, and the bigger at least since Daddy had owned it. But Mr. Crocker could sometimes come up with an odd item no one used any more, as though nothing had been discarded from his cellar for fifty years. He was older than Daddy, and would look smugly at Elspeth, and sometimes asked why she didn't work for a good store. But he had no stem for the gold-plated fishes.

At last she had driven to Boston and ordered them from Braman & Dow, but even they had had to send to Saint Louis. Meanwhile Elspeth put in other stems and plain handles on loan, so the Spectors could use the faucets while waiting, but Mrs. Spector had telephoned impatiently every few days for five weeks.

It was a hilly neighborhood of curving streets, cul-de-sacs and ranch houses. Elspeth knocked at the breezeway entrance. A long box she had carried from the truck hung from one hand. Mrs. Spector let her in, wiping her hands in an apron. She was a little woman with gaudy yellow hair, clipped and shaped. She led Elspeth to the bathroom, followed by her little girl Jody and a playmate.

A saucepan had been placed on the tiles behind the toilet to catch drippings. Elspeth removed the lotions and shampoos from the tank and put them on the sink. She lifted the porcelain cover. A thin fountain sprayed into the air. She put the cover back in place.

"See how it shpritzes?" Mrs. Spector said.

"We'll fix it," said Elspeth. A cat squeezed through the legs of her jeans. She crouched, near where she had set her long box on the tiles, and tried to close the shut-off where the supply pipe angled toward the wall beneath the tank. It was frozen and greenish, as though no one had touched it in twenty years. The bolt in the center of the handle was partly rotted into a whitish caked oxide, leaving no slot for a screwdriver. She feared it would crumble in her hand. The white-and-black cat brushed before her knees and under the tank seeking all the narrowest passages. Elspeth rose.

"I'm gonna have to shut off all the water," she said. "Why don't you fill up a kettle and some pots, so you'll have water meanwhile, and show me again where your cellar is, please."

"All the water in the house? Why do you have to shut off all the water in the house?"

"Well, there's a local shut-off here but I'd advise not messing with it. There's a little corrosion and I don't want to multiply your problems."

"Don't tell me my house is corroded! You said that before, and I don't like it."

Elspeth found her way with her flashlight in the basement, brushing invisible cobwebs from her face, stepping over a roll of screening, and closed the master shut-off.

When she returned the two little girls watched her flush the toilet to empty the tank. They were the same height. Jody's friend held a rag doll. Elspeth removed the porcelain cover from the tank again and studied the insides. Then she found Mrs. Spector chopping a salad in the kitchen. The girls followed her and the cat followed the girls.

"There are two ways I could go at this, Mrs. Spector. I could replace the whole ball cock assembly, which is probably quicker, and cost you less in labor and more in parts. Or this kind has a little leather bushing inside, which is probably all that's gone, and I could just replace that. And if that does it you get out real cheap. Except the float rod may not take another bending, and if it happens to shear off in the wrong place I'll have to drill a little and hammer with a prick punch to get the pieces out, and then thread it again with a bottom tap, which could take a little bit longer. Or if we're lucky, chances are we won't even have to. And frankly I'd rather go that route. It's almost sure to cost you cheaper. And with a new bushing and a new float rod I'm pretty sure that valve's gonna last another two or three years at least. Maybe five or ten. And it just goes against my grain to junk something that's got life in it. It's just my personal feeling. The whole United States is turning into a big garbage dump, and it's a crime. But you're the boss. It's your ball cock."

"What did you say?"

"I said it's your ball cock."

84

"Is that what you call it?"

"Yes."

"That doesn't sound very nice."

"Well, should I fix it or put in a whole new one?"

"Oh, put in a new one. I'd rather get it over with and be sure."

The children and the cat followed Elspeth back to the bathroom. She had put two ball-cock assemblies, a taller one and a shorter one, both of a model that used no leather bushing, into the long box she had brought from the truck. The sink had straight black marble siding running down to the floor, so that the floor space beside the toilet was quite small. She had no choice but to lie on the tiles and apply a wrench to the collar that fastened the supply pipe to the protruding lip of the assembly under the tank.

It was stuck tight. The wrench slipped. She held it in place above her face. It would not turn, though she strained with all the strength of her arm. The effort made her head throb. She rested, panting. The air was thick and humid around her face in the cramped space under the tank. There was some moisture on the floor and she felt it soak her shirt under her shoulder. The cat's litter box lay not far from her leg. She could smell that it needed changing. All her jeans had seemed tight at the waist the past few days. She undid the snap, and opened the zipper an inch. She strained on the wrench once more, tightening her whole face. Again her head throbbed. Above her Jody sat on the toilet and tinkled.

Elspeth felt the wrench give a little. She braced a foot on the opposite wall. Jody turned the flush handle uselessly. The wrench gained an eighth of a turn. Jody slid to her feet and stepped over Elspeth's leg. The other little girl dropped her pants, still clutching the rag doll, and climbed to the toilet.

The wrench handle hit the marbled wall of the sink. So cramped was the space that she had to stop, turn the wrench over, and refit it with every half turn.

At last the collar came undone and slid down, the supply pipe springing a fraction of an inch to the left. The dregs of clear water from the tank spilled through the opening onto Elspeth's cheek and neck, along with some granules of rust. The girl rattled the flush handle. Then she jumped down, a foot grazing Elspeth's hip.

The girls ran out, and Elspeth was glad. Her hand felt in her long box for a chisel, as the rubber washer had hardened, fragments of it, cracked and squashed, stuck to the underside of the porcelain. She scraped, using her other hand for protection, lest bits of dried rubber fall on her face or into the neck of her shirt. She raised a knee. She felt the cat rub against her jeans.

She reached a hand to the top of the sink, and pulled herself up. She stood, and caught her breath. With her forearm she wiped the perspiration from her forehead and lip.

She chose a ball-cock assembly of the right length. Its parts were of brass in various shades, glistening and clean. She knelt to fasten it.

Then she lay on the floor once more, her head in the humid space between the supply pipe and the black marble, her braids thrown across each other on her bosom to keep them out of the wet. She tried to fasten the supply pipe to the protrusion of fresh brass above her face.

The cat settled itself on Elspeth's stomach, closed its eyes and purred. The supply pipe, which had sprung a little to the left, resisted going back into place. The faint odor the children had left in the toilet mingled with that of the litter box. She tried to give her hips a shake, but the cat remained on her stomach, heavy and purring. She wished she had thought to open the high little window above the bathtub when she had been on her feet.

Mrs. Spector came to the door. Elspeth heard her, but the black slab of marble kept her from seeing her. "How much longer you gonna be?" said Mrs. Spector.

"It shouldn't be much longer."

"It's pretty long already. I don't know. Your father tells everybody you have golden hands, everything his little girl touches turns to gold, but I can't see it. You touched my gold faucets and I had to have old chrome ones for two months."

"Can you take the cat off my stomach, please?"

"Come on, Timmy. Come, Timmy. I'll give you your lunch."

The cat rose, and with a thrust of hind feet followed Mrs. Spector away. Elspeth had loosened the collar on the supply pipe and begun again five times, but each time it cross-threaded. She felt nauseated.

She reached up and grabbed the sink again and pulled herself to her feet. She climbed on the rim of the bathtub and flung open the high window just in time to vomit onto the grass.

She clung there to the sill, drinking in the fresh air, her sneakers on the tub. In the backyard Jody and her friend were playing in the sandbox. She was glad they didn't notice.

She wiped her lips with toilet paper. Then she settled under the tank again, pressing the pipe hard into place. Finally it threaded properly.

Then she found her way as quickly as possible to the master valve in the cellar, banging her shin on a lime-spreader in the dimness. She returned to the bathroom and tested the new mechanism.

When she had dried the floor, and wiped her footprints from the tub, she brought the old assembly to Mrs. Spector. "This is yours," she said, "but if you want me to take it, I'll see that it gets to the right salvage barrel at the dump."

"You take it."

On the way back to the store she kept both windows of the van open. The breeze refreshed her. The sun was hot on her arm.

The door jingled when she entered. A high pitched hum came to her from where Homer cut a key. So did the vibration of the mixing machine that shook a can of paint her father had just tinted for the elderly lady who towered over him. He looked at Elspeth.

"Go over to Our Lady of Mercy," he told her. "In the rectory. Father Foley called. The hot water's down to a trickle. Probably the pressure valve's clogged."

"Has he paid his bill?"

"Never mind. It's the Church. Get over there."

12

RIDING home in the van from the store Joe told Elspeth of inquiries he had made to various agencies. He had spoken to the Florence Crittenton League, to Hastings House, and to the Jewish Family and Children's Service. They were going to send some literature. If Elspeth wanted to get out of town during the later months there was even a facility where she could live in a complex of cottages with other pregnant girls.

"No, I'd rather just stay put." She was undoing the braids.

"I thought you probably would."

He had also been in touch with his attorney, Barney Rosenbaum, who was preparing to write Jared a tough letter and tell him it would be cheaper to get married. Elspeth said nothing.

Harriet suggested during supper that they call Dr. Edelstein, this time as an obstetrician. "We've got to make an arrangement with somebody," she said. "You're supposed to see an obstetrician regularly, from the beginning. They say he's really very good."

"He won't take me," said Elspeth.

"I think we should ask," Harriet said. "You got him very upset before, but this is different. This time it's definitely obstetrics. And I think this is the night he has evening hours, so why don't we call him tonight. If he can't fit you in I'm sure he'll at least recommend somebody. You shouldn't put it off, Elspeth."

"All right," she said drearily.

"Shall I make the call? Or would you rather call yourself?"

"I'll do it."

Elspeth helped Harriet clear the dishes, and brought a desert of stewed fruits from the refrigerator. Harriet talked about Diana's wedding plans. She had seen Frieda during the day.

"I don't know why they couldn't have it in a more neutral place," said Harriet. "Like the town hall. And go to a plain catering place afterward. Frieda and Harry both suggested that to her. But it's up to the kids, I guess. What they want."

"What's the difference," said Joe. "It's phony anyhow. They'll bring up their kids to believe in nothing ."

Harriet said Harry had already sent Diana a washer and dryer for a wedding gift, delivered from Jordan Marsh right to Diana's apartment. "And the card said 'from Dad and Mother Sylvia,'" Harriet continued. "Imagine! Frieda's so burnt up.

'Mother Sylvia!' The nerve. He really had no right."

"And why couldn't Harry have talked to me about a washer and dryer?" Joe said. "I could have gotten him the exact same thing."

"I know," Harriet agreed. "I know. People just don't stop to think."

"I'd have given him a good break on it."

"And Frieda told Diana, 'don't you dare ever call that woman Mother,'" Harriet went on. "And Diana told her 'don't worry.'"

Frieda had given Harriet a copy of the newspaper clipping, which was some weeks old, and Elspeth looked at it after supper. There was a starry-eyed portrait. Miss Diana Elizabeth Shoemaker, the caption said. Her forthcoming marriage to Donald C. Weaver had been set for midsummer, following Mr. Weaver's tour of duty in the National Guard. He was a graduate of Bentley.

Elspeth took out the garbage. When she had rinsed her hands afterward Harriet handed her a slip of paper with Dr. Edelstein's number penciled on it.

"Don't put it off," Harriet said. She spoke in her typical voice, dulcet, melodious, slow and very soft.

She went up to the master bedroom and closed the door. She lay barefoot on her parents' tufted wide bedspread with the pink extension at her ear, and massaged her belly where she had loosened her jeans.

Elspeth identified herself. She recognized Miss Spencer's voice.

"Oh yes," said Miss Spencer.

"Um, the reason I'm calling, Miss Spencer, is, well, I guess I've decided to have the baby, and give it for adoption. I can't explain it exactly, except the more I think of it the more it kind of suits me more. I know I should have had it all thought out before, and I would have saved everybody a lot of trouble. You, and the doctor. I'm sorry about that. But you can understand, it's sort of a hard choice. With school and all. Anyway it looks like I'm gonna be needing an obstetrician, and my mother thinks the world of Dr. Edelstein, so I was wondering if he'd consider taking me as an obstetrical patient. Strictly obstetrics."

"I'll have to check the doctor's calendar," Miss Spencer said.

Elspeth heard her put the phone down on the desk.

She waited. She drew up a foot. She massaged with a finger between her toes.

Then she could hear Dr. Edelstein himself, off somewhere in the background. "Oh, no! That crazy Baker kid? Please! Spare me that! Jesus, if she ever comes in here, warn me quick so I can run out the back! I've had it up to here with these crazy Jewish girls! I can't take it! I'm gonna hang out a sign, Practice Limited To Goyim! You think I'm kidding? I'll call the sign man! Practice Limited To Goyim! With a shikse, she looks at you, she listens, you're the doctor, she keeps her trap shut! These Jewish girls, they read, they think they know everything! They drive you up the wall!"

There was a second or two of silence. Miss Spencer's breath was briefly audible before she spoke. "I'm afraid the doctor's all booked up. Way into October. There's just not a thing. I can take your number, and let you know if there's a cancellation."

"Could he refer me to someone else?"

Miss Spencer did not answer immediately.

"Another obstetrician," said Elspeth. "Could he suggest someone I could call?"

"I'll ask him," said Miss Spencer. "We'll call you. Do we have your number?"

"My mother's number. Harriet Baker."

She went down to the living room. Her parents were watching television. They looked up.

"Did you talk to the doctor?" said Harriet. Joe took the cigar from his mouth.

"I talked to his nurse."

"What did she say?" Harriet asked her.

"Get lost."

"Get lost?"

"It's a free translation. They're booked up. Until hell freezes over."

"Did you ask them to recommend somebody?"

"I did. She says they will. Meaning they won't."

"What do you mean, they will, meaning they won't?"

"Mama, it's like I said. I'm unforgiven. If he recommends me to anybody it'll be to the dogcatcher."

Harriet sighed. "Do you want to ask Dr. Fleming to recommend somebody?" she said turning to Joe. He was puffing the cigar. Dr. Fleming was the man he had seen once or twice for his ulcer. He shrugged. "Or Dr. Morrison?" said Harriet. Dr. Morrison was the family doctor. Elspeth had known him as long as she could remember.

"Why don't you give Morrison a call tomorrow," Joe said to Harriet.

Elspeth went upstairs.

She collected her jeans and shorts and a skirt or two and took them across to the sewing room. She sat at the machine, and opened the waist of some faded jeans with a razor. In a while Harriet came to the door, and watched her pin and baste the seam. "Why don't you have your hair cut short," Harriet suggested, "while you're working in the store and going out on those repair jobs. You'd save time braiding and unbraiding every day. And all the combing."

"I like it long."

The phone rang. Harriet answered it in the bedroom but it was for Elspeth. Cindy Schaeffer suggested that they go to a movie. So Elspeth left her altering in the middle.

"Take my charge cards," Joe said. "If you're taking the car you'll need gas."

"Don't stay out too late," Harriet cautioned. "You're working tomorrow."

"She's never tired," said Joe.

"It's different now," Harriet said.

Cindy and Elspeth crunched popcorn together in the theater.

Afterward they walked together in their denim shorts to the Dart and drove to the big ice-cream stand, where they stood leaning on posts in its portico and licking their cones, Cindy with her shirt knotted to show her midriff. They said hello to a family that Cindy had used to baby-sit for, and chatted with some boys they knew.

Elspeth had always thought Cindy attractive in a unique way, though she knew

Cindy considered herself plain. She was taller than Elspeth and quite slim, with black hair cut short, and a face that Elspeth thought of as vertical, with a long descending straight nose that did not jut out far, a small pouting mouth, and eyes that always seemed pensive. She told Elspeth she had had a fight with her father, and had just had to get out for the evening and relax. She talked about it riding in the Dart. He had been unable to get her a summer job, though he had promised her one, but he had gotten a job for his lady friend's son, who was only fourteen. True, it was a loading-platform job she wouldn't have wanted, but even so.

All evening long Elspeth was on the verge of telling Cindy she was pregnant. Yet finally she returned Cindy to the big Victorian house with the long porch around two sides without having mentioned it.

The next day, when Elspeth and Joe came home from the store, Harriet had queried Dr. Morrison and received the names of a Dr. Goldwasser and a Dr. Hatch.

"Hatch?" said Elspeth. "Did you say Hatch? What a great name for an obstetrician! Hatch gets my vote."

"Well, I already made the appointment with Dr. Goldwasser," Harriet said.

Elspeth began to notice articles on pregnancy, childbirth, and adoption everywhere. In Harriet's Reader's Digest there was an article on the marvels of the womb. The newspaper had a letter in the Chit Chat from a woman who had given up twin boys for adoption six years before. It was signed Son Plus Two.

I have since married and have another little boy, and when people ask, 'Is this your first,' I force myself to say, 'Yes.'

I presume they'll be starting school in September, wherever they are, and I wonder how they'll get along. I wish someday I would get a letter that said: 'Your boys are fine. We love them very much!' How my heart would sing! Maybe someday we'll meet and I'll be able to tell them the circumstances. I keep a diary for them in case I die before we meet.

Just in case this reaches that 'special house,' I want to say, 'I love you boys, and the wonderful people who are caring for you. Be good.'

On the van's radio, while she returned to the store after setting up a vent pipe for a dryer in someone's cellar, a man with a British accent was interviewed about the horrors of American childbirth. The baby is born into an atmosphere of chemical odors that is supposed to be sterile; they then wash off the body coating, chemical changes in which would have been beneficial to the child had they let it alone; then they forbid the immediate nursing right after birth which would be of physiological benefit to the mother in several ways; and whisk the child away to the nursery where he has only the company of other newborns and busy nurses instead of someone reassuring, thus adding to the shock and fright of being born.

The Sunday newspaper had a big article on the increasingly wide choice of life-styles. But it said nothing new, and did not touch on what she would have liked to ask, which was how difficult any of the alternative styles really were in practice.

She filled the mower with gasoline and pushed it noisily back and forth, working her way from the backyard to the front.

It seemed to her that the right kind of commune, if she could find it, might be the easiest environment for an unmarried parent. The newspaper article had said only that it was impossible to know how many different kinds of communes exist, and that their patterns varied from puritanical to permissive.

Later she tied new strings to a couple of the tomato plants. Around the garden's edge, and at spots in its midst, she planted mint and chives to keep the insects away. She remembered having heard that in kibbutzes in Israel the children lived collectively in a separate hut away from the parents. But she didn't know how doctrinaire they might be, or whether they allowed singles with kids.

In a few days she took the morning off and drove to the city for her appointment with Dr. Goldwasser. She wore jeans. Harriet went with her. The office was in the district where Elspeth never knew precisely where Boston stopped and Brookline began.

After the examination Dr. Goldwasser chatted across his desk in the paneled inner office, rocking in his swivel chair, his chubby fingers together. He seemed well into his fifties, with gray hair curling over his ears. He said more than two thousand of the people on the face of the earth were his children. Some that he had brought into the world had babies now of their own. He wanted to see Elspeth once a month. She was to drink from a pint to a quart of milk every day, to make sure the baby did not drain her teeth of calcium. He squeaked forward in the swivel chair and wrote a prescription for iron capsules. Not that there was any deficiency, but he felt that an excess was a good preventive against anemia in both mother and child. He told her to nap for an hour every afternoon. He asked her if she thought she was likely to be having sexual relations during the next several months.

"I wasn't planning on it," Elspeth told him. She didn't look at Harriet. "How much risk is there for the baby if I don't get the nap? I work in a hardware store."

"None. It's just better for you, dear. If you can't nap, at least try to put your feet up for a while. In a few months, after the hot weather, you can wear surgical stockings, which will help you. And I may prescribe a corset for you."

"Don't you think she has a narrow pelvis?" said Harriet.

"No, she has a nice pelvis. I don't foresee any trouble."

"I was always wider than she is, even when I was very young, and I always had a terrible time. I had to have caesareans."

"Well, we have so many ways of killing the pain today. Caudal. Saddle block. Twilight sleep. We can knock her out completely if it's too bad." He smiled at them both, rocking back in the swivel.

"What do you think of natural childbirth?" Elspeth asked him. "Like Lamaze, and stuff?"

"Well, I never went along with it. It's nonsense, frankly. And the fad seems to have passed its peak now, so my initial judgment has been borne out. I think you'll find that most of these women you hear talking Lamaze and painless childbirth are just being fashionable. They may start off with their breathing exercises—huh

91

huh huh, huh huh huh, at the beginning—but as soon as it begins to get not so painless they all ask for a shot of something. Afterward they like to say they did Lamaze. It doesn't mean anything. There's no such thing as painless childbirth, my dear." He was smiling affably, his fingers locked on his rounded vest. "Or by chance are you one of these with-it types, that likes to be up to the minute, always into the latest fad?"

"No. Fads kind of put me off, actually."

"Then I see no problem, dear. I suggest you forget about natural childbirth."

Elspeth and Harriet had lunch at a soda fountain a few doors from the doctor's building. He said cheese or ice cream could be substituted for the milk.

"I'll get fat," Elspeth said.

"I put on weight with every baby," said Harriet. "You can't help it. You have to do what's best for the baby. You think you'll take it off, but you don't."

In Winslow Elspeth dropped Harriet off at the house and drove on to the store. Joe sent her to install a lantern in somebody's front yard. She dug the hole with a spade, and planted the post in rocks and cement, checking its straightness with a level. She became faint in the sun and sat in the van a moment, her head bent over her arms on the steering wheel. Her hair, which she had not had time to braid, hung loose. She recovered. She buried the cable in the front lawn, replaced the sod and watered it. Then, after warning the lady and her children, she undid some fuses, installed an extra switch inside the front door, dropped a wire through the wall, and made the connections in the basement. She asked the lady to say Joe had done the work if anyone should ask, because she did not yet have an electrician's license.

One morning, when the store was briefly quiet, she ran down the block to the public library, and collected three books on expectant motherhood. She also scanned the New Acquisitions shelf, and picked one by a British lady who had traveled in Borneo, catching animals for a zoo.

She tried to follow the doctor's instructions. However she never had a chance in the store to put her feet up for more than a minute or two. She had always drunk milk occasionally, but she was not used to quite so much. Dr. Goldwasser had suggested an iron capsule only every second or third day, but every day that she took one she got the runs, and the store's toilet was an unpleasant one in the darkness of the cellar, where even the gray stones and cement of the wall smelled of musty damp.

Besides, one of her books on expectant motherhood, the slimmest one and the one she liked best, disagreed with all Dr. Goldwasser's instructions. It said that she should eat no more than before, and be as active as she felt like. So long as her diet was reasonably varied the baby would take care of itself. It seemed to make sense, and the author was a professor of obstetrics. Without telling Harriet, she left off the extra milk, and stopped the capsules. Occasionally, when she thought of it, she bought a tiny box of raisins as a compromise.

Friday evening she shopped with Harriet for maternity apparel at the big mall between Winslow and Bradbury. There was a branch of a Boston department store, and one of a discount chain, and a specialty shop called Stork Town. There were tunics in a print that she liked, consisting of squares that looked like four strokes done casually and lopsidedly with a brush, superimposed off-center on other squares of a second shade, all on a background of white. The squares could be had in russets, oranges, greens, or rich grays that went well with her hair and eyes, and some had solid-color shorts to match, with stretchy tummies. "Some of these are darling," Harriet said. There were pop-art tunics and psychedelic ones. "Wild," Elspeth murmured.

She tried on her size in the dressing room and modeled the slanty squares before Harriet, smiling at herself in the mirrors, turning about, swinging her hips, holding the tunic out at the sides, and puffing her belly. She chose two of the patterns of squares, and black pants, and a darker tunic in a kind of paisley, that came with khaki shorts.

She also chose some underpants.

"Would you like to see the nursing bras?" the lady asked.

"She won't be nursing," Harriet said.

No, of course not, Elspeth thought. Since it'll be given for adoption. Too bad. They looked at bathing suits. But she didn't like any.

There was still the question of what to wear to Diana's wedding. They sat where the rows of shops intersected, watching the colored lights in the little fountain. Harriet massaged her feet. Elspeth had been asked to be a bridesmaid.

"I still think it doesn't make sense to blow good money on a dress I'll never wear again, and then right away have to alter it all out of shape," Elspeth said. "What about my senior prom dress? What if we let it out a little at the sides, and dye it yellow? When is it? Two weeks from Sunday? I don't really show yet, do I?"

"No. It doesn't show."

"Well, I say take that dumb white thing and dye it yellow. I don't need it for anything. And if that doesn't work, just tell everybody, and beg off as a bridesmaid, and the heck with it. This thing about not telling anybody is dumb."

At home she put on black shorts and a white tunic with sloppy squares of four orange strokes off-centered on brown ones. She hurried downstairs to the living room and stood before Joe.

"Aren't I cute?" she said.

He looked up from his chair darkly. She lost her smile. The cigar shifted from one side of his mouth to the other. He took it out.

"You make it like a blessed event," he said. "Don't you know it's a tragedy, for Christ sake? That's the trouble with kids today. They haven't got enough sense to be miserable."

"But I'm gonna need it, Daddy. And I might as well look nice."

He looked at the television and puffed the cigar. She swallowed.

"I decided not to get anything for the wedding," she explained. "I'll make over the senior prom dress instead. I didn't want to buy a dress for one time."

"What's the difference?" he said grimly, staring at the television, the cigar firm in his mouth. "Money comes easy. Like babies. Wear it once, throw it away. Have a baby, throw it away."

He took the cigar and blew smoke, not turning from the television. "Why don't you go to the wedding naked?"

"Daddy, please. You know I'm not like that."

Harriet had tears in her eyes.

Elspeth remained before her father awkwardly, one hand playing with the other. She glanced at the television, but seeing not the screen so much as the three hinged portraits on top. Eric, in the middle picture, had hair the color of her own. She turned again to Joe. "I was almost gonna get a dress, just so Mama would get one. Mama always gets a dress for a wedding, but she won't this time, because I'm not."

"I don't always," Harriet protested. "I just thought a new dress would be good for your morale—"

"Mama, you need the morale boost, not me. My morale's okay. You're the one with the long face—"

"Hear that?" Joe said as though over his shoulder. "Nothing wrong with *her* morale."

In the van Saturday morning Joe and Elspeth hardly spoke. She did her braids, trying to think of some conversation, but couldn't.

In the evening Cindy phoned. A boy had called her, so she wondered if Elspeth could sub for her on a baby-sitting job. "Okay," Elspeth said drearily.

She brought her book about Borneo. The children were in bed, so there was not much to do. She had begun washing the dishes before it occurred to her that it might not be Cindy's practice to wash dishes on baby-sitting jobs. She ought to have asked, lest she spoil things for Cindy. But she had started, so she went ahead and finished. It would be Cindy's own fault anyhow—she shouldn't still be baby-sitting at her age.

She opened the refrigerator, and took a slice of the cake Mrs. O'Meara had said she could have.

She kicked off her sneakers and put her feet on the coffee table. She lighted a cigarette. She did not open her book yet, but drifted through the evening paper. She found an item about an unwed father suing for custody of his baby. The girl was only fifteen and did not want to marry the father, and her parents wouldn't let her anyway. He was nineteen and worked with a crew that repaired telephone lines, and was already suing the family and the adoption agency though the child was not born yet.

I want my child, the paper quoted him as saying.

If only Jared were like that.

13

HOMER Lathrop left his car at Healey's one day for the brakes to be relined, so Joe and Elspeth took him there after work. When they had dropped him off and turned the van toward home Joe handed Elspeth her weekly envelope, just as she was lowering the window.

"I'm increasing your salary," he said.

"Why?"

"Because you're worth it. You're entitled. I'm getting a bargain. You're worth your weight in gold. Just for example, how could I give a customer a trade-in allowance on his old mower if I didn't have you there to overhaul it? For that alone you're worth it."

She held the brown envelope, but she did not look inside. "Should I pay more board?"

"That's up to you," said Joe. "You don't have to pay board, you know. I give Mama enough for the house. If you pay too much the raise is no raise."

"Well, I'll give Mama a third of the increase. I should contribute when I'm working." She still held the envelope unopened, but she was pleased. Customers wanting advice or instruction had begun to seek her out, instead of always asking for Joe. And one morning this week she had fixed a customer's relay switch in a moment, without charge, climbing over the furnace on a stepladder and bending a piece of metal with her thumb to make a better contact, after his oil man had told him a new switch was needed. She had brought the new switch back to the store in its unopened carton, saving the customer twenty-five dollars and preventing a few pounds of good metal from being thrown into the dump. Joe had remarked that incidents like that were well worth the few dollars of lost profit. They brought the store a reputation that money couldn't buy.

She crooked her elbow on the lowered window of the van. The breeze blew in upon her and kept the cigar smoke away. She had read an item that said breathing smoke could be bad for unborn children. She had thrown out a half-empty pack of cigarettes.

"I should file a tax return next year," she said. "Because I'm on the store's books."

"You should," he agreed. "I don't think you'll owe anything, but file it anyway. If it comes out you owe any tax let me know."

When they got home there was a letter for Elspeth. Wine-red penmanship on a powder-blue envelope. In the corner was the name of Ms. Roxanne Sweetser and a Pennsylvania address.

95

After supper she lay on the lower bunk, one heel dragging on the concentric ovals of the braided rug, and opened the letter. Roxie wrote that she had a part-time volunteer job helping summer-school children with learning disabilities.

> There aren't any real jobs around. I filled out the usual applications at the hamburger joints. I don't think they even look at them. If somebody quits they hire the next kid that walks in and the applications rot in the file. No guys around either. I've even been getting involved with my mother in the church picnic. That's how desperate things are. Cole slaw for Jesus. The Evangelical & Reformed is everything in this town. The good old E. & R. They've got a new young minister for the third time in five years. The usual beautiful set of teeth and all the right liberal ideas, but not too well endowed with gray matter.

The letter continued for several pages. Some relatives had visited, and she had had to take them to gawk at the Amish. She wondered how Elspeth had made out with the abortion. She envied Elspeth for living in New England, especially so near the ocean. At last she closed with some nostalgic recollections about the past year at college.

> I remember when you would bang away at the piano and we'd all sing.

The sentence about her piano-playing gave Elspeth a feeling of wistfulness. She missed that fellowship. She reread the letter. One hand unsnapped her jeans and slowly massaged the firmness of her belly. Even the crowd she had known around here in high school was already scattered. The end of schooling was a lonely time.

Even Cindy Schaeffer was not available much. She had a lot of baby-sitting customers and besides her father had gotten her a job finally in the stockroom.

Elspeth went barefoot to the varnished table. She locked one ankle around the other under the chair. Her hair hung to her forearm as she penned an answer to Roxie.

> I'm not that near the ocean. Anyway we don't think of 45 minutes or an hour as near. Would you believe I haven't seen it all summer? I guess when something is always available you don't take advantage of it like you should.
>
> About the abortion, I chickened out again. I don't know why. My parents think I'm nuts. They're probably right. Now I'll have to carry it the nine months and give it to an agency. I probably will never know if it's a boy or a girl as they don't let you see it. Maybe it's for the best. I even feel good about it in a way, because at least a life is being created.
>
> My father is horrified at the idea of my going back to Mt. H. with a big belly, and he pays the bills, so it looks like I may not be back till a year from Sept. though I will try for January. I may be a sophomore when you kids are juniors. I'm just sorry I didn't know sooner in time for you to arrange for a

roommate. This way they'll just stick you with somebody. I'm terribly sorry, and just hope they don't move some real stinker in with you. You and I were very lucky the way we hit it off from the beginning.

Anyway, my Tolkien posters I left on the wall are yours, to keep or give away, as you see fit.

I have written for the leave of absence and said I have to help in my father's store.

Sometimes I imagine my child as growing up a beautiful, intelligent, sensitive woman. I guess every mother does and really it will be just one more ordinary kid. Maybe the advantage of never seeing it is I can dream and hope. I just wish she will become something good like a medical researcher or something and make the world a better place. That would sort of justify everything. They say they give the babies only to excellent parents who have no emotional problems. I sure hope so. It will be just dumb if she makes my mistakes all over again and flounders around like me.

She sat there rubbing her forehead under the hair. She slumped back in the chair. There was a light breeze from one window to the other. She thought of writing a letter to Jared. She sighed.

Out the window a roof and treetops were nearly black against the red and blue of the sky. On the table her handwriting and Roxie's were shrouded in dusk. She remained there, in one posture and then another. At last she clicked on the light.

Jared honey,

You're probably surprised to hear from me. But my thoughts are with you and what's the use of pretending otherwise? I'm going to have the baby. The agencies will take care of the adoption and I'll never see it. My parents are much better about it than I thought they would be. I have to give them credit.

Just think, there will be a human individual on the face of this earth who is the result of our coupling. So I guess there was a purpose in it after all. Someone who would not have lived but for our loving each other. Someone neither you nor I will ever know, as we go our three ways, but you and I will always know that somewhere there is a whole separate person who is our child.

I bet by now you know the complexities of poor King Dick's character better than the Bard did himself. I know you'll be the greatest.

Don't let them work you too hard this summer. Maybe at one of your tables there'll be a famous producer and you'll get a break. Anyway get lots of tips. Good luck, darling.

She looked for his smiling face in the high knit cap, standing before the snow house in the corner of the middle mirror. It was gone. She moved the tissue box and brush on the vanity, and looked in the drawers, and behind the vanity against the wall, and on the floor, even under the radiator, every place it could have fallen.

97

That snapshot was the only one she had of him. Somebody must have taken it deliberately. Maybe Daddy had given it to Mr. Rosenbaum for evidence. Or maybe he just happened to see it, and crumpled it and tore it to bits. Or spit on Jared's face and ground it under his shoe. Though Mama had more opportunity to come into this room. Maybe she had quietly thrown it away, thinking it would help Elspeth to forget him.

Monday morning a lady asked Joe if he could fix her son's bicycle. "All right, leave it," he said. "Elspeth will get to it."

It was rolled in through the narrowness of an aisle. Elspeth removed the rear wheel and sat with it on the step of the open back door to the alley, jimmying the tire off with irons. The black telephone rang at the angle of the counter while Joe was high on the ladder up front. Elspeth sprang to it.

"Sawyer's Hardware," she said.

"Ellie?"

"Bob!" she cried, recognizing the voice.

Her cousin had driven up to Boston from Woods Hole. He asked if she could join him and Karen at one-thirty with a group from the Society for the Prevention of Cruelty to Animals to picket the rodeo.

"Oh, gee. I couldn't take time off, Bob. It's not fair to Daddy. Our other man's out sick."

"Well, if you can't you can't," he said. "I'm just calling everybody I can think of that might help. We've got a lot of the Audubon people. But we want to really make an impact. People just don't realize, you know. Well, okay."

"Are you really not gonna be at the wedding Sunday?"

"Who needs it?" he answered.

There was nothing to say to that. But neither could she end the conversation there. She leaned an arm on the cash register. "Do you ever take the ferry over to the Vineyard?" she asked.

"I haven't had a chance to. Why?"

"Oh, just because it's near you. I have a friend in Oak Bluffs. A guy I knew in high school."

Joe had come down the ladder and was approaching the register, catching her eye darkly, a customer following.

She stepped aside for him and he rang up a sale. "It's Bob Shoemaker," she explained.

"What's he want? Anything important? I'm waiting on five customers by myself here."

"Bob, I have to go."

That evening she opened the sides of the dress. It had to be let out more than she had expected. Harriet took several tries at pinning the seams. "Turn around to the other side like a good girl," Harriet said. "You always had such a cute little figure. Such a narrow waist. It's all gone."

"It'll come back," said Elspeth.

"Oh, it never comes back," Harriet said tearfully.

"It will, Mama. I don't go for this eating for two. I don't care *what* Goldwasser says. I read a book that said not to."

The reshaping of the dress troubled them a while. Elspeth suggested more flare at the hem to draw attention from the waistlessness. At last it hung from her bosom with an airy brevity that seemed stylish and right.

She turned before the vanity, looking at its angled mirrors over her shoulder. The drape was broken by a suggestion of buttocks. There was something provocative about short dresses that hung that loose. They seemed to say they could be easily lifted.

"There," said Harriet. "That's good."

"You're a genius, Mama."

"I'm not the genius. You figured it out."

They did the basting, and she tried it on once more. Then she turned it inside out for the last time and took it across to the sewing room.

Harriet went downstairs to prepare tea. Elspeth sat at the machine in her underwear. She threaded it, and bent to guide the stitch.

It didn't work right. She undid the tangle of thread, and began again. This time the sewing went smoothly. The seam moved slowly. The jumping bright metal and the noise were the engine of the turbotrain. She was en route to New York, with Jennifer on her lap. Jennifer was only two and did not need a ticket. We're going to see your daddy, Jennifer. Your daddy needs us.

For alas, Richard the Second, which was to establish him as one of the greats of all time, was a failure. They had loved his Falstaff, his Lear, his Hamlet, but the subtleties of wretched Dick were too far over their stupid heads. He had plowed his whole fortune into the production. He was a bankrupt, a laughingstock, without friends or self-confidence, his career a shambles. Janice had left him and was living with the most biting of the critics.

She found him in a ratty hovel on the Lower East Side, dying of malnutrition and grief. There wasn't even a phone. The refrigerator was empty. She stomped on the roaches and kicked the rats. Jared, look at me. Lift up your head. It's the real Jared I love, not the great actor. Meet your daughter. Jennifer, say hi to your daddy. Give your daddy a kiss. The smile struggled with the tears upon his face. She guided the cloth in the sewing machine, trying to hold her tears in check. In his humility he had a dignity and beauty she had never seen before.

14

ELSPETH stood with the one other bridesmaid and the matron of honor, ranged in their yellow gowns on one side of the altar with yellow bouquets. Elspeth was much the littlest and youngest of the three. Both were elder sisters of Donald, horse-faced with high gummy smiles. The best man and two ushers were on the other side with yellow boutonnieres. Beside the ushers Mr. and Mrs. Weaver took their places, lank, skinny, uncomfortable-looking people, Mrs. Weaver powdery under a wide-brimmed hat. Aunt Frieda stood by Elspeth. Uncle Harry stumbled a little on a wrinkle in the carpeting. He kept altering his pace, trying to keep to the slow rhythm of the organ. He stood by the Weavers, so he and Aunt Frieda could avoid one another. It made an imbalance in the arrangement.

Elspeth held her bouquet low to hide her stomach. For all the care in refitting, the gown did not fit right. Either it had tightened a bit in the dyeing, or she had grown perceptibly larger in the past several days. The perfection it had had when she finished at the machine had somehow vanished when she put it on this morning. The looseness that had hidden everything a few days ago now seemed the worst possible kind of drape, with the suggestion of bulge at its center all the more firm and round because of the absence of other breaks in the material. She had slipped out of the house and into the Dart before her parents, and they had noticed nothing.

Diana was radiant, and leggy in the shortest wedding gown Elspeth had ever seen. The minister was youngish and balding, with a stylish little beard. His sentences were a churchy monotone punctuated by a brief singsong lilt on the last accented syllable. It occured to Elspeth that she had never attended a Christian wedding before. Though perhaps in several years there would be many—Roxie and Fletch and everybody. Yet there had been so many in movies and on TV that nothing was unfamiliar.

Everything was beautiful. The wisp of veil, the flawless skin-colored hose above the white patent-leather high heels, the private little smiles that met sideways between Diana and Donald, the quiet sniffling of Aunt Frieda, the subdued sureness with which Diana said I do.

He kissed the bride. The organ pipes filled the soaring wooden rafters with triumphant Mendelssohn. The minister steered the bridesmaids down the carpeted steps after the couple.

"Is her underwear white?" Elspeth asked the other bridesmaid.

"I don't know," the horse-faced girl said from the side of her mouth. "Maybe she isn't wearing any."

Elspeth held the bouquet close and low in the stately march. She saw ladies on both sides wipe their eyes.

In the bustle of the wide crowded vestibule she stayed behind people. She saw her father kiss the bride, and her Uncle Normie from New Jersey did also. Diana stood at the center of the receiving line, smiling tirelessly, flushed with excitement. Elspeth did not care for Donald's looks. He pumped handshakes eagerly, his stoop thrusting his grinning upper gum into everyone's face. His eyes were close to his nose and the sandy hair rose high above the perspiring forehead. His mother and father were limp-handed.

Again Elspeth maneuvered to duck out and into the car ahead of her parents. The luncheon was to be a catering hall a number of blocks from the church.

"Elspeth!" Aunt Ada from New Jersey said on the steps. Her olive-skinned young son was beside her, toothy with braces. "Have you put on weight?"

"Well, a little, I guess. Does it show?"

She was settled in the driver's seat when her parents came to the car. Joe let Harriet into the front and seated himself in the back.

"Do you know where this place is, Daddy?"

He directed her, sitting forward and holding to the back of the seat in the front. He was not smoking.

"Sweetheart," he said as she drove, "you were the most beautiful one there, do you know that? Wasn't she, Harriet? Prettier than the bride. Some nerve you got. Don't you know it's not nice to be prettier than the bride?"

"Oh, Daddy. Stop."

They were among the first ones there. Elspeth still carried her bouquet with one hand. The fruit cups and nut bowls were on the round tables, but they had to go to the buffet line for their dishes, and then pass a row of Chinese-style concoctions in hot steel pans, behind which stood middle-aged waitresses in white who served with ladles. Elspeth stayed close behind Harriet. She saw the red-jacketed bartender over in the corner filling platoons of champagne glasses.

"What kind of champagne do you want?" Elspeth asked when they had chosen a table. "Pink or white?"

"I'm better off without that stuff. So's your mother."

"Oh, come on," said Elspeth. "It's a wedding. You have to take a sip. I'll get you some."

She mingled with the gathering at the bar. She drank a glass of the pink, and then a glass of the white. Both were good, but the white seemed stronger. The bubbles rose from her mouth to her nose, inside her head. A long-haired three-piece combo at the other end of the hall began plucking their electric guitars and pounding a drum.

Elspeth gathered up two wide glasses of the pink and one of the white. It was not easy to carry all three, but she maneuvered carefully. The place was already quite crowded. She remembered her belly, and lowered the three glasses a few inches.

As she arrived at her parents' table Aunt Frieda was joining them.

"I'll get you some champagne, Aunt Frieda."

"No, sit down. Enjoy yourself. I'll have plenty. I'm just table-hopping." Frieda pulled out the chair at Elspeth's plate. Then she looked about at the crowd. "Well, my little girl's a married woman." She sighed. Elspeth sat beside Frieda, and took a sampling of the food. It had rice and almonds and gooey sauce and bits of pork and greens. She saw Frieda look to where Uncle Harry was carrying a plateful to Sylvia. His hair was silvery and wavy. "Look at that," Frieda said. "Look. He had to bring her. Couldn't spare my feelings for one day of happiness. He had to spoil it."

Harry put down a piled dish before the frowning Sylvia and another one for himself. They were several tables away. He sat and shook out a napkin.

"Well, that's what he wanted," Frieda sighed. "Just goes to show you what a bleach rinse and a fourteen-dollar brassiere can do. I told him, it's too bad she could only afford the bra and the bleach. Too bad she couldn't afford to have her face lifted. I give it five years. He stayed with me for twenty-five. I bet you Sylvia doesn't last five. She stinks with powder and perfume. I don't know how he can breathe. I said to him, Harry, if you have to have an affair with your secretary, why don't you at least get a young one? Even Diana told him off. Diana said, how corny can you get, having an affair with your secretary?"

"Frieda, relax," Joe said. "Don't let it bother you."

"Oh, she doesn't bother me. She knows better than to bother me. I told her where to get off. I don't have to take it from her. She called me up, you know. She says, why don't you let Harry go, like a civilized person? Why do you have to take him for his last dime? Civilized person she says. Ha! The nerve! I said to her I said, why can't you get a man of your own?"

The bride and groom rose from the table they shared with Donald's parents, on the other side over by the tall red-draped windows, and moved onto the dance floor. A scattering of applause spread around the room. Diana and Donald danced before one another to the electronic thumping of the guitars.

Other couples came onto the floor and danced also.

"Well," said Frieda, "I should circulate and talk to my guests, I guess." She rose. "Harry's looking over here. He knows I'm talking to you. Oh, well. No fool like an old fool."

"Take it easy, Frieda," Joe said.

"Who knows," said Harriet, "maybe it's for the best."

"Come over to my place after," said Frieda as she moved away. "Normie and Ada are coming over and we'll all have a chance to visit."

"Okay," said Joe.

"Dance with me, Daddy," said Elspeth.

"Let me eat first. I'll save you a waltz."

"Oh, Daddy."

She tapped her feet under the table. She watched the groom and bride dancing lightly together among the other couples. They did not touch one another. Diana had plenty of underwear as white as her dress. There were lacy little petticoats that peeked when she turned.

Harry and Sylvia came to the table. He was holding two used glasses and an opened bottle of champagne. "Hi, kids," he said to Joe and Harriet, pulling two chairs out with a scrape. "You know Sylvia?"

"Of course," said Harriet. "We've met Sylvia. I've seen her in your office I don't know how many times."

"Oh, yeah, in the office," Harry said, as he and Sylvia sat. He filled his glass and Sylvia's. "Let me fill those glasses." He extended the bottle.

Joe covered his glass. "No, enough for me, thanks," he said.

"Right, bad for the ulcer," said Harry. "Too bad. Is it under control?"

"Well, pretty fair," said Joe. "Healing, maybe, if it gets a chance. I take stuff once or twice a day if I need it."

"And you," Harry asked Harriet. "You okay?"

"Considering," said Harriet.

"The old gray mare ain't what she used to be," said Joe.

"The colitis never came back?" Harry asked.

"Knock on wood," said Harriet.

Sylvia was dressed quietly. There were deep shadows around her eyes. Her filled glass sat before her. She didn't smile.

"Looks like you're the only healthy one," Harry said to Elspeth, refilling her glass. "Isn't she gorgeous?" he said to Sylvia, and Sylvia looked at Elspeth. "Ever see a face like that? Hair like that?"

"Uncle Harry," said Elspeth. "You'll spoil me."

"Spoil you?" he said. "How could anybody spoil you. You're too sweet." He raised his glass to his lips. "Cheers," he said to Joe and Harriet. He on the glass and smacked his wet lips. "I know what Frieda was talking about over here," he said. "Her favorite subject. Knocking Sylvia."

"No, she didn't say anything," said Harriet.

"She said I shouldn't have brought Sylvia, right? I told her go look it up in Emily Post. I've got every right to bring her. And who's paying for the God damn wedding? Me! Nobody's telling me what to do. A man's entitled to a little happiness. We're all losers. Only some of us are bum losers, that's all. All right, have it her way. That's why there's no head table. We couldn't agree who sits at the head table. So all the tables are unreserved."

"Dance with now, Daddy," said Elspeth.

"Wait for a fox trot," Joe said. "I can't do this rock stuff."

"Sure you can," said Elspeth.

"Sure you can!" Harry told him. "Think young! How can you say no to a pretty girl like that?"

"Come on, Daddy." She rose and pulled his arm. "The whole family says I twist you around my finger. You're not gonna spoil my reputation, are you?"

"Ha!" said Harry, slapping the table. "That's telling him!"

Joe rose. She led him onto the floor.

"Not the new stuff," he said. "I can't dance the way kids dance today."

"Try it." She faced him and danced. Her hands and elbows floated and bounced.

He danced opposite her, kicking out this way and that. There was a heaviness in his motions but his rhythm was good. She smiled and nodded her approval.

He tried to imitate her steps, and then improvised his own as best he could, working his hips and arms bravely, gesticulating, and keeping to the beat. Except when she spun about she did not take her smile from him. He did not slow down.

The music and the dancing came to a pause. Elspeth laughed and squeezed Joe in a tight hug. "You're great, Daddy! See, you could do it! My favorite fella."

She heard his breathing. They walked together toward their table. She knew suddenly from Harriet's face that the bulge in her dress was quite obvious. Then she was aware that Joe read Harriet's face and glanced at it too.

They resumed their seats. "Fill up my glass again, Uncle Harry," Elspeth said.

"Sure thing, honey." He reached and poured. "That's the spirit, Elspeth. You and me are gonna drink each other under the table."

Sylvia was still silent and unsmiling, her eyes shifting from one to another. She seemed to Elspeth more shy than unfriendly.

"Well, at least the cross was very subdued," Harry said to Harriet, as if resuming some discussion. "Not prominent. Just the one there. Tasteful. I would have preferred more neutral ground, if it was up to me. A civil ceremony before a judge. Or City Hall. I told Diana how I felt. Or at least have a rabbi up there to share the honors with the minister. Be fair about it. So Diana says to me, 'Dad, what's the difference, it's just a lot of shit anyway.' Isn't that a fine way for a girl to talk about her own wedding?" He took a drink of champagne and looked at everyone. "I ask you now. Sure, I know it's a lot of shit. She's been shacking up with him for a year, at least a year. So what. I still say it's a hell of an attitude. Damn crazy kid. She shows up at the rehearsal yesterday with a great big button that says Tax The Churches. I said to her, take it off! What's the matter, you want to get off on the wrong foot with your in-laws the first thing?"

He shook his head. He turned the stem of the glass, looking at the columns of tiny rising bubbles. He looked at Harriet and Elspeth and Joe.

"And my son," he began again. "There's another case. He isn't even here, you know. He's the opposite extreme. He's like a rabbi. Worse than a rabbi. It's been going on for a while, getting worse and worse. He comes to visit me and he's wearing a yarmulka. He wears it everywhere. In the street. Everywhere. In public. I said, Bob, please! Your mother threw you out. Don't come to me with this shtik! Take that damn thing off! It makes me sick! It's uncalled for! You're in the United States, for Christ sake, you're not in Israel. So he does me a big favor now. When he comes to my place he takes it off and stuffs it in his pants pocket when he rings the doorbell. And when he says good-bye, I'm sure as soon as he's out of my sight it's on his head again."

"At least that shows he respects you," said Harriet. "If he doesn't wear it where you have to see it."

"Look," Harry said, "my friends tell me their kids are on pot, I'm sure Bob's tried it too in his time, they all do. Diana—it's nothing new. I've got three different friends their kids burned their draft cards and went to Canada. But this stuff with the yarmulka, and the tefillin, and the tallis, and the tsitsis, and the rules, and the regulations, and every other day is some kind of festival or half-festival or a fast day or some new kind of shtik, one month you can't cut your hair, another month you can't go swimming, another time you have to sit on the floor and wail about the Babylonians burning Jerusalem— it's insane! It's lunatic fringe!"

"Everybody has to find their own thing," Elspeth told him. "How would you like it if he were gay or something?"

"God forbid."

The middle-aged waitresses were bringing desserts and pouring coffee. Harriet had caught the eye of Normie and Ada, and waved fingers. Harry watched the steaming coffee poured before him. Sylvia picked at the strawberry parfait with the tip of her spoon. Harriet explained to Sylvia who Normie and Ada were. The brother from Minneapolis hadn't been able to come. Harry stirred his coffee and watched the waitress go to the next table.

"You know why I hired this catering joint?" he said to Joe. "Because they said we couldn't bring liquor in the church. The Weavers said why don't we have a quiet luncheon in the church. In the parish hall, they call it. It's okay with me. And then I hear this thing about the booze. How'm I gonna make a wedding without liquor?" He tasted his coffee. He took another cube from the sugar bowl and stirred again. "That minister. A kid. A yingl. Wet behind the ears. 'You cannot bring liquor into the First Congregational Church,' he tells me. 'You cannot bring liquor into the First Congregational Church.' Did you ever hear of such crap?"

Normie and Ada and their son came to the table, taking a semicircular route to avoid the dancing couples.

"Hi," said Harriet. "We saw you over there. We were gonna come over."

They found additional chairs, but it made the table crowded. A sandy-haired young man who seemed to be one of the Weaver's guests asked Elspeth to dance. He was square-jawed. She rose and walked onto the floor with him.

She faced him and danced. All her joints responded to the drums. Her hips tipped forward and back. She danced with her wrists, her fingers. She danced with her shoulders. Her hair flew across her face when she turned. She saw that people noticed her belly. Her feet moved tirelessly as if they bore no weight.

"What's you name?" she asked him breathlessly when the music stopped. They remained on the dance floor.

"Douggie."

"I'm Elspeth."

"Are you Diana's sister?"

"Cousin."

The music resumed. They danced. Another boy, taller and darker, cut in on Douggie but Douggie did not leave. They all three danced facing one another. She saw Joe dance a little with Harriet, in the old gentle way, their arms about one another, while Harry and Sylvia and the New Jersey relatives remained at the table. The bridegroom with his gummy grin joined Elspeth and Douggie and the other boy. She turned from one to another without a break, sometimes rapidly, sometimes with sudden contortions at half rhythm as though possessed.

The musicians rested. Douggie returned with her to her table. The New Jersey relatives were not there now, but Joe and Harriet and Harry and Sylvia were sitting with a sandy-haired man who was apparently Douggie's father. They greeted one another. Elspeth and Douggie sat. Joe had lighted a cigar.

"You know I had to hire this catering joint because they don't allow liquor in the First Congregational Church?" Harry was telling Douggie's father. " 'We can't have spirits in the church,' he tells me. That snotnose, who does he think he is? I should have told them they can shove it. They know where. I'm a Jew, by God, and I'm proud of it! I hope to tell you. Both my wives were good Jewish girls. If it was a synagogue, I'd show 'em! In all my life, nobody ever told me I can't bring booze in the synagogue!"

The musicians had had only a minute's respite but the guitarists rose again and the tympanist began striking out jumpily all around him.

"Come on," Douggie said, and Elspeth rose.

"Don't make it long," Joe said. "We should be going."

The dancing exhilarated her. The vibrant amplified chords got into her arms, her legs, her hips, her head. The bride and groom had already left. There were fewer people on the dance floor and fewer at the tables. The waitresses were gathering soiled dishes onto steel carts.

She saw Harriet and Joe moving to the door. Joe beckoned to her with his cigar. Their former table was empty. She stopped her rhythms, and stood limply before Douggie. "I have to go, I guess."

"You're a good dancer," he said.

"You are," she said. "I'm not. I'm just in the mood."

"No, you've really got it," said Douggie.

She walked to the door through which her parents had gone. They were not in the big carpeted entrance hall. A few people were chatting and the girl at the checkroom gave a man a hat. A boy of about thirteen and a girl of perhaps twelve were talking together in low tones and staring at Elspeth's belly. They looked to be part of the Weaver crowd.

"Are you pregnant or something?" the boy asked.

"No, it's a pillow," Elspeth said, "I'm supposed to represent the fertility goddess."

She continued out to the parking lot. Joe and Harriet were waiting in the front seat of the Dart. Elspeth got into the back.

The car rolled onto the street in silence, the cigar clamped to the steering wheel in Joe's fingers.

"I don't know what happened with that dress," Harriet said unhappily. "You must have gotten bigger in the last few days."

"Well, I'm in my fourth month."

"It wasn't a very nice way to announce it," said Harriet.

"Well, it happened," Elspeth said, slumped alone in the middle of the seat. "We can't help it. We'd have to tell people around now anyway, if it's starting to show. I already told Bob. A long time ago."

"Him? What'd you tell *him* for?" Joe asked without turning. "There was no call to tell anybody."

"I don't know. I just wanted to. When he came with the tea wagon and stuff. I guess I told him I was getting rid of it."

"Well, now Frieda can tell him you didn't get rid of it," Joe said.

15

DR. Goldwasser lounged in the swivel, hands locked behind his head, his stomach expansive in the tattersall vest, the windows reflecting on his eyeglasses, and told Elspeth the itinerary of his forthcoming cruise of the Aegean. He forgot to examine her until she reminded him.

When she returned to the store it was after six. Joe locked up unhappily.

Joe drove the van. The air currents took the cigar smoke across her face.

He raised again his old idea of getting Jared to go through with a marriage and a divorce a few months after. She began to interrupt him but he continued. He also wanted Jared's agreement to always tell people they had actually been married before the baby was conceived and had kept the marriage a secret because they were in school.

"Dad, forget it. Forget the whole thing. He'd never consider it anyway."

"He'll consider it."

"Why should he?"

"Because he's got something to lose. He can be hit for child support."

"Not if it's given out for adoption he can't."

"Look, I'm trying to do something for you. You've got your reputation to consider."

"A stupid phony story like that isn't gonna give me any reputation worth having. Let me have a reputation for honesty at least."

"Sure, what do you care. Big shot. That's the God damn attitude that got you in trouble in the first place."

But he said nothing more. The wet stub of cigar was in a hand that gripped the wheel. It was dented with tooth marks.

At home Elspeth squatted in the garden and picked the newly ripe yellow squashes. She reached under the floppy leaves. A bee hummed near her wrist.

She made herself motionless, waiting for the bee to go away. Her thigh was pressed to the hardness of her belly. How natural and unnatural pregnancy was. Unnatural to have the tenant pushing all your innards out of place, till there was scarcely room for your bladder. Yet unnatural too to leave the womb untenanted, and the eggs dying month after month unfertilized.

The bee departed.

Harriet came to the screen door and said Cindy Schaeffer was on the phone.

"Tell her I'll call back," said Elspeth.

But she forgot about Cindy until she was in the shower. She wrapped herself in the terrycloth robe, lay on her parents' tufted bedspread, and dialed the pink phone.

Cindy asked her to come on a blind date with a couple of guys. They were touring New England on motorcycles.

"Where are they from?"

"New Jersey someplace," Cindy told her. "They know my cousin in Elizabeth. Can you get the car?"

"I suppose."

She went downstairs in the white terrycloth, brushing her hair. "I'm taking the Dart tonight, okay?" she asked.

Joe did not take his gaze from the television. He said nothing. His fingers and his jaw were tight on the stub of cigar. Little puffs came around it.

She ought to have told Cindy she was pregnant, she thought as she went back up the stairs. She almost had, but in the context of going out with these two guys it would have been awkward. It would have sounded as if she thought Cindy might want to call it off on that account.

She laid out the black shorts with the stretchy tummy, and the tunic with brown and orange squares. She stood looking at them on the bunk, still brushing her hair. She returned to her parents' pink phone and dialed.

"What are you wearing?" she asked Cindy.

"I was gonna ask you that. How about cut-offs?"

"Well," said Elspeth, "I'll be in some new shorts under one of these tunic things. You know, these tunic jobs. I'm sort of pregnant."

The phone at her ear was silent.

"Did you hear me?" Elspeth asked. "I'm kind of pregnant."

"That's what I thought you said. God, Ellie."

"I've been meaning all summer to tell you. But, you know, we sort of haven't had a chance to get together and really talk. Except that once at the beginning of the summer, and I didn't have my thoughts organized then. It's just that there's so much to tell."

"How'd you get pregnant? I don't mean that. What are you gonna do?"

"What am I gonna do? Have a baby, I guess."

"My God. I don't believe it."

"I'll tell you everything. I just wanted to make sure your mother wouldn't be too shocked when I walk in. Maybe you better just come out to the car."

"Nothing shocks my mother. Jesus, Ellie. Tell me."

"Well," Elspeth began, "it doesn't look like I'm getting married. It's a guy you met actually."

"I met him?"

"At a dance at the temple. In the dim past. Remember when we were thirteen, they invited kids from a bunch of other temples, and there was this boy you and I and Abbie kept fighting over all night?"

"Oh, ya. Sort of. Vaguely. It comes back to me. God, Ellie. You mean you were seeing him after that?"

"I bumped into him last fall. He was at Amherst. Five years later and all of a sudden there he is. He didn't even remember me. But I guess I made more of an impression on him the second time. Temporarily, anyway."

"God, I can't believe it. It's a small world."

"You remember him?"

"I remember. He was part of that bunch from the older group that weren't supposed to be there."

"That's right," said Elspeth.

"And his name was—?"

"Jared Blumenthal."

"Jared. That's it. Jared. And you can't marry him?"

"He doesn't even answer my letters. Look, I made a mistake. I'm stupid. Or unlucky. Or both."

"Well, gee, Ellie. I don't know what to say. What'll you do with the baby?"

"Oh, they'll find parents. An agency. Maybe they do it by computer. Everybody wants Jewish babies. Look, I don't want to talk about it anymore now, okay?"

"Okay, okay."

"I'll come by at eight then," Elspeth said.

The conversation left her nervous. For the first time since quitting cigarettes she craved one.

She came down to supper in the terrycloth robe, the hairbrush in her pocket. There was broiled fish and a huge salad of red beans, greens, and slices of yellow squash.

"Are you going out?" Harriet asked her.

"With Cindy. And a couple of guys, friends of her cousin. I think she met them when she was down at her cousin's." She wished she hadn't mentioned the guys.

"Does Cindy know how big you are?" Harriet asked.

"I don't care if it shows. What am I supposed to do? Be in confinement?"

"Did she tell the boys you're pregnant?"

"They'll see for themselves."

Joe ate without speaking or looking at anyone. Elspeth had no appetite. The fish was dry in her mouth.

109

"Did you see Dr. Goldwasser?" Harriet asked.

"Yes."

"What did he say?"

"He's going to Greece. For three weeks. He told me all about it."

"About you. What did he say about you, I mean."

"Oh, fine, fine, fine. I'm always fine, fine, fine."

She dressed after supper and sat at the vanity to finish the brushing. She heard her father's rapid double knock.

"Come in."

Joe tossed a couple of charge cards onto the vanity before her. "You may need gas," he said.

"Thanks." She saw him at three angles in the mirrors. In one her eyes met his. She kept brushing. He was not smiling.

"Comb and brush between your legs, too," he said. "So you'll look your best."

Her throat tightened. He turned and left before she could decide what to retort.

She went to the garden, still somewhat agitated, and filled a paper sack with vegetables for Cindy's mother. She carried it around the house and half jumped and half slid off the retaining wall into the driveway. The twilight was fading into darkness. A window was flung up suddenly and Harriet looked out. "Is that your radio playing out there in the garden? Out back?"

"It's my transistor," Elspeth told her. "Leave it there. It's to keep rabbits out."

"What's the idea?"

"You said a rabbit's been getting into the garden, didn't you?"

"The radio will keep him out?"

"I think so," said Elspeth. "Especially human voices will. I put it on the all-night talk-show station."

She tried to calm herself by accelerating once she was headed outward on Peacemaker Avenue. She raced the yellow light at Plymouth Road and it turned red as she crossed. I shouldn't have done that, she thought.

But she felt better as she approached Cindy's. The street lamp silhouetted some of the moving foliage. Something about those giant maples, the big gray house with its cupola and long porches, was good for the soul. She carried in the bag of vegetables with two hands.

"Gracious, what's this?" said Mrs. Schaeffer, a tall lady who always seemed to Elspeth stately and somehow unspontaneous.

"Vegetables," Elspeth said, as Cindy and Cindy's kid sister Adrienne watched her take the bundle through the dark varnished dining room to the kitchen. From the corner of her eye she saw Cindy and Adrienne take in the protruding front of her tunic, though she knew Mrs. Schaeffer's eyes would avoid it. She put squashes and cucumbers on the table. "I hope you can use them," she said. "They're from our garden."

"Well, you're very kind," said Mrs. Schaeffer. "I'm sure we'll enjoy them."

"Make a salad or something tomorrow," said Elspeth. "There's a flavor when they're real fresh. You never get it in store stuff."

"That's certainly so. There's nothing like freshly picked fruits and vegetables, or freshly baked bread. I've been meaning to call your mother. She's such a sweet woman."

"We've got more than we know what to do with," said Elspeth. "My mother wanted us to put a box of it for sale in the store, but we couldn't do that. It wouldn't be dignified for a hardware."

"You can make preserves."

"We may preserve some. But it's best fresh. We give it to all the neighbors."

There was a racket of motorcycles.

"That's them!" said Cindy. "Come on! I said we'd be out front." She hurried back around the circular table in the dining room. She wore faded denim shorts with raggedy edges and a pullover.

"What time do you think you'll be back?" asked Mrs. Schaeffer.

"Who knows?" Cindy said without turning.

Elspeth followed her onto the columned porch. Adrienne came out to watch and straddled the porch rail. Her braids were tied round her forehead.

"Hey!" Cindy called, and waved. The motorcycles had gone further down the street. Cindy ran across the lawn to the sidewalk and waved both arms. "Hey!"

The motorcycles leaned and circled slowly. Both men had beards.

The motorcycles approached and stopped. Each man had a sleeping bag rolled behind him.

"Hi. I'm Cindy. This is Ellie."

They took off their helmets. The one with the full beard introduced himself as Skip. The one with the Lincolnesque fringe was Ralphie. They were not bad-looking. They were perhaps about twenty or a bit more. Cindy said they could put the bikes and stuff in the garage.

But when Ralphie got off his motorcycle Elspeth slung a smooth leg over it and got on. She took the helmet from where he had hung it. "Brrrm! Brrrm!" she said, clutching the handlebars.

"Would you guys like to go to the drive-in?" Cindy asked.

Elspeth's hair hung out long under the white helmet. "This takes me back," she said. "I had one of these for a while. A piece of junk, but it ran. Remember, Cindy?"

"I remember. You never gave me a ride."

"I didn't? I must have."

"You never did. You said you would, but you never did. You were always tearing around with Sonny Elkin."

"Gee, I'm sorry, Cindy. I meant to. But I didn't have it long. I got rid of it again about three weeks after I got it."

"Why?" said Ralphie.

"Because my mother got so hysterical every time I got on it. It just wasn't worth it."

"Want to take it around the block?" said Ralphie.

"No, come on, Ellie," said Cindy. "Take off the helmet, and let's stash the bikes in the garage. It's late. If we're going to the drive-in we're missing half the first movie."

There was some discussion about whether to go to the drive-in, which was showing a double feature with the same comedian starring in both. Cindy was for it, and the boys were agreeable. It was a comedian that Elspeth had always found rather heavy-footed, but she did not say so.

The Schaeffers' garage was wooden with a pitched roof, to the back and side of the big old house. Elspeth and Cindy walked with the boys as they rolled the motorcycles toward it.

"Give the nice man back his crash helmet like a good little girl," Cindy said.

Elspeth bent to the mirror that extended from the handlebar. "It looks good on me."

"You look like an astronaut," said Ralphie.

At the garage she kissed the top of the helmet and gave it to Ralphie with two hands. Cindy secured the garage and they all walked to the Dart.

Ralphie got in front beside Elspeth.

"Fasten seat belts," she said. She revved the engine loudly. They moved in low gear. "Does it sound like a motorcycle?"

"Nope."

She zigzagged the stick shift forward to third. She yanked it back to high.

"Are you pregnant?" Ralphie asked. "Or is it some kind of a gag or something?"

"It's no gag."

Cindy asked the boys where they had been and where they were going. Skip said the Cape had been disappointing. He had expected something more picturesque. Not a bunch of pizza stands. Cindy said they should have gone to Nantucket and the Vineyard. Skip said they would have, but the ferry cost too much. They would be heading up to Maine in the morning. Maybe they would end up in Nova Scotia.

"Where'll you sleep tonight?" Cindy asked.

"Any suggestions?" said Ralphie.

"Nope. You could put the sleeping bags in our yard if you want."

They arrived late at the drive-in. They chipped in for the admission.

"Get a mosquito thing," said Cindy.

The comedian played a bumbling detective. The women had plunging gowns and short nighties.

On the way to the refreshment counter during intermission Cindy and Skip walked ahead, his hand on the rounded seat of the cut-offs.

"Our money will go farthest in popcorn," Elspeth advised Ralphie.

The second movie was duller than the first. Elspeth felt Cindy's feet push the back of the seat and knew she was nestling with Skip.

After a while Skip remarked that he had seen the movie before. He had forgotten.

"Want to go?" Elspeth asked.

"I don't care," said Skip.

"Let's go," said Ralphie. "It's not that good."

"We could take a ride somewhere," said Cindy. "Mosey out Reservation Road.

112

No, on second thought, skip Reservation Road. It's been getting full of high-schoolers. The lookout's a better place. Let's go up Firefly Hill to the lookout. There's never anyone there, and you can see all the way to Boston."

"Okay?" Elspeth asked.

"Let's go," said Skip.

Elspeth leaned out to restore the speaker to its post.

The Dart climbed the curves of Beaver Dam Road. In the little overlook there were no other cars. The headlights shone on a wooden rail over tufts of grasses. She turned off the lights and shut off the motor.

Before them the earth fell away. It reappeared as rolling black forest, expanding into the distance under an enormous sky. Here and there clusters of tiny lights and a feeble glow marked settlements, far separated from one another, or points of light were strung out to mark a stretch of road before burying themselves again in the gloom. In the north the Big Dipper was hung, the Little Dipper at an angle above it. On the horizon a small portion of sky was diluted reddish over a city. The lights of its towers were a twinkling constellation.

They did not leave the car. "Is that Boston?" Ralphie asked. "How far off is that?"

"Oh, twenty-odd miles," said Elspeth. "As the motorcycle flies."

They were silent a while. Then Elspeth asked Ralphie about the sandals he was wearing. He said he had bought them from a friend he had visited on the Cape, who had a job there making them and selling them. He took off a sandal and let her examine it. There was no talk from the back seat. They knew Cindy and Skip were occupied with one another, so they did not try to include them in their conversation or look around.

Ralphie asked Elspeth whom she lived with, and if she would keep the baby. He had recently finished college at Reed on the West Coast. He didn't know what he would immediately, except try to avoid the draft. He thought he would like to study forestry eventually. They talked about conservation. She told him about the hardware store. She said she thought sometimes she would like to have a bunch of kids. But she would like to be married to the right guy before having the next one. She said she guessed she was basically conventional and square. She was still fondling the sandal.

"Oh, the hell with it," Skip said in the back seat.

"What's the matter?" said Cindy.

"We can't do anything in the back seat, when they're not doing anything in the front seat. When they're just sitting there, trying to make conversation or something."

Elspeth looked around. In the darkness she could see Skip's face and beard, but could not make out his expression.

"Do you want us to be quiet?" she asked him. "Do you want us to go out for a walk or something?"

Skip said nothing.

"Maybe Ralphie and I don't happen to be in the mood for necking," said Elspeth. "Maybe we're in the mood for talking."

"Of course he's not in the mood," said Skip. "You don't neck with a pregnant woman."

Elspeth kept staring at him in the dark, her cheeks growing warm near the ears.

"What was the point of that crack?" she said. "If we feel like talking what's it to you?"

Skip did not flinch from her gaze. But he didn't answer.

"Ralphie and I will take a walk," said Elspeth, "and get out of your hair. Okay? Or we'll go sit on the rail there. Okay, friend? I'm taking a walk so you can enjoy the privacy of my automobile."

"Don't get mad," Ralphie said quietly. He was leaning back in a slump, looking toward the windshield.

"Yeah, don't go away mad," Skip said.

"Come on, calm down, everybody," said Cindy.

"Yeah, let's just enjoy each other's minds," said Skip, with an edge of sarcasm.

"Not a bad idea," said Elspeth.

"Do you go out with guys to enjoy their minds?" Skip asked her.

"I might," she said. "If they happen to have any."

"Oh, ho ho," said Skip. "Are you one of those? Right on, sisters?"

"Not exactly. But I'd like to know what's a pregnant woman got to do with it. If you want to make out, that's your business. And what Cindy does is her business. And my being pregnant is my business. Look, don't look at *me*. I'm not the one that's making trouble. I offered to get out of my own car." She pressed the door handle.

"Never mind," said Skip. "The mood's killed now anyway."

"Well, sorry. Did I kill it?"

"I know what he means," Cindy said to her. "Moods are contagious. The romantic atmosphere is a very delicate thing. You know that."

"Romantic?" said Skip. "Is that what they call it in this town?"

"Or amorous atmosphere," said Cindy.

"Jesus," said Elspeth. "If Ralphie and I have to make out to turn Skip on—I mean, it's sick or something. What kind of a hang-up is that? It's sick."

"What the hell," said Ralphie drearily. He had sunk lower, still looking at no one. His eyes were barely up to windshield level. "Let's laugh it off. Let's find a bowling alley. Or a tiddlywinks tournament. Or something."

"Let's count police cars," said Skip.

"Want to go back to the drive-in?" asked Cindy. "It probably isn't over for a while."

"Anything but that," said Skip. "What do people do for excitement in this town? Just drive up to the lookout and make girls pregnant?"

"Listen," said Elspeth, "once and for all, cut it out. Don't be nasty."

"I guess we should have driven to Boston to a disco place," said Cindy. "But you guys said you were on bikes all day and you want to get up early."

"Let's find and ice-cream stand," said Ralphie. "They say it's hard to be unhappy when you're eating ice cream."

"Are you serious?" Cindy asked him.

"Sure I'm serious. What can we lose?"

"Okay, let's go to Niccolo's," Cindy said tiredly.

Elspeth backed the car and turned it. In the bends of the descent the headlights picked out shrubbery and handsome house fronts. She drove slowly, trying to calm herself.

At the ice-cream stand there were teen-agers and families with kids. Ralphie and Skip and Cindy and Elspeth stood in line at one of the windows.

"Cranberry sherbet—that's a new one," said Skip.

"I'll stick to ice cream," said Elspeth. "When you're pregnant you need lots of calcium."

She had meant it as a pleasantry but it seemed to fall flat.

They sampled each other's cones, and hung about together under an end of the portico.

"Do you find yourself getting a craving for certain foods?" said Ralphie.

"Not especially. Not any more than before. I guess anybody can get a notion sometime that they'd like something or other."

The conversation was labored, sporadic. Elspeth shaped her diminishing blob of ice cream with her tongue, leaning against one of the posts. Ralphie was near her. He turned slightly away, almost imperceptibly. It was as if she could read his mind. She was certain it had just occurred to him that the people who looked at her belly supposed he was her husband. Cindy was solemn, with her pouting lower lip.

Skip said they would like to get back to the bikes. They wanted to get on the other side of Boston before bedding down.

"I want to get far enough north so we can flop in the woods alongside the interstate somewhere," said Skip. "And really cover some ground tomorrow."

"Won't you tour the city at all?" said Cindy.

"A city is a city," he said. "We're looking for the real New England."

Elspeth drove back toward Cindy's. No one spoke. She glanced in the mirror once and saw that Skip pretended to doze.

When she saw the cupola and long porches she turned in toward the garage. She halted with her lights on its doors.

Ralphie, Skip and Cindy ran out. The boys helped Cindy raise the door. The faded brief denim was skin-tight on Cindy's behind above long legs.

Elspeth backed up without saying good-bye.

She drove home slowly. She put the Dart beside the van between the retaining walls. As she walked around to the back she saw the kitchen windows suddenly darken. She went to the garden. The transistor was not visible in the darkness and the squash leaves but she heard it chattering, just as she had left it, very quietly but sufficiently to give pause to an animal.

She entered by way of the kitchen. The house was dark and silent. She turned on a light. On the maple-colored table a pot and a glass told her her father had taken milk for his ulcer. They were still warm and moist.

115

She washed his pot.

The yellow wall phone rang. She picked it up in the middle of the ring. "Hello?"

"Ellie?" She heard Cindy's voice.

Then she heard someone pick up the extension in her parents' bedroom. "It's for me," she said. She heard the upstairs disconnect. "Wait a sec," she said to Cindy. She closed both doors.

Then she sat with the wall phone at the kitchen table. "Hi, Cindy," she said.

"Well," Cindy said. Then Cindy sighed, and fell silent.

"I guess it was kind of a fiasco," said Elspeth.

"Fiasco is right."

"Ralphie was okay," said Elspeth. "But Skip was such a creep. What'd he have such a bee in his bonnet for?"

"Look, don't put it on Skip," said Cindy. "How'd you expect them to react? It's not exactly what they were expecting."

"You mean my being pregnant? So what? I think we had a right to assume they're reasonably liberated. I mean, what century are we in?"

"It has nothing to do with being liberated," Cindy said. "It's just unsexy. It couldn't be more unsexy. Just dumb. Crazy. The atmosphere was like lead."

"How is it unsexy? It's a perfectly natural process. It comes from screwing. What's unsexy about it?"

"Ellie, don't play dumb! Just to put the blame on somebody else. You know perfectly well. It's just unsexy, that's all. I don't know what could be more unsexy. For God sake, Ellie! A guy isn't gonna start feeling your tits when you're pregnant. Not when you're obviously pregnant, like you are. Unless he's some kind of a pervert."

"Fine! Maybe I don't want him feeling my tits."

"Ellie, did you ever see a pregnant girl in the centerfold of Playboy? Did they ever hand out a pregnant Playmate-of-the-Month, standing there bare-ass with a great big huge belly, for guys to drool over? Did they? Did they?"

"Screw Playboy. What's Playboy, the Holy Bible?"

"Ellie, I mentioned it to make a point, that's all, which you know as well as I do. You're not dense. You just won't admit it, that's all."

"Cindy, you just called me to go out. You didn't say you were billing me as Playmate-of-the-Month."

"Ellie, don't be obtuse. You know what I'm saying. I'm just using Playboy to illustrate something. They wouldn't put a ninety-year-old hag in the centerfold either. Or a three-year-old little kid. For the same reason. A pregnant woman is like that. I don't know, I never thought it through before because it's just so damn obvious, but maybe the species is programmed so the male is turned on by a female who's impregnatable. A woman past childbearing doesn't turn him on, and a preadolescent doesn't turn him on. I mean, assuming he's normal. And a pregnant woman is in that category. She's not impregnatable because she's already pregnant. But the bottom line is that sexy isn't pregnant. Pregnant isn't sexy. It just isn't."

"Tough," said Elspeth. "And I don't know if I like your theory. It makes out

116

guys pretty damn stupid. If you're impregnatable you turn them on, and once you're pregnant they're so turned off it kills the evening. I say if guys think girls shouldn't get pregnant, then they shouldn't screw them. I mean, be consistent. One thing or the other. If they want to get laid, then accept the fact that there's such a thing as pregnancy. And anyhow Skip was the one doing all the squawking, and you weren't pregnant. He was with you. In the back seat. If you had in mind slipping your pants off that's between you and him. Don't blame me. There was no pregnancy in the back seat."

"I didn't say slip my pants off. God, Ellie! I don't even know the guy. I just mean I could have used a little affection, that's all. It's been a dry summer. Jesus, you have such a dirty mind! But even if a guy is just sitting and talking with a girl, he wants to know it's a woman, that's all. I'm not very active sexually. You know I'm not. And I believe I can go out with a guy and just sit and talk, not do anything. Exchange ideas, like two human beings, like you and Ralphie were doing in front. Why not? But even so, even just talking, the guy wants to feel like he's out with a woman, just like the woman wants to feel like she's out with a guy. That's all I mean. And pregnant is like not a woman. Like an old lady is not a woman, and a little kid is not a woman. I mean, Ellie, if it's a woman, they can sit there and look at the stars and discuss Einstein and never touch each other, and it still makes sense to him. Because she's a woman. But if he's sitting there with somebody's ten-year-old little sister, flat chested, he feels like an idiot. Ellie, I keep coming back to Playboy and those magazines—not that I have any use for them. I don't. But they're a fact of life and they prove a point. I said centerfold before, but I mean the whole magazine. A guy can't have sex with the magazine. But it has photos of sexy women all through the magazine, and that's why a guy buys it. He looks at those bodies, and he feels like a guy. But you never, never, anywhere in those magazines, ever see a photo of anyone pregnant. Okay? Except in the cartoons. In the cartoons there may be an old lady, or somebody pregnant. In the jokes. Never in the photos."

"So what," said Elspeth. "Whether it's his hand in your drawers or whether it's just talking about Einstein, Skip wasn't stuck with the pregnant girl. Ralphie was. And he wasn't complaining. All the noise came from Skip."

"Because it's the whole atmosphere. We were together. Just like if you were at your best, you'd have turned him on. I mean, you'd have turned my guy on too. And since Ralphie had you, and he was stuck with me, I'd get the benefit too."

"Well, sorry Cindy. Sorry I wasn't the prop you were looking for. But I didn't go out to be a centerfold, and I didn't go out to be a cartoon, either. I went out to go out. And because you asked me. Two guys dropped on you out of the blue, and you needed somebody. I guess you shouldn't have called me."

"I wouldn't have. If I'd known."

"You did know," said Elspeth. "I told you. I called you back special."

"Yeah, after it was all arranged, and I couldn't do anything about it. And I didn't know how pregnant. I thought you meant it didn't show. I gave you credit for a little bit of sense."

"I said I was wearing a maternity tunic."

"You did?"

"Yes, I did."

"Well, you caught me off guard. I was flabbergasted, Ellie. I'd already invited you. And you'd already accepted. What was I gonna say? Don't come? Why didn't you tell me before? We've been on the phone a few times this summer. And at the start of the summer, when we went out to Niccolo's that time, just the two of us. Were you pregnant then? You must have been. You never said a word. I thought we were friends."

"I know," said Elspeth. "I guess I should have. I was sort of leading up to it. Waiting for the right time, when we'd have lots of time to go into it. In depth. I know you'd want to know everything. Like you said, we're friends."

"Well, that's true. I do want to know what happened. I mean, anytime you want to talk about it, Ellie. I'm here. I'm your friend."

Elspeth didn't reply. There was a silence. Elspeth laid a leg on a chair.

"You want to talk now?" said Cindy.

"No. Not now."

"You sore?"

"I'm not exactly cheerful," said Elspeth. "Are you sore?"

"No, I'm not sore. Look, Ellie, we've been friends all our lives. Friends can fight and they're still friends."

"Okay, but not now, Cindy. I'm tired. All of a sudden I'm tired as hell. I'm signing off. Okay? So long."

"So long," said Cindy unhappily.

Elspeth rose and put the phone in its place on the wall.

She went upstairs. When she stood at her open window, near the whispering maple, and listened carefully, she could still hear her transistor quietly down there in the garden.

Before undressing she sat nervously on the lower bunk in the darkness, staring at the moonlit braided rug. Cindy was okay in her way. But with Cindy you couldn't separate the sympathy from the nosiness.

Cindy would have had an abortion, probably. Except Cindy wouldn't get pregnant in a million years.

Elspeth made herself undress. She got into the lower bunk without hanging up her clothes.

Out there in the hall the long pendulum maintained its faithful slow tick.

Every time she tried to relax, and welcome sleep, her brain became busy again.

It was true that they don't put photos of pregnant girls in Playboy or any of those. They wouldn't put them in a skin flick or a nudie show either. Except the jokes, the cartoons. Cindy was completely right about that.

They jerk off over the Playmate-of-the-Month, but when you're pregnant they can only deal with you as a joke.

A professor at Mount Holyoke had said that we joke about the things that make us uncomfortable, the things we can't face. The human infant laughs when the parent sets up a situation of mock danger, such as tossing the baby in the air, or pretending to chase him. The baby knows it's pretended danger, not real. Biologically, laughter derived from crying; in its earliest form it was the enjoyment of escape from danger, and then the titillation of danger you knew you could lick, or that you knew wasn't real. And as adults we still try to use laughter in this same way— to persuade ourselves that something that troubles us isn't real.

There was truth in that. The professor had shown cartoons from the old Saturday Evening Post, circa 1931, in which black people were always jokes. Whites were uncomfortable, afraid to expose their attitudes about blacks to the light of truth. So they pretended that black people were something funny. Like girls who get pregnant. They wish you didn't exist, but since you do, their next defense is to pretend you're funny.

People are such phonies. Always telling themselves they've made such progress. They haven't.

In the olden days you had to go into confinement, and pregnant was a dirty word, and you had to hide indoors and be invisible, but now of course we're so enlightened and liberated. Oh, sure. If you're a pretty little housewife with your shopping cart, fine, fine, they let you show off your big tummy in your cute maternity outfit and they smile at you. And congratulate themselves how liberated and intelligent they are. Try to go out double-dating, though. You're a leper. You're poisoning the atmosphere. The same hang-ups are still there, only in different form. Only the names have been changed to protect the bullshitters.

Nothing makes any sense. These guys want you to be sexy sexy sexy, at the same time that they have to psych themselves into thinking pregnant is something they never heard of. To turn guys on, you have to pretend you don't have a uterus. Jesus. When a guy is penetrating you, what does he think is up there after the top of the vagina? What's he thinking girls are stuffed with? Ice cream? It's cockeyed.

Sometimes I'd like to just quit the human species. Resign from it. And join some species that isn't so phony, so sick. The whales, or something. Some intelligent species, that's not afraid to be aware of what it's doing when it copulates and isn't so full of crap.

She was nervous enough to smoke. But no. She'd sworn off it. She had no cigarettes. She owed the baby that much.

She went to the bathroom and came back. This time she tried the upper bunk. She still couldn't sleep.

The grandfather clock, bonging out there, at the head of the stairs. Does the baby hear that, in the womb?

She thought of a grisly article she had seen in Newsweek downstairs just a day or two ago, by some guest columnist who was against abortion. It said that saline solution burns the baby's skin off. In dilation and curettage, an instrument slices up the baby's body. In suction abortion, it is torn apart into a jumble of arms and legs. And in a hysterotomy the baby fights for its life and moves and even cries as they kill it. She didn't know if it was true or propaganda. It had made her sick to read it. She hoped it was lies. She wished she hadn't seen the article. She wondered if her parents had. She had not mentioned it to them. But articles like that always had that effect on her. She had read an article in Life magazine once about the yearly hunt for baby seal skins in Alaska. How they skin baby seals alive, and take their skins, and leave them alive, red, to die of shock and cold and bleeding there on the icy shore, in front of mother seals weeping and weeping and flipping around them on their flippers on the ice. She'd seen the article and its pictures years ago and she could still neither forget it nor bear to think of it. Why did they print those articles? All they proved is that the world makes no sense. The world is terrible, if only you knew. That's what the victims of the Nazis had found out. That was the real truth. But you couldn't let yourself think about it. Or you'd get the horrors. You'd vomit. You couldn't keep food down. You couldn't live.

Inside her the baby kicked. She felt it. It was the first time. She moved her hands on her abdomen.

She sat up, on the edge of the bunk, dangling her feet. She looked tiredly at the moon through the window. In a while she lay down, sleepily.

She thought of the postcard Diana had sent from her honeymoon. Did Diana really love that funnyface?

She wakened about ten in the morning.

When she came downstairs in shredded-edged cut-offs and shirttails her parents had had their brunch. Joe was on the sofa, with parts of the Sunday paper spread beside him, and puffing a cigar. Harriet was in a housecoat. Other parts of the paper were scattered about. The television was already playing under the portraits of herself and Eric and Mark.

She went out into the sunshine and turned off the transistor.

She fixed a cup of instant and wandered to the living room sipping it.

"It's a terrific day," she said. "Let's drive down to Woods Hole, the three of us, and go to the beach, and see Bob, and get him to show us around that Oceanographic Institute or whatever it is. Maybe it's like an aquarium or something."

"I'd be too embarrassed to be seen with you with that belly," Joe said.

"Nobody's gonna be staring or thinking about it. People have their own problems."

"No," he said. He reached behind him to squash out the cigar. He lay down on the sofa without shoes, and closed his eyes.

"If you're just gonna nap mostly, would you mind much if I drove down with Mama?"

"To Woods Hole?" he said.

"I don't think he's there anyway," said Harriet. "Frieda said he goes to his girl friend every weekend."

Joe's eyes opened a little and looked at Elspeth. "The doctor said you're supposed to have a nap too, didn't he?"

"No. Not if I'm not tired. Just so long as I'm off my feet a while every day."

"Frieda was down at Woods Hole," said Harriet. "She said it's not even open to the public."

"Well, I'd like to go to a beach," Elspeth said.

"You don't have a bathing suit that'll fit you now," said Harriet.

"I'll manage. I'll wear one of the old pairs of cut-offs I let out, and an old shirt hanging over it. Like I have on now. Let's go to Winthrop. We haven't been there since Gramps died."

"Too far," Harriet said.

"Well, Nantasket, or Duxbury."

"The traffic would be terrible," said Harriet. "On a day like this."

Elspeth wandered to the rear window. The upper half had been lowered. She leaned her arms and face on it and gazed through the screen.

Maybe she would go the whole summer without having gotten to a beach. There wasn't a lot of summer left. When Gramps and Grammy were alive, they had all had an excuse to go to Winthrop Beach every Saturday or Sunday. And even stay as guests in the little house for weeks at a time.

They had been staying there when Aunt Frieda bought her that teensy bikini. At age twelve she had refused to wear any bathing suit but modest one-piece ones. But Aunt Frieda gave her that horrible little thing and then made fun of her half the summer for being too shy to wear it. Till at last one Sunday in desperation and near to tears she went upstairs, though everyone else was fully dressed, and put it on. The bra would not fit right at the edges, no matter how she tugged. The ridiculous wisp of panties got smaller with every step. But she had had no choice but to go back down to the living room and prove she wasn't afraid to wear a bikini. Otherwise the teasing would never end. When she appeared in the living room Aunt Frieda and Uncle Harry and Diana had laughed and laughed and cheered and cheered. But Bob sensed her humiliation and blushed, which made her blush too, worsening the embarrassment for them both. She didn't dare run up to change too quickly lest they laugh louder. If she were to flee now Aunt Frieda would laugh forever. It seemed to her there was a mile of skinny nakedness from the circles of the bra to the twist of fabric at her crotch. They covered so little they seemed only to draw extra attention to whatever they covered. But she forced herself to remain, helping her mother to set the table and cut the pie, virtually nude among all these clothed people. Mama was no help. Mama never disagreed with people. Mama just passively assumed that whatever Aunt Frieda did was somehow reasonable. She felt as though she were showing everyone her navel. She felt as if she were showing them the creases under her buttocks. She knew of her ribs and the bumps of her backbone, moving visibly under tight skin, as though even her bones were naked. There was a golden fuzz of down on her lower back, tapering toward the cleavage of her buttocks, that she knew from the mirror, and she was aware of even this now being public knowledge. She dared not catch Bob's eye lest they both blush again. She was aware of him trying to finger a book, trying to neither stare or not stare, glancing out of a window, putting his hands in his pockets or adjusting his collar, faking nonchalance, moving about self-consciously. It was a good thing Aunt Frieda hadn't noticed his discomfort. Because that would have been a tremendous joke, with Aunt Frieda teasing both of them. It had been awful to be twelve. Especially if you had an aunt like Aunt Frieda.

Behind her part of the Sunday paper slid audibly from the sofa to the floor. She glanced around, still resting on the lowered window sash. Joe's eyes were barely open. He was nearly asleep. "I'm gonna put the hammock up, in the backyard," she said. "Did you ever replace that hook on the oak tree? I'm gonna put the hammock up, and put my belly in the bottom of the hammock, and take my top off."

16

ALL outside repairs had become Elspeth's job exclusively, but now Joe took her off it. He would not reconsider. It just didn't look good for a pregnant woman to come into people's homes and sprawl with a wrench under people's sinks. He did the outside repairs himself.

Many jobs that had been mainly Joe's Elspeth now did in his absence, like tinting paints to the exact shade. Duplicating keys was supposed to be one of Homer's specialties. But wise customers tried to wait till Homer was busy and give their keys to Elspeth, because Homer's keys sometimes had to be thrown away and redone.

"On Rosh Hashanah I'll be going to the temple," Joe said while he unlocked the cash register one morning, before any customers were there. "So you two will be here alone. That's a week from Thursday and Friday. Elspeth, you'll open up. The two mornings. I'll get here about twelve, twelve-thirty."

Elspeth had already turned over a bicycle and was loosening the bolts to remove the rear wheel. Her braids touched her hands. "I'd like to go too," she said.

"What do you want to go to the temple for?" said Joe without turning. "You don't believe in anything."

"You don't either."

He looked at her. "I wouldn't say that. I wouldn't say I don't believe in anything. As a matter of fact I increased my pledge fifty percent this year. I'm gonna be up there on the bimma with all the machers. I'm gonna open the curtain when they take the torahs out."

Elspeth lifted out the wheel and squatted again to lay it on the floor. Joe turned back to the register. He unwrapped a roll of coins. Elspeth pried tire irons into the rim. Grease from the chain had stained her fingers. "Don't say I don't believe in anything," she said quietly.

"Yeah? What do you believe in?"

"Well, for instance, I believe the Messiah has already come."

She watched what she did, the iron sliding with difficulty. But she knew her father and Homer were both staring at her. The sound of coins had stopped.

"You do?" Joe said.

She kept prying the tire, not taking her eyes from it. "Yup. But his mother had him aborted in the third month. And so there's an end of it, and there's no more hope for the world."

"Really?" said Homer. "Do you mean it? Where would you get a belief like that?"

"It's as good as any."

"Come on, can't you see she's pulling your leg?" said Joe. "I *told* you she didn't believe in anything."

"Maybe my soul needs praying for as much as yours," she said, still busy with the tire.

"Do you really want to go?" Joe asked.

"Well, I usually like to stop by, anyway. And see if any of the kids are hanging around out front."

"And hang around with the kids out front? With a big belly? That'd look great."

The door jangled and a customer entered.

On the way home, Joe took the cigar from his mouth and told her she was to be considered in charge whenever he was not in the store. "If there's any question. Like if I'm out on a plumbing call. And like those two mornings next week."

"Mm, no. I'd rather you put Homer in charge. Really, Dad. It happened once before. You said I was in charge, and Homer didn't say anything, but he was very hurt."

"Well, okay. We won't call it in charge, if you want. But if there are any decisions to be made you make them. Like if a salesman comes in."

"Salesmen? We could just tell them to come back when you're there."

The van had arrived in the driveway. Joe turned off the switch but did not get out. "Well," he said, "that louses them up. Sometimes they can't get back for a couple of weeks. And if it's any of the regular guys, you know whether to reorder or not. If we're low on something. And if it's a stranger with a new item, use your judgment if it's something you think we should carry, and if you like the price. I trust you. You've got a head on your shoulders."

Elspeth went up and showered. When she stepped out of the tub onto the bath mat she tried some calisthenics. She couldn't touch her toes anymore.

As she came down the stairs she thought she heard Joe in the kitchen mentioning his attorney. When she entered the kitchen there was a silence. Harriet was setting the table.

"Are you trying to make some deal with Mr. Blumenthal and Jared again?" Elspeth asked Joe. "That marriage-and-divorce baloney?"

Though she looked at Joe she noticed that Harriet colored slightly.

123

"Why do you think that?" said Joe.

"I just heard you mention Mr. Rosenbaum, that's all."

He was sitting at his place at the table. He had not met Elspeth's eyes. She began to help with the table setting.

"So what," he said. "Maybe you heard wrong. And if I did mention Barney Rosenbaum, what does it prove? He's on the high holy day seats committee."

"Okay. But if you're making a deal, I've got a right to know."

"Yeah. You and your rights. All you kids care about is rights. Do anything they God damn please. Rights, yes. Responsibilities, no."

Her suspicions were aroused again in the morning when Joe gave her the store keys and told her to take tha van and open up alone. He was taking the Dart to Boston for an errand.

He came to the store toward noon. "Did any salesmen call?"

"No."

The store was busy all afternoon. At the day's end she stood with Joe, undoing a braid while he locked up and set the burglar alarm, but he gave her not a word or a glance. They took the van and the Dart home separately.

Joe watched his fork turn in the spaghetti. He said he had met with Rosenbaum and with the Blumenthals' attorney, in the other attorney's office. The Blumenthals had not been there. But their attorney said their top offer was five hundred bucks and he could not in conscience advise them to pay a nickel more. Rosenbaum had said it was a good deal, to grab the five hundred and forget it. "The kid says you slept with everybody. And four of the kid's friends are ready to swear in court they had intercourse with you. That's what he said. Four of them. And they're willing to come into court."

Elspeth felt a debilitating chill go through her. Her eyes blurred. Her arms felt limp. She could feel her heartbeat, almost as though she heard it inside her. Across from her Joe still stared down at the fork he held in the spaghetti, but it was no longer turning. "Jared said that?" Her voice was dry and shaky. "He said that about me?"

She looked at Harriet, and again at Joe, catching his eye this time as he glanced up. Their expressions were as though her face frightened them, and she wondered briefly what it looked like.

Her lips kept moving. "He said *what?*" she said. "Oo, that turd. That stinker. He said *what?*"

"Maybe he didn't," Harriet suggested. "Maybe the lawyer made it up."

"But he'd know what the lawyer was gonna do," said Elspeth, her voice becoming stronger. "The lawyer must have talked to him. If Jared didn't want the lawyer to say that he could have written me, or phoned me. I wrote to *him*."

"I said," Joe explained, "I said, 'would you do a thing like that, bring in four punks to testify like that? What would you blacken my girl's name for?' And he says, 'it's not every girl in this day and age that would bring a paternity suit.'"

"I didn't bring it," said Elspeth. "You did."

"I said," Joe continued, " 'how do we know you're not bluffing about these guys?'

124

and he says, 'you want to take depositions? You'll see for yourself.' You know, cool as a cucumber. Smiling. 'Take depositions. Or go to court, it's your privilege. Mark it for trial.' And I said, 'what if these guys all turn out to have blood types that show they couldn't be the father.' But the answer to that is it doesn't make any difference. If they slept with you there could have been others. And I even asked Barney, suppose those four kids are lying. If they're lying, couldn't he ask them all kinds of questions in cross-examination and trip them up. But the bottom line is, maybe he can make them out to be liars and maybe he can't, but there's still no way a blood test can prove any particular boy is the father. It can prove he isn't, but it can't prove he is. So what can you do? Wait two years for the case to come to trial, and hope the baby's gonna look exactly like him, and maybe the court will order a student with no money to pay token support of five dollars a week? You won't even know where the baby is by then. The baby will have been adopted out already where it can't even be traced. The agency won't tell you. They can't. So the whole thing's ridiculous. The only way we can scare them is as long as they think you might keep it. The next three months, before it's born and adopted out. And no way is it gonna come to trial in that time."

"Why do you say, '*if* they slept with me,' and '*if* they're lying.' Do you believe them? Don't you *know* they're lying?"

He sighed tiredly. His eyes moved from hers. "I don't know what to believe."

Elspeth stared at him. Her lips moved wordlessly. Then she let out a wild shriek. Joe gave a start. Elspeth picked up her plate of spaghetti, her hand beneath it, and flung it with force to the floor. It smashed.

Harriet got down weeping to clear the mess.

Elspeth got down too, pressing her aside. "Don't clean it up!" she told Harriet. "You shouldn't have to clean it up! I'll clean it up." Joe had left the room, she didn't know where. Maybe to lie down. She sponged the food. She put wedges of china into the garbage. She worked quickly, trying to reach in all directions to leave nothing for Harriet. But though she had smashed it near her chair bits of ground meat and slivers of china had gone surprising distances. Some were beyond the linoleum tiles and were in the carpeting of the foyer. She rinsed tomato sauce from the sponge again and again and returned to the linoleum, the faucet running.

At last she ran upstairs. The slamming of her door shook the pendulum out of its rhythm, so that it seemed the clock would stop. She looked about for something more to smash. But there was nothing she wanted to break here. Through the closed door she heard the clock regain its regularity. She almost sprang onto the upper bunk and bit the pillow.

She heard her mother's footsteps and the opening of the door.

"Daddy didn't mean it," Harriet said tearfully. "He loves you."

Elspeth rose on her elbows and looked at her. Her mother was red from weeping. "He believed them!" Elspeth said, weeping too. "How could he!"

"No he didn't. He didn't believe them. You didn't hear him right."

"I heard him all right! Go away! Go away! Everybody leave me alone!"

Her mother hurried out.

"Close the door!" Elspeth shouted after her. Then she wept into the pillow.

She recognized Joe's knock. "Can I come in?" he said.

"What do you want!"

He came in. She lay clutching the pillow, her back to him.

"Sweetheart, I'm sorry. I didn't mean it like that."

"Don't call me sweetheart! I won't forgive you. I'll never forgive you. Never."

"Look, I've been upset."

"How could you believe them!"

"I didn't believe them."

She turned and rose on an arm. "But you didn't not believe them! Why? Why? I told you I only slept with one boy."

"I'm sorry. It's my fault. But they get you in a lawyer's office, and I'm upset and aggravated anyway, and he throws these four kids at me, and I never expected you to be pregnant in the first place. When I got out there to that infirmary and they said you were pregnant I couldn't believe it. I never expected anything like that from you. So how's a parent supposed to know what to believe these days? But I believe you now. All right?"

"They offered you five hundred dollars. Didn't that show you they had a guilty conscience?"

"Yes and no. The five hundred is just in consideration of dropping a claim, that's all. For nuisance value. They didn't have to agree to that."

"I'm nuisance value. I'm a nuisance to everybody."

"No, no. Come on now, Elspeth." He came over, and put his hands on the wood of the upper bunk. "Stop it. Give me a kiss."

"No."

He dropped his hands, but stood there looking at her. Then he turned to go.

At the door he turned again. "Look, don't make me out to be such a bum. You got yourself into this mess. You. Not me. I've been trying to help you. And so has Barney Rosenbaum. Barney was sort of pulling a fast one too, on the other guy, you know. He didn't tell him you're not keeping the baby. I think he sort of suspected it, but Barney gave back as good as he got. He said, 'you want to chance it? You want to see that baby on her lap in a courtroom?' And he got five hundred bucks for you. Half a thousand. You'll have the check in the mail. You'd have had nothing. Your expenses I'll pay for. Rosenbaum's share I'll pay for. But at least you'll get a little compensation for your aggravation—"

"I don't want his check! That lousy no-good shit, that stinker, telling those lies and throwing money at me! I'm not a prostitute!"

"That's not the idea. For him it's a lot of money. He's a kid, struggling to get through school. And money doesn't come that easy to his parents, either. So it'll be a damn good lesson for them. That kid'll stop and think before he mistreats another girl. What are you gonna do? Tear the check up and do him a favor? Put it in your savings account and forget it."

"I don't want it! I won't take it! Tell him to shove it up his ass!"

He sighed. She rolled toward the wall. She heard him sigh again. Then he went out, and closed the door.

After he had gone down the door unlatched itself. Elspeth let herself down from the bunk and closed the door securely.

She thought she might be sick. She allowed herself to collapse, in the middle of the concentric circles of the braided rug. She crawled to the back window and raised the screen. She gagged, but she couldn't vomit. She crawled to the bunk bed and took the lower one this time. It was growing dark. An arm lay on her forehead.

Sometimes a lie was just so preposterous that you didn't know where to begin sweeping it up. All you could do was sit down and cry.

The way that son of a bitch bragged to us in Symphony Hall there, about how every woman in Smith and Mount Holyoke and the U of Mass is panting for his son's cock. Young women, old women. Bragged! To listen to him you'd think his son was screwing everything in sight, the greatest swordsman of all time. Jared Blumenthal's stiff prick is God's great gift to womankind.

And now they have the gall to come with a straight face and point the finger at me. All of a sudden we're back in the Middle Ages.

And none of it was true. I was a virgin and Jared knew it. I was his great triumph. I only gave in because I was so sorry for him. The poor slob wasn't getting anything, for all his glib gab. He was starving. Really starving, for a piece of ass and some self-assurance.

And I was stupid, charitable. After that mixer, when the guys came down to look over the freshman class, I could have had my pick of ten times as many guys as I could remember the names of. And I picked him. Not because he's a great actor. Not because he's such a talker. He's not even good-looking. He wasn't even a catch. Something in him got to me, that's all. Something vulnerable. I though he'd really appreciate it. Being the winner, getting into the one they all had their eye on. Instead it just gave him a great big swelled head.

Guys can make you sick. Oh, sure, they're for the single standard. When they're talking. Especially when they're trying to talk you into it. And then when it suits them they can turn right around and stick you with the double standard.

She dozed, but awoke in darkness, hot in her clothes. She pushed off the slacks and extricated herself from the tunic without rising. She lay there in her underwear.

She slept again. She awakened to the sound of her father's groans. She heard her mother ask if he wanted her to call Dr. Fleming. She could not make out his answer. But in time they were quiet.

She wished she hadn't wakened.

It was all too possible that the best of life was behind her. She was eighteen, going on nineteen. She might never again be as pretty as now. Nowhere to go but down.

Once she had believed in love. Love made babies. But the truth was that a boy who had contempt for you could make you just as pregnant. Your getting pregnant was just like the mold growing on stale bread. People were isolated in their own private universes, fighting for survival, and they loved you only so long as they

127

thought they needed you. You reached out for love, and your own body turned on you.

Where there's life, there's stink. Why hadn't some philosopher pointed that out? Philosophers need beauty, or love, or truth, or faith, but everybody needs toilet paper. The emergence of the human species has made toilet paper the most important item on earth. You can survive without parents, without children. Without schooling. But not without toilet paper. And the forests are being cut down and the world made a desert to provide it.

She listened to the crickets. They were slower now. Their season was ending.

Next it was the clock that woke her.

"Bonggg—" she said together with the clock. "Bonggg—"

The reverberations died away.

She thought she had counted four. It was still dark. And humid.

She had married a kindly, older millionaire, a genius in commodity futures and a quiet philanthropist. Elspeth and Jennifer were the joys of his life. On Sundays in summer the formal gardens out back were open to the public.

Jared telephoned from California. Any chance of Jennifer spending the summer with me? he asked. I'll have Jennifer return your call when she comes in, Elspeth told him.

Poor Jared. So lonely. All the children of his various marriages had been born with syphilis and died in infancy. Occasionally he was still able to get a humiliating bit part in a grade-D movie.

Jennifer parked her Porsche beside the Alfa Romeo and strode through the magnificent entrance hall, drawing off her gloves. It was a great brick chateau of a house. How beautiful Jennifer was. The image of her mother.

Jennifer returned his call. Yes. Mother asked me to return you call. However, it's rather late for you to come into my life now, don't you think? A father I've never met, that I don't even know? To say nothing of the inconsiderateness of asking me to pack and fly to Switzerland with you on half a day's notice. I'm not trying to be unkind, but my plans for the summer were made months ago. I'm sailing with an expedition to the Arctic, to study the whales. Sorry. I said sorry. No. I can't help it. You're nineteen years too late.

This time Elspeth did not sleep again. She saw the creeping gray daylight. Why do the birds take this crazy time for their chirping? Her eyes hurt. She still lay in yesterday's underwear. At last, when the sun rose, she opened a drawer and looked for clean clothes.

On the way to work in the van, Joe said that if she wanted, she could go to the temple on the second day of Rosh Hashanah and he would work.

"That's okay," she answered. "You can go both days. On condition you pray for me."

"Yeah."

"I mean it, Daddy. You have to pray for me."

"Are you serious? Are you getting religious or something?"

"No, but I like the idea of you praying for me."

"I'll pray for you and you can still go the second day."

"No."

"You said you wanted to go."

"Well, I guess I changed my mind. I'd just as soon be in the store."

He shrugged. "Suit yourself."

Everybody in town knew she was pregnant. They had either seen for themselves in the store or heard from others. But why walk into that crowd at the temple, and stand at prayer with Mama and Daddy, and have people sneaking looks up the row at her and at Mama and Daddy, and glancing away the second you caught them?

She did not want to be mad at Daddy anymore. But some days now he would ride the whole trip between the house and the store smoking in utter silence, as if he did not know she was beside him. Sometimes, in the store or at home, he was his friendly self. But some days, or for whole parts of days, he seemed never to look at her, and her eyes would seek his unsuccessfully.

The Sunday before Rosh Hashanah Elspeth went with her parents to the cemetery. They stood without saying anything, looking at the graves of Mark and Eric. One of the granite markers had settled a little crooked. Their plot had room for six graves in all. Space for Daddy and Mama and herself and one left over.

They turned to leave. "Can we walk over to Gramps's and Grammy's graves too?" Elspeth asked.

"That's a different cemetery," said Harriet. "I went with Frieda last week."

"Oh."

"In Dedham," Harriet said.

They walked toward the gate. Elspeth had known Gramps's place was different. She wondered why she had forgotten. Well, Gramps probably wouldn't want me visiting with a big belly anyway.

Near the iron gate she started to cry.

"What's the matter?" Harriet asked her.

"I don't know."

Harriet cried too, which made Elspeth cry more. They walked to the Dart. Joe opened the door, the unlit cigar in his mouth. "A couple of weeping women," he said.

On Rosh Hashanah it rained hard. Elspeth and Homer tended the store. But most of the time there were no customers. In the afternoon Joe came. He said nothing and looked at no one. He rested his elbows beside the cash register and stared at the beating rain beyond the merchandise in the windows.

There was rain the second day too. She had brought her white raincoat. There was constant activity in her womb. She had never felt the baby exercise so continually like that. She sat on the tall stool by the register. If it were born now, she thought, it could live, probably. Just about entering the seventh month, actually.

"Northeasters always last three days," Homer said.

"I know it," said Elspeth.

"I mean, I was just mentioning it."

"It's probably the edge of the hurricane," she said.

Joe came again in the afternoon, chewing an unlighted cigar. His clothes were wet.

When it was time to go home the rain was heavier. Joe drove fast, in a way that seemed to her reckless in such weather. She leaned back, braced for a crash. She breathed with relief when they arrived between the retaining walls.

Joe ran out and flung up the garage door noisily. Elspeth slid behind the wheel and drove in.

They entered through the paneled basement. He threw his soaked hat onto the upright piano.

Harriet had stayed home the second morning because of the rain. "Was the service nice?" she asked during supper.

"The usual. If you've seen one you've seen 'em all. I had a discussion with the rabbi afterwards. I told the rabbi God is meshuggeh. I told him straight out. God is meshuggeh. I lost two sons for no damn reason. Life doesn't mean a thing. And girls can be impregnated like rabbits. We breed like flies and we die like flies."

He stabbed a piece of roast.

"I'm glad these holidays only come once a year," he said. "Yom Kippur I won't go. Except half an hour for yizkor, I'll run over. It's a Saturday and we need three in the store. The sermons, Rabbi Quint, I can get along without. He's no genius. And some of those hotshots around the temple I wouldn't care if I didn't see them till next year. We're having a shmooss out in the Donors' Lobby there, and it's like every guy's daughter hit the jackpot. I got sick listening to them. Lester Holtz's daughter got accepted in Harvard Medical School. Boy, is that guy on cloud nine! He's walking on air! You know how many girls they took? Two! Two, from the whole United States. From the whole world, actually. Can you imagine that? Summa cum laude. Phi Beta Kappa. And the Cohen girl, Lori Cohen, in her first year at the U of Mass she was elected to the Student Government already, and this year they're putting her up for vice president. She's in the Who's Who In American Colleges. And I'm standing there like a jerk listening. And thinking about my little sweetheart here. Veh's mir."

Hardly anything more was said for the rest of the meal.

Elspeth loaded the dishwasher.

"Hey! What's this?" she heard her father say in the living room. " 'Notice of attempt to deliver registered mail.' " He came back. "You know what that is? That's gonna be your check for five hundred bucks."

"I don't want that money!" She turned. "I told you to tell him to shove that check up his ass, and I meant it!"

"Crazy! You want to give it back to him? I don't understand kids. Morals are nothing, who needs it. Money's nothing, who needs it. Go wreck your life, who needs it. But all of a sudden they're on their high horse. 'I'm not a prostitute!' Man the barricades, comrades! Just so long as it's for some cockamamy lunatic reason that doesn't make any sense."

Elspeth shut her eyes, leaning back on the dishwasher and biting her wrist.

"It's not her fault," said Harriet. "It's the times."

"It's no excuse! She doesn't have to go along with the times! I blame her! And I blame you, too! Crazy! Like her cousin Bob Shoemaker, there's another one. She'd be better off if she was a religious nut. At least she'd know enough to keep her legs closed. Listen, you idiot." He advanced on Elspeth. "I can lead you to water but I can't make you drink. You're gonna need that money. Your childhood's over. You need money every day of your life, until you die. You know what a nightmare life is when you can't pay the rent? At least I cost that stinking son of a bitch five hundred. It was the best I could do. You want to make him a present of that money? After what he said about you?"

"I'll never touch it!"

"You don't have to touch it. You don't even have to endorse it. I'll mark it 'deposit to account of person named on face' and give it in at the bank for your account."

"I'll never touch it! It'll rot in the bank forever!"

"Money in the bank doesn't rot, sweetheart. They loan it out."

HER belly grew bigger. She spent a Sunday letting out the denim jeans she had let out before. She ripped up a denim skirt to get inserts for the jeans. In the store now customers' eyes fixed on her belly before her face. Often she saw Joe look at the customers look at her.

"You're huge," he said to her in a moment when there were no customers. "Are you sure you counted right? You can't be just six months, seven months. You must be in your ninth month already."

"No, I'm positive. I still have a ways to go."

In ten days or so she had to sit at the machine in the little sewing room and let out the jeans still further.

"Maybe you should ask Dr. Goldwasser if you're carrying twins," Harriet said anxiously. "Or triplets God forbid."

"Well, he said one heartbeat is all he can find. But I'll ask him again when I'm there. Tuesday."

Joe shook his head at her when she came to breakfast next morning. "I've seen pregnant women in my time. But never as big as you. God, if you've still got two months to go how much bigger can you get? Mama was never that big."

"Oh, I was big," said Harriet.

"Oh no you weren't. Look at her, for God sake. Don't tell me you were that big. Not like that you weren't."

The thought crossed her mind that she could be carrying a monster, like a pair of Siamese twins with one heart.

She was relieved when Dr. Goldwasser told her nothing was amiss.

"Maybe you look very big because you're a relatively small girl," he said, standing by the table on which she sat. His thumbs hung on the pockets of his white smock. "On a tall, big-boned girl it might not show at all. Or they can be enormous too. Individuals differ from one another, you know, in every part of the body. And this is no exception. The volume of your uterus may be no more than someone else, but instead of getting wider like some, or higher like some, all your increase seems to concentrate on projecting straight out forward. Something like those two breasts of yours. That's good, actually. It makes less pressure on you internal organs. If you held the baby more inside, so to speak, it would be less visible, but your intestines and bladder and everything else would all be pressed to the wall to make room. Maybe even your lungs. Carrying way out from you like that makes a more comfortable pregnancy. So far as all your other organs are concerned."

She put the wrap back on.

"It's very firm," he added. "You have good, strong tissues. That belly's as hard as a rock. Nothing sags."

"It's out way further than my breasts."

"Of course."

"Am I gonna have a big baby?"

"Not necessarily. No reason to think so."

At supper she told Harriet and Joe what Dr. Goldwasser had said.

"Well, I can't stand it," said Joe. "I can't look at you. I wish it was something I couldn't see. That stomach is the biggest thing in the store. All day long I have to look at it. If I go out on a plumbing call I dread having to come back and have that that God damn thing hit me in the face again. She's turned into a monster."

"Dad, if I was married it wouldn't bother you. Just try to forget I'm not married for the next couple of months."

"You're not the same kid. You're not even pretty anymore. And all I think about is I want to get a gun and go find that Blumenthal kid and shoot him. Shoot him. A big fat bullet right in the face. I want to stick the end of a pistol right up his nostril."

In the van each morning and evening they rode without a word.

The mowers that had not been sold in the end-of-summer clearance Elspeth took to the cellar, bumping them carefully a stair at a time. She uncrated the snowblowers. She put a leaf mulcher in the window.

"You guessed it, she pregnant," Joe said suddenly to a customer who she had not heard say anything. "Out of wedlock of course. The new fad, you know. The latest thing."

"It's not the latest thing! It's the oldest thing!" Elspeth retorted. She was red-faced, unable to look toward Joe and the customer. She tried to concentrate on what she was doing, squatting among boxes and rearranging and replacing the contents of a shelf.

"Yup," Joe went on. "Kilroy was here all right. It just goes to show you, they take morons in Mount Holyoke."

Elspeth saw that the garden-hose fittings she had meant to put away she had put out again on display where they had been before. She could not keep track of what she was doing. The customer left with his bundle, passing her. She did not look up. The door jingled behind him.

"Okay, so I was dumb!" she shouted at Joe. "Do we have to discuss it with the whole world? What do you have to embarrass customers for?"

But Joe was at the work bench behind the rear counter, putting together a storm window, and neither answered nor looked at her.

She was shaken and confused. She did not know if the customer had been a stranger, or some special buddy to whom he could talk like that. But it had been such a crazy thing to do anyway.

The store became busy again. When Joe had to ask her to get something or to take over a customer, he spoke to her quite naturally, as always. But at other times if she chanced to be near him it gave her a feeling as though she did not exist. He could manage for long stretches not to see her, not in a way that appeared deliberate or obviously or sulking, but with apparent naturalness not looking wherever she was.

She showed him a transparent shelf she had cut to order. "Dad, what'll I charge her for this piece of plexi? Twenty inches by six."

"Give it to her for nothing. You cut it from a scrap, didn't you?"

Elspeth taped wrapping paper around the glassy oblong. She came around the counter and handed it to the lady. "No charge," she smiled.

"Really? Nothing at all?"

"It's on the house. Our pleasure."

She had known Daddy would not charge for that. It was just that she had had to make him speak to her.

Then one morning when the cash drawer popped out against her he began commenting to the customer like the other time. "Notice her delicate condition. Not married of course. Who gets married anymore. To these kids it's nothing to be ashamed of. They're not ashamed of anything because they don't respect anything. They don't even respect their own bodies."

The customer blushed and Elspeth blushed for him. She gave him his change. He was a soft-spoken man of about thirty, and she had explained the difference between wood putty and water putty to him and how to get away with the cheaper stuff.

"There's no religion today," Joe continued. "The almighty cock. That's their religion. That's all. The almighty cock."

It occurred to Elspeth that her father might be going to have a nervous breakdown. The customer turned to go with his package. She wanted to warn him again not to use the water putty outdoors on a damp day like today with rain threatening, but to watch the forecasts and use it early on a dry day, to allow for full drying before the dew. But she couldn't speak.

"You don't read the papers?" Joe said to a different customer, an older man in a flannel shirt. "They're all doing it. Six different actresses, for God sake. They're proud of it. You want a baby, you have a baby. Who needs husbands. Husbands are for squares. Guys like you and me, you know, we're squares. We're out of it."

He left off, and let the man tell him what he wanted. Homer was busy with another and three more were waiting. Elspeth tried to work quickly and efficiently and politely. But on the way to fetch an item she would have to return to be reminded what she was looking for.

Once she even came back to ask a third time, apologizing in embarrassment and explaining that she was not herself. She kept trying to think of how to tell Harriet that they needed to get Daddy to a psychiatrist. It would do no good. Her mother would only be upset and confused. She was incapable of crossing him or disagreeing with him.

Every time Elspeth came to the register she dreaded that Joe would start in again. By eleven o'clock the store was quite busy, and he seemed to work smoothly. She hoped being so busy would keep his mind off her and prevent another outburst. But she feared that if he did sound off again it would be even worse before so many people. It would make him a public spectacle before the town. It would hurt the store. And it might need nothing more to set him off than a customer staring at her belly. And every customer did stare at her belly. They couldn't help it.

He had coped much better when her pregnancy was more restrained, when you could choose to either notice it or not. She wished the expansion had been more gradual. In these past few weeks it seemed to her too that she had suddenly become just about the pregnantest woman she had ever seen. Despite what Dr. Goldwasser had said, Daddy was right about that.

The new hurricane was expected to come inland instead of veering to sea, and some of the purchases seemed to reflect it. A man asked her for roofing tar. She got the big red covered can up the cellar stairs by herself, with two hands, but when the customer saw her he would not let her carry it further. He dragged it out and lifted it into his station wagon himself. A lady asked her for a new hasp to secure a swinging gate.

During the afternoon the sky grew darker and it began to drizzle. They had to turn on the lights. Elspeth brought in the two snowblowers and the galvanized cans that had been displayed on the sidewalk.

Joe hung up the telephone and said he was going out on an emergency. "Mrs. Luskin's toilet is blocked up. Problems, problems. Everybody's got problems."

That was not like him either. To broadcast to other people whose toilet was plugged.

After he had gone there came a moment finally when there were no customers at all. Elspeth sat on her father's old backless chair by the workbench. Homer straightened items on the shelves that did not need straightening, the way he did when he was idle.

"Do you think my father's losing his mind?" she asked anxiously.

"Oh, I don't think so," Homer said without turning. "He's been under a strain, you know. He takes things hard."

"He hasn't been right since Mark," Elspeth said, her eyes filling. "Mark happened too soon after Eric. I don't know how he managed. My mother either. Neither one of them are really okay, exactly. Sometimes I wonder what right I have to still be alive." Her voice choked.

"Oh," Homer said, "don't worry. He has a strong constitution."

She found her handkerchief and dabbed her eyes but they filled again. She blew her nose softly. She watched Homer even the spaces between the cans.

"If Daddy has a nervous breakdown," she said, and the tears were still in her voice, "and if he has to go to an insane asylum, what'll happen to the store? Everybody in this town loves Daddy. They need this store."

"He'll be all right. He gets excited, but he calms down. Joe has to let off steam. It's the way he lets off steam. Better than keeping it bottled up. Better for his ulcers."

The door jangled. She let Homer take the customer.

She had thought trade might come to a standstill with the sky turned so grim and ominous, but more customers came and again she was busy. She passed Homer going in opposite directions in one of the narrow side aisles, and he felt her up on the behind. She was sure of it. He just freely took a whole buttock in hand and gave the slacks an instant massage and let go. He continued down the aisle with a porcelain socket in his hand and never looked around. Is he going crazy too? she wondered. Is the whole world coming apart?

She knelt among the trays of nuts and screws. Somebody wanted twenty-four five-sixteenths wing nuts. And the bolts. Why such an odd size? Why not quarter-inch? And in brass yet. She was sure they didn't have that many. Could it have been her imagination that Homer did that? Was she the one that was going insane? No, it really happened. It was deft and quick, but his whole palm had been in contact, down and up again, and fingers in the seam. That slimy son of a bitch. And according to Ralphie and Skip pregnant women weren't even sexy.

Joe came back. "It's starting to blow," he said. She did not want to look at him. She did not want to look at Homer. She did not even want to look at customers. But they came faster than they left and she kept going.

She climbed the ladder and took a gallon of clear gloss from the top shelf.

"They have to live their own lives," Joe said over by the register. "That's all you hear. So look at her living it. Ya see that? See what I mean? The Chinese've got the right idea. They live on these little river boats together all across the whole Yangtse there, and when a baby's born, if it's a girl they just push a couple of boats apart to make a little space between, and drop it overboard."

Elspeth dropped the can of gloss.

"The Chinese," Joe was saying as she climbed down. "They learned the hard way. An old civilization. Boy, did I spoil that one. You knock yourself out to send her to a decent college. I should have given it to her on the tosh, where it hurts."

She brought the can of gloss to the customer.

"It got dented when I dropped it. Do you want me to get another one?" She knew there were tears in her eyes but she kept her voice steady.

"No, that's all right." He was tall and she didn't have to look at him.

"I'm fed up, God damn it to hell," she heard Joe saying. "I'm like a squeezed lemon. Wrung out. Used up."

"Are you all set on brushes?" she asked.

The man said he had brushes but needed some sheets of sandpaper.

"If I had to do it over again I wouldn't even have children. I'd have a dog. Or a fish tank to keep me company. It's crazy to have children! They're like a faithless lover. They put a knife in your heart. And if they see you're not dying fast enough, so they give it another twist. God, what you do for kids. You move heaven and earth for kids. They don't thank you, but you don't want thanks. You just want them not to wreck their lives."

Among the high racks she picked out squares of sandpaper, trying not to listen.

"I've buried two! But I was able to go on, because I had this one. This one, my favorite from birth, I used to bring her in here when she was three years old, she'd sit on the floor right here and play with the color charts, she's heart and soul to me. I don't want to live. I'm tired. I tried to get her out of this mess, I was willing to go to prison if necessary, and what does she do? Jumps off the table. I get a lawyer and make the boy give her a little money, and she practically throws it in my face. What can I do? Whatever I do for her she throws it in my face. I'm tired of wiping her ass for her. It doesn't help. If she wants to go around with shit in her pants it's her problem."

Elspeth collapsed to the floor in the long narrow aisle and wept, glad the high barricades of drawers and shelves hid her. His voice went on out there, to how many customers she didn't know.

"The hell with her. I've lost enough sleep for her. I'm not gonna have a nervous breakdown for her. I owe something to myself. I told her, look, before you get big, get out of town. They have these institutions for a pregnant girl to hide out and be anonymous, they take care of you. Who has to know? We'll tell people you went back to school. A ready-made excuse. She tells me no. You need me in the store, she tells me. Sure I need her in the store. Like I need somebody grinding a heel with spikes in my face. So I can brag about it to the whole damn town, how liberated my daughter is. It's a new age, liberation, don't you read the papers? I'm a thing of the past. I'm dead. I'm in my grave already, I'm just too stupid to know enough to lie down, that's all. In the old days a father could strike a minor child, right? Beat her up and give her a miscarriage. Do everybody a favor. I couldn't hit a pregnant woman. I'm too soft."

136

She sat on the floor in her hiding place with sheets of sandpaper in her hand. She wept silently and open-mouthed, her face drenched. She glanced up and saw a customer looking down the aisle at her, a tall, lean, middle-aged lady with eyes full of sympathy and compassion. Elspeth glanced away. Would Daddy keep talking like this till they came to take him away?

"Kids! They're the ones yelling about ecology and the environment, right? So who throws the beer cans and broken bottles all up and down Reservation Road? The same kids. I'm telling ya, they ought to be spayed. The Catholics've got the right idea. They do. The Catholics. They've got the right idea. They lock them up in convents. Kids wake up in the morning and think, let's see, what trouble can I get into today? My parents are recovering, they aren't miserable enough. What mess can I find to get into so I can really break their hearts once and for all?"

She couldn't sit here with the man out there waiting for his sandpaper.

She rose and came out of the aisle, the tears running on her cheeks. In a blur she saw customers look at her startled and then Joe looked at her.

She pressed the sandpapers into the man's hand without looking at him.

"How much?" he asked.

She hurried past him, still crying silently and open-mouthed. She dodged around some customer in the wide front aisle, tripped on a lime spreader and fell. The customer she had dodged helped her up.

"Where are you going?" Joe called behind her from down by the register.

She hurried to the door.

"Hey!"

The door jangled as she pulled it open, and it flew at her with the wind. In the rain she grasped at the door handle from the other side. She struggled against the wind. She got it shut. The rain was not heavy but the trees swayed. The cars splashed. Twigs with their leaves tumbled over and over in the street.

The van was parked a few spaces down, shiny in the wet. She could start it by crossing wires, even though she didn't have the keys. She even knew a way to spring the doors in back. But then Daddy would have no way home. And in this weather.

She hurried across diagonally, dodging two cars, toward the Veterans Taxi office. The rain was not like a rain but like part of the wind. It came not from above but horizontally, beaten to a fine mist. A gust stopped her and almost took her breath. Then she started again. She ran, though it seemed to her it was not like running exactly. With this distribution of weight you had to lean back more, and put your feet down more flat-footed.

The little storefront office was locked with nobody at the desk, the way it always was when the taxi wasn't there. She looked back at Sawyer's Hardware. The stores over there looked almost bluish. A lady on the sidewalk was pushing an umbrella into the wind. No one had come out to search for her.

She came to the curb and waved her thumb at the cars. She saw a middle-aged lady look at her as she sped past beside the driver.

Elspeth ran out and raised two arms to flag a car but it came so fast that she dodged back to the sidewalk. She waved an arm at the next one and raised a hand like a sign to stop, but it went on. The wind kept throwing one of her braids across her mouth.

Then a police car was coming around toward her in a U-turn, its blue light revolving. There were two officers and the side window was down. She pulled open the rear door before it stopped.

"Hospital?" the officer near the window asked.

"I have to get home," she said breathlessly. She got in. "Cabot Road."

"We can get you to the Lapham in five minutes."

"No. I have to get home. Please."

"Have your pains started?"

"I'm not in labor. Honest. Please. I'm not in labor. Just take me home. I live on Cabot Road."

They started off, weaving past cars, faster than she had ever ridden in the center of town. They let the siren rise and fall once. The officer on the right reported something on the microphone. Then he relaxed, and smiled over the back of his seat.

"I guess you never know just when the baby's coming, right? They give you a date but it don't mean nothing. You should have phoned us right from Sawyer's. We'd have sent the ambulance."

Her hands had begun undoing one of the braids.

"How did you know I'm from Sawyer's?"

"I know you," he said.

She knew him too, by sight. Her tunic clung wet and cold, especially on the shoulders. Her bra and skin showed through the white parts. Some falling leaves flattened themselves on the windshield and the wipers pushed them aside. She would have to get a furnished room somewhere. Or move to some outfit like the Crittenton House, or whatever it was. And stay out of her father's sight till she had had the baby and her shape was normal again.

Rounding up the slope of Cabot Road they sounded the siren again. It seemed scarcely two or three minutes. Only one of her braids was undone.

The officer who had spoken to her went up the steps and the walk with her. "You having the baby at home? My wife wanted to do that."

Inside the storm door Harriet opened the inner door, looking mystified through the glass, and unlatched the storm door.

"Okay," Elspeth said to the officer tiredly, turning and waving him away.

"What happened?" said Harriet.

"You all right?" the officer asked.

"I'm fine," said Elspeth. "Thanks. I could kiss you guys."

Harriet followed her up the stairs. "I've got to leave," Elspeth was saying. "I mean it's for my good and Dad's good and everybody's good but I have to get out."

"You're soaking wet," Harriet lamented, running after her into the bedroom. "You don't have to get out." She was weeping while talking. "Where will you go?"

"I'll keep in touch. I'll stay with Cindy overnight and then I'll look for a place."

She pulled her round blue valise from the closet. Then she ran to her parents' bedroom, Harriet following.

She picked up the pink phone.

"Who are you calling?" said Harriet.

"Cindy's house. Did Dad call?"

"No."

Mrs. Schaeffer answered. Elspeth said breathlessly she had to leave home. "Could I stay over just one night, till I get organized?"

"Of course. Longer if you like. What time will you come?"

"Now?" Elspeth asked her. "Is that all right? As soon as I pack a couple of things? The Dart keys are probably around somewhere. Or I'll jump the spark. I've got to get out before my father comes home."

"I'll come over and get you. I'll be right over."

"I'm imposing—"

"Not at all. I'll be there in fifteen minutes."

Elspeth looked at Harriet as she put down the phone.

"Why do you have to go? What happened?"

"If I stay Dad'll go nuts. Or his ulcers will tear him apart. Or something." She was hurrying back to her own bedroom.

"You don't have to go!" Harriet said anxiously, her voice rising. "Daddy loves you!"

"But I have such an effect on him that he'll need surgery." She had opened a drawer, and threw some things into the valise. "And your colitis will come back. I'll call you up every day, Mama. I promise. I'll be back after the baby's born and adopted and rid of. But the way I am I shouldn't be here."

Harriet was weeping, but helping to lay flat the underwear that Elspeth had thrown in. "Change your shirt," she managed to say. "It's soaking wet."

Elspeth lifted the tunic over her head with Harriet helping and took a fresh one. The bra was damp but she didn't change it. "And if I stay I'll start to hate him. I'm gonna hate him and I don't want to hate him. I love him."

"Change your shoes. Your socks."

"I'll change at Cindy's. Don't slow me up, Mama. I want to be out there waiting when she comes."

She opened the top drawers to decide quickly what she needed. She saw Eric's Junior Lifesaver certificate. She took her bankbook. Some cash lay in a corner of the drawer, forty-five dollars, and she took that too. She took the little transistor radio.

"When he'd jump on Mark and Eric, I don't know, I knew just how to handle him. It was so easy. I used to wonder why Eric couldn't, and Mark couldn't. I'd calm him down, and everybody said I could make him jump through hoops. And now that it's me, I can't do a thing." She grabbed her white raincoat from the closet. She tied a kerchief around her head.

"She isn't even here yet," Harriet said blubbering. "Wait inside."

"I want to be out. What time is it? Dad'll be home. He might close early."

Halfway down the stairs with the valise she debated momentarily whether to go to the bathroom, decided to skip it, then changed her mind and put down the valise and ran back up.

On the way down the second time she sneezed twice.

"Take an aspirin at least! You'll catch cold!"

"No! No aspirin! It's bad for the baby." She fastened the storm door behind her. The wind almost knocked her over.

Branches were swaying now, almost waving. The rain came in gusts.

The street was deserted. She watched down the hill. Water ran in the curving gutter. The white raincoat could no longer be closed over her belly. She put down the valise and started to undo the other braid.

She heard the door of the house open again behind her. The storm door got away from Harriet and banged against the iron railing. Harriet hurried down the walk without a coat, carrying an open umbrella. The wind caught it and raised it inside out.

18

MRS. Schaeffer gave Elspeth one of Cindy's bathrobes and hung her wet things in the big old-fashioned upstairs bathroom. She gave her a box of tissues, as she had wept in the car and had begun sneezing besides. She brought her a hot lemonade. Elspeth was shivering, and the tall glass warmed her hands. Mrs. Schaeffer made her take a vitamin C tablet and gave one to Adrienne also.

Elspeth found herself defending her father now, as Mrs. Schaeffer seemed to have the impression he had threatened her. "He wouldn't hurt me, or anything like that," Elspeth explained. But talking about it made her cry again and Mrs. Schaeffer told her not to try to discuss it now. She drew a hot bath for Elspeth.

The bathtub's curving legs stood not on tile but on dark uneven hardwood. The window over it was a design in red and yellow stained glass, the pieces joined by lead. Elspeth wound her hair under the bathing cap and lay in the hot water to her neck, listening to the plink of the dripping faucet, and the occasional fury of rain against the stained glass. What a godsend Mrs. Schaeffer was. She had always been different from the mothers of other kids. Odd in some ways, mannerly and never entirely at ease, as though choosing her words with care. She seemed gentile somehow, though she wasn't. But you could talk to her. She was always on your side.

The round blue valise had been opened on the extra cot in Cindy's room. The room was at the cupola corner and had a round bay full of windows, exposed to the storm behind drawn shades. Elspeth put on her nightgown, and over it Cindy's bathrobe hung to the floor. The slippers were large on her also.

Mrs. Schaeffer was preparing supper and Adrienne was setting the round grainy table in the dining room. Elspeth insisted on helping. Mrs. Schaeffer asked whether that police car that had picked her up on Main Street had just happened to come by, or whether somebody had phoned. Elspeth said she didn't know.

"Well, you should certainly write a thank-you note to the Police Department when you get a chance."

"I will," said Elspeth.

"You've gotten bigger," said Adrienne.

Cindy would not return from Boston University till the last bus of the evening. She had phoned, and Mrs. Schaeffer had urged her to stay overnight in Boston, perhaps with a friend in the dorms, because of the hurricane. But when she heard that Elspeth was there, Mrs. Schaeffer said, she insisted on coming home.

During supper Mrs. Schaeffer did not speak of Elspeth's problems or ask about her plans.

"Does your mother still do volunteer work at the Recuperative Center?" Mrs. Schaeffer asked.

"Yes. She goes in one day a week with another lady. She likes it."

"She doesn't drive, does she."

"No. It's lousy. She has to depend on rides. Or my father likes to take her if it's an evening meeting."

"She has such an agreeable-sounding voice," said Mrs. Schaeffer. "So soft. Gentle."

"I know," said Elspeth. "Her whole character is in her voice."

Elspeth complimented the meat loaf, though she had not eaten much. They would not let her help with the dishes. She retired up to Cindy's room, selected a volume from the low boards that served Cindy as a bookcase, and bundled herself into the iron cot, bathrobe and all.

She read a number of pages before she realized she had no awareness of what she had read.

There was a record player. She put on a folk singer's album with the sound turned low.

The windows rattled. The house even creaked in the storm. Once or twice the lights flickered, and she heard the flicker on the record player. Sometimes the radiator gave a brief hiss of steam.

She hoped Daddy was not having ulcer attacks. But she didn't want to phone. Maybe he would phone, and say he was sorry. Or ask Mama to phone and say it for him. He probably wouldn't though. Or in a few days he might find it too hard in the store with only him and Homer. But they had managed okay without her before. And it was a relief now to be away from him, actually.

She held a windowshade aside and looked down upon the headlights backing away in the rain when Mrs. Schaeffer went to meet Cindy's bus. The bus was very late. She went downstairs when she heard them return. Adrienne came down too, in pajamas.

"Hi. I hear your father finally went bananas," Cindy said, pushing off her shoes and hanging her poncho in the vestibule.

"I'll make some hot chocolate," said Mrs. Schaeffer.

They went to the kitchen. Adrienne removed some schoolbooks from the chipped enamel tabletop and put out mugs. Cindy raised a knee in her jeans, gathering a bare foot to her on the chair, and massaged it. "You've gotten bigger," Cindy said.

"I know it."

"Your father was always a kook. I don't know how you put up with him this long. I don't know how your mother stands him. Your brothers couldn't stand him. He's gonna find himself all alone someday."

"That's enough, Cindy," Mrs. Schaeffer said at the stove. "Elspeth loves her father."

"She does not."

"She does, and it's very natural."

"Well, I was just being sympathetic. You can stay here as long as you want, you know. You can share my room, or if you want your own we can open up one of the ones we closed off. There's two guest rooms."

"Elspeth knows she's welcome."

"I left for his good, actually," Elspeth began, but her voice became tearful in spite of her.

"And for yours too," said Mrs. Schaeffer, "and you shouldn't feel guilty about it. His conduct is unacceptable. The things you told me. That he said. Even though he's upset, but in a place of business? In front of customers? It's not rational. I'd think it could hurt the store."

"That's what I'm afraid of." Elspeth blew her nose into a paper napkin. "He loves me, but he hates me."

"Maybe if he didn't love you so much he wouldn't hate you so much," Mrs. Schaeffer said, stirring the pot.

"Maybe," Elspeth agreed, still tearful. "But he was really very understanding for a long time. He tried. He had a lawyer going to bat for me, and he set things up with doctors—he's really on my side."

Mrs. Schaeffer brought the pot to the table and poured the cocoa. Adrienne fetched a bag of supermarket cookies from the cabinets.

"Adrienne," said Mrs. Schaeffer, "have your cocoa quickly and go upstairs."

"Why?" said Adrienne.

142

"In case Elspeth wants to talk privately."

"I want to listen. I'm old enough."

"Adrienne. Do as I say."

"I don't care," said Elspeth.

"It's late, Adrienne," said Mrs. Schaeffer. "You have school tomorrow."

"So what," said Adrienne. She didn't move.

The hot drink steadied Elspeth. Her breathing grew calmer. She said she wanted to go to the city to try to get a temporary job, and a furnished room somewhere. There was the Crittenton League for pregnant girls, and Hastings House, but she didn't know much about it or whether she could get out again on short notice once she was in. And if her father lost his mind and had to go to an insane asylum she would have to come back immediately and run the store till he's better.

Cindy suggested coming to BU and just hiding out in the dorms. There were always kids staying elsewhere overnight so there were always empty beds somewhere.

But Elspeth said she didn't think she'd like that. She didn't want to live out of a suitcase. She felt she could work for a plumber, or an electrician. Only she didn't have a license. She had always done everything on her father's license. But she even knew all the adjustments and fittings in gas stoves. Maybe she could be a repair man for the gas company. Or she could go on unemployment or welfare for a while, if she had to.

Mrs. Schaeffer said she could lend her a little money, but Elspeth said she had savings to tide her over.

"I'm all he has left," Elspeth said. "I should have been extra super careful. With extra precautions and stuff. Or if you can't do it right you shouldn't screw, I guess. And I fell for the wrong guy. That was dumb."

"Everybody makes mistakes," said Mrs. Schaeffer.

"He thinks I'm ruining my life. Maybe I am. He thinks I do everything all without any sense. I was supposed to have an abortion while there was still time. It was all set up, with a good doctor and everything."

"Why didn't you have the abortion?" said Mrs. Schaeffer.

"I almost did. I was there on the table. And I changed my mind."

"Why?" said Mrs. Schaeffer.

"I just didn't feel like it."

"Well, everyone makes errors, Elspeth. And it's not the first time in history that a girl ever got pregnant. He still doesn't have a right to talk to you that way."

"Even if you don't mess up your life," said Elspeth, "everybody's life gets messed up anyway sooner or later. In one way or another. Just in the nature of things."

"You're too young to have such a pessimistic view," Mrs. Schaeffer said.

"Yeah, too young. That's like admitting it's true. When I'm older I'll know enough to be pessimistic, right?" She took a sip and let the mug rest again on the table, her hands around it. "Maybe Mark was dumb not to dodge the draft. Maybe my father was dumb to listen to a dumb doctor about Eric. Maybe we should all know better."

"Are you sorry you didn't have the abortion?" said Mrs. Schaeffer.

143

"I don't know. I don't know. I really don't."

All the lights went out. The sudden darkness seemed to heighten the sound of rain and wind.

"Goodness!" said Mrs. Schaeffer. "I hope we still have some candles."

But they could hear Adrienne already rummaging in the lower cabinets. The blinding eye of a lantern dazzled them from the black.

"Oh good! A flashlight. Have we got any more there, Adrienne?"

"I've got a little one up in my room."

"Maybe we should turn in," said Cindy.

"Are you ready for bed, Elspeth?"

"I've had a full day."

Adrienne swung the darting beam before them here and there and to the newel post and banisters.

As they mounted the stairs the lights came on. Mrs. Schaeffer murmured relief. She went down to switch off the downstairs lights and lock the doors.

In Cindy's room the windows of the bay still rattled. It was chilly.

"Gee, you're really into the pregnancy thing," Cindy said, looking at the adjustable belly corset with its lacings that Elspeth had thrown with her clothes on the chair. "Is that what you have to wear?"

"I don't have to. Dr. Goldwasser said to have it in case I need it. I use it if I'm gonna be on my feet a lot. Like in the store."

"Gee. When a guy makes a girl pregnant he sure puts her to a lot of trouble."

Elspeth was glad to be in bed. Her eyes closed of themselves. Her hands moved about on her hard smooth mountain. Both inside and on its surface she felt its stirrings.

She heard Cindy raise the shades and get into the other bed. Through closed eyes she saw the light become darkness. She opened them a little. The bay windows were toward the street lamp, each with a different angle and different silvery wetness.

"You're mother's a doll," she said.

"Well, she comes through sometimes in a pinch, I guess. I hope your figure comes back, after. You always had such a teensy waist."

Elspeth said nothing.

"You had a wild figure," Cindy said again. "Hourglass. Do you still have the convex areolas?"

"Yup."

"I remember when your nipple would stick out, the whole thing was like a projection in three stages."

"They're still like that. Jared said my tits rise like pagodas in Bangkok."

"Everybody starts out like that, but not like you. You'd think they'd level off by now."

"Maybe I'm retarded."

"Have you felt life yet?"

"I'm feeling it now."

"You are?"

144

Again Elspeth said nothing.

"Are you gonna have natural childbirth?"

"You mean like Lamaze?"

"Or whatever."

"Dr. Goldwasser says the Lamaze fad is past its peak, and he's not one for fads anyhow. I'm not either. Maybe I'll have twilight sleep or something."

"Honestly, Ellie, you're loyal to your father, and sorry for him and all that, but I always thought he should be put away. All smiles one minutes, and then mad at something out of the blue. Unpredictable. And it's your mother's fault, you know. Just totally passive, whatever he does. Like she never heard of women's lib."

"My mother wouldn't know what to do with women's lib."

"I know. That's what I mean. It would scare her out of her wits."

"*Your* father's no bargain either, you know."

"Well, that's true."

"Do you still not see him?"

"Well, a little now. When his girl friend and her brat aren't around. Adrienne sees him. She thinks he's Mister Wonderful."

"You don't know the good side of my father," said Elspeth. "You know, at Mount Holyoke all the kids used to brag about what terrible unhappy childhoods they had, and how their neurotic parents messed them up, and there I was with this idyllic childhood. Crazy. And he was good with Mark and Eric too. You don't think so, but he was, when they were small. Always making us a swing, or a sandbox, or a seesaw. And he'd sit down on the floor and play with my doll house with me, he'd be the man coming to read the gas meter and all kinds of things. And he'd say things like 'girls are the prettiest people,' and 'girls are much nicer than other people.'"

"That's pretty sexist."

"I don't care what you call it. He wanted me to feel good, and I knew it. And Mark and Eric followed his example, and they'd take turns pulling me around in the wagon. Like everybody thought the most fun was to give me pleasure. And he taught me things." She felt her voice threatening to grow tearful again but she kept on. "Even little things. Like sawing the cut deeper in a bolt to get it out, when the slot's worn and the screwdriver won't catch. And when I was twelve I was cutting and framing screens to order and he trusted me with that whole department. He taught me everything he knew, really. What closer relationship is there than that?" Her voice caught. She stopped, and suppressed a sob. "Just like my brothers taught me cars. There's such love in teaching. You impart what you know, and what you care about. Like sharing your soul. You'd be surprised what a good teacher he is. He knows just how to explain things. There's a customer that calls him professor. Did you ever see how he'll give a customer his time, and draw diagrams, and let them pick his brains, even when there's not a dime in it? A good hardware man like that is a necessity in a community. Without a good hardware the whole town would turn into a slum. The material culture would deteriorate. It would. I mean it. People in this town love Joe Baker. You ask around. Ask which hardware

145

they'd rather go to. He bought that store when it was failing and look what he's built it up into. And he's completely self-made, you know. When he was a kid he had to shine shoes for a nickel at bus stops." She wept. As silently as she could, but audibly. She buried her head in the quilt.

"Well, I'm sorry," Cindy said. "I didn't mean to upset you. You're upset enough already."

The rain sometimes could scarcely be heard. Then a thousand drops would strike the windows at once.

"My problem's the opposite of yours," said Cindy. "I'm still a virgin."

"That doesn't make you the opposite of me," said Elspeth. "You make me sound like I was the town pump or something. I made it with one guy. And goofed up."

"I didn't mean it like that. I didn't. Honest. I really didn't, Ellie."

"Okay. But being a virgin isn't a problem, anyway. If you think that's a problem I wish every problem was so easily corrected."

"No, it is a problem," said Cindy. "It's my problem."

"I'm sure there's plenty of guys around that would be glad to oblige."

"I don't let them. I go so far and I panic."

"So maybe you don't really want to, then. That's okay. If you want to be a virgin don't worry about it and don't listen to anybody. It doesn't mean you're sick. You've got a right to be a virgin. Lots of kids are virgins. Even guys are virgins."

"But I don't know if I want to be a virgin. I have a theory that I should get lots of sexing around when I'm young, so I can always look back on it and never envy the young when I'm older. And study hard academically and become a scholar, so I'll have scholarly pursuits to make life interesting when I'm too midde-aged for my husband to be interested in me."

"Why don't you?"

"I don't have the courage of my convictions. I'm inhibited."

"You'll get uninhibited when the time comes."

"I don't know. There were times when I should have gotten uninhibited and I didn't. I can't ever make up my mind. Maybe if I really had a boyfriend it would be easier to make up my mind."

"It would be harder," said Elspeth.

"Adrienne's six years younger than me," Cindy said, "and I bet she loses it before I do. And my mother's no help. She says if I have an affair with a guy I shouldn't be afraid to bring him here, I can bring him up here and lock the door—"

"She said that?"

"Yeah, she said that. So I don't have to sneak off to a motel. So I don't have to feel guilty about doing it behind her back. And she talks contraception till it comes out of my ears. And can you imagine what it would be like if I took her up on it, and had a guy here all night, and my mother having breakfast with us in the morning and going bla bla bla bla? I'd never get a word in edgewise. Joel Bricker came over once when I was thirteen, to play Monopoly, the first boy that ever came to see me, and my mother was going bla bla bla the whole afternoon. Art. Music. Politics. When I get married I bet my mother calls up every day on

146

the honeymoon and lectures us about sexual adjustment."

"She wasn't so talkative tonight. I thought everything she said was to the point."

"Oh, she's great to you. She's always on best behavior to you. She's in awe of you."

"In awe of me? Why in awe of me?"

"She's always been. You were smart, and gorgeous, and one of the leaders of the class, and on committees, and your picture in the paper, and Cutest, and the Most-Likely-To-Succeed kid was your steady. She's even impressed that you're pregnant. And especially by the son of somebody that plays for the Symphony. She thinks you have discriminating taste."

"Really?"

"She's something like your Aunt Frieda, actually."

"She's not like my Aunt Frieda. To Aunt Frieda everything is a great big dirty joke. Your mother's very serious. Solemn."

"My mother's scared to death, that's all. It's a big front. Inside she's just scared. Scared, scared. When I was eleven I'd ask like if I should play kissing games, for instance, and she'd say 'you have to decide,' and 'do what you think is right.' I mean, what a cop-out. I'd feel like saying 'if I could decide I wouldn't be asking you, you ninny.' Lean on her and you fall through. When you need something solid she's not there."

"You sure they can't hear us?"

"Not with the door shut. This place is built solid. You can't even rebel against her. She's all squishy. She's so liberal she doesn't know where she's at. There's just nothing in her I can't read in the Sunday Times Magazine."

Cindy sighed. The mattress or springs made a sound as though she had changed position. Elspeth hoped the conversation had ended. She felt ready for sleep. The activity in her womb had quieted also. It was good to lie here blanketed, hearing the rain. The radiator gurgled.

"And what happened to you scares me," said Cindy. "I mean, after being careful and everything. Are diaphragms that unreliable?"

"They're not supposed to be."

"Where'd you get it?"

"A doctor in Springfield."

"Maybe he fitted you wrong. Gave you the wrong size."

"I don't think so. Maybe it got loosened in the night in some way, and then we screwed again when we woke up in the morning. I don't know. I know it didn't leak. I water-tested it."

"Why didn't you use the pill?"

"I guess I should have. But the diaphragm really should have worked, and I was leery of monkeying with hormone balances, just in case they discover twenty years from now it throws something else out of whack. The body's a very finely tuned mechanism. Like a super Italian sports car."

A wet gust beat the windows again.

"You're so—I don't know. Courageous," Cindy said.

147

"I'm not courageous. I'm just dumb."

"But—I don't know. If it were me I wouldn't know what to do."

"I don't know what to do either."

"How was it with him? Did you like it?"

"It was okay." She rolled to the wall, buried in the quilt. "Good night."

"Good night," said Cindy.

She heard Cindy sigh and scratch herself. Outside there was a sound of a galvanized barrel overturning and its cover clattering.

Cindy was quiet only a few moments. "I wonder if I'll ever be pregnant," she said.

Elspeth did not answer.

"What's it like?" said Cindy. "I mean, like do you get nauseous?"

"Not too much," Elspeth said.

"Does it make you fart a lot?"

"No. I'm starting to pee more often though."

"Do you get backaches?"

"Once in a while. If I'm on my feet a lot."

"Do you ever wet your pants?"

"Not really."

"Is it hard to sleep?"

"Sometimes. You get used to it."

"Remember the time we shaved off each other's pubic hair?"

"Yup."

"Remember that prickly stage, when it was growing back? There was about a week or two there when it drove us up the wall."

Again Elspeth tried not answering. She let her breathing grow audible, slow, regular.

"I guess I should let you get to sleep," said Cindy.

"I guess we both could use it," said Elspeth.

Garbled, meaningless images began to float before her. But they did not continue. She was still awake. She thought the wind and the rain had stopped. Then she heard it again.

"Cindy?" she said.

"What."

"You're inhibited, and I'm inhabited."

19

MRS. Schaeffer drove Cindy and Elspeth to the Boston bus. Again the hurricane had spent its main strength in the ocean. They saw no damage except to small branches, which lay in the drying streets.

Mrs. Schaeffer insisted on lending Elspeth twenty dollars, stuffing it into a pocket of the white raincoat as the bus driver boosted Elspeth by the arm. Elspeth found a seat by the window on the sunny side.

After the grade crossing the bus made a few stops. Light and shadow sped across their laps, the valise, the backs of the seats ahead. The autumn colors had not been their brightest this year, and now the storm had stripped the woodlands half bare.

"I wish I could afford to live at school," Cindy said. "But my mother says 'you don't get your money's worth, a teensy little space, no privacy, I don't know how they study.'" She mimicked her mother's voice.

"Could you ask your father?"

"He'd say, 'hell no, I'm supporting two households now.'"

At the terminal Elspeth bought a paper, and on the subway she read the classifieds for furnished rooms. There were not many. A lot were by students who needed roommates to share overpriced apartments. Some specified coll. grad., or ages, such as 20-26. Some said female and some said either sex. For some you had to be bus. or prof. They asked as high as $150 a month, plus a month's security. And a hundred-and-fifty or so was all the savings she had.

But there was one for fourteen dollars a week, and all it said was nice room, nr park, transp.

Straphangers pressed on her newspaper.

In the central city Cindy waited at the phone booth by the underground fruit stand, her green bag and Elspeth's round valise by her feet. The subterranean walls and blackened ceiling amplified the roaring of wheels, the screeching of steel. Elspeth unfolded the door flat shut, and plugged a finger in her other ear. A great big park, the lady said. Near the subway, all the buses, all kinds stores. Elspeth asked what the neighborhood was like. Knock on wood, the lady said, the whole street was still white people. Almost all the way down till the end, by Mudd Street and Launcelot Street.

Elspeth folded the door open a little and asked Cindy to write down the directions. She relayed them. Some names were hard to understand, and the spellings seemed implausible, as if the lady were guessing. "Maybe you better ask if she minds if you're pregnant," Cindy suggested.

At last Elspeth hung up. "It sounds awfully good," Elspeth told Cindy. "There's probably something terrible, but I want to see it. And I told her I'm having a baby in January and I'd probably go back to college after that, and she said 'that's wonderful.' I think it's an old Jewish lady, the way she sounded."

"Well, good luck. If it's a dump come back in to the Student Center. I'll check at noon if you're there, and we'll look at listings."

Elspeth had to ride another stop and transfer to a different subway. After a few stations the train rose with her into sunlight and became an elevated, clattering past brick tenements.

At the station Mrs. Brody had mentioned Elspeth descended with her valise. Blocks of stores were empty and boarded shut, the boards plastered with torn remnants of campaign posters.

She decided not to wait there for the bus. She climbed a wide thoroughfare away from the trains, alongside a granite embankment that bordered the park. Her white raincoat hung open. Where the hill leveled off she put down the valise and rested. Here there were pedestrians, black mostly. An electric bus headed down toward the dark valley from which she had come, its slender trolley flexing and sparking. The park was indeed large. She could not see its further side. It rolled, with curving roads, the trees bare in their upper branches though bearing scattered yellow leaves below. Across the street, opposite the park, the buildings were dense and close. Squat apartments, fat gray houses with dulled bits of Victorian ornament.

She crossed over there to look for the side street. She found the address, a narrow wooden house amid others like it, three porches high, with bubbles in the paint. There were three unmarked bellpulls, knobs of old white ceramic, one above the other, beside a heavy door of carved wood, a glass panel in its upper half. She pulled the lowest of the little white knobs, drawing it from the woodwork on a steel rod. She pushed it in again, but suspected it had rung no bell. It had felt stiff. She pushed the heavy door, pressing the cold bronze handle, and it opened.

In the musty vestibule an angular staircase led up into shadows, but the one inner door on the bottom level had a bronze plate that read JACOB BRODY, the black mostly gone from the grooved lettering. Under the plate a little brass handle like a wind-up key was set centrally in the wood, perhaps another bell or signal device.

But before she could touch it the door opened. A big old lady with white hair extending out in all directions smiled at her. "I seen you from the window already. Come in, darling. Please, I got swollen feet, forgive me I didn't put shoes on. Mh!" She turned and led the way barefoot with short waddling steps. A nightgown hung lopsided from under the robe. "Forgive me I'm not dressed. I don't feel good. Mh! It's no good when you get old. Don't get old, darling. This is mine husband. He don't see but he listens. Come. I'll show you the room." The old man sat slack-jawed across from the television. The whole apartment smelled like the vestibule.

The living room merged through an arch with a dining room that looked long

150

unused. Yellowed lace drooped around the table. All the floors had a slant.

"You got privileges in the stove and the fridgeyaire," Mrs. Brody said in the kitchen. A striped cat slept under the table, its tail around its fatness. "Put it down, the suitcase already. And the newspaper. Me, I always keep kosher everything. So if you don't want to keep kosher, so you'll watch to keep on the side separate your own little pots, a couple of dishes. A fork, a knife, a spoon. I'll give you for your own place in the drawer."

The bed was of brass. There was no night table but a large mahogany bureau with a mirror and only a few chips in its veneer, and a wicker armchair. The walls were papered in intertwined rosebuds and shaded off at the corners to brittle tan. Mrs. Brody opened a closet. It was shallow but wide. Beyond the gauze curtains the blistered clapboard of the next house was scarcely six feet away.

"I'll take it."

"Of course. A nice room, why shouldn't you take it? It's very quiet here. Except the television you wouldn't hear nothing. Only the motor from the fridgeyaire and the old man snoring."

"I'd like to call my mother on your phone."

"Oh course, darling. That's a nice girl, every day you should call up to your mother. You should be glad your mother's alive."

Elspeth stood by the black telephone in the hallway and called Harriet collect. Harriet began weeping. Mrs. Schaeffer had phone her. Elspeth calmed her. She told her the Brodys' address and phone number, after making her promise not to rush over by bus or train or taxi but to wait for a time convenient to both. Elspeth said she was very tired and wanted to get settled first. Then she wanted to find a job locally. She asked how Daddy was. Harriet said he seemed all right. He had brought home her shoulder bag from the store.

"What did he say about me?"

"Nothing much. He said children grow up and fly out of the nest and fall on their heads." She wept again.

Elspeth put away her few things. She lay down to nap in her clothes. The mattress was on a kind of a chain netting such as Elspeth had never seen before, and it sagged far down under her. Yet it was not uncomfortable. It supported her much like a hammock, her hips sunk like the hinge of a jackknife and her feet high. She heard the muffled applause of the television through the closed door.

She awoke in midafternoon and combed her hair. She asked Mrs. Brody where the stores were.

"Take Brody along with you, he should tell you the places. You wouldn't mind? He's supposed to take a little walk every day, and me, I can't take him. One can't walk and the other can't see. Oy! Ih! Brody! Come! The girl is taking you."

His glasses magnified his eyes hugely. He put on his fedora at the coat-tree by the door, and a coat over his black suit. He took his white cane from another of the curling wooden hooks.

"Will I be having my own key?" Elspeth asked. "Would you like me to make a duplicate at a hardware?"

"You don't need no key, darling. I don't go nowheres."

Mr. Brody crossed the porch with Elspeth, checking the top of the steps with the tip of his cane.

She walked slowly with him toward the thoroughfare that bordered the park. He asked if she could lend him a cigarette. "No, I haven't got any. I stopped smoking. It's supposed to be bad for the baby."

Opposite the park they took the direction further from the way she had come. She held his arm lightly. He kept talking to her in Yiddish. Several times she asked him to tell her in English. She told him she only knew about a dozen words of Yiddish. But each time he lapsed again into Yiddish. Yet he did not seem to require answers.

At a large intersection, where some trolley buses turned and others continued straight, Mr. Brody stopped before a little store, apparently knowing precisely where he was, and said it was a good place if she wanted cigarettes.

It occurred to her that it was he who wanted cigarettes. And he knew enough to speak English when it mattered whether she understood. She asked his brand and bought him a pack. He lighted one, and gave her the pack for her pocket. Perhaps Mrs. Brody was not supposed to know he smoked.

Elspeth chose a shoulder bag and some kitchenware in the discount outlet.

She still guided Mr. Brody's arm lightly, but he disengaged it occasionally to take a puff. She asked him the location of a food market called Leo and Walter's that Mrs. Brody had recommended.

"Across the street," he told her, and motioned with his cane.

When the light turned green he tapped the curb and started across.

"Do you see some?" she asked beside him. "Did you see that light change?"

"A little I still can see. And I hear from the cars, when they start that way and they stop this way."

Elspeth bought lettuce, tomatoes, tuna and sardines, bread, cereal, cheese slices, peanut butter, soups, milk and orange juice, a small bottle of vitamins and iron. Mr. Brody waited by the fruit bins, smoking. The white-aproned man at the register with a pencil behind his ear asked if she was the Brodys' granddaughter. "I see you're expecting," he added. "Mazal tov."

"Thank you. I'm not related to them. I'm just staying with them a while."

"So, you had a nice walk?" Mrs. Brody said when they returned. "You see, it isn't so far. Everything is right near." She made space in the refrigerator, in a drawer, and on a shelf. Elspeth apologized for not having thought to ask if Mrs. Brody had needed anything from the store. "Don't worry, darling. Mrs. Peress goes for me in the butcher, and they deliver everything together. If I wanted, I wouldn't be bashful to ask." She insisted that Elspeth join them for supper. "Come on, don't be bashful, darling. Tomorrow you'll take by yourself, but tonight you'll be company. You took Brody for a nice airing. You're a roomer but we could be friends too."

A bell clattered at the front door. It sounded slower than an electric bell.

"I'll get it," Elspeth said. But when she got there Mr. Brody had already opened the door. An old man had come to take him to services.

152

She tried to help him into his coat but he nudged her aside and did it himself. She saw the bell now, a brass hemisphere dulled and darkened with an aged patina, affixed to the middle of the door on the inside. Apparently a twist of its little handle on the other side made a mechanical clacking. Mr. Brody reached into her white raincoat on the coat-tree and took two cigarettes.

Elspeth returned to the kitchen.

"He'll come back in half an hour," Mrs. Brody told Elspeth, "and then we'll eat supper. They daven minchah, that's all. They're afraid, they shouldn't be coming home in the dark. It's no good to be out in the street in the dark anymore. So maariv they don't daven." She said that for a long time he didn't go to the shul. He had a fight with some of the men there. "They told him he's crazy, he makes fights, arguments, he shouldn't come there no more, they don't want him. He's losing his mind, it isn't his fault. It's from the hit in the head. A shvartzer gave him a klap in the head and threw him down and took away his money, the watch, everything, and from the hit in the head it did something in his mind. So in the shul he was mixing up everything. Maybe he was already losing his mind before, I don't know. Hardening in the arteries."

"His mind seems okay," Elspeth said.

"Na, his mind isn't good. From forty years ago he remembers. From today, from yesterday, he don't remember. So when they only got nine men, and they need one so they can daven, for that he's all right. All of a sudden they want him. If one is crazy it don't make no difference. God don't care. Crazy, not crazy. Mr. Kablotsky said they didn't tell him he shouldn't come, they didn't tell him they don't want him, he imagined it. I don't know."

"My father said God is crazy," said Elspeth. "He said it to the rabbi. On Rosh Hashanah."

" 'God is crazy.' Maybe that's right. I don't know."

Mr. Brody returned within half an hour, as Mrs. Brody had said. He hung his cane on the coat-tree. "Good shabos," he said.

"It isn't shabos," Mrs. Brody answered. "You don't know what day it is? It's Thursday."

Coming into the kitchen he stumbled on the striped cat, and gave it a kick. "Du chazirsche katz!" The cat leaped over his shoulder and shot toward the living room like a cannonball.

He put a napkin on his front, stuffing an edge of it into his collar. Mrs. Brody cut his meat into small pieces.

The meat was brown and soft and grainy, and the potato and vegetables brown and sticky.

Elspeth tried to do the clearing and dishwashing but Mrs. Brody would not permit it. "No, darling. I didn't give you supper so you should be a servant girl. Go. A few things, it wouldn't take me long. Watch the television."

The living room had doilies everywhere. The marble fireplace had been shut with painted plywood. But a charming clock sat in a glass dome on the mantel, its works open behind a face of porcelain and gold. Elspeth sank in the velvety armchair. She did not turn on the television. On the sofa Mr. Brody held the newspaper an inch before his face. He passed the big headline slowly before his eyes. He wore cuff links and sleeve garters. The clock under the glass dome struck a quarter-to, four notes down, four notes up, four more down, lingering and blending. Her eyes went to it.

Mrs. Brody turned on the TV. She braced her hands on the stuffed arms of the taller chair and lowered herself into its depth. "Mh! Ih!"

Mr. Brody fell asleep, his head to the side. The fallen newspaper formed a tent on the carpet. Elspeth picked it up.

"You got such beautiful hair, such a color," Mrs. Brody said.

"Thank you."

Mrs. Brody would not let her concentrate on the newspaper. She talked of the people interviewed on the morning talk shows, and of the scandals she had read about in the newspaper earlier. Somebody had given birth and thrown the baby out in the garbage pail. The garbage man had found it, still alive.

"I see things like that in the paper a lot," Elspeth answered her.

"Mh!"

On the television an audience somewhere found something hilarious.

"I almost had an abortion," Elspeth said.

"You shouldn't kill the baby," said Mrs. Brody.

"No, I won't. It's too late for that anymore anyway."

"Six million they killed. It's enough already."

Mr. Brody awoke in his chair and yawned. The magnified eyes squinted and then opened wide, staring toward the television.

The sound failed. Elspeth watched the screen, aware now of every change of camera, every brief close-up, every movement of actors around the set. But without words it was all arbitrary, fatuous, purposeless. Maybe it did make sense for a blind man to watch television. More sense than for a deaf man. "Want me to change the channel?" she asked. But as she spoke the sound returned.

Mr. Brody began to talk to her.

"Tell me in English, Mr. Brody," Elspeth said. "I don't understand Yiddish."

He paused. When he resumed his tone was careful and precise. She guessed he was explaining or paraphrasing for her what he had said. But still in Yiddish.

"Brody!" his wife cut in. "Talk English! She's a young girl! The young don't know Jewish!"

He spoke a Yiddish sentence angrily to Mrs. Brody.

"What did he say?" Elspeth asked.

"He says he *is* talking English. See? His mind isn't good."

Mr. Brody fell silent.

Elspeth said she thought she'd go to bed early. Even though she'd napped this afternoon. She hadn't slept much the night before.

"Go ahead, darling."

Again she was cradled under the quilt, feet and head up, her middle in the depths.

154

The baby was exercising. Always at bedtime lately. Don't you know it's sleepy time? Why did you come to me, little one? Why didn't you find a home in somebody else's womb? This is the wrong address. The adoption agency is gonna give us a divorce.

She heard fire engines. They receded. More followed and receded.

Why were sirens such a lonesome sound? Even when they screamed together in bunches, so high and excited?

She thought of the houses she and Mark had been going to build for themselves someday, all with their own hands. They had studied a library book on how to pitch rafters, the math and the technique.

The Brodys awoke before her. She wakened to the creak of footsteps, the opening and shutting of doors, the flushing of the toilet. While she ate her cereal she thought of the hammocky chain-link netting on which she had slept. Clearly a relic of another age. It had let her hang like a slack rope. And no bed had ever felt better. Strange.

When Mr. Brody finished his tea he again slurped the spillage from his saucer. He wore suspenders over long-sleeved underwear that buttoned down the front.

Elspeth phoned Harriet, again collect.

"Are you all right?" Harriet asked.

"I'm okay. I just wanted to know if you're okay. And if Dad's okay."

"We're okay. When am I gonna see you?"

"Maybe we can get together tomorrow," Elspeth said. "Saturday. If I don't have a job by then. I'll call you. I need a couple of things from home. A coat. I don't know how I'll get into one."

"I don't know if it's good for you to be so all alone."

"I'm not all alone. The landlady's here. The landlady and her husband. What does Dad say about me?"

"He doesn't talk about you. I told him I heard from you, that you found a room, and he just listened. He didn't say anything."

Elspeth found a carpet sweeper in the closet and tidied her room. The she started on the rest of the apartment.

"Na, na, darling. You shouldn't do so much."

"You can't. With your feet," Elspeth said.

"Mine daughter will do it."

"When does she come?"

Mrs. Brody shrugged. "Sunday maybe."

"Well, she can go over it again."

Afterward Mrs. Brody invited Elspeth to come sit on Mrs. Peress's piazza upstairs. It had been Elspeth's plan this morning to open a checking account and case the neighborhood for jobs. But she postponed it and went up with Mrs. Brody. It surprised her that Mrs. Brody managed the stairs at all, though she gripped the rail and bent. "Mh!" She pulled herself another step. "Mh!"

Mrs. Peress and Mrs. Brody and Elspeth each occupied a rocking chair. A glider of steel and quilting was vacant. The porch had a railing all around, unlike the

Brodys' porch which was directly beneath and was crossed by everyone who went in and out of the house. A third porch above formed the ceiling of this one. Mrs. Peress's rocker and Mrs. Brody's rocker squeaked in conflicting rhythms and in disharmony. Several times Elspeth began to rock as though by contagion, but the additional discord made her stop.

On the street below she spied Mr. Brody tapping his cane against the sidewalk. "Does he walk by himself?" she asked.

"Yeh. He comes when he wants. He finds somebody to take him across."

Little Mrs. Peress narrowed her eyes and studied Elspeth. Mrs. Peress's hair was as white as Mrs. Brody's, but unlike Mrs. Brody's wild mane it hung straight and thin, the pink scalp visible though it. Though Elspeth did not understand their conversation she knew they spoke of her, and that Mrs. Peress referred to her as the shikse. It crossed her mind to explain to Mrs. Peress that she was not a shikse, as Mrs. Brody knew. But she let it go.

Their conversation turned to the blacks, and in English. They discussed a street that had become black within a space of a few months. Mrs. Brody called them shvartzers, and Mrs. Peress called them neegairss.

Mrs. Peress warmed enough to Elspeth to include her finally in the conversation. She told Elspeth she had six children. The youngest son was a professor in the University of Illinoyess. "He is teaching there the Romentic Poets."

Apparently Mrs. Peress owned the house and the Brodys were tenants. There was another tenant above. A goy. A Polak. He was all right, minded his own business. He took out the barrels.

Mrs. Peress had considered fixing up her own spare bedroom and taking in a roomer as Mrs. Brody had, but hadn't made up her mind.

"Somebody sick I wouldn't take," Mrs. Brody explained, the rocker creaking. "And it's no good to take somebody old. I'm too old myself."

"Sick is no good and old is no good," Mrs. Peress agreed. "And neegairss, to fershloomper me up the house, I couldn't take."

At length Elspeth excused herself, leaving Mrs. Brody upstairs with Mrs. Peress, and set out on her errands.

Several stores past the discount outlet she found a bank, the Eggleston-Uphams Bank & Trust, and sat there with a fiftyish but rosy-cheeked Mr. Hudson, the denim bag against the stretched furry sweater, to open a checking account. Mr. Hudson asked if the account would be joint with her husband or in her name alone.

"Just me," she said.

"Separate accounts are getting more popular," he said agreeably. "Especially when both work. Fewer arguments that way."

He showed her a large plastic folder that held not only green checks but a variety of other forms. He called it an all-purpose account. You could have money in savings by depositing it with one of the yellow slips, or in checking by depositing it with a white slip, savings and checking both having the same account number. And at any time you could shift any sum back and forth between checking and savings as often as you wanted at a moment's notice, by filling out one of the orange transfer forms, also supplied in the folder. It enabled you to get interest in savings temporarily while the money wasn't needed to cover checks. And in two months' time, Mr. Hudson said, his glasses reflecting recessed ceiling lights and the mustache smiling, if she maintained her minimum balance, they would also give her a Master Charge credit card.

He seemed disappointed when her initial deposit turned out to be only ten dollars. But she assured him she was on the way to the post office, and would have another hundred-and-fifty or so as soon as she mailed her savings book to the Winslow bank and closed it out.

"We can do that for you," he said.

So she made out more forms and gave him the savings book. She got the oversized folder into the denim shoulder bag. Mr. Hudson rose, the mustache smiling again. He was tall and slender, and though aging he was pink and baby-faced. She gave him her hand. "You'll need those checks when the baby comes," he said affably.

Elspeth located the post office, even though Mr. Hudson was writing to the Winslow Savings Bank for her. She also found the library nearby. Better start reading before another few evenings of Mr. and Mrs. Brody and the television drove her out of her mind.

A bit further down there was a hardware across the avenue, and two blocks further a competing one. She had noticed them the day before and sized each up at a glance. Both were busy, and big enough to need two or three people. One was more traditional, the other trying harder to branch into a variety of discount junk.

But as she approached the first one she grew uncertain. Her steps slowed. She stopped. Hardware stores didn't hire people off the street. They hired people they had known for years, or took in relatives. The more she thought about walking in cold, with a face even younger than her eighteen years, and enormously pregnant, and claiming to be a competent plumber though she had no license, and a competent electrician though she had no license, and a locksmith, the more certain she was that they would think her some kind of nut.

She could try. They could only throw her out.

Maybe there was a way to approach them. If she could think it through. But today she wasn't up to it.

20

IN the morning Harriet called, apparently as soon as Joe was out of the house. They worked out the shortest route. It was not necessary to go by subway to the center of the city, as Elspeth had done, and out again. Elspeth awaited her at the end of the street and met her as she alighted from the trolley bus. Harriet set down the bundles on the sidewalk and made Elspeth try on the old long tan belted coat at once.

"There, I think you'll get away with it," Harriet said. It had phony wool on the collar and was double-breasted. Buttoned wrong, with outer buttons to the outer buttonholes, it still had barely enough girth to meet itself, provided you didn't really fasten all the buttons, but relied on a twist of the long belt to hold the middle shut. "Too bad the big months didn't come out in the summertime."

"You didn't have to bring food, on top of everything," Elspeth said as they carried Harriet's old shopping bags toward the house.

"Bob is gonna call you. Did he call you?"

"No."

"He knows somebody that wants to adopt the baby. He wanted to talk to you, so I gave him your number."

"Who would he know that wants a baby? I don't know if it's such a hot idea. The agency is supposed to handle it."

"He seems to think it would be doing these people a favor. They're trying to adopt."

"Let them go to the agency. Everything I read says it's bad if you know each other. How is Bob? Does he like MIT?"

"It's very hard. He says he's working very hard. That's what Frieda said too. She hardly ever sees him. He doesn't have any money, and he has to teach two days a week, and so he studies all day Sunday, and Saturdays he's at his girl friend's."

"Has Aunt Frieda met his girl friend?"

"I don't know. I don't think so. She'd have said."

For lunch Harriet warmed some of the meat loaf she had brought. The Brodys had returned to the television. Elspeth and Harriet had the checkered oilcloth to themselves.

"I'm not crazy about you living here," Harriet said. "Frieda said you could stay with her. She's having the painters this coming week, but after the painters. And in the meantime maybe Diana and Donald could take you for a week or two."

158

"Well, I don't know. I'm gonna start looking for a job Monday. Now that I'm here—"

"What if you had to be rushed to the hospital all of a sudden?"

"I'd call a cab. Dr. Goldwasser said the first baby doesn't come that fast anyway. And I'm not in the mood for Aunt Frieda really. Maybe it'll do me good to be on my own for a couple of months. I've had a very sheltered life. Nothing could be more sheltered than the way I came home and went to work in Daddy's store actually."

She thought Harriet's eyes became misty.

"I hope you're planning to come home again once the baby's born," Harriet said.

"Well, I was figuring on it. For a while anyway. But for now I just want to hide out, and not with somebody like Aunt Frieda, that I'd have to talk to. I just want to get these next two months over with. The whole thing has been a bad experience. Mainly because Dad takes it so bad."

"You can't expect him to be overjoyed about it. He just can't stand to see you in this condition, that's all. But after the baby bygones will be bygones."

"Is that what he said?"

"I don't know if it's what he said exactly. But it's what he means. He loves you. But he wants you to straighten out."

"I'm not really so unstraightened. I made one mistake."

"But then you jumped off the doctor's table, and you argued when he got you the money from the Blumenthals. He had to deposit it to your account without your endorsement. He just doesn't know the way you act whether you realize how serious it is. Just because we're not old-fashioned and we didn't throw you out you don't act like it's serious." Harriet began weeping. Elspeth fetched the paper napkins from the cabinet and Harriet took one for a handkerchief. She wiped her eyes and blew her nose. "He says he just hopes you'll stop being crazy someday."

"Okay. Tell him I'll stop being crazy. I promise."

"I just hope you've learned your lesson," Harriet continued, still dabbing her eyes. "God forbid if anything like this ever happens again, have an abortion next time."

"There won't be a next time."

"In my time the girls I knew didn't get into these messes."

Elspeth had forgotten about that Blumenthal money. Her bankbook didn't show it. But it couldn't. The bankbook had been in her drawer. And now her new bank was sending her bankbook to her old bank to ask them to close it out.

Harriet left for home before dark. Elspeth walked to the corner with her.

"Pew," Harriet said, once they were on the sidewalk. "How can you stand it? Don't they ever air the place out?"

"Is it that bad?"

Harriet did not wait for the bus at the end of the street, but walked toward the big intersection where they ran more often. Elspeth watched her recede up the sidewalk. The sun had gone down and the air was cold.

When she returned to the Brodys' the laundry on the back-porch clothesline was still damp, so she left it there overnight.

But there was a frost, and in the morning the laundered tunic and socks and underthings hung stiff. She brought them in and bent them over the brass rails at the foot and head of her bed.

Early in the afternoon the Brodys' daughter Phyllis came with two of the grandchildren, a girl about eight and a younger boy. Phyllis seemed tired and fortyish. She had short hair, a mixture of black and brass. The children spent little time with their grandparents but worked in the kitchen at coloring books.

"Ma, put on some shoes," Phyllis said, raising her own feet to the leathery hassock. "Slippers at least. The doctor told her not to walk around barefoot in the winter," she told Elspeth. "These floors are cold. But my dad can't see what she does so she gets away with murder."

"It isn't winter yet," said Mrs. Brody.

"Ma, when you have catarrh all winter long I don't want to hear about it, okay? Would you turn off that television? It gives me a headache."

Elspeth turned it off.

"I'd like to get them out of here," Phyllis said. "Mrs. Peress raised the rent on them again. And it's worth your life to go out on the street around here."

"If they raise the taxes, so she has to raise the rent," Mrs. Brody said.

"They've got some nerve raising the taxes. Why don't they provide some police protection? My dad got mugged you know. A year ago June. Hit him on the head. Knocked him down."

"Your mother told me," Elspeth said.

"A lot of people saw it. He fought like a tiger. Didn't you, pa?" Her voice was louder. Mr. Brody, dozing open-mouthed in the tall chair, gave a start. Phyllis addressed herself to Elspeth again. "He gave one of them a jab in the face, and another one in the stomach. Teenage boys, a bunch of kids, like twelve, thirteen, fourteen years old. An old man like that. He couldn't see a damn thing, just swinging and jabbing all over the place with the cane. He chased two of them off. And the third one got him from behind. And took his wallet with one lousy dollar in it, didn't even leave him his papers. And not a cop in sight. An old lady helped him get up. Bleeding in three places. The old Polish man on the top floor carries a gun. You know, one of these armpit holsters. I don't know if that's good or bad. He fired it about a month ago. I was here. He thought it was prowlers out back, but I think it was dogs. He shot the garbage can and Mrs. Peress was yelling gevalt."

Elspeth went to prepare tea. Mrs. Brody at once came to help her.

"Oh, you're sweet," Phyllis said to Elspeth when they brought the tea. "My mother told me what an angel you are. You didn't leave me anything to do. Believe me, I appreciate it. I've had such a migraine."

While they drank tea Phyllis asked Elspeth what method of childbirth she would use. Elspeth said she didn't know yet.

"Tell him to knock you out completely," Phyllis advised. "Tell him to wake you when it's over. On my first two I didn't know a thing. And then with Jeremy they

160

talked me into twilight sleep and my God, was that torture. The most horrible memory of my life. I felt everything. I thought I died and went to hell. God, did I suffer. And that was heavily sedated. Imagine what the pain must be for these nuts that do it with nothing, wide awake. Lamaze. They have to be out of their minds."

Phyllis told Elspeth to figure on being very sick for two weeks afterward, even with full sedation. She said it took two months to really get your strength back.

"Did you nurse your kids?" Elspeth asked.

"No. I would have, but I had no milk. I had just this thin blue stuff and the baby lost weight. So with the second one I didn't even try. What woman has the strength to nurse after childbirth? Maybe in the old days when women were beasts of burden. They died like flies anyway."

After an hour Phyllis and the children left.

"Mh. Nobody has time for me," Mrs. Brody said when the door had shut. "She comes, she's in a hurry to go. Once, in the summer, she stayed the whole day. Such a nice time. There was a cannibal in the park, and the children enjoyed it, they went on all the merry-go-rounds, the rides."

Elspeth had noticed that Mrs. Brody sometimes confused words like that. In the morning she had told of a show on the educational channel, about the Gobi, the most bewildered place on the face of the earth, sand for miles, only the Mongrels live there, in tents, on the other side from Chiny. Then she had said the television needed a new area, and it was a minute before Elspeth realized she meant aerial.

Elspeth took the Yellow Pages from the telephone table and sat with it in the wicker chair in her bedroom. She looked up Employment Agencies. Then Employment Contractors—Temporary Help.

There was an outfit that supplied Harvard students for bartending and truckdriving. There was a listing that she thought must have been placed by a pimp. It offered girls for hire as masseuses, escorts, art or photography models. The biggest ads were for office workers. She wasn't sure what her typing speed was now. Nothing great.

She turned the pages back and forth. The temporary office help companies seemed the best idea. They sent you to a different place every day, which might be more interesting. Only the temporary outfits could take her seriously anyhow, since it was obvious that she'd soon be taking maternity leave. Even if they didn't know she'd be quitting after that.

The sun was still in the sky. She strolled to the avenue, and picked out a compact, lipstick and eye shadow at the drugstore.

Monday morning Elspeth arose early. She ironed a tunic and pressed a pair of black stretch slacks. She daubed the makeup carefully, studying the effect in the dresser mirror.

The moving staircase from the subway lifted her into the city about eight o'clock. She had always like the area of Tremont Street and the Common—the light and shadow of the rolling, sparsely wooded expanse, the brick and white spire and graveyard, the little men hawking newspapers, the short slope and iron fence and blazing dome, the sound of pedestrians' feet everywhere in a constant blend of rhythms. She wore the coat unbuttoned, the ends of the belt in the pockets.

The first agency on her list was down a narrow street and up one flight. The office was carpeted, the furnishings angular and modern like the cool, slim, stylish lady behind the desk. Her name was Mrs. Bunting. She was distantly polite and said that they did not need more girls just now but that additions were made to the active list from time to time. With a graceful gesture her long arm handed Elspeth an application on tinted paper.

The next place was only three doors away and up two flights. The room was small and messy. A man with a white shirt too full over his belt rocked behind a big wooden desk, a black phone at his ear, and sipping from a steaming paper cup. He clapped a hand over the mouthpiece. "Can you type?" he asked Elspeth.

"Yes."

"Sit down at that machine and type as fast you can without errors. Anything. Copy a page out of one of the magazines."

He resumed the phone conversation. There was no place for her coat. She folded it over the water cooler and pulled a wooden chair to a heavy old Smith-Corona. The pages were curling at the corners and the covers were creased or missing altogether. She opened one and pressed it flat. She saw no paper, and he was still busy on the phone. She took a sheet of memo paper from the wastebasket and rolled it into the roller, back side front.

The ribbon had holes and the letters smudged.

He hung up the phone. "Okay, okay, that's enough," he said, though she had only typed a line and a half. He did not rise from the desk and did not ask to see what she had typed. "How do you spell separate?" he asked.

She told him, still sitting before the typewriter.

"Spell commission," he said.

She spelled it.

"How do you spell decedent? The last syllable, an e or an a?"

"An e," said Elspeth.

"What's it mean?"

"A dead person?" she said. "No, I guess I'm thinking of deceased. I'm not sure."

He asked her name, address, home telephone and social security number and jotted in pencil on a pad. Elspeth spelled her first name but he became confused. She lettered it again slower.

"Do you know where Federal Street is?" he said. "You can walk it in five minutes."

He scrawled an address on a white form that had pink and blue and yellow copies attached.

"Get right over there. They're waiting for you. They're in a big hurry."

On the sidewalk it occurred to her that she ought to have asked who pays her and how much. But she did not turn back.

The place was a law office on a high floor. A homely, dark-complexioned woman led her to a typewriter in a small room that had sets of books covering the walls. There was a very fat wad of long pages, pierced and fastened at the top by a big aluminum clasp, that had to be copied with several sets of carbons.

"Are you sure you're up to it? The last time we hired a pregnant girl we said we never would again."

"Why?"

"Well, she was suffering, and we suffered with her."

"I'll be okay."

Elspeth was left alone. As she began she realized it was a record of a trial, or a court hearing. She had never seen one before. There were names and what each said, as in a play.

"Mrs. Berman, there's a sentence I can't make out," Elspeth called when she had gotten to the third page.

The homely lady came and looked at it. Then she took the entire wad, and Elspeth heard the lawyer say somewhere in the suite of little rooms that the whole transcript was to be copied exactly as it was, errors and all, whether it made any sense or not.

Elspeth worked alone, hour after hour. Sometimes she stopped to massage her fingers. The whole thing had to be copied today, because the lawyer was not supposed to have it at all, and he had to put it back where it belonged before eight tomorrow morning.

"Why didn't he just take it to a photocopy place?" Elspeth asked. "It would cost a lot cheaper."

"It's not out of our pocket," said Mrs. Berman. "The client pays for it."

"Even so."

"Well, I did stop at a copying place on the way, but they said anything that big would have to be left overnight."

Elspeth finished at a quarter to six, tired, her fingers aching. She checked the hours that Mrs. Berman had written on the forms.

It was dark when she got to the Brodys' neighborhood, which made her uneasy. But nothing happened. She relaxed in a hot bath.

In the morning she phoned Mr. Harris at Extras, Inc., and asked if he had anymore work for her. He asked if she would do filing at an insurance company and said she could go there directly.

"I don't have a form," she said.

"I should have given you a bunch of them," he said. "Come in and get some. And bring the slips from yesterday."

The insurance company was in a high building with lots of glass and recessed lighting. Elspeth worked in the claims department. All she had to do was find the folders of clients and bring them to the desks of men and women who had given her the names on slips. And put the folders back when they were no longer needed. During the afternoon coffee break she telephoned Harriet on a company phone.

Elspeth was a filing clerk there the next day too. But they told her at the day's end that they would need her no longer, because the girl who had been sick would be back tomorrow.

For the first time no one in the subway offered her a seat. Why did people on the subway always look so beaten?

Mrs. Brody told her her cousin had phoned. "Bob, he said. He said tell you Bob. He's coming here with his girl friend, you should meet his girl friend. Sometime in the evening, maybe nine o'clock. They wouldn't stay long." There was also a fat letter from the new bank. Francis McAlister Hudson, Vice President, wrote that her all-purpose account had a balance of $672.02, that they welcomed her as a valued customer and so forth. Her old book from the Winslow bank was enclosed, canceled with perforations, and sure enough it now showed a deposit of the Blumenthals' five hundred before an interest payment and withdrawal of the total.

So she had cost Jared a total of eight hundred dollars. Assuming those hippie characters never gave him his three hundred back after the abortion fiasco. Eight hundred was a lot.

"Did my cousin leave a number where I can call him back?"

"Na, he didn't leave no number. I told him you're always home, you don't go out nowheres."

"Does he know how to get here?"

"If he says he's coming, so he knows."

It was nearly ten when Elspeth, watching through the net curtains in the bay, saw Bob approach the porch with a young woman. She opened the door before he could twist the rackety bell.

He bent and kissed her and introduced Karen Slater. "You look great, Ellie. A little big around the middle maybe, but just great." Karen kissed her too. She had sloping eyes and delicate features that somehow gave her a feline look, but Elspeth felt warmth and openness in her smile. It was as though she loved Elspeth for being Bob's cousin. She was olive-complexioned, quite dark, with hair cut short, taller than Elspeth. Elspeth offered to take her jacket but Bob said they couldn't stay long. Karen threw it over an arm of the sofa and sat beside Bob, her tapering thighs and her entire posture somehow inclining toward him. Her hand and his entwined themselves together on his knee.

"I like your mustache," Elspeth said. "It fits your face, somehow."

"I may take it off. Karen isn't sure if she likes it."

"Not necessarily," said Karen. "I just want to see how he'd look without it. He had it when I met him."

"So you had to move out," Bob said to Elspeth.

"It was getting to my father," she said. "It just seemed better for me to get out of his sight till the baby's born. I'll go back after."

"When's your due date?"

"Dr. Goldwasser said it could be January first."

"New Year's Day," said Karen. "If yours is the first one born, like a second after midnight, they put your picture all over the papers."

"Just what I need."

"I've heard of a couple that's looking for a baby," Bob said.

"My mother said you knew somebody."

"It's not somebody I know—I know somebody who knows them. Ed Gordon. A fantastic guy that comes down and teaches a course. And Karen and I went over to his class Thursday night and we went out for tea afterward, and somehow I mentioned about my cousin having a baby, and he said there's this couple in his congregation going crazy trying to adopt a baby. He's rabbi of the temple in Wilmerding Crosswalk."

"Where's Wilmerding Crosswalk?"

"Sort of up toward New Hampshire. Sort of outer perimeter, like Winslow. About as far north of Boston as Winslow is south. He'd like to help this couple if he could. They tried for years to have a baby of their own, clinics and stuff, but nothing doing."

"Gilbert," said Karen. "He said their name is Gilbert."

"So he asked if you'd be interested, and I said I didn't know, I'd ask. And then I thought instead of just asking you I'd make it an excuse to come and see you. Karen's been wanting to meet you."

"You're his favorite cousin," said Karen. "His favorite relative, I think."

"I don't know if that's a compliment, considering what he thinks of his relatives. I hear he hasn't had the decency to introduce you to his mother."

"Eventually Karen will meet my mother. Okay? But every time my mother sees me she starts a battle. Not that I mean to stay away, but I don't get a lot of time. I'm up to my ears."

"Well, I'm flattered then. But my opinions aren't too much different from your mother's, you know. Or your father. Or Diana."

"You're more tolerant, though."

"That's because you're not my son. I don't know about this adoption thing, Bob. I've heard it's better to work through the agencies. It's anonymous, and professional."

"Well, Ed said this couple hasn't had luck with agencies. Babies are scarce. Could I let Ed Gordon tell them your name, and maybe if they asked the agency for your baby it would help. At least they'd know it's a beautiful baby. Good stock."

"I don't care if you give them my name, but I don't know if the agencies work that way. I think they don't want you to know whose baby you get. And I'm not even sure what agency—you'd have to ask my father. I think it's connected to the Jewish Family Service or something."

"Well, I'll just give Ed your name then, if it's okay with you, and these people can take it from there, if they think it'll help any."

Elspeth had noticed that a slim white cord of finely knotted macramé, from somewhere inside his clothing, hung down over his belt at the side of his trousers and ended in long separate strands that lay on the sofa. She supposed it was connected to the holy underwear that Diana had told her about. "You're not wearing your potholder," she said.

"Oh yes. I am." He turned his head to show it. It hugged so closely and so far back on his head that she had not noticed. "Karen knitted this one." It was black, with maroon zigzags bordering the circumference.

"And what's that tassel hanging out of your pants?"

"It's in the Bible," he said. He smiled. "'Tell them to put fringes on the corners of their garments throughout their generations.'" He pulled out another one on the other side. "There are four of them. On the four corners." He reached behind him into his trousers.

"Okay, I'll take your word for it," said Elspeth.

"Gramps used to wear it. He unbuttoned his shirt once and showed it to me. But in his generation they kept it hidden, inside. Today some of us let it all hang out."

"I think Diana mentioned it. She said it gave you trouble in the john."

Karen laughed. Bob colored. "Well, I did have a couple of accidents. Until I got used to it."

"And you wear that stuff in the labs at MIT and everything?"

"Why not?" He leaned and reached for an apple. "We all do. There's about nineteen of us, at last count."

"At MIT?"

"Sure. Harvard has more like fifty or sixty. Seventy. Maybe more." He bit the apple.

"Are you into this stuff too?" Elspeth asked Karen.

"Of course." But she wore nothing unusual that Elspeth could see.

"Karen's a lifelong froomie," said Bob. "She grew up to it. She and her sister and brothers. Day schools from kindergarten on up. I wish I had her background."

"Where are you from?" Elspeth asked her.

"New York."

"You don't have the accent," Elspeth said.

"Well, you don't have the Boston accent. Bob doesn't either."

"Accents are out of style," Bob said.

"He has it in certain words though," Karen added. "I think it's cute."

"What are you doing up here?" Elspeth asked.

"Studying for a doctorate."

"What field?"

"History. Cultural history of the Renaissance."

"Where?"

"Harvard."

Elspeth told about the temporary jobs, and about Mount Holyoke, and her thoughts of getting back there. They spoke of Bob's schedule. He was supported mostly by a teaching fellowship. It occupied two entire afternoons plus papers to correct. He arose early and studied late. But he and Karen got out to a concert every couple of weeks. Karen knew a lot about chamber music. And one night a week he went to a Talmud class somewhere. Usually he stayed at Karen's on the sabbath, sleeping over on the sofa. If he got tied up Friday afternoon and it was too late to take the subway or drive his car before the sabbath, he could walk it in an hour. It would be windy along the Charles River in winter, and especially on the bridge after sundown, but Karen was knitting him a big scarf and a woolen hat to pull down over his ears. Karen lived with her sister and brother-in-law and went to Cambridge by bus.

"They're terrific people," Bob said. "They give Karen free room and board, just

166

in return for an occasional night of baby-sitting. And occasional mother's-helpering. Besides feeding me every shabos."

The sister and brother-in-law had two children. They would probably have more. And Karen and Bob intended to have a big family.

"I want there to be lots of people like Bob," Karen said. "As many as possible."

"Aren't you concerned about population growth?"

"Bob's gonna discover a way to grow food on the ocean bottom," Karen answered.

"Bob always used to try to get me to join the Audubon Society," Elspeth said.

"I'm sure."

Elspeth told about Bob taking care of a squirrel that someone had injured with a BB rifle and a dog had mauled. He had been about fifteen. He had nursed it back to life.

"You never told me that," Karen said to him. "Tell me more," she asked Elspeth.

"Well," said Elspeth, "he always had a bird that fell out of the nest or something. And there was a time when they had the police out looking for him all night, and then his sister remembered a lean-to he'd built in the woods, and they found him sleeping there."

"Tell me more."

"Well, let's see. There was a time when his mother made me wear this disgusting bikini, and Bob was the only one that had the decency to be embarrassed. Do you remember that?" she asked him.

"Ya, I think so. It was at Gramps's house in Winthrop."

The mantel clock in the little glass dome chimed its melody down and up, down and up, and began slowly counting eleven. Karen turned to look at it. "That clock is gorgeous."

"We've got to run," said Bob.

"Can I make you some tea? Instant coffee?"

"No. Thanks." He rose. He was visibly tired. He helped Karen put on the leathery vinyl.

"Is your car running all right?" Elspeth asked.

"Ya. I don't use it much."

"Why do you keep it?"

"Well, in the summer I'll want it again. And meanwhile I rent it out most weekends, which helps with the upkeep."

"Your brakes okay?"

"I think so."

"Okay. Take good care of Karen."

"I will. Ellie, can we lend you some cash? Like ten or twenty bucks?"

"No, that's awfully sweet, but I'm okay. Really. We got five hundred bucks off the Blumenthals."

21

IN the morning she phoned Mr. Harris at Extras Inc. again, but this time he had nothing for her.

Most of the day she spent in Boston, and visited four more of the temporary agencies. A couple of them tested her typing speed, but she did not do better than about forty words a minute. At one place the lady said they were taking no new applications and that she thought the country was heading into a major recession. At another the lady said they stressed the appearance of their girls and that Elspeth should wait till after the baby.

She came home in the rush hour. On the subway a big shabby black woman offered her seat. Elspeth declined, but the woman insisted.

The next morning Mr. Harris again had nothing for her. He had had a perfect job for her, he said, if only he had thought of her, but he had just given it to someone else. It was for a shopping center Santa Claus until Christmas—with her pregnant belly she would not even need pillows and it was easy, just sitting on a chair in the inside mall.

She went to Boston to leave her name at more of the agencies. They were becoming further apart. One told her they did not want girls who were registered at several. Elspeth tried one more, which turned out to be taking no applications now unless you knew shorthand. She quit, and took the subway before the rush.

There was a phone call for her at the Brodys' before she had even taken the coat from her shoulders. It was Marvin Gilbert, the man Bob had heard about, who wanted to adopt a baby.

"I'm afraid I'm not interested in private arrangements, Mr. Gilbert. My cousin was supposed to explain that. I'm giving the baby to a regular adoption agency."

"Well," he said, "if we can talk it over, we're prepared to negotiate a generous payment. The agencies don't give you a cent."

"Now look," said Elspeth. "This baby is something that happened to me. It's not like a crop I'm raising for the market. Anyway it's already arranged with the agency. I had my father arrange it. Some time ago."

"Have you signed anything? Any document?"

"No."

"Then I think you're still a free agent."

"Even so, Mr. Gilbert. I'd rather go through a recognized agency. If you want I'll find out the name of it and you can talk to them."

"I know them all." She heard the discouragement in his voice. "I don't get anywhere talking to agencies."

"Why not?"

"Because they don't have enough babies for all the people that want to adopt. So they can afford to be very choosy."

"And I think they should," said Elspeth. "Don't you?"

She hadn't meant to talk so coldly. It was just that her baby was entitled to professional service. And what did you say to someone who persisted when you'd already said no?

When Harriet visited Elspeth told her about it.

"How much money did he want to give you?" Harriet asked.

"I don't know. I didn't discuss it. The baby's not for sale."

They walked in the park. The trees were black and bare now. Brown leaves sometimes rose from the ground in gusts and scattered themselves anew.

When they returned Elspeth asked Mrs. Brody if there had been a call from Extras Inc.

"Na. The telephone didn't ring the whole time."

"I thought I'd like the variety of a different place every day," Elspeth said. "But I don't like the uncertainty. I don't know from one day to the next if I've even got a day's work."

"The rental," said Mrs. Brody, "the fourteen dollars, if you don't have one week, you shouldn't worry. When you'll have, so you'll give me."

"She has parents who can help her," said Harriet.

"It's okay, I've got money in the bank," Elspeth said.

"It's a shame you didn't take in high school the business course," said Mrs. Brody.

"She took the college course," said Harriet. "I took the business course, but I didn't like it. I always wished I'd taken the college subjects."

"My girls," said Mrs. Brody, "I always told them, the business course. Take the business. For a shorthanded girl they always have a job. All the time."

After Harriet had gone home a dark lonesomeness settled upon Elspeth.

She took a book to the wicker chair, but her thoughts did not stay with it. Her life did not seem tragic to her, just stupid.

She should be in the middle of her sophomore year now, probably getting ready for a serious major in architecture.

Would the unknown child be a wistfulness, a hole in her heart? Like for that mother who wrote to the Chit Chat?

Always the bloom would be off the peach. Life can still be good, just not really right, that's all. But that was already true when they killed Mark. And more so when Eric—geometrically more so.

It was such a short span between birth and death. It was too bad not to make sense of your life.

She went to bed early. She was accustomed now to the two sets of false teeth immersed in drinking tumblers in the bathroom. And to the sound of Mr. Brody at the sink, trying to cough up phlegm. Aoop. Aoooopkh. Aaaak. And every night she heard fire engines. Days too, if she was there.

Sunday Mrs. Brody was depressed and complaining. Elspeth finished her library books and looked for things to do. How could they watch that television for so many hours on end? This must be what was meant by quiet desperation. You could scream.

Suddenly she burst into tears and sobs. It surprised her. Now, now, Elspeth, she told herself. Don't go insane just yet.

When it was growing dark Mrs. Brody called her to the telephone. It was Karen Slater. "How are you?" Karen asked.

"Oh, fine, I guess," Elspeth said standing in her robe, the big comb in her hand.

Karen said she and her sister and brother-in-law wanted to invite her to dinner next Sunday. A week from today, at five in the afternoon. Bob would pick her up.

"Oh, I'd love to. Gee. Thank you. That's awfully nice. I'll really look forward to it."

"We'll look forward to it too."

Elspeth returned to her room and her combing. It amazed her how different she felt. It was like a life preserver thrown to her from a boat whose approach she had not seen.

Monday she looked into the phone book for Job Centers of the State Employment Service, and went to one of them. She sat by the desk of a man who could scarcely have been thirty. He pondered her application through eyeglasses, resting his mouth on the back of his hand. She told him of her experience in plumbing and in electrical work and in locksmithing and in hardware. He was soft-spoken enough but there was something unpolished about his pronunciations. He seemed surprised that she was not on welfare.

"Should I be?" she asked.

He looked through one typed sheet after another, turning them back on a clipboard. At last he looked at her.

"Have you had experience working a cash register?" he asked.

"Sure. Lots. I was working a cash register when I was ten years old. There's nothing to it."

"Would you take a job at the check-out in a supermarket? It's not too far from you. Pays the minimum."

"Sure. If it's an early shift. The neighborhood where I live is supposed to be not too good after dark."

He wrote an address on a scrap of paper. He looked up the bus connections in a folder.

The store was large and bright, like all the supermarket chains. The manager, a young blond man with a big mustache, showed her one of the big registers and punched keys. It was easier than the one at Sawyer's Hardware. It calculated everything for you, including tax and change. He asked if she knew how to stuff bags, with heavy items on the bottom and squashables on top. He gave her a starchy red coat, reminded her that items other than food were taxable, assigned her a number, and told her to ask Lisa at the next register if she had questions. He told Lisa to keep an eye on her.

Several times during the day he came and watched from behind, but he seemed to have no complaints. The customers were white and mostly middle-aged or elderly. For a while trade was slow, and Lisa chatted with her about their hair, offered bubble gum, and told her the neighborhood was mostly Irish and German. She was plump and her hair was black and as long as Elspeth's. The hawk-faced older woman at the third register talked little.

The longer the line grew at her register, and the faster she worked to catch up, somehow the more restful she found it. It occurred to her that nothing was more relaxing than a simple job just complex enough to keep you from thinking about anything else.

It took half an hour to get back to the Brodys', with one change of buses. She placed a collect call to Winslow, eager to tell Harriet about her job. To her surprise it was Joe's voice that answered. When the operator gave him the message he called Harriet without another word. It gave Elspeth a pang of hurt that he did not speak to her.

"What's Dad doing home at this hour?" she asked Harriet.

"He had an appointment at the doctor."

"Is anything wrong?"

"No. It's an appointment from the last time. Dr. Fleming said he wanted to see him again about now. He seems to be doing fine."

"Oh. That's good. I was worried. Take good care of him. Does he eat the lunches you pack for him?"

"I think so."

"Okay. Tell him not to send out to the deli."

"No, he's been very good."

"And tell him not to skip lunch, no matter how busy it is. Skipping lunch is the worst thing."

"He knows that."

Tuesday she learned that the supermarket gave employees a discount. She took a few items home. The mail had brought a fat bundle of white deposit slips, yellow deposit slips, orange transfer slips and green checks, all with her account number in computer-style digits at the bottom and ELSPETH ANN BAKER and the Brody address at the top. She fastened them into their proper locations in the big folder and threw away the old anonymous ones. She asked Mrs. Brody if there had been any phone calls from Extras Inc., or from the other agencies that had taken applications. There hadn't.

Each day she brought home a few groceries, for herself or for Mrs. Brody. Harriet had agreed to time her calls at five-thirty, after Elspeth got home and before Joe did, but she did not expect to hear from her for the next few days. Wednesday Harriet's theater group went to the matinee and Thursday was volunteer day. On Thursday her check from Extras Inc., arrived. She had earned $51.25.

As she was cutting the bottoms off the cans to flatten them for recycling Mr. Gilbert telephoned again.

"I realize you want to have your baby placed through an established adoption agency," he said. "But please. Give me a minute. Just hear me out. We think of the agencies as impersonal and wise, and professional, as if they know just what to do. But in fact they're only ordinary human beings, like you and me. Just because they have a couple of degrees in psychology and social work, that doesn't mean they're not still fallible human beings, with their own problems. They make their mistakes like everyone else. They're only people. And you don't know that their judgment is any better than yours. Somebody can have diplomas all over the wall, and belong to all the professional societies, and still be a horse's ass. Between you and me, Miss Baker, I know you love your child. Your child-to-be. You made it clear to me that finding the best possible parents for that baby means more to you than any amount of money. And that tells me a great deal about you. Believe me, Miss Baker. That child is fortunate to have you for a mother. And maybe you think that because an agency has an impressive name they've got the perfect parents, the best parents in the world, waiting out there in the wings to adopt your baby. They don't. Look, is there anyone up there in heaven deciding which natural parents are most fit to bring children into the world? Because if there is, they sure make a lot of mistakes too. Most parents don't know beans, and some do okay and some do lousy. And adoptive parents are just the same—the only difference is that for some reason they couldn't have kids of their own, but that doesn't make them immune to mistakes. They goof up and have problem kids just like natural parents. Look, Miss Baker, my parents did all right, but they weren't perfect either. And no one told them whether they could have children. And I don't know your parents, but I bet you'd be the first to admit that they weren't always the perfect, all-wise, ideal experts either. Am I right or am I wrong?"

"Yes." His words about her loving her child, and the baby being fortunate to have her for a mother, had brought moisture to her eyes.

"Of course. Because the perfect human being hasn't been created. Unless you happen to believe in Jesus Christ, who never had any kids and I'm not convinced what a hot parent *he*'d have been either. In other words, agency or not, your baby is gonna have to take his chances in the human grab bag. With the available fallible material. And I'm not convinced that anyone's judgment or anyone's instinct is gonna be sounder or more stringent that yours. Because to you that child is the one and only. He's not just another case, a day's work. Your standards are gonna be higher than any agency's. And between you and me, Miss Baker, some of these neurotic bureaucrats are the prisoners of their own rules. If my wife and I were twenty years younger, we'd be at the top of their list. Our crime is that we tried too long to have one of our own. We didn't quit soon enough. But Miss Baker, we have a lot of love to give. You should see my wife with children. And when it comes to all the theories, books, she knows them all. She's an educated woman. I'm not a millionaire, but we're very comfortable. Well off. There's nothing that kid won't have. The best in schools, camps, orthodonture. Music lessons. Sailing lessons. All I ask is look us over. Let us show ourselves to you. If we don't pass muster, if you'd rather take your chances with an agency, then fine and dandy. We won't bother you again. But inspect our home if you want. Inspect my tax returns. Talk to our doctors if you want. I'll tell them to release everything."

"There's just one thing Mr. Gilbert—"

"Yes."

"With an agency, at least there's this anonymous factor. If I deal with you, then we know each other. And that's not supposed to be so good."

"All right. Well, first of all, if my wife and I adopt your baby, naturally we'd insist on an ironclad agreement that the adoptive parents have sole rights to the child, and that you're out of the picture. Every possible legal safeguard. Just the same as it would be with an agency. For the child's protection. Of course we'd know who you are and you'd know who we are. But do we know that this total anonymity is such a good thing? Theories change. Years ago they didn't used to tell kids they were adopted. Now they say tell them. So now they've raised a whole generation of adopted children, in their twenties and thirties, that are obsessed with finding out who their biological parents were. They travel the country. They spend years. Even though they love their adoptive parents. You've seen them on television."

That was true. He had a point there.

"Maybe it's better for the child to know that his biological mother isn't a great mystery, and a forbidden fruit to go on a quest for. Maybe it's better to know that she's ordinary and locatable and has a family of her own. What can I say, Miss Baker? All I ask is that you see us once. No obligation. If you don't like us we'll leave in twenty minutes. But for your child's sake. Just so you'll know you didn't leave this stone unturned."

"When do you want to come?"

"Well, we have your address. We'll put on our coats and come right now."

"No," she said. "Make it tomorrow. Say about seven."

"Seven o'clock, tomorrow evening. Thank you, Miss Baker. Thank you. Seven. We'll see you then."

"Call up and confirm it, like at six," she added. "Just in case I'm tired, or sick or something."

"Of course. Certainly."

22

THE telephone rang at exactly six. Elspeth knew it was Mr. Gilbert before she heard his voice.

"Miss Baker?" he said. "This is Marvin Gilbert. How are you."

"Fine, I guess. How are you?"

"We'll see you in about an hour, I hope"

"Okay. Do you know how to get here?"

"I think so. I know the street. I was brought up in that neighborhood."

Elspeth told Mrs. Brody that some people were coming to see her. She said she would take them to the kitchen so that Mr. and Mrs. Brody could watch television.

"Na, that's all right, darling," said Mrs. Brody. "Brody and me will sit in the kitchen. I'll read him from the newspaper. We don't look at the television on shabos. Only once in a while something special."

"It's a couple that want to talk to me about adopting the baby. So I thought I'd meet them and sort of see what they're like."

"That's very nice. That's good, darling."

"He sounds like a pretty intelligent kind of a guy. I'll introduce you and you can tell me afterward what you think."

"Na, that's all right, darling. I don't want they should see me with no shoes on."

Elspeth straightened the living-room doilies. She put out a bowl of fruit.

She heard them cross the porch and enter the vestibule, but she waited for the bell's slow jarring before opening. She gave Mr. Gilbert her hand. He was handsomer than she had expected, broad-shouldered, tall. When he removed his hat he was balding on top. "Miss Baker? This is my wife, Mrs. Gilbert."

"Amethyst," the wife corrected. She drew off a purple kid glove and clasped Elspeth's hand. She was lean, with sharply cut features. She wore a large-brimmed black hat, floppy on one side and raised high on the other. A silvery fur with a hint of blue hung about her neck.

It was hard to judge their ages. Mrs. Gilbert had pancake makeup and the brown upswept hair could have been dyed. They could even be fiftyish, within a few years of her own parents. She took their coats, and then laid them over the stuffed chair that Mrs. Brody usually used instead of putting them on the coat-tree or taking them to the closet. Mrs. Gilbert did not remove her hat and Mr. Gilbert kept his briefcase. They sat on the sofa.

"Well!" said Mrs. Gilbert. "You're quite beautiful. I like what I see."

"Thank you. I don't hear that as much as I used to." She took the tall chair where Mr. Brody usually sat. She rested her hands on its arms. "My father thinks my whole face has gone to pot."

"I don't know how he can say that. You're stunning. Isn't she, Marvin? And that hair! Marvin, did you ever see such a color? I hope the baby inherits it."

"There have been lots of redheads in my family. My grandmother had red hair. But I guess my brother and I were the only ones with this deep shade. I guess it's a mixture. But the baby might not have it. The father's hair is black. My father's was too. He's bald now."

"And such a beautiful name," said Mrs. Gilbert. "Elspeth. I love your name."

"Thank you. I didn't used to like it because it's odd. But this past year I've kind of gotten to like it."

They could be only a few years younger than her own parents, she thought. Though they had a style and youthfulness that her parents lacked. Even Mr. Gilbert with his deadpan. He had been studying her silently and did not smile even when she met his eyes fully.

"Do you know Rabbi Gordon?" Mrs. Gilbert asked.

"No, my cousin knows him. Rabbi Gordon's your rabbi, right?"

"Yes. He's the rabbi of our temple. Beth El of Wilmerding Crosswalk."

"Is that an orthodox place?"

"No. Of course not."

"But my cousin's orthodox."

"Oh. Well, everyone loves Rabbi Ed," Mrs. Gilbert explained. "He's just a beautiful person."

"Where is Wilmerding?"

"Do you know where Sparkstown is? It's near Sparkstown. But it's a lovely town, fantastic for children. Completely unspoiled. Except the Wilmerding Mills section. But the whole Wilmerding Crosswalk area is just beautiful countryside. Typical New England. Woods. Fields. Farms, even. The little tumbly stone walls along the roads. They say they go back two hundred years."

Mr. Gilbert half rose with his thick briefcase and reached to hand Elspeth a large photograph. "That's our house, Miss Baker," he said. He sat back.

"Call her Elspeth," his wife corrected.

"Hey, that's some house," said Elspeth. "I sort of have a thing about well-made houses."

"Nine rooms," he said. "Six-foot stone fireplace." He rose again and gave her another picture.

"This is the room that'll become the baby's. That's a flash shot. You can't tell too much. But it'll all be redone, with Mother Goose wallpaper, that kind of thing. Linoleum. Twelve by fourteen, lots of space for toys. Southern exposure. And if we bring over a European girl for a mother's helper she'll have the adjoining room."

He came with two more prints. "And this is our cottage in Chatham. And this is the beach."

The little clock in the glass dome sang its descending tune. Mrs. Gilbert looked at it. "I love your clock."

"It's my landlady's."

Elspeth went through the photos again, putting each behind the others. She handed them back.

"We've been wanting a baby for years," said Mrs. Gilbert. "Unfortunately Marvin has a low sperm count."

He colored slightly and cleared his throat. "That's not the whole story. I have more than enough. It only takes one. Miss Baker, I said on the phone that if you decide to go through with this, to give the baby a loving home and all the advantages, some present is in order on our part. A token of gratitude for your bringing the child into the world."

"Like how much?"

He cleared his throat and folded his hands. "Well, I haven't thought too much about it. My thoughts have been on what we'll do for the child, naturally. How much would you want?"

"Well," said Elspeth, "I've read they pay six thousand dollars for Greek babies on the black market. From Greece. So if a Greek baby is worth six thousand, a Jewish baby should certainly be worth about eight thousand. Your own flesh and blood, so to speak."

He cleared his throat again. "Well. Maybe we should sleep on that. We can discuss other factors and come back to that side of it."

"Really, Marvin. Are you going to haggle over a few thousand dollars at a time like this? And let this baby get away from us so we can kick ourselves for the rest of our lives? What good is money if we have no one to leave it to? If kidnappers stole the baby next year and asked fifty thousand in ransom you'd run to the bank without batting an eye. At least I hope so."

"Dear, please. Let me handle it."

"You don't know how to handle it. You only know how to file sealed bids and figure profit margins. I think Elspeth is being very intelligent. She's not being mercenary. It's not the money she cares about. She's testing us. She wants to see how much we really want a baby."

Marvin sighed.

"And she wants to see if we're really affluent. If we can really afford the best, like you said."

"I told her she could check our tax returns. They're right here in the briefcase. And a detailed statement of net worth."

"It's not how much you've got. It's your attitude towards it. What good is a million dollars if you're tight? How can she believe you'd pay five thousand a year to send the kid to Exeter if you won't even pay eight to get the kid in the first place? This girl is no dummy, Marvin. She's wise beyond her years. I can see that, even if you can't."

Marvin sighed again, reddening. He turned to Elspeth. "All right. I still want to ask a few questions, but if the answers are satisfactory we're talking about eight thousand. A thousand down, and seven on signing the adoption papers."

"Thank God," breathed Amethyst. "Marvin, you'll be the death of me. The last of the big spenders."

"Do you want to just shake on that until I can have my attorney draw up something?" he asked Elspeth. "Or should we put something in writing tonight? I think I'd rather put it in writing as a matter of fact."

"Yes, put it in writing," said Amethyst.

"I think you'd prefer it too, wouldn't you?" he said to Elspeth. "You seem to have an orderly mind. I think you'd prefer a businesslike way of doing things."

"It's fine with me," she said.

"Now, as I said, I still have just a few questions. And maybe you have a few." He took a yellow pad of lined paper from the briefcase. There were some notations on it. He took eyeglasses from his inside pocket and breathed on them and wiped them. He opened a pen. Then he looked over the glasses at Elspeth. "Who's your doctor?"

"I have an obstetrician. Morton Goldwasser."

"In Boston? And he's been taking care of you?"

"Since the third month, about. Start of the fourth, actually."

"Do you mind if we talk to him?"

"Be my guest."

"You'll instruct him to release information? He can't without your okay, you know."

"Sure. There's nothing to hide."

"Fine. And you'll supply us with names of your family physician, and any other doctors you've had. I'm also leaving you the names of our doctors with this other material, and you can feel free to talk to them. Have you had any major illnesses at all?"

"No."

"Do you take any medication?"

"Nope. Nothing. I even quit smoking."

"Any hereditary diseases, like hemophilia for instance? You understand that any agency would ask you these same questions, of course. It's just so we can provide the baby with every help it needs."

"No hereditary diseases that I know of," said Elspeth. "It could be that there's a jinx on the family though."

"What?"

"Well, my oldest brother got killed in Vietnam, and less than a year before that my other brother died of epiglottitis. My parents took him to the hospital because he couldn't breathe, and the dumb doctor said 'it's just a cold, take him home and put on the vaporizer,' and they took him home, it was like one a.m., and in the morning he was dead."

"That's terrible!" Amethyst exclaimed. "Horrible!"

"We think so."

"How old was he?" said Amethyst.

"Seventeen."

"Oh my God. Your poor parents. And you say less than a year after that, his brother? Are there other children? Or are you the only one?"

"I'm all that's left."

"Oh, and I thought I had troubles. You never know what troubles are until you hear about somebody else's. My God! Two children like that."

"Tragic," Marvin agreed. "I'm very sorry. Tell me, Miss Baker, you're not diabetic that you know of?"

"I'm not. My father has ulcers and my mother has a history of colitis, if you care about that. And my landlady has swollen feet."

"This is your first baby?"

"Marvin, you have a nerve," said Amethyst.

"It's the first," said Elspeth.

He cleared his throat. "Excuse me, no offense. Do you happen to know your IQ, offhand?"

"Marvin, really!" Amethyst said.

"Dear, in the agencies you have certain safeguards—"

"So a lot of good the agencies have done us! Here we're seeing her in the flesh. That's better than safeguards."

"All right, all right. Let it go. Tell us about the father."

"I really don't know my IQ, Mr. Gilbert. In the Winslow schools they don't tell you. But my SAT scores were pretty good, and I was a freshman at Mount Holyoke till my parents found out I was pregnant. You could call South Hadley and ask my grades. You forgot to ask me my age, Mr. Gilbert. I'm eighteen. Nineteen in February."

"Oh yes. Thanks."

"Why do you keep calling him Mr. Gilbert?" Amethyst said to her. "His name's Marvin."

"Because, dear, she realizes that if we have a successful transaction here this evening, the time will come, after the birth of the baby, when we and the baby go our way, and she goes her way, and we do not stay in touch. As a matter of strict policy. For the baby's well-being. So it won't do to get too chummy. Miss Baker understands that. Even if you don't. As you pointed out yourself, she's no dummy. Now. Where were we. Miss Baker, please, if you'll tell us about the father."

"What did you want to know about him?" Elspeth asked. "Do you need a release from him or something?"

"No, if you're not married he has no rights. That's my understanding. Just tell us about him. What's he like? His race, for instance."

"Well, I suppose he's what you'd call white. Theoretically."

"What do you mean by that?" he asked. "'What you'd call white? You suppose? Theoretically'?"

"Well, if you've ever noticed, some so-called white people are darker than some so-called black people."

"So is he white? Or not?"

"Well, his conscience could be some other color. But he's a nice Jewish boy, as the phrase goes."

"In other words he's white. Caucasian."

"Mr. Gilbert, his name is Jared Blumenthal, he graduated from Amherst College last June, he's in the Yale Drama School, he's brilliant, he's a sensational actor, he's an actor who's also a scholar, he knows all of Shakespeare ass-backwards, he knows the subconscious mind of every character in every play, he'll be famous someday, and I can assure you he's circumcised. And he's a shit. And his father plays a bull fiddle in the Boston Symphony and his kid brother's a math genius, and his mother works in Filene's Basement. And he's probably in some play at the Drama School right now, and all you have to do is drive down to New Haven and buy a ticket and have a look at him."

"Let's do that," Amethyst said to Marvin.

"Unless it's Othello," Elspeth said.

"No, we'll take your word for it," said Marvin.

"Marvin and his caucasians," said Amethyst. "We could have had a Vietnamese war orphan. They give them away like a litter of kittens. But Marvin said he didn't want any chinky-eyed children."

"Dear, those interracial adoptions have all kinds of problems. I heard about a couple that adopted a Korean child—the father was a black GI and the poor kid had completely oriental features and black skin. And by the time he was fifteen they were in and out of juvenile court like a revolving door. Stolen cars, drugs, psychiatrists—could you cope with that? You could not."

"Is there anything else you want to know?" Elspeth asked him.

"No, I guess we can draft an understanding here." He tore a sheet from his pad.

"When's the due date?" Amethyst asked.

"Goldwasser keeps changing it. Last time he said anywhere from January first to the tenth. He said first babies are usually late."

"I'm dying for a cigarette," said Amethyst. "Mind if I smoke?"

"Not at all. I gave it up on account of the baby but I know where there are some."

"That's all right. I have my own."

Marvin was in the middle of the sofa, writing. Amethyst was at his right. "I'm giving you a check for a thousand dollars tonight," he said, "that you can cash or deposit immediately. I'll call my bank the first thing Monday morning. And my attorney will have adoption papers all ready when the baby's born, which you'll sign preferably as soon as you've recovered enough to hold a pen, and at that moment you'll receive a check for seven thousand more."

Elspeth took a little gold-trimmed dish from the mantel and gave it to Amethyst for an ashtray. Then she sat on the sofa too, beside Marvin, and watched him write.

"And put in that you pay Dr. Goldwasser and the hospital and all that," she said. "It's your baby now so you pay the medical."

His writing paused. "All right. Any medical items connected to the pregnancy and birth and not covered by your insurance. Or by your family's insurance."

"Oh, Marvin! You're such a stickler. Are you going to investigate her family's medical insurance?"

"Dear, there's no reason why we should save money for an insurance company. But if Miss Baker wants to submit duplicate bills and pick up a little extra, very well. I won't question it." He wrote a bit more. Then he paused. "Now what if the baby is defective? Birth defects. Or if it dies."

"Marvin," Amethyst said reproachfully.

"Your tough luck," Elspeth said. "You pay me the eight thousand no matter what. I take my chances and you take yours. If you had a baby of your own you'd be taking that chance. And if the baby has something wrong with it, it'll need love and acceptance all the more."

"Well spoken," said Amethyst.

"The baby's born and it's yours," said Elspeth. "As is. There's no guarantee."

"She's right," said Amethyst. "A baby isn't like a car, with a twelve-month guarantee."

"Yeah, yeah, she's right. Okay. In the agencies they weed out the defective ones, but all right—never mind." He resumed writing.

"There's no reason why it should have birth defects," said Elspeth. "I've been super careful."

"You never know though," Marvin said.

"That's right," said Elspeth. "You never know. And what if I die in childbirth? I want a twenty-five-thousand-dollar life-insurance policy—if I die in childbirth you give my parents twenty-five thousand dollars. Plus the eight for the baby, dead or alive."

They were looking at her.

"Look, it's a very small chance that I'll die, and it's a very small chance that the baby will have a defect. But when you give birth there's a risk. If you want the baby without the risk it's not fair."

"Okay, okay. You're insured for twenty-five thousand by me. You're not gonna die." He wrote, reading the words aloud. "'If Miss Baker dies in childbirth—'" He made an insert. "'— in this childbirth, Mr. Gilbert will pay the parents of Miss Baker twenty-five thousand dollars within sixty days thereafter.' Okay? Does that do it?"

"Make it 'in the childbirth or as a result of it,'" she said. "Because it could happen after."

"'Or as a direct result of aforesaid childbirth.' All right now? It doesn't make any difference anyway, you know. Because you're not gonna die. Nobody dies in childbirth any more."

"If it doesn't make any difference make it thirty-five thousand."

He turned and looked at her again.

"You can't blame her, Marvin. It's her life she's talking about. It's just a way of making clear that there won't be any temptation on our part to cut corners on the very best medical care. I understand her very well. Make it thirty-five thousand. As you said, it won't happen, so it doesn't matter."

Marvin scratched out the twenty-five and wrote thirty-five. He continued writing.

"Can you imagine the effect on her parents if anything happened to her?" Amethyst continued. "After what she's told us? She's a dutiful daughter. She's a dutiful mother too. Was it very hard for you to give up smoking?"

"No," Elspeth said, "because I never cared that much about it. I just smoked for the way it looked."

"You're lucky."

"All right," said Marvin. "Anything else?"

"If it's a boy we give her a bonus of five hundred dollars," said Amethyst.

"Dear, I did not ask you. I was addressing myself to Miss Baker."

"I wouldn't accept that," said Elspeth. "On principle. Same price for a boy or a girl."

"Very good," said Marvin. "No discrimination on account of sex. Eight thousand dollars as agreed. Boy or girl."

"I have a feeling it's gonna be a girl anyway," Elspeth said.

"Why do you think it's gonna be a girl?" he asked.

"It's just a feeling I have. Would you love a girl as much as a boy?"

"Of course."

"My father says girls are the nicest people in the world."

"Well, I agree with him. I married one."

She watched him finish their contract. "Put in 'regardless of the health or condition of the baby,' " she said.

"You don't have to say that. If it states I pay eight grand, that's it. I pay eight grand. Period."

"Okay. I guess that's right. Put it in though. It can't hurt."

He wrote the phrase. She saw him add a sentence that the agreed price was firm and not subject to change.

"Put in that you agree to give the child the best possible education," she said.

"Look, enough's enough. On that you trust us. The kid becomes ours and obviously we're gonna do the best we can for it. The best we know how."

"So why not say it in the contract then?" said Amethyst.

"Because we put a clause like that in the contract and some lawyer can tell her she's got a legal wedge for bugging us the rest of our lives. That's not how it should be. When the baby's born, that's it. Good-bye. The natural mother is out of the picture. We go our separate ways. We've heard the last of each other. She doesn't stick her head in ten years later and tell us to send the kid to Milton Academy." He turned to Elspeth. "You're intelligent. Do you see my point?"

"Okay," she said.

"Okay? You see my point. Agreed?"

"Agreed."

She watched him write the date.

"I haven't been so unreasonable," she said. "I wouldn't take the extra bonus for a boy, and that's really a fifty-fifty chance. The thing about paying my parents if I die in childbirth is only a teensy little one-in-a-million chance."

181

"You haven't been unreasonable at all," he said. "You're a sweet kid. It's been a pleasure doing business with you. Here. Read it. Do you have a typewriter here?"

"No."

"I should have brought the portable. Well, read it over and if it's satisfactory as agreed I'll make another longhand copy. Is there anyone here who can witness our signatures?"

"My landlady can. My landlord's blind."

"All right. Read it over."

"I read while you were writing. It's fine."

"Okay, I'll recopy it as is then." He took a fresh sheet.

Elspeth rose, as though to stretch her legs. "Can I make you some tea or coffee?"

"Let me help you," said Amethyst, rising. But she approached Elspeth, tall, the black hat still on, its brim erect on one side and drooping on the other. Her eyes were visibly damp. She embraced Elspeth, the smouldering cigarette in her fingers. "You beautiful person," she said. "You're a saint, like Rabbi Ed. I know you are. I hope the baby looks like you. And you know what I'll tell him? I'll tell him we paid eight thousand dollars for him. And I'll tell him that if the price was a million dollars, we'd have found it some way." Her eyes overflowed.

Amethyst and Elspeth hugged each other, sobbing.

"All right, all right, that's enough," said Marvin. "Enough!"

23

"YOU see?" said Mrs. Brody, as Elspeth sat having tea with her across the red-checked oilcloth after the Gilberts had gone. "It all worked out very nice. Everything worked out." The white hair was sticking out in many directions.

"But they're so old," Elspeth said unhappily.

"So maybe they got more experience. Old people don't get excited so quick."

"What if they die?"

"They wouldn't die. Look, young people could die too. If he's a rich man he'll have insurance."

Saturday Elspeth was at her register at the supermarket, so Harriet visited on Sunday morning instead. She brought another meat loaf, a macaroni and cheese pudding, and a tuna casserole.

"Does Dad mind your leaving him alone on Sunday?"

"Well, I told him I'd be back early. He knows I visit you. He drove me partway. All the way to the terminal. So I only had one bus."

Elspeth told her about the arrangement with the Gilberts.

"Well! I'm so glad that's finally settled," said Harriet. "And so much money! I'm surprised."

Elspeth brought the thousand-dollar check to the kitchen table and displayed it to Harriet. She did not show her the handwritten agreement because of its reference to death in childbirth. "I hadn't meant to ask for money. He was the one that was hinting money, hinting he's gonna give me a present and stuff, it was kind of disgusting. So I socked him. I don't know where I got eight thousand. I thought, okay, mister, you want to get mercenary? Let's not be pikers. I just wanted to set him on his heels. I mean, even if my baby is top quality, so what? You don't sell a baby like a horse. And when they went for the eight thousand, just like that—Jesus! It was wild. His wife was like completely on my side. She'd come up with arguments for my side that I never thought of. She wouldn't let him open his mouth. I should have said twelve. I really should."

"Don't kick yourself. I think you did very well. There are black markets, you know."

"I know there are. But I don't know what they charge. I just made up numbers."

"I don't know either. I have no idea. But if you started asking too crazy an amount they might have looked for another girl. You aren't the only pregnant girl in Boston."

"And they pay all the medical besides. They've even got to pay Goldwasser. It won't cost Dad a dime."

"Well, I just can't get over it. I think most of the time girls don't get anything. The people just give the agency a fee, a few hundred dollars. I never heard of such prices."

Harriet cried a little, then made herself stop. She insisted on washing all the woodwork in Elspeth's room, even the closet shelf.

"Dad will be glad when you tell him about the eight thousand," Elspeth said at lunch.

Harriet left in early afternoon. She asked if it was tonight that Elspeth was having dinner with Bob's girl's family.

"Yes. I'm looking forward to it."

"Well, have a good time. That was very nice of them."

Elspeth expected Bob to call for her at six. "Are you sure you wouldn't rather I took a key?" she asked Mrs. Brody. "I'd hate to wake you with the doorbell."

"Don't worry, darling. I don't sleep much. I go ten times to the bathroom."

Bob and Karen came for her together. Elspeth put on the coat she could not button. They had Karen's brother-in-law's car, as Bob's was not running right. The guy he had rented it to for the weekend had said the radiator kept leaking, the taillights stopped working, and a cop had stopped him about the taillights. It also needed a differential, and the guy who had rented it knew a lot about cars and was going to get a differential from a junkyard and put it in.

"If he doesn't, I think I can," said Elspeth. "Mark put in a differential three times, and I was under the car with him two of those times. But for the radiator just buy yourself a can of sealer and dump it in."

"That's what I was gonna do."

"The lights are probably just a fuse."

Karen drove. They all sat tightly in front, Elspeth in the middle.

"I really appreciate this," she said. "It's so lonesome there at the Brodys'. Maybe lonesomeness is human condition. Do you think so?"

"Well, I guess it's part of it," said Karen.

"Maybe that's why God created the world," said Elspeth. "Because He was lonesome."

"It's been said that God created the world because He loves stories," Karen said.

Elspeth nodded slowly. "Ya, I like that," she said. "But I guess He must love sad stories best, then."

They drove in silence for a bit. Then she told them of the agreement she had made with their friend's friends, and how they had surprised her by agreeing to eight thousand dollars.

"And I feel so mercenary. As if I took advantage."

"Well, it does sound like kind of a lot," said Bob. "I wouldn't know, though."

"They didn't have to give me money. I mean, they seemed no worse than most of the parents I've come across. And they seem to have the means to provide a nice environment and good schools. And what more could I ask? But then he kept on assuming that I had to have my palm greased—I guess because he was just so desperate—but even so. He did it on the phone too, and I was starting to get ticked off. I should have said, okay, one million dollars. Then they'd have got the message and shut up about money. And we'd have talked like human beings. But I started playing along and the first thing I know he's writing an agreement. And then if I'd said, 'oh, here, I don't want your money,' they'd have started worrying that I might change my mind after and not give them the baby. That's how their minds work."

"Well, it's more money than I ever expect to see at one time," said Karen. "But they can probably afford it. Look, you'll have carried the child for nine months, and your college is disrupted and everything. You're entitled to something."

"And then I added the medical expenses onto that."

"You should have," said Karen.

"The one thing I'm really glad about with that money," Elspeth said, "is that it makes it possible to go back to Mount Holyoke. Daddy would probably want me to live at home and go to BU or Simmons, but now I can go back to Mount Holyoke no matter what he says. For a year anyway. And after a year he might relent."

184

"What are they like?" Bob asked. "The Gilberts."

"I don't really know. They seem basically okay. Marvin's a bit of a cold fish. And Amethyst is a little dizzy. But they'll do the best they can. That's all you can ask. My parents had their good points and their rotten points, and who says I'd be such a bargain as a parent? Kids are gonna have to deal with imperfect people all their lives, so they might as well learn young."

The apartment was up three flights in a structure of brick, not old. Avis answered the door with an infant at her breast. She had Karen's features with their leanness and mildly Tatar cast, but quite fair, in contrast to Karen's deep complexion. Her husband Steve, large and blond and smiling, took Elspeth's coat. She handed him the gift she had brought, a bundle of paper napkins imprinted with line drawings of Boston scenes. A little boy was underfoot.

Elspeth sat on the sofa. Logs crackled brightly behind the fireplace screen. The little boy told her he could do a somersault.

"Do we have time for a drink?" Steve asked.

"Everything's about ready, so let's drink after," said Avis. "Here, you change Jeannine, okay? I think she's had all she wants." She handed Steve the baby and buttoned her blouse. The little boy did a somersault at Elspeth's feet. His knit skullcap fell off.

"That's very good," said Elspeth. "How old is he?"

"How old are you, Mickey?" Avis asked him.

But he was into another somersault. "You know," he said.

"He'll be three in January," said Avis.

The dining area was an ell of the living room. Karen was setting a crystal bowl of salad in place. A tapering bottle of pink wine picked up the light. There were shaggy rugs in a design of bright Scandinavian explosions. The windows beyond the dining table were hung with trailing plants. The shelves of books nearest to Elspeth held mostly scientific texts. Bob had removed his tie and jacket, and the tasseled and knotted cords hung over his belt onto the dark trousers. He told Elspeth that Steve was a physicist.

Steve came back without the baby. "I changed her twice," he told Avis. "As soon as I changed her she had a b.m."

"Oh. So that's why she wouldn't nurse. She'll be up again, hollering for more."

"She seemed ready to sleep."

"Probably not for long. Okay, shall we wash?"

They went not to the formica dining table but past it, to the kitchen. Steve filled a two-handled mug at the sink and poured water first over one hand and then the other, and then over each a second time. He wiped with a hand towel, muttering a Hebrew formula.

"You want to wash, Mickey?" Avis asked. She lifted him and poured water from the mug onto his little extended wrists. She said a Hebrew word to prompt him, but he responded with a different one. Avis said another word, and Mickey said still another. It occurred to Elspeth that he was saying every second word, responding to each prompting with the word that came next. Avis put him down, and rinsed

185

her own wrists and said the blessing as Steve had done. Then Karen did it. Bob gave the two-handled mug to Elspeth. She filled it and wet her hands.

"Is there something I'm supposed to say?"

She repeated the strange words one at a time after Bob. Then he performed the same washing himself, and muttered and wiped. The others had already gone to the table, and Mickey was near his father on a jump seat.

"Did Gramps do this?" Elspeth asked Bob.

He didn't answer. But she saw Mickey twist around and look at her from his jump seat, a finger pressed over his tight lips.

When Elspeth and Bob were seated Steve said the blessing for bread. He cut the loaf, bit a slice and tossed another to Avis, who caught it at the other end of the table. He gave Mickey a piece and passed the tray.

Bob chewed a crust. "I never saw Gramps do it," he said. "But I'm sure he knew about it. He must have gotten away from it. Like a lot of things."

"Was I not supposed to speak before?"

"Well, the washing is for the breaking of bread. So we don't interrupt between. To connect the two."

Karen was serving brown rice with mushrooms from a deep steaming vessel, and Avis brought a tray of chicken pieces baked and coated. Steve cut Mickey's chicken into tiny pieces. Bob poured the wine. There was another vegetable mixture with marinated beans. Elspeth helped herself to salad. "Everything looks so delicious." Mickey ate with his fingers, looking only at his plate. I LOVE GRANDMA was lettered in red on his bib.

"Will you breastfeed your baby?" Avis asked.

"I can't. I'm giving it for adoption."

"Oh, of course. I'm stupid. Are you going to have Lamaze?"

"I don't think so. My doctor likes saddle block or twilight sleep. But somebody told me about a bad experience with twilight sleep."

"We had Lamaze both times. I'd never do anything else. It's the only way."

"Really? Well, they say it's not for everybody. I'm afraid it wouldn't work for me. I'm too skeptical to stand much of a chance with self-hypnosis."

"It's not self-hypnosis," said Avis. "It's very practical. You have breathing methods to hyperoxygenate yourself, and the massaging increases the blood flow. Oxygen is the best anesthetic, you know. And you also control your breathing to keep the diaphragm from pressing on the uterus between contractions. And you're so occupied with timing, and breathing, and massaging, and pushing, that you don't have time for anything to hurt. When you're busy enough nothing hurts."

"And you had no anesthesia? No pain killers or anything?"

"No."

"Nothing?"

"Nothing but nothing."

"That's the truth," said Steve. "I was there. She was like you see her now. In full possession of her faculties. Never more awake in her life."

"And didn't it hurt? You didn't feel anything?"

186

"I felt a lot. I felt contractions. That's not hurting. When a dentist sticks a drill in your tooth, that's hurting. A toothache, that's pain. Not childbirth. I'll take childbirth any time."

"But everybody says it hurts. My landlady's daughter had twilight sleep for the third baby, just a little bit awake. And it was the most unbearable agony of her life. So imagine how awful it would have been if she'd been completely awake."

"It hurt *because* of the anesthesia," said Avis. "She was knocked out just enough so that her muscles couldn't function, just when she needed them most. Here's her uterus needing to contract and push the baby out, and the birth canal needing to stretch, and her whole body so drugged that nothing can function. Like when your colon is so exhausted and tired it doesn't have the strength to take a crap, but you still have to go. Only worse. You're equipped with muscles for birth contractions. And to drug all that equipment into lethargy just when you need it is the dumbest thing you can do. Everything stops, the baby lies there aching, and you lie there aching, and finally the doctor has to dig into you with forceps and shlep the poor kid out. You wouldn't think of being anesthetized for intercourse, would you? If the vagina were put to sleep, it wouldn't respond and it wouldn't stretch. You'd have to be raped, in the most painful way. It's the same thing. If it's anesthetized it won't stretch for childbirth either."

"Well—" Elspeth began uncertainly.

"Go to at least the first session of a Lamaze course," said Avis. "Promise me you'll do that. For your sake and the baby's sake."

"I don't think there's time left for a Lamaze course. I'm due in six or seven weeks."

"That's time enough."

"Well, my doctor says some of his patients use a partial Lamaze," Elspeth said. "He says it's okay if you're not fanatic about it. They start without anesthesia, but when it starts to get painful he gives them something, so it's easier for her and easier for him."

"That's awful," said Avis. "I hate that kind of doctor. If there's a breech birth, or something abnormal, you're gonna need anesthesia, you can't help it. But if it's a normal simple childbirth, Ellie, stick to your guns. He just wants to drug you and make you weak and helpless so he'll seem like Superman. So be a fanatic about it. Because it's your first time, and he'll be encouraging you to chicken out. Make up your mind to stay with it. And do your breathing with each contraction. And if you think it does start to hurt, that won't happen till the contractions are only a minute or two apart. So if it hurts you know it's practically over. You hang in there, breathe, keep on top of each wave, and bang, it's over. And wow, do you feel great. And there's your baby. You just laugh and laugh."

"Well, my doctor says there certainly is pain."

"Oh, doctors can be impossible," said Avis. "Did your doctor ever have a baby? What does he know about it? We had one of those jackass doctors too. He said 'I am adamantly opposed to this so-called natural childbirth.' He said Steve would faint and get in the way. And if Steve saw the delivery it would ruin our love life.

And I said, 'why? Steve and I were there at the conception, why shouldn't we be there at the climax of the whole process?' And he said, 'if you want that, you're morbid.' And I said, 'you'll be there, so you must be morbid too.' So he said, 'but I have a job to do,' and I said 'I have a job to do too.'"

"How did you get him to go along with it?"

"We fired him. We got another doctor. Tell him if he needs an unconscious patient there's something wrong. Do you know what it is? It's Victorian prudery. I bet he's an old guy, right? There was a time when Victorian ladies were taught to faint at the sight of a man's balls. And now this neurotic so-called civilization we live in thinks it's accepted sex finally, but it still hasn't accepted childbirth. It hasn't accepted that our first view of the world is from between a woman's legs. And that's why it was such battle to get husbands into the delivery room, and that's why doctors wanted the mothers unconscious."

There was a wail from another room.

"There she goes," said Avis. "I knew she'd wake up." She rose and left.

"She certainly feels strongly about it," Elspeth said when she thought Avis was out of earshot.

Steve nodded.

"How did you like it?" said Elspeth. "Did you like being there?"

"Loved it," he said. "Not that what I did compares with what she did, but it helped her to have me with the stop watch, so she knew just where things were at."

"And it really didn't hurt?"

"Everything she told you is true. When she was in labor with Jeannine she did have some backache for a while. So she told me where to massage."

Avis returned with Jeannine sucking at her breast. She resumed her place at the table. Steve rose to cut her chicken and she ate with one hand.

"Yes, I feel strongly about it," she said to Elspeth. "I feel strongly about a lot of things. I feel strongly about organic gardening, and all the junk they put in our food. The one thing I hate about this apartment is that I have no place for a garden. The year we were down the Cape I had a garden."

Steve went back to his chair. "When my wife believes in something," he said, "she goes all out. She doesn't do things by halves."

"Of course," said Avis. "If I believe in something, why shouldn't I go all out? If I don't act on my beliefs, do I really believe them?"

"You've got a point," said Elspeth.

"It's a point that made that year down the Cape a pretty lively one," Steve said to Elspeth with a twinkle. "A lot of people were glad to see us get out of town."

"What happened?"

"I was opposed to an urban renewal project," Avis told her. "We lived there the year Steve worked for the nuclear plant. And there was this urban renewal scheme, supposedly, but actually it was just a dodge to move the Bravas out. Do you know the Brava people? They live all down through Cape Cod and around there. They're black. And the loveliest people. Industrious, very handsome, really stunningly good-looking. And they all have gardens, and they own their own little homes, lots of them have small businesses—they have white people working for them. The old folks speak Portuguese. They started from a mix of Africans and Portuguese in the Cape Verde Islands. And along comes this renewal project. But the real idea was to clear the blacks away from the tourist areas. To evict the Bravas from their homes."

"The way Avis took the Bravas to her heart is all the more remarkable when you realize how anti-goy she is," Steve said to Elspeth. "There she was exchanging gardening techniques over the fence, and having them in for coffee, and actually she's extremely anti-goy. Avis's idea is that Jews should have ten kids apiece and goyim should get their kicks from dirty movies."

"That was just a joke," said Avis. "I don't like to see anybody get pushed around."

"And did she let them know it. She was at every session of the town meeting. And every hearing. The board of selectmen, the zoning board, every other kind of board. And she was nursing Mickey then, and there was this old lady that said the last time she saw a woman nurse a baby at town meeting was sixty years ago, but this was the first time she ever saw a woman go up to the microphone with a baby at her breast."

"It was covered up. I had my jacket. What was I gonna do, let him holler? If I didn't take my turn the next speaker might move to call the question."

"And it wasn't just the Cape Verdeans and the renewal project," Steve told Elspeth. "If it wasn't that it was something else. She hit that town like a cyclone. It was always something. Once she wrote a letter to the local weekly—I don't remember what the subject was— but she starts off 'Fourscore and something years ago, our fathers brought forth on this continent a new nation, conceived in liberty, dedicated to the proposition that all men are created equal, and predicated on the extermination of the aboriginal inhabitants.' "

"The subject was the quality of life," said Avis. "I look at the litter all over the countryside, and I look at the commercials on TV, stretchier and stretchier girdles, more and more chocolate in the cereal, and I ask myself, was it for this? For this the Bay Colony put a bounty on scalps? For this we paid farmers to go moonlighting as murderers at so much per head?"

"And the response kept that little newspaper going all summer," said Steve. "Week after week after week. Letters for, letters against. 'Sorry we didn't have space for all your letters, we'll print more next week.' One old guy accused her of confusing the Plymouth Colony with the Bay Colony, so we learned some history. The basic problem was that we didn't have a congenial congregation to drain her energies. If we did, she'd have been up to her neck in fundraising and committees. But there was just this one temple, and it wasn't our style. We went once, and so Avis got into a fight with the rabbi naturally."

"I couldn't help it. He made me sick. I can't stand water in the whiskey."

"Okay, I don't like water in the whiskey either. But we knew before we went that it wasn't our kind of a place. We just went to be sociable. So we should have just smiled, and been polite, and been sociable."

"What they did to a four-thousand-year-old tradition," Avis said to Elspeth, "it's like you take good whiskey, old whiskey, and dilute it and dilute it till it's piss."

Karen was gathering up the dishes. Elspeth and Bob helped her collect them.

Avis shifted Jeannine to the other side. The baby went to work anew.

"Well, cooking must be one of those things you believe in," said Elspeth, "because you really went all out. Everything was fantastically delicious."

"Thank you."

"Yeah, she's a good cook," said Steve. "Like I told you, she doesn't do things by halves."

Karen brought out a dessert of gelatin and fruits.

"Mickey can't keep his eyes open," said Avis. "He's not gonna eat anymore. How about putting him in pajamas."

"Okay, young man?" Steve said. "Pajama time?"

"You can come back in your pajamas for the benching," Avis said to Mickey.

Elspeth spooned her dessert. The tea had a subtle flavor It was pale, with almost a grayish tinge. Bits of leaf, like black filings, had settled in a spiral.

"I love this tea," she said.

"It's from the Himalayas," said Avis. "The Himalayan foothills. There's just one store that has it."

Karen put out little finger bowls.

Steve returned with Mickey in pajamas riding on his shoulders. He set him down.

"Want to pass out the benchers?" Avis said to Mickey.

He opened a drawer of the hutch and took several booklets, of uniform size but each a different color. He turned and counted the adults quietly, pointing a finger.

"What color do you want?" he asked Elspeth.

She took a red one. A title was embossed on the fuzzy cover in gold. Grace After Meals.

Karen and Bob and Steve and Avis began to sing a rhythmic chant together. Apparently the booklets all had the same pages inside no matter what color the cover. Mickey was on Steve's knee. Avis sang from memory, still nursing Jeannine, not opening her booklet. Elspeth could not join in, since they sang in Hebrew. She tried briefly to follow silently in the translation, which was on each left-hand page, but she had no way of knowing where their place was. She occupied herself looking at the colored illustrations and decorations. They were in a modern zigzaggy style. A jumble of crooked buildings under an orange sun apparently represented Jerusalem. Sometimes the singing would end, usually after a loud refrain, and they would continue seeming to mutter separately. They would come together in something quite melodious, Karen's clear voice seeming to lead, and Avis harmonizing steadily and closely, two tones below. Elspeth saw Mickey's mouth shaping along with them in refrains he knew. At one point they all gave the table a sudden pound with a fist, not quite in unison, so that the teacups jumped, even Mickey attempting it on cue, and Karen's voice rose spiritedly and led them on without a break. None of it bothered Jeannine, who nursed with her eyes shut.

Finally Karen and Avis went into a slow melody so lovely and plaintive that

190

Steve and Bob stopped to listen. Elspeth glanced at Steve's booklet to see what page they were on. They were near the end. He will bless His people with peace.

Mickey slid from Steve's knee and raised his arms to Elspeth. "He wants to kiss you good-night," Steve said.

Elspeth picked him up and kissed him.

He made his way around the table. He kissed Bob, and then Karen. He kissed his mother. He even kissed his little sister, but she did not interrupt her sucking and put a tiny hand to his face as though to push him away. At last he departed, hand in hand with his father.

"I'll put Jeannine to bed and meet you all in the living room," Avis said, buttoning her blouse.

Elspeth returned to the sofa. The logs were now infused with silent intensity and redness, the flames small and blue. Heat radiated to her face. Karen put a bowl of nuts with nutcrackers on the coffee table. Then she put out a tray with little glasses, and a Dutch liqueur and a Swiss one. Bob, at the other end of the sofa, opened a bottle and filled a glass. Elspeth held out a glass and he filled hers too.

Steve returned to the living room before Avis did. He moved aside the fireplace screen and added two logs. The flames expanded crackling, yellow once more. She noticed that he wore a dangling white cord like Bob's, a column of precise knots and twists, ending in separate strands.

"What do you call those things?" she asked. "That hang out. Bob told me about it, but what's the word?"

"Tsitsis," said Bob. He was lounging with his liqueur in a corner of the sofa, an ankle across a knee.

"Tsitsis?"

"Or you could say ritual fringes, if you prefer," said Karen. "I've also seen it called a scapular."

"A what?" said Bob.

"Scapular. Because the garment hangs from your shoulders."

"Sounds kind of Archbishop of Canterbury," he said. "I couldn't call it anything like that. If I did I'd think I had to walk it to the De Luxe Valet Service. I'd rather call it tsitsis and chuck it in the hamper."

Steve hung the poker by the fireplace. He poured himself a liqueur.

Avis came to the living room and sat on the hassock, her slim knees leaning sideways together in the pale blue slacks. Steve poured her a drink too.

"I know the perfect Lamaze instructor for you," she said to Elspeth. "Especially if your doctor isn't a Lamaze man, then it's awfully important to have the right instructor. I'll find out if she has a class for you and let you know. She does them in her apartment and they're usually for couples only, but once in a while she has one for women whose husbands won't participate."

"Let Ellie make up her own mind," said Steve.

"She will," said Avis. "But she needs Mrs. Hasbrough. Because some of the hospital courses are wishy-washy. Too many doctors stick their heads in and the instructors are afraid of them."

"You don't even know if Ellie wants Lamaze," said Steve. "Stop bugging her. Maybe you'd make more converts if you didn't come on so strong."

"That's okay," said Elspeth. "I'd like to look into it. I may not end up doing it. But I think I'd like to begin the course at least."

"That's sensible," said Steve. "That's all we ask. Then you'll have a basis of forming a judgment."

"That's what I mean," said Elspeth. "The first session will tell me whether I want to hear more."

"It's awfully important," Avis said to her. "It's important for the baby especially, because anesthesia can reduce the oxygen supply to the brain. In a caesarean there's no harm done because the baby is taken out so fast. The anesthesia doesn't have time to get into the baby. But in a normal birth, if the baby's lying inside you doped, some of the brain cells are gonna start dying off for want of oxygen."

"Haven't there been any geniuses whose mothers had anesthesia?" said Elspeth.

"I'm sure there have." said Steve.

"But maybe they would have been even smarter," said Avis. "Steve, you can just see that Lamaze babies are brighter. They look smarter. You've said it yourself."

"Maybe that's subjective too," he said. Maybe we see what we want to see. Or maybe the parents that get into Lamaze are a bright crowd to begin with. But Ellie, if you do have anesthesia, make sure your anesthesiologist is a good one. Because if he happens to goof, certainly he can do harm. I can only tell you that what Avis said about her own experience is true. The babies were so alert, from the first moment. And her recovery was so quick. They couldn't keep her in bed, the first day even."

Avis nodded. "We've done it twice. And we're gonna keep right on."

Karen cracked a walnut. Steve again moved the fireplace screen. He gave the poker a twist between logs, and the flames sprang suddenly stronger, finding new drafts. Avis asked Elspeth what she did and if she had a job. Elspeth told about the temporary agencies and about her job at the supermarket. And about how she'd prefer the hardware business, which she knew, but how impossible that was just now.

"Bob said you know hardware backwards and forwards," said Karen. "You were practically born in it."

"Pretty much," said Elspeth.

"Why don't you ask your Uncle Lennie to give Elspeth a job," Avis said to Steve.

"Uncle Lennie has lumber yards, not hardware stores," Steve said.

"It's similar though," said Avis. "They have hardware up at the front counter. Nails and everything."

"Well, nails—"

"Not just nails. All kinds of things."

"A good lumber yard and a good hardware are a lot alike," said Elspeth. "I'd love to work in a lumber yard. They both have the same aspect of spending time with customers, and explaining to them how to do things. If it's a good place. There's tremendous overlap."

"Well, I'll call him," said Steve.

"He's got a whole chain of places," Avis told Elspeth. "I'm sure he could fit you in."

"I love lumber," said Elspeth. "And all the things that go with it. One of my brothers and I used to talk about building our own houses when we grew up. We were gonna do it all ourselves, with our own hands, inside and out."

Steve was refilling everyone's glass.

"Speaking of building your own house," said Avis, "I got this idea a couple of days ago about building a planet. Steve, I've got to tell you about this. We build our planet, with a viable atmosphere, little by little. Step by step. And then we go and live on it."

"You're ready to give up on this earth?"

"I mean as an alternative, in case things really get impossible. Listen. It's step by step. First we take all the junk, the solid waste, that towns are having trouble finding room for in their dumps. and we shoot it into orbit. The money we charge these towns for removing their solid waste pays for the rockets. Okay, so all this plastic and discarded refrigerators and stuff is thrown into orbit together around the sun. Several payloads, or several hundred payloads, but all near together, so they draw together and form the core of a new planet. At the same distance from the sun as the earth, but orbiting in a different plane, and crossing the earth's when we're on the opposite side of the sun, so they don't collide."

"You're gonna need some awfully inexpensive rockets," Steve said.

"That part I'm turning over to you. Okay? Your next assignment. Devise a cheapie-type rocket. Now then. We collect all the manure. And all the cesspool stuff. We'll start a cesspool-pumping business so we won't have any shortage of it. And all the dirty diapers. People will pay us to take it away. And we shoot all this stuff out there onto the orbiting core—till it's completely covered knee-deep with it. And it ferments, and produces an atmosphere of carbon dioxide and methane and ammonia. Okay? And next, we shoot out a load of plant microorganisms. And they multiply like crazy in the carbon dioxide, and the plant respiration transforms the atmosphere to oxygen and nitrogen and water vapor. Just like it happened on earth. And meanwhile we're shooting all the compost and grass clippings out there to rot and turn into a topsoil. And finally when there's enough topsoil and enough oxygen, we take some grass seed and a couple of goats and some chickens and go and live there."

"Can Bob and I come?" Karen asked.

"Of course," said Avis. "Naturally you'd be included. And eight other families. So we can have a shul."

"This planet would have to have a twenty-four-hour spin so the hours for prayer would come out right." said Bob.

"We could manage that," said Steve. "We get the right end-over-end tumble in the first payload on the way out, and keep that up."

"And speaking of twenty-four hours to a day," said Bob, "I'm getting up at six tomorrow. I hate to break this up, and I hate to rush Ellie, but I'm depending on you for a ride to Cambridge." He was looking at Karen.

"You want to go now?"

"I think I better."

Steve helped Elspeth with her coat. She thanked Avis, and complimented the meal again and the children. Avis said she hoped she'd come again.

She went out to the landing with Bob and Karen. At the door Avis put her arms around her. Avis's gray eyes looked at Elspeth earnestly.

"Did I come on too strong?"

"No," Elspeth said. "You were fine. I hope you're gonna call me and let me know about that Lamaze instructor."

"Steve thinks I'm a fanatic. It's just that I don't always know how to restrain my enthusiasms."

"Why should you?"

"Well, that's what *I* say. If I have but one life to live, let me live it as a fanatic. I mean, we only pass this way once. How can anybody live their whole life without knowing what it is to care about something with all your heart and soul? Don't ever be afraid to be a fanatic, Ellie."

ELSPETH deposited Mr. Gilbert's thousand-dollar check on Monday during her lunch break. There was a branch of her bank near the supermarket.

When she had returned to the Brodys' in late afternoon Harriet phoned. "Dad said you should take the eight thousand dollars in cash, not checks, so Internal Revenue doesn't know," Harriet told her. "And don't deposit the thousand-dollar check. Give it back and make him give you cash."

"It's too late now. It's already in the bank."

Harriet asked if she had enjoyed the evening with Bob and his girl's relatives.

"Ya," said Elspeth.

"I suppose they're all very religious."

"I guess so."

"Imagine, in this day and age. What could you find to talk about to them?"

"Oh, different things. Natural childbirth."

"Natural childbirth?"

When Elspeth had hung up Mrs. Brody remembered there had been a phone call during the day. "Somebody called up. She said tell you Avis. Avis."

Elspeth found the number and dialed at once.

"Hello?" said Avis's voice. "Mickey! Put that down! Wait a minute."

There was the sound of the phone being put somewhere, and household noises in the background.

"Hi," Elspeth said when Avis came back. "Are you busy? I could call back later."

"Ellie! No, that's fine. Listen, Steve called his uncle, and there's a lumber-yard job. And in the one that's nearest to you. His Dorchester yard. Get a pencil and note this down."

"Really? Wow! I've got a pencil. Shoot." The pad and pencil she had put on the black telephone table in the week of waiting to hear from Extras Inc. were still there.

"Steve told him you know all about lumber and you've got lots of experience."

Elspeth wrote down the address and phone number.

"He said to ask for Gus," Avis told her.

"It's so sweet of you to do this."

"It's nothing. I hope you get the job. And I called Mrs. Hasbrough, and unfortunately everything she's got starting around now is for couples. I was afraid that might be the case. But she's good to be in touch with anyway—she knows everybody. So why don't you give her a call. Maybe she'll have some ideas. She was one of the pioneers of it, teaching in her apartment back when ninety-nine out of a hundred doctors were dead set against it."

"Okay."

"Try to call before seven-thirty, because during a class she won't answer the phone. It's Mrs. Clarence Hasbrough."

Elspeth took down the number and the address. It was in the Back Bay. She tried to telephone at once but there was a busy signal.

She reached her after supper. Despite the English-sounding name Mrs. Hasbrough seemed to have a trace of a Continental accent. She said the next class for women doing Lamaze without their husbands would not begin for another three weeks. "I would say to wait for that if you have the time. But if you're due the beginning of January, then you don't have the time. Not quite. I have a group with husbands beginning next week, Monday, a week from tonight, if you would like to join us. And who knows? Maybe another without-husband will turn up, and then you will not be lonesome. At least you can come and see. And if you decide no, you don't have to pay for the first session."

In her lunch break the next day Elspeth telephoned the lumber yard. After work she went there directly. Behind the counter in the showroom was a frowning, stocky man in his thirties with bushy hair swept back. When she asked if he was Gus he nodded.

"I'm Elspeth Baker. I spoke to you on the phone today."

"Oh yes." He looked at the belly protruding from the open coat. Then he looked at her face. "I'll be with you in a moment."

He finished with a customer. Then he turned again to Elspeth.

"You know lumber?"

"Yes."

"Can you do a day's work? When my wife was pregnant she had to lie down a lot. You're supposed to take naps."

"I'll be okay. I don't need naps."

"You sure?"

"What would I kid you for?"

"What do you call that kind of edging? Those three pieces there tied with the sales slip."

"Clamshell," she told him.

"What's the difference between indoor and outdoor plywood?"

"It's in the glue."

"Give me another name for one-by-threes."

"Strapping."

"And two-by-threes?"

"Studs, of course. Anybody knows that."

"What's this kind of nail for?"

"Roofing," she said.

"What's this one for?"

"Sheetrock."

"How long is a tenpenny nail?"

"Three inches."

"If somebody hands you a Master Charge card or a BankAmericard, do you know what to do with it? You've used the machine? And you know how to verify?"

"Sure."

"You've worked in building supplies before?"

"No, but in a hardware. Almost ten years."

"Ten years?"

"Since I was a little kid."

"Are you Lennie's kid cousin or something? Or your parents are friends of his?" But he didn't wait for an answer. "Okay, when do you want to start?"

"How about Monday," she said, "so I can give the place I work for now a few days notice."

He nodded. "Lennie said to start you at the minimum."

"Okay."

"Be here Monday at seven a.m. sharp, for the early shift. You'll have Thursdays off."

Wednesday was her day off from the supermarket. Harriet arrived in midmorning, with another meat loaf, and a big old mayonnaise jar filled with chicken soup. She was so close to tears and red-eyed and nervous that Elspeth knew she had had a fight with Joe.

Harriet had wanted to invite Elspeth home for Thanksgiving dinner, but Joe had threatened that if Elspeth came he'd go right downstairs and out the garage and drive to a diner. He had said he had nothing to be thankful for.

"Mama, why did you suggest a thing like that? You know the way I look now drives him crazy. Literally. The last day I was in the store he wasn't even sane. I mean it. So if he doesn't want to see me till after the baby go along with that. Let him get himself together. You and Dad have your turkey. I'll be okay. There's no law that I have to be there that day, just because it's red on the calendar."

"But you're still our daughter no matter what—" Harriet blubbered.

"Mama, forget it! There's nothing sacred about Thanksgiving. It's not worth it. You take care of Dad."

The postman brought a fat letter from Marvin Gilbert. Elspeth read it, slung deep in the bed, while Harriet did laundering in the bathroom.

Dear Miss Baker,

Enclosed are two typed copies of our agreement, with my witnessed signature. Please sign the typed copies, with either your landlady or someone else witnessing and signing the appropriate line. Retain one copy and return the other to me in the addressed stamped envelope enclosed. We both have the signed handwritten agreement which is binding of course but I thought you might find typed copies more businesslike.

You will be pleased to know that I have been in touch with Dr. Goldwasser, who assures me that you are in excellent health, an excellent patient, and that there is every reason to expect a sound and healthy baby.

I will be in touch with Dr. Goldwasser regularly and if possible my wife and I will be at the hospital to await the good news. My attorney has been alerted and the adoption papers will be ready on time, as will your check for the balance of the $8,000. Dr. Goldwasser has been advised to send duplicate bills to each of us and the hospital also will be so advised.

I must say that you earned my respect and admiration the other evening. You are a very astute and capable person. I don't think an attorney could have represented your interests more efficiently. Despite one youthful error I am certain you will do well in this world. I don't know if you have set your mind on any particular profession as yet but I am confident you will succeed in your chosen field.

My wife shares these sentiments.

I am proud and happy that my child will inherit the genes of a person such as yourself. I am confident too that the father is as brilliant as you say, first of all because I have confidence in your judgment, and secondly because I am sure you would not have had anything to do with him otherwise.

Cordially,
Very truly yours,
Marvin H. Gilbert

MHG/ot

197

The signature over the typed name was the illegible curlicue and flourish she already knew from the check and documents. The compliments moistened her eyes. All Mr. Gilbert's stiffness was there, but also a warmth that had not been apparent face-to-face. She read quickly through the typed contracts. Nothing had been altered or omitted. She put them under clothing in a drawer.

She showed the letter to Harriet after they had hung the laundry on the back porch.

"That's very nice," said Harriet. "A very beautiful letter. Where are the agreements? He says they're enclosed."

"I put them away. They're like I told you. I'm not in the mood to look at them now. Let's make lunch. I'm hungry."

"I'd like Dad to see that letter," said Harriet. "When he's in the right mood."

"I'll show it to him someday," said Elspeth. "When it's all all over."

After lunch Elspeth persuaded Harriet to come for a walk in the park. It was windy across the rolling expanse and the open coat flapped.

"This park was beautiful when I was little," Harriet said.

"It's nice now," said Elspeth.

"Well, not like then. There was a nice zoo here then. I don't know what became of it. The Franklin Park Zoo was famous."

"Don't tell me the giraffes and the monkeys all moved away to Newton and Randolph and Marblehead when the blacks came in. That would be too much."

"No, I don't know what happened. I guess there was no money for it. It's terrible the way this neighborhood has gone downhill."

The blue sky shone. The bare twigs were black against it in infinitely branching patterns of line.

Harriet asked Elspeth if she always wore that supporting corset that Dr. Goldwasser had prescribed.

"No. Just when I need it. My belly's as hard as my head."

"You're supposed to wear it."

From the park they headed toward the library.

She told Harriet about the Lamaze method. Harriet said it was ridiculous. "You call that progress? That isn't progress, it's going backwards. That's how it was in my grandmother's day, when they didn't know any better. There's no reason to torture yourself like that, in this day and age. You've suffered enough."

"It's not suffering," Elspeth told her.

When they came out of the library the sun was low and the air was colder. Elspeth left Harriet at her bus stop and returned to the Brodys' alone. She found the Polish man from the top floor in the Brodys' kitchen, repairing a faucet.

"I could have done that," Elspeth said.

He worked in a soiled undershirt, the small pistol in its shoulder holster, the white hairs scrambled on his arms.

Monday morning Elspeth was at the lumber yard at seven. Gus showed her where to put the white slips and told her to give yellow ones to the customer for presentation to Pete or Turk out back.

In midmorning it was busy, but it slacked off toward noon. She ate her lunch sitting on a tall stool, her feet lifted to a rung. Afterward she had time to wander out back to have a look at the sheds, though she had not been told to work there.

"What the hell's that?" Pete said to Turk. She heard him despite the staticky jumpy music of the portable radio.

"She's working up front," she heard Turk answer. "Don't get too funny with her. She's a friend of the boss."

"Gus?"

"Naw, naw. The big boss. The owner. Lennie Kramer." They were puffing cigarettes.

In midafternoon it was busy again. She was off at four, but stayed a while to help Gus.

"I can't authorize overtime," he said. "You're free to go."

"That's okay."

She left at four-thirty.

At the Brodys' she phoned Avis. "Hi! I started today at On The Level Lumber," she told Avis.

"Great! How did it go?"

"Fine. I love it. And tonight I'm trying out a class with Mrs. Hasbrough."

"Good. I hope you stay with it."

She was glad to sink into the brass bed a while before supper.

Mrs. Hasbrough's class was in a middle-sized living room. The furniture had been supplemented with folding chairs along the walls. An oriental rug lay in the broad center. There were seven big-bellied women besides Elspeth, and seven husbands. Mrs. Hasbrough was fortyish and still pretty. She had a cultivated voice that the slight accent seemed to enhance. Her hair seemed a natural brown without a trace of gray. It was pulled tightly behind her to a bun. She wore tortoise-shell spectacles.

Elspeth was the youngest, but the others seemed no older than their middle or late twenties. It was the first baby for each.

They started with limbering exercises. The women lay on the floor, leaving their husbands on chairs. Like a chorus line they raised a leg, swung it to the side, up again, and down. The slacks were of a variety of colors. "You kids are cute," one of the husbands said. "We know," said one of the wives.

Mrs. Hasbrough had them sit crosslegged on the rug and press their knees down with their hands. She said it was to stretch the pelvic muscles.

Then there were relaxing exercises. The women lay on the rug again, while Mrs. Hasbrough gave crisp orders to contract the right arm, release the right arm, contract the left leg, contract the right leg, release the left leg, on and on. The husbands were to give such orders in practice sessions at home, and monitor that the released muscle actually did relax.

"This is a very important conditioning," Mrs. Hasbrough said. "If your husband sees in labor a certain muscle gets tense, an arm, a leg, he will tell you 'release!' And it will release, without thinking, because you have the habit. In Lamaze you are not going to be tied down to the table, with your arms in straps, and your legs in stirrups, like a prisoner on the rack in a torture chamber, like some obstetricians like to do. And if your doctor is not a Lamaze doctor, you must tell him, no stirrups, no straps. You must be free. So you must know to release all the muscles, relaxed, not tense, so your doctor won't be afraid you will kick him in the face."

They sat on chairs to practice a very slow breathing. They were to inhale no more than six times per minute. It was not easy. Elspeth found it dizzying, and on the first try had inhaled nine times before Mrs. Hasbrough said the minute was up. Some of the others said they had done worse.

On the next try they worked in pairs, each husband clocking his wife and Mrs. Hasbrough clocking Elspeth.

Mrs. Hasbrough showed them how to massage their bellies, in slow rotary motions. Finally they practiced the breathing and massaging together.

Mrs. Hasbrough lectured them. They were never to speak of contractions as pains. That word was absolutely forbidden. There were no labor pains. Only contractions. She said many old notions about childbirth were based on conditioning, tradition, ignorance. "Our great-great-grandmothers and our great-great-grandfathers, you know, they were conditioned to believe the wedding night was a terrible ordeal. And as a result the expectation could make it so. And the husband used to get drunk in case his bride would scream. And it was a mess. And we are all glad, thank goodness, all that is long gone. And so with childbirth. For centuries there was a tradition that childbirth was a terrible ordeal, and when women would feel a contraction they were already completely conditioned to think pain and be afraid. But now we are going to establish a new conditioning, based on knowledge."

Every couple and Elspeth received a red booklet.

Elspeth remained after the others and wrote Mrs. Hasbrough a check. She knew the others had paid in advance.

"For with husbands not participating, I like to advise a big wristwatch," Mrs. Hasbrough told Elspeth, "a very big one. If you know the kind with a big long hand for the seconds, going around all over the whole face."

"You mean a stopwatch?"

"A stopwatch. So you can see the seconds. Because you will be massaging, and at the same time you will be your own coach, to time the contractions, so you will know when is effacement, when is dilation, when is transition. It's easier if you have a husband or a girl friend to do that for you. To do everything yourself is more difficult, but you can do it. That's why with husbands participating and with husbands not participating are better not together in the same class. Because when the husbands see you can do it all by yourself, they will think they are not important, and I don't want them to think they are not important, because they *are* important, very helpful, helpful a lot. Too bad you didn't know to come two months ago, when I had a class for with husbands not participating. For three I'll make a class, even two sometimes. But you can understand, not for one only."

On the subway home Elspeth practiced breathing and massaging unobtrusively. In her room she lay on the floor alongside the brass bed and did the limbering exercises again. Then she sat in the wicker chair and repeated the massaging and the breathing. She read the two chapters that Mrs. Hasbrough had assigned in the red booklet. Then she read on ahead, through the chapters for the later sessions, all the way to the end of the booklet.

In the bathtub she read through it all a second time. With one hand she held the booklet carefully above the water, while the fingers of the other hand absent-mindedly made a soap bubble over each nipple.

The baby's kicks made visible momentary swellings on her flesh.

25

THANKSGIVING DAY was raw and sunless. The Brodys were taken by their son Marty to have dinner with his family, so Elspeth was left in the apartment alone.

She lay on the rug and practiced muscle-relaxing, ordering an arm or a leg to contract or release. She went to her wicker chair for the breathing and massaging. She knew the rhythm now, and could inhale six times a minute, without checking her watch till the end.

She pulled a knit cap about her ears and went out for a stroll in the grayness. The wind flapped her open coat. It tumbled a torn page of newspaper over and over in the park. In her pocket she found an empty crumpled cigarette pack. The newspaper store was open on the holiday so she entered and bought a new pack of the same brand. She slipped it unopened into her left-hand pocket, where she knew Mr. Brody would look for it.

She picked out a news weekly and three different magazines that had an article on babies or pregnancy. On her way home she detoured again into the park.

Three laughing slim girls were throwing a frisbee. It occurred to her that she had not come across a pregnant girl in the weeks she had lived here, and yet pregnancy out of wedlock was said to be statistically far more frequent among blacks. She was probably the only white teenager in the whole neighborhood. And another big belly certainly ought to catch her eye. Yet she did not recall having seen any. How come?

She scrambled eggs with mushrooms and heated some tomato soup. One of the magazines had a piece about the problems of working during pregnancy. It told of a secretary who vomited into the typewriter. Bits of vomit would appear in the enclosed part of an *e* or an *a* for days after.

An ad for tissues featured a portrait of an extraordinarily beautiful baby. The face of that child was by far the most interesting thing in any of the magazines. She kept turning to it.

In her room she found the pediatrics textbook with the broken binding she had bought at the discard table in the library. It was quite British, by a Dr. Illingworth of Leeds and London and Sheffield. On the second page he argued that the incidence of infectious diseases was lower in breastfed babies by startling percentages.

From the lumber yard the next day she took the subway to her appointment with Dr. Goldwasser. He told her while he examined her that Mr. Gilbert had been in touch, and had given very complicated instructions about the bills. The bills were to be made out to Elspeth but sent to Mr. Gilbert, who would pay them. And duplicates marked paid were to be sent to Elspeth. "I guess that's okay," she said.

At the end of the appointment she told Dr. Goldwasser she had begun a Lamaze course with Mrs. Hasbrough. He lifted his eyebrows.

"I took the first session sort of on trial," she said, "and it's only met that once so far, but at this point I'm about ninety-five percent sure I'll want to go through with it. So unless I tell you later I've changed my mind, I don't want you to give me any sedation. And don't let the nurses strap my arms down, because I have to massage. Be sure they're told that, in case they have to prep me before you're there. And I'll need my watch on my wrist, so don't let them take it off. And I'll have to be propped up on pillows, not flat. And no stirrups. So okay? I know you're a little skeptical but can you go along with it, for me? I have to know."

"As much as I can," he said, rocking back in the swivel. "You understand, dear, for your own safety, I must have the last say at every moment according to developments. I'll cooperate so long as circumstances permit. But my judgment is final. However, if you can get through the whole thing with no sedation that's fine with me, dear. It has been done. I didn't mean to give you the impression I have a closed mind. I even have another patient who's doing Lamaze. Due a bit after you. I've even agreed to let her husband be there. Again with the same proviso. That I have the last word."

"Of course," said Elspeth. "And thank you. I really appreciate it. I was worried you'd say no, and I'd have the problem of getting a new doctor this late in the game."

"Well," he said, "you won't have to do that. I don't go for fads. Fads come and go. I like to see if an idea stands the test of pragmatic use, over a period of time. And I like to have an open mind. 'Be not the first by whom the new is tried, Nor yet the last to lay the old aside.' Who said that? Shakespeare, was it?"

"Alexander Pope."

"Ah. Alexander Pope." His chubby fingers were locked on the vest. "It's a long time since I was in school. I've noticed it's the intelligent types that get interested in Lamaze. That speaks well for it. You might want to be knocked out at the very end though, so as not to see the baby. If you're giving it for adoption."

"Is it so terrible if I see it?"

"Well, you might want to think about that. All right. We'll see how things go."

Elspeth practiced the contraction-relaxation exercises lying on Mrs. Brody's sofa or sitting on a kitchen chair, mentally ordering the muscles of an arm or a leg to release their tension. In class Mrs. Hasbrough acted as her husband and felt her muscles, but here alone she was never sure it really happened. "Mrs. Brody," she said once, "feel the muscle of my forearm, and tell me when you feel it relax. See if you can feel the difference."

"What do you need muscles for? You want to be a ditchdigger? A bricklayer? A girl don't need muscles today." Mrs. Brody went barefoot to the stove and brought the kettle. "Mh. Ih." She refilled her cup, and dunked the same teabag. "Inside, the baby is listening already. Everything we say."

"You think the baby understands what we say?"

"I don't say understands. But listening. Listening everything, all the time. The heart is going boom, boom, the baby listens. You give a greps, a krechts, the baby listens. You say something, the baby listens. You ride in the subway, you take a bath, you turn the faucet, the baby listens everything."

At the lumber yard Pete was out three days when his father died and Gus asked Elspeth to help Turk at the shed some of the time. He told her to be careful of her condition, and not to lift.

She let customers do their own loading of heavy items. She worked the big circular saw. But she saw no harm in helping customers with light boards or rolls of insulation. And if they loaded on the roofs they rarely tied right. "Mister, that'll snap right in two as soon as you pick up a little speed and the wind gets under it." She cut more jute and passed it under the bumper.

She found dowels that had been put in the wrong bin and sorted them according to size. She collected scraps that customers sometimes requested for kindling. There was a vacuum cleaner in the shed with a hundred-foot extension cord, and once or twice she used it.

There was a light snowfall. It was a lot like being at Sawyer's Hardware, especially when customers were amateurs. A gray-haired man asked her advice about grade-A and grade-B studs. "Take the cheaper," she told him. "Don't waste your money. Some might have a twist, or knotholes, or an edge tapered off, but so what. They'll be inside the wall."

"Will they be as strong?"

"Sure. All the siding you put on them is gonna hold them in place too."

During idle times she loved examining the varieties of paneling, floor tiles, counter toppings, cabinets. She pretended that Mark was with her and that they discussed which they would use.

Every Monday evening she was prompt for Mrs. Hasbrough's class. The first part of labor was divided into three phases, called effacement, dilation, and transition, and together they brought the cervix to a full opening, five fingers wide. You used a different kind of breathing in each phase. You knew which phase you were in by how long the contractions lasted, and by the length of the intervals between them. It was an advantage to have a husband there, calling out fifteen seconds, thirty seconds, forty-five seconds, during contractions. And jotting down the time of each. But you could manage without.

Harriet told her on the telephone that she had heard Dr. Lamaze was a Communist.

"Mama, he ran a clinic for a French Communist labor union," Elspeth answered. "What of it? They sent him on a trip to Russia and he adapted it from a system he saw there."

"Russia!" Harriet exclaimed. "I knew it! A lot they care! They have the women cleaning the streets."

Harriet came to visit each Thursday when Elspeth was off. They would hang the laundry on the back porch, go to the library, shop for a few groceries at Leo and Walter's, and take the laundry in from the porch, sometimes with a fringe of icicles on the bottom edges.

Elspeth always asked how business was at Sawyer's and how her father was. Dr. Fleming had X-rayed him and the ulcer was smaller. Elspeth said that was wonderful. She even suggested Harriet could help out at the store. "He never stops to eat if there's customers waiting. And he's always pushing a sale at Christmas time, and between that and running out to fix people's toilets he's gonna skip lunch."

"Oh, he doesn't want me there," said Harriet.

Harriet had been to Diana's apartment finally. She told Elspeth about it. It was very cute, but they were paying a fortune.

Mrs. Brody shared Harriet's opinion of the Lamaze method. She knew all about childbirth without anesthesia. She remembered from when she was a girl in Europe. They didn't even have doctors, medicine, nothing. Just an old woman to help out. A lot of babies died. Sometimes the mothers died. You could hear them yelling, screaming. Terrible. Some people used garlic to keep away the evil eye.

Mrs. Brody was less and less cheerful as the weather grew colder. She said that her gravestone was all paid for, and that Brody's gravestone was all paid for. "We paid it ourself."

Then one day she told Elspeth casually over her teacup that she and Brody would go to Floridy for the winter, in Betty's condomimmium. "Betty wants we should come there."

"When are you going?" Elspeth said.

"December."

"It's December now."

"In the end of December."

"But my baby's due right after that. Is it okay if I stay here? I mean just a couple of weeks. I'll give you the rent ahead of time, before you go. And right after the baby I'll move to my parents'. But I'd hate to have to move to a new room for just such a short time. The baby could come early. I might move, and be in the new place only a day."

Mrs. Brody shrugged.

204

But a couple of evenings later there was a phone call from her son Marty. He spoke to Elspeth. "My parents are flying south on the thirty-first, and they won't be back till May. Frankly I'd like to get them out of there permanently, but at least they can't spend another winter in that dump. My sisters and I are in complete agreement. That steam heat there is lousy, one day you're freezing and the next day it's an oven, I don't know how you stand it yourself. But there's just no way you can stay on there in their absence. Phyllis will be taking them to the plane, and they'll spend the night at Phyllis's the night before, and you've got to be out with your stuff the day before that. The twenty-ninth. Noon at the absolute latest."

"Why? What's wrong with my staying another week or two? I'll pay in advance."

"Elspeth, it's not possible. It's in your own self-interest. I can't be responsible for your safety in that neighborhood. One pregnant girl, all alone."

"I'm not asking you to be responsible for my safety. Your parents aren't afraid of the neighborhood and I'm not either."

"My parents are afraid to go out at night. Now, it's just not practical. The gas man comes to shut off the gas on the thirtieth, and we lock up. I don't want to have to come back and close up a second time. I don't want it on my mind. It's for your own protection. My parents have valuables there. Suppose they mislaid something. You could be innocent and you'd be under suspicion. Do you want that? What if you go into labor in the middle of the night, and you don't even have a phone. I've got to disconnect that phone. If the phone company billed a long-distance call to that phone by mistake it'd be your word against theirs. It's just too complicated. You're getting plenty of notice, much more than the law requires. If I have to I'll send written notice so there'll be no argument."

What a nuisance.

Mrs. Peress had said something about possibly taking a lodger. Maybe she could go into Mrs. Peress's back room on a cot, even if it wasn't ready yet. Just moving upstairs would be easiest. Or she could call Cindy and Mrs. Schaeffer.

Elspeth asked Harriet to ask Cindy to phone her. When Cindy did, Elspeth told her about Lamaze. She also asked if she could move to Cindy's house on the twenty-eighth or twenty-ninth, for the final two or three weeks, if it turned out that Mrs. Peress couldn't take her.

Cindy suggested that she just move into a BU dormitory at that time. Most of the kids would be away for Christmas and there would be loads of empty beds. Cindy said she might even do that herself, for the whole vacation. She could get more work done.

It did not appeal to Elspeth, even though it would be much nearer to the hospital. But she did not say so.

She asked Mrs. Peress if the room she had talked about fixing up was available. Mrs. Peress shook her head. It was still used for storage. There was even a cot in it. But her son, the professor from Illinois, might come in the vacation and sleep on it. A couple days here, a couple days with his sister in Ipshvich.

Amethyst Gilbert telephoned. She said Marvin would be mad if he knew. She chatted about the wallpaper she had put in the nursery, and about the layette she was buying, the booties, the bassinet, the carriage. A marvelous rocking horse had been picked out, though the baby would not be ready for it for a few years. Elspeth told her about Lamaze. Amethyst said she had heard about it from Dr. Goldwasser. She thought it was marvelous.

Elspeth thought she could get no bigger, yet she seemed to. Gus sometimes urged her to resign. He said pregnant women shouldn't be working.

"I'd rather stay till the baby comes," she said. "It's only another few weeks. But I guess if you insist on firing me I can always get a Christmas job now."

"I didn't say that. I didn't say anything about firing you. Please. I was just thinking of you. You should rest. Take care of your health."

"I don't want to rest. My health is fine."

Her final visit to Dr. Goldwasser and her sixth and final class with Mrs. Hasbrough fell on the same day.

It turned out that Goldwasser meant to have her feet strapped in stirrups after all.

"You said you wouldn't. Mrs. Hasbrough wants us free to move around and find the most comfortable position. You promised!"

"I said I'd go along with arms unstrapped, so you can massage. You don't massage with your feet, my dear. I can't have you thrashing around. What if you threw yourself off the table? What if you knocked my glasses off?"

She was in tears when she arrived at Mrs. Hasbrough's class. For Goldwasser to let her down like that was like a blow to the stomach.

Mrs. Hasbrough was sympathetic. It would be somewhat harder, but she said Elspeth would still gain much from the massaging and breathing. She suggested asking the doctor at least for adjustable stirrups, to be placed in the lowest position, so that she could prop her back with pillows if she wished.

Mrs. Hasbrough told all the girls not to think in terms of success or failure. "If you do not do so spectacular as you want, this is not a disgrace. The Flemish people say a good motto, do well and see not back. In the future you will have another baby and you will try again." She asked them all to write her afterward and tell her how they managed.

When she walked to the subway snow was falling.

Amethyst phoned again. "Marvin's out in the garage tinkering with the snow blower. I'll have to hang up if he comes in. How are you feeling?"

"Rotten. Depressed. Goldwasser's insisting now on stirrups. Deep in my heart I don't trust that crummy bastard. He'll slip me a needle when I'm not looking."

The day before Christmas there was talk of closing the yard at three, or at two. But there was a trickle of customers. Turk and Pete came in to the front occasionally and Gus offered them a drink each time. They also had their own bottle in the shed.

For the second time that day she quietly practiced each kind of massaging and breathing, high on a stool. There was no one there but Gus, and he was used to her doing that.

For the dilation phase, when the contractions would grow stronger, there was a rapid shallow panting to keep the diaphragm high off the uterus. She finished the simulated contraction, with a prolonged exhalation and a glance at the big second hand jumping busily around the stopwatch on her wrist. Gus continued to stare at her belly, leaning on the counter, nursing his glass.

"Not much of a drinker, are you," he said quietly.

"Nope."

"Never touch it?"

"I wouldn't say that. I like wine with dinner once in a while. Or a liqueur. Or a beer. At parties, mainly. If I don't happen to see any I don't miss it."

His voice dropped lower. "Just confidentially, is Lennie Kramer the father of the child?"

Her lips parted slightly and she looked at him.

His cheeks colored, and his eyes avoided her stare. "Well," he said, uneasily, his voice still low, "I didn't mean to get personal. Don't get me wrong, I didn't mean to speak out of turn. I mean, what you and Lennie do, it's none of my business, it just sort of took me by surprise, you know. After all, knowing he's even got a daughter your age. So I didn't expect it. Older than you, isn't she? The oldest one? With the harelip?"

"Why don't you call him up and ask him?"

"Oh, sure, sure," he said. "And then where do I go look for a job?" He turned from her. He put down his glass. He played unhappily with the spiked pile of sales slips. Then he began again. "Listen. Please. I didn't intend any disrespect. I hope you're not gonna mention anything to him. That I opened my big mouth and butted in. That I was nosy. Lennie's a great guy. I think the world of Lennie. I just sort of put my foot in my mouth because I was surprised, but I don't mean to invade people's privacy. So please, I hope you won't say anything. I'm afraid he'd take it wrong."

"Okay."

"Okay? We can forget it then? Please. I've got a family to support."

"Okay."

"Thanks. I appreciate it. You're a good kid."

26

THE phone rang in the Brodys' center hallway.

"You still there?" said Marty's voice.

"You said I have till tomorrow."

"Tomorrow noon. At the latest. You gonna be out by then?"

"I expect it'll be about five-thirty. Before supper."

"Why not by noon?"

"Because I work. When I get home from work the people I'm gonna stay with are coming with a car to collect my stuff."

"Why can't you take your stuff along to work? And you won't have to come back."

"Because there's too much of it. What are you so nervous about? I'll be gone a whole twenty-four hours before your parents."

"Well, that's got to be the absolute latest. My wife and my sister are gonna be there early the next morning, both of them, to get them packed. And it's gonna take all day. You don't know my parents. Should I take this, should I take that, and changing their minds, and finding excuses not to go. They'll even use you as an excuse. That's why you've gotta be definitely out. I can depend on that then? Tomorrow by five-thirty?"

"Or thereabouts. Maybe six. If nobody has a flat tire. What's being done about the cat, by the way?"

"Cat?"

"Your parents' cat."

"I don't know. None of your business. Don't you dare mention the cat to my mother. That'll give her another excuse."

"If I want to mention the cat, I'll mention the cat. Don't crowd me, Marty. You're just a bit much."

Elspeth packed early. What did not fit in her round blue valise she placed in brown bags.

As soon as she returned from the lumber yard she began bringing her packages to the living room. She was to have dinner at the Schaeffers' and spend the night, and in the morning Mrs. Schaeffer would drive her and Cindy to Boston University. Cindy said they would have no difficulty moving in as squatters.

The clothes on hangers she lay over the arm of the Brodys' sofa. As she did so she felt her womb tighten. It was not the first time. She did her breathing along with the contraction. Mrs. Hasbrough had said to do that whenever they occurred, so the breathing response would be a conditioned reflex long before the onset of real labor.

It ceased. She put her valise by the door. She took Mr. Brody's pack of cigarettes from the pocket of her white raincoat when Mrs. Brody was in the bathroom and pressed it into his hand.

Mrs. Schaeffer had taken Cindy to her driving test, and they came directly from the Registry. Elspeth knew Cindy had passed because she was at the wheel.

"You got your license!" Elspeth said as she opened the door.

Cindy showed her the little document. Elspeth introduced Cindy and Mrs. Schaeffer to the Brodys. Mr. Brody rose from the tall chair, and Mrs. Brody apologized for her bare feet.

The suitcase they had brought was battered but large. They helped Elspeth finish the packing.

She embraced Mrs. Brody. "Have a good trip. Maybe I'll call you up sometime, when you get back from Florida."

"Good luck, darling. And don't worry. Everything is gonna be all right. You'll see."

"Are you taking your cat to Florida?"

"Na, the cat goes upstairs. I arranged with Mrs. Peress."

Cindy drove slowly, sometimes braking too soon. Mrs. Schaeffer kept offering advice. Again Elspeth felt a uterine contraction. She glanced at her watch, with its sweeping second hand, and breathed and massaged.

"Are you all right?" Mrs. Schaeffer asked her.

Elspeth nodded. When the contraction ended the massage ground to a halt, and she blew out the long cleansing exhalation. "It's what they call false labor," she said. "Braxton-Hicks contractions. I've had them before."

"Does it hurt?" said Cindy.

"No."

"How can you tell it's not the real thing, though?" Cindy said. "What if the baby gets born right here in the car."

"It's not."

"But how can you be sure. It could be. You hear about babies getting born in taxicabs all the time."

"Because for one thing," said Elspeth, "if it was the real thing they'd come at more regular intervals. I've been having this a few days. Off and on. You get it in the last two or three weeks before delivery. It's to get everything ready. It starts the cervix widening and flattening and all that."

"When are you due?" said Mrs. Schaeffer.

209

"January tenth. If I'm right on time."

"That's how many—that's twelve days from now," said Mrs. Schaeffer. "The baby could come any time."

"That's true," said Elspeth. "And on the other hand a baby can be way late, too. I just hope it's not so late they throw me out of those dorms first."

"We'll be okay there," said Cindy. "There's practically nobody around, and some kids don't get back till February. And I'll be there with you, if anything happens."

"BU is a lot closer to the hospital than the Brodys'," said Elspeth. "That's one good thing about it."

"That's a red light, Cindy."

"I saw it. Mom, will you let me alone?"

There were no more contractions all the way to Winslow.

At the house Cindy took the battered suitcase and Elspeth took her valise. Mrs. Schaeffer tried to take it. "No, please," said Elspeth. "You carried it out before, when I was saying good-bye to my landlady, but I'm not an invalid."

Adrienne followed Cindy and Elspeth upstairs to the corner bedroom with the big bay. She watched them unpack. "What are you hanging around for?" Cindy asked her.

"I'm not bothering you," said Adrienne.

"I don't hang around in your room," Cindy told her.

"Leave her alone," Elspeth said. She spread a rubberized sheet on the cot. "I've been using this," she explained. "So if I lose the waters all of a sudden it doesn't wreck the mattress."

When they had made up the cot they went down to the kitchen.

"Are we eating in the kitchen or in the dining room?" Adrienne asked.

"The dining room," said Mrs. Schaeffer.

Elspeth tore a length of foil from the roll and pressed it into the broiling pan.

"You don't have to help us," said Mrs. Schaeffer. "You should rest all you can."

"You always said I'm like one of the family," said Elspeth, "so why can't I do my share? I know where everything is and I know how you do everything."

"No, you take it easy. Cindy, you do that. Let Elspeth sit down. And help Adrienne set the table. Don't let Elspeth do it."

Elspeth sat and watched. They talked about going to the movie in Crowe, and whether they should make the early showing or the late one. Mrs. Schaeffer had read about the director and it was supposed to be his best so far. But it was rated R and she didn't know whether Adrienne should see it.

"What can it possibly show that I haven't heard about?" said Adrienne.

As they sat down to their soup Elspeth felt another contraction. She glanced at the big watch on her wrist. "Please forgive me," she said. She exhaled, then proceeded with the slow breathing and massaging. She turned her wrist to watch the seconds each time her hands rotated upward.

The contraction lasted under a minute. She blew a long exhalation.

"I'm sorry," she said. "But I just don't dare eat now. If this turns into the real thing I'm supposed to be on an empty stomach."

"Do you think it *is* the real thing?" said Mrs. Schaeffer.

"Probably not. It's just that if I'm wrong I'll be sorry I ate. When you go into labor digestion stops."

"Well, don't eat if you think you shouldn't," said Mrs. Schaeffer.

"The less you eat the more there is for us," said Adrienne.

"Adrienne," said Mrs. Schaeffer. "We'll keep yours warm in the oven," she said to Elspeth, "in case you feel up to eating later."

"I wish it hadn't started up again right at dinner time," Elspeth said. "If I'm gonna keep having false alarms like this it's gonna drive me batty."

"How long have you had these?" said Mrs. Schaeffer.

"Well, the first time was at work, the afternoon before Christmas, when we were hanging around waiting to close up. Nobody knew, because I practice the breathing at work anyway. But since then there's been some practically every day. And the last twenty-four hours it's been like almost constant, off and on. It stops for a couple of hours, and starts again. I even woke up in the night with it."

"It's wonderful the way you girls understand so much about your bodies," said Mrs. Schaeffer. "In my day we didn't know a thing. I never heard of Braxton-Hicks."

"Most still don't know a thing," said Cindy.

"How about letting me clear and serve," said Elspeth, "since I'm just sitting here."

"You sit still," said Mrs. Schaeffer.

Cindy collected the soup plates and brought the meat.

Elspeth told them what to do in case she did go into labor. She said everything she would need was in the round valise. She told them which hospital.

"Why all the way into Boston?" said Cindy. "Why not just over here to the Lapham?"

"Because I have to go where my doctor's connected. Goldwasser's a big shot and a professor. He wouldn't be with a dinky half-assed suburban hospital. And anyway the Lapham's the last place I'd go. They killed Eric there, don't forget. If I ever died there I think my father would dynamite the place. He'd get himself an Army-surplus tommy gun or something and shoot the whole staff. He hates that place. They called up my mother to do some volunteer work for them, some idiot got her name off a list I guess, and wow, did my father go through the roof. Don't ever go into Sawyer's Hardware collecting for the Lapham."

"I know," said Cindy.

"Oh oh, here it comes again," said Elspeth.

While she did her breathing they ate, but they were respectfully silent.

With the final cleansing breath she looked up from her watch. "In case I die in childbirth, there's one other thing you have to know."

"You're not going to die in childbirth," said Mrs. Schaeffer.

"I know I'm not. It's just a precaution. If anything happens to me the Gilberts have to give my parents thirty-five thousand dollars. So see that they do. It's in writing. That's what's in that brown envelope upstairs. Eight thousand for the baby dead or alive, plus thirty-five thousand for me. Less a thousand they already paid me. They'd owe my parents forty-two thousand. Plus all the medical."

"I'd like to see your belly bare," Cindy said. "I never saw a pregnant woman nude."

"You'll see it tonight, I guess. I think it looks great, actually. Like the more grotesque it is the more naked it is. I stand in front of the mirror and it's like seeing myself in three-D. My belly button will be right in your face."

"Can I see it?" said Adrienne.

"Adrienne," Mrs. Schaeffer reprimanded.

"Sure. You can all see it," said Elspeth. "If this false labor keeps up you might even see a contraction. You can actually see them, you know."

As they finished dessert Elspeth had another contraction. She sat breathing and massaging, glancing at her watch, while they cleared the table.

She watched them load the dishwasher.

"Well," Mrs. Schaeffer said, "I don't know if we should chance going to that movie under the circumstances."

Elspeth remained silent, somewhat downcast.

"What do you think?" Cindy asked Elspeth.

"I'd hate to wreck your evening. Especially if it turns out it's just nothing."

"The movie's not important," said Mrs. Schaeffer. "I don't think we should take a chance."

"Do you think it's for real?" Cindy asked.

"Probably not," said Elspeth. "There were a couple only twelve minutes apart, but then the next one was eighteen minutes apart. So they're not regular and they're not really getting closer yet."

"Maybe you should call your doctor," said Mrs. Schaeffer.

"I could, but I'd rather wait till I can tell him something more definite. He laughs if I call with something really dumb. After the last time he examined me I called up and said I had some show, and he said it was only because of the examination."

"Why don't we wait like till eight-thirty then," said Cindy, "and if nothing's happening there'll still be time to make the nine-o'clock."

"I was going to suggest the same thing," said Mrs. Schaeffer. "In the next hour or two the signs could get more definite, or they could stop entirely."

"They could," said Elspeth. "That's a good idea."

"Maybe you can fix our crazy faucet while we're waiting," Adrienne said to Elspeth. "You're good at fixing things."

"Don't bother her with that," said Mrs. Schaeffer. "It's not fixable anyway."

"What faucet?" said Elspeth. "What's wrong with it?"

"The hot faucet," Cindy said. She gave it a twirl. "It just goes around and around and around and doesn't turn anything."

"It can't be fixed," Mrs. Schaeffer told Elspeth. "We had your father here, and then we had Mr. Metcalf here, and they both said the same thing. This house is over eighty years old, and those sizes aren't made anymore. They'd have to rip out all the old plumbing and put in everything new."

212

"Mr. Crocker you mean," said Elspeth. "Metcalf is dead."

"Mr. Crocker," Mrs. Schaeffer said. "But he said the same as your father. And we can't afford it right now. This house needs repair from top to bottom."

"It's falling down around our ears," said Adrienne.

"No, it's not," said Mrs. Schaeffer. "But we can manage without that faucet."

"Can I see it?" said Elspeth. She went to the sink.

The handle spun ineffectually. She saw that it was fastened to the stem by a threaded set-pin in its side. It did not match the handle of the cold faucet.

"Somebody mickey-moused the wrong kind of handle onto it," she said.

"I know. The old one fell apart, oh, maybe six years ago, and it couldn't be duplicated, so my husband found that one and put it on. It worked all right until about a month ago."

"Have you got a little teensy screwdriver?"

"Daddy left his old tool box under the counter," said Adrienne. "In the cabinet."

Elspeth stooped and dragged out the tool box. "Oh, please don't bother with that!" Mrs. Schaeffer said.

Inside the box Elspeth found a jumbled mess. Nails, bolts, washers, and scraps of wire were scattered among tools and dust. She rose with a small screwdriver, and applied it to the set-pin in the side of the faucet handle. She took the set-pin completely out. Then she lifted the handle easily off the stem.

"Well, I can see what's happened. And my father told you right. It's unfixable. This set-pin was meant for a stem that had a little hole for it to fit into. And this stem doesn't have that—it's designed for a screw to go in at the top. But at first the set-pin pressed against the side of the stem tight enough to get a grip anyhow. But gradually it wore a groove all around the stem. See this groove? That wasn't there. It was worn there, by turning that handle with the set-pin. Till now when you turn the handle, the set-pin just slides around the groove without pushing anything."

"And we don't need the hot faucet anyway," said Mrs. Schaeffer. "For the dishes we have the dishwasher, and for coffee we have the kettle. Now that you're satisfied let's go to the living room so you can relax."

"Okay. I just wanted to see it." She washed her hands under the cold tap. She felt a contraction.

They moved to the living room and Mrs. Schaeffer turned the television to the news. The unseasonable warmth was expected to continue for tonight, with patches of local fog, and snow beginning in the early morning, possibly heavy, turning much colder.

The contraction had been mild, fading almost as soon as she sat, but she could not put her mind to the television. She went upstairs and came down with her pen and her spiral notebook.

When her next contraction began she jotted the time. Afterward she jotted the seconds of its duration, and the number of minutes from the last previous contraction.

The television was turned off for lack of anything worthwhile. She could not put her mind to Mrs. Schaeffer's talk either. She did effacement breathing when contractions came, and afterward she studied her notebook. She searched for a trend.

213

If only they would become regular. Like they were supposed to. Then she would know where she stood.

Mrs. Schaeffer talked of many things. It was as though Mrs. Schaeffer felt a responsibility to maintain conversation, or to see that everyone was entertained by intelligent discourse.

Cindy leaned back with eyes nearly shut and feet spread, her hands folded on her trim stomach. Adrienne turned the pages of a magazine. Mrs. Schaeffer discussed the pros and cons of celebrating Christmas. She did not approve of religious celebrations. But she did not feel that Christmas was religious.

Elspeth finished a contraction, the breathing and massaging decelerating together. Like an old-fashioned steam locomotive slowing and halting at the station, as Mrs. Hasbrough had put it.

"How do you feel, Ellie?" Cindy asked.

"We can fix that faucet. It just came to me."

She rose, Mrs. Schaeffer looking at her in astonishment, and returned to the kitchen. They followed her. She stooped to the cabinet. Cindy helped her drag out the tool box. Elspeth took the little screwdriver and a heavy file.

Again she removed the set-pin and took the handle off the stem. She rubbed the point of the set-pin on the file. She looked at it. She rubbed it again, vigorously.

"What on earth are you doing?" said Mrs. Schaeffer.

"It's simple. We file the point of the set-pin flat. Then file the stem. Make a flat place on the stem, just on one side. Then line up the set-pin against the flat spot, and it's a flat surface pressing a flat surface. No way can it slip around. When you turn the handle it'll take the stem with it." With one hand she gripped the faucet pipe, and with the other she filed briskly against one side of the stem.

"You've got no business doing that in your condition!"

"It'll only take a minute. It's brass. It's soft."

"Cindy, take that file away from her."

"No! When I get an idea I get inspired. Don't stop me."

"You're nuts," said Cindy.

Already the stem was losing its roundness. On one side a flat place was appearing, shiny and clean. A dust of brass was falling into the sink. Her underwear was becoming sweaty. She felt a contraction beginning.

She thrust the file at Cindy. "Here. Keep filing." She threw herself back on-to a chair and massaged and huffed, slowly at first, like a steam locomotive starting.

The contraction was fairly severe. At its climax the locomotive was racing. She kept glancing from her watch to Cindy, who filed busily.

Fifty-five seconds. A long exhalation, like a hissing of steam. "Be sure you keep that file at a constant angle. If you start rounding off the edges of what we did we're back where we started."

"I know," said Cindy. "I've got the idea."

Elspeth wrote the time and the duration. "I think I better call Goldwasser. They're still not regular, but they're closer. On average."

She went to the wall phone and dialed. She gave the Schaeffer's number to Goldwasser's answering service.

She inspected the faucet stem.

"Did I do a good job?" said Cindy.

"Yes." By now a little section had been cut quite deeply.

She took the tool from Cindy and filed rapidly to make the shiny new place flatter, pausing every dozen strokes to look at it.

The phone rang. Elspeth seized it before the second ring, still holding the file.

"Yes, my dear," said Dr. Goldwasser.

"I know I'm not due for another twelve days yet, but I've been having contractions for the last couple of days, like off and on around the clock, and for the last two and a half hours they've gotten pretty steady. I think they're getting closer together."

"How close are your pains?"

"They're not pains, they're contractions. Actually they don't have the kind of regularity I'd like to see—I had two eleven minutes apart and then it was sixteen minutes before the next one. Do you want me to read you the durations and the intervals?"

"No. Don't read it. You're not in labor."

"Oh. That's a relief. We were gonna see a movie. We didn't know whether to go or not."

"Young lady, go to that movie. That's my prescription for you. It's the best thing you could do. Some big lavish musical. Or a comedy. It'll take your mind off yourself. And then have a nice big glass of hot milk and go to sleep. Your trouble is that you've got a head full of this cult. Your voice tells me all. When a woman tells me 'they're not pains, they're contractions,' she's not in labor. And when she compiles figures and calculations, and wants to read me a list of numbers, that woman is not in labor. Now relax."

"What if the contractions continue?"

"If they continue? Call me when they're regularly under five minutes. Now enjoy that movie. When the baby wants out, you'll know it. And I'll know it. Give me a call tomorrow if you want, and tell me all about the movie."

She thanked him, somewhat crestfallen. She restored the phone to the wall.

"Okay, we can go," she said. "It's false labor."

"Goodie," said Adrienne.

"Do you want something to eat?" Mrs. Schaeffer asked.

"No. I'm not hungry really," Elspeth said. She put down the file.

"I'll drive," said Cindy.

"No," said Mrs. Schaeffer. "You've had enough for the first day. Don't push your luck."

"I'd like to try the faucet before we go," said Elspeth. She put the handle back on, careful to align its set-pin with the side of the stem they had flattened.

She gave a turn. Water gushed, splattering.

"Eureka!" cried Adrienne. "Hot water! Yay!"

"Wonderful," said Mrs. Schaeffer.

The stream kept pouring. Elspeth held a finger in it. "I'll send you my bill in the morning."

"What do you charge?" said Cindy.

"A cookie." She put her pen and notebook into her canvas shoulder bag.

No sooner had they set out in the car than a contraction began. Elspeth rode in back with Cindy. She massaged and breathed, but in the darkness she could not see her watch.

When they had left the settled parts of Winslow they meandered through wintry forest. The road was visible for stretches ahead before fading into the fog.

In Dowling, where two white churches stood at right angles, they forked up the hypotenuse of the common toward Crowe. Elspeth felt her womb tighten in a contraction more powerful than any she had yet known. The fierceness of it surprised her. She massaged and breathed faster. The increasing sharpness leveled off just as it had almost begun to frighten her. Then she felt it diminishing. She kept blowing. Another thirty seconds maybe, she thought.

"Are you still feeling labor pains?" said Mrs. Schaeffer.

"She is, Mom," said Cindy. "She can't answer. She's doing the breathing. This is the second one since we started."

Elspeth regretted that she could not read the watch. She suspected it had been the longest yet, perhaps close to seventy seconds. With its termination she blew the cleansing exhalation.

"Please, everybody," she said, a little winded. "They're contractions. Contractions. Remember that. Don't call them pains. Never, never."

The next contraction was absurdly mild, almost sensationless. She breathed with it, but it was gone in what seemed scarcely twenty seconds. She wondered if it had really been a contraction at all.

Among the misty lights of the parking lot Mrs. Schaeffer turned to Elspeth. "Are you certain you're all right?"

"I'm fine. It took us how long to get here, about twenty-five minutes, okay? And only three contractions during the trip, so they sure aren't anything like five minutes apart."

Mrs. Schaeffer sighed and shrugged. "We're a long way from Boston."

The theater was two-thirds empty. The film was strong drama. Cindy and Adrienne, on either side of her, dipped into their popcorn without taking their eyes from the screen. Elspeth sometimes found herself finishing the breathing and massaging of a contraction without having been aware of the beginning. The girl spun slowly as the big fist struck her jaw. She was flung to the couch. Cloth ripped sharply, loudly. The breasts shook like gelatin.

Elspeth's womb galvanized tightly, forcing itself upon her attention despite the fascination of the screen. It racked her in a way that made her want to twitch or kick out at the seat in front, but she breathed more deeply and massaged faster. When it ended she rose and went past Adrienne's and Mrs. Schaeffer's knees. She took the notebook from the shoulder bag and noted down the time. Then she watched the movie from behind the last row of seats.

216

Cindy came to her. "Is anything happening? What's the matter?"

"I'm okay. I just want to be out here where I can see my watch and write down the contractions. And maybe walk around a little. If it's false labor you're supposed to be able to walk it off."

"I'll stay with you. Maybe I can help write them down or something."

"You don't have to. Go watch the movie."

"I can see it from here. My mother wants me to stay with you. And I want to too. Sit down if you're okay. We'll sit in the last row here."

They sat and watched. Elspeth saw Mrs. Schaeffer glance around at them.

With the onset of the next contraction Elspeth handed Cindy the pen and notebook and showed her the big wristwatch.

But in the midst of massaging she stopped and gestured.

"What?" said Cindy.

"Nothing. Scratch out that one. I thought it was a contraction but it wasn't."

However the next was stronger. Again Cindy noted the time. Elspeth rose and walked slowly in the lobby as she breathed and massaged. Cindy gave her a supporting arm. The little old uniformed man looked at them askance and asked if he should phone for an ambulance.

"No, she's okay," Cindy said as they walked. "It's false labor."

The words struck Elspeth so oddly that she knew she no longer believed it. She might have a long way to go, but she had forgotten about false labor. Nor did she remember ever having believed it completely.

When she could speak she asked the little man if he could bring a chair into the lobby. He dragged a couple of wooden chairs across the dirty red carpeting. Cindy turned them toward one of the aisle entrances and they sat.

"Even money says I've had the baby by this time tomorrow," Elspeth told Cindy.

"Really?"

With each contraction they rose and walked, Cindy supporting Elspeth.

The prolonged wringing grew more intense. I'm not standing this too well, she thought. Maybe it would be better to switch to dilation breathing. But it was discouraging to have to do so this early. Mrs. Hasbrough had cautioned against switching too soon. You should stick with effacement breathing as long as you could stand it, and then with dilation as long as you could.

On the next contraction she switched to the shallow panting, massaging faster.

Between contractions, when she could talk, she studied Cindy's notations. Sometimes she glanced up at the movie, but she had lost the thread of what was happening. There were contractions as close as eight minutes apart, but others were still at longer intervals.

And sometimes between the severe ones there were little ones with no discomfort at all. She was uncertain whether to count the teensy ones, the nothing ones.

Counting those itsy-bitsy ones she was getting some now as close as six minutes. The rough no-nonsense ones that ground on and on for ninety or a hundred seconds were still thirteen minutes apart. Did you count them all, or what?

Mrs. Hasbrough had not said there would be such variation. It was unnerving

217

not to be able to calculate where she was at. They were supposed to get closer and closer and stronger and stronger in a uniform way.

"I'm wrecking the movie for you," Elspeth said to Cindy.

"Forget it," Cindy said. "And don't worry about after we get home either. I'll stay up with you all night if it continues."

It was good to hear that. "I'm afraid it might be all night," Elspeth said.

She used a couple of the intervals to go to the bathroom. Cindy went with her. She was glad she was between contractions when the movie ended. They pulled the chairs away from the aisle entrance.

"Well," said Mrs. Schaeffer, "how goes it?"

"They're getting closer," said Elspeth. "But not close enough to go to the hospital. But I'm phoning Goldwasser as soon as we get home anyway." She folded back the spiral notebook. "Look. Look at these intervals. They keep varying. Six minutes. Ten. Six. Seven. Ten. Five." Then she realized it meant nothing to Mrs. Schaeffer.

On the ride back Cindy took the watch from Elspeth and managed to angle it and read it. She kept recording the time each contraction began and how many seconds it lasted.

"How much did you two miss?" Adrienne asked, turning around. "Did you see any of the last part? Where they were throwing all these gasoline bottles and everything to catch the house on fire, and guys were breaking in all over the place, and he and his wife were running around trying to put the fires out, and he had to kill a guy with the poker?"

"I can't believe anything like that could really take place in England," Mrs. Schaeffer said. "It's not realistic. That director is trying to imitate the Americans."

"Why?" said Adrienne, "If things like that can happen here why not over there? What's so great about the English?"

"The English are polite, and they're socially oriented. They're a bit more civilized than we are."

"Oh phooey," said Adrienne. "Who said? It was a good movie."

Elspeth used the rapid shallow panting. The road home seemed slower and longer.

She was in the midst of a contraction as they came into the kitchen. She shook her head, panting, and massaging, when Mrs. Schaeffer asked if a hot cup of tea would help. When it ended she dialed the doctor.

"This is Elspeth," she said.

"Yes, my dear. Are you still having them?"

"About six minutes apart. There were two four minutes apart, and then it went back to six."

"I see. I see. And this has been going on ever since you called me before?"

"Yes. And it's down to six minutes apart. On my watch. My friend's got my watch."

"Well, maybe there's something going on, after all. Call me again when they're regularly under five minutes apart. I'll be here."

The next contraction was accompanied by a spreading backache. She tried walking about supported by Cindy, then decided she'd rather sit.

"Can you massage my back?" she asked Cindy. "Not there. Lower." She placed Cindy's hand at the small of her back and to the side.

"Why don't you get ready for bed," Mrs. Schaeffer said to Adrienne. "Adrienne. Did you hear me?"

"There's no school tomorrow," said Adrienne. She didn't move and didn't take her eyes from Elspeth.

The next interval was five and a half minutes. Then two minutes and a half-baked one. Then three minutes and a real one. Even if you didn't count the teensy one it was only five minutes. The next was another five minutes after that, with no teensy one between. Then another scarcely four minutes later. Then five and a half minutes and another.

"This is crazy," she said. "I have to call him."

Cindy dialed this time. She gave Elspeth the phone.

"They're just about five minutes apart," Elspeth told him.

Dr. Goldwasser chuckled. "Now, Elspeth, my dear, listen to me. And I'll tell you something. I've been delivering babies for over thirty years. Since long before you were born. I stopped counting after the first thousand. And believe me, I can tell from the sound of a woman's voice on the telephone precisely how far along she is. And I have yet to be wrong. Now, my dear, they are not five minutes apart."

"They are."

"You're very eager. And perhaps something is starting. But I know what a woman sounds like when they're five minutes apart. So don't tell me they're five minutes apart."

A contraction began as she hung up. It was short and mild, and when it ended she needed the bathroom. There was a water closet near the kitchen.

"Mrs. Schaeffer," she said when she came out, "will you come here please? I just want you to see something, in case Goldwasser doesn't believe me."

"What?"

"Look."

Mrs. Schaeffer looked into the unflushed toilet.

"Call him," Elspeth told Cindy.

She took the phone when Cindy handed it.

"I lost the plug," she told him.

"What did it look like?" said Dr. Goldwasser.

"Dark red. Shreddy."

There was a second of silence.

"All right." His voice was lower and different. "Get into the hospital. I'll meet you there. How soon can you be there? Fifteen minutes?"

"Fifteen minutes? I'm down in Winslow."

"Winslow. Winslow. What's near you down that way? The Lapham. Dash right over to the Lapham. I'll meet you at the Lapham. Get going."

"He says I should go to the Lapham, right away," Elspeth said as she put the phone on the wall.

"Adrienne, go up and grab that valise," Cindy said. "Mom, start the car."

She helped Elspeth into the coat.

Elspeth was panting and massaging as Cindy helped her down the steps.

"It won't start!" Mrs. Schaeffer called frantically from behind the wheel. The starter was cranking futilely.

"Oh no!" Cindy cried. "Mom! How could you! You flooded it! You always do that! What are we gonna do now!"

But Elspeth had made her way to the headlights and knelt to unlatch the hood. Cindy ran to her. "What are you doing!"

Elspeth rose and lifted the hood. She unscrewed the wing nut on the air cleaner. Adrienne came running with the valise and put it in the car.

"Not you," Mrs. Schaeffer told her. "Just leave the valise and go in the house. You're not going."

"Why!"

Elspeth lifted off the air cleaner. She pushed the flap wide open in the air pipe.

"Why! Why aren't I going! How come Cindy gets to go?"

"We don't need a crowd. Cindy's helping Elspeth."

Elspeth nodded to Mrs. Schaeffer through the windshield to try it again.

The engine roared lustily and lowered to a perfect hum.

"How did you do that!" Cindy exclaimed.

But Elspeth was fitting the air cleaner back into place, clumsily and unsteadily because she felt another contraction beginning. When she reached for the hood Cindy shut it.

Cindy helped her into the car and gave Adrienne a strong shove away from it. Adrienne kicked her.

"Bitch!" Cindy said, swinging to slap Adrienne, but Adrienne stepped back and she missed. Cindy pulled the door shut. Adrienne wrinkled her nose and rolled her tongue in a grimace as they rode off without her.

The contractions seemed hardly a minute apart.

"Oh God!" said Cindy. "The watch! I haven't got the watch! Have you got it?"

Elspeth didn't care about the watch. But she dared not interrupt the panting. The contraction was too big. When it ended she marked it properly with the long cleansing inhalation and exhalation. Cindy had the notebook and was desperately trying to estimate the time. She asked her mother for her watch. Before Elspeth could speak another contraction started. She resumed panting and massaging. But there was nothing she could do about the hurt in her back.

She saw the Christmas lights glowing in the mist before the darkened mall as they sped from Winslow into Bradbury.

The Lapham rose in the fog.

Cindy and Mrs. Schaeffer helped her up the walk to Emergency. The doors swung open of themselves.

"Call On The Level Lumber tomorrow," she gasped between contractions.

"Dorchester yard. Say I won't be in."

"Don't worry about that now," said Mrs. Schaeffer.

A rusty-haired powdered lady rolled a form with carbons into her typewriter. "Patient's name?"

"Can't we do this later?" Cindy pleaded. "Can't you see she's having a baby? Isn't there a doctor?"

The powdered lady looked at Elspeth. "I'll take her up," she said.

At the elevator she blocked Cindy and Mrs. Schaeffer.

"Sorry. You can't come up."

The doors slid together.

Elspeth had sustained herself with the knowledge that no contraction would last longer than a minute and a half, or a minute and three-quarters. No matter how awful it was she knew a few minutes of relief were just ahead. The longer a contraction tormented her, the closer she was to respite. She had only to concentrate on proper breathing to hasten it. But now a new contraction began as soon as the preceding ended, with no rest between.

In desperation she switched to transition breathing. Puff puff puff puff puff puff blow, puff puff puff puff puff puff blow, puff puff puff puff puff puff blow. She shouldn't have gone to transition without a doctor's assurance that she was at least half dilated. At least five centimeters dilated. It was a tiring breathing to maintain, and she would have nothing stronger to fall back on when things really got bad. But she couldn't help it. It was just too much.

The steel doors moved smoothly apart. She had expected them to open upon the face of Dr. Goldwasser, but he was not there.

A pudgy nurse with a tan sweater and a hairy mole rose from a desk. The rusty-haired lady had disappeared.

"Just have a seat," the nurse said.

The contractions were nonstop, with no interval. They rose and fell. Her womb seemed to convulse as if electrodes had been plunged into either end. Can the baby in there stand this?

The nurse with the hairy mole approached with a clipboard in which some papers were fastened and a fat pen. "You can fill this out while you're waiting."

Elspeth was massaging frantically. She tried not to see the nurse. If Goldwasser tells me I'm only one or two centimeters dilated, I'll die. I'll tell him to knock me out. I can't stand another three, four, five hours of this.

"Here! I said fill this out," the nurse said, thrusting the pen on her.

A lean, olive-skinned young man in white, his hair in a ponytail and a stethoscope about his neck, had appeared from nowhere. He seized the clipboard and flung it down the corridor. "Damn it, let her alone! Can't you see those contractions? Get the stretcher! Move!"

The nurse hurried off.

Elspeth saw his face. His features softened. "Hang in there," he said. "You're doing fine. Keep it up. As soon as she gets back with the stretcher we'll examine you."

He paced about a bit.

221

"Hell, we can't wait for that stretcher. We'll use the desk. Come on." He swept everything off the nurse's desk to the floor—telephone, calendar, books, paperweights. He spared only the blotter and pad. The phone lay open and humming on the linoleum.

Elspeth rose but couldn't walk. Her womb pressed in on itself with such force that she shuddered.

He helped her. Somehow he dragged her onto the desk. He undressed her from the waist. The slacks caught at her shoes. He tugged and the pants slid off with the shoes and underpants inside them.

"How many centimeters?" she gasped. She didn't know where she found the breath.

"Ten. You're fully dilated. The top of your baby's scalp is staring me in the face. You're just about home free." She could feel his busy hands. "If you can help it, don't push till I give the word. I want to avoid an episiotomy."

27

ELSPETH shrieked.

"Cool it!" the young doctor told her. "Take it easy."

She shrieked again.

"I said cool it!" he commanded more sharply. "There's nothing to scream about! It's just a simple childbirth, that's all! Not a nuclear holocaust! Not the end of the world. So don't panic, okay?"

Her whole body felt ready to burst like a pod.

"All right now," he said, "whenever you feel the urge to push, go ahead."

Fortunately the desk was large. He got her feet up. Elspeth grasped her ankles. She lowered her head toward her chest with rounded shoulders as Mrs. Hasbrough had taught, took a deep breath and held it.

The nurse came back wheeling the stretcher. "Hey, what's going on here?" she said. "She isn't even prepped yet."

When Elspeth could hold her breath no longer she breathed out quickly, filled her lungs and clamped her lips shut once more.

She saw the doctor's intense, lean face between her thighs. "Good," he was saying. "That's it."

The push ended. Elspeth gasped for air.

"Beautiful," he said. She could feel his fingers in a kind of relieving counterpressure. "That was a good push. Let's see if we can help the head around."

"Could we get some pillows to prop me up?" Elspeth asked. Mrs. Hasbrough had recommended at least three pillows, for the head, lower back, and knees.

"Get her into the gown," he told the nurse. "Quick. And then get behind her. Prop her up a little, to wherever she wants. Hold her under the arms."

The nurse got the rest of her clothes off and pushed her arms into the gown.

She still felt him working at the taut edges of skin. "A little lower," she told the nurse.

"If bacteria get to the baby because she's not prepped I'm not covering up for you," the nurse said. "Dr. Norris is gonna hear about this. Not even any antiseptic. There's plenty of young doctors that would like a residency here."

"Is the head out?" Elspeth asked.

"No, no," he said. "Not yet."

"I've got to push!" Elspeth exclaimed suddenly.

"Okay. Give me a good push. Lovely, lovely."

She gripped her ankles. Her chin pressed her collarbone. The nurse's hands supported her under her armpits. She wished they would raise her another few inches, but her mouth was shut tight against her expanded lungs. She refilled them quickly and held her breath till her temples pounded.

When at last she lay back against the nurse she looked to him for approval, but he was busy there and she did not catch his eye.

"And you're gonna owe me a new desk blotter," the nurse said. "The whole pad, too."

A new push welled up in her before she could warn him but he seemed to have expected it. "Here it comes. Fine. Fine. Just a little rip, a little one, we'll fix it with a stitch. Keep pushing. Bear down. You're doing great. Nice. Nice. Come on, honey. Beautiful, beautiful. That's the way."

She concentrated on the full lungs and the diaphragm pressing down on the uterus to help it. But when she came up for air she lost coordination somehow. Her foot slipped off the desk, and the nurse seemed to be supporting her under one armpit but not the other.

"Here's your baby!" he sang out.

He raised the child high for her to see.

She was breathless with amazement.

How complete, how real, how alive he was! How human! The little clenched hands, the bent knees, the male equipment, all so perfect, so miniature, so fine, so fully formed. Ears. Toes. A thatch of hair the color of her own and the little face, wide awake, staring at the light with an expression of intensity and puzzlement. Such big blue eyes. A knit brow.

The wrinkly gray cord dangled from him, looped in on itself in a knot, and trailed on down to her.

Elspeth heard her own laughter, involuntary and strange-sounding, a feeble ripple of it on each exhalation, and was not certain at first it was really laughter, because she felt the hot tears drenching her face. She raised her exhausted arms toward the child. They shone with sweat.

He placed the baby on her stomach. It swam on her as she put her hands to it, and buried its face in her flesh. Then it turned its face aside, the nose still pressed to the coarse cotton of her gown, but she saw the little nostrils.

"Let's get her onto the stretcher. I don't think you'll want a placenta on your desk."

She felt herself lifted by the legs and by strong arms under her shoulders, and was deposited on the comfort of a plastic mattress.

"Did you see that knot?" she heard him say to the nurse.

She traveled smoothly and head first, the pudgy nurse with the hairy mole pushing the stretcher, and did not see where she was going. A wheel was squeaking.

They banged through a pair of swinging doors and into a room that was lit brightly but not harshly.

They stopped, and she was aware of the doctor bending and working at her again. But she was looking at the baby, the familiar deep russet of his damp shining hair. She pulled him closer, up almost between her breasts, and he turned his face from side to side. She felt the doctor daubing her. There was a stab.

"Suture," he said.

She wondered if it was all right to kiss the baby. But it was more fun just to see him, to touch him. He was so soft. And when she lifted him to see him better he moved his arms in such a quivering way. Weren't newborns supposed to be all wrinkled and red and funny-looking? He was not wrinkly, not red. He was beautiful. Handsome.

The nurse took him from her.

Elspeth did not see where they went. The doctor had taken her wrist and silently counted her pulse. She looked at the ponytail that hung down his neck.

He placed the stethoscope against her chest. He moved it to another spot and listened.

At last he took it from his ears and it hung from his neck once more. He smiled at her. "How do you feel?" he said. "Like you just placed first in the Olympics?"

"Just wonderful. Wonderful."

"Would you like some juice?"

"No. I'm okay. I'm sorry I yelled."

"Don't be sorry. You really did great. Who taught you Lamaze?"

"Ursula Hasbrough."

"She's very good," he said.

"He's gorgeous, isn't he."

"He is indeed. You have a beautiful son."

"So beautiful."

"He has your hair. The exact shade."

"I noticed that."

"Why'd you wait so long to come in? You're lucky you didn't have the baby in the street somewhere."

"I don't know. I didn't think I was so far along."

"You were past labor and into delivery when I saw you. When did you start?"

"Gee. Sometime yesterday, I guess. Now that I think back."

The nurse was there again with a clipboard and pen. "This never did get filled out."

"Oh," he said. "Well, I'll help her. We don't want to make her sit up just yet, do we." He took the clipboard and pen. "Name? Last, first, middle?"

"Baker."

"Baker. First and middle?"

"Elspeth Ann."

"Elspeth, beautiful. I like that. Ann with an e or without?"

"Without."

"Address?"

She gave her parents' address.

"M? F? She looks like an F. Age?"

"Eighteen."

"Insurance? You don't happen to have your Blue Cross number tattooed on you anywhere? No. Married? Single? Widowed? Divorced? Separated?"

"Single."

"Single. Let's just put down none of your damn business. Nature of complaint? You don't have any complaints, do you? No complaints. Religion? Holy Roller?"

"Well, if it's for how to bury me if I die you better put down Jewish, because my parents would be upset, but usually I put down agnostic on those things."

"How about heathen," he suggested. "Or pagan. I'll put down pagan. That'll make two of us."

Dr. Goldwasser burst through the swinging doors panting and ruddy-faced, in overcoat and homburg. A scarf was wrapped about his neck.

"Dr. Goldwasser," he said breathlessly to the young man, extending a hand.

The young man gave a handshake. "Dr. Walker, doctor. Your patient seems okay. She tore about a quarter inch. I gave her a couple of stitches. The little guy was feeling kind of cramped in there, with all those contractions going on, so we decided to let him come out and play. But she hasn't delivered the placenta yet, so your trip hasn't been in vain. Would you like a gown?"

"Please."

"Second locker, doctor. Matilda, get the doctor some gloves."

"Where's the baby?" Elspeth asked.

"He's right over here, in his plastic box. You want to see him?"

"Can I have him again?"

She glimpsed the nurse closing the fastenings of a pale green gown down Dr. Goldwasser's large back, over by the sink.

The young man lifted the baby to her. This time he was in a little nightgown and he seemed to be trying to get his fist into his mouth.

The baby was cradled in her arm beside her.

He was more beautiful than before. The fist moved quickly away from his mouth. In his features she saw her grandmother. It was astonishing.

"Grammy! He looks exactly like my grandmother! My mother's mother!"

Through his nightie she could see the dark stump of cord, folded over and bandaged. She had not noticed the cutting of it. He worked his feet.

"I feel a push," said Elspeth. "The placenta's coming."

"Hurry, doctor," the young man said.

Dr. Goldwasser hastened to the foot of the stretcher, big in the pale green gown and a matching surgical cap. An antiseptic mask hid his nose and mouth. Only his eyes and spectacles showed. His hands were raised before his chest, glistening in rubber gloves.

"Steady, my dear. Easy does it."

28

THE stretcher rolled on its squeaky wheels into the elevator. The nurse moved to the other end of the stretcher, behind Elspeth's head. The doors slid together. Dr. Goldwasser stood facing the doors, beside her, in his coat and homburg now, the gray hair curling over the earpieces of his spectacles. The baby in his tiny gown lay cuddled with her under the blankets. Elspeth had seen the nurse produce the shoulder bag and the blue valise from somewhere, and she knew they rode under her now on the stretcher's lower level, along with her rolled-up coat and a plastic bag containing the clothes they had taken off her.

"That young fellow should have given you an episiotomy," Dr. Goldwasser said. "A clean cut would have been preferable to a tear."

Elspeth expected the doors to slide open upon the lobby, with Cindy and Mrs.

Schaeffer sitting there waiting, and she was eager to greet them. Hi, she would say as she was wheeled past, I'm alive! And I have a baby boy.

However she found herself not in the lobby but in a corridor. From the walls of gray-painted cinderblock she judged it to be at basement level.

Dr. Goldwasser held open a door and she was wheeled into the night, on a side of the building different from the one she had entered. The breeze was raw on her face.

The ambulance man helped the nurse lift the top of the stretcher off its frame, like a pallet. They slid it, Elspeth and baby and all, into the back of the ambulance. The shoulder bag and blue valise and coat and bag of clothes were put in and the metal doors shut behind her. Dr. Goldwasser got into the front beside the driver.

There were high curtained windows on either side. She could not see out. From flashing red reflections she knew the light on top was rotating. She felt the vehicle slow, make a turn, and accelerate.

It was good that Dr. Goldwasser was transferring her into Boston. It would have been hard on her parents to have to visit her at the Lapham. It was better to be where her doctor was on the staff and made his daily rounds.

The siren began whooping. She turned to the baby. Hey, little guy, you wondering what that noise is? That weeoo weeoo weeoo? It's telling everybody to get out of the way for you. Not that there's anybody around to get out of the way at this hour. But I never had a siren in my whole life, hardly, and you get one right away.

The speeding street lamps gave glimpses of the small face. The large blue eyes were still awake. The resemblance to Grammy was total, even while he was so clearly a person himself. Newborn, but in no way expressionless. He appeared to be trying to understand.

The street lamps ceased. It was hard to see him in the grayness. She half raised herself, meaning to pull the curtain aside and catch the flash of passing headlights, but her stitches gave a sharp hurt.

She was growing used to the darkness. The sleeve of his tiny gown trailed over his fist. It got to his mouth and he tried to eat it, but with the next quivering, nervous motion of his arm he lost it. Her hospital shirt was not made for nursing, but the ties had been left unfastened and she got it down from her shoulder. She put him to a breast. He turned his head from side to side, back and forth, his lips open, as if probing blindly for the nipple. His lips struck the nipple and clamped upon it. He closed his eyes, and sucked, his cheeks working.

Her hands enclosed him tenderly. He nursed, his eyes closed, even when the ambulance bumped over rails and cobbles. One of her hands held the back of his head, and played slowly with his hair. You getting some, little one? How come you know just what to do?

He left off sucking, and lay with lips resting open at the nipple, eyes still closed. Then he gave some more sucks, and rested again. He sucked again, and rested. He seemed so content.

Under his gown he had a bandage on his navel, and a paper diaper. It was dry. Of course it was dry. He was only just starting his first meal.

Weren't babies supposed to cry? It occurred to her now that he had not yet cried. Not even when he came out and the doctor had lifted him up for her to see. She had heard that doctors always had to slap babies, lift them in the air by a leg and slap them smartly to make them cry, because in starting to cry they started to breathe. If the doctor didn't slap them, they wouldn't breathe. Everybody knew that.

But that young doctor had not slapped her baby. She had not thought of it at the time, but she was sure of it. He had lifted the baby upright, with two hands under the baby's arms, firmly about his body.

He must have just breathed.

Because he wasn't drugged. That must be it. Mrs. Hasbrough hadn't spoken of it, but it tied in with everything Mrs. Hasbrough had said. Babies must have an instinct to breathe, as soon as they caught the first smell of air. That made sense.

You didn't have to whack them. Unless they were so anesthetized that you had to wake them from their stupor. No wonder they cried.

Why should a baby cry at birth? It wasn't a funeral.

She kissed his head. What a finely shaped head. His hair felt so silky. She laughed again, as she had in the hospital, tears running. It seemed a strange laughter, over which she had no control. She felt exhilarated, and her body just laughed of itself.

Dr. Goldwasser looked around from the front seat. "You okay, dear?"

"We're okay," she told him.

The ambulance stopped, the siren descending to a growl, though red reflections still flashed.

The doors behind her opened. The driver and another man in white affixed her stretcher upon a new frame. The air was sharply colder and snowflakes had begun sparsely, drifting and circling. She drew the blanket higher to protect the baby's head. The building was all around them, wings in every direction.

Glass doors opened almost silently.

Dr. Goldwasser stopped at the desk, but the stretcher glided forward.

In the elevator she felt no motion. Only the brightening of successive numbers above the door told her of their ascent. She strained her head back to see who was maneuvering the stretcher. It was a spindly black girl, her head expanded in an Afro.

In the corridors the lights had been softened for night. They stopped at a desk. A clock on the wall told Elspeth it was ten to two. The black girl handed a card to a tall lean-faced nurse whose lips remained parted, showing two big teeth like a rabbit's. She wore an unbuttoned black cardigan. A tiny starched cap perched on the top of her hair.

"Oh yes," said the rabbit-toothed nurse. "She's to have a private."

"And rooming in," Elspeth added.

"Rooming in?" said the nurse. "They didn't tell me that."

"Yes," said Elspeth. "Rooming in. The baby stays with me."

The nurse marked something at her desk. She told the black girl a number, and the stretcher resumed its glide.

It was a pleasant room, with Venetian blinds and flowered drapes. A beige telephone sat on the night table. The girl helped Elspeth onto the bed. The stitches gave a vicious twinge.

"You better hold the baby till I get his bassinet from the nursery. They should have told us you was supposed to have rooming in. So we could have had everything ready."

She lifted him to Elspeth. His eyes were wide open again.

"My God, Petey," Elspeth said half aloud. "Where did you get those eyes?"

The girl hung the coat in the closet, put the other things on the floor, and went out, steering the empty stretcher before her. Elspeth nestled with the baby. His expression fascinated her. It was a face that appeared to have the busiest of minds behind it. As if he were trying to sort out the welter of new sensations.

She had always supposed that infants' expressions were more or less blank, except when they smiled or cried, but this face was anything but blank. She had never seen a face so gripped in thought. Not even on an adult. Not even on a professor.

She studied one of his hands. It was no longer clenched. Its entire width, thumb and all, was less than two of her fingers. Yet its proportions were exquisite. Every line of its palm was there. Even the pinky, with its minuscule nail, had cameo perfection.

The girl returned pushing a bassinet with glass sides. She placed it alongside the bed and lifted the baby. Again his face seemed to register the lifting. The girl placed him in the bassinet. "I'll help you with the bedpan now," she said to Elspeth.

The stitches again pulled cruelly. When she got off the pan she was more gingerly about it. "Do stitches always hurt?" she asked.

"Oh, they hurt all right," the girl said.

The girl showed her the call button. It hung from a wire near the head of the bed. She showed buttons on another cord, which could raise Elspeth to a half-sitting tilt or lower her again. She demonstrated, whirring up a couple of inches and down once more.

And still another cord with buttons to work the television.

"Were you ever so happy you were sad?" Elspeth asked her.

"What you mean?"

"Well, I just feel so—so—I never felt like this. In the ambulance I started laughing all of a sudden. With tears. My doctor looked around like I was nuts."

"Maybe you was a little hysterical. Or maybe you was still high from the ether. What he give you? Nitrous oxide?"

"No."

She arranged Elspeth's few things in the top drawer.

"Could I have my pajamas and get rid of this white thing? This thing's no good for nursing."

"You ain't got no milk yet," the girl said. But she gave her the rolled pajamas. "It don't come in for two-three days."

"I have colostrum though. I saw it."

"Okay, you all set now? You'll sleep tonight. You won't need nothing to make you sleep."

"I'm fine. Thanks for everything. Is the phone connected?"

"Yep. All the privates get a telephone. You just dial nine for outside."

"One other thing—could you find me a sandwich, do you think? I didn't really have any supper last night."

"Well, I don't know if there's anybody in the kitchen. It's sposed to be closed this time of night."

When the girl had gone Elspeth moved to put on her pajama bottoms, but the first motion of a thigh was like a stab. Mrs. Hasbrough hadn't made it clear that stitches were this bad.

However she managed to ease herself into the pajamas.

The room was dark, except for the glow through the open door, a yellow paler glow from a night-light below her somewhere, and the gray of the window. The blind was halfway up. She could see the wind-driven snow beginning to accumulate against the stone alongside the window frame. She could almost hear its sweep.

The girl brought a cheese sandwich and a container of juice with a straw. Elspeth ate in the half-darkness.

From the baby there was no sound. She looked to the glass-sided bassinet. The little bundle in the dimness seemed motionless. Was he all right?

She edged herself by degrees out of the bed, respectful of the stitches.

She stood and looked down at him. He slept. She wished his breathing were visible, or audible. Or that he would give some sign that he was alive. Such utter stillness.

At last the soft lips parted, filled by the little tongue. It pushed out a bubble or two.

She lifted him. A hand gave a nervous wave when she disturbed him, but he did not waken. How light he was.

She took him with her to her bed, trying to lower herself into it in such a way that the stitches would not protest. She almost did. But when she lay back they nearly made her cry out.

At least it was only momentary pain, that eased when she lay still. She found the right cord and button, and tilted herself and baby up a few degrees. He slept in the curve of her arm, against the softness of her breast.

How much do you weigh, Petey? I forgot to ask them.

The nose, the nostrils. So fine. She kissed him. In his sleep he turned his face away, with an expression of avoidance or disgust, precisely like an older child.

Was there a design in the universe that had brought her and Jared together? Or if it was random, chance, senseless, then how remarkable that senseless chance had yielded up a new human being of such perfection.

How dumb of Jared to miss all this.

She did not sleep. Every stage of the labor and delivery was clear in her mind. She wished there were someone she could tell about it.

She heard a snowplow's slow passage.

For a long time she debated whether to go to the john. At last she did, leaving the baby in the middle of the bed, and moving cautiously. It hurt even to walk. Even so, the water closet seemed preferable to ringing for the bedpan.

When she returned she did not get into bed but took the baby to the armchair by the window. Snow curved up in the corner of the glass and flakes blew like a fog about the street lamps below. The street was already white.

The baby yawned and stretched, quite like a little adult. The big eyes opened wide. You're wondering where you are? You wonder what you're doing out here? Outside Mama's tummy?

She offered a breast. He turned his head to the right and left, right and left, eyes wide and mouth open tall, till he caught the nipple. His cheeks sucked and his eyes closed. You gorgeous creature. This is the first day of your life, little one, think of that. And what will your life be? Don't have a sad life, little one. Don't have a tragic life. You're too beautiful.

The tall rabbit-toothed nurse looked in once. "Are you still awake?" she exclaimed surprised. "Want something to make you sleep?"

"No, that's okay."

"I'll get you something."

"No, don't. Please. I want every minute."

Once, when the baby's eyes were open, she lifted him high above her in her two hands, and stared up at him.

For hours the only sounds had been occasional soft shoes in the corridor, the moaning of a distant patient sometimes, gusts on the window, the passing of a car, the steady progress of a plow, and once or twice the cry of a siren. But then, though it was still dark outside, the hospital grew noisier. The corridor brightened, there were sometimes more than one set of footsteps at a time, and she heard a cart and utensils. It must be morning.

Yet it was a long time before anyone came. At last a cheerful freckled girl pushed a cart into the room and switched on the light. She wore a pink-striped uniform. "Hi. I didn't know there was a baby here. Do you want to fill out the menu card? Or if you'll settle for cereal you can have your breakfast now. I'm way behind. The other girl didn't get in because of the storm."

"The cereal's okay."

The girl took the baby. "Wow! Those eyes! Is it a girl or a boy?"

"A boy."

"Wow! He's gonna be a heartbreaker." She lay him in the bassinet and looked at the card on it. "Did he get his bottle? Or are you nursing?"

"I'm nursing."

The girl changed the diaper.

"Were you ever so happy you were sad?" Elspeth said. "Like when something's so cold that it's hot?"

"I think I know what you mean, sort of," the girl said. She moved the one-legged table over Elspeth's bed and set out the cereal and utensils and milk and grapefruit and a couple of extra juice containers.

231

"How bad is the storm?" Elspeth asked.

"Well, it was already like five inches when I got here, and they're predicting twelve to eighteen. Where was it when we needed it? We could have had a white Christmas."

After breakfast Elspeth took the baby into her bed again. "Hi, sweetie," she said to him. "I love you."

When it had been daylight for a while Elspeth telephoned the desk and asked the time. Then she found that the chart on the bassinet had had the baby's birth weight all along. Six pounds four ounces.

It was still snowing. A middle-aged lady in gray came around with a form on a clipboard and asked Elspeth if she had a name yet to be sent in to City Hall on the birth certificate. "Let's see," the lady said, bending and squinting through her spectacles at the chart on the bassinet. "He was born at one o'clock sharp this morning?"

"I think it was earlier than that," said Elspeth. "That might be the time the doctor got there. He was born at the Lapham you know. In Bradbury."

"Oh. He wasn't born here in the hospital?"

"No, at the Lapham Memorial. In Bradbury. We came in by ambulance after. The Lapham might have sent in a birth certificate to the Bradbury town hall. I don't know if they did or not."

"Oh dear. We always send them to Boston City Hall. Well, we better send it too, I guess. Just to be safe."

Elspeth dialed the lumber yard. There was no answer.

When she was sure her father must have left for the store she telephoned her mother.

"Hi," she said to Harriet. "Did Dad have any trouble getting out of the driveway?"

"No. He was out there with the snowblower at six o'clock."

"I had the baby. A boy. I wanted to call you before the Schaeffers did."

"What?"

"I had the baby. We're both fine. We're at the hospital."

For a moment Harriet seemed incredulous. Then she cried. Elspeth waited. Then she said again quietly that she was okay. And that the baby weighed six four, and was beautiful and so bright, with hair like her own. Harriet asked tearfully if she had had a hard time. She said she hadn't.

"Well, so that's over. When do the Gilberts take him?"

"I don't know," said Elspeth. "I guess whenever Goldwasser says it's okay for him to leave the hospital. I haven't talked to them yet."

Harriet said she would love to see him. Just once. She had heard the roads were terrible, and it was probably impossible to get a taxi. She would try. But if she couldn't she'd come tomorrow for sure.

Elspeth asked her to bring some stationery. And she told how the baby had resembled Grammy. "So help me, the spitting image. When he was like half an hour old. But this morning he doesn't look like her anymore. He looks more like you now. And sometimes like Eric a little. And yet I never thought of you and

232

Eric as looking like Grammy. You seemed to take after Gramps's side more."

She dialed the lumber yard again, and gave Turk a message for Gus. She said she'd had the baby and would be out a few days, till the doctor said it was okay to go back to work.

In midmorning she dialed Mrs. Hasbrough but there was no answer.

She telephoned Cindy also. The bed had been adjusted to support her at a high tilt, and she lay with the baby in one arm and the phone in the other.

"We found your watch," Cindy said. "It was down in the upholstery."

"Oh. Thanks. I had a boy, you know."

"I know. They told us. Apparently we just got you there in the nick of time."

"Which was good, in a way. They didn't have time to shave me or an enema or any of that harassment."

"Let me ring you right back. Why should you pay a toll when we can call free? What's your room number there?"

"That's okay. The Gilberts'll pay for it."

Cindy said she had been out shoveling. They were snowbound.

She told Cindy how terrific the baby was. "Even the candystriper calls him a heartbreaker, and Handsome Dan and stuff. I just wasn't prepared for such beauty. Such personality in a newborn. You tend to think of an infant as a blob. But he's not. The expressions on his face. I see now that these first days and first hours of life are a very exciting time. He's trying hard to put together all the sensations, and make sense of the world."

"Too bad you can't keep him," said Cindy.

"I know, but what can I do?"

Early in the afternoon the snow stopped. Elspeth tried to dial Avis Kramer, but the line was always busy. A nurse came by with a hypodermic needle, and when Elspeth asked what it was for the nurse said it was to dry her breasts up.

"I'm nursing," Elspeth told her.

"It was prescribed."

"Well, he didn't know I'm nursing. Or it's a mistake. Take it away. Get that thing out of here."

The freckled aide in pink stripes brought stationery Elspeth had ordered from the gift shop. She began a letter to Mrs. Hasbrough. Tentatively the afternoon brightened. At last the descending sun shone yellow on the stone and plaster outside and inside the window. Sometimes she heard the futile shrill spinning of tires, despite all the plowing. Trucks lumbered.

Another middle-aged lady in gray stopped in, smaller and slimmer than the first one, and offered Elspeth a mimeographed information sheet with names and numbers she could call if she wanted her son to have a religious circumcision. She said they had begun giving this information if a Jewish person had a boy, and that the men on the list had been given permission now to operate in the hospital, provided her doctor approved.

Elspeth said her son was going to be adopted and it would be up to the adoptive parents. She told her the Gilberts' name and address. She watched the lady write

233

it carefully. How had she known to come here with that, if that young doctor had filled in pagan? Goldwasser must have filled out new forms downstairs.

Elspeth resumed her letter to Mrs. Hasbrough. But she interrupted it soon to feed the baby, and then to move him to the other side.

She got out of bed to change his diaper, even though her stitches hurt if she was not careful, and even though the head nurse had bawled her out about leaving the bed.

She got back into it and cuddled the baby sleepily, talking to him, her face close to his. He cooed in his throat.

They brought her supper, mashed potatoes and a thin slice of dry brown beef.

After supper she looked for her old watch, the little one, in her valise. She found it at last in the bureau drawer. She phoned the desk again for the time, and set it.

She tried once more to dial Avis, and this time Avis answered. The phone had been off the hook, she said. Mickey had spoken to one of his little friends early in the day and hadn't hung it up properly. Elspeth talked eagerly about all that had happened. The baby dozed at her exposed breast and as she spoke her arm emphasized her words from time to time by giving him a gentle hug.

"I can't thank you enough," she told Avis. "Steering me into Lamaze was the greatest thing anybody ever did for me. They're getting a bargain, these people. They're paying eight gees plus medical, but he's worth a million."

"I'm so glad," said Avis.

"This little guy is such a mensch," said Elspeth. "The minute he was born, as soon as you saw that face, you knew he's thinking, he's living it to the hilt, I swear. Like he sprang full-panoplied. I'm flabbergasted."

"Of course. He's a Lamaze baby."

"I wish you could see him. Such a busy little face, a real person, trying to figure out the scene. I don't know where he came from. The birds and the bees are insufficient to explain him."

Avis laughed.

Elspeth said she had done pretty well, but could have done better. It was partly her dumb doctor's fault. Just because she wasn't screaming in terror and crawling up the walls he refused to believe how close her contractions were.

"I did actually scream once. I'm sort of embarrassed about that. But you know, it wasn't because it hurt, actually. There were parts before that that hurt a lot more. It was more exhilaration. Like just that I had been wanting to holler for a long time, just to holler. Not that it hurt." The baby's hands moved on her breast and he was sucking again. She gave him another hug. She knew someone had come into the room but she paid no attention. "A theory kind of occurred to me this afternoon," she told Avis. "I wonder if maybe that holler was just instinctive. Like when our ancestors came down out of the trees, maybe women developed the instinct to holler to scare away the lions and leopards when they were defenseless and flat on the ground in childbirth. And also summon the troop together. And then when people built towns, and weren't prey to wild beasts anymore, they didn't know anymore why they had this hollering instinct, so they developed this

234

notion that the women must be hurting. Do you think that's possible?"

"I don't know," said Avis. "I never heard that. But I guess anything's possible."

"Like I read once that snoring started like that," said Elspeth. "When we came down from the trees, snoring evolved to scare away the lions and leopards while we slept on the ground. Did you feel an instinct to holler when you were having your babies?"

"No," Avis said. "But that doesn't prove anything. Maybe not everybody still has it. Not everybody snores."

The visitors had moved closer, and Elspeth looked up. It was Marvin Gilbert and Amethyst, in coats and scarves.

"MARVIN, look! Look at that hair. He has her hair. I was hoping he would."

"Avis, I'll call you again, okay? I have company." Elspeth leaned, holding the dozing baby to her breast, and hung up the beige telephone.

"Marvin!" Amethyst breathed. "Did you ever see? My God, how beautiful. Can I see him?" she asked Elspeth. "Can I hold him?"

"Of course you can hold him," Marvin said irritably. "He's yours."

"But she's nursing."

"Hold him," said Marvin. "Take him. She shouldn't be nursing, We'll talk about that." Marvin lifted him from Elspeth. The baby's eyes opened wide. Marvin gave him to Amethyst.

Amethyst held him to her furry coat, gazing upon his face. Suddenly his head tilted back with a start. His lip quivered. He shut his eyes and he cried. "Support his head," Elspeth told her. "Amethyst! Put your hand behind his head."

Amethyst did so. The baby continued to cry, in his high monotone, as if frightened. Amethyst tried to soothe him. She looked miserable.

"It's your fault, Marvin," she said. "Snatching him from his mother's breast like that."

"No, it's because he thought he was going to fall," Elspeth explained. "Their necks aren't strong yet when they're little like that."

"Aw, naughty Mummy," Amethyst said, looking at him miserably. "Mummy didn't hold your head. Poor thing. *Bad* Mummy!"

He kept crying. Marvin put a chair behind her. She sat carefully, one gloved hand supporting the back of his head.

"You'll catch on," Elspeth assured her. "I guess you haven't done much baby-sitting lately."

He stopped crying, though his big eyes looked troubled. His mouth searched for nourishment in the knitted scarf.

Marvin took off his coat, and hung it with his scarf and folded lambswool hat over the foot of the white bed frame.

"He won't wet me, will he?" Amethyst asked Elspeth.

"Well, he has a diaper," said Elspeth. "Just check for moisture once in a while. There can't be too much in him."

He cried again. Amethyst was flustered. "What did I do now?"

"Put him in the bassinet," said Marvin.

Amethyst rose uncertainly. Elspeth wanted to jump up and assist, despite her stitches, but she restrained herself. Marvin helped Amethyst lay the baby in the bassinet.

"Maybe we should call the nurse," said Amethyst.

"You have to have more confidence," Elspeth told her. "It's just that you hold him so gingerly like. If you're not sure of yourself he senses it."

"He doesn't like me," said Amethyst.

"Nonsense," said Marvin. "He's only a day old. Not even a day."

"He'll get to know you," said Elspeth.

He stopped crying. Through the glass side of the bassinet Elspeth could see the intense little face, and the sudden motion of his limbs in the gown.

"Marvin, look at him. Look at that face. Isn't he gorgeous?"

Marvin stood by Amethyst as she bent over the bassinet. His features softened.

"Our own baby," she said. "An answer to a prayer."

The baby yawned, his mouth opening narrow and tall.

"Look, Marvin! He yawned! Did you see that?" Marvin helped her off with her coat and scarf. She gave him her gloves but kept the high hat of gray felt that tilted up to a knife edge. She continued to stare down into the bassinet. "Scrumptious," she cooed. "Yes oo *are*. Scrumptious wumptious. Yes oo *are*."

Marvin pulled the other chair over from beside the chest of drawers, and sat a few feet from the bed and the bassinet.

"Marvin, he looks a little like your Uncle Leo. Come look!"

Marvin's slightly drooping eyelids drooped momentarily further. He did not rise. He crossed his legs. His face had settled once more into its dour expression of irritated boredom.

"Miss Baker, why didn't you call us?"

"What?"

236

"Didn't you think we were entitled to know? The baby was born what time? A little after midnight last night? And we finally heard of it about four o'clock this afternoon. And if my wife hadn't happened to phone Dr. Goldwasser we wouldn't have heard of it then. We still wouldn't know."

"Why blame *her*?" said Amethyst, turning on him. "Why didn't Goldwasser call us? Women are weak after childbirth. What did you expect her to do? Run to a telephone?"

"I can understand a doctor being busy," he said. "But she was chattering away here when we walked in."

"I should have called you," said Elspeth. "But I had a lot of people to call, and I was a little addled, I guess. I didn't sleep at all last night. I've been awake since when? Day before yesterday? No. Yesterday morning."

"You didn't sleep?" exclaimed Amethyst. "After giving birth? Couldn't they give you something?"

"I didn't want to sleep, really."

"Well, you should get some rest. Marvin, you ought to be ashamed. This poor girl—do you have any idea what a woman goes through in childbirth?"

"I heard it was a very short labor."

"That's not true," Elspeth told him. "I was in labor for two days, off and on, now that I look back on it. And really serious effacement from yesterday afternoon. I just couldn't get Goldwasser to believe it. You really ought to only pay him half, for the prenatal care. He wasn't there for the delivery, you know. The resident at the Lapham is the one that should be paid for the delivery."

Harriet came in breathlessly, and at once burst into tears.

"Mama! I didn't think you'd make it today!"

"I just had to have one look," Harriet blubbered. "Just one peek."

She bent over the bassinet. She found her handkerchief and blew her nose. Marvin had risen deferentially to offer his chair.

"Mama, this is Mr. and Mrs. Gilbert. This is my mother."

Harriet distractedly gave them her hand. "I couldn't help it, I had to have just one peek," she apologized again. "My husband said I shouldn't. He didn't want to. He says it would be better for us not to."

Marvin nodded slowly.

"Did you tell Daddy? What did he say? I bet he's glad it's finally over."

"Well, he didn't say much. He never talks about you much anymore. Since you moved out. If I talk about you he doesn't say anything."

"Look at him, Mama. Isn't he absolutely something else? Isn't he the greatest?"

Harriet turned again to the bassinet. Amethyst hovered over it with her. "He is a beautiful child," Harriet said.

"He has your daughter's hair," said Amethyst. "I'm so glad about that."

"Red hair always ran in my family," said Harriet. "Not as dark as Elspeth's. Hers was all her own."

"Precious wecious," Amethyst sang into the bassinet. "Yes oo *are*."

Elspeth saw him staring up at the faces as though puzzled.

"Wait till you see how he yawns," said Amethyst. "It's so cute."

Marvin had stepped into the corridor and returned with another chair. "Let me take your coat," he said to Harriet.

"Oh, I can't stay. The traveling's so bad. I left my husband's supper in the pot."

"Don't you think he looks like Gramps's whole side? And like Eric? It's so strange. And yesterday he looked like Grammy, but exactly. This morning, I mean. When he was born."

Harriet cocked her head and looked at him critically.

"I think he looks like Marvin's uncle," said Amethyst.

"There's a certain expression around his mouth," Elspeth said to Harriet. "You see what I mean? And the shape of his eyes."

"Yes. Yes." She wiped her eyes with her handkerchief.

Marvin was sitting with legs crossed. "You said you had a feeling it would be a girl, remember?"

"I know," Elspeth admitted. "I was wrong."

"Can I pick him up?" Harriet asked. "Just once?"

"Mrs. Baker, do you think that's wise?" Marvin said quietly. "Do you think your husband would recommend it?"

"No, you're right," said Harriet. She wept again. "Such a gorgeous child. Why can't the homely ones be illegitimate? What's the justice of it?"

"Why don't you sit down?" Marvin said gently.

Harriet sat. She sniffled in her handkerchief. Amethyst sat too. The little suitcase she had brought she now lifted to her lap. She clicked it open.

"I just have to show you these," said Amethyst. "There, isn't this darling?" She held up a tiny velvet suit of a rich brown, the shirt supporting the short pants with mother-of-pearl buttons about the waist. She turned it to Harriet and back to Elspeth. She lowered it and lifted a little visored cap of suede. It had an elastic chin strap.

Marvin cleared his throat. Elspeth saw him redden.

"Isn't that just out of this world?" said Amethyst. "And look at these booties." They were of red plaid cloth, with white lacings.

"Oh, those are just lovely," said Elspeth. "So cute. Let's try them on. They're still big, but let's try."

"Wait till you've seen everything," said Amethyst. "I bought girl things too but I'm giving the girl things back. These are the boy things. You should see his room. The cutest wallaper. Elephants, clowns, bunnies. Elves dancing over sleeping babies, just everything on it. Won't he be just cunning in this?" She held another suit, yellow and silky, with ruffles at the collar and down the front.

Marvin cleared his throat louder. "Dear, do you think this makes sense?" he said red-faced. "Put those things away. I didn't know you had those in there. I thought it was a bed jacket. Didn't you say you bought Miss Baker a bed jacket?"

"Of course. For Chanukah."

"So where is it?"

"In the car. Go get it, will you? It's in the back seat. In a white bag, with a Filene's thing."

238

"God almighty, close up that suitcase. Put those clothes away."

"Why? What's gotten into you all of a sudden?"

"Do you think it's fair to Miss Baker? And to Mrs. Baker?"

"Elspeth wants to see them. She wants to know the baby's well provided for."

"Dear, I insist! Do you hear me? I insist! It's tasteless. It's callous. It's stupid."

Amethyst refolded the suit and closed everything in the suitcase. "You're such an old phoof," she said.

"I'm sorry, Miss Baker," Marvin said more softly. She could see the blood vessels in his temples.

"That's okay."

"And that brings me to another thing, Miss Baker. That I have to discuss with you. I had formed the highest opinion of your intelligence, and your good judgment. So I must confess I was somewhat disappointed to walk in here and find you and the baby together. In a rooming-in situation. And breastfeeding, on top of it. I was just a bit shocked, actually. It's not the kind of good sense I had come to expect from you."

She felt herself coloring.

"I think you understand me," he said.

She nodded.

"You're perfectly well aware of the hazards in this kind of situation," he continued. "The emotional hazards. For the baby, for us, for your family, above all for yourself. For God sake, girl. You're giving up this baby, you've agreed to give it up. Why do you risk giving yourself an emotional attachment like this? All right, I think we understand each other. And if we understand each other it'll be corrected. I can understand how it happened. You were addled after giving birth. You weren't yourself. You never should have even seen it."

"How could she not see it?" said Amethyst. "She had natural childbirth."

"Natural childbirth? Did Goldwasser tell you that? He never told *me* that."

"Elspeth told me."

"Miss Baker told you? When? Why didn't you tell me?"

"Because it was none of your business. Natural childbirth is good for the child."

"It's *not* good. The great majority of children do perfectly well without it. It certainly wasn't called for here."

"I told her the same thing," said Harriet. "I didn't like it at all."

"Marvin doesn't care what's good for the child," said Amethyst.

He shook himself. "Miss Baker, I *appeal* to you. Get some sleep, and get your bearings, and then think it through. For your own sake."

He pulled a handkerchief from his hip pocket and mopped his brow, up into his baldness.

"Is there water in that pitcher there?" he asked.

"Yes. You want a drink?" Elspeth leaned to the night table and opened the gray thermos pitcher. She poured water into the plastic cup.

He rose and she handed it to him. "Thank you." He sat back with it.

"How did you stand it?" said Harriet. "You had no anesthesia at all? Nothing?"

239

"No. I think he gave me a shot for the stitches, but that was after the baby was out. I can ring and get you some juice," she said to Marvin.

"No, that's all right. Water's fine." He sipped it.

"Are you okay?" said Elspeth.

"I'm okay."

"You can open your collar if you want."

He loosened his tie and unbuttoned his collar. She could see his breathing. He took another swallow.

"Miss Baker, I just want to explain to you the papers I hope to bring you tomorrow, and then I think we should be on our way and let you start catching up on your sleep."

He drained the cup.

"Want some more?"

He shook his head. "I'll be here tomorow with papers for you to sign, saying you agree to our adopting the child and you give up all rights and so forth, as we agreed. And I'll bring you the certified check for the other seven thousand at the same time. Hopefully if my attorney can get it all drawn up early enough I'd like to get over here for your signature and get it back to him in time for him to make a court appearance with it tomorrow, as it's the last day of the old year and it's a question of a tax deduction. I'm not sure just how the law reads on the timing, and at just what point the adoption becomes official, but I'm advised to take the deduction anyway, and meanwhile try to get as much transacted before the end of the old year as possible. Just in case of audit."

"Our son's just a tax deduction to you," Amethyst said to him. "No room in your heart for anything but a dollar sign."

"Now, dear, really. That's not fair. You know that's not true. And there's no reason why we shouldn't have the deduction if we're entitled. Then there'll be that much more available to spend on our son."

"He doesn't want your money," said Amethyst. "He wants your affection."

"Why do we need another paper?" said Elspeth. "We already signed a contract."

"That was different. The baby wasn't born yet at that time. Now we need something that actually identifies the child. Exact time of birth, sex, attending physician and so forth. Do you understand?"

"Okay."

"And there'll be another paper, giving us permission to take the child from the hospital. Authorizing the hospital to let us take it. Just in case there's any delay in the court appearance, I'm advised it's better and smoother if the child is already in our physical possession at the time of the appearance. Now, Dr. Goldwasser tells me he'd normally discharge the child at the same time he discharges you. That's to say, in about a week. But he says he can shorten that to five days, if all goes well, and I'm asking him to do that. Even though our nurse won't be ready. We told her the tenth, so she's gone to help her sister. But I'm sure we'll manage. Even if we have to bring in someone temporary."

"What nurse?"

"Oh, she's absolutely marvelous," said Amethyst. "She was recommended. I had misgivings about a German but not after I met her. She's perfect with children. Just adores them. She escaped through West Berlin before the Russians put the wall up. I just hope she can cut her sister short, and come early. This having the baby early messed everything up. The curtains aren't even ready. I ordered everything way ahead, and they weren't done right and I had to send them back and now they're not ready. I could shoot those people."

"Dear," said Marvin, "the baby doesn't care if the drapes don't match."

"Even so. I'm so mad at those people. I paid good money, so things would be right when the baby comes home. They promised. It's good for the baby to know nice things from the very beginning."

Marvin sighed. He looked at his watch. "Well, dear, I think it's time we let this very tired young lady begin to catch up on her sleep. At long last. Mrs. Baker, can we give you a lift home?"

"Oh, you could take me to the subway," said Harriet. "That would be very nice."

"The subway?" He was buttoning his collar. "Which way do you go?"

"I take the subway all the way to the end, and then there's a bus."

They were rising. "In this weather? And at night?" said Marvin. "We can't let you do that. We'll take you home."

"Oh, no, that's too much," said Harriet.

"It's way out of your way, Mr. Gilbert," Elspeth said. "Just the opposite direction. Winslow's way south and Wilmerding's way north."

"No matter." He was helping the ladies with their coats. "My wife and I insist. We'll take you to your door. It's our pleasure."

Amethyst bent over the bassinet. Marvin picked up her suitcase. "He's asleep," said Amethyst. "Look at that. Are we allowed to kiss him?"

"Kiss him," Elspeth told her. "I kissed him a million times. Mama, next time you come bring a pair of my jeans and one of my flannel shirts, okay? All I've got is pregnancy stuff."

"That's another reason why we should take you home, Mrs. Baker. You can give us the things and we'll bring them when we come with the papers. Dear, just blow a kiss. It's safer." He buttoned his overcoat at the neck and put on the scarf.

Harriet's eyes were full again. She seemed to avoid the bassinet, but she kissed Elspeth hard and long, bending over the bed and clinging to her.

Elspeth watched them go out. Their footsteps grew fainter down the corridor. She even heard the doors of the elevator.

She swung her legs to the floor, keeping them together to minimize the strain on her stitches. She visited the bathroom.

She went to the bassinet. His eyes were shut tight.

When she lifted him he knit his brow and nervously waved his arms but did not waken. She got into bed with him.

Petey, you don't want a German governess, do you?

She detested German accents. They reeked of insensitivity, dumbness.

No, that was only prejudice, she chided herself. She shouldn't feel that way.

But that was how they sound. Military. Pedantic. Gross. My little guy taking orders from a German voice? Achtung! How could they do such a thing?

She dozed, and the room was replaced by jumbled images. She wakened. It could only have been a few minutes. She let herself drift back to sleep. She wakened again with a start.

Marvin Gilbert was in the room, in his hat and coat and scarf. He held a white paper sack on which a sprig of blossoms was imprinted. "We meant to bring you this, but we left it down in the car."

"Oh."

He made room for the package on the night table. "There's something else I wanted to say—I didn't want to mention it in front of your mother. I don't know if you've made plans, but if you'd like to go to school out on the West Coast, or spend a year in Israel, or somewhere else, I'd be glad to pay for it. I'm not making any secret of my motive—I just think it will be easier for you, and for us, if we're far apart. You don't have to answer now. I just wanted to leave that thought. I don't know how your folks would feel about you being far away, but it's the natural thing. You're not the type to be on apron strings. Kids go to Israel, or they go to Africa in the Peace Corps, or they bum around the world, Nepal—in my time it was Paris." He cleared his throat. "Okay. Well, good night." He cleared his throat again. "Don't you think he'd be better off in the bassinet? You might sleep very deeply—you said you didn't sleep at all last night. What if you rolled over on him—smothered him."

Elspeth put her feet together to the floor. Over the bassinet his eyes opened wide.

"I didn't mean to make you get out of bed," said Marvin. "I could have put him there."

She waved the baby's arm at Marvin. "Wave bye, Petey. Wave bye to Daddy."

30

ELSPETH wakened to the sound of the breakfast carts. Crystalline patterns of frost had formed in a sweep around the bottom and side of the window and glistened pink in the morning sun. She turned eagerly to see if the baby was awake or asleep and what expression his face wore.

He was gone, bassinet and all.

She slid to her feet, pressing the call button but not waiting for it. In the corridor a girl in pink stripes emerged from another room, a steel cart before her. "Where's my baby?" Elspeth cried.

The girl looked at her bewildered through oversized eyeglasses.

Elspeth hurried barefoot around the corridor's bend. Marvin Gilbert must have finagled this. Or maybe he had cried for a feeding and she hadn't wakened and he had become dehydrated, and they had had to rush him somewhere to try to save him. She ran a few steps, slowed for a bathrobed lady, and found the alcove near the elevator where the rabbit-toothed supervising nurse sat behind a desk.

"Where's my baby? They took him away."

"Is that the Baker baby? The little boy that's being adopted?"

"Yes."

"He was transferred to the nursery."

"Why?"

"Well, I suppose your doctor must have ordered it. It was before I came on."

"That's down back this way?"

"Don't go there now. They're having their six o'clock bottles."

"When can I see him?"

"You wait till visiting hours this afternoon. Then you can go to the window."

"I just want to see if he's okay."

"He's fine. Don't you worry."

Elspeth went back. Her room was the first after the bend, but she continued on past it. She had a notion of where the nursery was.

She found the broad window. Beyond the glass were a number of bassinets and a round-faced young woman with a cart was holding a bottle to one of the infants. Elspeth rapped on the thick glass. The woman looked at her unsmiling and shook her head.

Elspeth remained watching. She could not see the faces of most of the babies

243

but she could see that one was crying. It was not hers. They were in two rows, at a distance from the window, and arranged so the two nearest hid most of the others.

The lady moved to another bassinet and administered a fresh bottle. Elspeth beat the heavy glass with the flat of her hand, and when the woman looked she made an appealing expression. The lady wagged her finger, then turned her back. Elspeth watched a while longer.

The girl in pink stripes and big eyeglasses came, preceded by her cart. "Oh, here you are. I left your breakfast on your table. You shouldn't be down here."

"Why does my baby have to be in the nursery?"

"Oh, they like the nursery. They're all together, with other babies here. We even had a Santa Claus come to see them last week. The Santa from the Christmas party, he came up special from the party."

"There's one crying there, and she doesn't pay any attention. There might even be more crying in back."

"Crying is healthy for them. It's natural for babies to cry. You know that. That's how they develop their lungs, their wind."

"Well, can I find out if my baby had his bottle?"

"If he was supposed to I'm sure he will. When was he born? They're not supposed to have anything the first twenty-four hours."

"He was born night before last."

"Then I'm sure he'll get a bottle. He'd be on the list for the six o'clock."

"Why don't they get anything the first twenty-four hours?"

"They're not hungry. Now why don't you go have your breakfast before it gets cold. And don't worry so much. You'll make yourself nervous. We can take care of them better than you can."

Elspeth wandered unhappily toward her room. The stitches began to hurt now, though she was walking much slower than before.

Somewhere a woman was moaning. It was a groggy, almost drunken voice.

Elspeth eased herself into bed. She put a hand tenderly to the hurt.

She reached the one-legged table and brought it over the bed. The oatmeal had congealed into rubber.

She dialed her mother. Her father answered.

"Dad?"

He didn't reply. She heard him call Harriet.

"The baby's in the nursery," Elspeth told Harriet. "I haven't even seen him today. He was gone when I woke up. I can't even see him till visiting hours, and then I can only see him through the glass."

"It's for the best," Harriet said. "Mr. Gilbert was right about that."

She would not come in to visit today. She had given the jeans and shirts and some underwear to the Gilberts and they would bring them. She asked when Elspeth would come home.

"Are you going to come home?" she corrected herself before Elspeth had answered.

"If Dad will let me."

"Of course he'll let you. He loves you."

244

"Well, I'll be home as soon as Goldwasser lets me out. Find out if Dad wants me in the store, so I can give Gus notice in the lumber yard."

While talking to Harriet her eyes had fixed on the white paper sack with Filene's floral design that Marvin had left on the night table. When she had hung up the phone beside it she took it and looked inside. She drew out a quilted bed jacket, of a rich aquamarine color, with edging of whitish lace, and ribbon ties. She fondled the rounded thickness of the quilting, the deep furrows of the stitching. She put it on.

Why would Mama not come to see her today? It was not like her. The roads must be fully plowed by now and the buses running less tardily than yesterday. She sensed that her mother intended not to visit the hospital again, in order to avoid the baby. Having allowed herself one peek, she now wanted to put him from her mind. Maybe Daddy had bawled her out for letting herself see the baby at all.

From a labor room down the corridor somewhere she still heard that moaning. It was a dragging, uneven wail, a drugged cry. "God! Oh God! Mama!"

To shut it out Elspeth found the cord that controlled the television. Morning programs. She clicked from one channel to another. Only the advertisements attempted any creativity.

She strolled in the quilted jacket, in the direction away from the bend and the desk and the elevators and the moaning.

When she got to the nursery three other mothers were on the long bench opposite in bathrobes or housecoats. Elspeth pressed her face to the glass but could not see Petey.

She sat with the other mothers and listened to their chatter. They exchanged names. It was not a first baby for the others. One was surprised to hear that Elspeth had had her baby the night before last. "And you're up and around after only one day?"

"I was up and around yesterday," said Elspeth.

"You may be young and strong, but nobody's that strong," the woman said.

"Women in China have a baby and go right back to work in the fields," said a deep-eyed little lady of about thirty, whose name was Gail.

"This isn't China," said the first one.

"You must have had natural childbirth," Gail said to Elspeth.

"I did."

"I wanted to do that," said Gail, "but I couldn't. I had a breech birth."

They shared experiences and stories. The youngest but for Elspeth was a quiet woman of about twenty-five, with thick blond hair hanging in a loosely tied bundle to one side of her neck. She had had her second baby six days before. A girl. She was taking her home today. Elspeth asked about the first baby. He had died, the woman said. He had gone blind just after his third birthday. He had remained cheerful, as though he accepted the loss of sight as natural, and played happily as before, feeling about for his toys. When he died she had come home from the funeral, and his little cars and blocks and houses were still laid out on the floor there, and she had collapsed.

245

She told it in her gentle, barely audible way. She hoped her new baby would be all right.

Elspeth averted her face to hide her tears. She could not ask the cause of the disease or its name.

At eleven they went back to their rooms for lunch. The drowsy groaning still wafted from the labor room beyond the elevators. Sometimes it seemed to gurgle off into sleep but then it rose louder.

She finished the mashed potatoes and managed to break a piece from the overcooked slab of fish. Then she wandered toward the labor room. She met a nurse coming from it toward the desk. Her shoes squeaked and she waddled. It was a tall strangely-shaped nurse Elspeth had not seen before. The turretlike neck and head under the tiny cap were not fat, and she was narrow-shouldered, but she got fatter farther down. Her hips and legs were massive.

"You're supposed to be in bed," the nurse said to her. "This is just your second day isn't it? You shouldn't be down here." She seated the ballooning hips behind the desk where the rabbit-toothed nurse had sat in the night.

"I keep hearing that woman crying and calling out," said Elspeth. "I just wanted to ask if she was okay."

"Just labor pains. We'll be hearing that for hours. It'll get worse before it gets better."

"She sounds so miserable," said Elspeth.

"Well, the doctors don't like to knock them out completely anymore, until toward the end. Just shut your door if it bothers you." She shuffled through papers on the desk.

Elspeth half turned to go, but didn't. "Do they ever use Lamaze here? Natural childbirth?"

The nurse had taken a pen and worked at the papers. "Lamaze? Some do. I don't think much of it myself."

"Why don't you think much of it?"

"Oh, like chiropractic and Christian Science and all those things. All these mind over matter things. There was some Yugoslavian doctor up in Canada, said he was curing cancer, and it turned out he didn't even have a medical degree. There's always gullible people I guess. Mind-expanding drugs. Macrobiotic diets. They're killing themselves, these kids. Lamaze. The Lamaze ones are the worst."

"Why?" Elspeth asked.

The nurse kept writing, making check marks, turning papers.

"Why are the Lamaze ones the worst?" Elspeth asked again.

"They're all prima donnas, for one thing. Come in here, and they think they're the only ones that ever had a baby. Puffing and blowing. Their antics. And everyone's supposed to kowtow to them. I can't stand them myself."

"But some of the doctors go along with it, don't they?"

"Oh, there's always a few show-offs that like to think young, and play to the grandstand, as they say."

246

Elspeth watched her busy shufflings and markings. The desk lamp made shadows in the creases of her face.

Elspeth turned and went back slowly toward her room.

But at her door she paused. She continued on toward the nursery. Behind her down the corridor she could still hear the slurred voice of the woman calling for her mother. No doubt she had been shaved. And subjected to the indignity of an enema. And childless nurses would manhandle her in her stupor, and truss her arms to the bars and her legs to the stirrups. Bind her and immobilize her like a sinner in the stocks.

And then a pompous Herr Doktor Professor would pull on his rubber gloves and bring a baby into the world. Doctors don't bring babies into the world. Mothers bring them into the world.

She sat on the bench opposite the nursery to wait for visiting hours.

Inside the glass a girl in white sat inside beside a bassinet, reading a folded magazine and holding a bottle to an infant. But the baby had lost contact with the nipple and was crying. Elspeth rose and beat her hand on the thickness of the window. The girl seemed to hear nothing. She chewed her gum, absorbed in her reading, her wrist drooping over the glass, the nipple pressed to the baby's neck.

Elspeth waited, then rapped again, to no avail.

At last the girl glanced at her watch, though not at the baby. She restored the bottle to its place on the cart, as though not noticing it still was full, and drew the chair and the cart to the next bassinet.

Elspeth rapped once more and this time the girl heard. Elspeth pointed to the baby, and articulated so that her lips could be read even if her voice could not penetrate the glass. The girl looked at her in puzzlement. The girl shrugged, exploded a gum bubble over her lips, and sat with her back to Elspeth. She administered the next bottle to the new baby, settling into the magazine. This baby sucked eagerly. The first one still cried.

Elspeth went back toward the desk. Her stitches hurt but she did not slow down. She found the big-hipped nurse still working at forms.

"Is there a way to get a message to that red-haired nurse in the nursery?" Elspeth asked. "She missed one. The poor thing didn't get any lunch at all."

"They're not all supposed to. There's a schedule." She didn't look up from her papers.

"No, this is one she meant to feed, but the nipple wasn't in his mouth and she didn't see it."

"They don't all finish. They don't want much at this stage. Now, I'm sorry, I have a lot of work to finish."

"No, that's not what I mean—"

The nurse looked up. "Really, you can be exasperating. You're not supposed to be wandering all over the floor. You had a baby two days ago and you think it's your job to supervise the labor room and the nursery and everything else. Now go to your room and get some rest."

Elspeth reddened. She turned away, frustrated and angry.

She went around the bend to the door of her room, and stood leaning a while on the side of it. She walked to the nursery.

Two mothers in bathrobes were on the bench. They were not the ones she had met before. They seemed in their mid-thirties, and were chatting like old friends.

Elspeth sat at the other end of the bench. Beyond the glass the nurse with the magazine had progressed a few bassinets further. One of the women was telling the other that someone on the floor was giving her baby for adoption because she wasn't married. A high-school kid. The other mother was clucking.

"That's me," Elspeth told them.

"Oh. That's you?"

"It's me. My name's Elspeth. And I'm not a high-school kid."

They chatted. Elspeth told them about the baby who had missed his lunch.

"I just hope my baby isn't crying," Elspeth said. " I didn't have the heart to put him on a schedule when I had him with me. In the womb they're getting constant nourishment, and then all of a sudden they're regimented. And they don't know what clocks are, or what time is. If they're hungry and there's no food they think there's never going to be any. It's terrible."

The aide with oversized eyeglasses approached down the corridor.

"Here she comes," said one of the ladies. "Visiting time."

They told her the names of the infants to be brought to the window. "And would you tell the nurse in there that one baby didn't get fed?" Elspeth added. "I can show her which one."

The aide unlocked the door without reply and shut it behind her.

She wheeled a sleeping baby to the window and then another. The two mothers oohed and awed. The aide returned to the corridor without bringing a third one.

"What about the Baker baby?" said Elspeth.

"You're not supposed to see him."

"What? Who said I'm not supposed to!"

"Those are the instructions."

"I can't see my own baby? You've got a nerve!"

"I'm sorry. You talk to Miss Lovell if you have any problem."

"You mean that big pear-shaped one at the desk?"

"I think she's at the desk."

Elspeth hurried. At the bend she nearly bumped into a black man with a humming floor polisher. She dodged around. She found the same nurse still at the desk.

"Hey, what's this about I can't even see my own baby?"

"Those are the orders."

"Who gave that order? Marvin Gilbert? Who does he think he is!"

"Your doctor gave it. Now I've had about enough out of you. Go to your room and stay away from this desk."

"You want to know something?" Elspeth said. "This hospital stinks. It's a dump. It should be closed up."

"Young lady, this is one of the finest hospitals in the nation. In the world. They bring the classes from Harvard Medical over here."

248

"What for? To show them a horrible example? And the food I wouldn't give to a pig."

"This hospital is under the supervision of the faculty of Harvard Medical School! I don't have to take this! I don't have to take your big mouth! Members of royalty come from all over the world to be treated here! That whatsisname, the maharajah from India, with the racehorses. And the sultan of Borneo! They all come here, to Boston! Now you get straight into your bed and don't you dare get out of it again until your doctor says you're ambulatory! If you want the bedpan ring the button. Go on! I'm ordering you!"

"You're ordering me? Well, screw you! What *is* this, a concentration camp?"

The big nurse rose a few inches and fell back to her seat. "Do I have to call some aides? From downstairs? We have some men who can handle you."

Elspeth backed off. She turned back toward her room, weeping with fury.

A stitch gave a sting as she began to climb into bed. She turned and eased herself in backwards. She dried her eyes with tissues, blew her nose. She reached for the phone. Whom should she call? Cindy? Avis? She sighed. She wished she knew Avis better, so she would have more right to bother her more.

She had not finished her letter to Mrs. Hasbrough. She hung up the phone, reached for the stationery box, and pressed the button that made the bed raise her to a higher tilt.

The pen the aide had brought from the gift shop wrote purple.

> I have so much to tell you. The baby is an absolute genius. Only they
> won't let me see him. I really hate this place. If I ever have a baby again I
> think I'll have it at home. There is a lard ass supervisor that I hope gets
> cancer of the rectum.

She tore up the page. She watched the pieces flutter down among the crumpled tissues in the wastebasket.

Miss Lovell came in, holding a syringe.

Elspeth pulled the sheet higher. "What do you want? What's that?"

"Medicine. It won't hurt."

"What kind of medicine?"

"To make you feel better. A sedative. You won't even feel it."

"Don't you come near me with that needle! Unless you want my foot in your front teeth! You get Dr. Goldwasser over here first if you want to give me any needles! I'm allergic to sedatives! If I get a reaction to that needle—I warn you—there's gonna be one hell of a malpractice suit."

She saw the nurse's uncertainty.

"I reported you to my father already," Elspeth pursued. "And if anyone lays a hand on me, and my father's attorneys tangle with this hospital, you're gonna wish you thought twice."

The nurse stood there. She tightened her lips, but the arm with the needle had grown limp. She went out.

Elspeth shuddered. She felt perspiration on her forehead.

She thought she had frightened the nurse, but she could not be certain. There was just a chance she had gone to summon some goons.

Elspeth lay propped, waiting. Ten, maybe fifteen minutes passed. No one came. So far so good. Maybe it was a kind of truce. She would stay away from the desk, and Lard Ass would stay out of here with that needle.

At last she took up the stationery box again.

> My girl friend was a big help with the timing, even though she wasn't trained at all. It would have been a thousand percent easier if I had known how close to the finish line I actually was. When it is banging away hammer and tongs in transition and you think, my God, this is only effacement, it can be pretty demoralizing.

She looked up when Dr. Goldwasser entered. The broad, affable face smiled. "Well, my dear. You were sound asleep the last time I looked in."

"Hi."

"How are you feeling?"

"Well, the stitches are a pain."

"That's normal. It takes a week or two. There's a cushion you can get to sit on that should make you a little more comfortable. Sort of doughnut-shaped, inflatable. How are you otherwise, dear? Eating all right. Any bowel problems?"

"I'm okay."

"Let me just check your pulse while I'm here."

"When can I go home?" she asked while he held her wrist.

He waited till he finished counting. "Well, six days or so is the usual. We can shorten it a little if you're doing all right."

"And I want to ask you something," said Elspeth. "Who gave that order that I can't even see the baby at the window?"

"I ordered it. I think it's best for you, under the circumstances."

"And who do you take your orders from? The patient, or Marvin Gilbert? He doesn't own that baby yet, you know."

Dr. Goldwasser frowned. He cleared his throat. "Well, happy New Year. You seem to be coming along. I'll look in on you tomorrow. Despite the holiday. No holidays in my business."

"Oh, is it New Year's? I forgot."

"Yes, if you could have waited two days you might have had the first baby of the New Year. Your picture in the paper and all that. Tell me, dear, would you like a mild tranquilizer? Just something to relax you?"

"No. Why?"

"Well, I understand you've been under some nervous strain. Postpartum depression."

"Who said that?"

"It was on the report."

"They're out of their minds," said Elspeth.

"Well, I'll tell them you can order a cocktail later if you'd like to. Just to ring out the old year."

Elspeth napped. She wakened when the aide brought her supper. It was the cheerful freckled one that Elspeth had not seen since yesterday morning. "Where's your baby?" the girl said.

"He's been transferred to the nursery," Elspeth said. "I'm giving him for adoption, so my doctor thought it wasn't too smart to keep him here and develop a bond. He's right, really."

The girl murmured sympathetically.

"I'm glad I had him for one day though," said Elspeth. "I don't regret that." She sighed. "Am I glad to see this year end. It's been quite a year for me."

"That's how it always is," said the girl. "There aren't many years I'm sorry to see go. Let's hope the next one sees us out of Vietnam."

"Let's hope so," said Elspeth.

It occurred to her during supper that the shift must have changed. Perhaps Lard Ass was no longer on duty.

She was drowsy. After supper she let herself doze off.

When she wakened she felt she had slept a few hours. She was still in the propped position. The one-legged table had been moved aside and the tray of soiled dishes removed.

She sneaked to the corridor and peeked cautiously around the bend. Lard Ass was not there. The rabbit-toothed one sat at the desk. Further down, the elevator door opened and some people came out, Amethyst and Marvin among them. Elspeth ducked back to her bed. She smoothed the quilted aquamarine jacket on her front.

The Gilberts entered with another couple, Amethyst in front and holding a brown paper sack aloft. "Hi," Amethyst smiled. "We brought your jeans and stuff." She put the bag on the chair.

"The bed jacket's lovely," said Elspeth. "I've been wearing it all day."

"Marvin's got all kinds of papers for you to sign," said Amethyst. "He was at his lawyer's all day long."

Marvin introduced the couple. He and the other man wore tuxedos with shiny lapels under their open coats. Amethyst was in a sequined gown that showed her aging bosom. The coat had a bristling collar of gray fur. The other lady was a bleach blonde with glittering stardust sprinkled in her hair. "I'm sorry I couldn't get here earlier," said Marvin, opening his briefcase. He handed Elspeth sheafs of papers. "Sign each copy. There's four copies of each. And I have your certified check for seven thousand dollars right here." He handed her a pen.

"Seven thousand?" the other man said. He had a full head of hair but gray, and a square, lined face. "Did you say seven thousand? You're paying seven gees for the kid?"

"Eight," said Amethyst. "And he's worth it. Wait till you see him."

"That's a lot of jack," said the man.

"No it's not," said Amethyst. "We paid more than that for a car last year."

"Is that pen working all right?" Marvin asked Elspeth.

"Do you mind if I read it first?" said Elspeth.

"Come on, let's go see the baby while she's reading it," said Amethyst. "They're gonna throw us out. It's late."

"I'd like to get these signed first," said Marvin.

"Marv, you sure they're gonna hold our reservations?" the other man said.

"They'll hold them. I told them we'd be late."

"Well, I'll take Charlotte and Jase to the nursery meanwhile," Amethsyst said. "I want to see that scrumptious thing."

"No," said Marvin. "I want their signatures as witnesses."

"Come on, Marv," the man said. "Let's get on with it. You know what traffic is gonna be like down there? We need time to park. Leave the papers here and pick them up tomorrow."

"Jase, I want them signed tonight. It's December thirty-first. I'm counting the child as a deduction. And just in case I get audited I want to be able to say at least she signed him over before the turn of the year, even if we didn't get into court. If the documents are dated the thirty-first maybe we can ask the court to make it retroactive."

The freckled young aide looked in. "Visiting hours are over," she said.

"We'll be going shortly," Marvin told her.

"Is the nursery still open?" Amethyst asked. "Can we see the baby?"

"No, that stopped at eight-thirty," said the aide. She left.

"See what you did?" Amethyst said to Marvin. "I knew we should have left earlier."

"Baby," said Jase, "where Charlotte's involved, there's no such thing as leaving earlier. When you rang the bell she didn't have her ass in a girdle. Remember last year?"

"Oh sure," said Charlotte. "Always blame Charlotte. You know why it's Charlotte's fault? *This* guy uses all the hot water. I couldn't even take a bath."

"Come on, kid," Jase said to Elspeth. "read a little faster. We're missing a floor show."

"Don't rush her," Marvin told him. "Please."

"I really can't concentrate," said Elspeth. "There's so much of it. I'm very tired."

"Come on, Marv," Jase said.

"Jase, this is important."

"So date it back, shmuck. Sign it tomorrow and date it yesterday. I'll come in with you and witness it, first thing in the morning. We'll be up all night anyway. We'll come here for breakfast."

"They won't even let us up here at that hour."

"So at visiting hours. Whenever. One o'clock. I'll come back with you."

"Would that be all right with you, Miss Baker?" Marvin asked. "If we date it back?"

"Sure."

"I'm so mad," said Amethyst. "So I didn't get to see my baby today after all. I'd

252

have been here at one o'clock sharp, but he had to go to his lawyer's."

"Well, you know how Carl is," said Marvin. "I was supposed to be out of there in an hour. But you sit down with him and his phone rings. Interruptions—"

"I'd really rather read it tomorrow," said Elspeth. "My eyes are tired."

"It's exactly what we agreed," Marvin said. "Standard adoption papers. You can sign without reading if you'd as soon not bother."

"No. That's not how I do things."

"Come on, Marv," said Jase. "She isn't signing. You heard her. What are we waiting for?"

Marvin sighed. "All right. We'll be back tomorrow at one. Is that a promise, Jase? You'll come with me? You won't tell me you've got a big head?"

"A promise, a promise," Jase assured him.

"All right, we'll see you tomorrow at one, Miss Baker. Let me just ask one thing. You do intend to sign. Right? I don't want to go out of this room with any doubt about that."

"The nerve!" Amethyst exclaimed. "Marvin! You're actually paranoid!"

"Miss Baker?" Marvin asked.

"I assume so," said Elspeth. "If it's all in order like we said."

"It's a good thing Elspeth isn't as suspicious as you are!" said Amethyst. "Or she'd have a lawyer too! And then we'd have another twenty-five documents. Lawyers are just like businessmen—they think everybody else is as crooked as themselves."

"Dear, it's just that I want to be doubly sure you're not disappointed. Leave it to me, please! I don't want you to have a breakdown. You'll be right back in that sunny room."

"Do you think she's dickering with someone else?" Amethyst shot at him.

"No, I don't think she's dickering with someone else. But one thing does disturb me. Miss Baker, on the birth certificate. Why did you tell them Peter Baker?"

"Well, I'd been calling him Petey, and somebody came around and asked for a name, and I had to say something."

"You didn't have to say anything at all. You could have said Boy Gilbert, or Baby Gilbert. And why Baker? Why did you tell them Baker? You know his name's not going to be Baker."

"I didn't," said Elspeth. "I didn't say any last name. They must have gotten Baker from the records. Or from Goldwasser."

"See?" Amethyst told him. "It was an accident! You were all excited for nothing!"

"As a matter of fact," Elspeth said, "a lady came around with stuff about a bris, a list of cockchoppers and everything, and I told her to ask you. I gave her your address."

"That's right!" said Amethyst. "She's telling the truth. It was in today's mail. See, Smarty? Your suspicions were unfounded. And the birth certificate can be changed anyway. Carl told you it could. Elspeth, don't pay any attention to Marvin. He's just upset because he wants to name the baby after his father. Irving."

"Dear, I did not say any such thing."

253

"What a thing to do to a defenseless child," Amethyst went on. "Irving yet. Oyving."

"Dear, I said it before, and I'll say it again. You can name the baby anything you want. You can name him Richard M. Nixon Gilbert for all I care."

"So let's go, all right?" said Jase. "Before you kill each other."

The freckled aide had come back. "I'm sorry," she told them. "It's way past time. You have to go."

"Can't you let us see the baby just for a teensy minute?" Amethyst begged. Her dainty posturing became more coy than ever. "Bring him to the window? I've been waiting all day. Please, please?"

"Oh, all right," the aide said.

"Thanks again for the bed jacket," said Elspeth.

"Miss Baker, it's our pleasure."

"Amethyst," Elspeth called after them. They turned. "Amethyst, can I ask something of you? Please. And you too, Mr. Gilbert?"

"Of course," said Amethyst.

Elspeth wet her lips. She swallowed, while they waited for her to speak. "When he's older, you know, and he asks you what his natural mother was like—tell him I loved him. Okay? It wasn't that I didn't want him, or I didn't care. Tell him I loved him so much, all the time he was inside me. And the day I had him with me here. So much. This little while. Tell him that. Okay?"

Amethyst was wet-eyed. She nodded.

Marvin gave a nod also. "You have our word," he said quietly.

ELSPETH lay propped, her hands limp on the sheet, and heard their heels clacking down the corridor.

Then she found the switch cord and darkened the room except for the corridor's glow, the window's pale moonlight, and the dim haze of the night-light.

In five minutes or so she heard their footsteps returning from the nursery.

"I don't know if she would have taken less or not," she heard Amethyst's voice.

"But she was asking eight thousand plus medical and I wasn't going to argue. It's still not enough to compensate her for her suffering."

"We all suffer," she heard Jase. "And we don't all get compensated."

"The main thing is you have a beautiful baby," said Charlotte. "And you have a big home. It needs a child."

They passed her room and rounded the bend.

"Amethyst will spoil him sick," said Marvin.

The feet and voices receded toward the elevator. At last there was the sound of elevator doors, some laughter, and the voices stopped.

Elspeth slipped out of bed and went to the nursery. Perhaps Peter's bassinet would still be at the window.

She almost ran the last few steps. When she got there the freckled girl was wheeling him back to his place in the platoon.

Elspeth beat on the glass. The aide looked about in wonderment. Elspeth beckoned for her to come back.

Peter was wheeled to the window. He was asleep. The nursery door was ajar and Elspeth went to it. "Could I hold him?" she asked. "Just for a minute?"

"Oh no. I can't let anybody in. It's against the rules."

"Well, could you leave him right there by the window for a while, like until the next feeding? In case I want to come and look at him in the night?"

"Okay. That's no problem." The girl came out to the corridor, closing the door behind her. "Why didn't you come and see him with your company?"

"Well, I didn't want to intrude on their fun. They're adopting him. The sort-of-bald guy, and the one with green eye shadow."

"Oh, is that them? They looked older. I thought it was your parents or something. Okay, he can just stay near the window the whole shift. I'll tell Lula."

"Thanks," Elspeth said after her.

Obviously the message that she was not permitted to see the baby had not been conveyed to the night crew. Or not to all of it. Thank God for inefficiency.

She stood looking down through the glass at Peter. In his sleep he pushed the tip of his tongue through his lips. He drew it in again. A little bubble remained and then broke. She studied his face. There was milk in her breasts. They were wet. She massaged them in the bed jacket. They leaked more.

She blew Peter a kiss. Then she went to phone her parents a New Year greeting. She pulled herself backward into the bed.

She spoke to Harriet. "I don't suppose Dad would be willing to say hello to me," Elspeth said finally.

"Well, he's down in the kitchen warming his milk. I'm in bed already."

"You mean you two aren't gonna watch the New Year come in?"

"I don't think so. We're getting too old for that. I just hope it'll be a good year for you, dear. Better than the last."

"I hope so."

"I think you've learned your lesson."

"I think so. Did you ask Dad if he needs me in the store?"

"He says we'll cross that bridge when we get to it. You know how he is. You have to let him soften gradually."

Elspeth tried to phone Avis too. The line was busy. She tried Cindy. Adrienne answered. She said Cindy had gone to a New Year's Eve party. The girl giving the party was a creep, and there would not be enough guys there, but Cindy had decided it was better than nothing.

She tried Avis again. Still busy.

She returned to the nursery. Gail, the slight dark-haired mother with deep-set eyes she had met during the day, was on the bench now with another in a flowered kimono whom Elspeth didn't know. They greeted each other.

"I think that's your baby up front," said Gail. "It says Baker."

"Yes, that's mine." The intense big eyes were open and the arms and knees moved in the gown.

"Oh, is he yours?" said the mother in the kimono. "That's the one the girl calls Bright Eyes and Handsome Dan. He's a heartbreaker."

"He's been crying though," Elspeth said. "I can see he has. His whole expression is different. Even when he was asleep I noticed it."

"And he'll cry a lot more," said the lady in the kimono. "It's your first baby, I can see that."

Elspeth was still at the glass, her back to the two women on the bench. "Before they put him in there he never cried in his whole life. Except once somebody picked him up wrong."

The spindly-legged aide with the Afro arrived pushing a cart of bottles.

"Can you let the Baker baby stay by the window?" Elspeth asked as the girl unlocked the door.

"Yeah, Nancy told me."

"Why is *she* privileged?" said the lady in the kimono. "Put mine at the window too. Greenwald."

"And Perry, please," said Gail.

The girl drew the cart in and shut the door. The mothers joined Elspeth at the window. The two bassinets were positioned on display beside Peter.

"Yours is the prettiest though," Gail said.

The aide had moved among the bassinets further back.

"Lula and Nancy always go to the crying ones first," said Gail. "The daytime kids just take them in order, no matter who's crying."

They watched. The lady in the kimono said she had heard that martinis would be available at the desk later for ambulatory patients. Gail said drinks made her dizzy.

Elspeth hugged her bosom. "I have milk," she said. "I can feel it."

"You can ask your doctor for something to dry your breasts up," the lady in the kimono said.

Petey's lower lip pouted and quivered. His brow wrinkled. He cried.

"Come on, come away from the window and sit down," Mrs. Greenwald said. "What's the use of tearing yourself apart?"

256

She was right. Elspeth let Mrs. Greenwald put an arm around her and lead her to the bench.

"It's part of growing up," said Mrs. Greenwald. She shook her head. "Wait till you've had your third."

It was good the glass was thick, Elspeth told herself. You could not hear the sounds of the nursery. And from the bench you could not see the bassinets over the sill.

"They'll all be crying now," Mrs. Greenwald said. "It's feeding time."

"I know," said Elspeth. "I'm okay."

When Lula gave Peter his bottle Elspeth returned to the window. The big eyes were wide, and he sucked with concentration. Gail and Mrs. Greenwald joined her at the window.

"Well, I think I'll go watch a little television and turn in," said Mrs. Greenwald. "You two can stay up and see the New Year come in but I haven't got the strength."

But Gail left also, and so did Elspeth.

Televisions were playing in some of the rooms as they passed. When Elspeth had gotten into bed she turned on hers. Outdoors there was a hoarse bray as some celebrant blew a paper horn prematurely.

She clicked from channel to channel. There was a pastiche of events of the past year, narrated with sonorous circumstance. Crowds milling about in Time Square. The announcer mentioned that in Europe the New Year had already come. There was a shaking picture of Big Ben chiming midnight, and one of His Holiness blessing throngs from his balcony. She clicked it off, clicked it on again, clicked it off.

Would Petey be like Mark and Eric, rebuilding old cars for his own use, and always looking for after-school jobs even if he didn't need the money? And would he fight with Marvin the way they had fought with Daddy?

Too bad he would not have a little sister to adore.

She went back to the nursery.

Peter was awake, but the other two near the window were sleeping.

In a few moments Gail joined her. "Hi," said Gail. "I thought I'd find you here. I looked for you in your room. Just to visit."

They watched Peter work his feet. He had kicked the gown up.

"Are you gonna watch him all night?" said Gail.

"I don't want ever to forget that little face," said Elspeth. "How it looked. The shape of his ears. Those little wispy eyebrows. The way he moves his lips."

"Maybe they'll give you a picture."

Gail stood with her watching Peter, several minutes. Elspeth sighed. She wandered up and down, and Gail wandered with her.

Somehow Elspeth put her hand on the knob of the door. It opened. "Hey, it's unlocked," she said.

"Close it," said Gail.

Elspeth closed it. She opened it again. "I'm gonna go in and hold him."

"Don't! Are you crazy?"

257

Elspeth had gone in. She lifted Peter from the bassinet.

"Hey, come out of there! They'll kill us!"

"You stand guard. Tell me if anyone's coming." It seemed to her that Peter tried to focus on her face.

"Elspeth! Are you out of your mind?" Gail's voice was not much above a harsh undertone, yet high and excited. "You can't go in there! What if somebody comes? They don't just wait for feeding time! They keep coming through and checking!"

Elspeth had loosened her quilted jacket and pajama top and given Peter the breast. He turned his head once to each side, clamped and sucked. "Look at that," she said. "I remembered right. He takes the bottle with eyes open and the breast with eyes closed."

"Suppose the supervisor comes! What'll she say?"

"She'll put him back and yell at me. What else can she do? Come on, I'm taking him to my room. Grab some of these diapers and put them under your robe." Elspeth took diapers from a stack.

She thrust them on Gail, who hid them in her robe, giggling through her nose.

"Mind if I put your baby and the Greenwald baby back with the others? It'll make it a little less noticeable. Whoever comes by will think somebody else must have put them back." She rolled the Greenwald bassinet back to the double row, and Gail followed with her own, snorting giggles.

Elspeth shoved Peter's empty bassinet to the other empty ones at the side of the nursery. She peeked through the door, a flap of the bed jacket over Peter's head.

"The coast looks clear. You sort of walk in front of me to hide him a little, okay? Don't laugh so much. You'll give it away."

The corridor was empty. Elspeth pulled the door shut behind them.

Gail preceded her along the wall. A couple of patients came out of one of the rooms talking together but seemed scarcely to notice. Gail contained herself near them but giggled again when they had passed, clapping a hand to her mouth.

Elspeth ducked into her room and Gail followed. "Shut the door," said Elspeth. "And give me the diapers. He's slightly stinky."

She changed him on the one-legged table, and saw the redness of diaper rash. He had not had that before the nursery. She wiped him with tissues. Gail had doubled with half-suppressed laughter and sank into the chair.

"What's so hilarious?" said Elspeth. "Didn't you ever break a rule before?" She placed Peter rediapered on the bed. The big bandage was still on his navel. She rinsed the cotton diaper and left it rolled in a ball on the bathroom floor.

Gail had calmed somewhat. Elspeth got into bed and gave Peter the other breast. "That nursery is kept sterile," said Gail. "We might have spread germs."

"Everybody has germs. The nurses have germs."

Peter had given a couple of sucks and stopped, the breast still in his mouth. She did not take her eyes from him. He gave another suck, as though in his sleep, and stopped again.

"Can you really get away with it?" Gail asked.

"Of course I can't. They'll miss him at the next feeding. Or sooner. And they'll

258

come straight here. But meanwhile we'll have had this little time together. For five minutes, or an hour, or however long it takes them to notice."

"What if they kick you out of the hospital?"

"Let them. It's fine with me. I hate this dump."

Her hand enclosed the back of Peter's head. One of his clutching hands dug the side of her breast.

"You're really wild," said Gail. "You don't care about anything, do you."

"What do you mean? Of course I care."

"I mean, you've got a reputation around here as a tough customer. A wild kid. Undisciplined."

"Who spread that? Miss Lovell? That weirdo? I'm very disciplined. I quit smoking. Just like that."

For a while they were silent. Once Peter gave a little quiver. He gave another solitary suck and slept on, his mouth still holding the breast.

"Want me to put out the light?" said Gail.

"Okay."

The room dimmed to the night-light's glow. Gail sat again in silence, except for the muffled jumble of television from other rooms. There was another suck.

"I think I'll go see what's going on," said Gail.

"You won't say anything? If you tell just one person it'll spread."

"I know that. I can keep a secret. I'll just scout around and report back to you."

"Okay." Elspeth did not take her gaze from the downy red hair. Light from the door widened across him, narrowed and disappeared once more.

Outdoors there were another couple of horn blowings.

Going back to South Hadley, term papers, and starting all over to meet guys again—it would seem so insipid after this. So warmed over. A couple of guys would phone looking for blind dates, and a couple of girls would agree to meet them by the main gate. If you were pretty they came up smiling. If you were dogs you just stood there waiting. They drove past and took a look and disappeared. Sometimes a homely girl would ask her to just stand by the gate with them till the guys showed.

Marvin had suggested she clear out and go to Israel. Maybe that would be better. A kibbutz. She could maintain the tractors. She knew motors.

Gail came back. "Nobody knows a thing. They're all down on the floor below. They're having a party."

Elspeth said nothing.

"Want to sneak the baby back, and come down to the party?"

"No. Thanks anyway. I'll just stay here with Petey."

Gail sat watching her. But in less than a minute she rose. "I'm going back down to the party. I'll come and visit again after a while."

"Okay."

"Maybe I'll bring you a sandwich."

"Okay."

"You can trust me. Don't worry. I didn't breathe a word."

"Okay."

Gail left.

Elspeth felt under the sheet, and found Petey's big toe. How tiny it was. "Dis itty piggy went to market."

He withdrew his foot.

The various televisions joined in bells and Auld Lang Syne. Even the horns outdoors became insistent. She wondered if Gail had made it back to the party in time for the grand moment.

Hear that, Petey? That's the New Year. Aren't you ashamed to be born into such a disgusting species? Wouldn't you rather have been something sensible? Like a chamois in the mountains, or a porpoise, or a dignified gorilla sitting under a tree in the Congo?

The breast fell from his mouth. He must be really asleep. She stroked him.

Petey-boy, you're not sick, and I'm not sick, so what are we doing in a hospital? This is dumb. Let's get out of here. You want to elope with me, Petey? I think we should have a few more days together. Say three more days of titty. Would you like that? We'll hide out, for about three days, and then when they're all tearing their hair we'll say okay folks, don't get excited, we just took a little vacation. What do you say, Petey?

She lay patting him. She studied his face. She put her finger to his nose.

Then she left him on the bed and rose. She opened the drawer and found her underwear. Her wallet was gone. Instead there was a small manila receipt, stating that her valuables had been placed in the safe. But the big checkbook was there, with its various deposit slips and transfer slips. She took the valise from the closet.

There was not room for all her things. She put in the cotton diapers. And the clear plastic bag, with only the rolled-up rinsed diaper inside it.

The jeans fitted now.

The bed jacket would have to do as a wrap for Petey. There was nothing else. She spread it open on the bed. She wrapped his body in extra diapers and laid him on it. He wakened, with his concentrating, puzzled expression. "Quickly, quickly." She formed the quilted jacket so that it made a hood about his head, bundled him tightly, passed the sleeves around and around and tied them. The little face was almost hidden. "There. How's that?"

Her little transistor and Marvin's folded legal documents lay together on the night table. She stuffed them all into the valise. She could read those papers at leisure. She got her coat from the closet. She slung the shoulder bag on. She picked up Peter and grasped the valise.

She pulled the door open a little with the hand that held the valise.

Televisions still sounded but the corridor seemed empty.

Okay, men. This is it. Out of the trenches. She advanced with him to the bend and peeked around. No one. She could not see the whole desk because there was an alcove. She strained her ears.

A decisive beeline past the alcove to the elevators seemed best. She would chance it that no one was there. If anyone stopped her she'd say she'd been discharged. The other way was far around, through the cardiac unit.

She thought she heard Peter's heart, then realized it was her own. She did not glance right or left, but she knew as she passed the alcove that it was empty.

She pressed the down button.

Then she decided on the stairs instead. Somebody could walk into that elevator at any floor, or somebody could come out of it into her face.

As she ducked into the gray cinderblock stairwell she heard the elevator doors sliding open, but the maroon door of the stairwell shut tight behind her. She went down one metal flight after another, turning and turning. Petey-boy, old Marvin's gonna blow a gasket. He's gonna say, Amethyst you dodo, I *told* you we should have mounted a guard of United States Marines over that kid. She's rotten. You can't trust this generation today. Especially a girl who'd have a baby out of wedlock.

How would she get through the lobby? Somebody would surely be there. Just march through with confidence, I guess. If you make like you know where you're going, sometimes people won't bother you.

But at the level marked Main Floor the stairs did not end. She went down another level and another, till there were no more.

The basement corridor was of painted brick. A young man and a girl were wheeling a gray-haired woman on a stretcher. An intravenous bottle hung above her. They saw Elspeth but took no notice. She looked straight before her, pretending not to notice them either.

Corridors extended from corridors at right angles. She chose her turns almost at random, but trying to hold to one main direction. She did not slow her gait, and did not look back.

An exit sign appeared. She continued toward it, with no change of pace.

She leaned on the emergency handle. The riveted door swung away. The cold air made her gasp. She looked at Peter's sleeping face under the extended fold of quilting. She put down the valise on the ice, and pulled the quilting forward to shield his cheeks from the wind.

32

THE emergency exit had led into a narrow alley. At the end of it, on the main street, she saw a car or two speed past, headlights ablaze. Her feet slid suddenly on the ice and she sat with a cracking blow. Pain shot through her.

It hurt too much to cry. She had clutched Peter tighter when she had lost her balance, dropping the valise, and had been unable to maneuver to distribute the fall. She had come down on her behind in the most awkward way, so hard she had felt it in her teeth.

Peter stared from the depth of quilting, apparently undisturbed. She groaned, eyes half open, unmoving. It was as though a sledgehammer had cracked the base of her spine.

Yet oddly the stitches did not hurt. Her buttocks felt the cold pressing up through the coat.

She drew her feet slowly closer. Cautiously she raised herself, her arms guarding Peter, one bare hand pressing the quilting to his head, the valise hanging from the other beneath him. Though throbbing she seemed to be whole.

She made her way cautiously up the alley, not lifting her rubber-soled shoes from the soiled and bumpy ice.

At the main street a crosswind numbed her mittenless hands. Floodlights shone on the gray-white front of the hospital. Her long hair blew about. She shook it from her eyes, and shook it from her mouth. The sidewalk here was sanded, and in places it was worn bare.

She needed to hide somewhere and sort this out.

She looked at his face. He was falling asleep again. The wind was behind him, but against her hands and face. Her steaming breath blew back at her. But if she kept heading this way she would get downtown, and there would be hotels.

The pain had become bearable and brisk walking made it no worse. Her coat was closed, for the first time in months, and the exercise even warmed her except for her hands.

After a wide crossing, divided by a broad center strip covered with snow, the buildings became all connected and cut the wind.

The electric signs became closer together. There were as many pedestrians as by day. Young people in groups, older couples dolled up, evening gowns trailing out of coats, gray-haired men hailing taxis.

Yellow lights chased one another around the marquees. She came into a columned hotel lobby. Her hands were numb. Prosperous celebrants moved up or down short flights of wide stairs. One of the clerks at the desk, when she could get his attention, told her no rooms were available. Not a thing. Booked solid.

Elspeth returned to the sidewalk crowds. Of course the hotels would be booked on New Year's. So people could get smashed and not have to drive home.

From the entrance to a club she glimpsed a girl dancing in a G-string. She stepped inside to watch. A band filled the darkness with heady pounding. The girl under the spotlight was no older than herself, full of tireless motion. She thrust and rocked her hips, shoulders, feet, neck, hands, elbows as though weightless, in harmonious rhythms as free as the band was labored, her breasts bouncing in separate rhythms of their own. Her perfect gracefulness seemed an inborn talent.

A ruddy-faced man sipping from a tall glass looked at Elspeth, and at the baby sleeping on her shoulder, and at Elspeth again. He asked if he could buy her a drink. She shook her head. She left.

Beyond the crossing she saw the vertical bright sign of the bus terminal. Maybe she could sit with Peter in the warmth of its waiting room till morning, changing diapers in its bathroom, studying a newspaper for listings of furnished rooms.

The waiting room had a dreary brightness. A machine at the wall offered hot drinks—coffee, tea, chocolate—but she had no money, only her checkbook.

She put down the valise by the bank of telephones and felt inside each of the coin-return receptacles with two fingers. Sometimes people forgot to take their money.

All were empty.

She stood in line at the only ticket window that was open, the valise at her feet and Peter awake now at her shoulder. She had taken the checkbook from the valise and found the purple pen. She heard the priest behind her talk baby talk into the quilting. There was a woman with a crying infant still further ahead.

"Your baby fascinates me with those big eyes," the priest said. "Is it a little boy or a little girl?"

"Thank you. He's a boy."

"How old is he?"

"Two days."

"Two days! I was going to guess a couple of weeks—I was afraid to guess anything less. You don't often see them that young. So tiny."

"He's in his third day actually."

"He looks like you," the priest said. He was a handsome man, graying, with spectacles. "He certainly has your hair."

"He does. He doesn't have my eyes though. His are blue."

She patted him. She swung a little to the right and left to amuse him, turning her back once more to the priest.

She wondered if the priest would pry further. But he said nothing more. She was glad to ignore him. She watched the transactions ahead, and at last arrived at the window.

"Where?" the girl asked her.

263

"I'm not going anywhere," said Elspeth. "I just wondered if you could cash a small personal check for me. Like ten dollars."

"No personal checks."

"It's a good check," said Elspeth. "How about five dollars? Or just a dollar, so I can use the toilets and stuff? I'm stranded without any cash."

"I'm sorry." The girl shook her head behind her square of glass. "Next, please."

Elspeth stepped aside for the priest. "Harrisburg, round trip," he said at the window.

Elspeth bent to grasp the valise and went to the benches. She sat on the first one. At the other end of it a long-haired boy and girl, both in ragged jeans and short coats, dozed on one another's shoulders. The bench was of hard wood but its curvature made it comfortable, even though she felt again the soreness at the base of her spine. Her legs stretched before her. Without dimes for the toilets she would have to change his diapers at the sinks and throw the dirty ones unflushed into the trash barrel.

Even to find a furnished room she would need money for a newspaper and phones and subways. And she was hungry. Maybe in the morning some kindly storekeeper would cash a check. Not many would be open though. It was a holiday.

The priest sat beside her. "I can let you have some cash," he said. He threw aside the flap of the black overcoat and reached into the pocket of the black trousers. The veined hand came up with bills and coins. He counted it. "Eight dollars and seventy-one cents," he said. "That might help take care of things for a day. What do you think?"

"You can't give me everything you have!"

"I don't need it. I've got my ticket now. My niece sent me too much. And her husband will meet me at the station."

"But what if you have to change buses somewhere, and you miss connections? Or you get hungry? I can't take your last cent. I'm shocked."

"Well, five then," he said. "And take the change. You'll need change for the toilets, and the coffee machine. I'll leave myself three dollars in case of emergency."

She received it. "I'm overwhelmed," she said. "It's like you dropped out of heaven. I have cash at the hospital but it's all in the safe." She picked up her checkbook and took the pen from her coat. "How do you want the check made out?"

"Oh, that's all right." He raised a hand. "You don't have to give me a check."

"Of course I do. Don't be ridiculous. You can't just give all your money away."

"You don't understand, my child. I'm not supposed to have any money."

"Why?" Peter whimpered. His lips explored an inch or two of her coat. "Why can't you have any money?"

"Well, I've taken a vow of poverty."

"So I'll make it out to your favorite charity then. How about that? To your church. A donation. Five dollars and seventy-one cents." Her left arm supported Peter, and the open folder of checks and forms slid about on her lap.

The tinny voice on the loud speaker announced a list of cities. He hesitated. "All right, make it out to Saint Gabriel's Monastery."

Elspeth began to write. "I'll double it," she said.

"No, no. Don't do that. You might need it."

"There's over sixteen hundred dollars in this account. I'll have plenty of money when the banks open."

"Even so. Don't do anything rash. The five seventy-one if you want, that's sufficient for now. You can always give charity."

He had risen, picking up his satchel. She knew the bus being announced was his. "I'm adding a dollar anyway. I insist." She finished the check, tore it from the folder, and rose with Peter. "Thank you, father. You're a godsend."

He kissed her forehead. "Thank you, and bless you, child. What's your name?"

"It's on the check."

He looked at it. "Elspeth. That's a form of Elizabeth, isn't it?"

"Yes."

"Elspeth Ann. And what's the baby's name?"

"Peter."

"Peter. Elspeth Ann. Beautiful names. Good luck to you."

"Thanks, father. You're a doll."

She watched him hurry to the platform. At the door he looked back and waved. She blew a kiss.

She returned to her place on the bench. She laid Peter down to restore the big check folder to the valise, and he cried.

"Don't worry, Petey. Mama hasn't gone anywhere."

She gathered him and the valise and went to the ladies' room. She unbuttoned her coat and sweater quickly and lowered a strap of the bra. He nursed busily at first, eyes shut. But then he reverted to his dozing style, with only an occasional suck.

He opened his eyes when she laid him on the marble. She had to lay him in the quilted bed jacket on the tile floor while she rinsed the soiled diaper, wrung it and put it in the plastic bag. She sat on a toilet and gave Peter the other breast. His mouth held it unmoving. His eyes were closed. "Hey, Petey-boy, you think that titty is just an old pacifier. You've got to work at it."

In a while she returned with him to the waiting room. There was a cafeteria, locked and dark. The sign said it would open at six. She went to the hot-drink machine, and pressed the button for black coffee.

She sat on a rear bench this time, holding Peter with one arm, and sipped her coffee.

At the sandwich machine every column was sold out. The candy machine was out too. There was a machine for dispensing newspapers, but it was empty.

She found an old newspaper, mussed and creased, on a middle bench and took it to her place in the rear. She turned to the Furnished Rooms. She marked some in purple ink.

Would the hospital have notified Dr. Goldwasser of her disappearance already? Or would they wait for morning?

Were the police looking for her? Could Marvin charge her with kidnapping?

265

She hadn't signed the adoption papers yet, and Marvin had not taken the papers to court yet, so Peter really didn't belong to him yet. So how could he charge kidnapping?

She really ought to read those papers. She owed it to Marvin. He had been to all that trouble.

If Peter was still lawfully hers, why did she sneak out? She should have marched up to the front desk, Peter and all, and announced that she was discharging herself. And demanded her valuables from the safe. They couldn't hold you in a hospital against your will, could they? It was not an insane asylum. Maybe they could hold you till the bill was paid.

What about that contract she had signed? It said she would give her baby to the Gilberts, and she had received a thousand dollars as a down payment. Maybe Marvin could show it to a judge and get a warrant.

Anyway she had better telephone Mama in the morning, and tell her not to worry.

She had become very tired. She lay in the curve of the bench, Peter between herself and the back of it. But she could not sleep. There were lights on the ceiling. Peter did not cry, but neither did he sleep. He was squirmy.

She changed him again. This time she nursed him in the waiting room, on the back bench. Again he did not seem to take very much. It was as though the first suck made him drowsy.

Though the high windows to the outdoors were still black she knew when morning approached. Beyond the doors two buses came noisily to the platforms and discharged their passengers. The cafeteria was lighted, though its doors were still locked, and a white-clad black man and a black woman worked inside.

As soon as the cafeteria was unlocked Elspeth went in. She ordered a big orange juice, scrambled eggs, English muffins, coffee. She tried to hold Peter face down on her lap, but he spit up. She held him against her, and watched him while she ate. Sometimes he went cross-eyed, and sometimes he studied the proximity of her garments, and sometimes he stared with astonishment at the movement of lights and images all about.

She propped her newspaper on the emptied tumblers, folded to the classifieds. The room that sounded best said twenty dollars a week. It was more than Mrs. Brody's. And it was best to grab any bed quickly, with no commitment beyond a week.

It was after six-thirty when she phoned. She did not know what area the exchange signified but the man told her it was Chelsea. It took a while for him to explain how to get there, because she could not always grasp his accent. She thought it was Spanish. He said she must pay in advance.

On the underground trolley she drifted once into dreaming sleep, but the shriek of curving rails woke her.

A bus lifted her high on bridges and showed her the harbor. It descended into dense brick. The potholes and bumps agreed with Peter and jostled him to sleep.

The man who emerged from the bottom apartment was short and swarthy, a scowl seemingly carved permanently into his features. Elspeth climbed after him on worn stairs, pausing at the third flight to switch Peter to the other shoulder and the valise to the other hand. The air below had been thick with a kitcheny stench, but at the upper levels she recognized the odor of plaster. Some of the fourth-floor rooms were still being done. She saw exposed lathing, and dropcloths and tools. He showed her a room freshly painted in forest green. The sun had risen and on part of the green it shone pink. The bureau gleamed with varnish, as did a curtained wardrobe that stood not quite plumb. There was a sink in the corner.

"All new," he said.

"Where's the bathroom?"

He led her back to the brown hallway and opened a paneled door set at an angle in a corner near the head of the staircase. There was a water closet in a triangular little space, with an overhead tank and a pull chain.

She nodded. She returned to the cot and sat on it with Peter beside her to take the big checkbook from the shoulder bag. "You work?" he asked. "You got a job?"

"I work in a lumber yard," she said. She mentioned the name of it and the address. It crossed her mind that he was guarding against prostitutes.

He studied the check with his fixed frown. "You got no cash?"

"Just a couple of dollars. Till the banks open tomorrow. But that's a good check." She showed him the folder, with her imprinted name on all the checks and forms, and the register, with its calculations and balance.

"Driver license?"

"No. It's in my wallet, and I don't have my wallet. Look, trust me. Look right here in my check register. The last check I wrote is to a priest. A monastery. Saint Gabriel's Monastery. See that? If I were dishonest, would I be writing checks to monasteries?"

He looked at the neat small handwriting without change of expression. He accepted it.

Her eyes pained with sleeplessness.

She drew the fringed translucent shade against the sun, which was brighter now and no longer pink. She pushed off her shoes, but except for her coat did not undress. She took Peter under the meager blanket. He was still in the aquamarine quilting.

She closed her eyes. Before she slept, it came to her what she would do. She would keep Peter. For now, anyway. After three months, or six months, or after a year or two, she could still give him away then if she had to. To the Gilberts. Or to an agency. Maybe she wouldn't have to, ever. Times were changing, and anyway every case was different. If she never tried, she'd never know.

33

SHE slept deeply. Sometimes she half wakened to Peter's voice or his motions, but she would only roll over, lift him across to the other breast, and sleep would envelop her once more.

When at last she woke for good she woke slowly. She lay there with Peter. The light around the cracked edges of the windowshade was different now, afternoon light on the side hidden from the sun, bluish.

She tried to think it through again. Was there a way that Marvin Gilbert could bring the law to bear on her? Despite the contract, it must be that until she signed adoption papers Peter was still hers and they could not take him. Otherwise, why was Marvin so nervous and anxious about getting those papers signed? What if she just refused to sign? They can't make you, can they?

If they could, the contract would be self-executing. And if the contract were self-executing, you wouldn't even need adoption papers. There wouldn't be any. That was logical. But could she be sure the law was logical? She wished she knew a lawyer. It would be no use to call Daddy's lawyer. Mr. Rosenbaum. He, like Daddy and Mama, would consider keeping the baby sheer madness.

Certainly she was a better mother than Amethyst. Obviously Amethyst could not even change a diaper. That's why she had to hire a governess.

Better to send the Gilberts a letter as soon as possible, returning their thousand dollars, and entreating them not to try to find her. If they did have a lawful claim it would be no use to go into hiding. With hair like hers and Peter's they'd be recognized anywhere.

Maybe she could soften it for the Gilberts by writing that if she found she could not cope, and eventually had to give Peter up after all, they would be at the top of the list.

No. It wasn't fair to keep them hoping. She had hurt them enough already.

Unless perhaps a compromise deal? They could have the baby, provided they hired her to be her own child's governess? Forget it. The worst of both worlds, and a never-ending battle. And what would happen when she married?

She owed it to the Gilberts now to get out of their lives, quickly and cleanly. The only question was whether to include a letter of apology and explanation, or simply send the check alone, letting it speak for itself.

Her job at the lumber yard could lend itself to having a baby around. Especially if she were assigned out back in the big sheds. She would have to bundle him warm. There was plenty of slack time. She could breastfeed him out of sight behind stacks of plywood.

She raised the windowshade. She was on the top floor and the building was near the crest of a hill. The back of the flat-topped building opposite was already murky, and the alley far below was in twilight. But somewhere in the distance a dazzling window mirrored the sun. She could see over flat snow-covered rooftops to a bit of the ocean.

Elspeth spread a diaper on the floor and changed Peter on it, cleaning him with tissues moistened at the sink. She wished she had something for his rash.

She rolled up the dirty diaper and took it to the hall toilet for emptying and rinsing. But when she opened the door of the triangular water closet she reeled. She staggered back. Half-liquid excrement had been sprayed upon the white porcelain, upon the black oval seat, mostly to the left, on the wooden floor nearby and even on the yellow wall behind. It was as though somebody with explosive diarrhea and bad aim had disdained to sit down.

She slammed the paneled door shut, turned from it and gagged.

She ran down to the third floor. There was a triangular water closet there directly beneath the other one, near the head of the next stairs down. It was clean. She knelt, allowed the diaper to empty itself into the water. She pulled the chain. It flushed in its narrow gorge with a churning roar. Elspeth rinsed the diaper. The water was icy. It numbed her fingers.

She listened for Peter. But no sound came from upstairs. She shut herself into the water closet, dropped her pants and sat.

When she mounted the stairs she saw her landlord up there with a pail and a mop and a roll of paper toweling.

"Hey! You do that?"

269

"Of course not!" she told him.

"You see that?" he challenged.

"I saw it. I thought I'd retch." She walked past him, entered her room and shut her door behind her.

Peter was as she had left him, kicking on a square of diaper on the floor. She lifted him to the cot, fetched the quilted bed jacket, and wrapped him in it.

"We have to go bye-bye, Petey. Our first shopping trip. We have to find a laundromat, if any's open, and keep your diaper supply up to date, and something to eat, and some baby powder, and maybe some mittens for you and me, if we're lucky, and a knit hat to tie under your chin and keep your ears warm. Would you like that? And you need more nighties, sleepers. And more rubber pants. We have to find you so many things."

She put on her coat and buttoned it. The plastic full of rinsed diapers she folded tight and pressed it into the shoulder bag.

The landlord was still cleaning the water closet. The wastebasket was stuffed with a mountain of paper. With one hand he pushed a sudsy mop, and with the other he sprayed an aerosol disinfectant. Elspeth turned down the staircase carrying Peter.

"Hey!" he said after her. "You say not you. Who did it? You got the baby. Only you."

She stopped and looked back up. "That's not how a baby shits. He shits in his diaper. I couldn't make a mess like that if I tried." She turned and continued on down.

"One more," he called down after her, "and you go."

A bitter wind swept across the stoop. She went carefully down the icy granite steps, fearing to be blown off balance. It blew in Peter's face and he squinted. She pulled the quilting forward about his face. She hoped she had dried her hands thoroughly, lest the cold crack the skin.

The street sloped toward the remnant of sunset. The street lamps all clicked on in unison, yellow and at foreshortening distances down the hill. A dented galvanized barrel turned over, shedding snow, and rolled noisily, faster, then slower, then faster again, till a snow bank far down on the other side stopped it. The tin cans it had spilled along the way rolled on their own. The empty milk cartons and papers blew about.

Near the bottom of the hill the wind lessened. There were stores ahead, mostly dark, with grillwork locked over the windows, but at least one was lighted. She was hungry.

One of the locked stores was a laundromat. Too bad. There were two or three clean diapers left. They would have to do until morning.

The lighted place was only a cramped variety store on the opposite corner. The cross street was wide, cobbled and level, and she turned up it, hoping to find a drugstore and a luncheonette.

But except for the variety store everything was closed. Then the stores petered out. The buildings on her side turned into darkened warehouses stretching side by side to the piers. She could hear the lapping of the water.

270

She made her way back to the variety store. There was a customer, a lean elderly man, and a stout proprietress. The two were passing the time, chattering in Spanish. Elspeth allowed her fingers to warm. She opened a small carton of chocolate milk and ripped the packaging of a turnover.

"Do you have any mittens?" she asked the proprietress. "Mittens? Gloves?"

"No."

There were newspapers and a phone booth. She could check the rooming houses and begin looking for something better. On a shelf she saw packages of disposable diapers with the familiar prizewinning baby face. She took a box. The plastic sack in which her clothing had been transported from one hospital to the other, and which was crushed now in her shoulder bag with rinsed diapers inside, would do for a trash pail temporarily.

She bought a newspaper and turned to the Furnished Rooms. She sipped a second carton of chocolate milk and broke the wrapping of a fruitcake slice. There were fewer ads than in the old paper she had seen in the bus station. And no new ones, except one by young professionals seeking additional roommate age 23-28. It would be a wasted call to ask if they would tolerate a baby. The rent was too high anyway.

Maybe some of Mrs. Peress's friends had rooms. Maybe even Mrs. Peress would have her spare room ready soon, and maybe her son the professor had already made his visit and moved on to the sister in Ipshvich.

It was stuffy in the phone booth with Peter and the shoulder bag. She left the door open. She picked two nickels from her remaining money. There was not much left.

It occurred to her to find out first if the Brodys had really gone. If they had, it would cost nothing to learn that.

She dialed. She waited for a recording to tell her the number was disconnected.

"Mrs. Brody?" she exclaimed.

"Hello, darling! I recognize the voice. Everything is all right?"

Elspeth told her about the baby and that she was keeping him. She told how handsome and how intelligent he was.

"That's very nice. Of course. You're a nice girl, a pretty girl, so you have a nice baby."

"What about Florida? I thought you'd be gone."

"Na, na."

"Are you still going?"

"Na, na. We changed our mind. The children say go to Floridy, it'll be all *right*, you'll get used to it. They don't know what they're talking."

"Mrs. Brody, I've got to find a room. I don't know if you want me again. But if not, maybe you know somebody."

"So come here, darling, like before. For the baby I wouldn't charge you extra."

"Why didn't you go? I'm really surprised."

"How could we go? In all the rooms, Brody would be bumping in. If he goes down the corner, if he goes to look for cigarettes, so he'll get ferblonjet. Here he

271

knows. He knows the rooms, he knows the street, he don't bump in. From before, he remembers. Something new, he don't remember."

"I've paid my rent here for a week in advance," Elspeth said, "but suppose I come to you a week from today then."

"Any time, darling. You could come now if you want. Or next week, no difference."

Elspeth bought a package of cashews.

She sang to Peter and danced him this way and that above the soda boxes. "Bitty bitty bum bum, bitty bitty bum bum—"

She climbed the hill rapidly on the rutted frozen slush. At the top she was panting but she continued up the three flights. She dropped the shoulder bag and flung herself on the cot to catch her breath.

Al last she took off her coat and changed Peter. The rash was worse.

She took the diaper to the water closet.

"Oh no!" She felt a surge of nausea. Again the culprit had been too fastidious to sit. The mess was new, quite fresh, but not unlike the one before. Again the aim was rather leftward of center, but with a ubiquitous shotgunlike spray that rendered aim superfluous. She slammed the door.

She descended and rinsed the diaper on the third floor. She wrung it, her hands freezing. Then she returned to Peter.

She raised the sweater, dropped a strap, and lay on the cot to give him the breast. The radiator hissed.

She heard the landlord in the hall. He pounded on her door. She didn't answer.

He kept pounding. She rose, with Peter still at her breast, and opened the door.

"Hey! Come! You clean that up! I bring you the bucket!"

"You're out of your mind," said Elspeth. "I will *not* clean it up. I didn't *do* it."

"So who you blame?"

"I don't know your tenants. Somebody's sick in this place. But it sure wasn't me. I haven't even used that one. And I'm getting out of here, for your information. Right now. You give me back my check. I'll write you a new one for the day."

"No."

"You better. Or I'll just stop payment, as soon as the bank opens. You'll have zilch. I don't care."

34

FIRST that priest, just at the moment she was so desperate for a little cash, then the Brodys when she needed them—luck was with her. Like omens for continued good.

Mrs. Brody admired Peter's little face. "Brody," she told her husband, "I wish you could see."

She prepared a drawer of the bureau for him to sleep in, padding it with a blanket. It hung open at a slant. Then she dialed Harriet from the black phone on the stand in the hall.

"Mama, I hope you weren't worried—"

"With the things you do I shouldn't be worried?" cried Harriet's voice.

"I'm at the Brodys'—they're not moving—it's beautiful the way things have happened. And I'm okay. And the baby's okay."

"At the Brodys'? You're not okay. In the head you're not okay. You just think you're okay."

"I should have called sooner," said Elspeth. "But I slept most of the day. I didn't sleep at all last night—"

"It's a good thing you called when you did. I was gonna wait till eight o'clock and then call the police."

"I thought you'd figure out that I'd taken the baby and I'd be in touch—"

"Oh, I figured it out, all right. I was gonna give you till eight o'clock. Please, dear—you're at the Brodys'? I'll come there tomorrow morning. I don't want to talk about it now. I'll get too worked up."

"How's Dad?"

"Don't ask. He doesn't want to talk about it. And I don't blame him. I never heard of anything so crazy in my life. I could wring your neck. Such a stupid thing. Please dear, leave me alone. I'll see you tomorrow. I can't talk. I can't talk." Harriet hung up.

Elspeth went to her room. It was extremely rare for her mother to be angry. She could hardly remember the last time.

Peter was asleep. She considered whether to take him into the sheets with her. The spring mesh was so soft that there was no danger of his falling from the brass bed. He could only roll toward her.

But it was so hammocky, her hips so much deeper than her feet and head, that she feared he might drift down far into her blankets, lower and lower, and suffocate.

273

She went to bed without him. But when he cried in the night she took him. In the morning she found him still cradled in her arm, asleep, his mouth open and slack at her nipple.

She phoned the lumber yard when it opened and again after Gus arrived. "I'll be in tomorrow," she told Gus. "I'll have to bring the baby because I'm breastfeeding, but he won't be in the way. I'll stash him out back somewhere. Turk and Pete didn't like it that I was always the one that got to work up front, so maybe now it can be my turn to do my share in the sheds." Gus said little.

Elspeth had made the bed, but she was lying again on its spread and feeding Peter when Harriet arrived. Harriet had brought more of Elspeth's clothes. She arranged them in the drawers.

"Don't use the middle drawer," said Elspeth. "It's Petey's bed temporarily. Did the Gilberts call?"

"No."

"Not at all? They didn't call up the house looking for me?"

"No."

"I'm surprised. I guess they must realize the situation then. I didn't explain to you that I'm keeping the baby."

"Please don't explain," said Harriet. "I can see for myself. You just don't see what you're doing. Dad's right. We spoiled you."

"Mama, it's not the end of the world. It's not like when *you* were young. I can still get married. Lead a normal life."

"Married to who? Some hippie?"

"Not necessarily."

Harriet sat in the wicker chair and watched the nursing.

"And I suppose this means forgetting all about going back to college," said Harriet.

"I may take courses, when I get organized. But frankly the campus bit has lost its luster anyway. I never was too sold on it. College for the sake of college, and rah rah. Who needs it? *You* never went to college."

"Things were different then. Today girls think of professions."

"Well, the world's overprofessionalized anyway. And I'm family oriented. I want a family. It was more fun when there were five of us than three, wasn't there? Look, Mama, I'm sure I'll go back to school when the time's ripe. Maybe I'll study architecture. Or maybe I'll invent something, and get a patent, and go into manufacturing. I didn't mean things to work out like they did. But they did, and I'll have to take things in a little different order, that's all."

Harriet looked heavy in the wicker chair.

"Mama, I wish I could do what would make you happy, and Dad happy, and the Gilberts happy. But Petey's face was so different when they took him away from me. He was only a newborn, but his expression on his face was so eloquent. If you saw the look on his face in that nursery."

"You're so headstrong," said Harriet. "I can't talk to you."

Elspeth moved Peter to the other breast. He licked his lips, then went to work. "Isn't he a beautiful child?" said Elspeth.

274

"Yes. He certainly is. And I wish he wasn't. Maybe you wouldn't have kept him."

"No, I still would have."

When he stopped nursing Elspeth tickled his foot. He moved his foot but did not suck. Elspeth laid him on the bed to change him. He opened his eyes.

"This is the last of my diapers from the hospital. We have to go out to the laundromat. And we'll shop. He needs everything."

"That diaper rash is terrible."

"He got it in the hospital. In the nursery. And that's the truth."

"You have to get something for it."

"I know. It's on my list."

"You really should give him a bath."

"Not till his navel's healed."

Harriet watched how Elspeth bundled him in the quilted bed jacket and tied the sleeves. She shook her head.

They crossed the porch, Peter asleep at Elspeth's shoulder and a tote bag dangling. The snow was blackened.

"This is no neighborhood to bring up a child."

"You grew up here, right in these same streets. And so did Dad."

"But it was nice then. Not all full of colored."

At the corner Elspeth suggested that they cross to the other side of the big street and take the walkway along the park's edge.

Beyond the park's wall the fields extended white, undulating on and on.

"I don't know," said Harriet. "Not all kids are crazy. Pamela Holtz is going to Harvard Medical School."

"I'm not Pamela Holtz."

"And Lori Cohen's gonna be president of the Student Government. She's very popular. And she's not half as pretty as you."

"Tell me about Dad. What's with his ulcer?"

"Not bad, but not good. All this hasn't helped."

"I think if we could get him to lay off the cigars it might help."

"Dr. Fleming told him it doesn't make that much difference. And he says cigars is the only pleasure he has left."

At the big intersection where the trolley buses turned they waited for the lights. A huge yellow front loader was chugging smoke from a diesel chimney as it lifted a chunk from a pile the plows had made.

"What does ferblonjet mean?" Elspeth asked.

"Lost. What *you* are. Where did you hear ferblonjet? From the Brodys?"

Past Leo's & Walter's on the further side they found a laundromat.

They watched the diapers churn and splash in the round soapy window.

"Do you want me to come tomorrow?" Harriet asked.

"No. I'm going to work. I phoned them I'll be in."

"But you can't leave Mrs. Brody to take care of the baby all alone. It's too much for an old lady like that. She has foot trouble."

"I'm taking him with me."

"An infant like that in a lumber yard? He'll get killed."

"I'll stash him in a safe place."

"He'll catch cold."

"Not if he's dressed warm."

"I could come again tomorrow and take care of him till you get back."

"You'd probably sneak him away to an adoption agency or the Gilberts or somebody."

"Is that what you think of your mother? I don't think I could even do that without your permission anyway, could I? Maybe I could go to jail for that."

"I'm sorry." Elspeth reddened a bit. "But I have to have him with me. I'm breastfeeding."

Harriet shook her head. "Will they let you keep him there? Will your boss let you?"

"I sure hope so."

"So when shall I come again? You work Saturday. Sunday, I'll come Sunday."

They bought a flannel outer garment for Peter. It was blue, with a zipper, and the bottom was sewn like a bag, with room for his legs to kick. There was a hood that could be tightened with a drawstring, and the sleeves ended in flaps that covered the hands like pockets. They put him inside, first in his new waterproof pants and his new sleeper.

"He'll have plenty of room to grow in that," the little old saleslady said. "He looks like a little papoose."

Suddenly Peter went cross-eyed.

"He hasn't learned to focus yet," said Elspeth. "He does that sometimes."

Elspeth chose an inexpensive pram of chromium tubing with deep-blue canvas sides. The body of it, hood and all, could be lifted out of the metal framework and off the wheels and carried as a kind of canvas-sided box, like a car bed or a portable bassinet. "I could take that part right out and carry him in it on the bus," Elspeth said.

Elspeth wrote a check.

"Don't cash it till tomorrow morning, okay?" she said. "I've got lots of shopping and I don't know if I'll get to the bank today. I've got lots of money there in savings but not enough in checking till I write a transfer slip. Call the bank to verify if you want, but tell them to look at the savings balance."

They wheeled Peter in the pram. He did not take up much of it, and bundles were piled at his feet and beside him.

"I've got to phone the hospital to send my wallet," Elspeth said. "They've got my driver's license and everything."

They had sandwiches in a luncheonnette. They rocked the pram on its springs. "When I come Sunday I'll bring some decent food," said Harriet.

They selected a crib, and a hard waterproof mattress, and blankets. Harriet said babies didn't usually use pillows. The gray-haired black man took the vinyl-covered mattress to a faucet and wiped away the dust.

"There, that cleaned up real nice," he smiled. "He be mighty proud of that."

It had a pattern of puppies and kittens. "You want to pay installments?"

"No, I'll write a check."

He added the bill. "I don't charge tax on the blankets, and the sheets and the waterproof. I say bedclothes is clothes. Ain't no tax on clothes."

In the drugstore Elspeth turned the rack of books. "What do you need books now for?" said Harriet. "We've got so many bundles. Look at books another day. And I want to get home in time to make Dad's supper."

"I'm looking for Spock."

By four o'clock the light was waning. As they passed the bank Elspeth took the big checkbook from her shoulder bag and wrote a transfer slip moving some money from savings to checking. She dropped the slip into the night-deposit slot.

"You can't manage all these bundles yourself," Harriet said at the bus stop. The park rolled toward the sunset. Its snow was red and blue.

Elspeth lifted Peter to her shoulder and loaded the rest of the bundles into the pram. "I'm fine," she said. "Here comes your bus."

At the Brodys' she took a bath. It was her first since Peter was born. She lay in the warmth. The door was open, that she might hear him if he cried. When she had dried herself she did calisthenics on the bath mat. She was able again to touch her toes.

She put on pajamas and settled with her box of stationery in the wicker chair.

Dear Mr. and Mrs. Gilbert,

I guess the check for $1,000 which you will find enclosed speaks for itself. I find I can't give Peter up. If a time comes when I just cannot hack it all alone I will cross that bridge at that time, but for now my decision stands.

I will of course pay for the doctor and hospital bills in addition. I would also like to reimburse you for the new wallpaper in what was going to be the baby's room and now having to do that room again. Also if any of the things you bought cannot be returned I want to pay for any loss. I feel very badly about all the preparations you made.

I know every responsible person says adoption in a situation like mine is best for the baby, best for the mother, best for the mother's parents, and best for the adopting couple. I'm well aware of all the excellent reasons for adoption. It's just that my deepest instinct tells me that for me, and for my son, maybe what's right for everyone isn't right for us. I know I haven't reasoned it out. There isn't time to think it through. But sometimes, at the point of no return, something speaks to me loud and clear. Like with the abortion. I was already there on the table. I'd reasoned it through one way, and there was no time to re-reason it the other way, but it was the moment of no return, and I had to listen to my gut feeling. I don't regret that I did. Even if I gave Peter to you I'd be so glad I had him. Not just glad for me. So glad for him. I truly believe God never created a more perfect little boy.

My parents think I should have my head examined, and I'm sure you do too, and you're probably right. But when something inside has been telling me no no no, and finally I get to that moment of no return, I can't silence that voice. I only wish I could have seen far ahead what I would ultimately have to do, so I would not have hurt others so badly and disrupted other people's lives by making arrangements in good faith that then have to be suddenly reversed. Maybe that kind of total foresight is too much to ask in this world.

She mailed the letter with its enclosed check in the morning, on the way to work. She held Peter against her shoulder, and carried a beige-colored baby seat of molded plastic. It hung from her arm by its strap.

The snow had been bulldozed from most of the lumber yard and was piled high by the fence. She walked through the bays of the long shed, surveying for the safest spots. At last she set up the seat at its lowest tilt, on top of a waist-high pile of plasterboard. She fastened Peter into it. He was wearing his blue flannel, and the drawstring of the hood made a circle of his face. She gave him the yellow telephone-shaped rattle to clutch in one hand and the white dumbbell one in the other. He waved them a few seconds but lost one and then the other.

He seemed to want the breast. She unstrapped him. The nursing bra made things easier.

Out beyond the open platform the yard shone in sunlight. A gust raised a swirl of snow powder from the pile of four-by-fours. Another gust swept a cloud of it from the roof above her head. She saw it dusting down outside the wide opening. Some of it found its way in. Turk came past as she fed Peter, the coat still hanging from her shoulders. "Hi," she said to Turk.

Gus arrived earlier in the forenoon than usual and at once came out back to look at Peter. He was frowning. "You gonna leave him right there? On that stack of drywall? What if we need some sheets off it?"

"If we need it I'll move him. But we don't get calls for the five-eighths too often."

Pete worked up front with Gus, and Turk worked in the sheds with Elspeth. She helped Turk and a carpenter load the carpenter's pick-up with bundles of shakes. "Do I hear a baby crying?" the carpenter asked.

"Yes," said Elspeth.

The crying stopped. But afterward when she sat with Turk on the edge of the loading platform, their legs dangling, it resumed.

"Your kid's crying back there," Turk said.

"I know it. It's his first day on a schedule. I'm trying for two hours for starters. In the hospital they start them right off on a four-hour schedule. That's what I should have done, I guess. But he hasn't been on a schedule at all, so I'm starting with two and then we'll work up to four. He's got to get on some kind of a schedule or I can't hold a job."

The crying was a repetitive waa, always on the same note. But then he gave a louder, angrier one. It followed by some voiceless little gasps. Then he was silent. She hoped he had fallen asleep.

"You don't usually see a guy come in for a pile of shakes like that at this time of year," said Turk. "There isn't that much outside work. Now's more the time for paneling. Finishing basements and stuff."

Peter cried again.

"How long is it now?" said Turk.

"Ninety minutes. Ninety-three to be exact."

"Half an hour to go."

"I could go back there and play with him and try to distract him," Elspeth said. "I did a while ago but it made it worse. When he sees me he gets all excited and starts rooting around for the breast and it breaks my heart. I can't hold out on him."

"Sounds like it's worse on you than on him."

"No, it's worse on him. He's only five days old. Not even five days. It'll be five days tonight."

She could not wait the two hours. She gave in twenty minutes early. He locked onto the breast ravenously. She actually heard the milk gulp in his throat. She was sitting on the pile of plasterboard. Pete came to the shed with his lunch pail and sat on the rolls of insulation opposite. Turk joined him. Pete was ruddy and lean. Turk was swarthy. Pete threw his head and yellow locks back to drink coffee straight from his thermos. Elspeth thought it somewhat crude of them to park themselves opposite her and watch the breastfeeding. Still, between Peter and her coat they could not see much.

He stopped sucking and seemed to sleep, his mouth open large around nipple and areola.

"Is that all you wanted? After all that?" She jiggled him. He responded with one suck. She jiggled him again. He gave another of his lazy shut-eyed sucks. He dozed. "Aw, Petey. You're supposed to empty it, to stimulate lactation. And you've got to fill up. Or you won't make it through the next two hours."

She adjusted the coat and moved him to the other breast. He took it blissfully and slack-mouthed, eyes closed, without sucking. She knew she had milk. Some ran down and wet her. She gave him a bounce. It made no difference.

"Come on, Petey. Mama prepared such a nice lunch."

"She named him after you, Pete," Turk said.

"It has nothing to do with Pete. I just happened to like the name."

She gave up. She buttoned up and strapped Peter back in his seat. He slept.

"He's not used to a schedule," she explained, "and he just doesn't get the idea. He's been sleeping with me all night and taking one suck every five minutes. That's how he likes it."

"That's how I'd like it too," said Turk.

Pete snickered.

Elspeth had her sandwich, but she interrupted her apple to help a customer. In less than forty minutes Peter wakened, clamoring.

By late afternoon the intervals were down to an hour. Elspeth drew the line there, refusing to shorten them further no matter how desperately he cried.

If there were no customers she carried him about and sang to him softly, in and

279

out of all the bays and alcoves of the big shed. But as soon as she tried to lower him to his seat his eyes would pop open, his lip would quiver and the crying resume.

"Petey, I can't just carry you around all the time. I have work to do."

Sometimes she had to fasten him in his seat and let him holler while she attended to customers. She told herself that his distant yelling was easier to take when she was busy. But it was not. Sometimes it brought tears to her own eyes. As soon as she finished with a customer she would run to Peter. Then his crying would leave off with a little choke, the last tears running from the big eyes, as though he recognized her, though Illingworth and Spock both said babies did not recognize at that age. But if she didn't feed him he resumed the fuss with anger and outrage.

So long as customers came one at a time Turk went to them first and did more than his share. He did not complain. Elspeth said she'd make it up to him in a few days when the schedule got straightened out.

"Is that your wife and child?" she heard a customer ask him once.

"No. She works here."

The motion of the bus put Peter to sleep on the way home. But at the Brodys' the crying resumed. Elspeth dialed Dr. Goldwasser's answering service. She held Peter and tried to distract him while she ate. "I'm at my wits' end," she told Mrs. Brody.

"Maybe you should give a bottle, not the breast," said Mrs. Brody. "Everybody gives a bottle today, it's more easy. It's old-fashioned the breast. And in the daytime you could send him out for a few dollars. Sometimes somebody used to advertise in the bulletin on the wall in Leo & Walter, for a couple dollars she takes in babies every day in the house."

Dr. Goldwasser returned the call. "Well, my dear. So you took a walk. And how are you getting along?"

"Well, lousy, actually," she said into the phone. "That's why I called. I seem to have a problem."

"Yes," said Dr. Goldwasser, "I think you'll find it's not so easy."

Elspeth recounted her efforts to put Peter on a schedule. "He just won't take enough to last him. He yells for the breast but as soon as he gets a taste he falls asleep. It's like he wants a continuous dribble of nourishment, like it was in the womb. I can't go twenty-four hours a day with my breast always out, while he snoozes on it."

"Of course you can't," Dr. Goldwasser agreed.

"I guess it's my fault for not putting him on a schedule immediately, the first day," Elspeth said. "But you wouldn't think you could spoil a kid so in just five days."

"Oh, you'd be surprised," Dr. Goldwasser said. "He'll tyrannize over you if you let him." Then he lectured her. He told her to hold to a four-hour schedule, with no more compromises. By the clock, rigidly. And one breast only at each feeding. "Stick to your guns. You're bigger than he is, and he's got no choice but to play by your rules. Let him yell. It won't hurt him."

She asked Dr. Goldwasser about the diaper rash. He recommended a different ointment from the one the druggist had sold her.

It was a difficult night. Sometimes she got Peter to sleep by carrying him about and singing, but no matter how gently and slowly she laid him down into his bedding in the drawer he would waken and protest. She turned on her transistor. The station that played classical calmed him. He slept. She got him into the drawer and this time he continued sleeping, as though he thought the 1812 Overture was a lullaby.

But when the classical hours were over the transisitor was no more help. She gave him the left breast at ten o'clock sharp. He nursed somewhat longer this time, and went to sleep in his drawer. But in an hour he wakened her.

She sat with him in the wicker chair, patting him. Sometimes he dozed off, as though from total exhaustion.

At two o'clock Peter had the right breast. He worked a while till he fell asleep at it. Elspeth managed to waken him a couple of times and he took a bit more. He slept in his drawer. Elspeth sank into the hammocky springs and fell at once into deep sleep.

His next crying woke her dizzily. She staggered to the bureau to squint at the little watch. They had slept scarcely an hour. "Oh, Petey. What am I gonna do with you? You're an insomniac."

She dandled him in the wicker chair. She sang Where And Oh Where Has Your Highland Laddie Gone. She sang Mama's Gonna Buy You a Mockingbird. Whenever Peter took forty winks Elspeth did also.

At six she gave him the left breast. Out the window were the feeble beginnings of dawn. No sound but the distant cawing of crows in the snow-covered park and the slurp of milk in Peter's throat. It crossed her mind that she had forgotten to give the bank an orange transfer slip moving a thousand dollars from the savings part to the checking part, to cover the check she had mailed to Marvin Gilbert. And that had to be done, or her check would bounce. Today was Saturday. The bank was closed. She had better get to the bank as soon as it opened Monday.

Peter slept in his drawer while Elspeth had her coffee and cereal. Mrs. Brody faced her across the red-checked oilcloth, the silky robe a mass of wrinkles, the white hair wild. "He didn't let you sleep, the baby," Mrs. Brody said.

"Well, I got a couple of hours," said Elspeth. "Plus cat naps. Did he keep you up?"

"Na, na. I always get up three four times. When you get old you don't sleep much."

"Petey can't sleep because he's hungry. And then at feeding time he's so exhausted from being awake and crying that he can't stay awake to nurse. It's a vicious circle."

"So everything'll straighten out," said Mrs. Brody.

At the lumber yard Peter was worse than the day before. Elspeth was busy. It was harder to wait on amateurs than on carpenters. They often wanted things cut, and they tried to pick the best quality pieces out of the grade-B pile. And you had to help them tie stuff to the roofs of their cars.

Peter screamed back there in his tilted seat till he had no more strength, panted, dozed, woke again and screamed. Elspeth asked Turk if he could find some classical music on his radio. "Classical seems to put him to sleep," she said.

"It's AM only," said Turk. "The classical's all FM."

Her breasts kept moistening and her eyes did also. Poor Petey. What a way to begin life, in a torture chamber. He thinks I've decided never to feed him again.

The screech of the big circular saw seemed to fascinate Peter and he would pause to listen. But the saw did not run that often, and a minute or two after it stopped he would begin again.

"Is that your baby crying back there? I can wait a few minutes if you want to run back and see what the matter is," a customer said.

"Thanks, but I've been to him every ten minutes just about. He's just hungry. And I'm not supposed to feed him till ten."

A few minutes after ten she asked Turk to cover for her, ran to Peter's alcove, climbed onto the pile of drywall slabs. Peter stopped crying when he saw her.

"It's a long time between drinks, isn't it, Petey."

She heard his wail again at eleven.

At two he nursed at the left breast. But before three he wakened crying.

Gus came into the sheds, his broad shaggy head scowling. He was short but his strides were long. "Elspeth! Take the rest of the day off. Take your baby home."

She looked at him.

"Did you hear me?" he said. "I'm doing you a favor. Take off."

"It's just temporary, all this crying," Elspeth explained. "As soon as I get him adjusted to the schedule he'll be okay. Just give us a couple of days. Probably by Monday he'll be fine."

"I hope so. But right now I'm sending you home early. All right? I'm not docking your pay. Do yourself a favor. Do us all a favor. Go home."

35

AT night she carried him about and sang quietly at his ear. His only other diversion was the melodious chime of the gold clock under the glass dome. So she managed to be in the living room at each quarter hour. Every note hung long in the air till they all resonated together.

Were God and nature such lousy dingbat mechanics, that they designed a baby who's sleepy only when he's supposed to be feeding?

She fetched her copy of Spock and read in Mr. Brody's tall corner chair, though her eyes burned. She gave Peter bounces and jiggles. When he dozed she sat very still, scarcely breathing. She rose very slowly, and tried without disturbing him to wend step by careful step toward his drawer, and lay him down in slow motion. But he popped awake and threatened to cry.

"God damn it, you! I can't stand it! It's the middle of the night! A little nap is all I ask! It'a a quarter of one! You don't get fed till two! You had your chance at ten! When are you gonna catch on, stupid?"

She started over. She walked with him.

"Bim bully bum bum," she sang to him, "bim bim bum." She turned pages. She read again the part about colicky babies. It said they grow out of it in about three months.

Harriet arrived with a meat loaf as Elspeth sat in the wicker chair trying to prolong the ten o'clock feeding.

"Hi," said Elspeth. "How does Dad feel about you leaving him home all alone on Sunday to go off and visit his illegitimate grandchild?"

"Well, he doesn't approve. But I said I'll be back early so we can go out to a movie."

Peter's eyes were closed, his mouth open and motionless on the right breast. "Look at this," said Elspeth. "The one time he's supposed to stay awake a few minutes, that's the only time he sleeps." He was altogether limp. "Come on, Dumpling. Get it while it's hot."

She could not reawaken him. He slept while she placed him in the open drawer.

"The little guy is driving me bananas," she said.

Elspeth and Harriet moved to the kitchen. The red-checked oilcloth lay empty between them.

"Have you heard from the Gilberts?"

"No. I wrote to them. Why? Did they call you?"

283

"No. We haven't heard anything."

"They're too quiet. I keep thinking they're gonna all of a sudden slap me with a summons, or a court order or something. Or walk in with some policemen. And my wallet's still at the hospital. I'm afraid to ask for it."

"Oh. Your wallet came to the house yesterday. In the mail. The money in it and everything. I forgot to bring it."

"It did? Just like that? With a message?"

"No message. Just a brown envelope. I signed for it."

"Well. That's interesting."

"Dad wants to know if you'd be willing to sign yourself into a mental hospital. You'd be there for three months and then you could sign yourself out. He'd be willing to pay for a very nice one, like McLean's."

"And meanwhile the baby would be taken away."

"Well, that's part of it. But it would give you a good chance to get a rest, and get straightened out. You've been through a lot. It's a beautiful place, with tremendous grounds. It's like a resort. And it's nothing to be ashamed of."

"Why doesn't he sign himself in? He's as crazy as I am."

"That's not a thing to say about your father."

"But he is. You know he is."

"Who'd run the store if he signed himself in? Homer can't run it."

"I'd run it. I know the business from top to bottom, and he knows I do. Mama, if they come after me with a strait jacket that's one thing, but I'm not signing myself into any nuthouse. I'm amazed he'd ask a dumb thing like that. Tell him I've got his grandson to look after."

"Well, he asked if you wouldn't do that would you at least see a psychiatrist."

"What for? So the psychiatrist could sign me in? No thanks."

Harriet sighed. "Elspeth, you know you're doing a very foolish thing. And you're not doing that baby any big favor. You're just messing up your own life more and more. Everybody says you're one of the prettiest girls they know. And you have a nice personality—look at all the things they voted you in high school. And if you went to a good college in the normal way you'd have all the most desirable boys falling all over you. And I still think you could. Of course the man you marry would have to know sometime, but if he loved you he'd forgive you. Things are different now than how it used to be. Let me finish—don't interrupt. Don't pooh-pooh it. Who you marry is still very important for a girl. Whether you go in for a career or not. It makes a lot of difference in where you live, the opportunities your children have, everything."

"Mama, I still expect to marry in the normal course of events. The only difference is that it has to be a guy that loves Petey too."

"But being an unwed mother tied down to a baby all alone makes a big difference in how you rate in the marriage market," Harriet said. "Don't think it doesn't. I'm just trying to talk common sense to you. What kind of boys you have an opportunity to fall in love with depends on how attractive you're considered in the first place."

"Mama, I look at it a different way. Having Petey can even be an advantage. By eliminating all the guys who aren't serious, and all the Good Time Charlies. If a guy appreciates Petey and wants to be his daddy, that's a very good test."

"But not every man wants to start right off being serious on the very first date," Harriet said. "If you have a child, they know the first time they ask you out they have to be serious about you. And it makes them hesitate. A man has to get to know a girl more gradually. Without all kinds of commitment and seriousness on the first few dates. With a child you're too threatening."

She had not thought of that. It was true. You got to know guys more easily, more naturally, if beginnings were casual. And no matter how she would try, they would not be casual. There would be signs all over her: love me love my son. "Well," she said at last, "I only need one."

"That's right," said Harriet. "The right one."

"Even widows get married," Elspeth said. "Divorcees with kids get married."

"That's true," said Harriet.

Still, Elspeth thought, Mama had made a strong point, that had to be faced. On the other hand, she had read of women with kids who never married and raised their kids alone and got along okay without a guy. It was possible today. But it was not what she wanted.

"Okay," Elspeth admitted, "maybe you're right. Maybe I'll have fewer dates. Fewer guys. And I won't be Miss Popularity. Let's hope the guys I do get are of better quality."

Peter had slept a long time. She began to feel encouraged. But then she heard his cry.

She rediapered him and brought him to the kitchen. She waved his arm. "Say hi to Grandma."

She gave him to Harriet to hold. Peter turned his open mouth this way and that against Harriet's front as though frantically searching for a nipple.

"This baby's hungry!" said Harriet. "I don't care *what* you say. He's hungry."

"I know he's hungry. But he can't be fed till two."

He despaired on Harriet's front and wailed.

"You're gonna let him starve like this for an hour and a half? He'll be exhausted! No wonder he can't nurse!"

"Mama, what can I do? Goldwasser says let him holler. He has to go on a schedule."

She took Peter and kissed him. He stopped crying but he continued to be nervous. She rocked back and forth with him on the chair. She knew there were tears in her eyes.

"Is this what's been going on all along?"

"Day and night," said Elspeth. "It's been awful. But he's starting to improve."

"No wonder you look so tired. He looks terrible too. It's crazy. I'm gonna go out and get some bottles at the drugstore and prepare that child a bottle."

"Mama, no! It'll kill the breastfeeding!"

"What's so great about the breastfeeding? Did you ever stop to think that maybe you don't have any milk?"

"I do have milk! I've seen it. I feel it. It wets me. He only got unhappy when the schedule started. He can't figure the schedule out." She sobbed, hugging Peter. She kissed him and kissed him, all over his face. "Mama, what shall I do? I ran away with him because he got so unhappy when they stuck him in the nursery, and now he's more unhappy than when he was in the nursery."

Harriet shook her head. "And you're sure you wouldn't do better to give him up?"

"Mama, let's not mix up two separate problems. If I were married and had a husband there'd still be this feeding problem, wouldn't there?"

"I suppose so," Harriet admitted. "But let me give him a bottle betweentimes. You can still breastfeed."

"No no, Mama. You want me to show you in the books? If you expect to establish lactation you avoid bottles like the plague, at least for the first two months. A separate food supply is the surest way to make your breasts dry up."

"So let them dry up. What good are they if they leave the baby hungry?"

"Mama, what are breasts for? Just for guys to play with? That's all?"

"Well, you three kids were bottle babies, and I don't see that it hurt you. I didn't have any fixation that just because I had breasts I had to breastfeed. Bottles are a lot more convenient."

"Bottles are not more convenient. Breastfeeding is more convenient. You can take the baby anywhere anytime and the tit is always with you. You don't have to sterilize it, you don't have to warm it, you don't have to mix it. And there's no question that it's healthier."

Peter yelled, then panted. Elspeth raised him higher against her shoulder and patted him rhythmically.

Mrs. Brody came into the kitchen. She apologized for her bare feet, scratched herself, and sat down. "Mh! Ih!"

"Does the baby cry at night?" Harriet asked Mrs. Brody.

"So we close the door. We don't sleep anyways. She walks around with him. The whole night, walks around, walks around."

Peter gave several loud wails and panted.

"Maybe you don't have no milk," said Mrs. Brody.

"That's what I told her. When she was little she only listened to her father, and now she doesn't listen to anybody."

Peter yelled, giving it his all, and dropped his head, gasping for breath.

"I can't stand it!" cried Harriet. "At least compromise and give him some sugar water! Some sugar water, to hold him till feeding time! Be reasonable! Are you gonna starve that child to death, just to prove a point? Just because you're such a stubborn mule? You're worse than your father! You're stubborner than your father!"

"All right. Okay. Just sugar water then." Elspeth's eyes were wet. "We'll go to the drugstore and get a bottle."

"We don't have to go to the drugstore. I've got a bottle right here in my bag." Harriet produced a short plastic bottle. She unscrewed the cover and there was a nipple.

"You had that all this time?" said Elspeth.

"I brought it just in case. I didn't tell you before because I knew what you'd say."

"You sneaky thing."

She watched Harriet boil a little water and add sugar.

Harriet cooled the bottle under the tap, squirting droplets onto the underside of her wrist to test it.

Peter grabbed the rubber nipple, cutting short a yell in the middle. He sucked ravenously, eyes staring.

"I just hope it doesn't spoil his appetite at feeding time," Elspeth said.

"It won't," said Harriet. "You have to watch out a baby doesn't get dehydrated too, you know."

Peter choked and coughed. He guzzled again, eyes open.

"Poor Petey," said Elspeth. "The first night and day he stayed with me with no schedule at all. And then the nursery on a strict schedule, and then me again with no schedule. And then a schedule. So I suppose you can't blame Petey for being all mixed up. He does the best he can. He's only a week old. Not even a week. He was born a week ago tonight."

"What are you doing about having him circumcised?"

"I don't know. I don't even know if I want him circumcised."

"A Jewish boy should be circumcised."

"Mama, he has enough problems."

At two o'clock she bared her left breast. As she lifted him some fluid trickled down the underside of the breast.

"Is that what you call milk?" said Harriet. "That stuff? It's blue! And so thin! There's nothing to it! It's practically water!"

"It's human milk. Do you expect it to look like cow's milk? Every species is different."

Peter nursed. His eyes were closed.

"You probably never saw any before," Elspeth said to Harriet.

When Peter had finished he slept.

"Well, it's a quarter past two and I'm going home," said Harriet. "Your father works hard all week and on Sunday he's entitled to a little company."

"We'll go to the bus with you."

He did not waken, even when she placed him in his blue flannel and pushed his arms into the sleeves and zippered him up.

Along the sidewalk the snow piles were somewhat smaller, though blacker and harder. But the empty surface of the park dazzled in gold.

"Mama—" Elspeth said at the bus stop.

Harriet looked at her. The bus emerged beyond the park and began its turn, the parallel trolleys bending and sparking.

"Thanks for everything," said Elspeth. "You've been just great. I know you don't agree with me, and that makes it all the greater. You've been so loyal."

"What else can I do? We always spoiled you. Dad especially. But at least he's

287

had strength enough to stop finally. Maybe I'll come to my senses one of these days and stop indulging you." She turned from Elspeth with a great sigh, and stepped down from the curb toward the bus. "I wish I could wake up from all this."

Elspeth pushed the pram on the sanded walk. The sun struck Peter's face and he squinted in his sleep. She adjusted the hood of the pram.

Mama was not so dumb. Everybody thought Mama was dumb, and she even believed in her own dumbness. The old-fashioned clinging-vine act came so naturally to her that she believed in it. Daddy had twice tried to teach Mama the hardware business, and always he had had to give up and leave her at home because she couldn't remember one item from another and was more trouble than she was worth. She didn't know an Allen wrench from a stove bolt. Only Elspeth perceived what a brilliant cop-out it was. Poor Daddy never suspected. Mama had a good thing going.

And Mama had hit it on the head today about how Petey was going to make things difficult. Not that it wasn't obvious. But Mama had made it impossible to avoid any longer confronting the obvious.

For one thing single girls go in groups, just as single guys do. They hunt in packs. It was easier to throw parties, easier to maneuver at beaches and resorts, as part of a crowd. The girls set their bait together. You met your friends' guys, and you had girls for your guys' friends. But with a baby, the girls didn't want you in their crowd. You were a ghost at the feast. Guys at a party are supposed to think about how delicious the girls are, and you made them think about consequences.

That night Peter slept after the ten o'clock nursing till almost two. But at two o'clock her right nipple felt sore in the nursing. And afterward Peter slept scarcely twenty minutes. She walked with him. She gave him sugar water at half-past four. It helped a little, but not much.

When she heard the cawing crows at six she fed him again, but the left nipple was tender too. When he worked at it it hurt. There were cracks in the skin.

After the feeding and the diaper-changing she applied hand lotion to her breasts and nipples.

"So, it was a little better last night?" Mrs. Brody asked at breakfast.

"No. No better. I'm so discouraged. And now my breasts are cracked. The nipples are cracking."

Beginning at seven she dialed the lumber yard a few times till it answered. She asked Pete to tell Turk she would be in late, perhaps about nine-thirty, because she had an important errand at the bank.

She was waiting at the bank when it opened. Peter was awake at her shoulder. The plastic tiltable seat dangled from her arm. She had bought Peter a pacifier at the drugstore and tied it to her buttonhole by a length of string.

She gave a lady at one of the windows a transfer slip shifting a thousand dollars from savings to checking. The lady smiled at Peter even though his back was to her.

"Well, had the baby I see," tall Mr. Hudson said to her, his eyeglasses shining, his mustache smiling between the rosy cheeks. "A little boy."

"Oh, hi. Yes." She turned Peter about for Mr. Hudson to see. Peter crossed his eyes. "Oh, Petey. Don't do that."

"I'm expecting a fourth grandchild any day now. Hoping for a girl this time. After three boys."

"Mr. Hudson, I'm sort of concerned about something—maybe you can help me. I mailed somebody a check for a thousand dollars, and I forgot to put in the transfer slip. I put it in just now. I just hope that check didn't bounce."

He wrinkled his forehead. "What's your account number?"

She gave him the big folder. He opened it.

"Well, go sit by my desk a while. I'll see what I can find." He gave her back the folder. "You say a check for one thousand?"

Elspeth sat in the chair by Mr. Hudson's desk. She retrieved Peter's pacifier. She tried to interest him in a mechanical advertisement that had moving colors.

Mr. Hudson came back and sat in his armchair. "No, that check hasn't come in. When did you mail it?"

"Thursday. No, Friday morning."

"Where to?"

"Wilmerding Crosswalk."

"Wilmerding Crosswalk, Massachusetts? Well, if you mailed it Friday morning, there's no way the recipient could have received it before Saturday. So he couldn't get it to his own bank before today at the earliest. Which means we wouldn't see it here till tomorrow. So you're in good time. You're more than twenty-four hours early."

"Oh. You always have leeway like that?"

"Well, you could hand someone a check and he could walk in here with it immediately and ask the teller for cash. But assuming he uses a different bank, it takes at least a day to get here through the Boston Clearing House. Or if you sent a check out of state, to someone down in New York say, figure at least three days. You should allow a week to be sure, actually. But you've just earned yourself an extra three days' interest on that thousand dollars by waiting over the weekend, and not shifting it when you mailed the check on Friday. Actually you could leave it in savings, and come in tomorrow and shift it to checking still in good time, because our computer won't process it before three o'clock tomorrow. And that way you'll get still another day's interest on your thousand."

"Oh. Well, I've already shifted it. So I'll just leave it."

"Then it's off your mind," he smiled. The day's interest is only about fourteen cents."

"You mean, like if he puts my check in a daily interest account today, and I don't switch it out of savings to checking till tomorrow, he and I would both get a day's interest between today and tomorrow on the same thousand dollars?"

"That's right. For one day each bank would pay its customer interest on the same thousand dollars."

"Gee. There ought to be a way to exploit that. And get rich."

Mr. Hudson laughed. "Well, you'd go to an awful lot of trouble to pick up a few extra pennies. But you'll find that big insurance companies often pay a claim with a check drawn on a bank far away, so it'll take longer to clear. That way they still get interest on their money for several days after they've paid you. I guess for a big company it adds up. But not for you and me."

Elspeth smiled. "I guess not." She rose to go. He rose in his courtly way and bowed.

She ran for a bus, and the running hurt her stitches. She had almost forgotten about them.

The bus put Peter to sleep.

There must be some way, though, to tap that double interest. Suppose Daddy mailed me all his available free cash on Monday, by check. I receive it in Tuesday's mail, deposit his check in my bank, and at once mail the money right back to Daddy by *my* check. Daddy receives it in Wednesday's mail and immediately deposits it in *his* bank, the same day his own check gets back to his bank via the clearing house. So Daddy loses no interest at all. Meanwhile *my* check gets back to *my* bank on Thursday, and my bank credits me for two days' interest on Daddy's money, from Tuesday to Thursday. We each get interest simultaneously on the same money.

But it would mean an awful lot of trouble, me and Daddy both running to the bank every couple of days. Besides, the Winslow Trust Company didn't have those new switch-back-and-forth-from-checking-to-savings accounts. Mr. Hudson said his bank was pioneering them.

Gus's car was already at the lumber yard, beside Pete's and Turk's. She had not expected him to arrive before her. He usually came late, because he worked into the evening. She carried Peter around to the sheds. Pete was there with Turk, his lips parted, his breath rising in the cold. "Gus wants to see you up front," Pete said.

She found Gus busy with a customer. Elspeth began to unbutton her coat. "Don't take off your coat," he said.

He continued with the customer. When he finished he beckoned Elspeth to the register, unsmiling.

"I have a check for you," he said. "You won't be required any further."

"What?" She took the check he handed her. She gave Peter a jiggle. "You mean I'm fired?"

Gus turned his back and went to another customer.

Elspeth swallowed. So.

Clearly Gus understood now that she was nobody important, not Lennie Kramer's favorite and youngest mistress, and the baby was not Lennie Kramer's bastard after all. That she had never even met Lennie Kramer, had no idea what Lennie Kramer looked like. That she was only Lennie Kramer's nephew's sister-in-law's boyfriend's cousin.

It was easy enough to piece together what had happened. Gus must have contritely and discreetly mentioned her, perhaps in a phone call. And when Lennie Kramer learned that some employee kept a screaming infant in the shed all day he must have blown his stack.

36

SHE stood at the door with Peter, looking at the speckled snowbank and wondering where to feed him. He was fussing at her shoulder. The seat dangling from her forearm clacked against the buttons of her coat.

She turned back toward Gus. "I'm gonna sit over there on the two-by-threes and feed him for about ten minutes, and then I'll get out," she said. "If you don't like it call a cop and have me arrested for trespassing."

Gus did not turn from his customer. But she knew he heard because he colored.

Elspeth crossed the yard. She knew every inch of it. The grade-C eight-foot studs lay piled neatly in the sun about fifty high, but on the farther side of the pile from which they had been taking them they were down to seven or eight high. It was the sunny side, free of any remnant of snow. She sat there leaning on the wood and gave Peter the right breast. His every suck hurt the nipple.

Afterward she went down to the phone booth outside the doughnut counter and telephoned Dr. Goldwasser's office while Peter slept at her shoulder. Then she telephoned Harriet.

As soon as she tried to speak to Harriet she burst into tears. It took a while to regain control.

"Dear, what's the matter?" said Harriet. "What happened?"

"Well, I just got fired for one thing," Elspeth managed. "Not that that job was so great. But it would be the same problem with any job. Petey just won't go on a schedule, and I can't just hold him next to me twenty-four hours a day. And now I've got a new problem—my breasts are sore and cracked and they hurt whenever he touches them. So I can't even nurse, hardly. It's not just people against me—nature is against me. Breastfeeding is supposed to be natural, but it doesn't work."

"Isn't that what I told you?" said Harriet.

"You did, but it doesn't make sense for it not to work. If something's natural it should work. Anyway I'm going right in to Goldwasser's office. He's in the hospital all morning and doesn't have office hours till noon and his old crank secretary said he's all booked, but I said I don't care I'm gonna come in right now and sit there and wait. It's an emergency."

"What do you expect Dr. Goldwasser to do?"

"I don't know. Maybe he can tell me why my breasts hurt. And maybe the four-hour schedule isn't right for Petey. Maybe it should be two hours."

"Maybe Dr. Goldwasser will tell you to stop being silly and give him a bottle."

"Maybe he will. Mama, will you come in and meet me there? I'm just so depressed. So discouraged."

"All right, I'll meet you there. But I don't know what I can do."

"You can give me moral support. You can hold my hand." She began weeping again.

"It's all right, dear. Everything's gonna be all right. You haven't slept, and you were up and working a couple of days after giving birth, and you're very conscientious. But you don't have to feel badly. You did the best you could. Dr. Goldwasser will put the baby on a formula and that will give you a chance to get some rest."

Elspeth took the subway train and then the underground trolley, which swayed on the curves. Peter slept. She regretted that she had been a crybaby and imposed on Mama like that. She must be tired, as Mama had said.

Mama would have to take a taxi to the mall, and then a bus to the terminal, and then the subway train and the underground trolley.

In the doctor's office Peter wakened when she unzipped him and cried. There were no other patients. The middle-aged lady at the desk said she had given the doctor the message, and that he would try to get in by eleven-thirty and see Elspeth before his appointments. The waiting room had a couple of magazines about baby care, each with a beautiful smiling infant on the cover. There were National Geographics and the top one had a piece about the same oceanographic institute her cousin Bob had worked at. But she had no time to read. She changed Peter's diaper and carried him about and tried to keep him entertained.

Harriet and the doctor arrived at the same time, Harriet somewhat breathless. The doctor nodded to Elspeth on the way to his inner office without stopping to take off his scarf or homburg and said she could undress in the examining room and undress the baby too. Harriet went with her and looked after Peter. Elspeth put on a paper disposable gown and sat on the white paper that had been pulled over the soft table.

Dr. Goldwasser sauntered into the examining room, his plump fingers holding a styrofoam cup from which he drank steaming coffee. The gray hair curled about the tops of his ears. "Would anyone like some coffee?"

"I'd like some, just black," said Harriet.

"The same," said Elspeth.

He leaned out the door and told the secretary. Then he turned and sipped. "So. Problems, my dear? The little fellow seems a bit fussy."

"She insists on breastfeeding," said Harriet. "You know, the kids today think the more old-fashioned something is the more modern it is."

Elspeth told him how she had followed his instructions exactly, but how Peter seemed to tire himself out crying between feedings. Dr. Goldwasser sipped without answering. She told about her nipples. She had put hand lotion on them but it hadn't helped.

At last Dr. Goldwasser put down his cup and placed Peter in a basket scale. "The navel's healing nicely. My, my, look at that diaper rash. Did you get that stuff I told you?"

"Yes. I've used it every time."

"Well, he may be allergic to it. I'll prescribe something else."

He listened with a stethoscope. Peter began to cry again. He gave him to Elspeth to hold and looked into his ears and eyes with a tiny light.

"You should begin to get settled with a pediatrician," he said. "I'll give you some names."

He let Peter hang in the air like a monkey, clinging to Dr. Goldwasser's two forefingers. Peter swung forward. He didn't seem to mind.

"You have a high-strung child here," said Dr. Goldwasser. He gave him back.

"Is he colicky?" asked Elspeth.

"You could say that."

"Is he hungry?" Harriet asked. "He seems to always want something to eat."

"He's definitely hungry," said Dr. Goldwasser. He folded his arms, leaning back against a small table that held equipment.

"But why? Breastfeeding is supposed to be able to meet all a baby's needs, shouldn't it?" said Elspeth. "Isn't it supposed to be the perfect food?"

Dr. Goldwasser shrugged. "Well, maybe we weren't meant to be cows."

"What do you mean by that? It doesn't make us cows. We were meant to breastfeed."

"Well, in your case the breastfeeding has gotten into a kind of vicious cycle, as you said. He's too tired to take enough, and then he's too hungry to sleep. The question is how do you break out of it. Your baby is somewhat nervous, and that doesn't help. I could prescribe a tranquilizer."

"For the baby? Or for me?"

"Well, I had in mind some drops you can give the baby. To calm his tension. And you could do with something also, or at least some sleeping pills. Lie down, please. Let's have a look at you."

She gave Peter to Harriet. She swung her legs onto the paper-covered vinyl and lay down. Dr. Goldwasser pulled on a rubber glove. As he was examining her the lady brought two cups of coffee and set one on the cushiony table next to Elspeth's arm. That's dumb, Elspeth thought. There was no way she could drink the coffee lying down.

"Petey's awfully little to be on drugs and tranquilizers already," she said. "I'd rather not do that if there's another way."

"How are your stitches? How do they feel?"

"Well, they were awful at first. But I haven't noticed them as much lately."

"Your belly's doing well."

"I can touch my toes again."

"That child had an hourglass figure," said Harriet.

"Well, she may have again." He raised the tissue-paper gown higher. It bunched briefly against her face, then floated from her armpits. "Hm. Your nipples are abcessed."

"What's that mean?"

"They're cracked."

She knew that. She had told him that.

"The hand lotion is all right," he added. "But I'll prescribe something that'll do a bit more. All right, my dear. Just go stand on the scale a minute and then you can get dressed."

When Elspeth had put on her clothes she took Peter to her shoulder. He had cried while Harriet dressed him. She bounced him, and drank the coffee meanwhile. It was cold. Dr. Goldwasser had departed to his inner office.

"See?" said Harriet. "Dr. Goldwasser said the baby's hungry."

When they entered his inner office he was at the desk, writing.

"I'm giving you several prescriptions. Tranquilizer for the baby—you can use your own judgment. But you'll have the prescription on hand if you find you need it. You give it by mouth with a dropper. And sleeping pills for you. No mother produces enough milk when she's tired and tense. And a new ointment for the diaper rash. And an ointment for your breasts. And a baby scale. And bottles, nipples, sterilizer. Breast shield. And I'm giving you a formula." He gathered all the little papers together. He mentioned a big drugstore nearby that would have everything. He leaned back in the swivel. "Now, I won't tell you to give up breastfeeding if you want to continue. Breastfeeding is very in now. There's a whole mystique. And if it's what you want to do you certainly may. Just so long as the little fellow here gets his nourishment, which is the main thing. Now, you're to weigh the little fellow in the scale at the start of each feeding, and then again at the end of the feeding, before you change the diaper. Then you'll know exactly how much he took from the breast in that feeding, to the fraction of an ounce. It should be at least four ounces at every feeding. If it's less, you give him the difference directly after in a bottle as a supplement. He must get that four ounces. If he gets it from the breast fine, but if the breast doesn't have it, he still has to get it. The little fellow weighs less today than when he was born. Now, first things first. And the first thing is that child's health and happiness. Do you agree?"

"Yes," Elspeth said weakly.

"Thank you, doctor," said Harriet. "I know she'll listen to you. She wouldn't listen to me."

He locked his chubby fingers on the full vest, and tilted back till his eyeglasses shone. The swivel squeaked. "Now, you asked about going to a two-hour schedule. Absolutely not. One breast in alteration, every four hours. If you want your breastfeeding to have any chance of continuing, you've got to give those nipples a chance to heal. He's been so hungry his little gums have chewed you all up. Now the mother's state of mind is a major factor, and you cannot lactate if the nursing is painful. That's why I'm prescribing a breast shield. It's rubber. You only need one. You use it on either breast. He can nurse through it. But it keeps him from chewing you up."

He sighed. The swivel squeaked again.

"Get lots of rest," he said. "Keep a relaxed frame of mind. No anxieties. Drink a lot of milk. And you may find your breastfeeding succeeding after all, once you know and he knows that a minimum of four ounces at every feeding is guaranteed. All right? Now, don't feel you must succeed. If you find in a few weeks you have to give it up, don't feel badly. Sure, our great-great-grandmothers did it, but that was a relaxed age. And we also tend to forget that a lot of the babies died. These devotees of breastfeeding, they never tell you that. Just as they don't tell you how big and fat the wet nurses were either. Certainly, in most of the world today—Asia, Africa—breastfeeding is still the custom. And so what? Those very same areas are the areas of highest infant mortality. I don't think you'd care to bring up your baby in Calcutta."

"Doctor, I just can't thank you enough," said Harriet.

"I agree," said Elspeth. "Petey comes first. But if the scale shows he took four ounces from the breast, then he doesn't need a bottle, right?"

"That's right. For that feeding. You still have to check every feeding."

"But if it turns out he doesn't get enough and he needs supplementary bottles, can there still come a time, like after a week or two, when there *is* enough and we can chuck the bottles?"

"Elspeth—" Harriet began.

He put up a hand. "It's a legitimate question," he cut in. "Yes, dear. It's entirely possible. Of course as he gets bigger he'll require more than four ounces. And there's no guarantee you'll ever have enough. So don't be too disappointed if you don't. Don't be a fanatic." He rose. "Okay. Get your stuff. And good luck at the two-o'clock feeding. Which side is it at two o'clock?"

"Left," said Elspeth. She had risen with Peter.

"And use the shield."

Harriet gave the doctor her hand. "Can I ask you something else, doctor?" she said. "Do you believe in circumcision."

"Of course. As a matter of fact, is today the day? Yes, wasn't he born Sunday night, early Monday morning? So today's the eighth day. Having a bris are you?"

"We haven't made plans," Harriet said. "I mean, just asking you as a doctor."

"Oh yes. No question. Strongly recommended. Go to a mohel."

"A mohel?" said Harriet. "Not a surgeon? We had our boys done by a surgeon."

"Or a surgeon if you prefer. But I'd recommend a mohel. They do it best."

"I don't mean for religion," said Harriet. "I mean for health."

"I understand," said Dr. Goldwasser. "But no surgeon can specialize in that one operation the way a mohel does. Surgeons do other things. The mohels have experience. There's a couple around. We all recommend them. They do beautiful work."

The elevator descended noiselessly.

"Oh, you know what I forgot to ask him?" said Elspeth. "I forgot to ask if the Gilberts called him."

"You want to go back up?"

"No, never mind. Let's go get the stuff."

The sun was brilliant. Trickles of thaw carved rivulets in the ice.

"If the Gilberts had spoken to him he'd certainly have mentioned it," Elspeth continued. "Like if they really blew their stacks. Or if they said they're taking action. I can't understand why they're so quiet. It scares me a little."

The scale had a dial and pointer, not an arm and weights like Dr. Goldwasser's. But it had a basket on top. With the bottles and the sterilizer it came to considerable bulk. The man asked if they wanted it sent. "No, we'll carry everything," said Elspeth. "We need it right away." The bundles were tied and handles were affixed. Harriet suggested a taxi, but Elspeth said it wasn't necessary. "If you'll just carry Petey I can take everything else."

The midday subway was nearly empty. Elspeth set down the bundles.

"You see?" said Harriet. "Dr. Goldwasser believes in circumcision."

"Naturally. Because he's circumcised. He's been circumcised all his life. So he thinks that's the way to be."

"But he's in favor of it medically," Harriet insisted. "It's not just Jewish, you know. Lots of Christians do it. It's supposed to be healthy. Every doctor says so."

"Every doctor doesn't. I looked it up in Spock and in Illingworth, and Spock is for it and Illingworth is against it. So take your choice. Neither one is very convincing. Probably Spock's parents had him circumcised and Illingworth's didn't. I bet it's as simple as that. Just a matter of what he sees when he opens his own pants. Every guy is in love with his own cock, you know."

"Oh, you know everything, don't you."

"Well, my instinct is to trust nature. Natural childbirth, Natural food. Natural sex organs. Don't mess with nature and don't louse it up."

"I hope your going to take seriously what Dr. Goldwasser said about the feeding, though."

"Of course I'll take it seriously. I'm not gonna let my little guy starve."

It was not yet feeding time when they arrived at the Brodys'. The crib had arrived and so had the combination changing table and bath, and the other items. They had not been unpacked, and the wide flat corrugated cartons stood against the wall in Elspeth's room.

"Did they give you any trouble?" Elspeth asked.

"Na, na. They gave me something to sign my name, that's all. Two shvartzers. A short little shvartzer, and a great big shvartzer."

Elspeth ripped open the narrow ends of the cartons with a knife and peered in at the unassembled parts. Harriet prepared a water bottle to tide Peter over.

The changing table was a contraption of lightweight metal that unfolded. Elspeth stood it in the bathroom. The top lifted to expose a plastic sack in which the baby could be bathed. But the crib had many parts. There was wood and there was metal, springs, rods, bolts, a sheet of instructions with lettered illustrations. The Brodys had no screwdriver.

"Why didn't I think to get a screwdriver?" said Elspeth.

She telephoned the Polish man who lived on the top floor. He came down, squinting, crouching, looking this way and that, white-haired, chewing his gums, and loaned her a big screwdriver. He was in an undershirt and wore his leather armpit holster and pistol.

"Thanks. I'll bring it up to you when I finish," she told him.

"Isn't that dangerous?" Harriet said when he had gone.

"The gun? He doesn't use it much. Phyllis said all he ever did was shoot one of the trash cans once."

"But can't it go off?"

"Just like that? In the holster? In his armpit? I don't think so."

She pushed the bed a few inches till it pressed the wicker chair. Between bed and wall there was barely room for the width of the crib, as represented by one of its polished wooden ends. She sat on the floor and put parts together.

"Dr. Goldwasser said you're supposed to relax."

"I *am* relaxing. I'm always more relaxed when I'm doing something."

She dragged the big cartons across the back porch on their narrow edges, and down the steps. She stood them in the snow between clapboard and trash barrels.

"It's two o'clock," Harriet told her when she came in.

"I know."

The scale was on the bureau. They weighed Peter in its basket.

Elspeth lay in the hammocky bed. She put Peter to the shield on her breast. He took it, then drew back startled. He took it again, but once more he drew away, this time with an expression of disgust. His lip quivered, as if he would cry. He looked insulted, as though a trick had been played on him.

"It's okay, Petey. Try it. Come on." She pressed the rubber forward, toward him.

He made the best of it. He sucked, his face wary, one eyebrow lifted. But then he cried.

"Mama, I don't think he gets much through it. Take it to the kitchen and make the hole bigger, will you? Use a knife or something." She gave it to Harriet.

"Should I sterilize the knife?"

"I don't think it matters. Don't sterilize it. He's in a hurry."

When Harriet returned with it Peter was nursing shut-eyed at the unprotected breast.

"Don't bother him," said Elspeth. "Let him finish. I can stand it. I'll start the shield next time. It'll be a truer test on the scale anyway without it. I want to see how he's been doing."

At last he would suck no more. She rose. He opened his eyes when she laid him in the basket. She watched the pointer. She could feel the beat of her heart.

"Oh, no," said Elspeth.

"There!" said Harriet. "*Now* are you satisfied?"

"I can't believe it," said Elspeth. She jiggled the pointer. It returned to its place.

"Do you call that four ounces?" said Harriet. "He only got an ounce and a half!"

"An ounce and three-quarters."

"All right, an ounce and three-quarters. Can we make him a bottle then?"

"I guess we have to," Elspeth said sadly. "Two and a quarter ounces."

"No wonder he lost weight! No wonder he was crying all the time! I hope you're satisfied!"

37

HARRIET helped with some laundering and departed.

Before the six o'clock feeding Elspeth sterilized the shield and washed the ointment from her breast.

She did not like the shield. It was necessary to hold it in place. Peter didn't like it either. He latched on in the usual way, but at once spat it out, stiffening, his face unmistakably angry, indignant, disapproving. It struck her as remarkable that a week-old infant knew the facial expression for every mood. Neither Spock nor Illingworth had prepared her for that. He gave a wail. But he took it again and took a few more sucks. Then a wail, a few more sucks, another wail, and more sucks.

When she could no longer rouse him into activity she weighed him.

He had taken only half an ounce. She wiggled the scale. But half an ounce was all.

Without changing him she lifted him to the breast once more, with no shield, and he sucked busily and peacefully, eyes closed. It was several minutes before he stopped. This time the scale said he had taken two and three-quarters ounces, including the half ounce through the shield.

"Okay, Peteyboy, that's better. Much better." She changed the diaper, applied new slave to the rash, and measured the supplementary bottle.

She did not use the shield again. At ten o'clock Peter took two and a half ounces, and at two in the morning he took a full three.

The nipple did not hurt when Peter began, and she would begin each time to hope it was improving, but it was always sore when he finished.

Despite the supplementary bottles he was still fussy much of the night. Maybe spoiled from having already been carried about so much. Or maybe he was still nervous and insecure from the days of hunger.

She calculated how many hours he had slept in the past twenty-four. It was scarcely half as many as her books said he ought.

The six o'clock take was down a little from the three-ounce high.

She took her cereal sopping in extra milk, and read the Help Wanted.

There were no jobs listed that could be done with a nursing infant on hand. Except one, possibly. There was a listing for a mother's helper.

It occurred to her that night watchman might be convenient employment for a nursing mother. But there were no listings for night watchman.

The mail came at eight-thirty and Elspeth had a gray envelope from the bank. She ripped it open, expecting a letter to the effect that her thousand-dollar check had bounced after all, or that one of the tradesmen from whom she had bought baby things had cashed his check too soon.

But it was a Master Charge card, of gleaming plastic, with ELSPETH ANN BAKER raised in relief, and a long code number. There was a letter of welcome, stating that her line of credit was a hundred dollars.

Harriet telephoned.

"I just got my very first credit card," Elspeth told her. "I'm looking at it. It's very pretty."

"What do you need a credit card for?"

"I don't. The bank just sent it. I didn't ask for it. Maybe I'll give it to Petey to put teeth marks in when he starts teething."

Harriet said she'd come and help again. "I can't do it every day of course, but I thought just till you got started. If you insist on keeping that baby for a while. I'd hate to see anything happen to that beautiful child." She asked how the feedings and the bottles had gone.

"Oh, fine. I'm really encouraged, Mama. At two o'clock this morning he took three whole ounces. I just hope it gets up to four and stays there. So I can throw those bottles away."

"Don't throw them away. You never know. I thought you didn't like to waste things."

It was nearly time for the ten o'clock feeding when Harriet arrived breathlessly, bending in the vestibule to undo her overshoes.

"I'm glad you came, Mama. I can use the moral support."

"I'm not giving you moral support. I still think it's a very dumb thing you're doing."

She sat and watched Elspeth breastfeed.

"Don't you use the shield?"

"Petey doesn't like it. He only took half an ounce through it, and I took it away and he took two more ounces."

"Dr. Goldwasser told you to use it."

"I can't help it. I do everything else he said. But Petey objects to the shield."

"Petey doesn't know the difference. He's only an infant. Eight days old."

"He's not dumb though. Mama, I'd put on the shield and you'd see for yourself, only I don't want to torture him that much."

"Is the soreness getting better?"

"No, not really. I use the ointment."

"But you don't use the shield, so you see? When you try to fool your doctor you're only fooling yourself."

Elspeth wanted to change the subject. She told Harriet about the Help Wanted ads. She said the only opening in which she thought a nursing infant could be brought along was for a mother's helper.

"A nursemaid? Wiping the noses of somebody else's children? That's not for you. You're a college girl. What's the matter with you? You're the one that needs a mother's helper. Put the baby on bottles and give him to someone to take care of and go back to college."

When they weighed Peter he had taken an ounce and three-quarters.

"I don't understand it," said Elspeth. "He was improving. He really was."

She sat dejectedly in the kitchen and watched Harriet, who held Peter and prepared the bottle at the same time.

"I hate doing breast and bottle both like this. You get all the limitations of both and the freedoms of neither. It's awful."

"So give up the breast then. And you won't have to worry."

"As long as he gets something from the breast I'll keep trying. Look at him, Mama. Look at the expression on his face. He's always like that on the bottle. His eyes practically popping out of his head. He takes the breast with his eyes closed."

"That doesn't mean anything."

"It does too mean something."

Peter finished the bottle.

"See?" said Harriet. "He always finishes it. That shows he needs it." She lifted him against her shoulder and patted his back to burp him. "Boobeleh, get your bubble up," she sang, "Boobeleh, get your bubble up—" Her voice was melodious and rich.

"Where did you get that?" asked Elspeth. "That's cute."

"That song? I sang that to all you kids. Boobeleh, get your bubble up—"

Peter belched as loudly as an adult.

"Hooray! Atta boy!" Harriet sang out.

Elspeth climbed on her bed to lift him over the crib rail. The crib took all the space between bed and wall.

Harriet stood looking at him over the polished end of the crib. Quite suddenly the stirrings of his hands and feet stopped. He slept.

"We've got to get Daddy to see him," said Elspeth. "We have to find a way. If Daddy could only see how beautiful he is."

"No, he never will. And he's right. Sooner or later you're gonna have to give the baby up. For your own good. And he knows how stubborn you are. He says if the baby got sick and died it would be the best thing that could happen. It would be a blessing in disguise."

"He said that? Dad said that? Like as if I'd given birth to an incurable idiot or a monster or something? He's a beautiful, healthy child! How could anybody want him dead? What an awful thing to say! And a man who buried two sons?"

"He didn't mean it literally," Harriet said tearfully. "I know what he means—"

"But how could he even say such words?"

"He means he's thinking of *you*. He sees you making such a mess of your own life. He worries you'll end up having as little joy from your children as we had from ours. And I'm afraid he's right. He won't be a beautiful baby forever. And when he's big he'll resent you, he'll blame you."

"Gee, I hope not. Do you think he will?"

"It could happen. Bringing him up alone like this certainly isn't fair to a child."

"Petey is Dad's own flesh and blood too you know."

"But you're the one he cares about. He feels you're all he's got."

"If he thinks I'm all he's got it doesn't make sense for him to refuse to see me."

"Well, that's the only way he has to try to put some pressure on you. He means it for your own good. I told him he should try to talk to you. But that's not his way. He says I'm encouraging you."

Harriet sat, a few inches from Elspeth's feet. The bed sank under her. She heaved a long, drooping sigh.

"Mama, why don't you go home before Petey wakes up? You're tired, and you've done enough for a couple of days. I can manage now. And tell Dad I love him, okay? The child that's all he's got loves him."

"I do tell him."

"I don't know. Maybe I *am* selfish. I guess when you make a mess of your life you also make a mess of everybody else's. I'm gonna try to think things through the next few days."

Harriet stayed for lunch, and Peter wakened meanwhile. Elspeth bundled him into the pram and walked with Harriet to the bus stop.

At the two-o'clock feeding the take from the breast was even lower—an ounce and a half. She was glad Harriet was not there to see it.

She sat at the kitchen table and worked on the details of her budget. Her bank balance was nearly down to four hundred. Without a job it could be stretched for two months at the most.

And that was taking no account of the doctor and hospital bills and other reimbursements she had promised the Gilberts in her letter. She should have asked Mama to ask Daddy to what extent his Blue Cross covered her.

Maybe it didn't cover her at all, since she was over eighteen and not a student and not living with her parents. And it surely wouldn't cover a grandchild. She had better get Blue Cross of her own. She started on the budget anew.

At six o'clock the take was back to an ounce and three-quarters. But it was hard to take much encouragement from that. It would never get up to four ounces at this rate. And her nipples were more sore than before.

The Brodys' daughter Phyllis dropped in that evening. She admired Peter and asked to hold him.

"He's so light!" she exclaimed. "As light as a feather. You always forget from one baby to the next how light they are."

Elspeth told her about the breastfeeding.

Phyllis threw a hand. "Forget it. You're better off if you never even start."

Phyllis looked at the crib in the bedroom, at the changing table and diaper pail in the bathroom, the basket scale on the kitchen counter.

"Whatever you do, don't ask my mother to baby-sit," said Phyllis.

"I wasn't going to."

"My brother Marty says they should charge you more rent with the baby here," said Phyllis.

"Na, na," Mrs. Brody cut in. "What should I do, tell a baby he should pay rent?"

"I'm only saying what Marty said. That bathinette table takes a lot of space in the bathroom."

"Never mind Marty said it. I told her fourteen, and that's what it is."

Elspeth had meant to telephone Cindy, both to bring her up to date and just to have someone to rap with. But it was late when Phyllis left.

She thought of Mark and Eric. They would have stood by her now. They would agree she had done something pretty stupid, but they wouldn't take Daddy's attitude.

It snowed in the night and she heard plows. For a day all would be clean and white again.

At breakfast she read the Help Wanted but there was nothing new. The ad for a mother's helper was still there. She took a second cup of coffee. There was nothing interesting on the front page, mostly Vietnam. She had stopped reading about Vietnam after Mark died. Vietnam never changed anyway. She turned to Ann Landers and then to Chit Chat.

In the Chit Chat she found another letter from a young mother who signed herself Blue Bell and whose husband had left when the baby was three weeks old and whose earlier letters Elspeth remembered. She blessed God and the Democratic Party for the Aid to Dependent Children allotment. The baby needed a special diet. She had sold her hair. She moved in with her parents but they made her get out because there was no room for the younger brothers and sisters. She worked at telephone soliciting, and some days she didn't earn the cost of the phone. She walked to save carfare, but the neighborhood was awful and she kept the door bolted even in the daytime. The carriage was stolen. She ordered from the grocery by phone so as not to go out, but they sent her rotten stuff if she didn't shop in person. She kept the baby in heavy sweaters and told the super she would kill him if the baby died of pneumonia. The super said he was not afraid and showed her his gun. She had to give the baby some expensive penicillin but he threw it up. He vomited half a week's pay. She couldn't afford a photo of the baby.

It occurred to Elspeth to ask Mama if Mark's camera was still around. He had had it in Vietnam and she was quite sure it had been returned with his effects.

Elspeth had promised to take Mr. Brody on her errands today, but he declined because of the snow. So she wheeled Peter to the library. She stopped at the bank to inquire whether the thousand-dollar check to Marvin Gilbert had come back. The girl looked it up and told her it hadn't.

After the two-o'clock feeding she tried to nap. But she kept hearing the tittering of the television.

She rose and dialed the number in the mother's helper ad. It was a Mrs. Giddings. She had two little girls, aged three and five. Elspeth explained she had an infant she would like to bring. At last she agreed to be there tomorrow at nine-thirty.

She settled into the wicker chair with one of her library books. It was a symposium on children's intelligence. She read an article that told of whole families of indigent being railroaded into state institutions for the feeble-minded. Many of the children were normal when they entered but became feeble-minded in the institutions. A child might enter at six with a mental age of six, and at eighteen still have a mental age of six.

She dusted the apartment though it didn't yet need it again.

She was used by now to the fact that Peter's take from the breast rose somewhat at night and dropped by day. What was discouraging was that his total take in the past twenty-four hours was less than in the preceding twenty-four.

She thought of resuming her correspondence with Roxie. They had been able to open up to each other. But she couldn't write the letter. It was bound to come out like a plea for sympathy, and what could Roxie do about it?

When Harriet phoned Elspeth told her she had taken the mother's helper job. "I can't help it, Mama. I have to do *something*."

In the evening she dialed Cindy.

"You make fun of me for being too old to be still baby-sitting," said Cindy, "and *you* take a job as a mother's helper. A mother's helper is worse than a baby-sitter."

"But I have no choice. There aren't that many jobs you can take a nursing infant to. I got fired from the lumber yard because Petey kept crying for the tit all the time."

"What do you call him?" said Cindy. "Petey?"

"Petey. It's Peter, really."

"Why did you name him Peter?"

"I just liked it. I decided if it was a girl I'd call her Jennifer, and if a boy he'd be Peter or Timothy."

"But you didn't know you were gonna keep the baby."

"Even so. I couldn't think of it as just nameless. Or as Sanford or Jules or whatever the Gilberts would name it."

"I like Peter and Timothy." said Cindy. "And I guess my very favorite is Christopher or Barnaby. If *I* ever have a little boy I'll probably name him Christopher or Barnaby."

They were silent a little while, though neither made any move to hang up.

"Do you see any of the kids around town?" Elspeth asked. "I was just wondering if they ever asked about my being pregnant and everything."

"I don't see that many actually. They're all scattered."

"Do you ever run into Sonny Elkin?"

"I never run into him at all," said Cindy. "He's still at Harvard, isn't he? Living there?"

"I assume so."

"I don't think I've seen him since we graduated," said Cindy. "Where would I see him?"

"Didn't Rabbi Quint have a breakfast for all the college kids during winter vacation?"

"Oh, ya."

"Sonny wasn't there?"

"I missed it," said Cindy. "As a matter of fact I heard nobody showed up."

"I was just sort of wondering today if Sonny knows about me. He must have heard. He was away at the Vineyard all last summer, but anybody who saw me in the store towards the end must have told everybody else."

"You could call him up at his dorm at Harvard."

"I couldn't do that."

"Why? You were pretty thick together senior year."

"What would I say? Hi, guess who *this* is, and guess what *I've* been doing? Congratulate me, I've had a baby?"

"Don't tell me you're in love with him."

"No. We were never in love. It's just that all the guys I ever knew keep coming to mind. I wonder what they're doing."

"Do you think of Jared?"

"No. That's one guy I feel completely turned off of. If you didn't mention his name just now it wouldn't have occurred to me it's his money I've been writing checks against."

"Who else do you think of?"

"Everybody. You know who I dreamed about last night? That young doctor that delivered Petey at Lapham. I don't even know his name. I think it's something like Walker."

38

THE next morning Peter for the first time took less than an ounce. It's the beginning of the end, Elspeth said to herself.

But she would try again at ten o'clock, which would be at Mrs. Giddings's house, in the midst of her mother's-helper job, and try to stretch the breast feeding another day if she could.

For less than an ounce it was scarcely worth the weighing, and the soreness, and the double system.

Still, before giving up on it altogether, it would be good to have one more medical opinion. Maybe from a clinic at the Children's. Maybe she could go there at four when she finished at Mrs. Giddings's. Or even that young guy at the Lapham. Or just a talk on the phone with Avis Kramer.

Peter opened his mouth as she approached him with the bottle. Before she got there the nipple squirted in his face like a water pistol. He cried.

"I'm sorry, Petey. It never did that before."

She wiped him. Again she gave him the bottle. He took it, but at once turned from it and howled.

"Now what?" She squirted some onto her wrist. Too hot. "Oh dear. Your mama's just no good this morning."

She cooled the plastic under the tap. At last he drank, his throat working, his eyes round, the teardrops still sitting on his cheeks.

She checked the Help Wanted for new listings but there were none to which you could take a baby.

She readied him for the trip to Mrs. Giddings'. She put disposable diapers into the shoulder bag and two bottles to be transferred to the Giddings's refrigerator. That's how it was with bottles. You sterilized, put them in the refrigerator, reheated them. Heat it, cool it—what inefficient waste.

The scale was too bulky to take. She would have to estimate.

As she left, Peter at her shoulder and the plastic seat dangling from an arm, the postman handed her a letter from Marvin Gilbert. The envelope was of linen, the addresses typed.

She feared the contents. Yet it had the look of a personal letter. She would have expected a long flat business envelope with a firm of lawyers printed big and black in the corner.

She did not dare read it now. It would make her tardy the first day at Mrs. Giddings'. It was a long trip and she was not yet sure how much time it took. She dropped the envelope unopened into her shoulder bag.

She meant to open it on the subway. But the train was crowded. She needed one arm to cling to a strap and the other to hold Peter.

From the train she transferred to a trolley. It ran westward through suburbs that grew pleasanter and pleasanter, not along streets but speeding in a gully and stopping like a train at unfamiliar platforms that had snow-covered roofs and signs bearing their names.

The car was roomy and nearly empty. The baby chair and the shoulder bag sat on the seat beside her. Peter slept at her shoulder. She read the station names, watching for the one Mrs. Giddings had mentioned. It was a while before she thought again of Marvin's letter. She opened it gingerly.

Dear Miss Baker,

Thank you for the refund and for your thoughtful letter.

Your decision did not come as a surprise to me. The possibility was in my mind all along. From the very first I knew you are strong-willed, and that you listen to your inner promptings. Finally, when I walked into that hospi-

305

tal room and saw the baby at your breast, though I kept fighting to hold to our agreement, I knew that legally you could not be compelled to adhere to it and was certain that you knew it, and I had in fact little hope left.

As for your apology for disrupting our lives, as you put it, please be assured that I do not see this episode as your fault. After all it was not you who sought us, but we who imposed ourselves upon you. It was only after my re- peated urgings that you consented to interview us despite your misgivings.

The outcome is probably for the best. My wife for the past several years has not been a well woman, and with your perceptiveness I am certain you suspected that.

The clacking of the rails slowed and Elspeth saw the approach of her station stop. There was more to the letter. She refolded it into its envelope and restored it to the shoulder bag.

Mrs. Giddings met her on the platform, smiling, fluffy-haired and stylish in leath- er boots, a collar of fur and a dangling stocking cap of great length. Elspeth knew her by the little girls in snowsuits. Mrs. Giddings introduced Victoria and Felice. "Children, say hello to Mrs. Baker. And her little boy. Did you say it's a boy?"

"Yes. His name is Peter." The hood had twisted half across his face and hid an eye. She straightened it.

In the station wagon the girls stared runny-nosed at Elspeth and Peter over the back of the front seat. As wide as the car was it was full of clanking articles. A pair of skis slid against Elspeth. The car ascended between banks of sparkling ice and crossed a bridge over the tracks.

"Smoke?" Mrs. Giddings offered as she drove.

"No thanks."

"How old is the baby?"

"Ten days."

"Ten days! My! I *thought* he was a teeny-weeny, but I didn't want to say. My, and you're up and around *already*?"

"I was up and around right away. I had natural childbirth."

"Oh, *I* had that. I had saddle block. And some Demerol toward the end. I didn't get dressed for three weeks. I told my husband after what *I'd* been through I wanted to be waited on hand and foot. You look so young. Is your husband a student?"

"Well, Petey's dad is a student, yes. We're not together."

"Oh. You know I was really thinking you were someone more mature. Especially when you said you had a baby, you know. Well, we'll see how it works out, I guess. We tried one of the English girls and it didn't work out at all. That's such a racket. You pay their plane fare and they're supposed to stay with you a year. But they quit you after a few weeks and find another job and there's not a thing you can do. The courts say they have a right. And so snippity. 'I'm not Mary Poppins you know.' Now they're bringing Nova Scotia girls, I don't know if they're any different."

They passed snow-laden evergreens. The house was gabled, of stucco and stone, with eaves extending at their ends and swooping down to become archways over gates.

Elspeth knelt in the foyer to set up Peter's chair and fasten him into it. A huge malodorous dog, lean but flabby-skinned, came sniffing sadly.

Mrs. Giddings pulled off her suede gloves. "I hope that baby isn't going to occupy you every minute. *My* children have first claim, you know. They get overheated if you leave their things on."

"I just wanted to get him off my hands." She knelt in her coat to the girls, trying to keep herself between Peter and the dog.

Victoria and Felice sat leaning altogether limp at the baseboard, looking puffy-faced at Elspeth while she dug their legs out of the snowsuits. She wiped their noses with tissues from her shoulder bag.

"The car picks up Vicky for nursery at twelve-thirty, so you'll just have the one after you give them lunch. You be sure to have her all ready, because Mrs. Westrom doesn't like to wait. She just honks once. And then you'll put Felice in for her nap, so you'll have an easy afternoon."

Elspeth hung the snowsuits in the closet, trying to protect Peter with a foot, though the dog seemed gentle enough. The dog managed to sniff Peter's face with his wet nose. Peter blinked but did not seem to mind.

"Get up, girls," said Mrs. Giddings. "Don't let them lie there like that. Don't you know it's drafty on the floor?"

Elspeth knelt in her coat and lifted them to their feet.

"I hope you can stay to six the first day. I know it's supposed to be till four, but I want my husband to meet you. I never decide anything without my husband. The baby will be in the way there. Don't leave him there."

Elspeth had no intention of leaving Peter on the floor. She had knelt to take off his flannel, and was already picking him up seat and all.

"Why don't you take off your coat?" said Mrs. Giddings.

"I just want to get the bottles into the fridge."

She could see the kitchen through archways. The dog followed her, sniffing.

"Major won't hurt you," said Mrs. Giddings, also following. The girls brought up the rear.

Elspeth placed Peter and his tilted seat on a counter of formica speckled in gold. About her head were rows of scalloped cabinets. She took off her coat and gave her hair a shake.

Mrs. Giddings said she would show her the children's rooms. She followed, leaving Peter on the kitchen counter with misgivings, because it was near his feeding time and she knew he was wet. But he was quiet. The dog came too, sniffing her jeans.

Mrs. Giddings had a strange walk. Her buttocks in the rough woolen skirt went up and down in alternation. They all went up the staircase, Felice on all fours and Vicky grasping the uprights.

Each child had a large bedroom, sunny and chintzy with little maple rocking chairs.

"Very pretty," said Elspeth.

"We like it. Well, I guess you might as well start the breakfast dishes. Go with Elspeth, girls. Mama has things to do."

Mrs. Giddings followed down the stairs with more instructions. The dusting she had already done herself, but the dining-room furniture was to be polished today. If necessary it could be left till nursery and nap time, but it would be wise to get a head start, as it took long. Major was to be taken for his walk before lunch, with the plaid dog blanket, and of course the girls would need their snowsuits and boots again. Major's dish was under the sink and he was to get a whole dish of liver if he had a bowel movement on the walk. The girls' lamb chops were in the meat tray. They had their little table and chairs in a corner of the kitchen. If Major stole from their plates he was to be beaten on the nose with a tightly rolled newspaper and dragged out the back door by the collar. It occurred to Elspeth that the dog might weigh as much as she did.

In his tilted seat Peter was making noises and moving his arms and legs, but not crying yet. The shoulder bag was near him on the counter.

The sink had more than just breakfast dishes. Besides the coffee grounds and grapefruit rinds and dried egg there were larger plates, garbage, and desert dishes that could only have been left from the night before. There were big pots with glued messes. The dog nuzzled her behind. She turned and struck his mouth sharply with the back of her hand.

She pulled open the dishwasher, which was directly under Peter. But it was already full of unwashed dishes. She sprinkled detergent into it. Again the dog nuzzled up under the crotch of her jeans. She wheeled. "You do that once more, you stinking mutt, and you get this soap powder right in your eyes."

He backed off forlornly as though he understood.

"What did you say to Major?" Vicky asked.

"I told him to let me alone." She closed the dishwasher.

She turned the switch. Nothing happened.

"You have to kick it," said Vicky.

Elspeth kicked it.

"Not there," Vicky said.

"Where?"

"Here," said Vicky.

Elspeth kicked it near the right edge, as high as she could kick. The throaty rumbling began, and then the swish. Above it Peter seemed to listen.

She pushed the sink's meat scraps into the disposal. It roared viciously with a crunching of bones. Peter's eyes widened.

"Will you stop that? I'm on the phone!" Mrs. Giddings shouted from another room. Elspeth clicked it off. She rolled her sweater sleeves and began to scrub a pot. She could hear the whiny voice on the phone. "I don't know how she'll work out. It's so hard to get anybody."

"Do you know any songs?" Elspeth asked Vicky. "Would you like to sing to Petey?"

Vicky said she only knew one song. She sang it, and Elspeth said it was lovely. Then Vicky sang some more.

"Look, he's really listening," said Elspeth.

But he became fussy. She wiped her sudsy hands and felt his diaper. He was damp but he did not have a b.m. She decided to save time by letting the changing go until the bottle was warming. She sat on a stool she pulled from the breakfast counter and locked her feet into its legs.

Vicky watched Peter take the breast.

"Whacha doing?" she asked.

"Feeding Petey. And after he's fed, we're gonna give him a nice new diaper. So he'll be clean and dry."

"What are you feeding him?" Vicky asked.

Felice yelled from another room. Elspeth had scarcely noticed her absence.

"Are you all right?" she called. "Felice?"

The yell was repeated, louder.

"She made poo-poo in the potty," said Vicky. "You have to wipe her."

There were more yells, louder and impatient, rising to a squeal.

"I'll be there soon," Elspeth called. "I hear you. Just wait a few minutes."

Mrs. Giddings burst into the kitchen. "Don't you hear that child?" Then she saw the nursing. Her lips tightened. "Vicky, go upstairs."

"Why?"

"Right now, Vicky. Go to your room. Mommy is upset." Felice was hollering. "Mommy's coming, dear," Mrs. Giddings sang out, shoving Vicky gently before her into the hall. "Well, I never!" she said to Elspeth through her teeth.

Elspeth was shaken. Peter kept nursing, eyes closed. The nipple was sore, but she did not interrupt him.

Felice sounded hysterical by now. Mrs. Giddings was cooing and comforting her. Vicky was stamping on the staircase.

At last Peter stopped and let go. He opened his eyes. Elspeth laid him on the counter. She put paper toweling under him.

While she was changing the diaper Mrs. Giddings appeared at the door. She had the tight-lipped frown and her nostrils widened. "Well! It would have been just fine if my husband came home and you were exposing yourself like that. Wouldn't it. Just dandy. Number one, I made it clear to you that *my* children come first. And number two, I don't expect you to start undressing yourself in front of the children."

"I wasn't undressing myself."

"No. You were nursing the baby. I'd like to know what kind of affectation *that* was. You put two bottles in the refrigerator."

"The bottles are supposed to be supplementary."

Mrs. Giddings sighed, shaking her head. "It won't do. It just won't do. You get your things, and I'll take you to the station. I'm sorry. Like I told my husband, what we need is an older person. I'll give you half a day's pay and I think that's very fair, considering that you haven't done anything."

"Can I warm his bottle first so I can give it to him at the station?"

Mrs. Giddings sighed visibly. "You can warm it while I get the children's things on, I guess." She turned and Elspeth watched the up-and-down dance of the buttocks in the skirt as it receded. She heard Mrs. Giddings call the girls.

"Aa," said Peter.

"Aa yourself," Elspeth said to him. She dropped the wet diaper into the trash basket under the sink. Let it smell there. The dog smells worse.

She warmed the bottle. It was not losing the job that was depressing. The job was no good anyway. What was depressing was that there were no jobs. From the front hall came sounds of irritable fussing.

"You get all kinds," she heard Mrs. Giddings murmur under her breath while they got into the station wagon. The tassel of the stocking cap hung to her behind. "All kinds. It's a mad, mad world."

Elspeth sat on the bench under the roof at the trolley platform and gave Peter the bottle. She had the day to kill. It was only half-past ten.

It would be interesting to make the long trip to Bradbury and ask the resident at the Lapham for his advice about Petey. There was nothing to lose. And nothing else to do with a wasted day.

Peter slept without taking the last ounce.

When she boarded the trolley he still slept. She watched the wintry slopes pass endlessly, jagged brown twigs encased in brilliant ice.

Marvin's letter came to mind. The shoulder bag sat beside her. She fished the letter from it.

You kindly expressed concern about our expenses. Be assured that the baby things have been returned for full credit. As for the wallpaper, my wife redecorates constantly in any case. It is an activity she seems always to enjoy and is probably as good a therapy as any, so I ask you not to trouble your head or your conscience further.

I did have the foresight, once I saw you nursing the child, not to give the caterer an advance deposit for the bris. So there is no loss there. As for the medical and hospital bills, these have been paid in full, and I suggest you just forget them. Consider them my gift to you. It is my pleasure. I will treat them as tax-deductible anyhow. If perchance you can get your own family medical insurance to reimburse you in addition, just keep the money. With a child on your hands you are going to need every dollar.

It is very difficult for a young person like yourself to bring up a child alone. I am sure that to a great extent you realize that, and I am afraid you will come to realize it even more as you confront the reality. Yet I feel if anyone can do it, you are the one who can. You have spunk and resourcefulness, and I have the feeling that once you are determined there is no stopping you. My admiration and respect for you continue of the highest. For that reason I cannot say that I regret the entire episode. Meeting you and knowing you is an experience I would not want to have missed.

The whole encounter has given me food for thought. Had I had the courage to listen to gut instinct, and reverse arrangements made, as you put it, my life would have been less tragic. Much would have been different, had I

310

had your gift for the right stroke in the nick of time, trusting heartfelt impulse without agonizing or soul-searching.

In closing, may I wish the very best of luck and good fortune in this world to you and to the child. If I can ever be of assistance in any way, I beg you not to hesitate to get in touch.

I have typed this myself, as some of what I wanted to convey was too personal to entrust to my secretary. So please forgive the erasures and any further errors that escaped me.

As ever,
Marvin H. Gilbert

AN elderly lady was the receptionist this time at the Lapham.

"I'd like to talk to the doctor who delivered my baby, if I could, please," Elspeth asked. "I think he was the resident — I'm not sure of his name. It might have been Walker. It was about a week and a half ago, around midnight December twenty-ninth, or one A.M. on the thirtieth."

"Harlan Walker is the resident," the lady said. "But he's not in Out Patient today. Dr. Feloukis is in Out Patient."

"No, it's Dr. Walker I want to see. He wears his hair in a ponytail. Sort of olive complexion. Is it his day off?"

"No, he's not off," said the lady. "I think he's up on the fourth right now. I'll see if he's available." She plugged a line into the switchboard.

Elspeth strapped Peter into his seat and sat beside him on the couch. Beside her, beyond the end of the vinyl couch, a potted tropical plant towered, made entirely of plastic. It was remarkably realistic. The tiniest veins were molded into the green.

She rose as the doctor came into the lobby. She picked up Peter, chair and all. The doctor looked the same as when she had first seen him, dressed in white, his long hair tied behind him, a stethoscope hanging from his neck. He walked toward her.

"Hi. Remember me? I'm Elspeth Baker. You delivered my baby."

"Oh yes." His uncertainty had changed to recognition even before she spoke. "This is the baby with the knot in the cord."

"The what?"

"Weren't you the ones with the knot? I'm sure it was you. You came in around midnight, fully dilated. Ready to push."

"Yes, that was me."

"Right," he said. "You delivered on the desk upstairs. There wasn't even time to get a stretcher."

"That's right. You were great."

"I wasn't great. You're the one who was great. And you didn't see the knot? Didn't I call your attention to it? What we call a true knot. Like a plain overhand or single knot, looped and passing through the loop."

"Gee, vaguely. Yes. I did see it. Now that you mention it. In the cord. When you lifted him up."

He nodded. "So," he said, "what can I do for you?"

"Well, we're not doing so good. And I just thought if I could get your opinion, you know. You were so good that night Petey was born."

"What seems to be wrong?"

"Well, I'm breastfeeding. That is, trying to, and it's a big flop. I guess I don't have the milk."

"Nonsense. How could you not have enough milk?"

"Well—" She looked about the lobby. It was nearly empty. A middle-aged couple in their coats and boots had come to the desk and the receptionist was turning her rack of visitor cards. "Could we go somewhere and talk?" Elspeth asked. "Instead of standing here?"

"Sure."

She followed him to a door at the side of the lobby. He ushered her into an office that had a desk, bookcases, vinyl chairs. She sat, Peter and his chair upon her lap, and remembered as she did so that she had left her coat, the shoulder bag and Peter's flannel out there on the couch. But she did not go back for them. Dr. Walker closed the door and sat behind the desk.

When he fixed his eyes upon her she began to tell about the breastfeeding. He leaned, playing with a pencil he picked up from the desk. When she paused he said nothing, so she continued. She could almost remember the exact yield of each breast at every feeding.

"When did you start the weighing?" he asked.

She told him. She recounted how it had been at the lumber yard, before the supplementary bottles. He twirled the pencil idly, his eyes on hers, but said nothing. She told him about the hospital and about having Peter with her at first, and his transfer to the nursery, and their running away.

"That ointment you used. What was it?"

She told him. "I'm still using it," she added.

"Has it helped?"

"I wouldn't say so. Maybe it would have been worse without it."

"But your nipples are no less sore since you've used it?"

"No. They may even be worse actually."

"Has the shield helped?"

"Well, I didn't really give the shield a chance. I couldn't stand it. And Petey didn't like it either. It seemed like he wasn't getting much through it."

Dr. Walker put the pencil down and put his elbows on the desk, leaning forward. Peter sneezed.

"I'm sorry, what did you say your name is?"

"Elspeth. Elspeth Baker."

"All right, Elspeth," he began. "Not all doctors agree, naturally. So I guess you've got to pick your doctor and stick with him. But if you ask for my opinion, I'll give it. And my opinion is that you've had some good advice and some bad advice. But mostly rotten advice. And my advice is, if you want to breastfeed, take the scale and throw it out. In the trash. As soon as you get home. I don't care how fancy it is or what you paid for it. Or have a garage sale next Saturday and sell it for fifty cents. But get it out of the house. Don't ever weigh the baby again. And the same with the bottles, and the sterilizer, and the breast shield, and all that junk. Get rid of it. And the ointment. Throw it out. And throw your mother out. And your aunts, and your grandmother. And when you feel like nursing and the baby feels like nursing, nurse. And don't listen to anyone else. It just concerns you two. You and the baby. It's nobody else's business. One thing you've been told is true. You can't lactate very well when you're overtired. You've got to get your rest. Or when you're nervous, or worried, or anxious. If you're uptight, the breast knows it. And the baby knows it. It shuts off. So you can't have people around bugging you, and planting doubts in you, and arguing with you, and pushing bottles on you. And you can't have that damn scale around pointing a finger at you and telling you you failed. That scale is guaranteed to kill breastfeeding. It's poison."

"But what if he really doesn't get enough?"

"Don't worry about it. He'll get enough. Listen, kid. Elspeth. I'm telling you the facts because I know you want to breastfeed. And I saw how you handled the Lamaze, so I know you're smart. Elspeth, you have milk. Like you have functioning ovaries and everything else nature gave you. Sure, I suppose here and there there's a pathological case. Just like some people don't have enough insulin. Or some people don't have enough hemoglobin. They're anemic. But most are normal, right? And this widespread notion that in a few generations half the women or more have lost the capacity to breastfeed is nonsense. Evolution doesn't work that fast. If you're in general good health, I assume you can breastfeed. You haven't told me any evidence that you can't. The evidence is that you've done everything possible to guarantee failure. Number one, the schedule. Number two, the scale. Number three, bottles."

"What schedule should I use then? Two hours? My breasts would be even sorer."

313

"No schedule. Demand. Let the baby make his own schedule. You did all right that way in the hospital, didn't you? At the beginning?"

"That's different. In the hospital we had nothing to do but lie in bed all day. I have to have a job. I have to support myself."

"Oh. Well, yes, that's a problem." He was resting on his arms, his hands loosely folded on the desk. "What did you say you work at? A lumber yard?"

"I did. Right now I'm between jobs."

"Any chance you could just stay home with the baby till the nursing's established?"

"It just might work out that way because jobs are hard to find. But I don't dare get down to my last dollar. I've got barely enough for two months."

"Do you get unemployment compensation?"

"I hadn't thought of it. I probably wouldn't be eligible. I wasn't there very long."

"Well, you say you have enough for two months. Why don't you just take it easy for a month. Preferably the whole two months. Or maybe you could borrow, or go on welfare, and stretch it longer. But take this first month off anyway. Are you sure you want to breastfeed?"

"That's the idea. That's why I'm here."

"Well, that's what I thought. And my advice is, if you've got some money to live on for two months, then just lie back and enjoy the breastfeeding and cross the next bridge when you get to it. At least you'll have a month or two of breastfeeding. Which is a lot better than nothing. And who knows, maybe in the meantime you'll find some kindhearted boss who'll let you breastfeed in the office. Or some kind of work you can do at home. It's too bad you don't live in one of the countries where babies ride along on their mother's hip, inside her clothes. That's really the best way. The baby is upright, next to his mother's warm body, hearing the beat of her heart like he did in the womb, and whenever he feels like it he leans over and takes a suck. And meanwhile the mother is going about her business, in the fields or the market or whatever. Eventually, as the baby gets bigger, he takes larger amounts at longer intervals, and falls into a schedule naturally, and finally sleeps through the night without a feeding. And by then lactation is so firmly established you could go to work all day and leave the baby with someone with a bottle, because by then one bottle a day won't hurt that much. But at the beginning he needs smaller amounts more often. And the breast needs that frequent stimulation to get going. The breast responds to the baby. It'll produce as much as he needs. No more, no less. If he sucks less, it'll produce less next time. And if he gets hungrier and sucks at shorter intervals, it'll produce more. So absolutely no supplementary bottles, okay? Not during these early weeks. Which brings us to the next problem, those clogged-up ducts. Abcessed breasts, so called. And the sore nipples. That never should have been allowed to happen. You drove the kid crazy with hunger making him wait four hours, so then he's so overeager he chews the nipple to bits, and then like you said he's so exhausted he doesn't take much, so the breast assumes he doesn't need much, and produces less. All right, now how do you get rid of the soreness? Throw away that ointment, that goo. And go bare-breasted every chance you get. In the privacy of your room. In your apartment. Strip to the waist. Sleep topless. Eat your breakfast topless. Do your laundry topless. Answer the telephone topless. Topless all the time. Except when you have to go out."

"That'll cure it?"

"Of course it'll cure it. Smearing that crud on didn't cure it, did it? Give it air. Nothing cures a skin problem like air. I don't say sun necessarily. The sun thing's been overdone. But air. Just like if you never wear panties you'll never get vaginitis. Did you know that?"

"No." She was stroking Peter's hair.

"Women never wore underpants till the early part of the nineteenth century. Did you know that?"

"No, I didn't."

"Well, they didn't," said Dr. Walker. "They wore shifts, and petticoats, but no pants. And they never had vaginitis."

"It sounds kind of far out. How long do I have to go topless?"

"Oh, a few days should do it. Does the baby have a problem with diaper rash?"

"Yes, as a matter of fact."

"Treat it the same way. Exposure to air. When you think it's fairly safe for a while, let him go without diapers. With a bare bottom. Put some newspapers on the carpet, or a rubber sheet, and spread out a diaper on top, and let him lie on it. Do you have athlete's foot?"

"No."

"Well, if you ever do—"

"Go barefoot," she said in unison with him. "I don't know," she added. "I like you. I like what you say. I like a lot of what you say. Some of it's just crazy enough to be true. Maybe it'll even work, who's to say? I'm ready to try anything. God knows what I've done up to now hasn't worked."

"You do like I said. It'll work."

"I almost believe you. I think I do believe you. It has the right sound. I just hope it really works."

"It will. You just have to let it."

"If it does—gee—if it only does, you're a great doctor. I'll be grateful to you all my life."

He smiled. One cheek dimpled in a way she hadn't noticed before. "I'm only doing my job," he said. "If I can help you to do what comes naturally why shouldn't I?"

"You know what you said about those tribes where the baby is carried upright inside his mother's clothes? Petey loves being carried upright."

Dr. Walker nodded. "Sure. We must have carried babies like that for millions of years, I guess. And they probably cried a lot less."

"Maybe we should wear clothes like the Africans. And keep our babies in them."

"Maybe. It's been suggested. Anyway I think you're going to succeed at breastfeeding. There's just enough of the enthusiast in you, and that's what it takes in this society. You know some hospitals even have a rule against nursing for the first twenty-four hours? That's just when the stimulation is needed most."

315

"It's Victorianism," said Elspeth. "They invented bottles because breasts embarrass them."

"Maybe. But the nonsense that's been given out on this subject is just fantastic. Like this notion that a nursing mother has to drink lots of milk. How ridiculous can you get? Whatever you eat you turn into milk."

"Well, that's what I thought," said Elspeth. "Cows don't have to drink milk."

She kept looking at him. His eyes remained on her. She liked them. They had a languid intensity.

"Don't you want me to undress? Shouldn't you examine me?"

"It's not necessary. I couldn't here anyway. This is the administrator's office."

"Oh. Well, somewhere else?"

"There's no need. And I should get back upstairs."

"Oh. Okay. Well, what's your fee? I owe you for this visit."

"You don't owe *me*. Did the desk write this up as an admission?"

"No, I just walked in and asked for you. Do I owe the hospital?"

"Not if the desk took it as a personal visit. I guess you don't owe anybody."

"Let me pay you then."

"No, my pleasure. I don't have office hours. Not while I'm a resident."

"Is there a way you can be my doctor though? Or Petey's doctor?"

"Not really. And I'm not in pediatrics, actually. You should get yourself a pediatrician. Or for regular checkups and shots and stuff, you can try a well-baby clinic. At any hospital with an obstetrics department. Not here."

She gathered up the tilted seat, Peter and all, and rose. Dr. Walker rose too.

"Oh, I know what I wanted to ask. The cord. The knot. I mean, what about it? You mentioned it like it means something."

"Oh yes, the knot. That can happen in the early weeks of pregnancy, when the fetus is small enough to have room to drift around, and it drags the cord with it. And sometimes it makes loops and tangles in the cord, only usually they pull out later. But a true knot like that is comparatively rare. And when they do occur they're nearly always fatal. What happens is that during labor the knot is pulled tight, and the oxygen supply is cut off. So the baby goes to term but dies during labor. Your baby was very lucky. The knot didn't tighten."

"My God! I had no idea! What saved him? What kept it from tightening?"

"I don't know. It just didn't happen to get pulled tight, so it was harmless. Survivals like that are known. But they're extremely rare. One in a thousand."

"Wow!" She closed her eyes and shook her head, clutching the seat to her bosom while Peter slept in it. She opened her eyes. "Well, I'm keeping you. I don't know how to thank you."

"Good luck. I think you're gonna make it with the feeding."

"Are you like married or anything?"

"Well, I'm spoken for. I'm living with someone."

"Oh. That's good."

40

ELSPETH told Mrs. Brody what the doctor had said and asked if there was any objection to her going about the apartment bare-bosomed.

"Yeh, yeh, don't worry, darling. You don't mind I walk around with no shoes, no stockings, so I don't mind you should walk around with no blouse, no brazzeyair. And Brody can't see, it don't make no difference."

She did not actually throw out the scale and the sterilizer and bottles. But she climbed on a chair and hid them in the farthest corner of the hall closet shelf, behind Mrs. Brody's dusty hat boxes.

Harriet phoned in the late afternoon to ask how the mother's-helper job had gone. "Oh, terrible," Elspeth said. "Awful. You were right about that, Mama. I got fired in half an hour." She declined Harriet's offer to come and help the next morning. There's plenty of clean stuff. And I just want to lie around and rest a few days, and not even have to talk to anybody."

"I won't talk," said Harriet. "I'll be very quiet."

"No, Mama, please. I just want to be by myself a few days and wind down. Why don't you come like around Monday. And *you'll* have a chance to rest too. I spoke to a doctor who told me about a different breastfeeding method, and you're lots of help, Mama, but right now I just don't want company. It's hard to explain."

"What doctor?"

"Oh, a doctor. His name's Walker. I'll tell you when I see you Monday. Don't you ever just want to wind down?"

By midevening Peter's rash showed improvement. There was no doubt of it. She had not expected such rapid results. Whether her nipples were better she was not sure, but she thought they might be. The inflammation and cracks looked about the same, and she was not uncomfortable, even when nursing at frequent short intervals.

She wore an unbuttoned sweater, and Peter slept diaperless against her breast while she read in the wicker chair. She kept layers of cloth diapers on her lap. When he woke she sang to him.

> Ly,
> Do,
> Dydeedle do,
> Ly,

317

Do,
Dydeedle do—

When she went to bed she wore no pajama top.

Elspeth did not cover her breasts or Peter's bottom till the warmest part of the afternoon, when she got ready for a stroll with the pram. This time Mr. Brody decided to come with her. She eased the pram down the porch steps. Mr. Brody held to her arm and his cane.

"Watch out for the ice," she said.

But the sidewalks were moist and partly clear, and the walking was not bad.

He told her a meandering history, about coming to America at seventeen, and about the first boss he had worked for, a gonef, a mamzer, a shvinyak.

By evening her breasts were all but cured. Peter's rash was gone. He nursed often, with eyes closed and apparent satisfaction. "It's fantastic," Elspeth remarked to Mrs. Brody. "He said a few days, and it's only a day and a half."

She checked the Help Wanted. There was an ad by a mother, looking for someone to board a seven-month-old infant five days a week. How sad, Elspeth said to herself. That could be me, placing such an ad, one of these days all too soon. There were still no ads for night watchmen. She tried to think of other occupations in which on-the-job breastfeeding might be feasible. But no pratical ones came to mind. Disc jockey. Grape trampler. Maybe secretary to a very understanding professor, if he didn't require shorthand.

Elspeth went bare-breasted another day, as a few spots of irritation were not yet completely cleared, but the day after that she dressed normally. It was Sunday, and she had seen an ad for a singles get-together. It was sponsored as a fundraiser by a sorority of a secretarial school, and open to all unmarrieds nineteen to twenty-nine. Donation three dollars.

She found a skirt that had been brought to her with her stuff from home. She lifted the canvas-sided bassinet out of the chassis of the pram, swung up the two square metal handles that were usually tucked beneath, and carried it to the subway like an open canvas box with Peter inside.

There were not many people on the train. She nursed him while she rode.

The get-together was in a large seedy ballroom. It was crowded. There was loud recorded music. She set the bassinet on a chair beside her own, at the edge of the dance floor, and Peter slept in it. She asked a guy to get her something from the punchbowl but he said it was empty, unless she wanted an ice cube.

There must have been a few hundred people, but most of them looked at least twenty-nine and some were surely older, especially the men. They looked like rejects. A lot of the girls wore their hair piled high, and had too much makeup, and stank of perfume. She wished she hadn't come.

No one asked her to dance. A skinny mild-eyed bald fellow who seemed rather shy, perhaps in his early thirties, stood looking at her a while. "How old is the baby?" he asked finally.

"Two weeks."

Peter wakened and cried. She picked him up and gave him the breast. The bald fellow stood watching, as though trying to think of further conversation. At length he wandered away.

She left early.

She found Mrs. Brody watching television. "The party is finished already?" said Mrs. Brody. "So quick?"

"I didn't want to stay. It was kind of depressing." She sat on the leather hassock, putting Peter to her breast, and looked at the television. She recognized the educational channel. The voice told of cowboys in Argentina. Horsemen wore ponchos and flat Spanish hats. Mrs. Brody seemed fascinated.

"The most pasturized country on the face of the earth," Mrs. Brody explained. "All kinds of hay growing there, miles and miles, every direction you look."

When Harriet visited on Monday morning Elspeth did not mention the singles get-together. But she told all about the change in the breastfeeding. "This guy was absolutely marvelous," she said. "His name's Harlan Walker. And at the Lapham, of all places. He's not the same one that killed Eric. I guess they get a new resident every year or two. But he's like a magician. I don't know whether he's just a genius, or whether it's that the old guys don't keep up with the new stuff or what."

"Maybe you could make him your regular pediatrician," said Harriet.

"No. He's not a pediatrician. I don't think he takes patients of his own now anyway."

Peter wakened in his tilted seat on the kitchen counter. He yawned. Elspeth felt his diaper, took him to her chair, and opened her front.

"I like the name Harlan. Don't you?"

"I don't know," said Harriet. "I think it sounds sort of peculiar."

"The nursing is working. I'm pretty sure. Knock on wood. I mean it's actually the fourth day now without a supplementary bottle."

Harriet sighed. "Well, it's good to see you happier. But at the same time I'm sorry to see you settling down with the baby. In a life like this, at your age. Tied down. I don't know how long Mount Holyoke will hold a place for you. You shouldn't let that go. You have to begin looking toward leading a normal life. Including marriage."

"I will, Mama. I'll meet somebody. Somebody who doesn't mind Petey. Who loves Petey. I know I will. If you want something enough it happens. You make it happen. I'm only eighteen. Or almost nineteen, say nineteen. I'm not desperate."

"Well, I hope so. It's good that you're so confident."

When Peter stopped nursing Elspeth climbed on the step stool and took a can of soup from the cabinet. She picked up Peter again while stirring the soup.

"He's got a girl friend. He doesn't know I exist."

"Who?"

"Dr. Walker. Who else were we talking about? I wish he didn't have a girl friend. To him I'm just another case. Nice when he sees you, but then okay, you're cured, good bye, next case."

"You pick up the baby too much. Put him in the crib, maybe he'll sleep. You hold him too much."

"There's nothing wrong with holding him. He only wants company."

"He has to learn he can't have company all the time. You're always carrying him around."

"Oh, and I have to tell you about the knot in the cord. Don't let me forget."

"The what?"

"Something unbelievable. Wait till we're sitting down."

They set the table with soup and crackers, and a cottage cheese salad that Harriet had made. While Elspeth ate she held Peter and he nursed. She told about the cord, and how slim the chances were of a live birth in such a circumstance.

"Isn't that weird, Mama? That would have been what Daddy wanted, if Petey had been asphyxiated in labor. The blessing in disguise. Isn't it just typical of Daddy's bum luck that Petey happened to be the one in a thousand where the knot didn't tighten?"

Harriet shook her head but didn't speak.

"I mean, poor Daddy. My poor Daddy. Somebody up there hates him, like he says. The two sons he loved and that he wanted to live, they die. And Eric especially by such a fluke. And then the grandson he wanted to die, and who was marked for death, doesn't die. He escapes by a fluke. It's so strange. Crazy."

She saw that Harriet's eyes were wet. Harriet still said nothing and again shook her head a little.

"I didn't mean to upset you, Mama. But that knot, a thing like that, I couldn't keep it a secret."

"I know. Fate plays strange tricks sometimes."

"Do you think we should tell Daddy? I mean, maybe it would convince Daddy that God watches over Petey. Or that he was meant to live."

"No. I wouldn't say anything."

"I guess you're right. He'd probably just say that God has a sick sense of humor."

"Your father has suffered plenty on account of you. Just leave him alone. Don't talk about it."

They ate silently. Elspeth moved Peter to the other breast and ate with her left hand.

"Well," she said, "anyway tell Dad the money he got from the Blumenthals is what Petey and I are living on now. So tell him thanks. I appreciate it now, even though I didn't then."

"And what will you do when the money's gone?"

"Well, for the next three weeks I'm just taking it easy. Not even think about a job. Just relax. And then I'll start looking. And there's another idea I'm gonna look into, after these three weeks of relaxing. I've been thinking I'd like to support myself and Petey by having my own little fix-it shop. You know, fix irons, blenders, vacuum cleaners, mowers, all kinds of appliances, and umbrellas, anything. I'd be very good at that. And then I could nurse Petey at work. I thought maybe the Small Business Administration could help me get a loan. And I'll write to different manufacturers and see how many will give me a franchise as an authorized repair center. I already know where to get parts for lots of things. I'd seek out a good location, maybe like Brookline or someplace, where it's middle class but dense, and I'd be The Fix-It Lady. It would be a good business for meeting people, too. I just woke up with this idea this morning."

Harriet shook her head.

"And as an alternative to that," said Elspeth, "I'll apply to Sears Roebuck about a job in one of their service centers. Good skilled help can't be that easy for them to find, and they shouldn't mind a nursing mother out back in a repair depot."

"Elspeth, I don't know what to make of you. Next you'll tell me you're starting your own hardware store."

"I thought of that. A lot of towns don't have any. But a fix-it shop would take a lot less capital."

Harriet shook her head again. "You're in a dream world. Living like this, trying to raise a child like this. You insist on finding out the hard way. Things aren't like that. It's different for these actresses that are rich."

After lunch Elspeth gave Harriet Marvin Gilbert's letter to read.

Harriet held the letter long, as though rereading several times. It surprised Elspeth that the letter brought tears to Harriet's eyes.

"What's this erased here?"

"You mean at the bottom?" said Elspeth. "He wrote 'affectionately,' and then he erased it and changed to to 'as ever.' "

Harriet seemed to read it through again. "It's a beautiful letter," she said finally.

"I know. Whenever I'm low I take it out and read about how terrific I am."

Harriet left in early afternoon. Elspeth walked with her to the bus stop, pushing the pram.

At the bus stop Harriet's eyes moistened again.

"The house is so empty without you," she said.

"Wasn't it empty when I was at Mount Holyoke?"

"Yes, it was. But then we got used to having you again."

During the next several days Peter did appear to be moving toward a schedule. When he slept by day it was sometimes three hours at a stretch, and awake he occasionally did not bother with the breast for an hour or more at a time. At night, though, he took sucks at intervals in his sleep, just as in the first day at the hospital. She always took him to bed with her, to make up for not being able to carry him about all day inside her clothing like an African tribeswoman. Sometimes the stirring of tiny fingers on the softness of her breast felt remarkably sexy.

His face grew even more beautiful. One day he seemed to focus, and stared up at her face, fixedly and open-mouthed, as though marveling at it.

"Hey," she said.

"Look, those eyes," said Mrs. Brody. "He looks like he knows what he's looking."

"Peteyboy, you're so alive," said Elspeth.

How could people refer to a baby as an it? Clearly that little face was far more alive, far busier receiving and sorting impressions than any adult she knew. People thought of infancy as such an empty time, yet you had only to look at Petey to know it was the busiest, most intellectually occupied time of life. Every moment you processed floods of data, figuring out by trial and error that the patterns you saw represented objects, that this hand was part of you, that a tit meant food, that images of a certain kind implied a certain distance, or spatial relationship, that day alternated with night.

"God, Petey. You're so alive. You're so nice. You're the most wonderful thing I ever did. I love you so."

Maybe the real times were the beginning and the end of life. When all was new, fresh, like for Petey, and when you faced the grave as Gramps had. Maybe at these two times you really saw. You had the clarity that artists struggle to glimpse. In between, for the long middle of your life, you fumbled around, highly impressed with your own wisdom, and made every kind of asinine error.

The park benches were clear of snow, and she had a favorite one where she sometimes sat with a black girl whose baby was a few weeks older than Peter. It was on a hillock, just inside the wall, and before them lay a vista of snow fields.

"Your baby don't cry much," the black girl said, rocking her pram. "You better take him to a doctor and check that out. It could mean he's retarded."

"I don't think he's retarded," said Elspeth.

"Well, I wouldn't be so sure, if I was you. When a baby don't cry, that's a sign. A baby is sposed to cry. You take *my* baby, he cries a lot."

"My baby used to cry," Elspeth said, "but now I carry him around next to me a lot at home, and keep him next to me at night, and I guess he's happier. Like if you ever notice pictures of babies in Africa, like in the National Geographic, they're in their mother's clothes, next to the mother's body, with only the head out, and they're not crying."

"What's Africa got to do with it?" the black girl said.

As Elspeth strolled home Peter lifted himself upon his arms in the pram, and stared forward into the whiteness of its plastic lining under the canopy.

"Hey! Petey! You're too young to push yourself up on your hands like that. The book says seven weeks for that. What's the matter, didn't you read that book?"

Harriet visited every few days. Once she raised the question of circumcision again. "Mark and Eric were circumcised," she said.

"So what? What's that got to do with Petey? I like him the way he is."

"Well, they never complained about it," said Harriet.

"They didn't have any choice about it. Who did it? Some rabbi? A mohel, I mean? Or in a hospital?"

"It was in a hospital."

"Well, I don't want to stick Petey in a hospital again if it isn't necessary. And I don't want him tampered with."

Another time Harriet told her that Daddy was thinking of going to court to have the baby taken away.

"Can he do that?" said Elspeth.

"I don't know. He asked Mr. Rosenbaum, and Mr. Rosenbaum said he'd have to show you're an unfit mother. I suggested talking to Rabbi Quint. Or that Rabbi Quint talk to you and Dad both."

"Well, if Rabbi Quint can bring us together it's fine with me. I want to be reconciled."

"I know you do."

And on another occasion Harriet remarked to her that her figure was coming back nicely.

She got around finally to answering Marvin Gilbert. She wrote at the kitchen table.

Dear Mr. Gilbert,

Thank you. I guess I never did realize what a beautiful person you are. When Petey is older I will tell him about you.

I really hope Amethyst is okay.

Best,
Elspeth Baker

She wrote to Harlan Walker also.

Dear Dr. Walker,

I want to tell you the advice you gave me worked beautifully. The diaper rash and the nipple problem were both gone within two days, and I mean completely gone, with no ointments or medication. Petey is nursing okay and not crying. He is going longer and longer periods like you said he would and I think he is really getting on a schedule by himself.

You certainly know whereof you speak. Either you are a medical wizard or else the training has certainly improved since my other old doctor went to school. Anyway I can't thank you enough.

Your fiancee is very fortunate. So are all your future patients. If you ever settle down to private practice anywhere in the greater Boston area or southeastern New England please let me know, so I can be your first patient. I mean that. So do let me know.

Sincerely,
Elspeth A. Baker

Her bank statement arrived. The canceled checks included the thousand dollar one. Her interest for the month was five dollars and three cents.

At the beginning of February there was a thaw. Mrs. Peress invited them to come up and sit on her porch. Around the roof of the porch, which was the floor of the Polish man's porch, a fringe of great icicles dripped and shone.

Mrs. Peress squinted at Elspeth suspiciously through her two magnifying lenses. The baby seemed to puzzle her.

"Your husband died, or what?"

"I didn't have a husband."

The three rocking chairs kept creaking in perpetual disunison. Elspeth tried to bring them into harmony, but she could not, because Mrs. Peress and Mrs. Brody rocked out of phase.

Elspeth knew when Mrs. Peress discussed her in Yiddish with Mrs. Brody, though she could only guess at the gist of it. Mrs. Peress seemed to refer to her always as the shikse.

"I'm not a shikse," Elspeth said after a while.

This silenced Mrs. Peress for a time, as though she were uncertain now whether Elspeth understood Yiddish or not.

Next morning a bunch of colossal icicles fell past her window. She heard them shatter.

After breakfast she went strolling with Peter. At the curbs the wheels of the pram descended into swirling rivulets. A light breeze played with torn ends on the billboards. The sky was a cloudless blue. The shadow of the pram's canopy was sharp on the blanket, with Peter's face in the shade.

She crossed the avenue, and took one of the main streets leading out of the intersection, that she never explored before. She had awakened that morning with an idea about how to squeeze extra interest from her checking account, almost as though she had dreamed it. She had pondered it while she nursed and during breakfast. She tried to reason it through now while she walked.

Suppose I open another checking account far away by mail, in California, or Alaska. And meanwhile keep the account I have here, in the Eggleston-Uphams Bank and Trust. Now, suppose I write a check on each bank and deposit each bank's check in the other bank, in equal amounts. Ten dollars each or a million dollars each, it doesn't matter, so long as both checks are for equal amounts. Nothing happens. They cancel each other out.

The two checks cross the country in opposite directions. Each bank credits me with a million dollars when I give it the other bank's check for the deposit. Tentatively of course—neither bank would let me walk in and draw hard cash against the uncollected funds. But then each bank receives its own check back through the clearing house, and in each bank the computer subtracts a million dollars from my account. I'm back where I was at the start. In each bank my balance is the same as it was at the beginning. No profit, no loss.

Each bank adds a million and subtracts it again. How long would the whole thing take? How long for my deposit by mail to cross the country and for both checks to come back to their own banks? A week? Ten days? Now, suppose my check on the faraway bank is deposited in the savings part of my account in the Eggleston-Uphams. They credit me with a million. But I've also mailed an Eggleston-Uphams check to the faraway bank, and before the clearing houses bring it back to the Eggleston-Uphams I have to give the teller a transfer slip moving the million from savings to checking so the computer will have it to subtract.

And for the days that the million was in savings, the computer also credits me with daily interest.

What's a week's interest on a million dollars? It seemed to be well over nine hundred, as she figured now in her head. The phony million would evaporate in a week, but the week's interest would remain. Could she really make nine hundred dollars like that? There had to be a catch.

Before her the street turned downward. Far off, beyond the hill's bottom, she could see storage tanks, and a thin curve of empty beach, and tiny whitecaps on the blue ocean.

She descended. A smelly bus climbed past her. Streams split around dirty melting chunks and joined again.

The slope leveled finally, but down here she could no longer see the ocean. None of the stores here were boarded up, and at the intersections there were taverns. The people were white. Some blocks ahead a high expressway crossed above the street on fat pilings. Peter had awakened. "Hey, Stinkypoo, you did something," she said to him.

In front of a corner gas station a lady in a green denim jacket and green denim trousers was chipping with a shovel at the half-frozen edge of a black-speckled old snowbank, as though trying to widen the approach. Elspeth asked if she could use the washroom.

"Sure. Wait a minute. I'll get you the key." She tried to plant the shovel in the snowbank, but it struck ice and clattered to the muddy pavement. She seemed to curse under her breath. "My man goes and plows all night for the city when they need him, and for his own place he does a half-assed job."

Elspeth followed her with the pram to the door of the office. The lady was slight, with graying blond hair cut short and a lined face. She opened a drawer in an ancient rolltop desk and Elspeth saw a fat pistol in it. She gave Elspeth the key.

Elspeth wheeled the pram around to the washroom door and locked the brake.

When she had cleaned him she shut herself in and gave him both breasts. She heard the continual whir of tires on the elevated expressway nearby. Through the cinderblock wall she heard a metallic hammering in the repair bay. When Peter finished he smiled, still at the nipple. She saw his gums. She had seen his smiles before. The books said they were only gas smiles, not to be taken seriously at his age, but she had been doubting that more and more. This one she was certain was real.

She brought back the key. She was holding Peter. The lady in green denim was lounging in the swivel chair. A small electric space heater sat on the floor, tilted to throw its glow at her. On the rolltop's upper ledge stood a small potted plant and a picture of two children. "All set?" the lady said. "I thought you must have fell in."

"I was feeding the baby."

"Oh. Out baby-sitting, are you? Or is that your little brother? Or sister?"

"He's my son."

"Come on, now. How old are you?"

"Today's my birthday as a matter of fact. I'm nineteen. I know I look younger. A couple of times people in the park thought I was a sitter."

"Nineteen? I took you for about sixteen. Are you married? Or maybe these days I should know better than to ask that."

Elspeth had loosened the hood. "See? Look at his hair. He's really my baby."

"He's a beautiful baby, that's for sure. The eyes on him. But he ought to be, with a mother like you. You're one gorgeous kid."

"Thanks. I'm not bad but I'm not in the gorgeous category."

"Well, I sure wouldn't mind looking like you. I'd be an actor or a model or something. I'm an ugly duckling myself. But like I tell my daughter, it's what you are inside that counts. Everybody gets middle-aged and ugly anyhow."

Elspeth handed over the key. "Thanks for the bathroom and the compliments," she said. "You've made it a happy birthday."

"Oh, yeah, happy birthday." She opened the drawer and shut it, dropping the key and its holder across the pistol. "You don't happen to know a good boy that'd like a job pumping gas, do you?"

"What are the hours?" Elspeth asked.

"Twelve-thirty to eight-thirty. A five-day week. Monday to Saturday, and he'd be off Wednesdays. All we pay's minimum wage. But with hours like that he could even go to school mornings if he wants. And the evening's not exactly shot when he gets off at eight-thirty, like if he wants to go out once in a while. Do you know somebody?"

In the repair bay someone shouted at someone else.

"Well, *I* know something about cars," Elspeth said. "Does it have to be a boy?"

The woman's steel-gray eyes narrowed. Elspeth saw them go to the baby and back to herself.

"I can change tires, do a lube. A tune-up if you want. And anybody can pump gas and wash windshields and stuff."

"Where'd you learn?"

"Helping my brothers, mostly."

"Well, I don't know," the woman said. Her arms rested on the arms of the swivel. "Actually it seems to me it's against the law anyway not to consider a girl. Or it should be. It's discrimination. I'm with *you*, kid."

"There's just one thing," said Elspeth. "I'm breastfeeding my baby. I'd have to bring him. But he's a happy baby, and I have a little baby seat he'd stay in—I could put it on the floor in the office here, like in the corner there out of the way, and I could feed him a few minutes now and then when it doesn't interfere. Like if a customer came I'd put him down and run out."

"Well, I don't see what's wrong with that, just between us girls. Yeah, I know those seats. You could put him right up on the desk here if you like. Well, why not. Lemme just ask my husband. Vinnie!" she bellowed through the open door that separated the office from the repair bay.

Nobody came.

"You mean like you'd give him a couple of licks between cars. I don't see anything

326

wrong with that," she said to Elspeth. "Hey! Vinnie! C'mere a minute!" she yelled again. "I'll tell you kid," she said to Elspeth, "the main thing is, we need somebody we can depend on. If you're one of these characters that calls in sick all the time, or just don't show up, forget it. But if you're dependable, then I say how a woman feeds her child is her own business. Just turn your back to the window, that's all."

A big man with a flat smeared face filled the door of the repair bay. He stepped up into the office. A screwdriver hung in his hand. He had bushy reddish hair, lighter than Elspeth's, swept back on either side of the bald part.

"You got any objections to a woman taking the Hennessy kid's place?" the woman asked.

"Well, I've got nothing against women. I've put up with *you* for sixteen years." His voice was almost a drawl. He looked at Elspeth. "Worked in a gas station before, have ya?"

"I worked in a hardware mostly, and I've done electrical work and plumbing professionally. What I've done with cars has been in the family mostly."

"She says she can change tires," the woman said. "Do tune-ups, even."

"I can do a lot of things," said Elspeth. "Adjust brakes. Replace a muffler, and without wrecking the whole exhaust line. You know, some guys, every piece they take off, it wrecks the next piece. I do it right."

The man gave a slow nod.

"Are you gonna need references?" Elspeth asked him.

"Naw, I don't need no references. If you're no good we'll fire you fast enough. Just give Chrissie your name and address and social security. And phone." He turned to go but then turned again. "Chrissie, start her next week. It makes the bookkeeping easier." He stepped down to the repair bay.

The woman wrote all the information on the desk blotter. "Okay, snookums, looks like you got yourself a job. Pleased to meet you. I'm Chris O'Banion. Okay. We'll see you Monday then, twelve-thirty, and let's hope you work out. Us girls have got to stick up for each other, that's my opinion, or nobody else will."

As Elspeth came outdoors a massive trailer truck lumbered on the overhead expressway that came within feet of sheltering a far corner of the garage. She steered the pram back toward home. But after a few steps she turned and looked again at the gas station. SALTMARSH SERVICE, the sign said. In smaller letters below it said VINCENT DE P. O'BANION, PROP. Beyond the further cinderblock wall the front of a dark red tow truck stuck out. She checked the location. Saltmarsh Avenue Extension at Smelter Street. She felt good.

She turned away and pushed the pram. On the way up the long hill she panted, but she enjoyed the effort. It seemed to cleanse her lungs.

The million-dollar checks came to her mind. It couldn't possibly work. But why not? It didn't even seem illegal. No check bounced. Each bank added a million to your account, but before any problem of collecting funds could arise they had already wiped away the million. Their books balanced, and they were happy.

41

THERE was an agreeable tiredness in her legs when at last she dragged the pram backwards up the porch steps. A birthday card with a pretty teenager embossed on it had come from Harriet. Two crisp ten-dollar bills and a five were enclosed.

She broke crackers into her soup and told Mrs. Brody about her new job.

The interest for one week on a million dollars would be nine-hundred-and-sixty-one dollars and eleven cents. She calculated it in the evening. Would two checks really cancel each other out so neatly, without bouncing?

Better not to find out. It wasn't worth going to jail. She didn't need that kind of money. Her wages at the gas station would be more than enough.

She took her checkbook and a bank statement with canceled checks from the drawer and looked at the sets of computer digits that lined the bottom of every check. Two sets of computer digits were the same on all her checks. Sometimes she had helped Daddy balance the Sawyer's Hardware checkbook, and she had noticed them before.

The second string of computer digits she recognized as her account number. The third set, at the bottom right, appeared only on canceled checks returned with her statement. That third set of angles and blots was recognizably the value of each check. Some bank must have put it on in transit. Probably the first bank to see it. But always a long row of zeros, ending at last in the amount. On the fourteen-dollar rent check it said ⑈000000 ⑋400⑈ . . Apparently the computer was designed to handle any check up to $99,999,999.99. Provided of course that no subtraction resulted in a negative balance to set off blinking red lights and alarm bells.

She did her calisthenics. The long uphill walk had made it easy to sleep.

Sometimes she dozed, aware of the touch of Peter's lips and fingers. She heard the steady groan of a plow and the clank of its chains.

When she awoke in daylight she lay without stirring.

Maybe she could open a faraway account with a small balance, and cancel out two little-bitty checks against each other that wouldn't hurt anybody. Just to find out. And then close out the faraway account.

Because how could she go through the rest of her life not knowing the answer to this?

Maybe afterward she would tell Mr. Hudson what she had discovered, and explain to him how a flaw in the system left banks open to losing hundreds and thousands.

She would be a heroine of the banking industry. They would hire her as a junior vice-president.

She would lecture on it at a convention of bankers and all the banks would plug the leaks. The chairman of the Federal Reserve would praise her for averting catastrophe. We have located a major hidden cause of inflation that we never knew about, the President of the United States told a press conference. It took a nineteen-year-old woman to call it to our attention.

Peter's eyes popped open. She was certain he looked right at her. He smiled. She saw his gums. She laughed, and stretched her arms, lifting him high above her.

She lowered him, and put her feet to the cold floor. "Okay, Stinkums," she said, and carried him to the bathroom.

Elspeth pushed the pram to the library.

She asked the librarian if there was a book that listed all the banks in the United States. The young mulatto one didn't think so, but searched the reference shelves, and asked the older lady. There wasn't.

Elspeth steered Peter to Leo & Walter's. She placed grocery bundles around him in the pram.

On the way home it occured to her that in every major city there is probably a First National Bank of wherever. All she had to do was pick a city and confirm through telephone information that there was a bank by that name. You could dial Directory Assistance anywhere in the country for free.

When she had taken off Peter's flannel and strapped him into his seat she took the directory from the black telephone table. She studied the map of area codes on its back cover.

She dialed Directory Assistance in a city on the West Coast and asked the number for the First National Bank.

"What branch?" the lady said. "I show about twenty branches."

"Oak Street," she said.

"I don't show an Oak Street," said the lady.

"I guess I better check again, thanks," said Elspeth.

She tried another West Coast city. This time she asked for the Pacific National Bank. The operator took a while. "I have a Pacific Northern," she offered.

"That's it," said Elspeth. "The Pacific Northern."

Simple. She had the name of a bank and knew what city it was in. She collected Peter in his seat, and the rattles he had dropped, and placed him on the kitchen counter.

Dear sirs:

I wish to open a regular checking account in your bank for my convenience as I make frequent business trips to your area.

My check for $100 is enclosed as the initial deposit.

Social Security and other vital statistics are listed below.

Maybe she shouldn't tie up so much money out there. But the hundred sent west would not be lost. She could always get it back by writing a check.

She put her letter into the drop.

She bought a fresh pack of Mr. Brody's brand and put it in her coat.

She strolled by display windows. At the store where she had bought the crib she remembered a mobile she had seen there then. She went in and bought it, and the black man helped her clamp it to the rim of the pram.

The little painted cow-jumped-over-the-moon figures dangled on their strings above Peter. At the curbs they swung wildly and she stopped to untangle them.

As she approached the house the sky was beginning to brighten. The snow chunks made shadows. Peter was asleep. She sat on the porch steps, with the pram braked on the walk.

Maybe the West Coast bank would simply return her check and advise her that new accounts must be opened in person.

Or maybe they would ask the Eggleston-Uphams for a reference. And Mr. Hudson would grow suspicious.

Maybe she had better just forget this whole thing. Just wait a while, and ask for her hundred dollars back.

It's because I'm alone too much, she told herself. When you're isolated from your contemporaries, you start to get off the beam.

Behind her the carved door opened. Someone stepped out onto the porch and stopped. She looked around.

"Elspeth!" the pudgy figure said. He wore a well-cut suit of gray flannel, with vest, and a pink shirt without his overcoat. The little goatee was trimmed neat and square. "I've been waiting inside for you."

"Rabbi Quint! For goodness sake! Who sent you? My father or my mother?"

"Well, the thought just grew. Why don't you come in? Let's talk."

"Gee, I'd rather not wake Petey just yet. We'll come in soon, and I'll make you some coffee. Why don't you wait inside. Are you in an awful hurry?"

But he didn't go in.

"How's my Dad?" she said. "What do you think?"

"I think you know how he feels," the rabbi said quietly.

"Poor Daddy," she said. "He'd be a terrific grandpa if he'd let himself. He loves kids."

"Your mother's the one I'm worried about. Your father at least has the ability to express his feelings. But your mother bottles everything up. She represses."

"Do you think so? I thought she was pretty good, considering. Rabbi, I wish you'd go in. Or at least get your coat. You'll catch your death."

"Elspeth, what do you intend to do?"

"What do you mean?"

"Bring up this child? Without a husband?"

"I'll find a husband. Somebody will marry me. Look, living my life over there are things I'd do differently. I guess I was pretty stupid. But one thing I'm sure of, if I give up Petey I'll regret it someday. And if I marry the right guy, who loves

Petey, and have more kids—there has to be somebody like that. Even if it takes seven years to find the right one I'll only be twenty-six. It'll be like a happy ending. And Mama and Dad will be so glad then I kept Petey. They'll be so glad. They'll love him so. They'll thank me."

"And until then what? Welfare checks?"

"I'm not on welfare. I'm able-bodied. I'm starting a job on Monday."

"What kind of job?"

"Well, I'll tell Mama directly. I don't want her to hear secondhand. It's a respectable job. And I'll be able to take Petey and feed him during the day."

"Elspeth, I'm sure eventually you'll find a husband. But isn't it common sense that your choice of husbands would be far greater if you weren't encumbered?"

"Maybe. I suppose."

"And as far as work goes, wouldn't your options there too be far wider if you finished college? And wouldn't the baby be far better off with adoptive parents who want him and can afford the proper home, schooling, advantages?"

"Maybe. Maybe not."

"Why not?"

"There's no guarantee."

"There's no guarantee of *any*thing in this life. but what advantage is there to you *or* the child in the present setup?"

"Well, breastfeeding, for one."

"Which I hear isn't working too well."

"It's working now. It wasn't, but it's okay now."

"And mustn't you admit there's one great immediate advantage in turning the child over for adoption, if it gives your parents some peace? You're breaking their spirits. I don't say either one is going to get sick tomorrow, God forbid, but a broken heart does shorten life. They're strong—God knows they've shown fantastic fortitude in the face of heartbreak in recent years. But how much more can they take? How do we know which straw is the last? Elspeth, we can't bring Mark back. We can't bring Eric back. But this present situation is one that can still be corrected. Or at least much improved."

She tightened her face.

"Have you considered psychotherapy?" he asked behind her.

She didn't answer. Above the pram the mobile figures jiggled. It meant Peter was stirring, though he was hidden from her in the pram, and would waken soon.

"There's not one of us that can't profit from psychotherapy," he said. "Consider, Elspeth. Is it guilt? Are you punishing yourself? Do you feel that because your brothers' lives were taken from them, that you're not entitled to a happy life? That because *their* lives were smashed, you owe it to them to make your life a shambles?"

"No, it isn't that. First of all it isn't just Mark and Eric. There were brilliant kids in Europe that ended up in gas chambers. Sure, sometimes I say, look, everybody in the world has some kind of snafu happen to him, why should I expect to be the exception? I got off relatively light. I have a beautiful child. I just want to try damn hard to avoid any more mistakes in the future."

331

The figures on threads over the pram jiggled again, the crescent moon with a grinning face in profile, the cow, the cat with his fiddle, the dog, the dish, the spoon, the smiling stars.

"Do you think," Rabbi Quint said behind her, "that you're giving your parents a little replacement for Mark or Eric? Mark and Eric can't be replaced. They can't be brought to life. Your parents accept that. What they want is for Elspeth to be brought back to life."

"Look, Rabbi, it isn't that at all. I thought of that too."

"What is it then?"

"I had an accident, that's all. I got knocked up, and with the wrong guy. And then I had such a terrific baby I couldn't part with him. I took one look at Petey and I thought, my God, this could be the most fantastic kid I'll ever have."

"You think it's so simple? Nothing's that simple."

"I think it's that simple, yes. If it were these deep, dark subconscious hang-ups I wouldn't have thought of them myself, would I? It's just that I look at Petey and I think, wow, if I was put on this earth for anything it was to be this kid's mother."

"Why didn't you go through with the abortion? You didn't know then it would be such a fantastic baby, as you put it."

"Are you in favor of abortions?"

"That's not what I said. I asked why you didn't go through with it."

"Because I didn't feel like it."

The rabbi sneezed. She looked back at him. He had produced a handkerchief. He wiped his nose. He wiped his goatee.

"Look," said Elspeth, "you're trying to give me advice, and you haven't got any more sense than to stand out here in freezing weather without your coat."

"You're right. I didn't expect to be out here so long."

"It's my fault." She got up. "I'm sorry. Come on in. Petey's waking up anyhow."

She drew the pram backwards up the steps. Rabbi Quint tried to help with one hand. Grocery bundles slid against Peter and he gave a cry.

"Here," said Elspeth, giving the rabbi two bags of groceries. "Take these."

In the vestibule she chained the pram to the newel post and shut the lock.

She gave the rabbi two more bundles. "Here, take this stuff to the kitchen like a good kid while I take Petey and change him. I'm sorry, I didn't mean to call you a good kid."

She lifted Peter and displayed him in his flannel.

"Look," she said. "Isn't he gorgeous? Look at that face. Those eyes."

The rabbi's nose dripped. A tear ran down the side of it. He turned and she followed him into the apartment. Pink stripes of the thinnest sort were woven into his gray flannel. He was not much taller than herself. It struck her that he was actually youngish, probably still in his thirties. Then when she had first known him, in her childhood, he must have been in his twenties, though he hadn't seemed young to her then.

"Have you met my landlady and landlord, Mr. and Mrs. Brody? This is Rabbi Quint."

"Yeh, yeh, he was in here already," said Mrs. Brody. Her white hair zigzagged in every direction. "Here, give me. I'll put away the stuff. Some she got for me anyways." She took two of the bundles. "Mh! Ih!"

"Mrs. Brody, can you do me a big favor and make Rabbi Quint a hot drink? Tea with lemon or something? He's catching cold. I want to change Petey."

"That's all right," said the rabbi.

"Sure, sure, darling. As soon as I put away. You fix up the baby."

Elspeth undid the flannel and buckled Peter to the changing table. She draped her coat over the rim of the bathtub. She bent to Peter and kissed his face.

"Are you a Petey pishuks? Or are you a Petey poo?"

The rabbi helped himself to tissues. He blew his nose. Elspeth sang while she cleaned Peter.

"Petey poo, I love you—"

"Elspeth, I'm very late for another appointment. So I'll have to make this brief. But I think you should be informed that your father intends to petition the courts to remove the child from your custody. He's quite serious about this. He's told Mr. Rosenbaum to go ahead."

Elspeth said nothing. She took fresh cotton balls and continued swabbing Peter.

"Now, if you'll agree to undertake psychotherapy, I'll do my best to dissuade your father from this court action. Psychotherapy can't hurt. You can only profit, and gain new insights. We can all use it. I've spoken to your father, and there's no doubt that psychotherapy is desperately needed here. If you were separated from the child by force, without self-understanding, it would be very traumatic for you." He blew his nose. "Will you make a commitment to therapeutic counseling?"

"And if I don't?"

"Then it's too bad. Your father will instruct Mr. Rosenbaum to take immediate action. And if the baby's taken away before you're ready I'm sure you'll become very depressed and then you'll seek counseling on your own. It's better to do it sooner."

"Mr. Rosenbaum can't get Petey taken away, just like that."

"He can try. A lawyer can always try. And being pulled into court is never pleasant. What's your objection to therapy?"

"Because the whole idea is for some shrink to talk me into giving up Petey. And if he doesn't succeed Daddy will go ahead with his court action anyhow. It's a waste of time. I don't need it. It'll only get me upset and when a nursing mother gets upset it interferes with the milk supply. What does Daddy know about it anyway? Daddy hasn't even seen Petey. He's afraid to see Petey. He's afraid he might love him."

"But I've been here. What if I'm asked to testify? This place is squalid. Filthy."

"I dust. I vacuum. I do what I can."

"The wallpaper's falling off the wall."

"In a couple of spots. I'm gonna fix that."

"The odor when I walked in was overpowering. Why do you think I was so ready to stay out on the porch?"

"Well, elderly people don't like to open windows much. They want to save the heat. And it's very hard for them to climb in and out of the tub."

"This isn't a filthy place!" Mrs. Brody called from the kitchen. "Since June, I didn't see one cockroach. We went away the whole day, to mine daughter and he cleaned them all out, the exterminator. He went all around. You couldn't find me in here one cockroach."

"See? She heard," said Elspeth. "You hurt her feelings."

"And the smell," Mrs. Brody continued, "they explained me they can't do nothing. I complained it already. It's from rotten in the wood. When a house gets old, it's like a person gets old."

Peter grunted and pushed, his face briefly wearing an exaggerated expression like a constipated adult straining on a toilet seat.

"Oh, look at that! I just put a clean diaper on him, and he has another b.m.! Peteyboy, that is a dirty trick." She unfastened the diaper.

"Is the baby receiving proper medical care?"

"Of course. We have an appointment tomorrow, as a matter of fact. I'm taking him for shots."

"Elspeth, listen to me. There's no doubt Mr. Rosenbaum will ask me to testify, and I would have to give my honest opinion that in your case some psychotherapeutic attention is indicated. I've known you nearly all your life, Elspeth, and you've always seemed to me somewhat strange."

"What about Daddy? Don't you think my father needs a shrink?"

"With that I certainly agree. Heartily. Your whole family has always struck me as somewhat disturbed. But your father hasn't moved into a slum to try to raise an infant all alone. From the court's point of view the child's interests are paramount."

"You mean to say you'll go into court and help them get my baby away? And you came over here to collect evidence and say the place is dirty and stuff?"

"It's not why I came over."

"You'll say it though. And if my father tells Mr. Rosenbaum to ask them to commit me to the McLean Hospital or someplace so they can get the baby away you'll testify I need it. Won't you. You sneaky son of a bitch. Get out."

"Not right away. Just relax a bit. Let's consider your choices realistically and get them in perspective."

"I've made my choice. And if your perspective is that I should give up Petey we have nothing to talk about. I don't need to justify it to you."

"Calm down."

"Don't tell me to calm down. You get out and I'll calm down. I told you to get out. Who invited you here anyway?"

"I'm here to help you."

"You're here for my father. Tell him to come here and make his own threats. Tell him to come and see his own grandson first. If he won't even look at him I don't want his opinion on what should be done with him. And I'm about to breastfeed Petey as soon as I rinse his diaper, and I don't want you here getting me mad. The madder I get the more you'll tell Mr. Rosenbaum I need psychiatric treatment, right?"

"Young lady, you're headed for trouble."

"And you're headed for a shitty diaper right in the face."

"You wouldn't react so violently if you didn't sense some merit in what I'm trying to say."

"I could call a cop and have you arrested for trespassing."

"Go right ahead," he told her. "Call the police."

His display of cool seemed to her calculated. "I'll do better than that," she said. "If you're not out of here when I count three you get this in the face. One!" She swung back the arm that held the diaper.

He moved as though to grasp the arm. She gestured with the diaper and he hesitated. He withdrew from the bathroom, trying to shut the door. She extended a foot to hold it.

She followed him into the hallway.

"If any of that gets on my suit," he said, "you'll pay for the cleaning."

"*Me? Me* pay for it? Daddy said you're good for thirty-two gees a year!"

"Well, your Daddy exaggerates."

"In the face! Two!"

"If that gets in my eyes—if I get an infection from that—"

"Here it comes, Fatso! Three!"

But he had grabbed his overcoat from the arm of the sofa and fled, slamming the door.

SHE nursed Peter on the living-room sofa, her feet on the hassock.

"I shouldn't have lost my cool, but he really got me," she said to Mrs. Brody.

"Everybody wants to put somebody in the insane asylum," said Mrs. Brody. "Brody too they wanted. Maybe we should all go in the insane asylum. Maybe everybody would be happy there."

Mr. Brody had started briefly from a doze in the high-backed corner chair when the door had slammed, but now he slept, his head to the side, his jaw slack.

"I guess he meant well," Elspeth continued. "My father got to him first so I suppose he started seeing it all from my father's point of view." She stroked Peter's head. "But can they really have Petey taken away like that? Can they? Would the court do that? There's no law against illegitimacy. I don't *think* there is."

"I don't know, darling. Why should they take it? If the baby has a black eye and bleeding and a broken arm, and the mother and father is a couple of drunks, so they take away, married, not married. But if they see a nice baby and the mother is a nice girl and she's taking care of it, they wouldn't take away."

"Would you come as a witness and tell the judge I take good care of the baby?"

"If it's necessary, and my feet is all right, and I could walk, so I'll come. But I don't think it would be necessary. Tell the judge he could call me up on the telephone, I'll tell him you had a mistake, you had a baby, but you're a nice girl, he should for a daughter-in-law have such a nice girl, you take Brody for an airing, you clean up with the vacuum, everything."

When Peter had been put to bed Elspeth brought in the cow-jumped-over-the-moon mobile that had been on the pram. She fastened it to the crib rail. Peter stared up at the figures. They bounced lightly in the air.

Harriet did not phone her that evening, so she knew her parents had not yet heard from Rabbi Quint. She did not phone Harriet either. She called Cindy.

Cindy was cramming for a Saturday morning exam and cut her short. But they agreed to meet for lunch at noon near Boston University, after Cindy's class and after Elspeth had taken Peter to the well-baby clinic.

The temperature Saturday morning was six degrees, but on the windy sidewalk and on the platform of the elevated it seemed far below zero. However the clinic's waiting room was steamy, full of wraps and scarves. Peter slept against her while she gave information to a delicate-featured receptionist as young as herself. She drew off her mittens with her teeth and tried stiffly to massage the numbness.

Only one seat was available, so the canvas bassinet, which she had removed from the pram and brought with her, remained on the floor at her feet amid wet boots. Elspeth scanned the faces of the other babies. A couple were interesting, but none compared with Peter.

"Mrs. Baker," the girl called to her finally.

Elspeth undressed Peter in a little windowless room. The doctor was in his twenties or early thirties, with hair precisely combed, and seemed either shy or very businesslike. He talked little, not even acknowledging what she told him about the breastfeeding, and his rimless glasses never met her eyes. He worked with his stethoscope and his probe light as though there were not a moment to lose. He weighed him, measured his length, and lifted him with his two index fingers, which Peter grasped and hung from.

"He seems like a healthy baby," he said, lowering him to the table.

"When do you recommend solid foods?"

"The breastfeeding seems to be doing all right. What's the hurry?"

"There isn't. I was just asking."

He took a blood sample, which Peter seemed not to mind, and put on a little bandage. Then he stabbed with a small syringe and Peter cried.

"Okay," the doctor said. "Come back in about three months for smallpox." He checked off diphtheria, tetanus and whooping cough on the card he slipped between two of her fingers while she held and patted Peter.

Cindy had gotten to the hamburger place first and taken a booth by the window. She was already holding coffee before the long pensive face. Elspeth put the bassinet on the bench and unzipped Peter once more. He kicked.

"Let's see him," said Cindy. "Hey! Wow!"

"Who does he look like?"

"He looks like your mother. On him it looks good though."

"Don't you think he looks like me?"

"He's got your hair, but mostly like your mother. And those eyes are his own."

Elspeth settled into the bench. Ice had formed on the inside of the windowglass. She held Peter. Cindy continued to stare across the table at him. "How was your exam?" Elspeth asked Cindy. "You probably got an A."

"Nobody gets an A in that course. Popes, emperors, the marriages of the Hohenstaufens, the rise of the scholastics, there's no end to it. Did you really mean that last night? You actually threatened Quint with a shitty diaper?"

"Well, he made me mad. I never liked him, even when I was little. It always sort of offended me that a man of God let himself get fat like that. If the body is the temple of the soul he should take better care of it."

"What did you do actually? You picked it up like you'd throw it?"

"Ya. And I said I'd count to three."

Cindy laughed. "I wish I'd seen it. What'd he look like?"

"Scared. I never saw him move so fast."

Cindy laughed again. "Like hard shit, was it, or all wet like?"

"It would have been pretty splattery. When they're breastfed it comes out soft."

Cindy laughed harder. Elspeth laughed too.

"Come on, it's not that funny," said Elspeth.

Cindy seemed to control herself, and lifted her coffee. But she snorted into it and laughed uncontrollably. It made Elspeth laugh again. She saw people beginning to look at them.

"Let's not get hysterical," said Elspeth. "They'll throw us out."

Cindy reacted as though that were hilarious too. The girl came for their orders. Cindy was shaking and snorting voicelessly.

"Double hamburger with onion and ketchup, coffee black," said Elspeth.

"Same," Cindy managed, red-faced, but burst again into snorts. Elspeth laughed but stopped. Cindy kept on, trying not to look at anyone.

The girl left. Gradually Cindy calmed herself, after a few last nervous outbursts.

"Well, what else is new?" Cindy said at last.

"What else is new? Petey had his first erection this morning."

Cindy laughed.

337

"No, I'm not kidding," said Elspeth.

"You're kidding."

"I'm not. The first one I observed, anyway. While the doctor was examining him."

"Is that normal?"

"I guess it must be. I'll look it up. I know the doctor saw it and he didn't even say anything. I wanted to say 'Peetah! I'm surprised at you!'"

"Would you believe I've never seen how that happens?"

"You will, one of these days. Didn't you ever see it happen to any kid you babysat for?"

"No. I guess I was never there at the right time. I mean how does it do it? Does it pop up all of a sudden, or like gradual, or what?"

"It doesn't pop. It's gradual, but not so gradual. It's pretty fast. Usually you just notice that it's already there."

"You mean not like a spring, but like when you blow up a balloon sort of."

"Sort of. I guess. Next time you're out with a guy ask him to demonstrate."

"Oh sure."

"I remember once when we used to go to New Hampshire Mark and Eric were skinnydipping around a bend in the lake, and I was sitting on the bank in case anybody came, and guarding their clothes, and Eric had an erection while he was floating there in the water."

"What did you do?"

"Nothing. They laughed, so I laughed. He just kept floating there with it sticking up like a periscope on a submarine. I'll never forget that."

"How old were you?"

"About eleven. Ten maybe."

"Didn't you go in with them?"

"No. In my family girls were something special. They didn't take their clothes off."

"Didn't your brothers ever see you?"

"Not usually. In my underwear maybe."

"But you saw them?"

"When they went skinnydipping."

Peter squirmed and whimpered. She raised him higher against her shoulder and patted him. Then she unbuttoned. She lowered him to nurse.

"What does that feel like?" Cindy asked.

"Nice. Want to try it?"

"Massachusetts legalized abortion finally," Cindy said.

"I know."

The girl brought the hamburgers. Elspeth held Peter with one arm and ate with the other.

"Did I tell you about my job? I go to work for a gas station on Monday." She told Cindy the details.

"What about Quint," Cindy said finally. "Will there be any repercussions?"

"Well, if my father takes me to court and gets Quint to testify it'll be all the worse now, I guess. My father's talking about asking the courts to take Petey away."

"Can they do that?"

"I don't know. I don't think so. Do you think they can?"

"How would I know?"

"I know I'll fight it. Or maybe I'll run away. But if they do they do. I'll enjoy Petey as long as I can."

"Your father's a crumb."

"No, that's just his way. I'd love to be friends with him again."

"You're sick."

"Okay."

"That's two of us, of course," Cindy added.

"How's your love life?"

"Lousy. I'm still mixed up."

"Don't worry about it."

"I go out with guys," Cindy said, "and I tell myself tonight's the night. I'm gonna let it happen. But then if I sense the least unsureness or self-consciousness on the guy's part, it makes me even more unsure and self-conscious. And then I freeze up. And I start getting nasty. And if the guy *doesn't* have any unsureness or self-conciousness, you know like he's completely sure of himself, then it's even worse. All of a sudden I get scared and fight him off. Maybe I need a guy who'll go just a tiny bit further each time, and stop when I say stop."

"I think a lot of guys would agree to that if you ask them."

"A guy did," said Cindy, "but he didn't understand me or something. He started going further, or I thought he was, and I panicked again."

"Well, forget it. Some guy will marry you *because* you're a virgin. Some guy that wants a virgin. And he'll work on you slowly the whole honeymoon."

"That won't make it any different. I don't want to wait that long anyway."

"Ask a guy to just lie there, and you get on top."

"No. If I didn't do it right he'd be like grading me on my performance. I'd feel like I was going through the steps of some lab assignment."

"God, Cindy. You're exasperating."

"I know. And if my best friend can't even stand it when I talk about it how will a guy ever stand it to do it with me?"

Elspeth gave Peter the other side. She rearranged the sweater and blouse to keep her skin hidden. Cindy picked up a crescent of onion and chewed it.

"If I can't afford to live at school maybe at least I should live with some guy on weekends," Cindy said. "Just to get away from my mother and my mother's half-assed intellectual act. It never stops. Day in and day out. She thinks she's so intelligent, you know. So enlightened, so above being Jewish or parochial or anything like that. Only she doesn't realize how Jewish she is. Still a yakity-yak talker. Bla bla bla bla bla bla bla. If there's anything Jews like better than herring it's talking."

"You could go to your father weekends," said Elspeth. "Except for the girl friend, I guess."

339

"And the thing."

"What thing?"

"The brat. Her darling fifteen-year-old son. If you can picture a bushel basket full of pubic hair, that's what his head looks like. And picking his nose."

Elspeth buttoned up, and laid Peter down in the bassinet between herself and the ice-encrusted window.

"Are you seeing anybody?" Cindy asked. "Any guys?"

"Nobody."

"You don't go out?"

"With who? I'm out of touch. I'll get around to it, I guess. Maybe I'm not ready to. Or maybe it's next on the agenda, I don't know."

"Do you miss not having sex?"

"Sometimes. Petey sort of keeps my mind off it a lot. But sometimes I wish there was a guy to hold tight, and be in his arms. Only not a guy who could make me pregnant and walk away."

"He has to love you," Cindy said.

"I guess. But the main thing is an awareness, that's beyond loving. Even if we both used every kind of contraceptive. Even if neither of us wanted a baby. Even if we just wanted to make love. I'd still have to know that if there was an accident against all the odds and I conceived, he'd want that baby, because it's mine, and because it's his. It can't be okay-what-the-hell-let's. Not for me. Not anymore. I'm not sure it ever could. But I know now it can't. It has to mean everything for me. Even if it's just a lay because I'm horny. Potentially it still has to be everything. If later that's asked of it." She put the crumpled wet diaper into a plastic and looked at Cindy again. "Through Petey, and Petey's descendants, Jared and I are tied together through all eternity. And yet it was such a casual thing. Of course we didn't intend to have a baby. And we took precautions. But the potential is there, even when there's no conception, even when there's no intention of any. Even when the moment and the joy and the partner is the whole thing. Even if the potential doesn't come to fruition it still gives it a whole dimension, just because it's a potential, and if you don't know that, then you don't know where it's at. You're insensitive. Petey proved it."

"You mean," said Cindy, "like if Petey's great-great-grandchild discovers the cure for cancer, or converts the human race to the ways of peace, or settles a colony on some weird planet in another galaxy, it's all because you and Jared screwed each other in some dinky squeaky bed in South Hadley."

"Yes," Elspeth said. "Watch Petey while I get rid of this and wash my hands, okay?"

43

HER hours at Saltmarsh Service were to be from twelve-thirty to eight-thirty, but she arrived early. She had lifted the bassinet out of the pram's framework, packed Peter and her lunch and the plastic baby seat and a box of disposable diapers into it, and carried it with two hands onto the bus. An airtight diaper pail hung from her arm. Her hair was in braids, the way she had worn it at Sawyer's Hardware.

Chris was behind a car at the pumps, the nozzle in her hand. "Why so early?" said Chris. "You're not due till ha' past."

"Well, I didn't know how often the buses run. And I thought I might as well have time to look around. So if somebody needs a quart of oil or a can of dry gas or a new wiper blade I know where it is."

"Well, suit yourself. Go introduce yourself to Edgar Clish. He's the only other one we've got on the payroll now."

Elspeth put the bassinet and the pail in a corner of the office, next to a stack of cartons of oil cans, and changed Peter's diaper. The door to the repair bay was open and a radio played loud music. Out front more cars pulled in and waited at each side of the pumps. Chris wore gloves and a long quilted olive-green jacket and her breath was frosty. Elspeth fastened Peter into his tilted seat. His staring face was small in the hood. The overlong blue flannel sleeves waved or quivered with his arms, their closed mitts drooping. She tucked a little blanket over him also and set him down, seat and all, on the plank bench against the whitewashed cinderblock to watch her at the pumps.

Chris was on the further side of the pumps so Elspeth went to the first car on the near side.

"Hey, you don't have to do that," Chris said. "You're not on duty yet."

"That's okay."

The tissue dispenser was empty, so she wiped dipsticks with her fingers. There was nothing to clean windshields with. But Chris was not doing windshields, and the customers seemed not to expect it. If anybody did ask, she thought, she would fetch a disposable diaper from the office.

She had to step into the office after each car to use the cash register, and sometimes to use the credit-card machine, and each time she crossed the threshold she glanced down at Peter. He had fallen asleep in his seat, his head to the side, cheeks puffed, the oversized hood rising to a point. Most customers did not notice him, but occasionally she saw someone look at him and smile. "Is that a baby over there?" one gray-haired lady asked her.

341

"I'm going in and have my sandwich and coffee," Chris said when traffic slacked off. "I didn't have any breakfast."

"Let me take your rag," said Elspeth. She took the oil-blackened reddish cloth that hung from Chris's pocket. Chris offered the cigarette pack. "Smoke?"

"No thanks."

For a long time there were always one or more cars at the pumps.

Peter wakened and cried. She knelt to unstrap him.

"Want me to take over?" Chris asked from the swivel chair.

"No, he'll be okay." Elspeth unbuttoned her sweater and put him to her breast, fixing the flap of her coat tight about him. She fed gasoline into the rear of a car, holding Peter with one arm and the nozzle with the other.

Business quieted. She saw Vinnie drive away in the high seat of the dark red tow truck. She stepped up with Peter into the office. Chris was in the swivel, tilted back so that her feet no longer reached the floor, and sipping steaming coffee.

"Want to sit here?" Chris offered.

"No. I'll just wander around and get familiar with where parts are and stuff."

"I need hot coffee to get my blood circulating again when I come in," Chris said. "It freezes in my veins out there."

Elspeth laid Peter in the bassinet and changed his diaper. But he was not inclined to sleep so she lifted him to her shoulder. She stepped down with him into the repair bay.

Edgar Clish was working there at the front end of a car. Tools and parts lay about him on the concrete. He was a stocky young man, perhaps not more than a couple of years older than herself, florid-faced and short, but solid, almost squarish. She saw him work with concentration, breathing heavily, and squinting under his straw-colored locks. It was hard to tell if he even heard the radio's frenzied rhythms.

She came near and watched him, stroking Peter.

"Bet you're gonna ask what I'm doing," Edgar said without looking up.

"No. Does it bug you to have me watch?"

"Watch all you want. You might learn something."

He was replacing a water pump and had already bolted the new one in place, still shiny-clean. Now he was refastening the fan before it, though he had not yet attached the hose to the pump. He lifted the radiator from where it had rested on the floor against the bumper. He dropped it into position before the fan. That's dumb, Elspeth said to herself, stroking Peter. Hasn't this guy ever done a water pump? Now he'll go nuts, trying to get the plug out and the nozzle attached, in a spot practically impossible to reach behind the radiator and fan.

Hey, friend, she wanted to say, put the fitting on the pump while it's easy to get at. The fan and radiator can wait. But Edgar was perspiring, with an air of stern efficiency, and she feared he would take offense.

Elspeth wandered by the shelves, studying the labeled boxes. Edgar was bending and straining over the radiator now, struggling with a fitting he could not see in a space where his fingers had no room to maneuver. Without looking she knew it

342

from the grunts and sighs. She knew he would attempt it also from underneath and find it no easier.

Elspeth took the push broom and began cleaning the part of the bay furthest from Edgar. She pushed the broom with one hand and held Peter with the other. After a while she glanced at Edgar. He was about to slam down the hood.

"Hey!" she said. "Don't forget the air cleaner."

"Oh," said Edgar. "Ya. Thanks."

She stepped up into the office. Chris's hands hung limp on the arms of the swivel, one of them holding a cigarette.

"Do we often get slack time like this?" Elspeth asked.

"Oh, it tapers off. And all of a sudden you get as busy as a one-armed paperhanger. You'll see. Edgar's off at five, and I go home about four if I can, and fix the kids' supper, and if Vinnie gets a road call in the evening you can find yourself all alone here with five cars lined up at the pumps."

Elspeth sat on the stack of corrugated cartons.

"We should have another chair," said Chris. "Actually we did have, but it fell apart." She blew smoke. "That baby's prettier than the baby on the diaper box."

"I know," said Elspeth. "My mother said that too."

"I've got a mind to tell Vinnie to bring his good camera in and take some pictures of him. Would you mind that?"

"Oh, I'd love that. I don't have any pictures of him yet."

"Well, I'll tell Vinnie. And color film to get that hair. I'd just as soon have a picture of that kid myself. Maybe a shot of you too. Is everybody pretty in your family?"

"I don't know. When I was little I was this skinny little snotnose with eyes like saucers. I think my father made me pretty by always telling me I was."

"I don't believe that. That's not possible."

"Honest. That's how it happened."

"Naw. You may think it, but it ain't true. You're naturally pretty."

"No, because when I was little he was the only one, and then year by year more and more people said it."

"Well, maybe you blossomed gradually, and he saw the possibility first." She drew on the cigarette, looking at Elspeth. "How did you get interested in this business? I mean to be ambitious to be around a service station?"

"My two brothers were into cars a lot. And I was helping them all the time. They taught me all kinds of things. Like, do you know how to cheat Sears Roebuck on batteries?"

"No. How do you do that?"

"You don't know that?" said Elspeth. "Like if you have more than one car, like my father had his regular car plus the store truck, and my brothers always had one or two junks, you outfit them all with the best battery, with the five-year guarantee. But bought at different times naturally. And when a battery conks out you always bring in the newest guarantee card. You come in with a battery you had for four and a half years and a guarantee card that says you only had it for eigthteen months.

So they give you a new forty-dollar battery for like twelve bucks. And the new five-year guarantee card from that one you bring in in a few months with the next old one that wears out."

"Hm. Never thought of that. I wonder if Vinnie knows that. Sounds kind of dishonest though."

"Oh sure, it's dishonest," Elspeth agreed.

"I like to be honest," Chris said. "Especially when you run a business, it's a good policy. For instance Vinnie will never tell a customer he needs a new battery if the old one will hold a recharge. He'd rather tell the truth and pass up a sale."

"I like that," said Elspeth. "My father's that way too. My father will take anything for repair. Even a toaster. And a toaster is a real pain to fix. Throwing it in the barrel would be a lot more lucrative."

"Well, I see what you mean," said Chris. "Cheating a big company is one thing. But the poor shmo that comes into your store as a customer is something else again."

The pay phone rang. Chris pulled herself out of the swivel and went to it.

She spoke, and then yelled into the repair bay, holding the phone. "Edgar! Are Mrs. Kimball's snow tires on?"

"Not yet," he said.

"Why not? Hop *to* it."

"You want to pull me off Mr. Ingram's car? Vinnie said give it top priority."

"How's it doing?"

"It's all apart. They brought the wrong throw-out bearing. I thought I'd ride over myself."

"I'll mount the snow tires," said Elspeth.

"You sure you can?" Chris asked.

"If I can't even change a tire I shouldn't be here."

The lift in the repair bay was not available because Edgar had left the taken-apart car sitting on it, though the lift was not up. So Elspeth wheeled the hydraulic floor jack out to the pavement. She saw her breath in frosty puffs as she raised and lowered the handle in deep bends. Edgar was a jerk to have tied up the lift uselessly like that.

The hub caps clanged to the pavement. She found the electric bolt tightener, but there was no extension cord long enough. She took an angular hand wrench.

The bolts would not budge. She drew off her gloves in the bitter wind. But the bolts seemed frozen in place.

She fixed the wrench onto a bolt, and stood on its handle with one foot, her other foot off the ground. Even with all her weight on the wrench the bolt didn't move. She gave a little jump, holding to the car, and the bolt loosened. Once when she jumped she slid off, and the end of the wrench handle scratched her ankle through the sock. Meanwhile cars had come to the gasoline pumps and Chris was tending them.

Chris looked over, holding the nozzle. "The baby's okay," she said. "Don't worry."

When Elspeth finished with the car she found Peter still sleeping. Chris sipped coffee. Vinnie had come back and stood in the office in his leathery windbreaker. He put coins in the soda dispenser. He threw back his bushy mane and raised the can to his lips.

"How can you drink that stuff in this weather?" Chris said to him. "Brrrr. You must have Eskimo blood. My bones couldn't take it."

It was twilight when Chris left. Chris pulled a felt turban over her ears. "Good night, everybody. Take good care of Elspeth."

"You sure you trust me with her?" said Vinnie.

"I trust ya. You're too old. Elspeth, if he gets fresh with ya, take his old service revolver out of the desk and shoot him. Like an old hoss."

She asked Harriet on the phone the next morning to look for Mark's and Eric's automotive tools in the cellar. Chris and Vinnie had not mentioned it, but she knew most garages expected you to have your own tools.

"Rabbi Quint told us about his visit with you."

"What did he say?"

"He said he found you hard to talk to."

"Is that all he said? Just that I was hard to talk to?"

"I think so. Why?"

On Tuesday she nursed Peter on the bus as she rode downhill on the way to work. She was directly behind the driver, where the long seats faced one another across the aisle, forward of the seats that faced front. The bassinet, with its blankets and diaper box and lunch bag inside, was beside her. When Peter stopped sucking she tickled his face with the end of a braid. He smiled and squinted.

A passenger beat suddenly on a window with the flat of her hand. "Officer! Officer!" She banged the glass again. "Driver! Stop the bus!" It was a bulging lady in a cloth coat, in the first of the forward-facing seats on the other side. The man beside her had glasses and earmuffs under the brim of an old gray hat. "Officer! Officer!"

The door folded open. There was a police car alongside. An agile policeman climbed aboard, his breath visible in the cold. He was young, beak-nosed, with earmuffs, a holstered pistol at his hip and bullets around his waist.

"There she is, officer!" The lady rose, chunky and ruddy, and pointed at Elspeth. "Arrest her! Indecent exposure!"

Elspeth glanced down, closing her coat more tightly.

"She was nursing the baby, officer!"

Elspeth's jaw dropped. Then she closed her mouth and swallowed. Everyone, white and black, was looking at her. She felt herself redden.

"I saw skin!" the lady said. "Ask my husband! He saw it!"

"That's right. I saw it, officer."

"They're crazy!" said Elspeth. "I was feeding the baby, so what! I was covered up!" Her face felt hot.

"Let's get on with it," the driver said. "I'm on a schedule." He was a black man with Abraham Lincoln whiskers.

"Okay, okay, off the bus," said the policeman. He waved them toward the door, seeming to mean both Elspeth and the man and woman. "Move it."

"Do your duty, officer!" the woman said. There were curlers under her kerchief. She had two chins, with a few black hairs twisting from them.

Elspeth put Peter into the bassinet and he cried. She buttoned her coat. "They're a couple of dingalings!" she said, her voice shaking. "They're the ones that ought to be locked up!"

"We'll discuss it on the sidewalk. Come on. Off. You too. We can't hold up the bus."

"Don't you grieve, child," a wrinkled black lady who had been sitting next to her said softly. "They won't do nothing."

Elspeth passed an arm through the strap of the baby seat and picked up the canvas bassinet, a hand at each end. Peter kept crying.

"Want me to carry that?" the policeman said.

"No."

She stepped down before him, turning sideways with the bassinet, the tiltable seat dangling. The blue light on the police car was turning. She passed before it and set the bassinet on the speckled snowbank. The other policeman came out. He was even younger, and his close-cropped hair was almost orange. He wiped snot with his glove. She saw the man helping the lady down. "Step lively, lady," the driver said. The end of the man's scarf was blowing. His gray hat flew off and rolled to Elspeth in the wet. She handed it to him. The chunky woman was carefully lowering her foot, testing the depth of the step, clutching her shopping bag. The policeman was behind her. Peter kept crying. Elspeth picked him up. Suddenly the bus excreted stench and fumes noisily.

"What are you gonna do, officer?" the woman said. They all collected near Elspeth and the bassinet at the snowbank. "Are you gonna arrest her or not? What do the police do when citizens stand up and be counted? We shouldn't have to see things like that on a public bus! She had her breast exposed!"

"I did not! It was covered up! You want to see how it was?"

"Cool it, cool it," the beak-nosed policeman said.

"They're a couple of dingbats! They've got my baby all upset and I'll be late for work!"

"All right, let's have your names," the policeman said. He produced a small notebook.

"You want *our* names too?" the woman's husband said.

"You too. You were gonna stand up and be counted. Show me some identification."

The man unbuttoned his overcoat to find his wallet. Elspeth took hers from her shoulder bag, and Peter cried nervously again.

The policeman copied from the licenses. "This lady is your wife?"

"Yes, officer. How about the other passengers? They saw it too."

"What did you want me to do? Clear everybody off the bus?" He kept writing.

"I have to be at work," said Elspeth.

He handed back the licenses and gave the man a slip of paper on which he had written something. "All right. Let me explain the procedure. I'm giving you my name and her name. You two are the complainants, right? Because you're the ones that saw it."

"Everybody saw it."

"Okay, but we need a complainant, right? I can't be the complainant because it was before I got on the bus. So you two have to sign a complaint, and then she'll be issued a summons."

The man and the woman nodded.

"Okay," the policeman said. "You go up to district court in Codman Square and tell Lillian in the clerk's office you want to sign a complaint. Whenever it's convenient. It don't have to be today. Dorchester district court. You know where it is?"

"Officer, can't you see they're crazy? I didn't do anything. Nobody else on that bus was complaining. Just tell them to bug off."

"That's not for me to say, miss. If they want to sign a complaint that's their right."

"Then what happens?"

"If a complaint is filed you may have to appear in court."

"Most citizens wouldn't go to this trouble, officer," the lady said. "I hope you know that. Most people don't want to get involved."

"Lady, you're a good citizen. You did your duty. You all squared away now, sir?"

"The courthouse," the man said. "I know where it is." His wife waddled off with him, dragging the shopping bag and looking for a cut through the snowbank.

Peter had stopped crying, more or less, but now he gave another tentative wail. She patted him. "This is dumb," she said. "I mean it's just so cockeyed stupid. I could throw a hunk of ice at somebody. Now I even have to pay another bus fare to get to work."

"Where do you work?" said the beak nosed-officer.

"Saltmarsh Service Station. It's on Saltmarsh Avenue Extension, corner of Smelter."

"You mean Vinnie O'Banion's place?" said the orange-haired younger officer. He had not spoken before.

"Yes," said Elspeth.

"We can take you there," the first policeman said.

They took the bassinet from the snowbank and put it in the back seat. "Thanks," said Elspeth.

The younger man drove. Here I am in a police car again, Elspeth said to herself. He didn't use the siren. There were voices on the radio. The darker officer looked back at her. "Buck up, kid. They'll probably forget about it before they get to the station house."

"I never heard of a complaint like that," the driver said. "I thought there was a pickpocket aboard. Or somebody'd been knifed, or a heart attack or something."

"You wouldn't think anybody would still be uptight today about nursing a child," said Elspeth.

347

"That's right," the driver agreed. "It's no sin. Our Lady nursed God at the breast."

"They even have entertainers that take everything off," said the other officer. "G-strings, everything."

"Sure," said Elspeth. "Let them go pick on that. Not on me."

"My sister nursed her kid," said the younger officer.

"On the bus?" said beak-nosed one.

"Not on a bus though," the younger answered. "Not on the bus, not on the subway."

The beak-nosed one turned back again to Elspeth. "Okay, kid? Don't worry. But don't nurse the baby on the bus next time, okay? Don't look for trouble. Do it in a powder room or something. People are funny, you know. There's all kinds."

"Maybe it'll make them happy that we took her off in the squad car," the younger one said. "I wonder if they saw that. We should have told them we were taking her to jail."

"You should've," said Elspeth. "Then they wouldn't file a complaint. Why didn't you do that?"

"Well, we can't do that," said the older one. "Don't worry. They'll never get to the courthouse. She'll tell the old man her feet hurt."

Chris was at the pumps and stared squinting when the police car drove up.

"Chrissie, I understand this young lady's a friend of yours," the darker one said from the window.

"Yeah, she is," said Chris. "What happened?"

"Nothing much. She was in a little disturbance. I guess she'll tell you." He got out to help with the bassinet.

"That's okay, I've got it," she told him.

Peter was crying again when she brought him into the office. She changed his diaper. At last, when she was able to hang her coat and sit on the corrugated cartons with Peter, he stopped, but she burst into tears herself.

Chris came in. "What happened, kiddo? You want to talk about it?"

Elspeth nodded but she was weeping too much to speak.

Chris went to the repair bay and came back with a styrofoam cup of milky coffee which she handed to Elspeth.

"Thanks," Elspeth said, controlling her tears.

"Want to sit here?" Chris offered.

Elspeth shook her head. The hot coffee helped her calm the occasional heaving of her shoulders.

Chris sat in the swivel.

Elspeth told her the story. Vinnie entered, in his vinyl windbreaker, and Chris told him. "Can you imagine two people doing a thing like that?" Chris said.

"A couple of cranks," said Vinnie. He put coins in the soda machine and a can clunked down.

"I better not nurse him out at the pumps anymore."

"If you want to nurse him out at the pumps, you nurse him out at the pumps," said Chris. "This is private property. And if some crank wants to make anything

348

of it I bet we can get the women's organizations to defend you."

"I don't know if women's organizations get into that," Elspeth said.

"I gave my kids the bottle and the hell with it," said Chris. "But if you've got the patience to breastfeed I say more power to ya. And on these premises at least, nobody's gonna bother ya. You tell them it's on my authority."

"I always kept the coat all around Petey's head so his lips don't get chapped. I don't expose anything."

"I know you don't," said Vinnie. "It'd freeze." He swigged from the can. "I don't know how it'll be when summer comes. But even then I'd say the tit is good for business. The ladies will say, oh, what a pretty picture, and the guys will crane their necks."

ON Elspeth's day off Harriet arrived with a set of straight wrenches, a ratchet wrench, and a set of sockets, all under the pan of macaroni pudding in the bottom of her woven shopping bag.

"Wasn't all that too heavy?" said Elspeth. "You could have left half till next time. You didn't have to polish them. They'll only get dirty again."

"I know. But they were so dirty."

They took the pram down the avenue and shopped for a quilted jacket, which would be more practical than the coat at the gas pumps.

"Your figure's really come back very nicely," Harriet said while Elspeth tried it on. "I think your waist is as little as it was before."

"It is. And the breastfeeding helped. It makes you secrete a hormone that pulls your belly in."

"Is that so? Are you kidding me?"

"I'm not kidding."

"Well, I don't believe it."

Harriet insisted on paying for the jacket.

"I thought things were cheaper in a colored neighborhood," Harriet said when they came out.

"They're not," Elspeth said.

Harriet had brought a Reader's Digest article, and another she had clipped from the Sunday supplement. Elspeth read them, nursing Peter in the wicker chair with one foot resting on the bed, after Harriet had gone. The Reader's Digest piece said attitudes toward unwed mothers were improving. Many cities now kept pregnant teenagers in high school instead of throwing them out as they used to, and even provided special facilities. It told of a black girl who had had an illegitimate child in high school and was now on a scholarship in a prestigious eastern college.

That's nice, Elspeth said to herself. But it didn't say if the girl had kept the baby. She probably hadn't. And it didn't say what college. Radcliffe maybe? She had heard that Harvard and Radcliffe liked to have some far-out types around, to enhance their cosmopolitan image. Why not apply for a scholarship at Harvard-Radcliffe, and take Petey along to class?

It seemed more interesting somehow than taking Petey back to Mount Holyoke in the fall, a year behind her old classmates. It made more sense, even. Sonny Elkin had chosen Harvard-Radcliffe because it was the least small-townish of colleges, more urbane than the largest city.

The Sunday supplement was in a similar vein.

The stigma of unwed motherhood is fast disappearing. Studies show the bringing up of children by unmarried mothers is now more common and accepted. It does not seem to harm the child. Moreover, statistics indicate that a third of the mothers marry within ten years, half of these marrying the father.

Hey, now, how about that. It had been sweet of Mama to bring her those articles. She hoped Mama had shown them to Daddy.

She pulled the wicker chair about, rested her other foot on the bed, and gave Peter the other breast. Wet snow slid from the roof. It sounded like a ton of it, all at once. But its thud did not bother Peter. He sucked with eyes closed.

Despite the cheerful tone of that article, its statistics became less encouraging as she reflected on them. If a third married, two-thirds did not. The marriages to the father were the shotgun cases and occurred soon after the birth. The article sounded so upbeat. But what did its rosy figures really say? If the baby's father ditched you, chances were four out of five you'd never marry.

Chris complimented her black quilted jacket.

She liked Chris and Vinnie. Chris said they were trying to build the place up as a general repair garage. "When we really get to that point," said Chris, "you'll be in charge of the parts department. Vinnie and I both think you make a good impression."

The customer for whom Edgar Clish had replaced a water pump drove up before the office and complained that the battery light kept going on. Elspeth adjusted the fan belt. She reached deep to the bottom pulley, her feet off the ground. It only took a moment. Vinnie came over as she finished.

"Good," said Vinnie.

"You'd better watch it, the way you lean over a fender though," Chris said to her. "Somebody's liable to give you a goose."

After Vinnie had gone a woman drove a car in with its hood open and said she could not close it. Somebody had not latched it properly, and the wind had suddenly caught it and flung it up before the windshield.

Edgar stood in the sunshine, near the frozen snow at the fence, and tried again and again to slam down the hood. Chris stood by commiserating.

Edgar paused, his face sweating and panting. He examined the tightened edge, where the hood would not go into its groove. He tried a few more times to shut the hood.

"It's no use," he said. "When the wind blew it up like that it sprung the hinges. It's all out of line. You're gonna need new hinges."

"Oh dear," said the lady. "Is that a big job?"

"I'm afraid so. It's gonna take a few days to get a pair of hinges. And then they're riveted in."

"Have we got a rubber hammer?" Elspeth asked. "A soft hammer? Like for body work?"

She went under the raised doors to the repair bay, found the hammer and returned with it. She whacked the hood a few times on the tight side, up near the hinge, and the fender alongside it, and the body above where they joined.

She tried to shut the hood. It closed almost. She brought the rubber hammer down a few more times, where the hood and fender met. The hood slid into place. She gave more whacks for good measure. Yet there was no ripple, no dent, no indication on the enameled metal that the rubber hammer had touched it.

"Can you open it?" said Edgar.

Elspeth opened the hood. She closed it again.

"Oh, that's lovely," said the lady. "Thanks so much. What do I owe you?"

"On the house," said Chris.

"Oh. Thanks."

"Our pleasure," said Chris. "Any time."

At the first slow time after her arrival each day Elspeth swept out the repair bay with the push broom.

In the slack part of the afternoon there was usually time to sit chatting with Chris. Chris would lounge in the swivel, smoking, her feet not reaching the floor, and Elspeth would breastfeed on the corrugated cartons.

"I notice you pick him up a lot, and dandle him a lot," said Chris.

"Well, I might as well make him happy when he's a baby. That's when his wants are easiest to provide."

"You won't fuss so much with your second baby," said Chris. "With my Kathy I changed the carriage bedding ten times a day. And then when Kevin came along he never got washed, and the carriage was full of leaves and dead bugs, and he

351

had less rashes than the first kid." She blew smoke through her nostrils, watching Peter suck. "Where do you get all those little songs you sing him?"

"They're just nonsense syllables," said Elspeth. "Whatever comes off my tongue."

"Yeah, but you've always got a song for him. One day you're dancing him back and forth with 'higgledy piggledy buggledy biggledy,' and the next day it's 'diddle di diddle di bim de bom.' If it was me, I wouldn't know where to find the words. Every day I go home singing your stuff and my kids think I'm nuts."

They talked day after day of many things. Elspeth said what worried her about that indecent exposure complaint was that it might be held against her when her father brought her to court as an unfit mother.

"I wouldn't worry," said Chris. "One thing's got nothing to do with the other. Did you ever hear anything on that exposure thing?"

"Not so far," said Elspeth. "Knock on wood."

Some days Chris sat on the cartons with an ashtray beside her and insisted that Elspeth relax with Peter in the swivel. Elspeth told Chris about the knot in Peter's umbilical cord.

"Yeah, there are miracles all right," said Chris. "There's mysteries we can't fathom. That's why I send my kids to the sister school. If they don't shut the place down on us. They don't get the sisters they used to. Same way with seminarians. They aren't getting the vocations. I don't know. Well, if they shut down the sister school, they're gonna have to go to school with the blacks, that's all. It's the Mass in English that's doing it, if you ask *me*. The whole frigging Church is going down the drain."

"Well, a lot of things that used to be taken for granted are going by the board," said Elspeth.

"Kiddo, you can say *that* again."

"But what good are the old values if they don't work anymore?"

"That's right. The old values got frigged up somewhere. I sure don't know what the answer is. It's a brave new world, only there's nothing brave about it. Like take these communes. There's a commune in my neighborhood. Okay, long hair and beards is one thing, but here there's about ten guys and girls all living together in one house. They've even got a little kid there, about three years old. One of them's his mother, I guess. And maybe five of them's his father."

"They aren't necessarily all sharing each other," said Elspeth. "A commune doesn't have to mean group sex."

"You mean they're like paired off? Not all sharing wives in common?"

"Well, I was never in one," said Elspeth. "I think probably they're not all the same. I'd expect they'd pair off, mostly."

Chris shrugged. "Well, I don't know what they do. I'm out of it. I was brought up different." She drew on the cigarette. "Are you for women's lib?" she asked.

"Of course," said Elspeth. "Do you realize how tough it would be for me to get this kind of a job, if I hadn't run into you?"

"I realize it. I'm with *you*, kid."

"Sexism is sexier, though," Elspeth added.

352

"Hm," said Chris. "I'd have to chew on that. You can't have it both ways, though."

"Why not?"

"Hm," said Chris.

Peter wakened. Elspeth unstrapped him from his seat. "You know what I'd really like?"

"What," said Chris.

"I'd like to be a carpenter. And you know what else I'd like? I'd like to be a farmer. Build my own house, and wire it myself, and have a few acres out back to grow my stuff. And no hunting allowed. All the wildlife would pass the word around that Baker's farm is a sanctuary."

LARGE snowflakes were falling in the nighttime glow of the high fluorescents, dusting the black frozen puddles about the pumps, and wetting Elspeth's face as she held a nozzle to a customer's tank. She had pulled the nylon hood of the black quilted jacket over her head. Her braids trailed out of it.

"Did you know one of your taillights is out?" she asked.

"I didn't," said the man in the car.

"I can probably replace it in a minute if you can wait. If you'll open the trunk I'll see if it's just a connection."

As he climbed out she ran to the repair bay. She returned with bulbs in her pockets and carrying a flashlight and screwdrivers. The middle-aged man was standing in the wet somewhat gingerly, big snowflakes clinging to his overcoat.

Elspeth lay in the trunk of the car, her legs dangling out, and worked at the taillight assembly from the inside.

"Getting colder," the man said.

"Yup. They say the snow won't be much though."

She heard Peter's high-pitched wail. She had left him in the office with the door ajar.

"Could you go into the office and sing to my baby or distract him for a minute till I can get in there?"

The man went. She heard his wet footsteps. She had thought he looked like a grandfather, somewhat portly, with his kidskin gloves.

Another car drove up for gas. It shone against the raised trunk lid above her. She finished with the bulb. She crawled out of the trunk, slammed it, and ran to the office. "Thanks," she told the man. She made change and gave him the sales slip. She picked up Peter and took him to the new car. A lady sat at the steering wheel, her head low in a tawny luxuriant fur. "Fill it?" Elspeth asked.

Elspeth felt the wet flakes on her face. Her hand squeezed the gas nozzle. From the way Peter moved his opened lips to the right and left against her jacket she knew he was hungry.

"No titty out here, Petey. Some creep might come by and make a fuss."

"Did you say something?" the lady asked from the partly lowered window.

"I was talking to my baby."

Vinnie returned, hauling a disabled car. He alighted from the tow truck into the wet.

Elspeth settled into the swivel and nursed Peter. Vinnie came into the office. Snowflakes lay on his bushy hair. He inserted coins into the soda machine. "Was it busy?"

"Barely enough to cover the overhead, I guess."

"Well, let's hope the phone don't ring. I'll take over for a while if anybody comes for gas." He swigged from the can. She had noticed that he always averted his face from her when she breastfed.

He stepped down to the repair bay.

Peter nursed blissfully, eyes closed. His tiny fingers played on her skin.

She reached to her little transistor that sat on the desk, in front of the leather containers of Vinnie's camera and light meter and long lens, and dialed in search of the classical music that Peter liked. Vinnie had taken snaps of Peter during the day, but they were still in the camera. If they were good, maybe she would send one to Roxie Sweetser.

She rested far back in the tilting swivel, till her toes no longer reached the floor. She half closed her eyes, hearing the soft music.

She was Harlan Walker's secretary and nurse. His practice had grown far too big. Teaching and hospital rounds all morning, running three hours late for appointments all afternoon and far into the evening, then more hospital rounds, never done till midnight. Peter's crib was in a corner of Harlan's office, next to the electrocardiogram machine. She brought Harlan his supper at his desk. Poor darling. I rewarmed that stew three times. You look so tired. Dearest, I worry about you looking at those naked women all day. I know I have no need to. It's naughty of me. You're so strictly professional and puritan. But when that Mrs. Astor with her fantastic figure was stretched out on the examining table there with nothing on but her diamonds, I worried. I couldn't help it. Please forgive me, darling.

Out amid the illuminated snowflakes at the pumps a bearded young guy in a knit cap whacked Vinnie on the head with what looked like a short crowbar. For the briefest instant Elspeth gaped. She sprand forward with Peter from the swivel to the glass of the door. She saw Vinnie crumple to the pavement. She screamed. Peter's eyes had popped open but he did not wail till she dropped him into the bassinet and yanked open the desk drawer, which came out completely and clattered down, knocking over the electric space heater and stopping its hum. She retrieved the heavy revolver and opened the door. The guy with the yellow beard and knit cap and crowbar was already coming toward the office, but he hesitated when he saw the gun. It took both her thumbs to cock it. For an instant she debated whether or not to scream again.

He turned and ran back toward his car.

"Stop!" Elspeth shouted.

He ran faster. She heard Peter screeching behind her.

"Freeze, you bastard!" yelled Elspeth, stepping forward into the snowflakes. "Or I'll put a hole through ya!"

The girl in the car moved across to the wheel. The door had opened and he dove in. Elspeth pulled the trigger hard but it resisted her. The gun was straight out before her and she sighted along an arm, squeezing the trigger with all her strength.

The rear wheels skidded briefly and the car sprang forward. The bang was deafening. The gun and the hand that held it flew high over her head. The car spun with a skid into Smelter Street and disappeared.

She ran to Vinnie. He was sitting groggily on the edge of the curbing that surrounded the pumps. He bled from the little bald spot behind the bushiness and the wound looked nasty. She tried to help him to his feet. "Vinnie!" she said. He was heavy. When he looked at her his eyes seemed unfocused, and he spoke a syllable or two without coherence. He toppled forward. She screamed. She heard him moan.

She ran to the office. Peter was yowling in the bassinet. She grabbed the wall phone but her whole right arm stung when she raised it to dial. She dropped the receiver and dialed with the left, but there was no dial tone.

She left the phone dangling and stumbled over the desk drawer that lay on the floor. She paid no attention to Peter's hollering but rummaged in her purse. The first coin she felt was a quarter.

She dropped it in the phone and dialed again.

"We need an ambulance!" she told the operator. "Emergency!" She began to say more but a ring interrupted her. She heard a sergeant identify himself. "Send an ambulance!" she said. "Police! Vinnie's hurt! They walloped him with a crowbar!"

"Where are you?" the voice asked.

"Saltmarsh Service! The gas station, corner of Smelter and Saltmarsh Extension."

"Stay right there," the voice said.

The transistor radio still played softly. She looked out at Vinnie. He lay with his cheek on the pavement, his eyes open, and worked one leg futilely. "Oh shit," said Elspeth. She began to cry. She knelt to Peter, but every movement of her right arm hurt like a knife. She lifted Peter with her left arm alone. His head fell

355

back, and his wailing which had stopped a moment at her approach grew louder. "I'm sorry, Petey," she wept.

She pressed him to her and ran with him toward Vinnie. She saw the revolver lying on the glistening pavement, the snowflakes on it melting into droplets.

46

CHRIS, her face haggard, came down to Emergency with a plainclothes officer while the doctor was taping the cast on Elspeth's arm. "This is Detective Walsh," Chris said to her.

"I know," said Elspeth. "We talked before. How's Vinnie?"

"Still in surgery. We won't know anything for a while. They have to replace a hunk of his skull." Her eyes filled. "The priest's up there."

The detective was standing hatless, a bit to the side and rear of her, his dark overcoat open. He had a flattened nose.

Chris controlled her tears. "I hear the kick on that damn thing broke your elbow."

"Never mind me," said Elspeth. "I'll be okay."

"It's a fairly clean break," the doctor said, not looking up from his work. "Considering where it was. She was lucky." He was bending over Elspeth's chair, short and white-smocked, with heavy rimless glasses.

"Where's the baby?" Chris asked.

"Right here." Elspeth indicated the young social worker, also in a loose smock, who sat holding him in a corner of the windowless little room. The girl smiled, round and somewhat pimply-faced. Peter slept against her.

"A slug out of that thing would stop an elephant," Chris said. "Did you see how fat the bullets are? Vinnie used to shoot tin cans with it on vacation."

"It's a forty-five," said Walsh.

"You have to know how to hold it, I guess," Chris told Elspeth. "Vinnie's arm would fly straight up when he fired it. I couldn't even pull the trigger." Her body seemed to shudder. "The police think they caught the guy," she added.

Elspeth looked past her to the detective.

"Well, somebody smashed himself up in a car in South Boston," said Walsh. "We don't know yet if it fits your description."

"What did he have to hit him for?" Chris said. "Vinnie would've have opened the cash register and given him anything he wanted."

"I think he was stoned," said Elspeth.

"I wish the son of a bitch had carried a gun," said Chris. "Then he could've pulled a plain holdup and nobody hurt. Instead of thinking he had to sneak behind people and hit them on the head."

"Tell me again what the weapon was," Walsh asked Elspeth.

"One of these short crowbars, like you pry open crates with. Cast iron. You know, with a curved end like. And divided prongs, like for pulling nails out."

"Where is it now?" said Walsh. "Did you retrieve it?"

"He took it with him. He never let go of it."

"Then how did you manage to see it in such detail?"

"I saw it. I know what those are. I used to be in the hardware business. Everybody knows what they are."

"Was he black or white?"

"White. I told you. With a beard. A yellow beard."

"Did he threaten you?"

"I didn't give him a chance to."

"Did you know the revolver was loaded?"

"I don't know. I didn't think about it."

"Why did you shoot if he was running away?"

"I didn't *want* him to get away. When he hit Vinnie I got mad."

"Why didn't you shoot sooner? When he was coming toward you?"

"I don't know. I think I tried to. It took me that long to pull the trigger."

"Don't be hard on her, Jim," Chris told the detective. "She defended my Vinnie and she defended her kid. She could've been hit in the head too. She's a brave kid, bless her heart."

"Don't worry, I'm with you, Chrissie," Walsh said. "It's just routine. You say there was a woman in the car?" he said to Elspeth.

"Yes."

"Tell me again what she looked like."

"I said I couldn't tell you. She wasn't the one I was looking at. I think she had a knit hat. A red knit hat."

"I'm going back up," said Chris. "I can't sit still. I want to phone the kids again. Look for me after," she said to Elspeth. "I'll give you a ride home."

When the doctor had finished, Elspeth took Peter in her left arm. He squinted in his sleep and waved nervously, then nestled against Elspeth and relaxed. Her right arm hung in a dark blue sling under the unzipped quilted jacket. The social worker stuffed the end of the empty sleeve into the pocket. She hung the plastic seat from Elspeth's good arm, buckling its strap. The detective had gone.

Elspeth went upstairs. Just as she found Chris and the priest a pair of doors banged open and Vinnie was wheeled out on a stretcher. His face below the bandage-

357

swathed head was unconscious and ashen. The intravenous bottle swung high above him. The stretcher moved rapidly away down the corridor.

The old priest's arm was about Chris. "All right, my child. There's nothing more we can do until morning. Why don't you go home and get some sleep."

"Yeah, I guess so," said Chris. "I better go home. And see if the kids went to bed like I told them. They'll just have to get themselves off to school themselves tomorrow. I want to look in on Vinnie the first thing and then go open up and mind the store."

"Maybe you should take the day off," the priest said.

"And leave that clown Edgar by himself?"

"Or close up for a day or two."

"Naw. Vinnie would hate that. He'd feel worse. If he thought we couldn't even function."

They found the elevator. Chris's red eyes were wet.

"Are you sure you can drive?" Elspeth asked her.

"Sure I can drive. Why not?"

On the ride they said little. The snow had stopped. The streets were empty and the pavement shone under the cold dampness. Elspeth directed her to the Brodys' street.

Chris got out of the car with her. "That's okay," Elspeth said. "I can manage."

"What do you mean you can manage. How the hell are you gonna unlock the door with your good arm holding the baby."

"My landlady's waiting up. I phoned her. She never gave me a key."

"Well, I'll go to the door with ya. Which floor you on?"

"The bottom."

Chris accompanied her onto the porch, and grasped the lowest of the white knobs. "Jesus. A bell-pull. I haven't seen one of these in thirty years."

"It doesn't work. Just push into the vestibule, and there's another door with a bell that goes clunkety clunk when you turn it."

Elspeth threw a nod at the little bronze handle on a pivot. "You turn that."

Chris gave it a twist. "Jesus. This house is an antique."

They heard an unlatching of bolts.

Chris did not wait for an introduction but descended the porch steps.

"Mh! Gott in himmel," Mrs. Brody muttered, looking at the sling.

Using one arm and still wearing her jacket, Elspeth got Peter onto the changing table. The plastic seat slid from her arm to the floor. Mrs. Brody kept swaying her tangled head.

"Should I help you?"

"Well, let's see how I make out first. I've got to learn to do this."

She slipped out of the quilted jacket. Changing the diaper quickly with one hand was not difficult. Mrs. Brody watched from the door. "Mh."

Elspeth lowered Peter into his crib. He looked so little draped on her hand, his hands and feet hanging, his eyes shut.

Getting her sweater off was difficult. They had rolled the sleeve above the cast.

On the phone she had said only that she had cracked a bone near the elbow and that her arm was in a sling. She was glad Mrs. Brody had seemed to recognize she was not ready to recount details.

She lay in darkness, slowly undoing her braids.

She closed her eyes, and tried to relax the cast away. But it grew heavier and sweatier. She could work her hand. But she couldn't roll over, at least not to any position that was tolerable.

Poor Chris. Poor Vinnie.

One thought led to another, endlessly. She remembered how Eric had once run away from home after a fight with Daddy, and how they had looked for him frantically for hours. After midnight the police cruiser located him walking along Pumpkin Hill Road. There was a dog following him. We can take the dog too, the police offered. So Eric and the dog got into the police cruiser. When Daddy came to the police station to take him home the police said hey, don't forget your dog. Eric said, it's not my dog. The policeman said, why did you say it was your dog? And Eric said, I didn't. You wanted to take him to the police station so I said okay.

Mama and Daddy didn't think it was funny, but at home Eric and Mark and Elspeth thought it was hilarious.

Things would be different if Eric were alive. Or Mark. They'd mediate between her and Daddy for her, as she used to do for them.

Eric would be at Northeastern now probably. He had wanted the cooperative program, where you left school every three months for a job.

The thought of applying for transfer from Mount Holyoke to Harvard-Radcliffe crossed her mind again. It would be crazy if she were accepted. Just crazy enough to happen. Daddy would brag about her.

She tried lying on her side. But she remained conscious of the cast.

She was still awake when the brass balls of the bedposts became visible in the gray morning twilight, and then the intertwined rosebuds and vines of the wallpaper.

The cow-jumped-over-the-moon figures of the mobile shook above the crib, indicating that Petey was stirring. At last he cried.

Oh shut up, you stinkypoo. Her eyes were heavy.

At breakfast Mrs. Brody said people who work around cars, machines, always have accidents. Even before cars, with horses, there were accidents. In Europe her uncle had had a wagon, and the horse stepped back on his foot.

The grapefruit rocked and slid from the spoon. She lifted the heavy half-stiff elbow and laid it cast and all on the table. Her thumb and third finger steadied the grapefruit. Even so, it was awkward to hold the spoon in her left hand. It was as though the spoon were a strange new instrument.

She had never realized the extent to which the world discriminated against the left-handed. Even the placement of the handle on the toilet tank. She couldn't anymore just reach behind and flush.

When she was sure her father would have left for work she telephoned Harriet. She took the plastic seat with Peter in it under her arm, and knelt to set him on the floor by the telephone table. To dial she had to lay the receiver on the table.

"I had a slight accident at work," she told Harriet. "I don't want you to worry. My arm's in a sling."

"What happened?"

"Oh, just a dumb accident. It's too complicated to explain. It would never happen again."

"Is your arm broken?"

"Well, sort of. A kind of crack at the elbow, down a long bone. But the doctor said it'll be fine. I just have to wear a cast for a few weeks and it'll heal completely."

"Oh my God. How did it happen? Which arm?"

"It just happened, one of those freaky things. Don't worry, okay? I don't want to go into a long story. There's nothing to worry about."

"What doctor took care of you?"

"City Hospital. They X-rayed it and fixed it and I'm okay."

"Who pays for the hospital? They should pay for that."

"I have Blue Cross. A family plan for me and Petey."

"Is Petey okay?"

"Of course. Can't you hear him? He doesn't like it that I can't hold him when I'm on the phone."

"How did it happen? I hope a car didn't bump into you at the pumps there."

"No, it didn't. It's too complicated to go into detail. Just take my word for it that it won't happen again in a million years."

"How do you take care of Petey with one arm in a sling?"

"It's not so bad. I'm getting used to it." He dropped the rattle. She put the phone on the table and stooped to unstrap him. Then she took the phone and lifted him, all with the left arm, holding the phone to her right ear and cocking her head to keep it in place. She had missed something her mother had said. "What?"

"I'll come and help you."

"No. Not today, Mama. I'm going to work early. Mr. O'Banion's not well and his wife needs all the help she can get."

"I'm sure Mrs. O'Banion doesn't expect you to show up. Not with a broken arm."

"Maybe she doesn't. But I'm okay and I'm going. Pushing gas just takes one hand. So does checking tires. Or putting oil in. I can't do any big stuff, but there's lots I *can* do." She kept up her gentle twisting, the top of Peter's head at one cheek and the phone at the other.

"I think you're out of your mind," she heard Harriet say. "I really do. Then come home and live here a while, so I can help you. You can commute to that gas station from here if you insist on it."

"I can't come home. You know that."

"I'll fix it with Dad," said Harriet.

"You can't fix it with Dad."

"Then at least let me come to the Brodys' and take care of the baby while you're at work."

"Well, maybe," Elspeth considered. "I suppose. The breastfeeding is established

360

enough so that I guess one bottle a day wouldn't wreck it. But my hours go into evening, Mama. You have to get Dad's supper."

"So I'll go home in time for supper. Or I'll leave him something he can warm up."

"No, Mama, never mind. I appreciate it, but I'll manage with Petey. If I left him with anyone I'd have to pump my breasts out manually and that's a pain. And Dad would want to come when I'm not here and take Petey to an adoption agency."

"Don't you trust me?"

"I trust you, Mama. Believe me I do. But he'd pressure you and you'd have to fight with him and it's just no good. When I need help I'll yell for help, I promise. Petey's not hard to take care of now. He's been sleeping through the night and I'm a lot less tired."

"He sleeps right through?"

"The last four nights he slept through. And he's such fun these days. The expressions on his face. He's like a little grown-up. When I put him down in the seat before he wants, the way he looks at me and puts his lip out, and looks like he's insulted. He's not even two months. And sometimes he has such dignity. Such aplomb. I think he knows things that we don't."

ELSPETH'S good arm held Peter and the dangling seat. Mrs. Brody pulled the door open.

In the vestibule only the empty tubular frame of the pram was chained at the bottom of the banister. The bassinet had been left behind when the ambulance had taken her with Vinnie.

When the bus flung open its door she let the young men crowd ahead of her and climbed carefully. A stout lady with a wide black face reached and helped her. "You all right, honey."

"Thanks. Would you take the fare out of my pocket, please?"

She found the nearest seat and fell into it as the bus started. When her stop approached she rose and braced her feet with care. The driver slowed gently, glancing back at her, and she thanked him.

As she descended she saw Chris staring at her from the pumps.

"What the hell are *you* doing here?" said Chris.

"Don't you want me?"

"Course I want ya. I need all the help I can get. I'm just surprised you felt up to it."

"I can't change tires," Elspeth said, "but I can push gas."

"Well, that'd be *my* attitude," said Chris as they went to the office. "Hang in there and fight. If you've still got one arm left use it."

Chris took Peter and lowered him to the bassinet, but he wrinkled his brow in disappointment and thrust his lower lip.

"Put him in the seat," said Elspeth. "He wants to be where he can see."

Chris took the seat from Elspeth's arm and strapped him into it on the desk surface.

"Your hair looks nice long. That's how it was that first time you walked in here. I'd practically forgotten. I'm so used to seeing you in braids."

"I know. But I can't braid it with one arm. And it doesn't matter now anyway. I won't be lying under any cars for a while. Any word on Vinnie?"

"Well, I wangled my way in to see him this morning." She lighted a cigarette. She leaned on the side of the desk. Her eyes were bloodshot. "They say he'll pull through, but I don't know in what kind of shape. His whole right side's paralyzed, and he can't talk. He understands everything I say, but he can't answer. He tries, but it just comes out noises. He looks at me with tears in his eyes. I haven't the heart to let the kids see him yet."

"But he'll get better, won't he?" Elspeth had sat on the corrugated carton.

"I sure as hell hope so." Smoke blew down her nostrils. "The doctors say sure, some get completely better, and some get partly better, perhaps, maybe, I don't think they really know. They say there has to be a long process of therapy, learning to talk and walk and all. He'll be glad you're still working for us. And Edgar's brother is gonna come to work for us starting next week— that'll be another hand."

Without Vinnie the place seemed disorganized. Chris left in her faded green car to get a part that Edgar needed, and was gone a long time. Elspeth kept busy at the pumps. Her left arm never stopped. The figures her left hand wrote on the charge slips came slowly, and were big and childish. The roads were filthy with salt and patches of brown snow, and she cleaned windshields with the squeegee. She sat on the curbing that surrounded the pumps with an oil can steadied between her knees, and punched it open with a spout. She was delayed in feeding Peter, and could feel the wetness in her clothes when her breasts dripped.

When at last she could get to him he stopped crying and his big eyes glared at her angrily, a tear sliding down his cheek. She settled back with him in the swivel chair.

But in a minute or two another car tripped the bell hose.

362

"Can you get that one, Edgar?" she called. She leaned further back in the swivel until she could see him in the repair bay.

"It's *your* job, ain't it?" he answered. "Or are you paid to sit there on your ass?"

"I have to feed the baby."

"That ain't *my* lookout. I'm in the service department. Somebody's paying ten bucks an hour to get this buggy fixed. If I walk away from it and push gas for somebody else on a customer's time, it ain't fair to the customer now, is it. It ain't honest."

Elspeth put Peter into his seat. It was hard to fasten the strap on him while he squirmed. "I'll be right back, Peteyboy."

While she was out there she heard the wall pay phone ringing in the office. She heard Peter crying there too. In the repair bay she saw Edgar still bent over his running engine under a raised hood. He did not answer the phone.

It stopped ringing. It started again. She put the customer's ten-dollar bill between her lips. She felt in her pocket for the coins she needed.

As the car left she hurried toward the office. Edgar stuck his head out under the raised door and yelled at her as she ran. "Answer the God damn phone!"

She grabbed it. "Saltmarsh Service," she said. Peter was still crying.

Edgar came to the doorway between the repair bay and the office, his face still flushed, the small eyes fuming. "Answer the phone! And if it's the President of the United States, tell him I'm taking a crap."

It was the lady whose car Vinnie had towed in late yesterday afternoon so that a frozen brake could be thawed. It was ready, Elspeth explained, but there was no way they could send someone to give her a lift. "Our best man's out sick and we're undermanned."

She took up Peter again and sat back in the swivel. Edgar had returned to his running engine in the repair bay.

"What did you mean by 'our best man,'" he demanded. "You think I don't know cars?"

"I didn't mean anything by it. I just meant the boss."

Detective Walsh came by just as Chris returned. He showed Elspeth some photographs of a man and of a woman, the man bruised with eyes half shut but staring. Elspeth said she couldn't be certain of the woman but the man looked like the one. He was dead, Walsh told her. A police car had begun to chase him because he was speeding. He skidded in the wet, careened off a street lamp, then turned upside down. The girl had minor injuries. There was no sign that Elspeth's bullet had hit him or the car. "It's probably right out here in the snowbank," said Walsh. "You'll find it when the snow melts."

"If it had hit him you'd find part of his brains across the street," said Chris.

"How's Vinnie doing?" Walsh asked her.

"Right now I'm just thankful he's alive. Father Nugent gave him last rites when they brought him in, you know."

"I know," said Walsh.

After Walsh had gone Chris sat brooding in the swivel, one toe to the floor.

"I'm gonna close early today," she said about four-thirty. "Come on, let's lock

363

up. Tomorrow's another day. Edgar! We're closing early!"

Edgar said nothing. He began putting his tools away.

"Come on, kiddo, I'll take you home," Chris said to Elspeth. "We're gonna have new hours around here. I thought it all through. No more evening hours. You and me, we'll come in together and go home together so I can drive you. I've got my mother coming starting tomorrow to look after the kids after school and get their supper. So starting tomorrow we can stay to six. Is that okay with you? Eight to six?"

"You don't have to keep giving me rides."

"I'm giving you rides. No argument. I'd think you'd be scared to be on the street in that neighborhood anyhow. Are the hours okay? Eight to six?"

"Sure."

"It's longer hours for you. I'll make it up to you. Or adjust your pay, or give you time off, or something."

Chris put the bassinet into the car.

"I'll bring it back in the morning when I call for you."

"You don't have to do that."

"Well, you used to take it back and forth. You use it here sometimes, when he sleeps. You said it's part of your baby carriage, isn't it? You might want to wheel him when you go shopping."

They headed first to Chris's house.

"I hope you don't mind," said Chris. "I just want to get the kids' supper together, and then I'll take you to your place, and then I'll go see Vinnie. Hey, how about having supper with us. Take pot luck with me and the kids. Come on. I don't take no for an answer."

It was not far. It was a wooden triple-decker like the Brodys'. Chris introduced Elspeth to Kathleen and Kevin. Both were very freckled. Kathleen looked about thirteen and Kevin was younger.

"How's Daddy?" said Kathleen.

"Well, not bad, but not good. It's gonna be a long road back. They said by Sunday he can have more than one visitor at a time, so I'll take you then. And they might let him graduate to a wheelchair by then too, and we'll give him a little ride up and down the hall."

"Can he talk?" said Kevin.

"Not much. He tries. He said 'Chrissie' this morning."

"I wish you'd killed the guy that did it," Kevin said to Elspeth.

"Now, you're not supposed to say that," Chris said. "You're not supposed to wish harm to anyone."

"I don't care."

"Anyway they told us today the guy's dead," Chris told him. "He crashed his car, maybe an hour after. So I guess God punished him."

They shared spam and beans. On the wall above the stove a cottage covered with tinsely snow was framed in relief, with the glittering legend God Bless Our Home. The picture above the table was a three-quarter view of a Nordic bearded

Jesus gazing up bemused, his Sacred Heart somehow visible in his chest, thorn-bound and oozing. Under the table a dog was sniffing and begging food. Kathy was taken with Peter, who had been placed awake in his seat upon the counter. She kept turning to him. "He's so cute."

"Yeah, he's cute all right," said Chris. "But it ain't easy to raise a baby out of wedlock. See how a smart-aleck boy can wreck a girl's life? So let it be a lesson to you kids. Kevin, when you get older, you ever do anything like that to a girl and I'll cream ya." She showed him a fist. "Understand? Ya have to respect womanhood."

"Is it okay if I feed him?" Elspeth asked.

"Well, I guess you have to. Just turn around. Listen, you kids. Starting tomorrow Nanna's gonna come and give you supper every day, so I can work to six. And I better not hear you gave her a hard time."

At the Brodys' Chris lifted the bassinet and set it into the frame of the pram.

The next day was easier. Chris did not go away much, except once in the high seat of the tow truck to get someone's car started.

The day after that Elspeth even had time to sweep the repair bay, pushing the wide broom with her left arm. She began her project of making an inventory for a parts department.

On Saturday Chris decided to close at noon. Elspeth took Peter marketing, and used a bundle-holder she had bought that hung from the handle of the pram. Dragging the pram back up the porch steps was not much harder with one arm than with two.

By Sunday it was as though the cast had always been there. The same arm that held Peter would push her shirt aside. He did not mind the stretched sling pressing on his head. He sucked resting against it.

She remembered not to screw the lid of the mayonnaise jar tightly, because if she did it could not be opened with one hand. But she found no way to work the can opener. So Mrs. Brody opened cans for her.

Nor was there any way to turn a knob holding Peter. Often she asked Mr. Brody, who would shuffle over with baggy trousers covering half his union suit, the suspenders hanging about them.

She did not wash dishes as much as before but she still did her own, which were few, rinsing them under a blast from the faucet and standing them in the rack to dry. She still dusted the apartment and pushed the vacuum. "No, darling, you shouldn't," said Mrs. Brody.

"I can do it," said Elspeth.

On Monday morning Chris went around the building knocking icicles off the overhang with the broom handle. The little ones tinkled and shattered. She broke a huge one and stepped back as it plunged. Edgar said his brother would be there, and presently he arrived. He was younger than Edgar but resembled him strongly— short, beefy, muscular, square. His complexion was even lighter than Edgar's and he was not so red-faced. His name was Puff.

"Puff?" said Chris. "That ain't your real name, is it? What's your real name? Like for the withholding and all."

"Everett. Everett Clish. They call me Puff."

There was a backlog of repair and servicing jobs. Chris prepared to get the parts. "You guys tell me what you need."

It was midmorning before the list was compiled and Chris could leave. By then Elspeth was less busy at the pumps. Peter wakened.

She fed him. Twice within a few minutes Puff came through the office while she nursed.

"Puff, would you close the door again, please? It's cold."

He closed the front door. "What's the matter? Afraid that tit'll freeze off?"

He went down into the repair bay.

"The milk's liable to freeze," she heard Edgar say.

"Yeah, the kid'll get a popsicle," said Puff.

They seemed to think this very witty. Puff said it again, and they laughed a second time.

"How'd she bust her arm?" Puff asked. She could hear them back there, despite the radio that played beyond them.

"She fired off Vinnie's old MP revolver when the guy tried to rob him. And the kick busted her arm. She thinks she's a hero."

"Did she hit anything?"

"Are you kidding? She couldn't hit a barn door. She's lucky she didn't hit the pumps and blow the place up."

They lounged all the rest of the morning and into the afternoon, waiting for Chris to bring the parts. Sometimes Elspeth went into the bay to get quarts of oil, and once to get a wiper blade. Each time they stopped talking and their eyes followed her.

When she went into the bay to sweep she was there longer and they talked, ignoring her. Puff asked Edgar about a car that was fixed and waiting.

"It was a squeaky bushing," Edgar said. "In the A-frame."

"Why don't you tell him he needs a ball joint," Puff suggested. "Or tell him the shocks are gone."

"Naw. I could. I thought of that. But I'll play it straight. He's a good customer. He knows the O'Banions. And he knows his way around."

"Did you charge Mrs. Eardley for the alternator?" Elspeth asked Edgar.

"What do you care?"

"I just wondered."

"Why?"

"I was feeling sort of sorry for her," said Elspeth. "She looked so sad."

"So what? I'm sad too when I have to pay a bill. I replaced the alternator. She needed it. Her alternator was burned out."

"But you're the one that blew the alternator. You put the battery in backwards."

"So I made a mistake. It happens to everybody. Everybody's gonna put a battery in ass-backwards sometime."

"Why should she pay for your mistake?"

"So who's gonna pay for it?"

366

"You should."

"You crazy? You know what the things cost?"

A car tripped the bell hose and she went out front. She checked the oil while the pump was running. But the oil rag had somehow found its way to Edgar's back pocket and she did not want to ask him for it. She fetched a disposable diaper from the office.

Chris returned. Edgar and Puff got busy. But up front it was quiet. Elspeth and Chris sat in the office, and Elspeth held Peter on her knee, bouncing it under him. "Yuckita kuckita kookita kuckita," she sang.

Edgar came to the opening between the repair bay and office. "There's a piss smell from that pail," he said.

"Watch ya God damn language, you stupid goon," said Chris. "Can't you see there's ladies present?"

"That pail has a very tight seal," said Elspeth. "And the diapers in it are tied in a plastic bag besides."

"I don't care," said Edgar. "I can still smell it."

"Stay out of the office then," said Chris.

"We can smell it way out there. And my brother's allergic."

"I don't believe it," said Chris. "I can't smell it. Ya probably smell each other. Ya baboon ya."

Edgar turned and went back to the repair bay.

Chris rocked, her hands on the swivel arms. "If his brother don't like that diaper pail, then just wait till summer. The smell off those mud flats at low tide when the wind's right will kill him. Especially at rush hour, when they're churning out exhaust up on the expressway there."

At the Brodys' that evening two pieces of mail awaited her on the telephone table. There was a fat little brown envelope from her new west-coast bank that she knew must be packets of checks, and a long white envelope from the Municipal Court with no stamp. Mrs. Brody said a policeman had brought it. The back of Elspeth's neck seemed to freeze.

She left them unopened while she changed Peter and fed him. It was probably that dumb indecent exposure thing. Maybe it would only ask her to send in a ten or fifteen-dollar fine or something, like a parking ticket.

She tried to lower Peter into the crib but she did it awkwardly and he cried. So she did not put him down.

She carried him when she went to get the letters. With a dip of her knees she picked them up with the hand that held him. She climbed onto her bedspread and laid Peter and the mail before her. It was not so difficult to open an envelope with one hand as she might have thought. She dug with fingernails at a corner and at last pulled, destroying the whole front of it unevenly. The document said she was commanded to appear on Thursday at nine o'clock in the forenoon until the action hereinafter named is heard by said Court. The action was a complaint of Child Abuse. The name of Joseph Baker was typed in as complainant. Hereof fail not, the document went on.

Daddy, how could you? How could you?

Fury made her eyes fill. She pictured herself holding up Peter for Daddy to see. Look at your grandson, that you refused to see!, she was telling Daddy, while the judge looked on. What do you know? You never saw him before! If I lose my child you'll lose yours, because you'll never see me again! Never, never, never!

Petey reached to Daddy and smiled. She saw Daddy's face become uncertain, hesitating between a tentative involuntary smile and tears. Your honor, Daddy said confusedly, I think I better give this some more thought. You would be wise to give it a great deal more thought, the judge said augustly, high on the bench. Why don't you and your daughter and grandson go out together and get acquainted?

She tore apart the brown packet. Tidy blocks of checks fell out, and also flyers about car loans and home-improvement loans. The checks were pink, with her name and address square and neat. At the bottom, on a stylized range of mountains, was the name of the Pacific Northern National Bank and the faraway city that meant nothing to her. Opening an account away out there seemed now an insane thing to have done.

She took Peter to the living room, wanting to hear Mrs. Brody's assurance again that the court would not separate a baby from his mother if he appeared unharmed.

But the Brodys were preoccupied with the television. She did not interrupt them.

She looked at Peter, trying to memorize his eyes, the ears, the beginning of a curl in his hair, so as to remember him always in case he were taken away.

Elspeth showed Chris the summons next morning. Chris held it out before her, tilting in the swivel and blowing smoke. "Don't that beat all, though," Chris said.

"Do you know any lawyers?" Elspeth asked.

"Not any I'd trust. Lawyers cost a lot of money, and I don't know what good they are. Vinnie went to court with a lawyer once, and he said the lawyer told it all wrong and he'd have done better without him. The way I look at it only crooks need lawyers."

"Maybe I should just take Petey and run away to another state."

"I wouldn't. Then you look in the wrong. It says it right here. Hereof fail not, or they throw the frigging book at ya. You've got nothing to hide. Any judge can see that kid ain't abused. Christ, every time I look at ya you've got a tit in his mouth."

"What if the judge is stupid?"

"He can't be *that* stupid."

Elspeth sighed. "It makes me sick that my father would do this. Even if he doesn't succeed it makes me sick that he'd try. He's so mad at me. So awful mad. It's because he loves me so much. You only get mad at people you love."

"I never heard that one," said Chris.

"If you don't love them you don't care enough to get mad," said Elspeth.

"Well, speak for yourself. I can get mad at people I'd just as soon would drop dead."

After supper Elspeth opened the Yellow Pages on the red-checked oilcloth. She had her day off tomorrow, and maybe she could interview two or three lawyers.

368

There were pages of closely packed tiny names.

Maybe it was better to forget lawyers, and use her day off to apply to Harvard-Radcliffe. They would not answer her for weeks or months of course, but Thursday she could tell the judge she had applied, and any judge would know that the type of girl who applies to Harvard-Radcliffe is not the type who abuses a child.

Harriet was planning to visit her on her day off, but she phoned Harriet and told her not to come until noon. She said she had an errand in the morning.

"What kind of an errand?"

"Oh, inquiring about possibly taking some courses in the fall. Broadening my horizons."

She did not mention the summons. Neither did Harriet. It occurred to Elspeth that her mother did not even know of it.

There was a freezing rain in the night, and when she set out to the subway with Peter the trees in the park were a world of blazing crystal. A forest of chandeliers, hewn of diamond, every twig magnifying the yellow-white morning sunshine and sending it out tenfold.

"Wow, isn't that something, Petey? I bet there's nothing brighter. Unless we get blown up by an H-bomb, and we'd just as soon skip that, wouldn't we."

She was in Cambridge before nine. The streets that surrounded the subway exit were clogged with traffic. A girl on a bicycle with books in its carrier threaded between trucks, pedaling slowly. From beyond the iron fence and long brick dormitories came the clanging of a steeple bell.

She supposed something like the admissions office would still be up in the old Radcliffe area. So when the lights changed she turned her back on Harvard Yard and carried Peter before the waiting traffic to the other side, where the shops and high buildings were. Among the sidewalk crowds everyone she passed seemed to notice her—middle-aged ladies with bundles, young bearded guys who might or might not be students. What if she happened to run into Sonny Elkin along here? Or any of the other Winslow kids who'd come to this place? It just might happen. She wasn't sure if she'd welcome bumping into Sonny just at this moment. If she did, the sling and Petey would certainly be a couple of conversation pieces.

After the shops the sidewalk became uneven brick, and she was walking alone with Petey between a churchyard and an old snowbank beginning to soften in the sun.

Anyway Sonny was probably living with somebody by now. He was an easy mark. He was too busy studying and achieving to look after his love life properly. It was no problem for a girl with perception enough to understand what a great guy he was to just move in and take over. And as long as she understood him, and didn't bug him, he'd rather have it that way. He'd much rather have the girl take the initiative, and save him the trouble. He'd probably go on after college to the Harvard Graduate School of Business Administration and make a mint. And as long as you sent his laundry out and matched his socks, and gave him a bit of affection to rock him to sleep, and left him alone when he was hard at work, which was most of the time, he'd be loyal to you forever. And never stray.

And do what you told him. He'd always been like that. You drove the motorcycle and he rode behind. You decided where to go on dates, and how far the making out would go.

Sweet, no meanness in him, Most Likely to Succeed, and a pushover. He'll be quite content someday with a beautiful division of labor, in which he'll be in charge of making millions of dollars and his wife will be in full charge of spending it. Some smart Radcliffe had probably grabbed him in the first two weeks and written her name all over him. A guy like Sonny Elkin you don't let out of your sight. It's like leaving your wallet on the sidewalk. Going to Mount Holyoke and letting him go to Harvard had really been dumb.

In a setting of neo-Georgian brick she asked the first person who came down a shoveled path for directions to the admissions office.

She found it on a first floor. The plastic seat dangled, its strap looped around the strap of her shoulder bag. The curly-haired young woman at the reception desk laughed.

Elspeth asked if she could have an application form.

"You mean for next fall's class? It's kind of late."

"Well, is there anybody around who's free to interview me?" Elspeth asked. "Or that I could talk to? Even though I don't have an appointment?"

"Somebody just might. Let me see."

She telephoned.

"Mrs. Vanderkruik-Gray will talk to you," she said as she put down the phone. "Second door down." She smiled. "You're kind of loaded up."

Elspeth found a lean, thirtyish woman wearing a suit, small-jawed and long-necked, her hair pulled back tight, who smiled coolly across a desk. The room was tiny.

"Let me just get the baby into his seat first," Elspeth said. She knelt in her jeans and quilted jacket and laid Peter on the carpeting. She slipped off the shoulder bag and opened the strap of the seat, using her teeth.

"You've got quite a handful, haven't you," said Mrs. Vanderkruik-Gray.

Elspeth slipped off the quilted jacket, from which a feather floated, and sat. It was a wooden captain's chair and she leaned on its curving back. Her arm itched in the cast. On the carpet in his tilted seat Peter passed wind and the noise startled him. His eyes widened.

She explained how she had withdrawn from Mount Holyoke, and about working in a gas station. She hoped she could combine a program in architectural studies with a general education.

Mrs. Vanderkruik-Gray said it was rather late to apply for the oncoming year, but she would take it upon herself to make an exception. Her Mount Holyoke grades and her Winslow High School grades would be sent for, and also her SAT scores.

After a quarter hour Mrs. Vanderkruik-Gray rose to end the interview, still maintaining a distant and noncommittal cordiality. Elspeth hung the jacket across the shoulder bag and squatted to gather the plastic seat under her arm with Peter in it.

"Can you manage?" Mrs. Vanderkruik-Gray asked.

"I'm fine. Can I fill out the application right out there in the office? And just leave it?"

"If you wish. If you feel ready to. But there's an essay to write. You may want to give it some thought."

"Well, I'll start it, anyway. Just don't hold the penmanship against me, please. I'm not used to writing with my left hand."

"I'll remember the broken arm," said Mrs. Vanderkruik-Gray. "It won't be held against you."

In the reception area the curly-haired young woman again looked at Elspeth with amusement.

"She said I could stay and fill it out right here," Elspeth said to her. "Is it okay if I use that typewriter there in the corner? The covered one?"

"I guess. I won't be using it. Can you type with one hand?"

"Well, it's faster than struggling with a pen. I've still got four fingers that know the keyboard."

Elspeth gave Peter a fresh diaper, kneeling on the carpet. She knew the receptionist watched from the desk as she positioned the first page in the roller.

Presently the irregular clacking seemed to lull Peter to sleep. Elspeth filled in the names of teachers she thought might give a passable recommendation. She paid no attention to persons who came and went behind her. She filled out the Financial Aid form.

She paused to give her fingers a rest. She scrawled a check for the fee. Then she began a draft for the essay question.

"Would you like some coffee?" the curly-haired woman asked.

"Oh. Sure. Thanks very much."

"Milk? Sugar?"

"Just black, please. And listen, if the bank questions the left-handed signature on my check, let me know. So far they haven't."

Elspeth turned again to her essay. She wrote about natural childbirth. She entitled it The Importance of Being a Fanatic.

She said most doctors did not know much about having a baby, just as they always lagged behind the informed section of the public when it came to polyunsaturates or just plain common sense. Even breastfeeding was a snap, provided you didn't listen to your doctor or your mother. Most doctors were stupid just like most mechanics, most clergy, most professors, and most Presidents of the United States. Medical schools served mainly to make them more pompous.

She paused to drink the coffee, reading what she had written so far.

She tore it up. She had to use her teeth.

She wrote instead about building one's own house, all by oneself. She said she had wired a basement room when she was twelve. No fuses blew, and her father had praised her to everyone. It had given her enormous satisfaction. She wanted to study architecture, but even more she wanted to build her own house and live in it. And over the lintel she would inscribe a phrase she had heard her grandfather

371

quote once: I will walk in my house with an honest heart. She thought it was from the Psalms.

48

AS she crossed to her own street she met Harriet coming the other way from the bus.

"Just *look* at you! You get yourself into such situations. All that to carry on one arm. Let me take the baby."

"I'm okay, Mama. Just let him be. Everything's in place and you've got a bag to carry."

They walked together toward the Brodys'.

"Well, did you look into the courses you wanted? What courses are you going to take?"

"I don't know yet. Maybe I won't be taking any. Did you bring me some more tools?"

"No. What do you need tools for? You can't fix cars with a broken arm. And I know how you broke your arm, by the way. I figured it out."

"Oh?"

"It was from cranking a car. Somebody brought an antique car to be fixed with a crank in front. I know because it happened to my Uncle Maxie when I was a little girl. He was cranking and all of a sudden it spun around the other way and broke his arm."

They stepped over a low place in a hardened snowbank, and crossed the glistening street diagonally.

"Well?" said Harriet. "Was that it?"

"I'd rather not say."

"See? It came to me. You kids don't know everything about cars. You think your mother doesn't know anything but I could have warned you about cranking a car. You probably never saw one. They don't make them like that anymore."

Elspeth laid Peter on the bed and began to unzipper him but Harriet took over. Peter's eyes moved to Harriet.

"How do you bathe him with a broken arm? I bet you haven't bathed him. I'm giving that child a bath. And then I'll wash his things."

In the bathroom Harriet raised the top of the changing table to expose the soft tub that hung beneath. She filled it, mixing hot water from the kettle and cool water.

His head rested upon Harriet's hand, the water lapping at his ears. He stared up at her face with total concentration.

She cooed at him. "You know Gammah. Don't you. Petey knows Gammah."

She splashed water over his belly. He did not take his eyes from hers. At last he crinkled and laughed, showing his gums.

Elspeth had never heard her refer to herself as Grandma before. She was certain now that her mother was unaware of the summons.

"Elspeth, I've got to mention something again. You really should have him circumcised. You shouldn't let that go. It's not right."

"Mama, I've looked it up, and nothing about it really makes any sense. I went into it at the library. It's just one of those anthropological things. It's not just Jews. There are different tribes all over the place that make a thing of it. They've even found aborigines in Australia or Africa or someplace that practice circumcision of girls. They cut out the inner labia. It's disgusting. I mean, what's the point?"

Harriet dried Peter in his terrycloth wrap. He never took his eyes from her.

"Such a face," said Harriet.

Elspeth fed Peter in the wicker chair while Harriet changed the bedding and prepared lunch. Then Harriet lowered him into the crib. She flinched from the bouncing cow-jumped-over-the-moon figures.

In the kitchen Mr. Brody was finishing his soup, raising the bowl with two hands. From under the stove the old cat glowered. Harriet watched Elspeth eat with her left hand.

"This place is like a home for the handicapped," Harriet said when Mr. Brody had left. "The three of you are really something. How can you manage? How can you peel a banana?"

"With my teeth."

"Or a grapefruit, how can you cut a grapefruit in half? It must roll away."

"I can't. I ask Mrs. Brody."

They heard Peter cry. Elspeth started up.

"No!" said Harriet. "You're gonna wear yourself out. Just sit and eat your lunch, like a good girl. I'll go in if you insist."

Harriet brought Peter to the kitchen. She ate holding him.

"He wasn't even wet," said Harriet. "And did you notice he stopped crying as soon as he heard my footsteps? I felt him and he was dry, and when I started to leave he cried again. That shows he's spoiled."

"It doesn't show he's spoiled," said Elspeth. "It shows he's intelligent."

"It shows he didn't have any good reason for crying. He just wanted company."

"Doesn't everybody?" said Elspeth.

373

When he slept Harriet did the laundry.

She brought Harriet the mending.

"I hate to give you more work—you do so much," said Elspeth. "But I haven't been able to sew, obviously."

"Work is what I'm here for," said Harriet.

Harriet sewed by the kitchen window.

She urged Elspeth to drop the breastfeeding now that her arm was broken.

"You don't understand, Mama. That's all the more reason to continue. How can I prepare bottles with one arm?"

Peter was sleeping when Harriet left. Elspeth saw her to the door.

"Thanks again for everything," said Elspeth.

Harriet kissed her.

"Mama, did you know I have to take Petey to court tomorrow? Daddy got Mr. Rosenbaum to file an action."

Harriet gave a start. Then her face turned heavy. "No. I didn't know. He didn't say anything." Her eyes moistened, though she didn't weep. A long sigh shook through her. "I'm attached to him now too," she said. "I don't know what's best. I guess Dad's more hardheaded. Practical."

She stood there in her buttoned coat, as though debating whether to return to the bedroom and look at Peter once more. She blinked. She swallowed. Then she turned hurriedly and left.

A SIGN said Courtrooms Upstairs, so Elspeth climbed the wide staircase, about twenty steps of marble, worn and soiled. There were already many people, though it was scarcely quarter to nine. Boots and galoshes had muddied the gallery. The long high radiator hissed. Men and women stood about, conferring in twos and threes, or just waiting. Some rested against the rail that surrounded the huge open stairwell. A black man heavily bandaged leaned on a crutch. Elspeth wandered with Peter and the dangling seat and the shoulder bag around the whole circuit of the gallery. She did not see her father or Mr. Rosenbaum, or any sign that told her where to report. There was a big room marked First Session, full of people waiting on benches. She went in. There was a half-enclosed high place up front, as for a judge, but no judge was there, and a desk below it faced the benches, but no one sat at the desk. A middle-aged man in a policeman's uniform but hatless stood at the wall with feet apart. Under the tall many-paned windows there was another desk, and a man in a jacket and tie busied himself there with papers. White people and black people sat in various degrees of shabbiness. Some read newspapers. There was a heavy odor of damp clothing. A young man talked to two young women with high-piled hairdos, gesturing earnestly.

Elspeth returned to the gallery that surrounded the great stairwell and looked for a place to nurse Peter. She had cut the six-o'clock feeding short so he would be ready again before nine, and would not have to be fed in midmorning.

With her shoulder she pushed open the washroom door. The stench was unbearable. She backed off.

She went further around the gallery to where double doors marked Second Session faced the First Session across the chasm of the stairwell. Through a little window she saw a courtroom much like the other, with not a soul inside, and clean benches.

"Could you open these doors for me, please?" she asked a uniformed man who passed.

"Can't go in there, miss. Everybody in First Session." He didn't stop.

Opposite the wide staircase there were doors lettered with the names of judges. The stairwell also contained two more marble staircases, narrow ones, beginning on each side of the summit of the wide one, and rising back the other way to yet another open gallery overhead. From here it looked as though no one was up there. But she had better have herself checked in as present before hiding somewhere to breastfeed.

She returned to the First Session and made her way across to the man at the side desk under the windows. Peter was squirming and chewing her hair. He thrust a hand into her eye.

"I'm supposed to be here at nine—" she began.

"What's your name?"

"Baker. Elspeth Baker."

He turned the papers on his desk. He was about forty. "That's Mr. Rosenbaum's case," he said. "Who's your attorney?"

"I don't have one. Do I have to have one?"

"It's up to you. Would you like the court to appoint an attorney?"

"I don't know. Who would you appoint?"

"Well, the judge would assign someone. Are you indigent?"

"I'm not exactly indigent. But do I need a lawyer?"

"That's up to you. But you might be better off. You'll be up against a lawyer."

"Okay, then. Try to find me an honest one."

"All right. After the sessions are split up we'll see who's available."

"And is there a place where I can nurse the baby? The ladies' room in this place is sickening."

"Well, wait here. I'll ask." He left, apparently through a door behind the high fortress up front.

Peter kept squirming. She hummed in his ear, turning this way and that where she stood by the desk, and it quieted him.

"If your man broke your arm you won't have no trouble getting a restraining order," a thin black woman said to her.

"Oh. Thanks," Elspeth said.

At the other desk, below the judge's place, a young man sat now and also busied himself with papers. A couple of older men who may have been attorneys went to speak to him and he looked up.

"Is that a little boy or a little girl?" a pockmarked white woman with no upper front teeth asked her.

"A boy," said Elspeth.

"Course he's a boy," said the black woman who had spoken to her before. "Can't you see his thing is blue?"

"What a shame, to waste such good looks on a boy," the white woman said.

The man she had queried returned to his desk. "The judge who'll have your case says as soon as he comes into the courtroom you can go to the Judges' Lobby. And use his office. Just have a seat meanwhile."

"All rise!" the man over at the desk below the high place shouted just then. Everyone shuffled to their feet and the judge appeared above, the robe swelling behind him. Elspeth was struck by his appearance—old with snow-white hair but big and erect, with an overhanging brow and piercing gray eyes.

"Come on, I'll take you now," the man who had spoken to Elspeth said. He led her quickly across the front of the courtroom and out.

She followed him a quarter of the way around the gallery, the plastic seat swinging against her jeans. It came untied and dropped with a clatter. He turned and picked it up.

At last he opened a door to a small office. He placed the seat in the middle of a cluttered desk. "Shall I strap the baby in the seat?" he asked.

"No, I have to change him." She laid Peter carefully on the desk and pulled the zipper.

"You'll have complete privacy here," the man said.

"Thanks."

He left, closing the door.

She had dropped the shoulder bag to an old chair that smelled of real leather, worn at the wrinkles. Peter smiled at her while she changed him.

"Don't smile, Petey. How am I gonna bear it when they separate us, if you smile at me like that?"

Through a half-open door she saw a small windowless water closet. Around Peter on the desk there were family photographs in frames.

She sank with Peter into the worn leather. The door opened and a tall, slim young man looked in. He wore a vest of gray velveteen with flat brass buttons, and long brown hair down to his shoulders.

"Elspeth Baker?" he asked.

"Yes."

"My name's Alfredo Castorini. You can call me Alf. If you're looking for an attorney I've been asked to defend you."

"Oh."

"Are you indigent?"

"I can pay something. Not a lot."

He nodded. "Who's the abuse victim? Not this infant?"

"Supposedly."

"He doesn't look abused."

"I'm glad you can see that. He's not."

"*You* look like the one that's been abused."

"Oh, my arm. I had an accident."

"Look, I've got another case, but I've asked to have it called early so I can have some time to confer with you before lunch. Amsterdam takes short lunches. And then maybe we can get you called right after lunch, so you don't have to hang around with the baby."

"Okay."

He put his hand on the knob, but turned and smiled down again. "How do you rate using the judge's chambers?"

"I asked some guy in the big courtroom there, and he arranged it."

"Murphy, probably. The probation officer."

He left.

Elspeth shook a breast out of the flannel shirt. Peter latched on eagerly. He closed his eyes and sucked.

"Get all you can, Petey. It may be nothing but bottles after today."

Besides the soft odors of Peter and leather there was another smell. It was like salami. It occurred to her that it came from a little brown paper bag with its top twisted shut, that sat on a corner of the desk. She wondered if the judge's lunch was in there.

In a short time Peter stopped sucking. She tickled the wrinkled pink sole of his foot. He drew up the foot and grinned, his mouth still half around the wet nipple and his cheek resting on the breast. But he did not suck and did not open his eyes.

She sang to him slowly and softly.

> "Lye dye,
> A sleepy eye,
> Hi fi,
> A lullaby—"

She closed the bra and shirt. He dozed.

She wondered if Daddy and Barney Rosenbaum had arrived yet, and were sitting in the courtroom, or conferring out in the gallery. Maybe Mama would even show up, and sit in the courtroom crying.

She pictured Petey smiling and cooing across the courtroom to Daddy, while Daddy's embittered features grew milder and milder, his eyes trying to avoid Petey but returning to him again and again. Till at last Daddy would rise and say, I'm sorry, judge. This is the first time I've seen the baby, and I didn't know what an outstanding baby he is. Of course she can't give him up. And neither can I. I want my daughter, and I want my little grandson—my heart's been empty since I lost my two boys. The voice choked. She would rush to him. Tears on her cheeks. Tears on Daddy's cheeks. Tears on the judge's cheeks.

Elspeth sank deeper into the stuffed cracked leather. Her hand stroked Peter's round little head, his soft hair.

But things don't happen the way you fantasize them. Life isn't like your dreams. But if you can't make dreams, how can you bear to live? When they've taken you away, Petey, I'll make dreams about you. Year by year.

The kind of dreams you'll dream for yourself, I'll dream for you too. And that'll be a kind of togetherness of us, though you don't know. And when you're old enough to read, I'll write to all the Chit Chat columns all over the country, and tell how mothers dream for the children they've given up. So maybe someday you'll know.

With each foot she pushed the muddy shoe off the other. She rested her heels on the edge of the judge's desk. She sighed.

What if the judge should come in here, for a midmorning coffee break or something? He'd probably knock first.

She would offer him his leather chair but he would tell her not to disturb herself. He would show her the pictures of his grandchildren. By the time her case came up, the judge would be her friend.

She dozed fitfully, while Peter slept on her front.

The knob turned with a sharp click, giving her a start. She took her feet from the desk.

But it was not the judge. It was Alf, looking down at her. Alfredo Castorini with his shoulder-length hair, pink shirt and handsome vest. A black raincoat hung on his arm.

"Hi," he said. "It's now ten-twenty, and your case is down for one o'clock. What do you say we go sit at the tavern, and you can tell me the story, and we'll have a bite."

"Okay."

He picked up Peter, who wakened and blinked. Then he lifted Peter high over his head with two hands, looked up at him and smiled. Peter smiled down at Alf open-mouthed, and gave a whooping laugh. Alf laughed heartily.

He held Peter to his shoulder and patted him.

"Are you married?" Elspeth asked.

"No."

"Have you ever been married?"

378

"No."

"You seem to like children."

"Well, I used to be one."

"But most people have forgotten."

"I don't like all children, anymore than I like all adults. I guess I react individually."

She had stepped into her shoes. She felt Peter's bottom under his gown. "He's dry," she said.

Alf laid him on the desk and zipped him into the flannel. He held the quilted jacket while Elspeth slipped her good arm into it. He hung the shoulder bag upon her.

"Thank you. I didn't realize lawyers were such gentlemen."

He put on his raincoat, picked up Peter and the plastic seat, and opened the door for her.

She preceded him down the broad marble staircase.

They crossed the intersection together in the mist.

At their booth in the tavern Alf pushed the sugar and napkin dispensers and ketchup aside, and set up Peter in his plastic seat on the table against the music selector.

Elspeth faced him across the table. She took the white dumbbell from the shoulder bag and gave it to Peter. He waved it.

"Would you like a beer?" Alf asked.

"Okay."

He signaled a tired waitress and ordered beers. Peter dropped the dumbbell. Alf enclosed it in the little hand. Peter dropped it again.

"How much is your fee?"

"Well, let's see what happens first. And then we'll see what you can afford."

"What do you usually get?"

"Sometimes nothing."

"How do you make a living?"

"Well, I don't. I'm only out of law school eight months. And still living with my parents. If I defend an indigent the Defenders pay me."

"Watch Petey while I go to the john, okay?"

In the bathroom she combed her hair. The cast had grown dirty. She spread the sling to cover it. She put cold water to her eyelids to make them open wider. She turned, and smoothed the fit of the jeans upon her behind.

When she returned Peter was wearing a little pretzel as an armband. The beers had come, and a bowl of pretzels.

Elspeth told her story, going back a full year to Jared. She sipped beer. Alf listened a long time without asking a question. She told of the people who had been going to charge her with indecent exposure, but he said nothing would happen if it hadn't by now. It was his first comment in nearly an hour. Peter slept now, the pretzel still on his arm. Alf didn't think much of the Harvard-Radcliffe idea. He said the judge would consider it immaterial. But he might mention it anyhow if the occasion arose. He studied her across the table. She met his stare.

379

"Do you love the baby?" he asked. "Are you determined to keep him?"

"Of course. Isn't it obvious?"

"It's obvious enough. But I wanted to hear you say it. Elspeth, I spoke to Mr. Rosenbaum this morning. I think he knows he hasn't got a leg to stand on."

"You think so? Really? I don't think they even served the summons legally. They gave it to my landlady. Maybe we can even quash the whole thing on a technicality."

"No, it was legal. They delivered it to your residence. Elspeth, it's risky to predict. In a court of law crazy things can happen. But frankly I'm not worried. I think Mr. Rosenbaum would rather not be stuck with this, except your father probably insisted."

"Is my father here with him?"

"No, your father won't be here. Rosenbaum says he won't call any witnesses."

"Are you sure he's not bringing any witnesses? What about the rabbi? There's a rabbi. I chased him out with a shitty diaper."

"He didn't say anything about a rabbi. What would the rabbi testify about?"

"The apartment smells. The wallpaper's peeling."

"Has he observed your treatment of the baby?"

"He didn't have a chance to. I kicked him out."

"We're gonna be before a Jewish judge."

"Oh. Could we get a different judge?"

"I wish we could. I'd rather have Cunningham. The black guy. Or Muldoon. But Amsterdam assigns the cases, and he always takes the first part of the alphabet for himself. But anyway Rosenbaum said no witnesses. I don't think he'd double-cross me."

"What's the judge like?"

"An old guy. He's one of the reasons they're pushing the mandatory retirement bill."

"How old?"

"I've heard he's eighty. I wouldn't say he looks eighty, but he's seventy easy."

"Is that the one I saw this morning? He looks like God in the Sistine Chapel."

"Don't kid yourself. Sometimes he can't put a decent grammatical sentence together. Elspeth, Rosenbaum offered us a deal of sorts. He'll drop the charge here, on condition we agree to a hearing in Probate Court."

"What do you say?" she asked him.

"I say no. The Probate Court has much broader authority to take children away. In Municipal Court he's got to show a crime. He just brought you here with a phony charge to persuade you to go there willingly. And once you go there willingly it's like you've admitted there's an issue. He'll ask the court to appoint some busybody to investigate and complicate everything. I say no way. Let him try to persuade the Probate Court to take jurisdiction if he can. If we ever have to go there we'll go under protest, and we'll claim harassment."

Elspeth nodded.

"Let's have some lunch," said Alf. "They have little steaks here that aren't too bad. It comes with a salad."

"I can't cut a steak."

"I'll cut yours for you."

He beckoned the slumping waitress again. She wrote the order.

"Oil and vinegar," said Alf.

"Same," said Elspeth.

He sat looking at her when the waitress had gone. "How can you work at a gas station with one hand? Pump gas, raise the hood, check the oil, clean the windshield, all that."

"Easy. It's a lot easier than opening a cereal box with one hand."

He nodded slowly.

"Easier than getting dressed too," she added.

"Listen," he said. "When we're in court, I don't want the baby in this little seat. Just put the seat away on the floor somewhere and I want you holding the baby in your arm, your one arm, every minute the judge is in that courtroom. Never put him down. Not for anything. Don't even change him if he's wet. Just keep holding him. Right up front there in the front row. We're gonna play the angle that you've never been apart. And if he cries, no matter what he's crying for, right away you take your breast out and give him the breast. Can you do that with one arm? Take it out without putting him down?"

"Sure."

"Okay then. The second he cries, you give him the breast. Right in front of the judge. And I'll say, 'your honor, can we tear this child away from its mother's breast?' "

Alf slipped the pretzel off Peter's arm. Peter still slept in the seat. Alf nibbled the pretzel.

50

IT was the same big-shouldered, hoary-headed judge as before. There were not many people in the courtroom now. Outdoors the mist had cleared, and the sun from the many high panes reflected too brightly off the side desk, from which the man had gone. The younger man, who had the desk below the judge's place, called her name without looking at her. Alf motioned to her to remain where she was. From her seat on the front bench Elspeth watched Alf and Mr. Rosenbaum go forward together. Mr. Rosenbaum appeared short and shapeless beside Alf. The back of his head had a bald space, and plastered black hair lay around it in circles. With one hand he grasped the seat of his pants and wriggled, as though his underwear gave him some discomfort.

"Okay, fellers," the white-haired judge said, looking down at them. "What's this about?"

"This kid is charged with child abuse, judge," Mr. Rosenbaum said. "Abuse and mistreatment of a seven-and-a half-week-old infant. The baby's grandfather lodged the complaint in the child's interest. But before this defendant is tried on a criminal charge, I move that she be committed to the Psychopathic for ten days of observation. To give her a break. It's the least we can do."

"We oppose that motion, your honor," Alf cut in. "First off, Mr. Rosenbaum never advised me he intended to make such a motion. If he intends to try this case let it be tried. The baby's right here. The court can see for itself it hasn't been abused."

"That's for the court to decide after hearing evidence, Mr. Castorini," Rosenbaum said. "Meanwhile there's nothing unusual in committing a defendant for psychiatric observation first. If she's mentally defective we avoid a useless trial, and if she's not there's been nothing lost."

"Your honor," said Alf, "may I explain the background of this case? The baby is illegitimate. Born out of wedlock. So the girl's father has disowned her. He's an old-fashioned guy, taking it awfully hard, and he won't see his daughter or the baby. And meanwhile this case is nothing but a misguided ploy to have the baby taken from her. So we can all pretend it never happened, she never had a baby, and everything's like before. And I contend if that's what Mr. Rosenberg is looking for he's in the wrong court. If a custody decision is what he's after he should be in Probate Court."

"Are you offering a motion that the case be remanded to Probate Court?" Rosenbaum asked him.

382

"No, I'm not. My position is it shouldn't be in any court. But I'm curious as to why my brother Mr. Rosenbaum didn't go to Probate Court by the front door. If he's really so concerned about the baby's welfare he'd have more leeway there. He wouldn't have to prove a criminal charge."

"Judge, young learned counsel here is casting around for a delaying tactic. Stalling. We're hearing a motion for ten days of observation at the Psychopathic."

"But why didn't you go to Probate Court, Mr. Rosenberg?" the judge asked.

"Judge, you know how they futz around in Probate Court. All they'll do is appoint an investigator. Somebody not psychiatrically trained, just some attorney looking to make a few bucks. And he'll just lay it aside for weeks or months until he hasn't got enough cases of his own to keep him busy. And when he finally has an evening free to go investigating she'll take him to bed with her and he'll write a favorable report."

"Objection," said Alf.

"There's no jury here," said Rosenbaum, "and no stenographer. We can talk man to man. Without formality."

"Even so. My client doesn't have to take these insults."

"You're defending her honor?" said Rosenbaum. "She *has* had an illegitimate child after all."

"But there's no allegation here that she's a prostitute or that she has no visible means of support. My brother Mr. Rosenbaum owes my client an apology."

"I'm not this young Lochinvar's brother and he knows it. And he knows I don't like his fancy law-school language. This kid thinks he's still in school."

"Okay, okay, boys, hold your hosses," the judge said. "Don't fight. I won't make you apologize. But don't tell me stories about what she's gonna do with an investigator. You could ask them to appoint a woman for an investigator."

Peter wakened and the sun from the windows made him squint. Elspeth kissed the top of his head, and slid herself a foot or two along the bench into shadow. She tried to turn so that Peter's face was toward the judge, but they didn't notice.

"Can we have a ruling on the motion? This girl doesn't have all her marbles, judge. Why does young learned counsel here object to letting the Psychopathic check her over? What's he hiding? What's he worried about?"

"Your honor, this is a college girl. She's within one one-hundredth of a point of an honors average."

"So what? I wish I had a dollar for every college kid that ends up in the booby hatch. This kid's unstable. She went running out of the hospital with the baby in zero weather when the baby was two days old, didn't even check out, just sneaked it out against doctor's orders, and that was after she promised some family they could adopt it, and after she drove the whole maternity ward crazy for two days. The head nurse had to threaten to put her in a strait jacket. My client offered at that time to provide the best care at a first-class private mental institution if she'd sign herself in. And now she's dragging the baby around with one arm in a gasoline station where she's broken her arm already, and we're lucky it's only her arm. Not the baby's head. Okay, everybody has a right to be stupid, but not where

383

the health and welfare of a young child is concerned."

"How did she break her arm?" the judge asked.

"Your honor, she fired her employer's Army pistol to scare off an intruder that attacked her employer, and the gun had a bad kick that threw her arm up and cracked her elbow. The police have a complete record of the incident and no charges were filed against her."

"Well now, that I didn't even know," said Rosenbaum. "I thought she busted it trying to fix a car. Bullets flying around. I suppose by young Mr. Castorini's standards that's a delightful environment to bring up a baby in."

"Her conduct is perfectly rational," Alf said.

"Isn't it best to let the experts decide that, Mr. Castorini?" said the judge. "That's what we have the Psychopathic for. They have the best professors from the Harvard Medical. There's no use two lawyers arguing about whether somebody's crazy or not."

"If she goes to the Psychopathic for ten days, your honor, where would the baby be during that time?"

"Children's Hospital," said Rosenbaum. "Or the Little Wanderers."

"Which amounts to removing the child to the jurisdiction of the court. That's not something to be undertaken lightly without grounds and without evidence, on the mere whim of Mr. Rosenbaum. This young mother is breastfeeding, your honor. You separate mother and child for a ten-day period and that kills the breastfeeding. Even if they let her out after ten days, as I'm sure they would, and she gets the baby back, her breasts will be all dried up."

"Believe me, judge. I'm not trying to dry anybody's breasts up," Rosenbaum said tiredly. "And breastfeeding isn't the most sanitary thing in the world anyhow."

"What's unsanitary about it?" said Alf.

"Well, you can't boil the female breast and sterilize it, like you can a bottle. She isn't pasteurized."

"Why don't you send my father to the Psychopathic?" said Elspeth, though her seat was a distance from where they stood. "He's crazier than I am." She saw Alf motion her to be quiet.

"Listen to that, judge," said Rosenbaum. "You hear that? Is that a way for a girl to talk about her father?"

"It's true," said Elspeth.

"Okay, so it's true. Between you and me and the lamppost, judge, the whole family's a little flaky. Maybe she inherits it. But the old man isn't the one that has the health and safety of a helpless infant in his hands."

"And its a good thing too," said Elspeth. "Because I'm a much better parent than my father is a grandparent. That was a laugh, Mr. Rosenbaum saying the complaint was lodged by the baby's grandfather in the baby's behalf. Daddy just wants to get rid of his own grandchild. He's been trying ever since I was pregnant. He even tried to make me have an abortion. And that was before they were officially legal, even."

"Is that true, Mr. Rosenberg?" the judge asked.

"Well, that's a technicality. It wasn't his fault it wasn't legal yet. What did you expect him to do? Can you blame him? He tried first to make the guy marry her. He did everything a father can do. But somebody, somewhere, sometime, has got to finally say no to this trend of getting more and more permissive. Of giving in to whatever kids do. Before society falls apart completely. A girl done wrong by a boy—that you can understand. Not a girl bringing up an illegitimate kid, brazen and proud of it."

"Okay, so he hasn't got a father," said Elspeth. "Just because he doesn't have a father does it make sense to deprive him of his mother too?"

"Judge," Rosenbaum said, "may I suggest that the bench caution the defendant against these outbursts, and that she speak through her attorney?"

"Well," said the judge, "who says lawyers have to do all the talking? I'll shut her up if she talks too much. Like you said, we're informal."

"And why does Mr. Rosenbaum have us assume her baby will be forever fatherless?" said Alf. "Look at her, your honor. The face of a Madonna. In the flower of her youth. Demure. A mother. A homemaker. I'll give you odds she'll have a husband within a year. Now, if your honor please, this whole thing has gone far enough. My client was summoned here on a charge. If Mr. Rosenbaum isn't prepared to produce witnesses to give sworn testimony, then it's nothing but harassment and abuse of process. If this charge is only a gimmick to provide a basis for ten days at the Psychopathic, in order to force the premature weaning of a nursing infant, then I move it be dismissed. Look at the baby, your honor. Bring him closer, Elspeth. Do you see any signs of abuse?"

Elspeth had already tried to nudge Peter around to a position facing forward, but she had not succeeded. She rose and came forward with him. Alf took Peter from her. He rested Peter against his arm and chest, supporting him in front and underneath, and faced the judge.

Elspeth regretted that he was wet. The judge leaned forward and looked down at him, putting on black-rimmed eyeglasses which he continued to hold at the hinge. Peter returned the judge's stare.

Suddenly Peter broke into an open-mouthed smile.

"She looks pretty good to me," the judge said.

"He's a he," Elspeth corrected him.

"What?"

"He's not a she. He's a he."

"She's a he?"

"A boy," said Elspeth. "He's a boy."

Alf handed him back to Elspeth. He wiped a damp hand quickly and unobtrusively against his jacket and indicated Peter with a gesture. "Does he look undernourished, your honor? Do you see any bruises? His mother took him to one of the finest clinics in the city for a routine checkup and inoculations not so long ago. Perhaps Mr. Rosenbaum would like to know what the findings were on that occasion. Maybe his client would like to foot the bill for a deposition."

"Okay," said Rosenbaum, "so he doesn't have any black-and-blue marks. Abuse is a lot of different things, judge. Keeping an infant in a gas station to be in the fumes all day. A baby that age crawling around under cars in the grease. Putting everything in its mouth. That's some environment for an infant, judge. And now we hear she's even been in gun battles there. She thinks the baby is a toy, or a doll. Not only does it wet, it even nurses. She may be the natural mother, but she's irresponsible. If she wants to play around gas stations, garages, why doesn't she leave the baby with a sitter?"

"She can't," said Alf. "She's breastfeeding."

"Well, what about crawling around in the grease, in the dirt there?" said the judge. "Like Mr. Rosenberg said. Putting everything in its mouth. Never mind, Mr. Castorini. I want to hear her answer."

"Petey's not of crawling age," said Elspeth. "And when he is he'll have a playpen. He stays in the office. And my boss there is a mother of two children and sometimes she helps take care of him. He stays in the bassinet from his carriage, or strapped in his seat, except when I'm holding him."

"Your honor, if I may be heard," said Alf, "where is a child safer than under the watchful eyes of its mother? This is a serious-minded young woman. On the Jewish New Year she was very anxious to go to the temple, but instead she worked in her father's store so her her father could go. Your honor, this girl has no boyfriends. She has nothing to do with men. She doesn't date. She doesn't run around. She doesn't drink or smoke. She devotes herself solely to the good of this unfortunate child, trying to make it up to him for bringing him into the world fatherless, and giving him the love only a mother can give. She read somewhere that natural childbirth is healthy for the child, so no pain was too much for her to bear. She readily suffered torment, refusing even the mildest pain killers. She read that mother's milk has special qualities, and again, no inconvenience is too great if it means some advantage for her child. He's never out of her sight. Your honor, I know that you yourself were deprived of a mother's love at an early age. I think every attorney in this city knows the inspiring story about how your honor was raised in an orphanage, and yet rose to eminence even without the priceless ingredient of parental encouragement. Your honor, this poor infant was rejected by his father. And rejected also by his grandfather, Mr. Rosenbaum's client. Don't deprive him even for an hour, even for a day, of his most precious blessing, this devoted mother who loves him more than anything on earth. She's all he has. I can understand that my brother Mr. Rosenbaum had to make a show of court activity to mollify a long-term client and old friend, but what we have here is basically a family matter, between father and daughter, and they're gonna have to resolve it between themselves. Just because his little girl is too big to spank anymore he can't go running to the courts of the Commonwealth, making a farce of lawful process."

"Mr. Castorini, I'm inclined to agree. I'm sorry, Mr. Rosenberg. Mark it dismissed, Mr. Doyle. But don't call the next one yet. I want to talk to this young lady a minute. Come here, young lady. And you can go sit down, Mr. Castorini and Mr. Rosenberg. Or go out and have a smoke. I don't need you."

Elspeth stepped closer. She kissed Peter on the top of his head.

"For a youngster you sure can sling it," she heard Rosenbaum say to Alf as they walked away.

"No, wait, Mr. Castorini," the judge said. "Why don't you take care of the baby for her for a couple of minutes. You seemed to hold it all right before."

Alf came and took Peter gently.

"All right, young lady. Come up close. You can come around Mr. Doyle's desk there. That's good. So I don't have to holler."

She rested her free arm in the sling, on top of the cast. The judge leaned forward, resting on his robed elbows.

"Now listen. Don't think I'm condoning you. Mr. Rosenberg has a very good point there, that you should go get your head examined. Your attorney did a very good job for you, you should thank him. But never mind that, I can see for myself if you didn't love the baby you wouldn't be in here fighting to keep the baby, and nursing with a broken arm. But you just better watch out. This time you're getting the benefit of the doubt. If any harm happens to that little baby, God forbid, you could be in court again and that time the next judge might see it different. Never mind what your attorney says. Every attorney that comes in here is defending a saint and the victim of society. I heard it all before. I knew it all by heart, before Mr. Castorini was even wetting his pants yet. Long before. You're no bargain. If you were such an angel you wouldn't be here. So get yourself straightened out. For your own sake, and your poor parents, and that little baby. Just because the world's all messed up, that doesn't give you the right to mess it up a little more. Tell me, did you ever have any religious education?"

"A little. The usual."

"Well, let me give you a little advice. It's very hard to bring up a baby all alone, without a husband to be the man in the house. I want to advise you you should get married as soon as possible. Find a nice feller of your own religion that likes children. Or a widower even, that's looking for somebody. I don't have anybody special in mind. I just mean you should go out and look around, look the fellers over. With object matrimony. As soon as possible, and make a normal family life, for the little baby's good, and so your parents can be happy. And the next thing I want to advise you, is see that the baby gets a good religious education. People have the tendency to forget all about religion nowadays, but it's important, because a man can't live by bread alone. It says right there in the Bible, 'come unto me, all ye that are heavenly laden, and I will give you the rest.' Even if some rich feller is heavenly laden with all kinds of Lincoln Continentals, and all kinds of stereo playing hi-fi in the dashboard, he still hasn't got everything, and only God can give him the rest. All right. I gave you good advice. I don't know what's the matter with kids. You're your parents' whole life. And look at the mess you made for them. You just weren't thinking or what? Or maybe you saw your parents hurt *their* parents, hurt your grandparents, and that's where you learned it. That's usually how it is. But believe you me, for the aggravation you caused your parents, that little baby is gonna grow up and pay you back good. Like it says in the Bible, 'in pain you will bring forth children.' Right in the pit of your stomach. Till you're sick in your heart. They all do. Human beings are like that. You think your little baby will have sense enough to stay out of trouble? No. He'll get a little older, and he'll say, stay out of trouble, eh, that isn't interesting enough. All right, young lady. Go home." The black-framed eyeglasses were in his hand and he gestured slightly with them toward the door. "Enjoy the baby now, while he's too little to make trouble yet."

"Thank you, sir," said Elspeth. "Your honor."

"Never mind, don't thank me. I just do the best I can. You spoiled my day already. Call the next case, Mr. Doyle."

The man rose and cried out a name.

A tattered black man shuffled forward handcuffed to a black police officer. Elspeth saw that Alf stood just inside the door of the courtroom and had zippered Peter into the flannel. He also held the shoulder bag and the plastic seat and her quilted jacket. Rosenbaum stood there too, unsmiling. He turned and preceded them out. He walked from them along the gallery.

"Mr. Rosenbaum!" Elspeth called after him on the gallery. "Hey! Take a good look at this baby and when you see my father tell him how gorgeous he is. And tell him how much like Eric he looks."

Rosenbaum did not look back but kept walking away.

She turned to Alf. She looked up and he gave Peter to her. "I love you, Alf. You're the greatest."

"I was only doing my job," he said, putting the shoulder bag on the wrong side, the strap under the sling, the seat dangling. "And besides, I thought it was a pretty rotten trick they were trying to pull on you. I changed the baby. I found diapers in the bag." He hung the jacket upon her shoulders.

"I'm sorry Petey was wet. It happened just the minute before, I swear. I took him into the courtroom dry."

"That's okay."

"How come you're so good with babies?"

"I help with my sister's kids a lot. They live with us too."

"And what would have happened without you? Would I have been sent to the Psychopathic?"

"It's hard to say. You spoke up pretty well yourself there, and Rosenbaum was leaning on a pretty flimsy reed. I suppose Amsterdam might have figured he couldn't go wrong in letting the Psychopathic check you over. I don't really know if he would. He's not as stupid as he sounds. Or he might have passed the buck to Probate Court."

"What would have happened in Probate Court?"

"I don't know. Maybe not much. They have their own psychiatrist on premises."

"Well, I'm so glad I had a lawyer. And I'm glad it was you. What about your fee? Will you send me a bill?"

"Have you got any cash on you?"

"Gee, I'm sorry, I don't really. Just six bucks. You're worth more than that. And

I didn't think to bring my checkbook. Send me a bill, okay? Don't worry, I'll pay it."

"I hope so."

"How could I not pay it. After what you did for me. I'll be glad to pay it."

He shrugged. "Okay. I'll have to send a bill then."

"I'm really sorry I didn't bring more cash. You know, everybody keeps saying don't carry money in this neighborhood."

"Want me to call you a cab?"

"Let's go have a drink somewhere. I want to buy you a drink, and celebrate. I have to wind down."

"Are you kidding? I just told the judge you don't drink."

"I never said that. Or let's have coffee then. I'm all wound up."

"I wish I could, Elspeth. I can't. I don't have the time. I'll get you a cab."

"That's okay. The bus is good enough. Oh, wait a minute. Could you do just one more thing for me, Alf? Hold the baby while I phone my mother?"

SHE heard Harriet weep a little, then blow her nose softly. Through the glass of the booth she watched Alf and Peter. He was not looking at her. "I'm glad, I guess," said Harriet. "I don't know if I should be. I'm glad and I'm sorry. I just hope it's for the best."

"They practically laughed Mr. Rosenbaum out of court. He made a farce of lawful process—that's what my lawyer said."

"Where did you get a lawyer?"

"Oh, I had a sweetheart of a lawyer! The court appointed a lawyer for me. I've got to run, Mama. I'll call you again."

"Are you going to the Brodys'?"

"No, it's only two-thirty, and Chris needs help. I can still give her a few hours. But phone Mrs. Brody and tell her I won the case, will you? She predicted I would. Will you call her for me?"

"I'll call her. I hope you dressed up at least to make a decent appearance in court. I hope you didn't go in blue jeans."

"As a matter of fact I did."

"Oh! What did the judge think of that?"

"I don't know. He decided in my favor. I'm keeping Alf waiting. I have to go."

"Keeping who?"

"My lawyer. He's holding Petey. Bye."

She emerged. Alf was no longer smiling.

"Come on, I'll see you onto the bus," he said.

The bus came almost as they reached the stop. He gave her Peter.

"Send a bill," Elspeth told him again. "I could kiss you."

When she decended from the bus at Saltmarsh Service Chris was cleaning a windshield. Sunshine beamed from a curve in the chrome.

"Well!" said Chris. "You must have made out okay. You've still got the baby. And you're smiling."

"I had a terrific lawyer and a terrific judge. It restores my faith in something or other."

In the office Elspeth dropped the shoulder bag and the baby seat. In the repair bay Puff was banging a fender with the rubber hammer. Peter widened his eyes. Behind the unrhythmic hammering the radio played. She settled into the swivel to feed him. She raised her heels to the windowsill. Chris came in, picked the smoldering cigarette from the ashtray, and leaned against the rolltop desk. Elspeth told her about the hearing.

"Your father really sounds like a skunk," Chris said at last. "You ought to disown him too, like he disowned you. Not make excuses for him all the time. I'd tell him to go straight to hell."

"He's there already."

"Hey, you remember the pictures Vinnie took the day he was hit? I finally took the film out of the camera this morning and took it to the drugstore. I thought in case they took the baby away at least you'd have the pictures."

"Thanks, Chris. I appreciate that."

Elspeth talked much during supper, reliving details of the hearing.

"Yeh," said Mrs. Brody. "The judge told you right, darling, you should look for a husband to get married. It isn't good the baby should be housebroken. I heard it on the television, the same thing. All the housebroken children were sorry, even when they growed up. They said it themself, and the psychology said it. It isn't good."

"Housebroken? You mean broken homes?"

"Broken homes. Yeh."

After supper Elspeth nursed Peter in bed.

What would you think of Alf for a daddy, Petey? Is he your type? And then we'd be Italian. And eat calamari al sugo. Would you like that?

He had said something in court about anybody could see she'd be married within a year. Of course he had said it for the judge's benefit, but he didn't have to put it quite so vehemently, if she didn't also turn him on some.

If the phone rang and he said let's go out—well, we have to just wait and see. After the first mixer in South Hadley, so many guys called and she honestly hadn't been able to remember which was which or connect names with faces. One pathetic guy had said, a toll call, forty-five cents, and you can't even remember you met me.

That seemed so long ago. A year and a half.

Elspeth Castorini. It had a better rhythm somehow than Elspeth Baker.

One of the things he had told the judge she hadn't liked. That she didn't care about men, was frigid practically.

Did he really see her like that? He couldn't. Not if he thought she'd be married in a year.

Unless he only meant married to some creep for Petey's sake.

But he had said something about her being pretty damn easy on the eyes. Look at her, your honor. Only how had he put it then? Did he say beautiful?

Face of an angel, or something like that. Face of a Madonna. Oh, shit, no! Why couldn't he have said she had tits rising like pagodas in Bangkok?

Petey Castorini. It sounded so perfect. Petey Castorini.

In a day or so Chris told her Vinnie was home from the hospital, but helpless. His whole right side was useless, though a therapist was to come in a couple of times a week. "It was real sweet of you, sending that plant."

"Well, I wasn't sure I should," said Elspeth, "because a plant is one more thing to take care of, when there's so much on your mind. But I figured, watching something grow is good for morale. It helps you believe in life, sort of."

"No, you did right, kiddo, God love ya. He appreciates it. His mind is clear, just like you and me. That's the trouble. It breaks your heart just looking at him. Sometimes he gets a word out, and then the next minute he just can't make words. He knows what he wants to say, and we guess this word and we guess that word, and he keeps shaking no. Poor guy. He cries. He can't even steer himself in the wheelchair, because he can only push on one side. It just goes in a circle. I'm telling ya, you want to cry. They fixed up his skull bone with this plastic piece, but he had some pretty bad brain damage. That iron must have come down on him with the curved prong end—it went in deep."

Chris would go home now for a couple of hours every day about noon.

"I give him his lunch, and I empty the piss bottle. And then I help him get on the toilet, and help him get off again. And you know how big he is. It ain't easy. Yesterday we almost fell over together. I'm gonna tell him, we just have to stick to the bedpan. As much as he hates it."

"Would he like me to come and visit sometime?"

Chris shook her head. "He doesn't want visitors. Nobody. Just the family. And Father Nugent. He's embarrassed for anybody to see him like this. But thanks, kiddo. I told him you ask for him. Father Nugent's been great, God love him. Climbs all those stairs, and he's no youngster. And hears his confession, even though the poor guy can't even talk."

The Clish brothers' grandfather had taken to hanging around the gas station almost every day. He would sit in the repair bay by the radio, watching Edgar and Puff and sucking his pipe. Chris paid no attention to him. He was not on the payroll and did no work, except to hand a tool to one of the boys when it was asked for, and apparently had no purpose in coming there except to pass the time. He was a scrawny thin-haired old man by the name of Alton Tingley, blinking through crooked eyeglasses. Sometimes he had his dentures and sometimes he didn't. If Edgar or Puff took the wrecker Mr. Tingley usually went along for the ride. Elspeth tried always to have finished nursing Peter before Chris made her midday trip home. But sometimes it couldn't be helped, and if she was nursing when Chris left Mr. Tingley was certain to know it and to come to the office to stare.

Once a boy of about eleven came in with a bicycle whose chain had come off its sprocket. She could not repair it with one arm, but she sat out front in the sun and told him what to do, and watched while he turned it upside down and made the adjustment.

"It's early in the year to take a bike out," she told him. "You'll get it rusty."

"The roads are pretty clear," he said.

A car came to the pumps, and it was an instant before Edgar saw her. "Get that car! Jesus! Laziest white woman I ever saw. Sits on her ass all day with a tit hanging out."

Each evening she asked Mrs. Brody if there was mail for her. But Alf's bill did not come. She began to hope it was because he intended to phone her instead.

And if no bill came and no phone call either, then in a week or two she would phone him.

On Elspeth's day off Harriet visited, and put a cooked chicken and a pan of baked macaroni and a jar of thick soup into the refrigerator.

"Why so much, Mama?"

"It'll keep. You can't cook with one arm."

"Well, thanks. I can't cook as good as you can even with two hands. But, you know, what I really can't do one-handed is loosen the cover on a jar. I hope it isn't screwed too tight."

Harriet have the cover a twist.

"Those snapshots you sent came yesterday," Harriet said. "Who took those?"

"The O'Banions."

"Some of them are very good. But I don't think any picture can do justice to Petey. Or you either."

"Did Dad see them?"

"He wouldn't look at them."

"How is he?"

"Oh, he's all right. Working hard. The same."

"How's his ulcer been?"

"Well, knock on wood. He's disgusted with Mr. Rosenbaum though. He says Mr. Rosenbaum is a bonehead. When he saw he was before a Jewish judge he should have brought out that you refused to have the baby circumcised."

392

"A judge can't make you circumcise a baby."

"Well, Mr. Rosenbaum said that, but Dad says he should have mentioned it."

"Maybe Mr. Rosenbaum didn't know it."

"He says he didn't, but Dad says he told him."

"Why don't you leave the pictures where Dad will have to see them?"

"Well, I had them on the kitchen table, and he kind of sneaked a glance sideways. I guess he couldn't help it. And there was a letter in the Chit Chat I meant to clip out and show you. I'll bring it next time. This woman had a little girl out of wedlock when she was sixteen, and then she married the father because she thought it was best for the baby, but they had an awful time and got divorced, and then she married somebody else and got divorced again, and it was a mess, and now the child has behavior problems and has to be kept in a special school for disturbed children. And now the mother's married a third time, and the third marriage and the new baby are okay, but she wishes she had given the baby for adoption when she could have, and not tried to raise a family before conditions were right."

"I know," said Elspeth. "I saw that letter. It was signed Chimney Sweep."

"Yes, I think it was."

"Mama, I'm not sixteen, and anyway so far so good. It's only a couple of months. If things get to where I'm doing Petey more harm than good I'll give him up. I promise."

The mail came while Harriet was giving Peter a bath. There was the bill from Alf. The return address in the corner said **ORZO, CASTORINI & McDERMOTT**.

She took it to the bedroom and opened it with one hand, placing the ball of her thumb on it and digging with a finger. She did not want to ask Harriet to open it, or even to call Harriet's attention to it by asking Mrs. Brody, in case he had included a personal note.

The was no note. Under the black letterhead he had written the bill by hand, in blue ink. Services rendered, $75. Please make out check to Alfredo Castorini.

Her budget was already close to deficit spending this month, because of the twenty-dollar check she had given to Harvard-Radcliffe. But it couldn't be helped.

She could hear Harriet singing to Peter, and the splashing of the bath. Without seeing them she knew the way he stared up at Harriet in wide-eyed fascination when she sang.

Harriet brought him diapered and wrapped in his hooded bath towel to be nursed.

"That cast is filthy dirty," Harriet said. "How can you wear it like that?"

"I know. But there's no way to clean it. At least the sling hides most of it. It itches inside, too."

Afterward Harriet did the laundry. Elspeth sat on the bed with her checkbook and her pad of linen notepaper. She had by now developed a left-handed penmanship that was not too scrawly, with parallel downstrokes slanting backwards.

Dear Alf,

Fee enclosed. Thanks again for

She crumpled it. She considered phrases.

Dear Alf,

I like your style.

Affectionately,
Elspeth

She folded it, with the check inside, and licked the envelope. She knew how to tear a stamp from the roll with one hand. You bent it back and forth at the perforation a few times.

She calculated her new balance in the checkbook.

She heard the harsh draining of the bathroom sink. Then the sounds of her mother hand-wringing clothes. In the crib Peter stirred, jiggling the mobile, but he did not waken.

The hundred-dollar deposit sent to the west coast, and now these unexpected fees, had cut her reserves.

Elspeth took her most recent bank statement from the bureau drawer and restudied it. The check to the Pacific Northern had arrived back at the Eggleston-Uphams nine days after she had mailed it.

If she really meant to experiment with that million-dollar trick, she had better get on with it. If not, then write a check against the Pacific Northern account and close it out.

If two checks were deposited against each other, each in the bank on which the other check had been written, and they simply canceled each other out, leaving no net gain in either account, what could they do to you?

It wasn't forgery. The signatures would be her own.

It wasn't theft. The banks never paid the million. Each bank's check came home through the clearing house to wipe out the deposit cleanly without your having gotten a penny of it.

If one of the banks incidentally paid interest from date of deposit before funds were collected, that was the bank's own affair. She had not asked it to.

Mr. Hudson had even told her of insurance companies making checks travel as far as they could, to stretch paper balances to the longest time, and the banks could not care less.

She carefully wrote out a Eggleston-Uphams check to herself for a million dollars. It looked nice, even with her left hand. She signed it. She turned it over and wrote For Deposit Only, and the Pacific Northern account number. She sealed it with a Pacific Northern deposit slip into the long gray no-postage-required-if-mailed-in-the-United-States envelope.

Now she took the Pacific Northern checkbook and began again. It looked as good on a pink check as on the green. PAY TO THE ORDER OF Elspeth A. Baker $1,000,000 $\frac{\#}{100}$ One-million exactly DOLLARS. She made out an Eggleston-Uphams deposit slip and put it and the check into a plain white envelope. She meant to drop it into the Night Deposits slot to avoid facing the teller.

She lay on the sagging bed and closed her eyes.

When at last Peter wakened, Harriet tiptoed in and took him. Elspeth did not open her eyes.

Harriet brought him back when it was time to leave.

"You had a nice nap," said Harriet.

As usual Elspeth walked with Harriet up the wide street to the trolley-bus stop, pushing the pram. Waiting there she watched Harriet gaze into the pram at Peter. She could read the whole mixture of her mother's thoughts and emotions.

"Give my love to Dad," she said when the trolley sparked and the bus circled around.

Harriet gave a nod, saying nothing.

Afterward Elspeth pushed the pram back across the street. The black snow and ice were nearly gone. She dropped the envelopes to Alf and the Pacific Northern into the fat mailbox at the corner. Then she continued down the avenue to the Eggleston-Uphams Bank and Trust.

The Night Deposit slot closed with a steely clunk.

She did not feel uneasy until she steered the pram back toward the Brodys'. When she rounded the corner it got worse.

Maybe she should have tried it with only a hundred thousand. Or ten thousand. Or an odd number instead of a round one. Anything that attracted attention might cause trouble.

Who fed deposits into the computer? And did they do a double take when they saw a big one, and show it to the vice-president?

What the judge said was true. Sometimes it was as though making trouble was a human instinct.

What would she answer if Mr. Hudson called her in and asked her why she had sent those checks?

Why? What's the problem, Mr. Hudson? They just canceled each other out, didn't they?

Yes, they just canceled each other out, precisely. So would you kindly tell me what the purpose was, young lady?

Well, no purpose. For kicks, obviously. To see how it feels to write a check for a million dollars. Pretending. So what? Credit a million, debit a million, back to the starting line. I didn't take any money.

And the interest, young lady?

Interest? What interest? Oh, you mean interest? Was there interest, for those couple of days? I never thought of it. Take your old interest. I don't want interest.

And she would call Alf. Hi, Alf. This is Elspeth. Remember me? I'm in trouble, Alf. I need a lawyer.

52

SEVEN mornings later Elspeth dropped an orange transfer slip into the Night Deposits slot of the Eggleston-Uphams Bank and Trust, shifting a million dollars from five-per-cent savings to no-interest checking. On the way home she did her shopping in the aisles of Leo & Walter's, steering the pram carefully around the slow-moving old ladies.

In the afternoon, clutching Peter in her left arm, she took the bus to the hospital. The doctor studied her elbow under the fluoroscope. He said they would remove the cast in another three weeks.

There was a day of heavy rain, then some bright days, warm and blowy. The last patches of snow were gone.

Chris said she had begun leaving Vinnie in the wheelchair after the midday break. "I tie him in tight with the bathrobe cord, and stuff a pillow on his bad side so he won't slide over."

"How's his mood?" Elspeth asked.

"Sometimes I think he wishes he was dead. His old man was a suicide, you know. I tell him he's got to keep his courage up, for all of us. And his faith. And I tell the kids, listen, he took care of *you*. Now we've all got to take care of each other."

One day the wall phone rang just as Chris returned, but Edgar had not seen her and bellowed with the first ring. "Answer the phone! Move!"

Elspeth grabbed it.

"For you," she said, and gave it to Chris. "I think it's your mother."

Chris spoke a while, discussing a roast. When she had hung up, she went over to the door of the repair bay, halting just inside the office, hands on hips.

"Hey! Droopy Drawers! Edgar! Front and center!"

He came over. As little as Chris was she was nearly as tall as Edgar, and because of the step from the office to the repair bay she now looked down on him. But he was broader, thick, square.

"Who told you to yell at a lady in that tone of voice?"

"I wasn't yelling at you," said Edgar.

"I know. You were yelling at Elspeth, weren't ya. Is that how you talk to ladies?" She turned to Elspeth. "Is that how he talks to you, Elspeth?"

"Oh, he's okay," Elspeth said.

Chris turned back to Edgar, and a finger gestured down at him. "Listen, you stupid misbegotten monkey-face. Don't ever let me hear you ever yell at a lady in

396

that tone of voice again. Understand? Don't even look at her in that tone of voice. Or I'll knock you on your ass."

Edgar stood silently. Then he went back to work. Chris pulled open one of the side drawers of the desk and took a cigarette.

Once Edgar told Chris that Elspeth had plugged up the men's toilet. "She probably threw a diaper in it."

"I've never been in the men's," said Elspeth. "I use the ladies'."

"She could have used the men's when the ladies' was in use," said Edgar.

"I didn't," said Elspeth.

"Did you see her?" Chris asked Edgar.

"No, I don't say I saw her."

"What's your proof?" Chris asked him.

"I just think she did, that's all."

"Never mind what you think," said Chris. "I know what she does with diapers."

Peter did something new every day. She woke one morning to find him on his stomach in the crib, but raised up on his arms, staring at her through the bars.

He discovered his hands. He lay in the canvass bassinet, hands above his face, watching his fingers as he moved them.

She sat with him on the plank bench, outside the office door.

"It's going to be spring, Petey. The trees are still bare, but they're gonna have leaves before long. It's gonna be green. You've never seen that. You'll play on grass. Did you think it's winter all the time, Petey?"

Alf obviously wasn't going to call. Maybe he had a girl friend. With anybody any good, you always had competition. Too bad he wasn't divorced or something, with a kid of his own. She'd have a good chance then.

Daddy would squawk about her marrying somebody that wasn't Jewish, and Mama would get weepy. They'd tell her that intermarriages don't have a good chance of working out, even though they knew it wasn't true. There were intermarriages every day. They had gone to Diana's wedding and had let her be a bridesmaid, even in a church, though at first they complained that Uncle Harry and Aunt Frieda shouldn't have stood for it.

If she and Alf determined to get married, Daddy would let Mama convince him that it was better than having a kid and no husband at all. You can't have everything.

Italians were usually Catholic. She hoped Alf didn't care too much about it. Intermarriages worked best when you didn't care what you were. The more you were undefined, the weaker your ties were, the easier you could make a new tie.

Anyway it was Daddy's fault. If he hadn't tried to get Petey taken away, she wouldn't have met Alf.

The boys had left the wide door up, and a woman who had driven up told them her car had been stalling every time she took her foot off the accelerator. "Could you look at it, please? I just can't drive it. If I move my foot to the brake to slow down, it stalls out. And everybody starts honking."

"You'll have to wait a while. We'll look at it as soon as we can."

"What does it sound like to you?"

"It could be a lot of things. Sorry ma'am, the less you bother us the sooner we can squeeze you in."

The woman waited. She was fairly young and stylish, just a bit chubby and matronly. She leaned on her car, holding the enormous brim of her hat so it wouldn't blow away.

Elspeth sang to Peter, still sitting on the plank bench. When he was asleep she strapped him into his seat.

The woman was looking at her by now. Her eye took in the baby and the sling. Elspeth walked over to her. "Let's see what we can see," said Elspeth. She released the hood and raised it.

Her hair hung down toward the engine. She flung it back over her shoulder. Then she reached down and put the loose end of a blackened hose in place.

"Look," she said to the woman. "The vacuum hose from the brake booster to the intake was off. So cold air was getting sucked into the engine. Try it now."

She closed the hood. From the shady indoors beyond the wide raised door Edgar stared with disapproval. So did Puff behind him, and so did Mr. Tingley, munching his gums, his eyeglasses cockeyed.

"I found it, guys," she told them.

"You mean it's fixed?" the woman said.

"I think so. Drive it. See if it's okay."

The woman began to open her handbag.

"No charge," said Elspeth.

She remained standing in the sunshine. Edgar and Puff and Mr. Tingley kept staring from the shade, motionless. The car circled, and paused at the end of the apron, waiting for a chance to cut into traffic, but did not stall. Then it drove into Saltmarsh Avenue Extension and disappeared behind the pillars where the overhead expressway crossed.

"I thought you weren't supposed to fix cars when you arm's in a sling. And what's all this no-charge shit. You think this is a charity clinic?"

"It only took me a second. I'm sure Chris or Vinnie wouldn't have charged."

"How do you know you fixed it. There could be something else. A million things can make a car stall. We should have gone over it."

"If I didn't fix it she'll be back."

"Yeah? Or she might stop at another place and give *them* the job. You don't kid *me* with your saint act. I know all about you cheating Sears Roebuck, swapping battery guarantees around."

She said nothing.

She was off the next day. Harriet visited. Mrs. Peress called down and invited them all to come upstairs and sit on her porch. Her son was home from the University of Illinoyess. Apparently it was spring break time. They told Mrs. Brody to say they'd be up after lunch, when the baby had been fed.

Eventually they made their way up the brown musty stairwell that rose from the vestibule, except for Mr. Brody who had gone out for a walk. Harriet carried Peter.

Mrs. Brody held to the wall, bending. "It's a wonder I'm still alive. Mh!" She wore slippers flattened at the heels.

Calvin Peress was well over six feet, and had a big frame. Elspeth looked up at him, and he nodded gravely, taking the pipe from his mouth. His great proportions surprised her as his mother was so shrunken. She judged him to be in his middle or late twenties. He had bushy hair and wide sideburns stuck out of his cheeks, adding to his immensity. He wore a dark blue turtleneck pullover of thick but close-fitting knit, and she saw he was not fat.

They went out to the slanting floor of the porch. Elspeth sat alone on the glider. Calvin sat on the porch rail, one hand lightly holding the corner post. Harriet, Mrs. Brody and Mrs. Peress took the three rockers, Harriet still holding Peter.

"You'll fall off from there," Mrs. Peress told her son, her eyes huge in the thick lenses.

"I always sit here," said Calvin. "I haven't fallen yet." His voice was the deepest Elspeth had ever heard, in such a low register it practically rumbled.

"Heart failure he'll give me," said Mrs. Peress. "Zetz doch! Vi a groysse mensh on the glider! Nit vi a ingeleh on the railing!"

"It *is* dangerous," Harriet added. "Especially on the second floor."

He humored them. He sat beside Elspeth on the glider, rested an an arm along its back, and crossed his legs.

"Watch down the street," Mrs. Brody said to him. "In case you should see Brody, you should tell him we're on the piazza."

Calvin was looking at Peter. "That child has remarkable eyes," he said.

"Doesn't he have an intelligent face?" Harriet said.

"He does indeed," Calvin agreed.

"He's figuring out the world," said Elspeth.

One of the rocking chairs began to creak, and then another. The wild strands of Mrs. Brody's white hair stirred in the wind. Mrs. Peress said Calvin was the youngest from six. All lived far away, except her daughter in Ipshvich.

"And between the fifth and myself there's a sixteen-year gap," Calvin rumbled quietly to Elspeth. "I was an accident. A postscript. I have a nephew three months older than myself."

"Are you getting your doctorate at Illinois?" she asked him.

"I'm there on a teaching appointment," he said. "But my doctorate will be from Yale, when I complete my dissertation."

"Where did you do your undergraduate work?"

"Bates," he told her.

"Elspeth had a year at Mount Holyoke," said Harriet.

"And what was your main field of interest?" he asked. He spoke softly, confidentially, almost as though he preferred that the three women not be included in their conversation, but even in quiet tones the low pitch was somehow ponderous.

"Well, I hadn't started majoring yet. But I was thinking of physics and more math, and some art history, and maybe architecture eventually. How do you like the Triumph?"

"The Triumph?"

"Your car. That's yours, isn't it? Across the street there with Illinois plates?"

"Oh. Yes. I guess I like it. I haven't had it long. I bought it from a colleague."

"What's your dissertation about?"

"I'm tracing the influence of British letters on American, and the subsequent influence of American literature on the British, and how the shift came about. The literary influence seems to follow political ascendancy. Not entirely though. And you still find embattled pockets of the authentic British tradition. In New Zealand. Even in England."

"You mean you could teach a course called Brit Lit?"

"As a matter of fact, I do teach one you could call Contemporary Brit Lit."

Mrs. Brody and Mrs. Peress had meanwhile begun a separate conversation, in Yiddish. Harriet seemed to be included in it, though Harriet's comments were in English.

"What are you smiling at?" he said. "Does something amuse you?"

"I'm always fascinated by the squeaks of those rocking chairs whenever I'm up here. Your mother's rocker squeaks together with Mrs. Brody once, and then they get more and more out of phase, until your mother and my mother squeak together just once. And meanwhile my mother and Mrs. Brody squeak nearer and nearer together each time, till they squeak together, and then little by little they widen. Try to listen to the three separate rhythms and sort it all out. Isn't it maddening?"

They listened.

"I see what you mean," he said.

"A mathematician could have a field day," said Elspeth. "Of the three possibilities of simultaneous squeakings, which one recurs after the shortest interval? And how many squeaks does each chair need from simultaneous squeak to simultaneous squeak?"

"Do they ever all three squeak at once?"

"I suppose. I haven't heard it. I've tried to listen for it but I go nuts too soon."

Peter gave a cry and squirmed. Harriet sang and he quieted.

"Look, how careful he listens," said Mrs. Brody.

Harriet changed her rocking to conform to her song, and Mrs. Brody and Mrs. Peress held still.

After some minutes Peter grew squirmy again.

"We have to take him down for his nap," said Elspeth. "If he's not still when somebody sings it means he's had it. He didn't sleep this morning."

"I'll take him down," said Harriet. "You can stay here."

"No, I'll go down." She rose.

"I'll walk you down," said Calvin.

Elspeth and Calvin followed Harriet.

As Harriet got to the turn in the stairs Mr. Brody burst in below from the downstairs porch. He looked up at the footsteps, then moved his cane in an arc that struck the chained pram.

"Your wife's up with Mrs. Peress," said Harriet. "Do you want to go up?"

"Na."

With his key he tried the bolt but found it already unlocked. He let himself in to the apartment.

"Look at him," Calvin muttered to Elspeth. "Blind. Senile. Useless. If I ever reach such a condition, I'll put my head in the oven."

"Why?" Elspeth answered. "Why should he? We'll all have billions of years to be dead in. So what's the rush?"

"Calvin!" Mrs. Peress called from upstairs. "Take me down the garbage!"

Elspeth went to help Harriet with the diaper but Harriet did it all. Peter thumped his heels.

Outdoors there was a sound of galvanized metal. Harriet was by the window. "Calvin's putting trash in the barrel," she said.

His heavy tread died away on the wooden backstairs.

"He seems like a nice boy," said Harriet. "And he's very interested in you."

"Forget it, Mama. He's too tall. He's too big."

"Give him a chance. What difference does a little flesh make if people love each other?"

"He must be double my weight. He's a whole head taller. And he's a lot older. Maybe ten years older."

"I don't think that much. Maybe five years."

"More."

"Don't be too picky. Beggars can't be choosers."

"Oh, Mama! Come off it. I'm not a beggar. Calvin's not my type."

"How do you know he's not? What *is* your type?"

"A certain type."

"Tell me. Do you know what you want? What kind of a man *do* you want?"

"Don't laugh. But I want the kind of a guy that wouldn't mind changing diapers."

Harriet did not laugh. "Well, I know what you mean," she said more quietly. "Daddy was like that. He always helped. But you don't even know Calvin. How do you know he wouldn't change diapers? And *you* have to make allowances too, just like *he* has to make allowances for the baby. Lots of very pretty girls think nobody's good enough for them and they end up getting left out."

"I won't get left out."

Toward twilight, after Harriet had left, Calvin came down to the Brodys' door. He had a fat manila envelope, somewhat battered at its edges, tied shut.

"I thought you might like to read some of my writings," he said, standing at the threshold. "Why don't you start with my novella."

"Oh, gee," said Elspeth. "I don't think my criticisms would be worth much."

"No matter. Years hence you'll be able to say you read me in manuscript."

She had books from the library. But there was no way to refuse.

She let him give her the fat envelope. But he lingered at the door.

"I've never known an Elspeth," he said.

"It's the Scottish form of Elizabeth."

"I'm aware of that. How do you come by it?"

401

"My mother found it in a what-to-name-the-baby book. Thanks for the novella, Calvin. I've got to go."

After supper she sat in the wicker chair and unwound the red string from its clasp.

The title page was soiled. It was called What God Hath Joined. The next page said Book One: Lead a Snot Into Temptation.

It took place in Switzerland, apparently late in the nineteenth century. There were two boys, Siamese twins, joined at the side of the head. They could have been separated by surgery in infancy, but their father was a grim Calvinist minister and he forbade it. Because Our Lord had said, what God hath joined let no man rend asunder. Now that they had grown it was too late, and separation would cause the death of at least one, maybe both.

They hated each other. They were both in love with their governess. The governess loved one of them, and would have sex with the one she loved while his brother slept. At last she and her lover conspired to murder the other brother and cut him away.

But sometimes a thought would leak from one brain to the other, where they were joined. So the intended victim knew the whole scheme, and just when it was to take place.

He did not let on that he knew. On the appointed night he forced himself to stay awake, and while his brother snored he managed to roll to the other side.

The governess entered the pitch-black bedroom at three in the morning and stabbed the wrong one.

When she turned on the light she was aghast. Aha, said the survivor. Never fear. We will cut him away, as you would have cut away me. And I will be your lover.

They disposed of the dead brother, piece by piece. But they were afraid to cut too near to where the heads had been joined, lest the living brother die also. They pared away as much as they dared to, in smaller and smaller slivers. Still, the surviving brother had to keep a sizable hunk of the dead one's head attached to his own head, for a margin of safety. He had to wear an enormous turban to hide it. He and the governess fled together from Switzerland.

Elspeth read about two hours. Then she put it into the bassinet of the pram, thinking she would finish it at Saltmarsh Service in the morning if business was slow.

But she and Chris were busy all morning. She told Chris about it.

"Do you like it?" said Chris.

"Not too much," said Elspeth.

Things did not grow slack till after Chris had gone at noon. Elspeth settled into the swivel chair and tried to read further.

He was known as the man in the oversized turban. They were in Argentina. A garrulous pest on the train befriended them and they could not get rid of him. They suspected he was a police agent.

Elspeth could not keep her mind to it. She found herself listening instead to a conversation Edgar and Puff were having with a customer about an overhaul.

"A car that's only got fifty-odd thousand miles shouldn't be ready for a ring job," the customer was saying unhappily.

"Well, I only know what you tell me," Edgar answered. "You tell me it burns up a quart of oil every hundred and fifty miles. You want to check it again? Maybe you made a mistake."

No, I've checked it and I've checked it. Damn it. I don't know *what* to do. I can't afford eight hundred bucks to take the whole engine apart and put new rings in. I can't afford to trade it in either."

"Except you trade it in and then you finance it and pay installments. That could be easier."

"I know how you feel," said Puff. "But what can you do? You burn oil that fast and it's a warning. You drive with worn rings and it's your risk. The pistons get more and more clearance to rattle and they get worse and worse till a piston goes flying through the head."

"Oh, I know, I know," the customer said. "I agree. I just don't understand the rings being gone in only fify thousand miles. I put ninety thousand on the last one."

"Well, every car's different," said Edgar.

Elspeth put Calvin's manuscript on the desk and went to the repair bay. "Guys, can I make a suggestion?" she said.

The customer was a fiftyish little man. They looked at her. She walked over.

"Let's run it up on the lift," she said. "I want to look at something. Drive it onto the lift," she told the customer.

When the wheels were secured in place and the customer stood beside her she threw the switch. The smooth greased column rose slowly from the floor and the car approached the ceiling. When it stopped she walked beneath. She looked up.

"Come here. Look." She pointed to the freshly wet black area on the bottom of the engine. "You're not burning oil. You're leaking it. You see where?"

"Yeah. It's the sending unit," said Edgar. "The oil-pressure sending unit. It works the indicator on your dash."

"So what do we do about it?" said the customer.

"Replace it," said Elspeth.

"We don't have that in stock," Edgar said.

"We can order it," said Elspeth. "It's a two or three-dollar item, that's all. And about fifteen minutes of labor."

The customer sighed and wiped his brow.

"A lot better than an eight-hundred-dollar overhaul, isn't it, sir," Edgar said. "You want us to order that? We'll be happy to. Give us a call in two or three days. Glad we could be of help. Our pleasure."

Elspeth was busy at the pumps again for the last part of the afternoon. She saw Edgar confer with Chris.

Chris spoke to her of it while she drove her home.

"He feels you made a jerk out of him," Chris said. "He thinks you're trying to be a smart ass. And when you make *him* look bad, it makes the whole place look bad. He's got a point there."

"How should I have handled it, then?"

"Well, he'd sort of like you to stay out of the repair bay. A guy on a job doesn't like somebody kibitzing. He said he'd have found that leak. He just hadn't got to it yet."

"Well, gee. Stay out of the repair bay? I was hoping I could do repairs too when my arm's better."

"Well, I know it," said Chris. "Okay, when your arm's better."

"You want me to stay out of there till then?"

"Well, not completely. It's good to keep an eye on those guys. I don't say they're dishonest, but I don't trust them completely. The two of them are a bad influence on each other. It was better when it was just Edgar, and Vinnie kept tabs on him."

53

WHEN Calvin phoned next evening the comment Elspeth offered on his novella was only that she found it very strange. But he seemed to take that as not uncomplimentary.

She did not mention that she hadn't finished it. He came downstairs for it, and brought a corrugated carton with more manuscripts.

"What's all that?"

"Oh, various things I've written. That I thought you might like to look at."

"How can I read all that? You won't be in Boston that long."

"Just dabble in it. Browse. There are some reviews, and articles of criticism, and a play, and my novel in progress. See what catches your fancy. And if you do get into something big, like the novel, just return it to my mother when you finish. These are copies I keep here. They don't go back to Illinois with me."

"You write reviews and plays and a novel and a doctoral thesis all at the same time? And teach?"

"It's mostly the dissertation now. Except for a few reviews and articles to keep my name in circulation. I did the play three years ago. And the novel's in abeyance, till the dissertation's done."

She had to let him carry the box to her room and place it on the bureau. But before he could settle down comfortably in the bedroom she said she had been about to make tea. He followed her to the kitchen.

He rested an elbow on the red-checked oilcloth and sucked his dead pipe.

"I've been trying herb teas," said Elspeth. "This one's a blend of lemon grass, whatever that is, and spearmint, blackberry leaves, rose hips, orange blossom, clover and eucalyptus."

"A veritable witches' brew," he pronounced deeply. "I believe you're trying to cast a spell on me. Or turn me into a frog."

When the kettle boiled she poured. "Does Illinois give you two weeks for the spring break?" she asked. "Most places only give a week."

"I took off a week early. I just gave my students reading assignments and canceled classes. I'd just bought the car, and I wanted time to drive instead of flying."

He sipped the herbal blend.

He suggested that they go for a drive in the Triumph on Saturday.

"I can't. I work."

"Sunday then," he said.

"I'm not certain of Sunday. There may be some family activity."

"An evening then," said Calvin. "Dinner at a Chinese joint. Or the Theater Company. They're excellent, you know."

"They were, but the original company's gone to New York. Anyway I'm so tired evenings. It's having my right arm in a sling, I think. When I try to use a fork or a spoon or a knife I'm so awkward. Conspicuous. Thanks, Calvin, but I don't really want to go out till they take the cast off. So don't pressure me."

They dawdled over a second cup of the brew.

Then she got rid of him, with the excuse that she would have to be up early for the six-o'clock feeding. She added that she might read some of his things in bed before putting out the light.

However she did not get around to it. Nor did she take any along Friday morning to read at Saltmarsh Service.

Friday evening she stood at the curved table in the center hallway and opened the telephone book. The only Castorini was a Giosue Castorini. But Alfredo had said he lived with family.

She dialed. If it was a wrong number she could try his office number on Monday. She wondered what his family was like.

"Is Alfredo there, please?"

She heard the lady call him shrilly. Then she waited. There was a background of household noises. At last she heard him.

"Hi, Alf. This Elspeth Baker. Remember me?"

"Oh. Sure. Thanks for paying the bill so quickly."

"You were entitled," she said.

"How's the baby? And the arm?"

"Fine."

"Has your father tried any more court action?"

"No. I guess you taught him a lesson. Look, I don't know how else to say it, so I'll just come right out with it. Let's go out together to a movie or something sometime. You and me. I thought I'd like to know you socially."

She thought there was the briefest hesitation before he answered. "Okay."

"My cast comes off Wednesday," she said. "We could go out after, and celebrate."

"Well, Wednesday evening I'm tied up. But how about Thursday? As a matter of fact I think the Honky Brothers are in town Thursday. Do you like folk singers?"

"Oh, I'd love to hear the Honky Brothers," said Elspeth. "That song of theirs is so great. 'Sins are Biodegradable.' Will they sing that?"

"I hope so. How could the Honky Brothers give a concert and leave out 'Sins Are Biodegradable'?"

"Have you got a car? If you don't I can meet you downtown."

"I can probably borrow my brother-in-law's car. If you don't hear from me otherwise, I'll pick you up Thursday at seven-thirty."

"Great." She reminded him of her address. She gave him directions. "The name on the door is Jacob Brody. Don't try to pull the white bell knob on the outside, because it's busted. The vestibule is unlocked."

When she had hung up she remained there, her hand on the phone. She could ask Mrs. Brody to baby-sit. Or maybe she should hire Chris's Kathleen. She might have to leave a bottle.

The telephone rang under her hand.

It was Calvin. He wanted to come downstairs and sit again over witch's brew. But Elspeth said no. She offered the excuse that she was busy reading his stuff.

"You can read it when I've left town," he said. "And write me about it."

"No, I want to read as much as I can while you're here. In case I want to talk to you about something. While it's fresh."

"What have you read?"

"Some of the reviews." It was a lie. "And I was going to read the play tonight." Now she had to read the stuff. But she would have had to anyway.

She sat in the sinking middle of the bed and looked at the reviews. They were pasted clippings. Most of them were witty, though always merciless. It seemed to her that the authors would hardly dare show their faces in public afterward, let alone ever write again.

There was also a longer article, filling several pages in a magazine. Unlike the short pieces it was reverent in its praise and made no attempt at humor.

Elspeth took the play to bed, and read propped on a pillow. It was called Ten Shillings for a Blow Job. The male character was exceedingly garrulous. His erudite blabberings went for pages on end, brooking no interruption.

Saturday night Calvin phoned again. She did not let him come down, and made the same excuse as the night before. But she had to promise she would let him drop in Sunday afternoon if the family plans did not materialize.

She spent three hours plowing through his novel at the kitchen table, while the television murmured and laughed at the apartment's other end. It was of monumental proportions. Though he had said this was only part of it, she got through only a fraction of that. The name of it was The World of Pig McGoon.

Elspeth was never certain what was happening. Pig McGoon had been sunk into the harbor minus his genitals by Shmuckbucket O'Toole, who had taken over the pinball machines. But yet he kept reappearing and functioning as though nothing had happened. She could not determine if these were flashbacks or if he had returned whole from the dead somehow.

Pig was only a short fragment of his nickname. His associates often addressed him by its full three syllables, which were an obscenity. He didn't seemed to mind, and would even use the unabbreviated form in introducing himself.

His girl friend was Nutcracker Sweet. She was constantly unfaithful. One of her lovers was the editor of a black newspaper called the Afro-Disiac.

Sometimes a single sentence went on with torrential verbosity for a page and a half. His vocabulary was enormous. Her paperback dictionary had some of the words but not all. After a while she stopped looking them up. There were too many. And even finding the meaning of the word did not always make the sentence intelligible.

On Sunday she flipped pages to see if there were more interesting parts further on. It wasn't much fun.

"Shmuckety buckety," she sang to Peter when she changed his diaper. "Shmuckety buckety, kaka de kuckety."

When she had put him into his crib she drew the windowshade and lay down to rest.

She heard somebody rotate the old bell in the front door. She knew the Brodys had not heard it over the television, though they were closer to it than she. She went to answer it.

But instead of Calvin she found Bob Shoemaker and Karen Slater. She embraced Bob with her left arm, and then Karen. "Gee! It's just great to see you!"

"We heard about your arm," said Karen. "Forgive us for not coming sooner. You know we've never seen the baby?"

Calvin appeared descending from the bend in the stairs, frowning upon his pipe. He wore a gray turtleneck this time.

"Hi, Calvin. Meet my cousin and his fiancée." She was glad it now appeared that she had told the truth about family plans, though in fact she hadn't expected Bob and Karen.

She made the introductions. Calvin nodded gravely, bending slightly at the waist.

"You took off the mustache," Elspeth said to Bob.

"Karen decided she didn't like it."

"Well, come on in, everybody," said Elspeth. "You remember Mr. and Mrs. Brody."

"Mh." Mrs. Brody did not rise from the low overstuffed chair but began to apologize for being shoeless. The old man stared blindly from his corner.

Karen was carrying a paper plate covered with plastic wrap through which some pastry squares and fruit-jelly slices showed, along with peanuts in their shells and chocolate mint patties. "We brought you shlach manos. Happy Purim."

"Is today Purim?" said Elspeth.

"Yeh. Today is Purim," said Mrs. Brody.

"Did you ever hear of shlach manos?" Bob asked Elspeth. "I bet you haven't."

"What is it?"

"On Purim you send goodies to your friends. Ready-to-eat stuff, at least two different kinds per friend. And it has to be in the daytime, on Purim, and it's supposed to be sent, so it's from me to you by way of Karen. I never heard of it either till three years ago."

"I never heard of not hearing of it," said Karen. "We always did it."

"Shlach manos, yeh, years ago they used to do that," said Mrs. Brody.

"Well, it's awfully sweet of you. Have you heard of it, Calvin?"

"I can't say that I'm familiar with it."

"We should have brought a baby gift too," said Karen. "And we will. We've just been impossibly busy."

"Well, let's adjourn to the kitchen and sample these butterscotch squares," said Elspeth. "They look scrumptious. Did you make them?"

"Avis made them," said Karen.

In the kitchen Elspeth put the plate of goodies on the red-checked oilcloth. She brought out various herb teas. She filled the kettle. Karen helped set out cups and saucers.

"Did you know your cousin Elspeth was into witches' potions?" Calvin said to Bob.

"What do you mean?"

"He means the herb tea assortment was on sale cheap," said Elspeth.

"How long do you have to wear the cast?" Bob asked.

"They're supposed to take it off Wednesday if the X-rays are okay. I can hardly wait. It itches, and I can't do calisthenics—I'm just so sick of it. And it gets dirtier and dirtier. It picks up grease from cars—I don't know how. It hasn't touched anything."

Calvin cleared his throat and took the pipe from his mouth.

"I hear Uncle Joe tried to get the courts to take the baby away," Bob said.

"He didn't succeed."

"I heard."

"I had a wonderful lawyer. His name's Alfredo Castorini. And we had this lovely old white-haired judge, this beautiful old man with a face like a painting. Amsterdam. He threw the case out and told me to get married."

"Adam Amsterdam?" said Bob.

"I think so. Something like that."

"Is that Buzzy's grandfather?" Karen asked Bob.

"Yes."

Calvin cleared his throat. "If they take the cast off Wednesday, suppose I give you a lift there. And then we'll go out and celebrate."

"I thought you were leaving tomorrow."

"I can stretch it to Wednesday. I'll leave Thursday morning. I don't have a class till the next Monday."

"Calvin teaches at the University of Illinois," said Elspeth.

The kettle whistled. "Let me," said Karen. She poured.

"So how about it?" said Calvin, dangling his bag of herbs gingerly above the steam. "I'll give you a ride to the doctor, and we'll spend the day celebrating."

"I have to think about it."

"It's settled," he insisted. "I'm staying till Thursday morning."

"What do you teach?" Bob asked him.

"English."

"He's also a writer," said Elspeth. "He's planning to be among the immortals."

"I hope you make it," Bob said to him.

"I've been reading his stuff," said Elspeth. "And I'm sure it's good. It's over my head sometimes, but anything of the highest order of excellence would naturally have to be over my head part of the time."

"Well," said Bob, "our children will understand it. Somebody will do a doctoral dissertation on myth and symbol in Calvin Peress."

"Calvin's doing a doctoral dissertation too," said Elspeth. "Not at Illinois though. At Yale. And Bob's studying for a doctorate at MIT. And Karen for a doctorate at Harvard."

"What field?" Calvin asked Bob.

"Biology. Oceanography, actually. Karen's in history. We've both just started course work. We're not into dissertations yet."

"I didn't know MIT was into biology," said Calvin.

"We've been broadening our horizons."

"I applied to Harvard too," said Elspeth. "I just got the rejection in yesterday's mail."

"Oh, I'm terribly sorry," Calvin said quietly, in his basso profundo. "But they're horribly overapplied, you know."

"Are you serious?" Bob asked her. "I didn't know you applied there."

"Nobody knew. I applied late, and I didn't tell anybody, except the teachers I called for recommendations."

"Well, it's Harvard's loss," said Bob.

"I don't really care that much. I just applied because it was there." She bit into a butterscotch square. "Hey, these are great. Yummy."

Bob raised his teacup with a nod to Calvin. "To your place among the immortals."

Elspeth and Karen clicked cups with him.

"Thank you," said Calvin.

"Or then again, maybe literary immortality is out of style," Bob added. "It seems to me some of the people who were still immortal when I was a freshman in high school are already forgotten. What do you think, Calvin? Even the classics of English literature. Is my impression correct that every generation fewer and fewer people read them?"

"It could be correct. I hadn't thought of it that way."

"And if you go back just a few centuries," Bob continued, "is anything read? I don't mean by students. I mean does anything older than that still have a public? Do you see what I mean, Calvin? Every novel is tied to its time. And part of its appeal is its language, which grows increasingly out of date. It may fade in a season, or a generation, or it may last a century or two. But it has to fade."

"There are exceptions," said Karen.

"Well, sacred literature is an exception," said Bob. "That's true. You're right. Because tens of thousands hear the stories of the patriarchs read aloud every year. Maybe hundreds of thousands. And Joseph and his brothers, and the whole Pentateuch, a little each week, and talk about it, and discuss it, and find nuances and connections in it, beyond what they saw the year before. Or the psalms. The psalms are alive. Calvin, have you ever heard the Twenty-third Psalm sung in the original? Have you? That's really something. The psalms in the original have a terseness, and rhythm—the translation loses all that. And on shabos afternoon, before sunset, when we sit around the long table in shul and eat and drink, and some tenor or baritone begins to sing a psalm, and the rest of us join in—I'll tell you, Calvin— the magic of it is something the Whiffenpoofs at the tables down at Mory's could have taken lessons from." He took a slow gulp of the tea. "And yet, you know, we don't truly know who wrote any of that stuff. All we know is that they wrote it for its own sake. Not for honors and prizes. And not to make a buck."

"I assume the baby's asleep," Karen said, "but can we have a peek? There's another place we have to get to this afternoon."

"I can wake him," said Elspeth. "He doesn't have any special pattern at this time of day."

"No, don't wake him. Can't we just sneak in on tiptoe?"

"Okay. Want to come, Calvin?"

"I'll pass. I'll wait here. I've seen him." He sucked the pipe.

Karen and Bob followed Elspeth into her room. The windowshade was three-quarters drawn. In the crib Peter was on his cheek and his knees, his bulbous pants in the air. His eyes and mouth were shut tight.

Karen drew in a breath, raising a hand to her mouth. "How beautiful!" Her voice was scarcely above a whisper. "Wow! Look, Bob. Look. Look at him."

They stared. Peter was motionless, except for an almost imperceptible widening of his nostrils at each breath.

"He's gorgeous," Karen said in her hushed voice. "No wonder you can't give him up. No wonder. But if you ever do, if ever you can't hack it, offer him to us first. We have dibs. Okay? Look, Bob. Wouldn't you love to have a baby like that? Five like that? Ten like that?"

"Sure."

"I mean it, Bob. He's the prettiest baby I ever saw in my life. Really."

"I mean it too," he said.

"And he looks so like you, Ellie. If I saw him anywhere I'd know he's yours."

"I think he looks like my brother Eric. Do you see it, Bob?"

"Yes."

"And he has one expression sometimes that's just like my father."

"Well, I don't know your family," said Karen, "But I'm so glad you had him. And I'm glad you didn't give him away."

Peter wet his lips.

They stood there, gazing silently.

They filed back to the kitchen. Calvin was looking bored.

"How are the Kramers?" Elspeth asked Karen.

"They ask about you. We're all going down to New York together for Passover. At our parents'. Otherwise Avis would invite you for Passover."

"We're going to New York so my future parents-in-law can look me over," said Bob. "It's time I met them."

"I adore Avis," said Elspeth.

"She likes you too," Karen said.

Elspeth thought Calvin wore a sullen and left-out expression, as though he found her visitors tedious, and their discussion of persons unknown to him even more so.

"I wish there were more hours in the day," said Bob. "We should get together more. Aunt Harriet said you're working in a gas station."

"Yup."

"We should have called Ellie last Sunday," Karen said to him, "when we did the ladybugs. Maybe she'd have liked that."

"The what?" said Elspeth.

"Tell Ellie about the ladybugs."

"Oh, it's something we did for Audubon," Bob said. "For a fundraiser. And to show people how to get rid of aphids without spraying. You can get Australian ladybugs in big sackloads from an outfit in California—they'll ship it to you by refrigerated plane in a wooden crate, each sack in a crate, you know, so they don't get squashed, and then we spent all last Sunday putting up medical bottles with corks, and tubes for air, and then filling up each bottle with ladybugs. They'll sell for about a dollar a bottle."

"It was crazy," said Karen. "We were covered with them. You reach into a sack and your whole arm comes out completely covered with ladybugs. They're nice though. Harmless. We must have packed over a million bugs. Easy."

"Easy," Bob agreed.

"And who is it that buys these?" said Calvin.

"People that want to get rid of aphids without poison," said Bob. "You buy a bottle of about a thousand ladybugs and put it in your refrigerator, and as long as they're cold their metabolism goes down to suspended animation and they don't need food. And then on a cool night you throw a handful in the garden, and they'll hang around there for a week and eat up all the aphids. And after the aphid population builds up again, you throw out another handful."

"Interesting," said Calvin.

"This year I dressed for it," said Karen. "Last year I had ladybugs in my armpit and in my bra and all over the place."

"Well, last year was the first time," Bob said, "and we learned by experience.

We learned you have to have the shades drawn, for instance, when you pack them. Because they'll all fly to the light. And we learned to print up an instruction sheet and give one with every bottle. Because some people last year put them out in daylight, and they'd immediately fly away to the sun. And then people called us up yelling at us."

"And some accused us of selling homing ladybugs that came back to us so we could sell them over again," said Karen. She drank the last of her tea. "We have to go in a few minutes. We have a party. We'll have to come again. When the baby's awake."

"How are Aunt Frieda and Uncle Harry?" Elspeth asked Bob.

"You know, I don't see them that much. I'm commanded to honor my mother and my father, but it's easier to honor them if the visits are few and far between. And I think that's how they want it."

"It can't be," said Elspeth.

"It's true. If I pay a filial visit to my mother's place or my father's place, okay, I hide the yarmulka in my pocket before I ring the doorbell. But I still get the same harangue every time about why won't I eat in their place. So I eat an apple. And the harangue continues. It bugs them. Why can't they just accept it that I'm a nut? And drop it? My father's wife is okay. She's quiet, and she lets me alone. But my mother and father can't stand me. Maybe it's my face—I remind them of each other. I can't help it. I try to be low-key, you know, and never mention anything controversial, but we've got so little in common. It's a generation gap or something. If my mother had her way I'd be sleeping with a different girl every night and telling her about it, so she'd get a vicarious thrill. She thinks the younger generation is having a high old time she missed out on. I should be prowling Cape Cod with a station wagon with a mattress in the back."

"Do you see Diana?"

"Not if I can help it. If you want to know the truth I feel closer to Karen's sister than my own sister. But Diana sees my parents though. I have to give her credit. She's on good terms with both of them."

"It's too bad for religion to divide people like that."

"I'm not so sure religion is what's dividing us. Let's face it. If you believe in something, somebody's gonna disagree with you."

"I agree with you about Karen's sister. Avis really steered me right with Lamaze."

"Diana's very broad-minded, you know," Bob added. "The only trouble is she's very narrow-minded when it comes to choosing what subjects she's gonna be broad-minded about."

Karen put her hand on Bob's hand. "We have to go," she said to Elspeth. "We're going to a party and we're bringing the potato salad."

They rose. Elspeth and Calvin went with them to the door.

"Tell me," Calvin asked Bob, holding the bowl of his pipe, "how did you get onto this religious kick?"

"I guess it was my grandfather mostly."

"Your grandfather brainwashed you with this stuff?"

412

"No. Gramps never leaned on anybody. And I wasn't into it much in his lifetime, actually. But what I mean is, you come to God through another person who's known God. Or whose life seems to have been touched by God, or whose commitment to God has made him good and admirable. Like the people at Sinai did through Moses. For me it was Gramps. For some it's a parent, or a friend, or a teacher, or somebody they meet whose example kind of plants a seed in them."

"Our grandfather was a very lovable guy," said Elspeth.

"He was a guy you could love," said Bob. "And I loved him."

"He doesn't seem to have had the same effect on Elspeth," Calvin said. "Or on your sister, I gather, or your parents."

"Everyone's different," said Bob.

"One more question," said Calvin. "If you'll permit me. If you put the ladybugs in the garden at night, what keeps them from flying away at the first sunrise?"

"Because they've discovered the aphids by then. As long as the eating's good they'll stay."

Karen smiled, her eyes crinkling in the smooth olive face. Elspeth kissed her, and then kissed Bob. Calvin had turned back toward the kitchen.

"Is your car running okay?" she asked Bob.

"Well, it got us here. I guess it'll make it through the spring inspection."

She watched them go down the porch steps.

She found Calvin preparing more of the herb mix that had become his favorite. It was the kind with licorice.

"Sick," he said. "That boy is sick. Sick, sick, sick."

"Bob? He's a very sweet guy. He's a saint. You should see him with an injured bird. Or an injured squirrel."

Calvin stirred a deep whirlpool, the edges of which rose to the rim of the cup.

"A strange duck. He's hearing voices, as they say. A candidate for the couch if I ever saw one."

"You probably wondered what those knotted tassels are that hang out over his belt on each side."

"I know perfectly well what they are," said Calvin. "I know what tsitsis is. I think it's disgusting."

"It's in the Bible," Elspeth said.

"I'm aware of that. I'm well aware of it. 'And you will have it for a fringe, and you will see it and be reminded to do all the commandments of the Lord.' This is a secular world, and a secular century. How can he involve himself in that atavistic tribalism?"

"Well, that's his thing."

"It's pietism, flagrantly flaunted. It's worse than pietism. It's tribalism. And especially for a man scientifically educated, a graduate student at MIT—it involves a kind of schizophrenia. A compartmentalization. Emotional illness. He has strange needs."

"Look, everybody has their thing. Your thing is reinterpreting the literary trends."

"I don't see how you can make a comparison. What *I* do is valid, like your cousin's scientific work. There's no contradiction. It's not as though I wrote a reappraisal of Emily Dickinson and then danced around with a loincloth and a spear."

"Well, Thomas Stearns Eliot was into the Church," Elspeth said.

"That's different."

"How is it different?"

"It's different. It's part of the whole fabric, the history of Western civilization, from which he drew his allusions, his sources, his references."

54

THE evening before her day off, when Chris gave Elspeth her usual ride home, Elspeth told her it was the last such ride she would need. Tomorrow the cast would be taken off, and with two hands it would be easy enough to take the bus, as she had at the beginning.

Wednesday morning Calvin spun the old mechanical bell just as Elspeth had picked up Peter to change him. Mrs. Brody unbolted the door. Elspeth caught his eye from the center hallway.

"Are you ready?" he asked. He wore the gray turtleneck.

"I'll be ready in a few minutes. Why don't you come in and wait."

"Anything I can do to help meanwhile?"

"You could change Petey's diaper for me while I comb my hair. He's got a load in his pants."

"No thank you," Calvin said. "Excrement offends me."

"It does? I wouldn't have thought so, after some of the descriptions in your novel."

"Don't make the mistake of confusing the writer with his work. I also described how it feels to be swallowed whole by a python, as I'm sure you recall. But I'm sure you wouldn't conclude it's what I do for kicks."

"Okay. Have you had breakfast?"

"I have."

"Well, sit down and watch television with the Brodys then. I won't be long."

"No, I'll wait in the car, out front. Take your time. I always have reading matter with me when I call for a woman."

Elspeth strapped Peter to the changing table in the bathroom.

"How's Petey the kaka artist today? Do you know Mama's gonna have two arms pretty soon? All the better to change you with?"

At last she came down the porch steps with Peter and the shoulder bag and got into the bucket seat of the low-slung orange sports car beside Calvin. The upholstery was worn.

"Why are you bringing the baby?"

"Why not? I always bring him."

He started the motor. Peter's eyes widened at the roar.

At the corner where buses turned they waited for a light.

"Your engine's running choked," she told Calvin. "Do you know how to adjust your carburetor?"

"I can't say that I do."

"I'll look at it after. An eighth of a turn with a screwdriver should do it."

At the hospital Calvin again waited in the car because there was no place to park.

The cast was brownish gray by now, thoroughly soiled. A young doctor cut it away while a social worker held Peter. The skin was pale where the cast had been. She massaged it. "The color will come back in a day or so," the doctor said.

Holding Peter seemed so easy now.

At the car she gave him to Calvin while she looked in the trunk for a screwdriver. There was none. She raised the hood and adjusted the carburetor anyway, using a nail file. "It's such a luxury to have two arms," she said.

Calvin suggested they spend the day together. "We could explore the rockbound coast. Or the dunes. It should be interesting at this time of year. Deserted. The geese beginning to migrate north. Lobster for dinner."

"I can't, Calvin. Take me back to Mrs. Brody's. I leave all kinds of chores for my day off and now that I've got two arms there's tons to catch up on."

"They've waited this long. They can wait another day."

"They can't. Anyway I didn't bring Petey's bassinet or seat or anything. We'll go out tonight like we said."

He drove her home.

"I'll be down about six," he said. "Incidentally, I trust it's not your intention to take the baby along with us. I think he'd be rather a distraction."

"No. I was gonna leave him with Mrs. Brody. Make it about seven, okay? Thanks for everything, Calvin." She thought the bushy sidewhiskers looked funny when he frowned. "As a matter of fact, there *is* something you can do for me now," she added gently. "I've been waiting for somebody with a car to get rid of all my cans and glass. Come on." She touched his arm.

He followed her uncomprehendingly. She undid Peter's sweater and lowered him to the crib. She gave the mobile figures a twirl.

Mrs. Brody said there was mail on her bureau. She saw it was her monthly bank statement in its long gray window envelope. It would surely tell her what had happened to the million-dollar checks. But she didn't open it. She led Calvin out to the back porch.

It was lined end to end with cartons filled either with glass jars of all sizes or with flattened steel cans.

She loaded a corrugated carton into his arms and took another. He followed her down the backstairs and up the narrow walkway past the trash barrels to the street. She told him meanwhile how to find the recycling plant. It was several towns away.

They returned to the porch for cartons again and again until all were stuffed into the little two-seater. Loose cans and bottles filled crannies. "Why don't you come for the ride," he said, "and direct me?"

"No room."

"We'll unload some and do it in two trips."

"No. You'll find it. I gave you good directions." She gave him a pat. "See you at seven."

She returned to Peter. Not till she had changed him and strapped him into his seat on the bureau top did she take up the bank's envelope. She began to open it with one hand, pressing with the heel of her thumb and digging with her third finger at the corner.

She remembered suddenly that that method was not necessary anymore. She ripped it open with two hands. Checks, deposit slips and transfer orders fell out. She stooped and gathered them, studying the statement.

She shrieked a laugh and fell back onto the bed. It sank under her, its steel undermesh squeaking. Crazy! She laughed again and kicked up her legs. It had worked! Those ninnies!

The balance at the beginning of the period was barely over a hundred dollars, but at the end it was more than a thousand. In between, among salary deposits and checks to Mrs. Jacob Brody, Blue Cross, Alfredo Castorini, Leo & Walter's Market, and Radcliffe College, there was a credit of a million dollars in savings and a debit of the same amount, then a credit of a million in checking and the same debit. But the interest box showed $961.85, and they had credited that to her balance.

She sat up again. The great check itself was there among the others, stamped red and blue with all sorts of clearing houses and dates. "Petey, I don't believe it! It's too beautiful."

She fed him in the wicker chair. The account was in balance. The computers were happy. And for the investment of a postage stamp she had netted more than nine hundred and sixty dollars. She laughed again. Peter kept nursing and did not open his eyes.

She strapped him into his seat and sat him on the changing table while she took a leisurely bath. She lay in the warmth.

No dates for all these months, and now suddenly two guys two nights in a row. There was a problem of what to wear. There was only one dress here, and if she

416

wore it for Calvin it wouldn't be quite fresh for Alf. She had wanted to save it for Alf.

She didn't even have a pair of dress-up slacks. All the good stuff was in Winslow. If she wore her usual frayed jeans, it would be like telling Calvin he wasn't worth dressing up for. He wasn't, actually.

She sat up in the bath and added from the hot side. Peter yawned.

If I canceled a million against a million every week, what would my yearly income be? At five percent, that's fifty gees a year. Wow, Petey, this is too big for both of us.

And some teller would surely start to get curious.

Don't be greedy. Lay low a couple of months.

Better still, quit when you're ahead. Maybe it was a fluke.

She climbed out of the tub. Peter was asleep, his head to the side. It was good to be able to swing arms again and do calisthenics on the bath mat.

She took Peter marketing in the pram.

Maybe the bank would still catch her, belatedly. Some auditor, in the bank out west, or in the clearing house.

Maybe she should go to the bank and confess before that happened. Tell them it was only a prank.

And maybe they would ask her to kindly keep the nine hundred and sixty, because if she gave it back it would gum up the computers.

Maybe she should just let well enough alone. Don't mention it, but don't draw against it. As long as it still lay there in the bank, she could argue that she hadn't taken anything.

Calvin was prompt, a few minutes before seven, as she had known he would be. She was in the dress, which was gray, with a shirt collar and buttons down to the belt. She had left a relief bottle in the refrigerator in case Peter woke, with instructions to Mrs. Brody on how to warm it and test it.

"Don't be afraid, darling. I warmed plenty bottles already. Children, grandchildren."

Elspeth hoped Calvin would not suggest a place far away.

"Where are we going?" she asked him in the car.

"I found a Chinese place about three miles down the avenue," he said. "It pretends to be Polynesian, but it's Chinese. If that appeals to you."

"Oh, good."

He was wearing a black turtleneck this time, with a tweedy jacket. His bushy head was its usual thick mess of scrambled curls, but the sidewhiskers seemed freshly groomed. She thought she detected a scented lotion.

An Oriental young man led them through dimness and bamboo to a corner table. Calvin took Elspeth's white raincoat and hung it.

He sucked his pipe while he studied the tasseled menu. Then he suggested cocktails containing pineapple and coconut and appetizers of chicken wings. He snapped his fingers to call the waiter.

He kept smiling across the table at her. His gaze made her glance to see if her top button was undone. It was not. The cocktails were in huge frosty glasses,

417

decorated with a garbage of fruit and paper umbrellas. He raised his ceremoniously, and they swallowed, looking at each other over the rims.

Elspeth pulled apart a marinated wing and dipped it in sauce.

"You have magnificent breasts," said Calvin. "Like the figurehead supporting the bowsprit of a beautiful ship. A clipper, of grace and elegance. If you raised your arms together high above your head, and leaned with the wind, I could just see you rounding Cape Horn."

"No I don't. They're too pointy for a bowsprit. Bowsprits have very round ones. There was a girl on my floor at Mount Holyoke like that. Belinda von Schmertzing. Perfect hemispheres. Majestic."

Then she excused herself to telephone Mrs. Brody.

"We only just got here," said Calvin.

"I know, But I'm a nervous mother. I never left him with anybody before. And she's so old. She can't really carry him around if he fusses. She has bad feet and everything."

"Maybe you'd be a better mother if you smothered him less."

"Well, I just want to give her the phone number where we are."

She found the booth. Mrs. Brody said he was good, fine. Sleeping. She just this minute went to look.

When Elspeth returned the main dishes had come. Calvin raised a silver cover. The tangle of moist vegetables steamed through button mushrooms, almonds, pale strips of pork.

"It looks delicious," she said.

"I'll order another round of drinks."

"Oh, not for me, please. I think there was more vodka in it than meets the taste."

He served her, first from the rice bowl, then from the serving dish.

"How'd you ever come up with a name like Shmuckbucket O'Toole?" she asked him.

"I just cooked it up."

"I think your play Two Shillings might have some off-Broadway possibilities. At least I hear they've been doing stuff like that. And especially where it doesn't need scenery, and very few props. It wouldn't need much budget. Maybe if you could rewrite it so there was a little action. It's really just right for theater in the round. The only thing was, I thought it was just a teensy bit static."

"Ten Shillings."

"What?"

"Ten Shillings. Not Two Shillings."

"Oh. Of course. I'm sorry. I didn't mean to devalue it. I guess I was thinking of the two acts. Or the two characters."

They ate some mouthfuls in silence. He was looking at his food now, frowning.

"You're certainly very versatile," she said. "Do you consider yourself primarily a novelist or primarily a playwright?"

"Primarily a critic. However I plan to do novels and plays from time to time if only to demonstrate that I can. A serious critic should not be open to the charge that the critic is a novelist or dramatist manqué."

"You're certainly a critic of very high standards. I mean, there's not much that pleases you."

"As you say, my standards are of the highest."

"I wonder if sometimes they're *too* high. For instance, a book like A Fireplace In Winter. That book said something to me. And you tore it to shreds. Okay, I may not have your perceptions, but that woman was so real—I loved every page of it. I cried over it. Maybe because it's a woman's story it doesn't appeal to men as much. But I know it wasn't a total loss. And if you damn a book like *that*, then what's left to say when a book is really rotten?"

"A Fireplace In Winter was shlock. Derivative. Utterly predictable. Transparent."

"Well, okay, I guess it's corn actually. But I loved it. It's *good* corn. U.S. Department of Agriculture One. You always bring out the worst possible side. You're so cruel. All your reviews. You sneer at everything."

"Not all. Granted, my praise is rare, sparing. One must know whom to praise. Indiscriminate kindness would scarcely mark me as a man of taste. Better to destroy the maladroit quickly."

"Well, I guess you do that. You go for the jugular, kind of."

"I employ wit, if that's what you mean. You can't blame me if I put my stylistic skills on display. I'm young, after all, on the way up. And whenever I get a chance to appear in the right publications I make the most of it."

"So how are your doing?"

"Some individuals in the right circles are beginning to notice me. The important thing is to be in favor with certain persons of influence. The most prestigious are getting along in years, and there'll be a battle for the succession."

"It sounds so competitive. Cutthroat."

"It is. For those who rise to the top in any field. Only the best survive."

"Dog eat dog, as they say," said Elspeth.

"As they say." He sprinkled some of the black sauce.

"Actually it sounds more like snake eat snake."

"My dear lady, do you understand the purpose of literary criticism? The function of the critic?"

"Sure. To show that the critic is smarter than the writer."

Though the light was subdued and the sidewhiskers hid part of his cheeks, she thought she saw him color ever so slightly. He chewed. "The critic is an intellectual," he said.

"Aren't novelists and playwrights intellectuals?"

"Frequently not. Sometimes even the greatest are not. Often they don't know what they're doing. If they did they couldn't write. They write out of their neuroses, and their times. They need the critic to explain what they've done."

Elspeth took a second helping.

"Let me," he said.

"No, I want to. It feels so good to have a right arm."

He helped himself to a smaller portion, and picked out additional almonds, unsmiling. For a while they ate without talking. The waiter poured tea.

Elspeth opened a fortune cookie.

" 'Chairman Mao say Comrade Brezhnev is capitalist bandit,' " she said.

"Does it really say that?"

"No. It says, 'All heiressess are beautiful.' "

"Dryden. They simply go through books of quotations."

She opened another. "Hey! This one is true! It says, 'You are going to receive a large sum of money.' I played a trick on my bank's computer and it gave me over nine hundred dollars."

"How did you do that?"

"Well, I wrote two checks, each one backing the other one. So it was imaginary money that evaporated into the nothingness from whence it came, but meanwhile I got interest on it."

"Imaginary interest?"

"No, real interest. Imaginary money pays real interest."

"I'm sure. But even if you did, the cookie would still be wrong. You say you received it. The cookie says you will receive."

"But I haven't received it yet. It's only credited to my account. I don't receive it until I draw against it."

"A likely story." He took a fortune cookie. "Hm. 'Better to have one wife and two cars, than two wives and one car.' What idiot do they pay to write these?" He ate a piece of it. He broke another. He smiled. "Now then. This I like." He handed her the little paper.

> It is easier to find an antonym for antonym
> than a synonym for synonym.

Calvin had put money on the corner of the table even before the bill came, but the waiter observed him and brought the bill and the tipping plate at once.

"Let's go to my mother's place and have a brandy," said Calvin. "Then you'll be near the baby in case of any emergency."

"Okay. That's a good idea."

The avenue was wide and straight at this end and there was little traffic.

"I guess it *would* be sort of interesting," Elspeth said, "if you make it to the top. The greatest authority on American and English letters in our generation, and your mother can't pronounce Ipswich."

He was watching the road.

"It can make it easier to comprehend a culture if your roots are outside it," he said.

"I'd think it could also make it easier if your roots are inside it," said Elspeth.

When he pushed open the heavy carved door to the stairwell Elspeth wanted to check on Peter at once, but he persuaded her to come upstairs directly and phone from his mother's apartment.

420

She found the wall phone in Mrs. Peress's kitchen. Mrs. Brody told her everything was all right. Peter had not waked up.

She returned to the living room. Calvin lifted her chin and kissed her.

"I kind of wish you hadn't done that," said Elspeth, turning from him.

"Exquisite," he said. "Eminently kissable." His voice was so low it seemed to reverberate in the depth of his chest. He took her white raincoat, and slid a hand lightly over the roundness of her buttocks. The room was as dark as the restaurant had been, lighted only by a single sconce on the far wall. On the coffee table were two snifters and a bottle of brandy.

"Isn't your mother here? Where's your mother?"

"I took her to spend the evening with Mrs. Cream," he said. "Do sit down."

"Mrs. who?"

"Cream."

"Cream? Like ice cream? Like the cream in milk?"

"Or in your coffee. That's how she spells it. I suspect it means Crimea, actually."

"Oh."

"So, we have complete privacy."

To avoid the sofa would be too obvious a rebuff. She sat in the middle of it, opposite the bottle and snifters, so that wherever he sat she would have room to move away from him.

"Have some brandy," he said, and sat beside her. He laid his pipe on the marble surface of the coffee table. He poured. "It has a lovely bouquet. Hennessy. My favorite."

Elspeth held her glass by its stem. She breathed liquor.

He sipped, and crossed his knees. "When I get back to Illinois we'll have to correspond."

"We will? What about?"

"You'll hear from me often. And I'll suggest some reading."

"I thought you thought I was a hopeless Philistine."

"Why? Because you enjoyed Fireplace? Your tastes are unformed, perhaps, but you're not unintelligent. I'm certain that you're quite educable. Under my tutelage, in a few short years you'll be a connoisseur of current trends."

"Oh. That's good to hear. You really think it's worth taking all that trouble?"

"I'm certain that you're worth educating. I find something very charming about you."

"From the direction of your gaze I'd say you find two things very charming about me."

He sipped brandy. "You put that very well. That's what I mean. There's an openness, a directness about you. In your eyes and in your speech."

His big arm came slithering behind her. His hand rested upon the dress, his fingers tapping gently, exploring the shape of her shoulder. They descended upon the short sleeve, swept the arm below it, then lightly cupped a breast.

She thrust away his hand. "Hey! None of that. Back to square one."

"What's the matter?"

421

"Nothing's the matter. Just forget it, Calvin. I'm not interested."

"You object to my arm on your shoulder? Have I offended you?" The large hand was half on her shoulder, more conservatively than before, and perhaps half on the back of the sofa.

"If it can stay on my shoulder that's one thing. But let's not start what we're not gonna finish."

"Meaning what?"

"Meaning I don't believe in getting laid on living-room sofas."

"There's the back bedroom."

"I don't get laid with guys in their mothers' beds, either."

"I didn't say my mother's bedroom. The further bedroom's mine when I'm here."

"Your mother could walk in on us."

"She can't get back till I pick her up and give her a ride back. Anyway, we could even lock the door and spend the night. She's an old lady, but she's got more sense than to say anything."

"You force me to put things in one syllable, Calvin. Just plain no, that's all. I know you've been here a week, and tomorrow your vacation's over, and you've been hoping to slide down my cellar door for the grand finale, but I just can't. A woman has a right to say no and not give a reason."

"You're being absurd."

"Why absurd? Are you one of these types that thinks a date has to end in a lay?"

"No, indeed. I do not. No truly enlightened person believes today that a date ought to end with getting laid." His thumb and middle finger rotated the stem of his glass back and forth, but the hand at her shoulder was creeping again. "Quite the contrary. Optimally a date should begin with it. Get laid first, then get dressed again and go out. A much sounder approach. It makes for a more relaxed evening."

"Oh great. Next time a guy calls for me I'll just answer the door naked. Leave my tits alone!" She thrust the big hand away. "Keep your cotton-picking hands off! Calvin, I'm sorry to have to disappoint you. Maybe you think I'm emasculating you. Maybe you think I'm a nutcracker like that girl in your novel, but I can't help it. That's how it is. So accept it. Okay? You can't win them all. Maybe it's that you don't appeal to me, or maybe I just can't psychologically go to bed with anybody right now. It's not your fault. But anyhow it's hopeless. So let's turn to another subject."

Calvin reached for his pipe. "You're determined to be difficult."

"Yup," said Elspeth.

He lighted the pipe. He crossed his legs, and blew smoke before him. He let an arm lie along the top of the sofa behind her, not touching her. "Why don't I appeal to you?"

"What's the difference? Maybe you're too tall."

"Does my height threaten you?"

"Maybe I don't trust writers."

"Why don't you trust writers?"

"I don't trust guys that think they're gonna be famous. I'm gonna find some guy

422

that's not on an ego trip, and marry him. I loved an actor once, and it was a bad trip."

"You had a bad experience with an actor, so you distrust writers? That's not very rational, now, is it?"

"Well, actors and writers are sort of the same. All the preoccupation with words and expression. I mean, like sometimes it's hard to tell a wordsmith from a bullshitter. It's a very thin line. Okay, maybe I'm square. You think a book like A Fireplace In Winter isn't literature because it doesn't have all this obscurity and beautiful language that's hard to understand. But obscurity and veiled references, and allusions and allusions, showing how sensitive they are—that isn't everything. Maybe the reason some of these guys make their books so hard to understand is that if people could understand it, they'd know it's just a bunch of crap. You know what I mean? I think sometimes the verbal fireworks and imagery and virtuosity and far-out similes are used for the purpose of obscuring that nothing very new or substantial is being said. When somebody really has something to say, he doesn't have to be afraid to say it plain and clear. Like the poems of Robert Frost, for instance. But I guess there aren't too many that really have something to say. I think most writers are dumb. Just dumb, and conning themselves and other people into thinking they know what they're doing. Just like doctors and Presidents."

The corners of Calvin's mouth dipped in a wide, tight-lipped frown. He pretended to smoke the pipe, though it was out again.

"I'll have to educate you," he said quietly.

"Don't bother, Calvin. I'm not worth it. I'm not for you. You wouldn't want to screw a lowbrow, would you? It would be beneath you. I'm sorry—I didn't mean that to come out as a pun."

"You're not a lowbrow. It's quite apparent that you're not. And you know you're not. Your effort to present youself as such is a defensive mechanism. Because you fear me sexually."

She didn't answer.

He leaned back, legs crossed, and played with the pipe against his teeth. "And after that line of defense, your next line of defense would no doubt be fear of pregnancy. Would it not? Look what happened to me, I had a child, you'd say. I don't dare, lest I have another. Once bitten, twice shy. Even though an unwanted pregnancy is virtually impossible, if it's genuinely unwanted. Elspeth, has it ever occurred to you that your baby itself is a defensive mechanism? That perhaps unconsciously you had the baby in order to set up a defense?"

"How do you mean?"

"Elspeth, you mentioned that you once loved an actor. Tell, me, was the actor the baby's father?"

"Yes."

"I gathered. I'll wager he's the only man you've ever slept with. Correct?"

"Correct."

"Correct, of course. As you can see, Elspeth, you've been on my mind constantly all week, and I've gleaned some insight into you. I'll venture further that your

423

couplings with the child's father were invariably limited to the so-called missionary position."

"Wrong, wrong, wrong. You couldn't be more wrong. Not that it's any of your business."

"Oh? In any event I'll wager odds that the affair was of short duration."

"Depends what you call short."

"But it came to an end as soon as you were certain you were pregnant."

"Well, things were coming apart around then."

"Of course. Elspeth, you used the pregnancy, and now you're using the child, the way a fat girl uses her obesity. You fear sex, and you fear men. In a way the baby is a more secure defense than obesity. Because the baby proclaims that you did have sex once, and enables you to avoid seeing your fear. And it throws your friends off the scent, so they won't lecture you about your fear and keep badgering you to get help, the way fat girls are constantly lectured. Where your fears came from, I don't know. Somewhere in the recesses of your childhood. But you worked out an exceedingly clever defense. Shut your eyes, force yourself to do the hated thing once, get yourself pregnant, and you'll never have to do it again. You'll be free of sex forever. You carry the child about with you everyplace you go, nursing at the breast, playing the mother, a bag of diapers on your arm, and what does this proclaim? Look, fellows, I'm a loser. Danger! Don't touch me, lest you find yourself saddled with a family."

"Hm," said Elspeth.

"You've never seen it in that light, have you."

"Interesting. No, I guess I never thought of that. I never looked at it that way."

"I'm sure not. The truth is always hard to face."

"And a ten-foot-high pile of horse manure is even harder to face."

"Meaning what?"

"Meaning I don't buy it. I don't know what I believe, Calvin. I started off like other kids, thinking life is a bowl of cherries, and concerned about what's in and what's out. And now at nineteen I don't know where it's at. I don't even know what questions to ask. All I know is, there's got to be more to this dumb world than meets the eye. I just don't understand it. Petey's daddy screwed me, and now there's Petey. And his daddy doesn't want to know from him—he's not even curious. To his daddy Petey was just something to be scraped out. Wiped away. Flushed down the toilet. Petey's daddy knows all there is to know about Richard the Second. And about his own little boy he knows nothing. He doesn't even know if I had a boy or a girl. And yet maybe his son is a better man than *he* is. Petey's life is a whole world. Poor kid. Who knows what good and what evil is in store for him? These people who talk so much about the naturalness of sex, it's natural natural natural so we have to have so much of it, why do they so rarely make the same fuss about the naturalness of breastfeeding? Or the naturalness of giving birth fully conscious? Guys are so disjunctive."

"Disjunctive?"

"I once had a guy point out to me that you never see pregnancy in Playboy, except in the jokes. And it's true. It's disjunctive. I mean, you guys think your prick is so great because you get a hard on. That's nothing compared to what a vagina can do. I saw Petey come out of me. I felt him, and I saw him. There's a connection that's been made for me, and I can't be disjunctive about it. I don't mean I have to be thinking about having babies every time I get laid. I hope I have a lot more babies, and that for every baby I have a thousand good screws. But the fact that it can give me a child makes it something more. The joy will be more for me even. Enhanced for me. Because it has an aura, a mystery, something marvelous I don't understand. I guess it's harder for a man to make the connection, because he doesn't give birth. Copulation is all you experience, so you think that's all that counts. I mean, what do guys know? All your prick is good for besides to have fun with is to piss through. Most guys. Maybe not all. I hope not all. My cousin told me he stopped screwing a girl once, because he didn't want a child of his to be aborted. He knew he didn't want her to be part of his life forever, but he knew that if she accidentally conceived his child, he'd want to know his child. He made the connection."

"That religious nut I met Sunday?"

"Yes, that religious nut you met Sunday."

"And that girl?"

"No, a different girl. That he knew before."

"Elspeth, do you know what you're doing now?"

"Let me make my point, Calvin. I listened to you. And you're helping me to clarify my thinking. I want the guy that screws me to understand what he's getting into, literally. I want him to understand what a vagina is. And if there's a baby, I want him to want the baby, and take the Lamaze classes with me, and coach me in labor and delivery, and be pregnant with me vicariously. I want him to think my belly's beautiful when it's big and hard, and not think diaper is a dirty word."

"Elspeth, you poor girl, don't you grasp what you're trying to accomplish with this kind of talk? It's yet another defensive mechanism. What you're endeavoring to do is make the atmosphere as unsexy as possible. The soft light and the brandy bottle frighten you. Though you can't admit it. So you invoke babies and pregnancy and childbirth to drive eroticism from the room. It only bears out what I was saying."

"You don't make the connection."

"I know that I'm terribly fond of you. Even though you're terribly neurotic. And I insist upon helping you. You need to conquer your fears, and a gentle and understanding friend is required. Someone who will only guide you, restore your confidence, and not push you, or pressure you. So let me suggest that you relax, rest upon my arm and shoulder. I'll simply caress you, cradle you, and it need go no further. I assure you that until such time as you yourself feel ready, it will go no further. Come on. Lean back."

"Nope." She hunched forward, away from his arm.

He edged closer.

She edged further away.

"Elspeth, I gave you my word. You have nothing to fear."

"Lay off."

"Aren't you being a bit childish? You're behaving like a twelve-year-old."

"How much more blunt can I be? I mean, Christian charity is all very well, but I still owe it to myself not to get cozy with a guy that doesn't appeal to me. So let's just say I'm too stupid to appreciate you and leave it at that. Okay, Calvin?"

"Elspeth, if you persist in behaving like a child, I'll be forced to treat you as a child."

"Meaning what?"

"If it becomes necessary to up-end you across my knees, and administer a smart slap to your exposed buttocks, you'll be quickly sobered. I assure you."

She looked at him in amazement. "You're threatening to spank me?"

"A proven remedy. I've had startling results. Women find it electric, or soothing, or even refreshing, but always sobering. You'll be brought back straightaway to earth and to reality."

"You're not serious!"

"Elspeth, I'm never anything but serious. I warn you. Don't exasperate me."

"I don't believe this. Good night." She rose. "And thank you for a lovely evening."

The big hands seized her and yanked her down flat across his lap. She twisted, and thrust a hand up into his face with all her force.

The heel of her thumb was stopped sharply by the bottom of his nose. He gave a cry of pain and raised a hand to his face. Elspeth scrambled from him and tumbled backward over the coffee table to the carpet. The stoppered brandy bottle tottered but didn't fall. With both her feet she kicked over the marble-topped coffee table against his shins as he rose. She heard the clump of the bottle and the smash of a snifter and his yelp all at once. She fled first on her knees and then on her feet.

"My nose is bleeding! Elspeth! Look!"

She glimpsed him as she slammed the door. He was standing behind the overturned coffee table, hands spread out, his mouth, chin, hands and black turtleneck jersey all streaked and bloody.

She ran down, clasping the banister post to swing faster around the bend in the staircase. She gave the doorbell several twists. She beat on the door with both hands. She glanced back at the stairs to see if Calvin was coming. He wasn't.

"Wait, I'm coming," she heard Mrs. Brody say.

She entered breathlessly when Mrs. Brody opened.

"So? You had a nice time?"

"Ya. How's Petey?"

"Don't worry, the baby's fine. You'll see. He didn't wake up. I got the bottle still in the fridgeyaire."

Under the bathroom light Elspeth took off the dress and looked for a stain of brandy she was sure had spilled against her. She found it. She rinsed the stain under the cold tap a while.

426

Her breasts were full. She went to the crib and lifted Peter. He nursed without seeming to have wakened.

She went with him to the telephone table in her half-slip and opened bra. She looked up the Peress number quickly and dialed. It rang several times. When it was picked up she heard it put down somewhere, and there were more stirrings before Calvin finally answered.

"Calvin? Are you okay?" she asked.

"I'll be all right."

"Have you had nosebleeds before?"

"I have. But that was a nasty wallop you gave me."

"It was one of my defensive mechanisms. What you should do is lie down with your head back, and some ice cubes in a towel on your forehead."

"That's approximately what I'm doing. I'm lying on the kitchen floor with a cold compress under my neck."

"Is it still bleeding?"

"It's slowed down considerably. It's the right nostril. It's always that one. Why don't you come up and look after me, and help change the compresses? I promise I won't touch you. I assure you I'd do the same for you if you had a nosebleed."

"I can't, Calvin. I'm feeding Petey. My breasts were full to bursting when I came down. Even if he doesn't wake up my breasts know when it's time."

"I could help relieve you of some of that pressure, you know. I'd love to have a suck. I was going to suggest it, before you got so touchy."

"Sorry, Calvin. Only Petey dines at this table."

"I didn't mean I'd deprive the child of his supper. Just the excess. Whatever you have to spare. I don't recall that I've ever sucked the breasts of a woman who was lactating. And it's an experience I ought to have. Don't you agree? A writer should experience everything possible, within reason."

"You didn't talk that way when I asked you to change a diaper this morning."

The big jerk. So self-centered it never even occurs to him that there might be competition, that maybe there's someone else. If I'm ready for a man again it's gonna be Alf, not him.

"You still have a coat up here you know."

"I know. You can leave it on the banister in the morning. Or I'll get it from your mother. Thanks for dinner, Calvin. Have a good trip back to Illinois, and drive carefully. And if the idle makes that urr, urr, urr again, just give that big screw in the carburetor a teensy twist."

55

WHEN Elspeth opened the door next morning to put Peter in the bassinet she saw her white raincoat draped over the banister rail. She took it in and hung it on the clothes tree.

She lifted the bassinet from the frame of the pram, with Peter inside it, and set out for the bus.

All the way down the side street she saw no sign of the orange Triumph, though there were plenty of empty spaces. Calvin must have risen with the sun and already gone.

"Look! Two arms!" she said to Chris when she brought the bassinet into the office.

Edgar and Puff and Mr. Tingley did not remark on it, though they watched her sweep the repair bay.

She reminded Chris that she hoped to do some real repair jobs now that she had the use of both arms.

"Well, I know, kiddo, but we're gonna have to be kind of tactful about that. They've gotten kind of used to thinking of you as the one in charge of pushing gas. Well, I'll have to speak to them, I guess. It's only right for you to get a chance once in a while."

During idle moments she thought of Alf. She imagined him returning her to her door and asking, What would you do if I kissed you? I guess I'd kiss you back, she answered.

Toward the end of the day Chris asked her to remove a customer's snow tires. "Don't get discouraged. I have to give them first call on the rush jobs. But there'll something you can work on. When the pumps aren't busy."

She was glad Peter had again been awake most of the afternoon. It meant he would probably give Mrs. Brody no trouble while she was out with Alf.

She fed him as soon as she got home, and before opening the thin white letter from the Eggleston-Uphams Bank and Trust that Mrs. Brody had placed against the bureau mirror. They've caught on, she said to herself. While he nursed she carried him about, drawing her bath meanwhile, and shedding most of her clothes.

Peter was asleep before she finished changing him. She ripped open the letter. It was a printed form, except where figures and her name had been typed in.

Dear Mrs. Baker,

In view of the admirable way in which you have managed your account consistently over a period of time, we are increasing your line of credit for automatic loans and for Master Charge from $100 to $500 effective at once.

As one of our valued and preferred customers, we stand ready always to serve you.

Sincerely,
Francis McAlister Hudson
Vice-President and Credit Manager

Beautiful. I bilk them out of nine hundred and sixty bucks and they love me for it.

She took only a minute's bath. She ironed the dress. There was no time for supper. She combed her hair before the mirror. Did Alf like long hair? He must, since he wore his own to the shoulders. Or did guys who wore it long prefer girls to cut theirs short?

From the kitchen Elspeth thought she heard Alf mount the front porch.

Elspeth took her raincoat from the coat-tree as she opened the door. "Hi. I'm ready."

He had no overcoat. His jacket was open and he wore the velveteen vest. "May I take your arm? Just to emphasize that there's no cast on it?"

"Oh. I've already forgotten about the cast."

His brother-in-law's Chevy was parked in front. He opened the door for her.

She saw a child's jump seat in the back with a plastic steering wheel attached, and a dirty stuffed dog.

"I didn't get time to pick up tickets for the Honky Brothers," he said, "but we can try at the box office."

"Okay," she said, and they started.

"How's the baby?"

"Fine. Asleep."

"He's a beautiful child. He has such a sharp way of looking at you. It makes you wonder what's going on in that little head."

"I know. Thank you."

They seemed to talk easily. He had begun to try a workingmen's compensation case that would involve more witnesses and testimony and preparation than any case he had had so far.

From the crowd milling before the concert hall it was apparent that the SOLD OUT sign had just gone up.

"Can't win them all," said Elspeth.

He suggested a movie. They studied the listings in a newspaper he retrieved from the back seat. The one they chose was at a cinema complex in a suburb she had never seen.

While they rode he talked of his sister's kids. They were four and two. He told

429

her something cute his niece had said. Elspeth asked what his family was like, and he told of the household and the grandparents who lived with them. His mother had been a war bride.

"Do you speak Italian at home?"

"Both. Not to my sister and brother-in-law."

"It's good to know an ancestral language. There was a Chinese girl on my floor at Mount Holyoke, and she couldn't speak Chinese. It wasn't her fault, but it was sort of too bad. She wanted to take a course in it."

"Italian's a great language," he said. "It's no wonder they wrote the greatest vocal music ever written, ten times better than anything north of the Alps. It was made to be sung, more than any language in the world."

"How?"

"Take the word for rocking chair. Sedia a dondolo." He sang it out loudly in clear measured syllables as though it were la donna è mobile. "Sedia a dondolo!"

The sweeping gesture of his left hand struck the window. Elspeth laughed. "I can see it rocking," she said.

"Doesn't that cry out to be sung?" Alf asked her. "It sings itself. The whole language is like that. It's like a mouthwash. It invigorates."

He sang again, loudly and full-voiced, still to the tune of la donna è mobile.

"Sedia a dondolo,
Avanti indietro—"

A grandiose gesture struck the sun visor. He opened the window to give himself more room. The wind blew his hair.

"Grande capitombolo,
Sconvolgimento—"

He dropped his voice dramatically, the gestures now flowery.

"Teste sono rotte,
Uova strapazzate—"

Again his lungs surged, and Elspeth joined him shrilly in the chorus. They flung gestures. She saw passersby look.

"Sedia a dondolo,
Sedia a dondolo,
Se-e-dia a dondolo-o-o,
Sedia a dondolo—"

A vision of Mrs. Peress's three squeaky and out-of-phase rockers uniting in such a resounding chorus made her break into laughter.

430

"See what I mean?" he said.

"I see what you mean." She laughed again. "I wish I were Italian. It must be fun to be Italian."

"It's been said that Russian is for swearing, German is for giving orders, and Italian is for singing."

"What's English for?"

"I don't know," he said. "Maybe arguing cases at law."

"Hereof fail not," said Elspeth.

When they arrived at the cinema complex the film they wanted still had twenty minutes to run. Elspeth telephoned Mrs. Brody. Peter had not waked.

She caught up to Alf at the ticket counter. "Can we make it Dutch?" she said.

"No."

"I should pay all of it," said Elspeth. "I called *you*."

"But then I invited you to the Honky Brothers, so it became *my* invitation. The evening's on me. All you get to pay for is that phone call you just made."

They went to the counter in the wide glassy lobby and ordered ice-cream cones.

"Vanilla," said Elspeth. "I like ice cream to taste like ice cream."

He followed her lead. He lapped his ice cream, looking at her. "You're right. It does taste like ice cream. Do you also take your hot dogs without mustard or relish by the same reasoning?"

"I put sauerkraut on hot dogs. I didn't say I like meat to taste like meat. Maybe I'm not really a flesh eater at heart. But I like ice cream to taste like ice cream."

The theater was suffused with dim bluish light. It was not a weekend and the place was all but empty. When it darkened and the film began she sank far down. Alf laid his arm across the back of her seat. She rested her head on it, and then on his shoulder.

His hand hung nearly to the crook of her elbow. She had rested her head on guys' shoulders in theaters many times, but did not recall that the arm enclosing her ever came so far down. From there, if he were to take advantage, not just the nearest breast would be in easy reach but both. But the hand stayed on the skin of her arm, unmoving. She must have somehow leaned on him in a new and different way, for his arm to get around her so completely, and so comfortably.

"Sedia a dondolo," she murmured. "How do you say, 'rest your head on my shoulder'?"

"Posati la testa sulla mia spalla."

"Sulla mia spalla," she repeated, imitating his intonation. "It's so fluid. You're right. You don't even have to try to say it, it speaks itself. No wonder it sings."

The movie was good.

There were Irish accents, and British uniforms. The turn-of-the-century costumes were striking, and so were the panoramas of hillsides, where sheep came bleating down, and mist and seacoast. The heroine was lovely in her big Edwardian hat, turned up at the side and back. And when she undressed, the old-fashioned underwear, long plain shapeless bloomers and black stockings, became surprisingly erotic.

Her skin was beautiful as she lay, behind grasses that swayed somewhat out of focus in the near foreground.

Alf's hand moved to a breast. Under his slow massage the dress rubbed on the satiny stuff beneath. She glanced to see if anyone observed them. But the nearest were far away, over a field of seats, and watching the screen.

She put a hand gently on his, as though to stop him. His hand went back to her arm, and was still.

She wondered how far he meant to go. If necessary she would have to explain to him after that she wasn't prepared to go all the way, not this first night. She needed time to get fitted for a new diaphragm, one that fitted securely. She could not risk even the tiniest chance that she could end up with two babies, abandoned by different fathers. It wouldn't be fair to Petey, for one thing.

But her periods hadn't resumed yet, so presumably she was not ovulating and would be safe as long as breastfeeding continued. Except that some of the books said you couldn't always depend on that. And since you couldn't have a period until two weeks after you ovulated, you got no warning the first time.

And the pill—she was leery of swallowing things. Even if there was nothing else wrong with it, it would probably kill her milk supply.

Maybe he was equipped with condoms. Would he mind terribly if she insisted that he use two condoms?

His hand returned. She raised her hand to his, as though again to restrain him. This time he did not take his hand away. Her hand rested on his, and his rested on her breast, unmoving.

In time she dropped her hand to her lap. Her head remained on his shoulder, watching the movie.

His hand departed from her breast and again she felt his fingers on her arm. The retreat surprised her. But his other hand went to her lap. It held hands with her briefly, then rested on the fabric of her dress.

She thought of raising her feet and tucking them in the back of the seat before her. Then her skirt would fall back.

She didn't raise her feet.

Her eyes did not move from the screen. But it was his touch that occupied her. It was under her dress now, on the goosepimples of her thigh, the fingertips moving as though wanting to trace it all, the firm part and the fleshy part. Sometimes his pinky was down again to her knee, but the ellipses of fondling reached higher each time, like the lapping of an advancing tide. Her leg gave a shiver. She had not meant it to. He paused. His thumb lay perhaps a quarter-inch from her underpants.

The hand withdrew from that area altogether. It straightened her hem discreetly. Then it went to the armrest on the further side of his seat. She stole a glance and saw that he was watching the screen. The screen darkened, and the theater with it. The conspirators were in the undercroft of a church, with only a candle in a copper lantern.

The first hand slipped down her shoulder and visited her front. It undid a button, and a second, and a third. It moved in and stroked the filmy smoothness of her bra.

"How do you say bra?"

"Reggipetto."

"Reggipetto," she repeated. "Petto me on the reggipetto."

Maybe she should tell him the clasp was in front.

He did not need the clasp. The hand in the dress found a strap. Imperceptibly she moved her shoulder for him. He eased the strap away and dropped it into her sleeve.

A breast was lifted, and quivered back into place. It was lifted again. It was as though she could almost feel the ridges of his fingerprints, at once warming and cooling. The nipple swelled against them.

She hoped he understood this was specially for him. That it was not just routinely for everybody. It was hard to know if a guy understood, because they pretended to understand, to be polite and keep it going, even when they didn't believe you. Sometimes being easy and unresistant was the dumbest thing you could do.

Courtship was so complicated for a woman. It was so much easier for a guy. He knows what he's expected to do—just try to go as far as he can. It's so simple for him. A girl has to figure out yes or no, the timing, the effect upon him. She has to arouse him, lead him, set the price exactly right, not too high and not too low, and judge the right moment. She has to be a strategist and a psychologist. Why should it be like that? Why should love be a matter of anxiety? She wished she could just say, I love you, do you love me, and get a truthful yes or no.

Milk came drooling from both her breasts. It did not just leak, it poured. He took his dripping hand out of her clothing. "Jesus," he muttered. "That never happened to me before."

"It never happened to *me* before either. Not like that." The cloth clung to her, almost sopping enough to wring. Tears filled her eyes. She tried to forestall the sobs but she couldn't.

She found a package of tissues but kept sobbing.

"Are you okay?" said Alf.

"I'm okay." But the crying wouldn't stop. She rearranged the bra and buttoned the dress. He was not touching her. He was sitting as though he had never touched her.

Both layers were drenched and stained, and seemed to grow wetter still. And the tears and quiet sobs went on with their own momentum. She could not control it. I'm just a bunch of secretions, she thought of saying.

He was sitting far down, legs crossed, elbows on the arms of his chair, chin resting on his folded hands, as if trying to concentrate on the movie.

The more she tried to end the sobbing the more it continued, though almost soundlessly. Her shoulders shook, her eyes flooded. It was as involuntary as hiccups.

"Are you all right?" he asked.

She nodded. "I cry easily," she managed. "It's nothing. It's something I inherit from my mother."

She thought she had brought it under control, but it began again. She kept using tissues.

Maybe she should go to the ladies' and wait there for it to subside. But then she would have to parade her wet front through the lobby, unless she put on her raincoat.

She tried to concentrate on the movie. The little convulsions kept coming, and her eyes kept filling. Crying easily was one thing, but it didn't usually go on and on forever like this. She knew Alf was as ill at ease and confused as she. But every apology that came to her mind seemed too dumb. She watched scenes, grim faces close up in the moonlight, then a card game in the barracks, but she had lost the thread of the plot. The sobs persisted. They seemed far more awkward than the stupid accident that had brought them on, which ought to have been laughed off somehow, except that it was too late to now.

"Do you want to go?" Alf asked her. "Shall I take you home?"

She nodded.

He rose. She reached for the white raincoat.

In the car they scarcely spoke. And still the dumb weeping would not go away. It would die down enough for her to speak, but she could think of nothing good enough to say. And then it would start again. She wished Alf would say something.

"I feel so transparent," said Elspeth.

"How do you mean?"

She was breathing irregularly. She had run out of tissues.

"My waistline's the same as before," she said, "but my head's different. I can't get back into the old boy-girl thing."

On the Brodys' street there was the rotating blue flash of a police car. Then with a start she saw it was before her own house.

"What do you suppose is wrong?" she said.

"Isn't that your house?" said Alf almost in the same instant.

He halted behind the police car and she sprang out.

The door from the porch hung open. As she ran up the steps she could see that the inner door was open also. A policeman stood there. She heard Mrs. Brody wailing and thought she heard Mrs. Peress in there too, talking hysterically in Yiddish.

"Are you the daughter?" the policeman asked Elspeth. "Granddaughter?"

"I live here. What happened?"

"The old man had an attack. We're waiting for the ambulance." As he spoke she heard the approaching siren.

"Let me get my baby, and I'll go with them."

56

SHE didn't think of Alf until she was in the back seat of the police car, with Peter sleeping at her shoulder and Mrs. Brody sighing and wiping her eyes next to her. She was sure Alf had gotten out of his car with her, but at what point in the confusion he had disappeared she didn't know. She had not even thanked him for the evening. She could not recall if he had come into the house. She had changed clothes, zippered Peter into his flannel, grabbed the shoulder bag and baby seat and tied Mrs. Brody's shoes all as speedily as she could, and Alf had not been in her mind.

The car raced after the ambulance. She saw it ahead, flashing like a Christmas tree. What if she had not come home just then? Had Mrs. Peress come downstairs in order to stay with Petey? Or would they have gone out and forgotten him? There was no point in asking. Mrs. Brody meanwhile had calmed considerably. "I didn't put on a corset, God will forgive me," she said.

Elspeth caught a glimpse of Mr. Brody as they wheeled him quickly through the emergency doors. He lay under blankets, and someone held an oxygen mask to his nose and mouth. His skin was lavender gray.

Mrs. Brody walked with her tiredly, sighing heavily and exclaiming half under her breath. A rosy-cheeked girl led them to Intensive Care and showed them where they could sit.

"Should we call Phyllis and Marty and everybody?" Elspeth asked. "Or wait and see how he is in the morning, or what?"

Mrs. Brody seemed to have heard, but only murmured as though undecided. But presently a beefy curly-haired man in white stood over them with a stethoscope dangling.

"He's holding on, but his vital signs are weak. He's suffered a coronary and a stroke. Apparently one set off the other."

Elspeth waited for Mrs. Brody to speak, but Mrs. Brody only listened, saying nothing.

"What are his chances?" Elspeth asked, not altogether sure if she should.

"He could linger a week. Two, even. Or he could go anytime."

"Don't go by the way his eyes look," said Elspeth. "He's blind, you know."

"I know that."

"You think we should call his children?"

435

"I would."

She turned to Mrs. Brody. "Want me to call?"

"You can use this phone," a woman with abundant black hair said at the desk.

Mrs. Brody was dry-eyed now. She seemed only tired. "You got a pencil? I'll tell you the numbers."

Elspeth set up Peter in his seat upon the bench. He slept.

"Would you like to see him?" the doctor asked Mrs. Brody. "I don't know whether he'll know you're there. But he might." Mrs. Brody rose heavily.

Elspeth rang Phyllis, standing by the desk, watching Peter. Her throat felt dry, her stomach queasy.

Phyllis sounded as if she had been wakened.

"Phyllis? This is Elspeth Baker. Look, I'm sorry to wake you, but I know you'd want to know. Your father had a coronary. We're with him at the Boston City. Your mother and me."

"Oh God. Is he dead?"

"No. Not yet."

"Oh God. How does it look?"

"Well, not too good, actually."

"I can't leave the children. Alan's on the road. My husband's on the road. I'll be over in the morning. As soon as I get the kids off to school."

Elspeth rang Marty. His wife answered. Marty was at a lodge meeting. The installation of officers. She would try to get to him. She thanked Elspeth.

The Florida call Elspeth asked to have charged to the Brodys' phone. Alongside the desk and the black-haired lady a row of monitoring instruments sat on a table. Elspeth only half saw them. Betty's voice at once expressed anxiety, as though she knew the meaning of a call at night from Boston.

"My name's Elspeth Baker. I rent a room in your parents' apartment."

"Yes. I know about you, Miss Baker. What's wrong?"

When she was told her voice cracked. Then she said she would come up right away, on the first plane. For a few seconds she seemed to struggle to get her voice under control again. She asked about Marty and Phyllis, and how her mother was taking it.

"She seems pretty calm," said Elspeth, her eye on Peter. "I'll stay with her, at least till somebody gets here."

Elspeth asked the black-haired lady if she could look in on the patient briefly. His room opened directly on the desk area. Elspeth pushed aside the plastic curtain and went in.

Mrs. Brody was near his bed in a canvas chair. Elspeth told her the results of the calls. Mr. Brody was lying open-mouthed, wired to a beeping electronic device that pictured his green jumping heartbeat on a little black screen. There was a tube to a nostril and another was bandaged into an arm.

She pressed his hand, but detected no response. "This is Elspeth, Mr. Brody. Your children are gonna come and see you. Betty's taking a plane. You have to get well, so we can go walking again." She didn't know if he heard. Her eyes moistened. She left the room and sat by Peter on the bench. He did not waken when she took off his flannel.

She was glad she had shed tears for Mr. Brody. But why wasn't she sobbing out of control, the way she had with Alf in the theater?

It was so dumb, the way things had happened tonight with Alf. The mortifying thing was the way her crying like that must have displayed all her wants and fears before him. And probably she embarrassed him with the ethnic thing too. Why had she kept insisting on it? Telling him she wished she were Italian—what a stupid thing to say. She had wanted to convey that their roots, their origins meant nothing. Instead she had protested too much. To him it probably sounded just like guinea wop guinea wop five cents a lollipop.

Mrs. Brody came out, dry-eyed, and said the chair in there wasn't comfortable. She sat on the bench. Elspeth took a comb from the shoulder bag, and Mrs. Brody allowed her to untangle the wild white hair.

Soon Mrs. Brody dozed. Elspeth sipped coffee the black-haired lady had given her, looking at Peter.

Was Petey dreaming? Or were three months too little for him to have enough experience yet to dream about? Still, the mechanism that makes you dream must make you dream, experience or no. Did he dream about breasts? Maybe he dreamed he was in the womb, hearing his mother's drumming heartbeat, and feeling the sway and tilt every time she walked or changed position.

It was hard to grasp that Mr. and Mrs. Brody had once been infants like that, adored by their elders, and with all the future before them. Of course you knew it. But you couldn't grasp it.

The doctor came again and looked in on Mr. Brody. When he came out he said there was no change.

Elspeth borrowed the newspaper on the desk. She turned to the Chit Chat. There was another report from the woman who called herself Blue Bell. She wrote that she had placed ads, and finally boarded her baby with a lady who charged too much and was very quick and not-listening and know-it-all. Three times in a row, she found her baby crying exhaustedly. At work she would wonder if her baby was crying. So she had to quit.

Marty arrived. Mrs. Brody was at once aware of it, as though she had not really been asleep. He was tall and stooped, with thinning hair. His coat hung over his tuxedo. Elspeth thought Mr. Brody must have looked like him once. He carried a moist cigar. The lady at the desk made him throw it into the basket.

"It's not even lighted."

"I'm sorry. We can't take chances. There are oxygen tanks here."

He looked in on his father and came out again. He talked a little, sat, stood, walked about. He said it made no sense to hang around. But just then the black-haired lady hurried in to Mr. Brody, as though in response to an electronic signal. In a moment the doctor appeared, with long strides, and went in also. Elspeth looked at Mrs. Brody and at Marty. Mrs. Brody closed her eyes and her lips moved. Marty peeked in around the curtain.

After some minutes the doctor and the nurse came out, and from their faces and their unhurried manner Elspeth knew Mr. Brody was dead.

"I'm afraid he's gone," said the curly-haired doctor. "I'm sorry. There was nothing more we could do." They had left the curtain open.

Mrs. Brody rose, unsteadily. Her son supported her. "Are you all right, Ma?"

Elspeth rose too. She saw Mrs. Brody go in with her son and bend to kiss the dead man on the forehead, slowly. Marty followed her example. Then they turned to come out.

"What do we do now?" Marty asked the doctor.

"Get some sleep if you can. And we'll wait to hear from your undertaker."

Marty nodded. He held Mrs. Brody. She was small against him, looking vacantly at the floor.

"Can we have your signature before you go, to give permission for an autopsy? It's routine, and we encourage it."

"Na," said Mrs. Brody.

"Any special reason?" Marty asked the doctor.

"Well, it's useful to us to trace precisely what occurred."

"Why not, Ma? If it helps science?"

"Gornisht helfen. Pa wouldn't want it. He was old. He died."

Marty shrugged to the doctor. He caught the eye of Elspeth, who had put on the shoulder bag and picked up Peter, seat and all. He shrugged to Elspeth too.

They walked down the corridor together.

"So let him rest in peace," said Marty.

At the car Marty first helped his mother in, then opened the rear door for Elspeth.

Before he turned the switch, he put his fingers to his eyes, and bent over the steering wheel. He emitted some choked sobs. Mrs. Brody sat beside him quietly.

He sat up, breathed deeply, and wiped his eyes.

They drove through quiet cold streets, past lonely street lamps.

"I know you go to work every day," he said over his shoulder. "But could you stay with my mother tomorrow until somebody gets over there?"

"Of course."

"Ma, you're gonna come to live with one of us. I'm gonna insist on it. You can even live with me and Shelley if you want. Well, you know how Shelley is. I know you'd feel more comfortable with Phyllis or Betty. That's up to you. But you can't stay there alone. The two of you should have been out of there long ago. Don't get me wrong, Miss Baker. I know you've been a lot of help to my parents. But you go out to business every day, and anyway it's not like family."

"I know."

"So we'll see," said Mrs. Brody. "Maybe by Betty in the winter and by Phyllis in the summer."

"That's right, Ma. And Miss Baker, you'll have to look for a new room, obviously. Obviously, I'm gonna give Mrs. Peress notice. As soon as we can make arrangements."

"I'll try to get a place by the first."

"Good, good."

438

"You have to bury Pa strict orthodox. Everything orthodox."

"Okay, Ma. Whatever you say. A shroud, his tallis, his tefillin, everything."

"Everything. The shroud he bought already. I'll show you. He bought it himself, four, five years ago, just in case."

Mrs. Brody did not go to bed right away. She sat with tea in the kitchen, and Elspeth sat with her.

"Poor Brody."

Elspeth slept fitfully. Often she heard Mrs. Brody arise, and she would lie and listen.

In the morning she phoned Chris that she would be late.

While she waited the mailman came. She received her statement from the Pacific Northern, and tore it open. As she knew, this account paid no interest. It merely showed her initial deposit of a hundred dollars, then a deposit of a million, a debit of a million, and again a balance of a hundred. They had enclosed the canceled million-dollar item, the only check she had ever written on this account.

Phyllis arrived about nine-thirty, looking drawn, with dark hollows under her eyes. Elspeth prepared to go.

"Is that what you do every day?" Phyllis exclaimed when she saw Elspeth lift the bassinet out of the chained pram with Peter in it. "How do you get to work with that?"

"On the bus."

"That's crazy. Let me drive you."

"Stay with your mother. I always take it like this."

"She'll come for the ride. Come on, Ma."

They gave Elspeth and Peter a ride to Saltmarsh Service. Elspeth did her braids in the car.

During the morning she checked the listings in the newspaper. Two girls needed a third roommate, and her share of the rent would be no more than she paid now. She had always assumed girls rooming together would not want a baby around. But she telephoned anyway and had a chat at the wall phone with a girl who identified herself as Corky McGrath and sounded quite congenial. She was twenty-three and worked as a waitress on a rotating shift. She saw no harm in a baby if he really cried as little as Elspeth said. The bathroom was big enough for a changing table, and the room which Elspeth and Corky would share had a pair of beds made to stand either side by side as twins or set one upon the other as double-decker bunks, in which case there would be lots of room for a crib. The other girl had a little bedroom to herself. And Corky's brother, who slept there sometimes, used the daybed in the living room.

"Why don't you take my car and go over and have a look at it," Chris offered. "I'll watch the baby."

She did. It was on the ground floor of a brick building at Two Corinthian Place, on the edge of Chinatown. From Saltmarsh Service by subway it would be five or six minutes, and the direction was the reverse of rush-hour traffic. Corky was sandy-haired, very freckled, taller than average, shapely and cheerful. Her real name was

Clarissa. The rooms were large. Corky's brother Neal was not there. Neither was Joyce, the other girl. Together Corky and Elspeth lifted one bunk bed onto the other.

Elspeth agreed to move in on the first, and wrote a check for a month's rent. "Make it out to C. Joyce Jencks," said Corky. "It's really her place. Her name's on the lease."

"Can you make the decision to take a baby without asking her?"

"Sure. She trusts me. If it doesn't work out, you'll split. No sweat."

She got back to Saltmarsh Service in time for the prenoon feeding. Chris gave her the swivel and went out to the pumps.

At six-thirty when Elspeth arrived at Mrs. Brody's Phyllis was there, with her two younger children now, Marty had come back, and Betty had arrived. The eight-year-old and her little brother chased each other from one end of the apartment to the other. What's the matter with those kids, Elspeth asked herself. Don't they care that their grandfather has died? I was no more than eight the first time I lost a grandparent, but I knew I'd lost someone.

She changed Peter and sat in the wicker chair to feed him. There was a knock at her door.

"Come in," she said.

Betty looked in. She was thinner than Phyllis. Her hair was straight and cut short, black mixed with gray. "Oh. I'm sorry. I just wanted to ask if you'd join us for supper. When you're ready. No hurry."

"That's okay. You don't have to bother. I've got stuff. I'll eat later."

"No, we'd love to have you. We've got plenty."

"Well, okay. Thank you. I'll be in as soon as I finish with Petey."

"Can I come in and visit with you meanwhile?"

"Sure. Come in."

Betty sat on the bed. It drooped under her. She had round gray eyes and her face was long and sad. "I've heard what a beautiful baby you have."

"Thank you. When he finishes you'll get a look at him with his eyes open."

Phyllis's kids came through the open door. Phyllis called them from the kitchen. "Come out of there, children!"

"We want to watch her feed the baby," the girl said.

"I don't want you to watch. Come here this instant! You'll be sorry if I have to come in there."

They left reluctantly.

"We're all grateful for all you've done," Betty said to Elspeth. "The phone calls. And the help you've been to my parents all along."

"Gee, it wasn't anything."

"No, it was a lot. Cleaning the place up, and taking my father on walks."

"Oh, once in a while. I liked your father."

Betty's eyes watered. "My dad was a great guy," she said. "I wish my kids could have known him when he was younger. I was the closest to him, and yet I lived the furthest away. My husband's business took us south. We used to talk of having them live with us. And a few months ago we were really set up finally, in a position to do it. We begged them to come. But by then they were too old to make the change, I guess. I guess it was better for him to die in peace, in familiar surroundings. That's what he wanted. It's so sad, all the things we hoped to do. We do such a fraction of what we could, and should. Every life is such a parody of what it could have been."

Her tears brought tears to Elspeth.

"When he was younger," Betty said, "when he had his eyesight, he saw everything. When I was little he worked long hours and I wouldn't see him all week, but on the weekend he'd take me for a walk in the park, and he'd see everything. He'd see a bird a hundred yards away, pulling a worm from the ground, and he'd stop, and point it out to me, and we'd watch. And if I'd cry about something, he'd tell me, don't worry, don't cry, you won't have to live this day again. And he'd say, you have to enjoy the rain, the snow, the heat, the humidity, the cold. You have to enjoy your troubles, you'll have plenty. There was no one like him. Once he picketed the laundry. Our neighbor had a fight with them, they lost her pillowcases and they said they never had them. So my father picketed them with a sign. I don't know what it said. But they paid."

Elspeth closed her front. She turned Peter about, and he stared at Betty.

"Such eyes. God bless him. I hope you have lots of happiness from him."

"Thank you," said Elspeth.

She put him down in the crib. He kicked his feet, and watched the swaying cow-jumped-over-the-moon figures.

She went to the kitchen. She saw that Mrs. Brody had lighted her sabbath candles as usual. There was a supper of chicken and vegetables. The two children had eaten and were running in and out of the kitchen. Phyllis shouted at them. From under the stove the hunched cat stared, hostile and sullen.

"The cemetery is all paid," Mrs. Brody said. "We paid it ourself."

Marty and Phyllis talked about funeral plans. Phyllis had phoned people all day and Marty's wife Shelley had helped. Alan had been reached and would be back for the funeral, which would be Sunday. It had been agreed to have the rabbi from Phyllis and Alan's temple, and the shiva week would be at Phyllis and Alan's house. "Okay, if you want it at your house we'll have it at your house," Marty said, "or we'll switch, a couple of days at your house and a couple of days at my house if you want—I'll talk to Shelley. But we can't have it here. People are afraid to come to this neighborhood. Even in the daytime."

In the living room the kids had turned on the television.

Elspeth saw that tears remained in Betty's eyes. She had seen Marty break into sobs last night, and Phyllis must have cried too, in her home or on the way here. Nobody can cry constantly, not even Mama, even when a stone weighs on your heart. You face what has to be done.

You're born, you die, you're mourned and spoken of. How long? Petey will know me, and he'll hear of my brothers. And after Petey? Maybe some that will remember me as a grandma, or have heard some little story to know me by. And after them? Even the memory of you dies, when those who knew you die. Generations.

They find an album of faded snapshots in the attic, and no one can tell them who those people were. They know their parents. They don't know you. How can they? For the billions of years that follow, you're as unremembered as a spider sucked into the vacuum cleaner. For a short span there are survivors to visit a grave. Then soon they're as dead as you, and for the long haul you're no more than the calf that was slaughtered to make your sandwiches.

Bob had told her how at Gramps's funeral he felt as if he himself were transported ahead to age ninety-one, and looked into the pit. And then given a brief reprieve back to his present age, but all shook up, because next time there would be no reprieve.

Someday the whole photo album, you and those you loved and who loved you, will be taken down from the attic and offered for a dime and then a nickel or a penny at a yard sale, but there'll be no takers, so it will be hauled away with the trash and bulldozed under the landfill.

"How soon do you think you can find youself a place, Miss Baker?" Marty asked.

"I've found one."

"Already? Good."

"I'm moving on the first."

"The first? Any chance you could arrange it sooner? We'd like to lock the place up. My mother's leaving tonight. If not to my sister's then to my house. I don't want her here alone."

"With Elspeth here I wouldn't be alone," said Mrs. Brody.

"Ma, Miss Baker goes to work in the daytime. You've got a heart condition. You have to be with your children."

"So Ma comes to me," Phyllis said to him, "but what's the difference if Elspeth's still here? If she's here a few days during the shiva?"

"If she's here," said Marty. "But if she can leave sooner I'd rather lock the place up. She doesn't have a key, we'd have to make a duplicate, it's just simpler. The sooner we get stuff out the better. There are valuables here. We have to sort out what we want and what goes to the Hadassah, and shut off the phone and the electric. The gas should be off."

"What valuables?" said Betty.

"The clock on the mantel. There's gold in that."

"So what do you think Elspeth is gonna do?" said Phyllis. "Steal it? What's the matter with you, Marty?"

"No, no, no. I didn't imply anything like that. But the neighborhood's rotten. It can be broken into. She's not safe here herself. There are pieces here that are antiques. The glass cabinet, in the dining room. With curved glass. The oak table. You can't buy that today."

"When do you want me out?" said Elspeth.

"Well, I was thinking, tomorrow's shot anyway. They don't bury on Saturday. If it's convenient for you I could come over tomorrow and move your stuff for you."

"Marty, you're terrible," said Betty.

442

"Yes," said Phyllis, "it's like you want to throw her out. After what she's been to Ma and Pa."

"I didn't say she has to. I said if it's convenient."

He irritated Elspeth. But she was not inclined to fight him. Without the Brodys, it would be like a cemetery here at night. The empty living room, the tall chair in the corner with its yellowed doily—it would all reek of death. Every piece of furniture would seem like a tombstone. Even the gold clock in its glass dome, and the marble slab on which it sat. Its quarter-hour chimes would be futile sounds in the land of emptiness. And the crib and changing table could be transported more easily in Marty's car than Chris's. Better to impose on Marty's time, and make him help her carry.

"I work tomorrow," she said. "But what if I could move tonight?"

"Tonight?" said Marty. "Now?"

"If I can. Why not? Let's get it over with. Everything will fit in your car."

"Where is the place?"

"Downtown. Corinthian Place. Near Chinatown."

"Okay. If that's what you want."

"And what about the cat?"

"Do you want it?" he asked her.

"No. But I want to be sure he isn't just tossed out without a home."

"I'll take the cat," said Phyllis tiredly. "I'll take Ma, and I'll take the cat."

"I'll see if I can reach my roommates," Elspeth said.

She went to the telephone table in the center hallway.

"Corky? Hi. This is Elspeth Baker. What if I moved in *before* the first. Like right now, for instance. Is that possible?"

"Sure," the voice said. "Come on."

"Does your roommate know about me yet? Does she know about the baby?"

"No, she hasn't been home. She won't be home till late. It'll be okay though."

"You sure it's okay?"

"We'll give her a surprise. Come on. I told you it's okay. What time shall I expect you?"

"Say in about an hour and a half? Two hours at the most. Somebody's helping me with the crib and stuff."

"Fine. Just ring the bell."

Elspeth went back to Marty.

"Okay. We're all set. Let's go to work on the crib and stuff and I'll pack my valise."

"Now?"

"Now."

Marty pushed back his chair. "Phyl, call Shelley for me and tell her I'll be late."

"I'll call her," said Betty. "I want to say hello."

"Actually," said Elspeth, "I have to take some manuscripts up to Mrs. Peress first. So you have time to call."

443

57

THE living room had a large rya rug in flaming colors, circular and shaggy, that Corky said she and Joyce had made, working on it together. There was a daybed with a soiled green cover along one of the longer walls, next to the door to the entrance hall. One of the short walls had a broken-down overstuffed armchair and hangings that looked Indonesian, and the short wall opposite had a pair of windows with a dinette table nearby and its matching chairs. The other long wall had one door and one doorless arch. The arch was to the kitchen, which had a window but was too small to eat in, and the door opened upon the larger bedroom. Joyce's little bedroom was beyond the larger one, and the bathroom, which had one window and two doors, was beyond the kitchen. Joyce's bedroom could be approached either through the larger bedroom, or through the kitchen area and the bathroom. None of the paint was fresh any longer or of uniform shade, but the big bedroom was tan, the little one blue, the bathroom white, the kitchen a deeper tan, and the living room a dark green. Someone liked arm lamps that hung out from the walls, because the kitchen had one and the living room had two. All the windows faced only on brick and other windows, the width of a paved footpath away.

Corky helped Elspeth assemble the crib. Elspeth set the spring and mattress a notch lower than before. Then she took Peter from his seat and laid him in the crib without waking him. She fastened the mobile once more to the crib rail.

Corky sat on the upper bunk, legs dangling in jeans, and watched Elspeth hang clothes in the closet. "You better have the lower," Corky said, "in case you have to get up for the baby in the night."

"Okay."

"Your baby looks like you a lot."

Elspeth laid out her things and Peter's in the drawers that Corky had assigned to her.

In the kitchen she handed up her few groceries to Corky on the stepladder. In the spacious bathroom they set up the changing table. At last they relaxed together at the dining table. Elspeth offered her herb tea but Corky was already knowledgeable about herb teas and brought out other flavors of her own.

They chatted. Corky said the Chinese were good people. Smart. Industrious. She worked with them at the restaurant. Elspeth talked about Mr. Brody and his death. Then she talked about Alf.

They boiled the kettle anew and refilled their teacups.

"I'll send him a postcard with my new address and phone," Elspeth continued, "so he'll know where to call me if he wants, and so his list of clients will be in order. And then, if he doesn't call, I don't think I should chase him. After all, I don't really know him. I know he likes children, but that doesn't mean he's ready to take on any. And maybe after that crying jag he thinks I'm a depressive. Or maybe he thinks the crying was on purpose, and that I'd throw crying fits to make him do what I want. If he thinks that, it's just too bad. I mean, I called *him* last time, and now he's got to show some interest before I'll chase him. I know there's such a thing as persistence, and keeping after a guy, and then being his long-term mistress, and trying not to get mad at him too often, and maybe he'll get used to you in a few years and eventually marry you, but I don't know, it seems sort of sleazy. I'm not ready for that yet. I'm used to being pursued. Maybe I'm not realistic, but I'm not ready to go begging for crumbs."

"Maybe he'll surprise you and call," Corky said.

"Maybe. But my instinct tells me he won't."

"Do you want to get married?"

"Sure. I want to get married, and I want to have more kids. I don't want Petey to be an only child."

"Well, I don't know about lawyers," said Corky, "but stay away from actors."

"Don't tell me about actors," said Elspeth.

"Oh. You know then. They're all ego. They don't know anyone else exists."

"Were you in love with an actor?" Elspeth asked.

"Well, I've known a few."

"Actors and writers," Elspeth said. "Boy, do they adore themselves. I guess they have to. Otherwise they wouldn't have the nerve to pour out their fantasies into books, or get up on a public stage, and let the whole world see what idiots they are. If they weren't so head over heels in love with themselves they wouldn't dare chance it."

"I was trying to break into theater for a while," said Corky. "And I was into drama workshops and stuff. But it's impossible. I took tickets at the Charles Street Playhouse, and understudied a few parts, but I never got on stage. And when the Pilgrim Burlesque reopened I even applied there. I thought I could get to be in skits or something. But when I saw what they wanted me to do I walked out. It wasn't even like porn. It was more like gynecology."

"Petey's daddy was an actor."

"Oh. Were you into theater?"

"No. Just young and trusting, I guess. He wasn't just all ego—he was also always playing a role. Always. And very convincing. He came over to me at a mixer, walked straight across the room with his eyes on me, and the first thing he said was, 'I wish every woman in the world looked like you.' And he could put so much into his eyes and his voice, that your heart bled for all the women that weren't me. I knew it was a line, and I knew he'd met me five years before and didn't even remember, and still my heart swooned. Stupid. My father always sweet-talked me when I was little, so I guess I was sort of addicted to it. Only my father meant it. He loved me more than anything."

"Is your father still living?"

"Sure. Why?"

"I don't know. It sounded kind of past tense."

"Well, he detests me now. Though he's only mad at me because he loves me, actually. He thinks I'm ruining my life."

Corky sipped her tea. "I don't have a father problem," she said. "Mine flew the coop when I was ten. I don't even remember too well what he looked like. But you know, Ellie, if you're that eager to get married, and make a home for the baby and all that, you could get some middle-aged millionaire to leave his wife for you anytime. You're real cute, you know. You could go out and get one tomorrow. Look through Dun and Bradstreet, and pick one out, and saunter through his office, baby and all, and drop your eyelashes."

"Except it's not what I want."

"Well, I know. You're like me. You want to love somebody. But don't worry, Ellie. It'll happen. You'll live with different guys, and eventually you'll marry one of them. Maybe even the first. Maybe you'll get lucky. I don't see that the baby makes all that much difference. Unless it puts pressure on you. In your own thinking. I think most guys are gonna like your baby. I mean, what do they care? They love you for yourself. They don't have to change the diapers. Unless they want to be helpful, but they know they don't have to. They just figure the baby's your thing. Like, what do they care, whether you've got a baby, or whether you're into needlepoint, or flower arrangement, or whatever."

"You're probably right," said Elspeth. "I hope so." She yawned, covering her mouth.

Corky yawned too.

"Well, that's life," said Corky. "We goof, we get punished, but we get a consolation prize. We're losers, but we get a consolation prize. That's my philosophy."

There was the sound of a key in the lock.

"Here's Joyce," said Corky.

Joyce was immaculate in her dress and grooming. Under her coat she wore a suit.

"Hi," said Corky. "Meet our new roommate. Ellie Baker. She works in a gas station."

"Hi," said Joyce. She was small and dark-haired, with a face somewhat pinched but pretty.

"Have some herbal brew with us," said Corky.

"What flavor? Wait till I go to the john."

"Camomile."

Joyce threw her coat to the daybed. She disappeared into the bathroom. Corky set a third place at the table. She got the kettle from the stove and poured.

The sound of flushing came loudly. Even the kitchen drain gurgled in response. Joyce reappeared.

"Hey, what's the thing in the john?"

446

"It's a changing table. I forgot to tell you, Ellie has a baby. His crib's in my room."

"Oh, no!" Joyce collapsed into one of the chairs. "Jesus, Corky! This time I draw the line! It's the last straw."

"Take it easy. It's a nice baby. He hasn't cried or anything. He's been asleep the whole time since she brought him."

"And some dark night I come in here and step right in a blob of shit."

"Joyce, he doesn't go on the floor. He's a baby, not a dog. He wears diapers. Look, Joyce, honey, what's she gonna do? Her landlord died and she had to get out. Where's she gonna go? I don't believe in this 'no children allowed' crap. It's discriminatory. Give it a try. She's a nice kid."

"Forget it," said Elspeth. "I'll find another place. Just let me stay tonight, okay? I'll find a place in the morning."

"No, you're staying. Joyce is okay. Her bark's worse than her bite."

"Well, I'll give it a try," said Joyce. "What time does the kid wake up mornings?"

"About six, and I take him into my bed and feed him. He doesn't cry."

"We never sleep late anyway," Corky said.

Joyce lifted her tea and blew on its surface.

"I like the place spotless clean," said Joyce. "I know you wouldn't know it to look at it right now. But I can't stand filth. And I can't stand slobs. We dust and tidy up every weekend. All of us."

"Corky told me."

Joyce ventured a sip, and blew on it again. "So that carriage I saw in the entry was yours."

"Yes."

"I thought it must be the Yangs'. I'm sorry, the way I reacted. I didn't mean to make you feel unwelcome."

"Well, it's your place. You have a right to refuse people."

"Okay, but we'll see how it goes. Meanwhile I'm sorry if I overreacted. It's just that Corky has such a soft heart for strays. Especially for her brother. He's the world's worst. I've been ready a hundred times to heave him out. Or put poison in his coffee. Or buy a gun and shoot him. And Corky always stops me. But it would be justifiable homicide. I've really had it."

"Neal's a little hard to take sometimes," Corky agreed.

"I brought my parents here once," Joyce said, "to show them the place. And we come in, about two in the afternoon, and there's Neal snoring right there on the daybed, stark naked. I mean, Jesus. My parents come to visit, and the first thing they see is a male cock. I just about died."

"It was hot. And he didn't know you were bringing your folks."

"Even so. And the girls he brings in here. The most disgusting females in the world, that's for Neal. There was this fat one, he used to give it to her in the ass, because it helped her with a constipation problem she had. Big-hearted Neal. You should have seen her. I don't think she'd had a bath since puberty. And she'd wear these cut-offs, torn off way too high, so they didn't cover her big fat ass. You had to see it to believe it."

"Does he work?" Elspeth asked.

"Mostly he's unemployed. Sponges off his sister."

"He does carpentry," said Corky. Works for different builders. But it's seasonal."

"He'll show up in the afternoon when nobody's here, and crawl into somebody else's bed to take a nap. The daybed's not good enough for him. I came home one night and got into my brand-new clean linens, that I put on fresh that morning, clean sheets I hadn't even slept in yet, and my heel goes right into a blob of sperm. I mean, after all. If a guy wants to pull his wagon let him pull his wagon, but not in somebody else's clean linens."

"How do you know it was sperm? Nobody even saw Neal here that day."

"It was sperm! I know that smell. And he admitted it. When I yelled at him he says 'oh, don't be afraid. You can't get pregnant from it. They don't live that long outside the body.' I mean, Jesus. Someday I'll kill him. What a turd."

Elspeth laughed.

"You think it's funny. Wait'll you meet him. You'll move out." Joyce sipped again. She shook her head. "They never should have let him out. They didn't even want him for Vietnam."

"He's no crazier than the people who wanted to send him there," Corky said.

"Let him out of where?" Elspeth asked.

"He was in a mental hospital for a couple of years," said Joyce.

"It was only six months," said Corky. "Don't exaggerate."

"Him and his terrible childhood," said Joyce. "You had the same childhood he did and you're not crazy. You even had this congential thing with rights and lefts, and you don't do the nutty things he does."

"Well, it's harder for a boy," Corky said.

"Did you ever meet anybody who's absolutely good for nothing?" Joyce asked Elspeth. "Just useless? He promised he'd grow us some marijuana in the kitchen window box. So naturally it just wilted and died. Wouldn't you know?"

"Well, it wasn't his fault," said Corky. "It didn't have enough room. And the sun never reaches there."

"He didn't even water it," said Joyce. "Everything he touches turns to shit."

They all drank tea a while, saying nothing.

"Well, I've got to be up early," said Joyce. "I'm turning in."

In the unfamiliar bed Elspeth slept intermittently. Corky had loaned her sheets and a pillow and a blanket. She would wake in the night to hear Corky talking in her sleep in the bunk above, not loudly and not intelligibly.

When Peter stirred in the morning she fed him, lying on the blanket, her knees raised. She stared sleepily up at the bulge of Corky sleeping overhead, silently now.

Still half shut-eyed she carried Peter to the bathroom, by way of the living room and kitchen. She thought she saw Joyce crosslegged and motionless in bra and underpants on the rya rug, hands folded on the top of her head, eyes closed, face trancelike, abdomen sucked far in, as though practicing yoga.

But when she returned from the bathroom Joyce had apparently already left. The door that connected the bedrooms was ajar. Corky still slept.

The subway was rapid. Peter widened his eyes at the unfamiliar sound, till the whites showed above the pupils. There were few passengers and she lay the bassinet beside her on the long seat.

She attended to the first customer with her braids half done. Then Chris allowed her time to complete her braids, and to telephone and bring Harriet up to date. Elspeth dialed from the pay phone on the wall and Harriet rang her back.

"The funeral's at a bad time," Elspeth said. "I'd end up breastfeeding right in Levine's Chapel, or have Petey crying in the middle of the eulogy."

"I wouldn't even think of going," said Harriet. "After the way they were in such a rush to get you moved out."

"But that wasn't his fault. I liked the old man. And I don't see how I can pay a shiva call either. They're gonna sit at Phyllis's, and she lives in Wellesley or Weston or someplace, and I've got no way to get there."

"So make a contribution in his name if you want to. I'll send something to Hadassah for you."

"No, make it some outfit for the blind. Or even some Jewish outfit for the blind, if there is such a thing. Ten dollars. I'll pay you back."

By evening Elspeth was quite sleepy, as though the hours at the hospital with the Brodys two nights before were catching up with her. She shared an omelette aux fines herbes with Corky and Joyce. They had a system of keeping their groceries in separate bags, marked with their names, whether on the shelf or in the refrigerator. Apparently it was to make certain that Corky's brother would limit himself to Corky's food if he came to scrounge. Yet the roommates regularly invited each other to meals at their own table, sometimes sharing Joyce's food if the brother wasn't there, and sometimes Corky's.

After supper Elspeth helped with the cleaning. They scrubbed windowsills, though it seemed to do little good. Old black streaks were embedded in the paint.

In the morning Peter had wakened before her but had remained quiet. He was raised upon his arms, staring through the bars at her in the dawning light.

She took him into her bed. She thought of Mr. Brody. There must be an old man sitting near him, who had remained through the night quietly reading psalms. Mrs. Brody had insisted on hiring someone. A few more hours, and he would lie under the earth, ready to begin rotting away.

From the living room came a low rumbling snore. She heard someone thump down Sunday newspapers in the entry. The snore continued. But it became intermittent, and at last it stopped.

Peter needed changing. She rose and dressed quickly in shirt and jeans.

On the green corduroy covering of the living-room daybed a young man lay fully dressed, with eyes closed, not snoring now. It had to be Neal McGrath. His long hair and his full beard were uncombed and shaggy. He wore a heavy dark blue sweater over a green sweater that showed through the holes, jeans with the color rubbed from stiff wrinkles, and even reinforced workshoes, laced over his ankles.

Elspeth locked herself in the bathroom and fastened Peter onto the changing table. "Okay, Mister McKaka. Let's clean you up."

449

When she emerged she found Corky in a nightgown puttering in the kitchen.

"Oh, hi," said Elspeth. "I hope I didn't wake you."

"No. I never sleep late. Would you like pancakes?"

"Why, sure. Thanks."

She found Peter's seat in the living room. She strapped him into it, on the radiator cover, and gave him his white dumbbell. He opened his mouth tall and tried to put the dumbbell in, but he was off target. Elspeth began setting the table.

"Set it for four," Corky said.

Elspeth cut the grapefruits.

Neal sat up on the edge of the daybed. He yawned. He rubbed his eyes. He stared at Elspeth.

"This is my brother," Corky said. "Neal, this is Ellie Baker."

"Hi, Neal," said Elspeth.

"Hi." He picked his nose. The beard spread in wide tangles. He wiped the finger in it. He kept staring at Elspeth. He picked the other nostril. She completed the place settings. Neal did not take his eyes from her.

Elspeth sat at the table, facing across it toward the kitchen, and rested her chin on her clasped hands. When she glanced sideways Neal was still staring.

"Forgive me for staring," he said. "It's just that you're extraordinarily beautiful."

"Oh. Thank you."

He took a seat at the table, facing the windows, and dug into his grapefruit.

Peter exercised his legs. He dropped his rattle.

Joyce came from the bedrooms in white underpants and bra and sat crosslegged and Buddha-like in the hairy reds and oranges and yellows of the rug, soles up, looking at no one. She entwined her fingers together on top of her head. She half closed her eyes, which seemed to turn inward.

Neal's back was to Joyce. He looked again at Elspeth. "You interested in a piece of ass?"

"Thanks, but no."

"God, Neal," Corky said.

He turned his attention back to his grapefruit, squeezing the juice from it.

Elspeth could not help but watch Joyce. "Can she hear us when she's in that trance?" she asked.

Neal half turned and looked at Joyce also. "She hears," he said, "but she won't answer you. Watch. Her stomach will get smaller and smaller. I don't know how she does it. Her guts just disappear."

From where Elspeth sat Joyce was at a three-quarter angle. Her entire abdomen seemed to roll in on itself, as though it were hollow. From time to time it shrank and hardened further, like convoluted muscle. Each time it did the waistband of her panties fell another inch.

"See?" said Neal. "Isn't that fantastic? She could get a job in a circus. I don't know where her entrails go."

Joyce's abdomen in fact had sunk in so far that the skin made a sharp tight angle over the bottom ribs. It seemed to recede, navel and all, till it must press against

450

her spine, as though her innards had vanished. Her face was red. The pulse throbbed visibly in her neck.

"Have you ever seen anything like that?" Neal asked.

"Never," said Elspeth. "Wow. How does she *do* that?"

Then Joyce's stomach returned to normal, in a few hesitant stages, as though her viscera rolled into place. She took her hands from her head, hiked up the waistband of her underpants and uncrossed her legs, raising her knees. She remained there resting, eyes half closed, catching her breath.

Then she rose and headed toward the kitchen and bathroom. But as she passed the dining table Neal hooked a finger into the waistband and yanked quickly downward. Joyce reacted with a sudden crouch. She caught the panties near her knees and pulled them up. "You son of a bitch." She continued through the kitchen past Corky and slammed the bathroom door.

"Neal, you just better watch it," Corky said. She brought the pan from the kitchen and placed some pancakes on Elspeth's plate and some on Neal's. She returned the pan to the stove and spooned more batter into it.

"Does she do that exercise every day?" Elspeth asked.

"Usually," said Corky.

Elspeth and Neal poured syrup. They ate. Elspeth complimented the pancakes.

"Would the baby eat a teensy piece?" Corky asked. "A crumb?"

"Better not try it. I'm afraid he'd choke. He hasn't had solid foods yet."

Corky brought the next batch of pancakes just as Joyce came from the bedrooms, fully dressed now in a suit and hose. She threw a blue coat onto the daybed with a matching hat of dyed straw, and took her place at the table, opposite Neal, her back to the windows. She started her grapefruit without looking at him.

"Good morning, Cicely Joyce Jencks," Neal said. "And how is Mr. Harrington Fawcett Flatley?"

"He's fine."

Corky put pancakes on Joyce's plate and on her own. She sat. Peter dropped the rattle a second time and again Elspeth returned it to him.

"Tell me, Cicely Joyce Jencks," said Neal. "Is his middle name really Fawcett? Or do they just call him that because he's a drip?"

"It's his grandmother's maiden name. It happens to be a very distinguished name."

"Ah," said Neal. "You see, Ellie? He comes from a long line of drips."

"For your information," Joyce told him sharply, "the first Fawcett came over with Sir Richard Saltonstall on the Arbella."

"Now, Cicely Joyce, please. That is a whopper. You know he wasn't on the Arbella. Ellie, don't believe a word she says. Actually he was trash from Liverpool that a Mormon missionary picked up in the eighteen-fifties."

"Ellie, he's lying. He made that up just now. He doesn't know a thing about it."

"Look, I don't care," Elspeth told them. "I'm not exactly the Queen's cousin myself, you know. My grandfather came over from Russia in a bottle of borscht."

"In a bottle of borscht?" said Neal. "Not even in a can of caviar?"

"No, in a bottle of borscht. With a bagel around his waist for a life preserver."

"Interesting," said Neal. "Well, fortunately you've risen at last into more distinguished circles. Cicely Joyce is a very important person. She has a big job. She's Administrative Assistant to the Assistant Administrator."

Joyce was drinking her coffee.

"You see how she's all duded up?" Neal continued. "Can't you tell she's distinguished? In a few minutes she'll put on gloves, and go out to the front stoop to wait for Mr. Harrington Fawcett Flatley. And man, talk about distinguished, that cat walks like he's got a ramrod up his ass. Like a sentry at Buckingham Palace."

"Harrington has perfect posture," said Joyce.

"If you saw them together," Neal said to Elspeth, "they look so respectable you'd swear they were going to the Young Republican Club. But they're not, though. Actually they're going to church. I'm not kidding. They actually go to church. They're high Episcopalians. High-stepping high-ass Episcopalians."

"Neal, shut up," said Corky. "Lay off. Joyce doesn't have to put up with you. She doesn't have to let you flop here."

"You're right, Corky. I'm sorry. She's all heart. You're right up there with the saints, Cicely Joyce Jencks."

"Your apology is accepted, creep." She had risen. She took the coat from the daybed and put it on.

"Too bad her tits aren't as big as her heart," he added.

"One of these days you're gonna get a foot where it hurts," Joyce said. "Why don't you shave? I'm afraid come hunting season some hunter won't realize you're human. You look like a yak."

"I told you, I can't shave."

Peter had flung down the rattle and was making noises.

"Corky talked me into getting a shave once, for a job interview," he said to Elspeth, "and you know what happened? The razor cut the whiskers all right, and it also shaved the tops right off every pimple and blackhead. It leveled everything. My face was a bloody mess."

Joyce opened the door to the entry. She picked up the Sunday newspaper, wrapped in its comics, and put it on the daybed. She put the curly-brimmed hat on the back of her head. She took white net gloves from her coat and drew them on. "Ellie, if you need any groceries, just give Neal your list and he'll go to the supermarket and shoplift the whole list for you."

"Cut it out, will ya? I didn't shoplift."

"I sent him marketing with a twenty-dollar bill and a shopping list, and he brought me back the groceries and the money, intact."

"Which proves I didn't shoplift, right?" he retorted, turning in his chair. "Because if I were dishonest I wouldn't have brought you back your money. I could have got change somewhere."

Joyce turned and left, shutting the door hard.

"That bitch! Anything to malign me!"

452

"Cool it, Neal," said Corky. "You started it."

"But she doesn't have to tell Ellie I'm a shoplifter."

"I don't care," said Elspeth. She picked up Peter and felt him. He smiled at her. "Dry. He just wants some loving."

"But I want to explain," Neal insisted.

Corky wiped her mouth with a napkin. "Leave everything," Elspeth said. "I'll clear and I'll wash. Okay? Leave everything right where it is. Please."

"Okay. I'm gonna do some laundry then. If nobody needs the john for a while."

Elspeth rose, cuddling Peter, as Corky left. She took Peter across the living room and sank into the overstuffed chair. It sat low because its stubby legs were broken. Neal stayed at the table but turned to face her.

"Listen. She gave me a list and twenty dollars, okay? So I went into the store, and there was nobody there except these two young clowns that work there, and they're just taking it easy shooting the breeze together over behind the meat counter. So I took a cart and went around and got all Joyce's stuff. Then I come to the register and there's nobody there. So I yell over to the two guys at the meat counter. Hey. How about checking me out. And they said, we ain't open yet. And I said, when are you open? And they said, eight-thirty. And I said, shit, man, you gonna make me stand here like a jerk for fifteen minutes? How come the door's unlocked if you ain't open? And they don't say anything. And I said come on, guys. I'm just standing here. Take the money, will ya? You're not doing anything. And I waved the money. And they don't move. Just sat there. So I said, hey you guys. You don't give a shit, I don't give a shit either. And I start pushing the cart toward the door, with all the stuff in it, slow like. And they just watched me. They couldn't care less. They didn't own the place. And I brought Joyce the cart full of stuff and gave her back her money. You understand?"

"Okay." She danced Peter from side to side upon her jeans. Neal watched her.

In the bathroom Corky had turned on the hot water. The pipes banged and shuddered.

"Deetle deetle deetle doat," Elspeth sang, dancing Peter.

He chortled. She laughed with him.

She danced him again. "Hoodle deedle dum bum—"

"You have a very pleasant voice," said Neal.

"No I don't. I'm just singing nonsense syllables."

"I know. But there's a tone about it that's, I don't know, sweet to the ear."

She shrugged. "Well, thanks, Neal. Who's older, you or Corky?"

"She's my twin sister."

"Oh. I've always thought it must be nice to have a twin."

He took a cigarette from his pocket. It was somewhat bent. "Would you like to share a joint?"

"No thanks."

"You sure?"

"Pot always gives me a headache."

"Oh. Will I bother you if I smoke? Or will it bother the baby?"

453

"I don't think so."

But he returned it to his pocket. "Well, I'll save it."

"I gave up tobacco when I was pregnant," Elspeth said. "And I bet in another twenty years the Surgeon General's Office is gonna come up with the discovery that pot is just as bad as tobacco. Smoke is smoke."

58

EDGAR CLISH, riding high in the dark red tow truck, dragged in an old black foreign four-seater that had become disabled somewhere in the midst of the city. From the swivel chair Elspeth saw its owner climb down with Edgar and Edgar's grandfather from the tow truck. Edgar disengaged the car. "If you want to wait around I'll take a look at it as soon as I have my sandwich," Edgar said to him.

"What do you think it is?" she heard the owner ask.

"Could be a lot of things," said Edgar.

Elspeth tickled Peter's face with the end of a braid. Had he not been nursing he would have smiled, squinted, turned his face. But when he sucked he noticed nothing. He did not open his eyes and his mouth worked without pause.

The owner of the black four-seater stepped up aimlessly through the open door from the repair bay into the office. He seemed an undernourished academic type, with owlish glasses, not quite young nor quite middle-aged, and sad-faced as people always were when their cars had broken down. He stopped short when he saw Elspeth breastfeeding. "Oh. Sorry."

"No problem," she assured him.

But he went quickly out onto the apron. She would have like to ask him about his car, which she had taken for a Morris Minor, or perhaps a Hillman. She hadn't thought there were any still on the roads. Through the window she could see him out there in the sun, looking at it forlornly by the fence. The elbows of his jacket were reinforced with patches of suede. In the repair bay Edgar and Puff and Mr. Tingley ate an unhurried lunch, their radio screaming.

Elspeth laid Peter in his bassinet to sleep, took the diaper sealed in plastic out

454

to the trash barrel, and walked toward the pumps to relieve Chris. Chris waved an acknowledgment without waiting for her, shut herself in her dusty green car, paused briefly for traffic, and was gone.

Elspeth set a car to drinking gas on one side of the pumps, and filled out a charge slip for another customer on the other side.

"How long do they take for lunch?" the undernourished academic asked her. "Not a whole hour, I hope."

"Well, maybe like half an hour or so," she said. "I know it seems long when you're waiting."

He wandered away again.

When the pumps became quiet she returned to the office, sat in the swivel and unwrapped her apple and hunk of Swiss cheese. The potted plant that sat by the pictures of Kathleen and Kevin above the pigeonholes of the rolltop desk was not doing well. She reminded herself to water it. Chris usually did, but with Vinnie on her mind she sometimes forgot.

"Do you think it could be moisture in the gas line?" she heard the academic ask against the blaring of the radio.

"Could be," Edgar answered him, his mouth full.

"Sell me a can of dry gas. I'd like to try that."

In a few moments she saw him empty it into the tank.

He got in. The engine started. She saw him brighten. He raced the motor. He let it idle. He got out, leaving it running, and returned to the repair bay.

"It's running," he told Edgar. "I guess I owe you for the tow."

"You sure do. Ten bucks for the tow and a dollar and tax for the dry gas."

When he had settled he got into the car. Elspeth watched him wait for the traffic. Then the car crossed Saltmarsh Avenue Extension and turned left. It stopped, mysteriously.

She could see him trying to restart it. But as far as she could tell there was no sound—the starter didn't even turn over. Cars honked, and veered around him.

Then he got out, leaned on it with one hand to the steering, and managed to push it to the curb.

When he could he walked across the street to the repair bay.

"It conked out again. Dead. Same as before."

She saw Edgar stir his coffee without rising or looking up. "Well," he said, "want me to tow it back here? That'll be another tow charge."

"Could we just push it in? It's only across the street."

"I don't push cars. What do you think I have a tow truck for?"

"Could you look at it over there?"

"Are you kidding? That's a public way. I work on premises. You want it towed again or you want to forget it? Make up your mind. And let me know when I finish my lunch. Do you like people interrupting your dinner?"

"Maybe I can push it back here myself."

"No you can't, sonny," Edgar said, though the man must have been ten to fifteen years his senior. "Not in this traffic. You'll be obstructing a public way.

455

And at that little slope at the curb it'll roll right back on you. And some truck will come along and knock you on your ass."

"Well, how much to tow it?"

"Ten bucks. Same as before."

"Just across the street?"

"Ten bucks. Same as before. You were here. What'd you drive away for?"

"Because it seemed okay."

"Sure it's okay. Until it conks out again."

"Why is it doing that? It was running beautifully, then all of a sudden nothing. Then it started again just now like nothing happened. Then it's dead again. Do you have any idea?"

"Sure, I have an idea. It's temperamental. It's old. It's senile. You want my advice, sonny? Take that bucket of bolts to a junkyard. It's had it. The car isn't even worth the price of the tow. Do you read me? It's junk. It's not even worth what they'll charge you to drag it to the junkyard. Buy yourself a car."

"I gave my wife the good car."

"Thumb a ride then. Walk away from it. Abandon it. Take the plates to the Registry. You know what I'll do for you, just because you're breaking my heart with that sad expression? I'll take it for junk, and I won't even charge you to pull it off the street. Just because it's right here, and I'm sorry for you, and I don't want to see them arrest you for littering. But I lose money on the deal, because it's worth nothing to me. Not even as spare parts. There's no call for those anymore."

The man frowned. He sighed. From her chair Elspeth saw him through the opening to the repair bay.

He walked slowly away. He waited for traffic, and crossed the street again.

Elspeth came out and watched. He got into his car. She saw his cautious surprise when the engine started. It purred healthily. He looked across at them and shrugged.

Slowly he began to edge outward, watching the traffic. This time he had scarcely moved three feet when it went dead.

Elspeth walked over to him. He was desperately turning the key in the switch but nothing responded. "It's crazy," he told her. "I don't get it. It goes, it stops. It goes, it stops. It never acted like this before. Do you think it could be a loose wire somewhere?"

She had put her head in. "Try it again."

He turned the key. It clicked futilely.

"For one thing," she told him, "Your water temperature is way up. Look at your dash."

"You're right. So it is. I didn't see that."

"Have you looked under the hood? Release your hood."

She went to the front and raised the hood. Slowly and carefully she unscrewed the radiator cap.

"Bone dry," she said.

"It needs water?"

"Water, or antifreeze. You were overheating. Metal expands, you know. And when the pistons expanded so much they couldn't even move in the cylinders, well, nothing moved. And when you let it sit, it cooled a little and the piston heads contracted until they had clearance, and you could start. But in a few minutes everything would heat up again and expand. We can try it with just water and see where the leak is."

He waited there while she returned to the gas station. A couple of cars came to the pumps before she could return to him. But when she was free she brought a jerry can of water and poured it into his radiator.

"Now try it," she said. The hood was still up.

The engine started. A fountain shot up from somewhere in its midst drenching the underside of the hood and filling the air around it with rain.

Elspeth backed away from the shower. "Okay, shut it off. That's it. A leak in the hose."

He turned off the engine. The rainstorm ended. Everything was wet.

"What's the problem?" Edgar asked her when she came into the repair bay. "Sixty cents' worth of hose?"

"Yes."

"That's about your speed," said Edgar. "I don't have time for this penny-ante stuff. Why don't you tell him it's the fuel pump? Make it worth your while. Sell him a twenty-dollar fuel pump. Keep the car overnight, call it four hours of labor. Make yourself a piece of change."

"And where would I ever find a Morris fuel pump?"

"So what. He wouldn't know if you put one in or not. Where's your imagination?"

She crossed the street once more, with a length of one-inch hose and a knife and screwdrivers, and made the replacement.

"You should be okay now," she said. "It's a real cute little car."

"Miss, I'm much obliged to you."

"You don't have any antifreeze," she told him, "so get some at a discount place. Not at a gas station. And until you do, watch the weather forecasts very carefully for the next couple of weeks. Say till the first of May. We could still get a bad freeze, even in April."

Edgar and Puff were shouting to her. She hurried across the wide avenue to the customers waiting at the pumps.

Elspeth rarely got repair jobs of any size to do. Edgar and Puff maneuvered to keep the big jobs to themselves as the hours spent as mechanics were paid at a higher rate. However she did not contend with them. Chris had confided to her that she was thinking of dropping Puff anyway, and was going to tell the grandfather to stay out as the insurance didn't cover him. Meanwhile the brothers let Elspeth do a lot of the spring inspections, especially if they were busy, and that sometimes involved replacing a bulb, or adjusting a headlight, or fixing a horn. She also removed snow tires and did oil and grease jobs, and flushed radiators. Once it even led to welding a radiator that rattled. She turned Peter's seat so that his back was to the sparks, and raised her mask frequently to glance around at him.

She was mounting a wheel when Chris returned from giving Vinnie his lunch.

457

"Be sure you get those tight," Chris said. "We don't want to kill somebody."

"They're tight," said Elspeth. "When the wrench won't turn any further I jump on it."

"That's the hard way," said Chris. "Use the pneumatic. Here." She handed Elspeth her ring of keys with a flat rust-spotted one extended. "In Vinnie's workbench. Down the bottom."

Elspeth found the tool amid the clutter. She fastened it to the air hose. It turned the bolt with a noisy battering.

"Hey!" said Edgar. "How come she gets to use Vinnie's stuff and we have to use our own stuff?"

"You've got one of those," Chris told him.

"I've got an electric, not a pneumatic. And Puff hasn't got *any*. I thought all Vinnie's stuff was supposed to be so sacrosanct. Nobody could touch it. Y'afraid I might swipe an item here and there? *She's* no saint, you know."

"Mind your business," said Chris. "You don't own the place."

"I've got seniority though. If you let anybody into Vinnie's bench it ought to be me first. I been here three years before that dumb broad walked in. Has she got seniority now or sumpin?"

"Yeah? Well, ladies first! Don't they teach you no etiquette where you come from? Or ain't you heard about women's lib yet?"

Elspeth kept her eyes on her work. The machine-gun racket of the last bolt kept her from hearing whether Edgar said anything more.

In the evening Elspeth told Corky and Joyce about the little old car with the bad hose. She told them automobiles were like a Rube Goldberg invention, with about a hundred different crazy parts—four different pumps for instance, and electrical gadgets, and cooling and warming gadgets, and mixing gadgets, and timing gadgets, all setting each other off in different ways—and if something or other wasn't always out of whack it was a miracle.

She liked Corky and Joyce. They had added E.A.BAKER in the rectangle on the mailbox, under C.J.JENCKS and C.L.McGRATH. She had replaced the washer in the hot faucet, which stopped its howl and its shuddering, and they were much impressed.

Corky demonstrated her mirror-writing for Elspeth. She had to put her watch on the wrist nearest the wall each morning, otherwise she could not tell right from left. It was a congenital business with a Latin name. She wrote from left to right or right to left with equal ease, and in the same hand. Once she had written a whole college paper the wrong way by mistake, and the professor had had to read each page in his bathroom mirror. But he gave her an A.

Elspeth did not learn about yoga from Joyce as she had thought she might. You could not talk philosophy to Joyce. Joyce was into the feel of things, apparently, and ideologies did not touch her. Each morning she turned to stone, her stomach shrinking and and her panties dropping till the matted tangle showed, but it seemed to be without credo or theory, enjoyed in the same way she enjoyed pulling on her gloves on a Sunday morning and tying the dyed straw hat under her chin, and seeing crucifers and acolytes in solemn procession while organ music filled the Gothic heights.

They often sat up late together, and knew one another's problems. Elspeth had told them about her father, and about the Clish brothers. Corky too had trouble at work. She was the only Caucasian and the head cook did not like Caucasians. The others were nice to her, but the head cook would do her orders last and do them wrong. At best he would laugh at her pronunciation of menu items, and at worst he would pretend not to understand her accent at all, and she would repeat and repeat till one of the Chinese kids came to the rescue.

Joyce's friend Harrington was starting a little computerized dating service after working hours, in partnership with one of his colleagues from the Raytheon Corporation, and Joyce urged Elspeth to try it, especially since it was clear by now that Alf would never call.

Corky said Elspeth should get herself some stylish clothes first. But Elspeth said she didn't like miniskirts.

"I know," said Corky. "I've never seen you in a skirt. But you should. You've got the legs for them. You really do. I've watched you do your calisthenics mornings. You think I'm sleeping but I'm not."

"Oh, I've got skirts," said Elspeth. "They're most about two inches above the knee."

"That's out," said Joyce. "Everybody's wearing them six now. Four at least. I wore them four last year, and I've had to shorten them all. And you've got better legs than I have."

"Well, I don't care that much about being in style," Elspeth said. "The whole mini thing has gone too far, when you can't bend over or climb on the bus without putting your underwear on public view. I mean, nursing a child when he's hungry is one thing, but having your ass out like the Folies-Bergères just because some Paris designer got horny is another thing. There's gonna be a reaction. And skirts will get longer again."

"No," said Corky. "The trend is to more and more exposure. Maybe down an inch one year, but then up three inches the next year. We'll wear less and less."

"It's the wave of the future," said Joyce. "People don't have hang-ups about the body anymore. Nothing's more powerful than an idea whose time has come."

"And what's the great brilliant idea whose time has come?" said Elspeth. "Hemlines shorter every year? When there's no more skirt left, what'll the designers do for kicks then? Cut down our blouses till our bosoms are out?"

"Probably," said Corky. "Eventually."

"Well, I don't believe it," said Elspeth. "Styles shift. Next year they'll get a brainstorm that long skirts are feminine and sexy, and hiding is provocative, and hemlines'll plummet to the ankles."

"Never," said Joyce.

"Never," said Corky.

"Skirts'll never cover the knees again," said Joyce.

When they woke next morning Neal was there, after an absence of several days.

"Ellie thinks one of these years styles will reverse," Corky said to him at breakfast, "and skirts will go below the knee again."

"You do?" said Neal.

"I think so," said Elspeth.

"Well, I hope you're wrong."

Elspeth liked Neal. He seemed to have read widely, and when he was in the mood he could talk about all sorts of miscellany. Sometimes she danced with him. He danced well, even in the heavy shoes. They would roll up the rya rug, and put a record on Joyce's turntable, and thrust their joints to rock rhythms, without touching.

"My sister told me a beautiful story about you," he said to her once. "About this rabbi came over to bug you, and you smacked this shitty diaper right on his face, and wiped it all around." He chuckled. "Sometime when you get a nice shitty one, you know a real juicy, pungent, fermenting one, there's a certain priest I want to bring you to. He's got just the perfect face for it. Wait'll you see. This round cherubic red face, always with this unctuous, sweaty, shit-eating smile."

"Corky's got it wrong," she told him. "I didn't put it in his face. I just threatened to."

"Ellie, Neal's in love with you," Joyce said to her one morning at the breakfast table, in Neal's presence. "No kidding. He really is. He's in love. Did you ever hear of anything so ridiculous? Neal, don't you know there's no way Ellie could possibly go for you? Any more than she could go for a leprous porcupine. Or a three-toed sloth, with fleas. Or a stinking, worm-eaten corpse."

"Sure," Neal said quietly. "Naturally I'm in love with her. She's a beautiful person. And Ellie loves *me*. Because she loves everybody. That's the kind of person she is. She can say no to me, and there's no meanness in it. You're kind and generous in your way, Cicely Joyce Jencks, but you could take a lesson from her. There's no hostility in her. No sourness."

"Take it easy," said Corky.

If Neal was around when Harriet came he was polite, even attentive, so that Harriet liked him in spite of her disapproval of his appearance. Sometimes Harriet advised him that he could surely get a good job, because he was intelligent and had such a nice personality, if only he would shave and get a haircut and buy some decent clothes. Neal would nod as though taking her quite seriously.

Often he was not there when Harriet came, so it never occurred to Harriet that he lived there. No one saw any reason to mention it.

Corky always made conversation with Harriet. "She's very easy to be with," Harriet told Elspeth once. "She makes you feel at home."

For a time Harriet and Joyce did not meet, because Joyce's secretarial job had quite regular hours. But once Harriet found Joyce in bed with a cold, and spent her time there taking care of her. "You're mother's a doll," Joyce said to Elspeth afterward.

"I know."

Elspeth took Harriet marketing in the places that Corky had showed her. Groceries in drab back streets of Chinatown, away from the restaurants and the lights, featured such apparent inedibles as dried seaweed, and Elspeth showed them to Harriet only as a curiosity, without buying. But near Faneuil Hall was the wholesale district, with stall after stall where meats and fruits were cheap. The pram bounced on the cobblestones. A few blocks away were piers where fish could be bought from the incoming boats.

"It would pay me to do my own shopping here," Harriet said.

A few blocks in another direction were the Common and the Public Garden. The swanboats were not yet in the pond, which reflected the gray bridge. But the gardeners were already setting flats of daffodils in full bloom into the ground. A few species of trees had embryo buds, though others seemed still entirely bare. But the grass was already green.

They brought back baby foods and fed Peter with a spoon. The purees made him eager for more. He waved hands and feet. He opened his mouth tall, but sometimes closed it too soon, or turned his head at the wrong moment, so that half or more ended on his face or on his bib.

But he still closed his eyes when he nursed.

Elspeth bought a teething ring shaped like a pretzel and another shaped like a bottle opener. But he didn't like them.

"Do you know what a Jewish bagel is?" Chris asked one day, leaning in the swivel and flicking ashes.

"A bagel?" said Elspeth. "Sure." The office door was open and she was sitting on the doorstep in the sun.

"Well, try that on him," said Chris. "It's the best kind of teething ring. Go to the delicatessen and get some. Somebody told me that when Kathleen was teething. They like it better than rubber. And when they get too dirty you chuck it in the garbage and give him a new one."

Elspeth speculated with Chris about which would appear first, the leaves on the trees or Peter's tooth.

"The leaves," said Chris.

They did, almost with suddenness, minuscule in a dozen powdery shades, from reddish to gray-green. Then there was a warm spell. Elspeth worked in shirt and jeans.

"When you lay down under a car there," Chris told her, "make sure your shirt don't come out of your pants. You'll be giving the customers a show."

"I guess they've seen midriffs before."

"Well, your hip bone was kind of sticking out over your blue jeans when you were on your back draining that radiator yesterday. Your whole stomach and belly button and everything. I guess you must wear those small little bikini panties or something. I finally put coveralls on the guys last year. Every time Edgar used to squat down in jeans the top of his hairy ass would show, and I got sick of looking at it."

Often in the late morning lull, when the shadow of the overhead expressway had moved aside, Elspeth would sit in the sun with Chris on the plank bench in front of the building, Peter in his seat beside her.

"That Mrs. Iverson just raves about you," Chris said. "She says three different places told her she needed a new transmission—half the time the damn thing wouldn't shift up out of low gear till she hit forty miles an hour, and then sometimes it wouldn't shift down again. And then she mentioned it to you when she was getting gas, and you just reached under the hood and fixed it in a few minutes, and charged her nothing. And it's been perfect ever since. She thinks you've got magic or something. And it sure sounds like it. What's the story on that? How the hell did you fix a no-good transmission in a couple of minutes? It's not possible."

"The linkage was hung up, that was all. The same thing happened in my brother's car. So I just bent it a little."

"Oh. Well, I knew damn well a transmission isn't something you can fix with a bobby pin. Or chewing gum. But you sure made us a friend."

A motorcycle passed before them on Saltmarsh Avenue Extension. The sun gleamed on the colored helmets.

"That's a sure sign of spring," said Elspeth, "when you see kids on a motorcycle."

"Yeah, I guess so," said Chris. She drew on her cigarette. "And did you ever notice, whenever you see a motorcycle, the guy's always in front driving, and the girl's always behind, hanging on to him? It never fails. In spite of all the women's lib."

"I've noticed that too," said Elspeth.

At last Elspeth allowed Joyce to give her name and particulars to Harrington for his computerized dating service. Joyce said it was very scientific.

Then on her day off she shopped for clothes. Corky came with her, and they pushed the pram through the department stores. Elspeth tried on miniskirts. "You're right," she said to Corky. "They do look good on me."

In the apartment she modeled them for Joyce and for Neal.

The computer service found a Saturday-night date for her. Joyce said that Harrington knew the man and that he was a great guy.

"He gives it out to his friends?" said Corky. "What's so scientific about that?"

"He's not his friend. He just knows him," said Joyce. "The computer made the selection."

Joyce was helping Elspeth comb her hair Saturday night when the young man came to call. They had left Corky in the broken chair, holding Peter, offering him a bagel to bite on and trying to amuse him. They heard Neal let the caller in.

"My name's Neal," he said to him.

The young man must have looked at Corky. "Elspeth Baker?" they heard him ask anxiously.

"No, I'm Corky, her roommate. She'll be out in a minute."

"Sit down, man," said Neal. "Loosen up. Don't let *me* turn you off. I'm just the roommate's brother."

"Oh." He sat on the daybed. The doors were open and they even heard it squeak.

"Like a beer meanwhile?" said Neal.

"No."

462

Elspeth entered from the bedrooms, Joyce hovering behind her. The caller didn't rise. He was scrubbed, blondish, ill at ease. He had unbuttoned his overcoat but had not taken it off. It bunched. "Hi," she smiled, standing before him. "I'm Elspeth. I see you've met Petey already." She took Peter from Corky, and as her arms enfolded him his drowsy eyes closed. "Look, he just fell asleep." She kissed him. "Corky's volunteered to be his baby-sitter so we can go out."

"The baby lives with you?"

"Of course. Didn't they tell you about the baby?"

"I knew you had a baby. But I didn't know it was with you. I mean—"

He fell silent.

"Does it bother you?" she asked. "I thought you knew. I thought that was supposed to be the whole point of the computer."

"Well, ya, he told me. But it wasn't all that clear."

He looked unhappy. There was a pall.

She still stood before him, Peter sleeping at her shoulder. "If it bothers you," she said, "would you rather just forget the whole thing?"

"Well, I guess so. If it's all right with you."

"Okay," she said.

"She's got two roommates," said Neal. "Take your pick."

"Stow it, Neal," said Corky.

The visitor rose. He went to the door, awkwardly and self-consciously. He turned, gave a slight nod, then quickly shut himself out. They heard the outer door shut also.

Elspeth sat on the stuffed arm of the broken chair. "Well, so much for that," she said.

"The jerk," said Corky. "What a creepy attitude."

"Wait'll I tell Harrington," said Joyce. "He'll blacklist him."

"Well," said Elspeth, "better to get to the point than waste an evening, I guess." She stroked Peter, who still slept.

Neal was sitting on the rug. "Ellie, don't feel rejected," he said. "Okay? He didn't reject you. He rejected the kid. He didn't even see you. Any time you want guys, you can have guys around you like flies around shit. You're beautiful. Only when you come on like that, holding the baby, that's all he sees. It's not the baby itself—guys don't mind women with kids. They don't even mind women with husbands. As long as the husband's not around. Like when a woman introduces a guy to her husband, he knows she was just playing games. And when you show a guy a kid before he's got time to get used to you, it's like you're laying out the ground rules. He doesn't have room to maneuver. Especially the way you flaunt the kid. Know what I mean? You don't hide it. Two people meet, they want to start out with a variety of options. But any guy can see right off who's number one in your life. You don't want a guy. You want a daddy for the kid. It's written all over you."

"Do I flaunt him? Did I flaunt Petey?"

"It was my fault," said Corky. "I should have put him to bed before."

"No it wasn't," said Joyce. "You have to be honest."

"Another guy said something like that to me," said Elspeth. "He said I was using Petey as a defense. I was using him to keep men away. You don't believe that, do you, Neal?"

"Me? I don't know, Ellie. I don't question people. If you want to take a vow of celibacy, that's your right. I always respect the next man's bag. Like take these clowns in the Krishnas. They only get laid once a month."

"Let me put him to bed for you," said Corky. "And you have yourself a stiff drink."

"I don't want a drink."

Corky took Peter.

"I don't know if I've got things all wrong, or if other people have got things all wrong, or what," said Elspeth. "It's so damn hard to think straight."

"The hardest thing in the world," said Neal. "That's why nobody does."

In a moment Corky returned.

"I used to have guys around me like flies around shit," said Elspeth. "As Neal so quaintly put it. A couple of weeks after I started at Mount Holyoke they had this mixer, for U Mass and Amherst and Hampshire, and like for days after, the whole floor was sick of calling me to the phone. After a while I told the kids if it's for me just hang up, and for anybody I wanted to hear from we had a code, ask for Roxie's roomie. I don't mean I was the only one—there were other girls that had that problem. But three hundred guys would meet two hundred girls at a mixer, and they'd all zero in on about five girls. Like gnats."

"You could have it like that again," said Neal.

"It's been a long year," she said. "Like a century. But it's a new world when you're a parent. I didn't conceive him on purpose, but there he is. He's not just my thing, like needlepoint or something. He's a human being. And I'm his mother. He comes way ahead of any stranger that walks in that door. My two parents would have fought the whole world for their kids, and I guess it's in my blood. I can't play games anymore. I can't play games like I used to. Pretending to be interested in a guy when I'm not. And pretending not to be when I am."

59

THE weather turned warmer, but apparently Vinnie's recovery was heartbreakingly slow. "He still can't get out of the wheelchair, or stand, or use his right arm," Chris told Elspeth. "Sometimes he can get a word out real clear, but more than two words at a time and it comes out just noise. He knows what he wants to say, and it just kills him. If he don't start getting better real soon, maybe we'll sell out and move to Florida or sumpm."

"Are you really thinking of selling it?"

"I don't know. I don't know what I'll do. The boys said they'd like to buy it. Edgar and Puff."

Elspeth was shocked. "Really? Are they serious? Could they raise that kind of money?"

"I doubt it. I don't see how. They're just a couple of punks. Don't worry, kiddo. I haven't decided anything anyhow."

"Well, I hope you don't sell. At least if you do decide, let me know before you do anything, okay? I mean, keep me informed. Don't all of a sudden give someone an option."

"Okay."

Elspeth considered buying it herself. Crossing big checks week by week till the interest amounted to enough for the down payment. Then seeking a mortgage. And a loan from the Small Business Administration.

It wasn't feasible. A continuing flow of such big checks, without the banks ever plugging the leak—it was pushing her luck too far.

And even if she had the down payment, she'd never get a mortgage in six figures. She was nineteen and looked younger. What bank would take her seriously?

The weather grew warmer still, and Chris did not do anything about selling or moving. And the Clish brothers were apparently in no rush. Once or twice she heard them dream aloud, but it had the ring of empty talk.

Corky was fired from the Chinese restaurant. She began waitressing at a place on the wharves, called Fishes Delicious. But the pay was less and they only needed her Thursday through Sundays.

Elspeth missed the doggy bags Corky had used to bring home almost nightly, leavings from the covered serving tureens that customers left half full. There had been tremendous variety. Corky brought stuff from the fish place once or twice. It did not reheat well. And the salads wilted.

But the roommates had less ambition to cook instead of more. When Joyce didn't work into the evening she had a dinner date with Harrington. Corky on her nights off was content with a spoon and an opened can, without bothering to warm the contents or get a plate, unless her brother was there to cook for.

And on nights when no one else was cooking Elspeth now felt too tired to cook for herself alone. Chris frequently didn't come to the gas station at all, or stayed only for an hour or two, and Elspeth found that the long day with Edgar and Puff would leave her emotionally drained. She would kick off her shoes, doze in the broken chair, and wake with a start to find Peter asleep at her breast.

Nor did she go to bed early, though Peter woke her every morning at six. After the day with Edgar and Puff she needed congenial society, and would stay up as late as Joyce or Corky or Neal, which was usually midnight, or if no one was there she would wait for one of them to come in, and they would talk till one.

"You should quit that job," said Corky.

"I know. I'm gonna have to have a talk with Chris. I know she's depressed, and at the end of her tether. Her mother isn't helping her anymore. Her mother had to go help her sister and then she hurt her knee, and Chris has her hands full. The kids get in a squabble and she has to interrupt the bookkeeping, and the younger one is flunking math, and there's no end to it. But I can be running around all alone with six cars at the pumps, and Puff will sit over there in the repair bay and just watch. I know they don't do that on Wednesdays when Chris is alone. Don't think I haven't looked at the Help Wanteds. Because there's got to be some changes made. I'd give Chris time enough to get a replacement if it came to that. But there aren't too many jobs where you can bring a baby along. And I'll be damned if I'll take a job like telephone solicitation. It would drive me bananas."

They made tea.

"Spring is a depressing time," said Neal.

"What do you mean?" said Elspeth. "It's not supposed to be."

"It's not supposed to be," said Neal, "but it is. In winter you hope for spring, but in spring your hopes don't materialize."

"If you have such a dismal view of life," Joyce said to Neal, "why don't you commit suicide?"

"Don't say that," said Corky.

"I thought of it," said Neal. "But I tried a dry run first to see how I liked it. I went to the cemetery and laid down. Just laid there still. Day and night. And after about nineteen and a half hours I decided I didn't like it."

"It's not where the action is," said Elspeth.

"Right," he said. "It was real peaceful at first. But then it got boring."

Corky was thinking of signing up for a schooner cruise that toured the coast of Maine and the Maritime Provinces at two-week intervals during the summer. You had to reserve space far ahead. She thought the ratio of guys to girls would be better on a sailing vessel. On a conventional cruise it was rotten.

But Elspeth was not interested. "I've got to start looking into courses. Evening courses. Practical stuff this time, like business administration. And I've got to get

466

my electrician's license and my plumber's license. This Wednesday I catch up on my sleep, and the following Wednesday I start visiting schools, and plan a course of action."

However Wednesday Chris phoned not feeling well, and asked Elspeth to go to work on overtime.

Harriet had brought a few more of the tools from home each time, so Elspeth had been able to build up her own supply in a locked drawer that Chris had assigned to her.

If Chris showed up, and stepped down into the repair bay, Edgar frequently took the opportunity to complain about Elspeth.

"She drives trade away," he said. "She doesn't stick up for the place. Today she told a customer to go to the Volvo place for a thermostat," Edgar continued. "Ours ain't good enough."

"The service manual called for a one-seventy," said Elspeth. "We only have one-eighties."

"She gets her hands on a service manual and she thinks it's the God damn word or God," said Edgar. "So what if it runs ten degrees hotter? It don't hurt. It's good for it. It keeps the valves clean. Mrs. Iverson thinks she's such a frigging magician because she saved her a transmission job, and it went straight to her head."

"All right, back to work. And don't tell tales out of school so much," Chris said to Edgar.

A few afternoons later Elspeth saw the old Volvo again. The little white-haired lady she had sent to the Volvo place for a thermostat parked over by the fence. She stepped out in flat shoes and a cotton crew hat and a belted suede jacket hanging open and went into the repair bay. The wide door of the bay was down, closing it off, and she used the little door set into it.

Elspeth was busy at the pumps. The lady came out of the repair bay, noticed Peter in his seat on the plank bench, and sat near him. Elspeth saw her bend to Peter and talk to him, and he responded with smiles and gurgles, exercising his arms and legs.

When the last of the cars left the pumps Elspeth walked over to the bench. "Hi," she said.

"Oh, hello. Is this your little brother? Or your little sister?"

"He's my son."

"Oh. Well, the resemblance is certainly strong. He's quite a charmer, isn't he."

"He has quite an outgoing personality," said Elspeth. "He likes people." She took a box of throat lozenges from her jeans, put one in her mouth and offered the box to the lady.

"No thanks. How old is he?"

"Five months. Did you get that thermostat okay?"

"Oh yes. Thank you. No trouble. I think I've got a bigger problem this time. I can't move the shift stick a lot of the time, and it's gotten worse. But that's how it is with an old car. It comes in bunches. I keep my fingers crossed. But I'd rather

467

fix something than buy new cars every two years. They don't make them like they used to anyway."

"I'm with *you*," said Elspeth. She unstrapped Peter. She danced him on her knees.

"Mr. Clish is going to give me a ride home as soon as he's free," the white-haired lady said. She had a gray pullover under the suede. "I hope he's not long. And then I guess I'll be without a car for a few days. If it's the clutch or the transmission he'll have to have it two or three days."

"That's a big job," said Elspeth.

"Oh, I know. I took automotive repair last summer in the adult education, so at least sometimes I know what they're talking about. But I don't think it could be the clutch. I had a new clutch put in last year. Not here. Somewhere else. And I've been awfully careful of it, like they told me. I don't use the clutch pedal for a foot rest, and I put it in neutral at stop lights. Except today, I couldn't budge it."

"Did they replace all parts of the clutch at that time?" Elspeth asked. "Disc, plate, throw-out bearing?"

"Oh. Dear me. I'd have to look up the bill. It was over a hundred dollars. But if it's the transmission now that's even more than a clutch, isn't it?"

"I'm afraid so." She cradled Peter in her arm. She took a bagel from the shoulder bag that stood on the bench beside the baby seat. She gave it to him to bite.

A car pulled up at the pumps. She strapped Peter into the seat again.

For a while cars came as quickly as they left. She saw that Peter had fallen asleep. The lady went into the repair bay briefly and came out again.

When the pumps were quiet Elspeth returned to the bench.

"I hope Mr. Clish can give me my ride soon," the lady said. "You don't think I'll have to wait till he's off duty, do you?"

"What did he say? Did you look in on him just now?"

"He said be patient."

"You say you can't move the shift?"

"Oh, sometimes I can. If I jiggle it a lot, and push very hard. I got it from first to second today, but that's all. I drove all the way here in second."

"Let me look at it," said Elspeth.

They went to the car. Elspeth sat in it. There were four forward speeds, with the usual diagram on the knob. She gripped it. The stick was indeed stiff. She got out and looked under the hood.

Then she went to the office and returned with a couple of cans and an opener.

"What is it?" the lady asked.

"Well, it needs a dose of castor oil, believe it or not. There's a hydraulic system, and in these foreign cars they use castor oil. These are our last two cans." She opened one. The thin stream of pouring liquid was both orange and lavender as the sun struck it. She emptied it into a little aluminum reservoir in a corner behind the engine. She screwed the cap back onto the reservoir.

She got into the car once more. Her foot pumped the clutch pedal again and again.

The wide door of the bay slid up rattling. Edgar came toward her scowling. Puff watched from the bay with a scowl like his brother's.

"Just what the hell do you think you're doing?" Edgar said.

"There wasn't any fluid in the master cylinder reservoir, so I filled it." Her left foot kept pumping the pedal.

"Oh. I see. The great transmission expert is back at work."

He glanced at the white-haired lady.

"I can give you a ride home now if you want," he said.

"Well, I think I'd rather wait now and see how this comes out," she said.

He stood there, his flushed face dark. Suddenly he turned and walked back to the repair bay. Once inside, his thick arm pulled the wide door down with such force that when it struck the pavement it almost bounced.

"Is Mr. Clish your husband?" the lady asked.

"No."

"Oh. I just thought he might be. The way he spoke to you."

Elspeth got out, with the other can, and looked into the little reservoir. The level of fluid had gone down somewhat. She filled it to the brim.

"Okay, I think your car has a self-bleeding system, so pumping the pedal should get the bubbles out. Help me count another hundred times."

She got in and pumped and pumped.

"Ninety-nine, a hundred," the lady said. "Isn't your foot tired?"

"Let me just look underneath and check your clutch adjustment."

She climbed out and leaned over the fender to peer into the reservoir a third time. Then she stuffed the ends of her braids into her shirt and got down and lay on the pavement, her head and hands under the car.

"Oh, you've got lots of clutch left," she said. "You're in good shape." She scrambled up, slid onto the seat again, pressed the pedal, and her right hand shifted the stick into each of its positions. She started the engine, and again slid the stick into each position. It moved easily. "There. How's that?"

"You mean it's fixed?"

"Well, let me show you something." She got out. "Did they tell you about the master cylinder and the slave cylinder in the adult education?"

"No, I don't think so."

"Well, the pedal pushes one, and that pushes the castor oil, and the castor oil pushes the other, and that pushes the clutch." She showed her the little reservoirs for the clutch and for the brakes. "Keep these full. And if there's a slow leak, like a quarter inch in a couple of weeks, don't worry about it. Just watch it and fill it. If there's a fast leak you'll need a new master or a new slave, which is like about twenty-five bucks for a rebuilt, plus labor. But I don't think there is. It might have just evaporated over the years. But keep checking those reservoirs. And my baby's waking up. Okay, you owe four bucks and twenty cents for two cans of fluid."

"And your labor?"

"I can't charge for fifteen minutes of labor." She was on her way to Peter and the lady followed. He stopped crying when he saw her. She made change from her pocket, already kneeling to change the diaper. She had begun singing to Peter and only half noticed when the lady drove away.

She left him in his seat and took the old diaper to the barrel.

As she returned Edgar emerged from the office, his two hands holding the pram bassinet. "Well, you did it again, Stardust," he said.

"Edgar! Where are you going with that? Put that down!"

He did not look at her and did not speak. He rounded the pumps and continued toward the avenue. She hurried after him.

"Hey! What's the matter with you? Have you gone crazy?"

He threw the bassinet into the street. It struck on its side near a manhole cover and bounced over on the pavement. The mattress and bedding and the package of disposable diapers fell out. A pickup truck swerved to avoid it and continued down the avenue without reducing speed. Edgar was heading back toward the repair bay, not looking at Elspeth.

"You creepy son of a bitch!" she said. "Wait till Chris hears about this!"

Cars kept dodging around it. Flaps of blanket stirred in the breeze. She watched for a chance to step into the street.

Then she gathered everything up, beating off the grainier dirt.

As she returned with it a car pulled in for gas. She put down the bassinet on the pump island and tended to the customer. She could scarcely keep her mind to what she was doing.

The customer drove away. Edgar came out of the repair bay, his little red eyes on Elspeth. He held his biggest combination wrench, with a box end and an open end, down at his side but somewhat out at an angle, gripped tightly. It looked almost two feet long. He moved toward her.

"You better hope I don't find any damage in that bassinet," she said. "I've got a lawyer that knows how to take care of you."

"Get out of here," he said quietly. "Do you read me? Get out. Split. Take your junk and bug off. And don't ever come back." He moved the wrench. Sunlight gleamed on the nickel-plated steel.

"Put down that wrench. And don't you tell me to get out. I'm on duty. Who do you think you are? You don't hire and fire."

"I'm the service manager. And I say get out. And you better believe it." He stepped slowly nearer, his big fist clutching the wrench. His knuckles were white.

"Don't be a jerk, Edgar. Do you really think you can get away with this? Chris'll have your head."

"You were a little bit easier to get along with when your arm was in a sling. Maybe it'd be still easier, if you had two arms in a sling."

"Let her get the baby, Edgar," said Puff. She hadn't noticed him. He stood far behind, near the repair bay door.

"I'm not stopping her," Edgar said without turning.

She did not believe he could be so unwise as to hit her with the wrench. Still, there was no advantage in forcing him into a corner where he might do something stupid to save face, when Peter could be injured. Chris was the one to handle this.

Behind him she saw Peter in his seat on the bench, with his white bonnet, his solemn round eyes watching her and Edgar.

She passed very close to Edgar to go to Peter, and he stepped back. She put on the shoulder bag, unstrapped Peter, and slipped his empty seat over her arm. Passing again close to Edgar, as though without seeing him, she lay Peter gently in the bassinet face down. He kicked his feet and raised himself up on his hands.

Then she lifted the bassinet with both hands and walked unhurriedly toward the street, without once glancing back. She thought of her tools. But they were safe under lock and key. And if she took them with her it would seem as though she did not intend to come back.

She paused for traffic, then crossed.

She did not look around till she reached the bus stop at the opposite curb. Edgar and Puff were not in sight. They had gone inside and closed the doors. Suddenly she felt exhausted. She wept.

She was about to sit on the granite curb and lay the bassinet on the brick sidewalk for a moment's rest, but a bus was approaching. She had been intending to go into the tavern and call Chris from the phone booth. But she decided instead to go home.

She checked her sobs, picked up the bassinet and backed away from the stop, allowing the bus to pass.

Then she walked toward the subway, tears running on her cheeks. Her throat was sore. Her head ached.

When she got home Corky was there. She told Corky, still tearful, still exhausted, blowing her nose and undoing her braids.

"I know you're not a drinker," said Corky, "but I'm gonna mix you a gin and tonic. And then I want you to go soak in a bath, and when you feel better call Chris. I'll watch the baby meanwhile."

Elspeth was somewhat refreshed by the drink and the bath. She dialed Chris from the brown telephone on the kitchen wall, but Kevin said his mother and sister had gone to buy a bathing suit. Then she fed Peter his puree. Neal arrived, and Corky told him what had happened to Elspeth.

"Some decisions are gonna have to be made," Elspeth said.

Joyce came home and Corky told her too.

"Are you gonna call the police?" said Joyce. "You could press charges."

"Not yet," said Elspeth. "I want to talk to Chris first."

Joyce suggested they cook a good dinner to cheer Elspeth up.

Elspeth wiped the puree from Peter's face and moved him with his seat to the rug.

Corky and Joyce were busy in the little kitchen, so Elspeth dragged the long spiral cord into the bathroom and sat on the toilet cover with the telephone at her ear. The door was open, and she smelled the onions and peppers, and heard the bubbling of the macaroni and the sizzling of beef slices.

"And I just can't continue there under those conditions," she told Chris. "I'd be afraid for myself. And afraid for the baby."

471

"Well, he tells it a little different, which is to be expected," Chris answered her. "He says he didn't threaten you with the wrench. He just had it in his hand because he'd been using it, but you were arguing with him and all of a sudden you looked at the wrench and you got hysterical. And then he helped you carry the bassinet because you said you were leaving, and you dropped it and then you got mad at him about that."

"Do you believe that, Chris? It's bullshit."

"Well, I know, he can stretch a point. Frankly, Elspeth, I know what you mean. You've been a good worker and I'm sorry to see you go. But if you kids can't get along with each other something's got to give. I depend on those guys. Good mechanics are hard to find. And who've I got to send out on the tow truck? I can't send you on a road call with the baby. And in a little place harmony's important. We've got to have a smooth-running operation. So I'll sure miss ya. We been good friends together, you and me. I really like ya. But if you're gonna be fighting with the guys all the time what's the use. It's conflicting personalities, I guess. Cats and dogs. If I can't even leave the place for an afternoon without a battle breaking out, well, Jesus. There's enough fighting in Vietnam, and the Middle East, and all over the damn place. I don't need it in my business. I can't be spending all my time adjudicating disputes."

Elspeth came into the kitchen, holding the phone at her side. She looked at Corky and Joyce and Neal. They looked at her. She hung up the phone.

"I don't believe it," she said. "I just don't believe it."

She went to the dining table, and sat heavily. She summarized the conversation.

"I'm speechless," said Corky.

"I've never felt so betrayed," said Elspeth. "Well, that's not true. I have."

Corky and Joyce brought dinner. They all sat.

"Okay, tomorrow you put in for the food program," Neal said. "And rent subsidy. And unemployment. And aid to dependent children."

"Maybe Chris'll still let you stay," said Joyce. "She didn't actually fire you. It's more like she was accepting your resignation."

"Are you nuts?" said Elspeth. "After the way she put it? I wouldn't lower myself." She picked at her food, without appetite.

"There's no way I could harmonize with those guys. Not and keep my self-respect. I'm not gonna let a little old lady wait around for a ride when she doesn't need a ride, and sit there worrying whether it's gonna be a hundred-and-fifty bucks worth of clutch or three hundred worth of transmission. When not a thing is wrong except the fluid's down."

The air turned foul. Elspeth glanced at Neal, but he was looking only at his dish. His face and beard were low over it as his fork scooped food into his mouth.

The stench grew overpowering.

"Pew!" exclaimed Joyce. "Jesus!"

"God!" said Corky. "Neal, was that you?"

"Of course it was Neal!" said Joyce. "Who else?" She jumped up and flung both

472

windows high. "Pew!" She fanned the air before her face. A chill breeze moved the curtains.

She opened the kitchen window too, and went on to the bathroom, stumbling noisily over the sealed diaper pail, and opened the window there.

"Christ, Neal," Corky said. "Right in the middle of dinner. You ought to be shot. Joyce, open the windows in the bedrooms too. Let's get some cross ventilation."

"Why does everyone blame me?" said Neal. "It could have been the baby."

"It's not the baby and you know it," said Corky.

Joyce came back to the living room by way of the bedrooms. "I'll open the door too," she said. "Maybe some of the stink will blow up the stairs."

"I couldn't help it," said Neal. "Why is everybody so uptight about a simple bodily function?"

Joyce returned, knocking her chair aside, and leaned out the window.

"Put some more onions in the pan," said Neal. "It'll help kill the smell."

Joyce turned. "Jesus, Neal. You are an unmitigated turd. You know that?"

"I'm just trying to offer a suggestion," he said. "Trying to be helpful."

"Neal," said Joyce. "Take a little walk. Pretty please? Just get out of my sight for a couple of hours. Or a couple of days. Or a couple of years. I mean it. Before I start picking up everything that's loose and throwing it straight at your head."

He rose, without protest. He left. They heard the outer door close behind him. Joyce sat. She rested her forehead on a hand. The curtains kept billowing.

"Maybe the peppers made him gassy," Elspeth said.

"The peppers didn't seem to affect anyone else," said Joyce. "And whatever. Unless somebody is a lazy stinker with no consideration he controls those things."

"And I thought he was improving," said Corky.

"Not really,"said Joyce. "The only thing is that since Ellie's here he doesn't bring his girl friends around. At least now he goes to their place."

"Why doesn't he bring them since I'm here?"

"Because he loves you."

"I don't care what girls he goes with."

"I know it. You couldn't care less. And he knows it. But even so."

Elspeth bent to Peter's seat and unstrapped him. She lifted him to nurse.

She felt the cold from the window on her face and breast, though the radiator was hot by her feet.

Corky suggested they go out to a movie. "Come on. It'll cheer Ellie up."

"I'm okay," said Elspeth.

"But it'll get your mind off your troubles."

She buttoned Peter into his sweater and tied on his hat, and carried him sleeping against her shoulder.

The movie was about college kids. She watched, but could not put her mind to it. She shared her throat lozenges with Corky and Joyce. A new plan was in her head for purchasing Saltmarsh Service. She kept going over it, refining the details. Tomorrow morning she would open accounts in several banks. And then start huge checks canceling each other out back and forth, odd amounts in hundreds of thousands and millions chasing their own tails in round robins and complex patterns, but not for interest. Interest was not the point. She would even stick to accounts that paid no interest. She would not gain a penny. What she would get instead would be a fantastic credit rating.

Each bank would be so impressed by all these checks in the millions that never bounced, and these average daily balances in the hundreds of thousands, that they would fall all over themselves in their eagerness to lend her money. They would fight for the privilege.

How much did Chris want? Two hundred thou? A mortgage was no problem. And the down payment? Another loan from another bank. All perfectly above board.

But what if she took title, and then found her monthly gross was not enough to meet the payments? They'd foreclose. So the bank would acquire a gas station, that's all. Maybe she'd stay on, and run it as an employee of the bank, or as an employee of the new owner. The important thing is that she'd have gotten rid of Edgar and Puff meanwhile.

And maybe the monthly gross would meet the payments. Why shouldn't it? It was meeting them now. She'd be the owner of a going business. In time she'd expand. By the time Petey was nine, he'd be climbing up on fenders and hoods to wash windshields.

After the movie she went to the ice-cream parlor with Corky and Joyce, Peter sleeping on the other shoulder now. The ice cream soothed her throat but seemed to intensify the headache. She scarcely listened to the conversation. She would call Chris in a few days and make her first offer.

Before taking title, she would purchase ample insurance and also have the alarm system checked over. The O'Banions had friends in the police district and she would ask for introductions and try to inherit that relationship.

She returned with Joyce and Corky to the apartment. "Do you think Neal came back?" Joyce asked as she unlocked the door. "Neal!" she called.

"He's not here," said Corky. "He always stays away a few days after you get mad."

"If I find him asleep in my bed," said Joyce, "I'm really having him committed. I give you fair warning."

"He's not," said Corky.

They went to bed. But Elspeth lay awake, even when the city was silent. A staff of three would be enough to start. Herself, one experienced mechanic, and a kid to help. She'd need a lawyer for the real estate deal, and thereafter. Alf of course. Maybe it would be wise to get a precautionary court order enjoining the Clish brothers from any vandalism.

Sonny Elkin kept intruding on her thoughts. Till she went to South Hadley, he had eyes for no one else. And as the owner of a successful business she could call him again, without sounding desperate. And find out what Cliffie had discovered him. Begin to get a line on the competition. I'm doing great, Sonny. Paying off a quarter-million mortgage, and looking to buy the right foreign-car agency. Or a distributorship. Yeah, I'll be the youngest in the country probably.

Her neck was itching. Scratching didn't help. Itches came on the sides of her face, her ankles.

Then everywhere. She squirmed in the sheets. She did not have hands enough to keep up with them. Every second she was tormented in a new spot. And she found bumps, swellings.

She felt her way through Joyce's room to the bathroom and clicked on the light. The image in the mirror startled her. There were great swellings, flat like mosquito bites, but the size of dimes, quarters, half dollars, and they moved about, changed shape, new ones appearing and growing before her eyes. Everywhere. Her forehead. The backs of her hands. When she tore open her pajamas they were on her shoulders, her breasts. Gnawing, burning, stinging. She scratched her behind, she scratched her knee, she jumped.

She ran back to the double bunk and turned on the bedroom light. "Corky! Wake up! Corky! Please! I'm sick!" She twitched, writhed, danced, her hands racing about to clasp whatever new stab had become most piercing.

Corky squinted sleepily. "What is it?"

"I don't know! I don't know! It's getting worse!"

Corky looked at Elspeth, and her eyes widened. "My God!" said Corky. "My God!"

IN the examining room Peter slept in Corky's arms. Elspeth tried to lie still on the table, but she clasped suddenly at her leg and her knee almost struck the young doctor in white who bent over her. "I'm sorry," she said. The biggest of the flat welts on her thigh looked two inches across. Amorphous arms were moving out from it as from a giant amoeba.

"Roll over, please," he said. He had glasses and a big mustache.

She turned to prone. "Can you do anything? I never itched like this in my life. It's something awful."

"I'm pretty sure we can give you something to relieve it. But I'd like Dr. Culp to have a look at you first."

She felt the light touch of his fingers.

"Have you eaten anything unusual?"

"Not really."

"Or been near any unusual substance?"

"Not that I know of."

"How long did you say you've had the symptoms?"

"Gee, I don't know. How long is it, Corky?"

"She woke me about twenty minutes ago. We came right over."

Dr. Culp arrived. He was past middle age and exceedingly lanky, with a receding chin and a prominent Adam's apple. His hair was the color of rope. He wore a gray, narrow, vested suit. His melancholy face looked down at Elspeth, while the young white-frocked man explained that it appeared to be acute urticaria, except that he'd never seen so severe a case, and that the causative allergen was unidentified. He proposed one CC of something that had a long name.

The tall old man nodded. "Make it one-point-five," he said. "And find her a bed. I want to watch it for a day or two." Then he mentioned some things he wanted done, all of which sounded like strings of initials or syllabic abbreviations.

"Thank you, doctor," the young mustachioed one said. Dr. Culp turned to leave, lofty and round-shouldered.

"What is it?" Elspeth asked.

"Hives," said Dr. Culp, without looking back, and went out.

"What are those things he wants done?"

"Just some blood tests," said the mustachioed man. "They'll do that in the morning. Turn toward the wall, please."

She lay on her side. A spot on her buttock was daubed with something moist. Then a needle stabbed it.

"Now I've got to have you admitted," he said.

"If you're keeping her here the baby has to stay too," Corky told him. "She's breastfeeding."

"Oh. Well, I'll see what I can do. That may mean a private room."

"Can she get dressed now? Or do you have a gown or something?"

"Oh. Sure." He opened a metal drawer. Then he left.

The itching was less. But now Elspeth was very sleepy. Her eyes would not stay open.

"Come on, honey," Corky was saying. "Sit up. Slip this on."

"Where's Petey?"

"He's right here. Right next to you. Come on."

Elspeth wondered which hospital this was. She didn't think she had been in this one before. There were so many in Boston. She saw her clothes as Corky folded them into the round blue valise.

A stretcher on wheels intruded into the room.

"Okay," said Corky. "I'll carry the baby."

476

Elspeth felt befogged. In one instant her surroundings were distorted, as though she dreamed, and in the next she was aware of Corky and a big girl with two chins sliding her from the table to the stretcher.

"That stuff he shot into you really worked," Corky told her. "The bumps are gone. How do you feel?"

"Tired."

"The baby goes to pediatric," the big girl said.

"Oh no," Corky contradicted her. "The baby stays with her. I spoke to the doctor."

"I'm sorry, miss. I've got my instructions."

They argued. The big girl left, and when she came back the young doctor with the glasses and mustache was there too. He was telling Corky that if a private became available in a day or so they could be together, but the only available beds now were in wards, and there was no way they could put the baby in that ward. They weren't equipped. He wouldn't get the care there.

"You're not separating them!" she heard Corky say. "I'm not letting you! This is a nursing mother! Now come off it, mister! There's no such thing as can't! If you don't have authority let me talk to the director. Who's the director? Culp?"

"No, he's not. Dr. Culp's gone. The director will be in at nine."

They argued some more. Then Elspeth felt herself being wheeled. "Corky?" she said.

"I'm right here," she heard Corky anser. "And Petey's here. Don't worry."

Elevator doors opened and closed.

At last the big girl was helping her into a bed. Somewhere in the ward a woman was sobbing and moaning. There were windows, and Elspeth saw it was already daybreak.

"I'm putting your valise on the chair," Corky said. "And they're bringing a crib for Petey. He'll right next to your bed."

Almost as she spoke a white crib arrived, a boy pushing it. Peter waved his hands nervously but did not waken when Corky lifted him into it. Then Corky drew the curtain all around bed and crib and night table and chair. She still heard the sobbing and moaning. It seemed to come from down the ward on the other side.

"You'll have to leave now, miss."

"I'm leaving. Ellie, get some sleep. You're okay."

"You get some sleep too. You're so good, Corky. I'll love you all my life."

"I'll try to get back and see you during the day."

Elspeth saw Peter in the gray light, through the bars of his crib. His diapered behind was in the air.

She slept.

When her eyes opened they still ached with tiredness. The ward was astir. Her curtain was closed but she heard soft footsteps and wheels. The same woman was still sobbing. But she knew that what had wakened her was simply Peter's six-o'clock feeding time. He was biting the sheet, his forehead against the bars, his eyes staring up at her.

She got out of bed, found diapers and swabs in the valise, lowered the crib rail and changed him. Then she cranked her own bed to an angle and took him into it. She reached to undo the top tie and lowered the gown from a shoulder.

She leaned with Peter into the pillows. Her eyes ached and she closed them. She even let herself doze while he sucked. But she knew when to move him to the other breast, and she knew when he had finished. She restored the slight cotton garment to her shoulder, rose, laid him down in the crib, and again gave him a fresh diaper.

The curtain was yanked open and a doctor appeared, a quick-moving, tight-lipped little man, youngish, with a stethoscope dangling on a plaid jacket. "Get this child up to pediatric!" he said sharply to an aide. "Right now, please. Stop what you're doing. I just can't believe Dr. Brokaw gave permission, without an examination or anything!"

The girl left the breakfast cart and came over, very young, with a face cherubic but dumbly staring, an amplitude of curls tumbling about it.

"He's on the breast!" Elspeth said. "We do have permission—"

"He'll be on the bottle temporarily," the little doctor said, "at least till we can check him over. It won't do him any harm."

"You don't have to check him over. I'm the one that's sick! He's not sick."

"You don't know that. It's for his protection, madam. As well as everyone else on this ward. We can't just put someone on a ward without examination."

"Examine him here."

"Madam, we have a department set up for it, with trained staff, and equipment. Take him out," he told the girl. "I don't want an infant on this ward."

The girl began to lift Peter.

"No, no, no!" he said. "The crib and all!"

"Now just a minute!" Elspeth said. "I want my baby *with* me! That's the only reason I brought him! We're not your prisoners!"

"That's right, you're not," he said sharply. "You came here voluntarily because you were sick, and you brought a friend with you, and you gave everybody a difficult time. I saw the report. And you can leave whenever you wish. All you have to do is sign a form that you discharged yourself against advice, and absolving us of all responsibility. We have rules in this hospital! We're busy. And we don't have time for cranks."

His calling her a crank left her for the moment without a reply. She was not convinced he was entirely right, though he clearly thought he was, but he did have some points.

"Take it away," he told the girl, and she raised the crib rail. Elspeth watched her pull the crib into the aisle and angle it. Peter was raised on his arms, looking at Elspeth.

The girl pushed the crib down the aisle. The doctor walked quickly around them and left the ward. Elspeth watched the crib till it disappeared. She climbed into bed.

She had come to the hospital because she had needed it, after all. It did not make sense to antagonize everyone as she had in the other place after Peter was born. The welts and the itching were gone, and maybe they would discharge her this morning anyway.

And if they wanted to observe her a bit longer, a bottle or two at this stage would not jeopardize lactation. Peter had just been fed. Maybe she could even ask at noon if they'd mind her going up to pediatric and feeding him there.

When she had been to the bathroom she tried to sleep, but in a moment breakfast was brought to her by the same expressionless cherub-faced girl that had wheeled Peter's crib away.

"Hi. How does my baby like it in pediatrics? Did he cry?"

"No."

The cereal was cold by now. It irritated her throat. Afterward she closed the curtain and slept, but she was awakened by a tall black girl, taut-skinned and handsome. "Sorry to wake you, but we have to take a little blood for the lab."

Elspeth offered her arm, looking away. She felt the cooling antiseptic.

"What's the matter with that woman down there that keeps moaning and crying all the time?" she asked. "It's awful. She was going at it like that when I came in and she hasn't stopped."

For a second or two it seemed as though the girl wasn't going to answer. But then the reply came, quietly. "She just found out yesterday she's going to die soon. Forty-one years old. In the midst of things. It came on very suddenly. Busy on committees, very active, four children, in the middle of projects, and then a death sentence out of the blue."

Elspeth scarcely felt the needle.

When she did look back three tiny vials had been filled. The girl plastered on a small round bandage and smiled. "Okay, that's all. Go back to sleep." She drew the curtain closed as she left.

But it was parted again by Dr. Culp. About eighteen or twenty students were with him. They gathered about her bed inside the curtain. "Well, now," said Dr. Culp. "How are the hives today?"

"Gone, I think," said Elspeth.

He drew off her sheet. Then he bent over her, his nose and Adam's apple pointing and the unruly locks hanging before his forehead, and untied the gown behind her neck. He took it off. "Itching all gone?"

He touched her here and there. Except for one bespectacled girl with hair pulled tight the students were male.

"Mm hm," said Dr. Culp. "Mm hm. Good." He described the size and extent of the welts that had been there during the night. Sometimes he called them eminences and sometimes he called them wheals.

Some of the students including the girl had notebooks in which they jotted. Some of the guys stared deadpan. But others let their eyes wander appreciatively, and she felt herself redden. Dr. Culp asked her to turn over. He poked about, apparently at spots where he thought he remembered swellings. He told her to lie on her back once more. He lifted her knee and checked under a thigh. One of the guys met her eyes, smiling lazily. It seemed to her that her entire body blushed.

At last Dr. Culp led them out, the smiling guy almost backwards, as she grabbed for the sheet and the gown.

She lay a long time, her eyes and body seeming too uncomfortably tired for sleep.

But she must have drifted off and slept for some time. She was aware for a while of the lunch carts without altogether wakening, and when she did waken and ask the time it was nearly one o'clock. Her breasts were full and leaking. They must have already given Peter his lunchtime bottle. She hoped so. If they hadn't he'd be ravenous by now and distraught at her absence.

She slipped her bare feet onto the floor. She felt feverish when she stood, but she did not return to bed. She checked the knots of the gown, all the way down her back.

Then she set out to look for pediatrics. Maybe they would not let her get there, but there was no harm in trying.

As she left her ward she came face to face with Harriet.

"Mother!"

"Elspeth! What's the matter! What happened to you!"

"How'd you know I was here?"

"Corky called me."

"I don't know what happened. I got these terrible hives in the middle of the night, and I was itching like crazy. But I'm okay now. I'm fine now."

"So how long are they gonna keep you here? And where's the baby?"

"They stuck him in pediatrics, just because of their dumb regulations. I'm just on my way to see if I can see him. I don't know why I didn't just check out as soon as the hives were gone. But I was tired, I guess, so I listened to them."

"You're supposed to be in bed, miss," a small fiftyish nurse said. "Your company can visit with you there."

"I was just taking a little walk," said Elspeth. "I need the exercise."

"The doctor said you're to have total rest."

"He did? Which doctor?"

"Go ahead," Harriet said to Elspeth. "Go to bed, like a good girl. I'll go and see Petey and I'll come back."

Elspeth turned back slowly to the bed. They'd let an outside visitor into pediatrics sooner than a patient from another ward anyway.

They brought her lunch. She rested in the pillows afterward, feeling drowsy again.

Suddenly Harriet was there though Elspeth had not seen her approach.

"Did you find him?"

"Yes. He was asleep and he looked fine."

"They must have fed him then," said Elspeth. "Or he wouldn't be asleep."

"Yes, they said they did."

"Was he dry?"

"He was wet, so I changed him. They said they just changed him, but I changed him again."

"I bet he has diaper rash when I get him back. What's it like up there? Children of all ages I bet. Some in bandages, some in traction—"

"Of course. What do you expect? It's a hospital."

"Can you stay around a while, Mama? It would be good if somebody could look in on him every so often. And if you could find one of the doctors so I can ask if I can get out. I don't know if they're afraid the hives might come back or what."

"I was planning to stay for the afternoon," said Harriet.

"That's good. If I get out maybe you can come to the apartment with me. I'd like to just get into bed and sleep all afternoon."

"Maybe you should stay here another day and rest then. You're in bed now."

"That's true. But I hate hospitals. Petey went into that pediatric ward well and he'll come out sick."

"Is there anything you want meanwhile, that I can get you? From your apartment? Or from a store?"

"Well, you could get Petey a bagel to bite on. In case his gums bother him when he wakes up. And something for my throat."

"Your throat? You have a sore throat? Ask the nurse for something. The doctor. You're in a hospital."

Elspeth lay propped when Harriet had gone. The talking had hurt her throat.

She hoped Edgar and Puff hadn't yet jimmied into her drawer to take her tools. When she phoned to make Chris an offer, she would also ask her to take those tools home with her for now. It was not the value of them that bothered her so much. But they had been Mark's and Eric's.

Harriet seemed gone a long time. Maybe she had had to walk far to find a bagel.

Chris wouldn't accept the offer right away. She'd probably say she wanted to think about it, sleep on it, tell Vinnie. For days. And the struggle of Vinnie trying to talk about it. Meanwhile Elspeth would increase the offer.

At last she heard Harriet speak to her from outside the curtain. Harriet opened it. "Good, you're awake. Do you remember Mr. Snyder, from Winslow? And his sister, Miss Snyder?"

There were two people with her. The man was smallish and balding, with a jacket of dazzling blue. His sister had dark pockets under sad eyes. Her hair seemed fixed in a spectacular permanent, black except for a stripe of gray that rose at a corner and curved back through it.

"Naw, she doesn't know me," he smiled.

"I may have seen you in the store," said Elspeth. "I think. I'm not sure."

"Yeah, I've been in the store. Your father buys fixtures from me. I watched you grow up. I remember your brothers too. When the three of you were little. Waiting outside the temple for your father to come and pick you up. You remember her, Cele?"

"Sure, I remember her as a little kid," the woman said. Her voice was deep, throaty. "Who could forget that red hair? And now the baby has the same hair."

"We bumped into each other upstairs," said Harriet. "Mr. Snyder's son is near Petey."

481

"Did you find a bagel?" Elspeth asked.

"Yes, and I held a half of it for him to bite on for a while. I still have it in the bag. I didn't want to leave it, because he'd lose it and they'd throw it out."

"How's he doing?"

"Well, he seemed all right. They were giving him a water bottle when we left."

"Did you say you have a son up there?" Elspeth said to Mr. Snyder. But he seemed to be staring at her, his mind elsewhere.

"Yes, my nephew Bradley," Cele said. "He's recuperating from an appendectomy."

"Yeah," Mr. Snyder said, coming to himself. "Brad had his appendix out."

"Is he okay?" said Elspeth.

"Yeah, they let him get out of bed and walk a few steps today. We'll be taking him home in a few days."

"How old is he?"

"Ten."

"That woman moaning like that, on and on," said Cele, turning her head, "how can you stand it? She should get a grip on herself. Or they should give her something."

"She's dying," said Elspeth.

Another doctor appeared, a big man, of Dr. Culp's generation, but portly with a buttoned vest rounding on his front. The sunshine reflected on his glasses. "Miss Baker?" he smiled.

"Yes."

"I'm Dr. Plunkett. I'd like to examine the patient, if you folks will just step outside for a minute. It won't take long."

Harriet and Mr. Snyder and his sister backed away, and he closed the curtain.

He put a thermometer in her mouth. He put his hands into her hair and fingered her neck, slowly and carefully. He lifted the gown and pressed fingers into her stomach.

He read the thermometer.

"The lab test shows mononucleosis, and there may be something else. So we'll want to keep you a while—observe you at least a week."

"What do you mean, 'something else'?"

"Well, I wouldn't want to say at this point. Something showed up in one of the tests, and we want to keep a watch on it till we're certain. Nothing to get alarmed about yet at this point. It may be nothing."

61

AT suppertime Elspeth expressed milk from her breasts. She worked with two hands at a time on each breast, bending over the ward's little toilet. It was an unpleasant process at which she had had no practice, and it took long. But she had no choice. If she did not keep emptying her breasts manually lactation would diminish and even cease irrevocably, unless Peter were returned to her fairly soon. The toilet could accommodate only one person, so she left the door ajar and got out frequently to let others use it.

Even after an hour she was not sure it was all expressed.

In the evening she was examined by a Dr. Folts, whom she had not seen before, and before she went to sleep there was another one, a Dr. Drinkwater.

In the morning she expressed milk again. At this hour the toilet was in demand, so after a while she left off. It was reassuring that her supply seemed as abundant as ever. She returned to her area, closed the curtain, and did calisthenics.

But the little elderly nurse stuck her head in. "Now you stop that! You know the doctor said complete rest!"

"I can't even exercise?"

"No. You're not to have any exertion."

Elspeth thought of commenting that she wasn't dead yet. But she got into bed. It was the windows on the other side that got the morning sun. It streamed across. They probably knew what they were talking about—calisthenics lately had winded her more than they used to. And no doubt the mono explained it.

The tall smiling black nurse with the queenly posture came again for a blood sample. "Hi," she said. "Shall we tap the other arm today?"

Again Elspeth looked away from the needle.

"What are they testing for now?" she asked. "Was one of the tests yesterday not clear? Or are they watching the progess of something?"

"Well, it could be either. Or it could be because I got you after breakfast yesterday. Fasting we might get different readings."

"Where's the lady that was crying yesterday? Is she dead?"

"No. Not yet. Her family took her home."

The cherub-faced girl arrived with breakfast as the nurse left. But as Elspeth settled to eat it another two doctors came in and drew the curtain.

"How many doctors are there in this place?" she asked during the examination.

"Oh, a good many."

"What's your name?"

"I'm Dr. Hilliard. And this is Dr. McNulty."

Afterwards she returned to the john to finish expressing milk, but a Dr. Rawlston came looking for her, and before he left he was joined by a Dr. Malouf.

She went to the john when she could, but every so often still another doctor came to see her and she would have to return to her bed and draw the curtain. There was a Dr. Tucker and a Dr. Frenning. But each examination was brief, and milking herself over the sink was such a slow and disagreeable task that she almost welcomed the interruptions.

There was a Dr. Kalyanasundaram, a sprightly little fellow with the complexion and delicate features of southern India.

"How many more have to examine me?" she asked while his fingers pressed her midriff.

"Oh, I think they've all seen you now," Dr. Kalyanasundaram said in his clipped accent. "Your spleen feels good. No complication there. So far so good."

"Do you have everybody examined by the entire staff? You're like about the seventh this morning. And that doesn't count yesterday. What do you guys do? Decide by majority vote whether I'm sick or not?"

"Oh, no, no. Nothing like that."

His fingertips probed behind her jaw and under her ears. She swept the long hair aside for him.

"I mean, if it's only because I'm young and female, well, that's one thing. I just hope it's not because I've got some rare disease nobody can figure out. Dr. Plunkett said the test showed mono and something else besides, and he wouldn't say what."

"I wouldn't worry. When you've got Dr. Culp consulting with Dr. Plunkett you're getting the very best of care."

"And that's what scares me. Why do I need the very best of care? Is there something mysterious in those blood tests besides mono?"

"Personally, I think there's no cause for alarm. But sometimes the body rebels against prolonged fatigue, and registers a protest, and organs behave peculiarly. And till we're certain it's good to be thorough." He closed his satchel. "Cheerio."

"You can leave the curtain open," she said. "So I'll know if the volunteer comes with the library cart."

She lay there. The sunshine had retreated from her bed and was compressed now on flooring and bedding close to the windows opposite.

She knew she hadn't succeeded in emptying her breasts entirely. She should go down there and work on it some more. But it was so tedious.

She saw Mr. Snyder enter the ward. He carried a bundle that could be a bouquet of flowers covered with paper, and wore a wine-colored jacket this time instead of the bright blue.

He approached, smiling.

"Hi," she said. "I thought visiting hours weren't till this afternoon."

"They're not. But I come when I can, and usually nobody stops me."

"I see you've got some flowers for your son."

"They're not for my son. They're for you. What would a boy want with flowers?"

"Me?"

He unwrapped them—small white and yellow daffodils in a green ceramic bowl, which he set upon the bedside table. "You're sick in a hospital. So why shouldn't I bring you flowers?"

He pulled a chair over and sat. He slung an ankle over a knee. His trousers were pressed with a sharp crease.

"Well, that's sweet," she said. "They're very beautiful."

"How are you today?"

"I wish I knew. Sometimes I feel great, and then I get tired. They keep taking blood tests. I'd like to get out of here."

"But at least you're getting some rest. That's the most important thing with mono." He put a cigarette in his mouth and opened a book of matches, but the little elderly nurse told him smoking was not permitted. He stuffed the match back among the others without striking it. He pushed the cigarette slowly back into its pack.

"I'd get more rest at home," said Elspeth.

"Nobody rests at home. Here you're forced to rest."

"No, here I'm forced to work. I have to keep expressing milk to keep the breastfeeding going, because they took my baby away and stuck him upstairs. And it takes all day and it's hard work. Of course I could just drop the breastfeeding. But why should I? He's had five months of it, and I wanted him to have about eight. He likes it, and I like it."

"What's wrong with the baby?"

"Nothing. You saw him up there yesterday. I brought him so I could take care of him and breastfeed. I didn't know they'd separate us."

"So why don't you have him brought down here? They could put a crib next to your bed."

"I did. But it was against their stupid rules."

"You probably didn't talk to the right people."

"Who should I talk to?"

"I'll talk to somebody," he said.

They were silent a while. His persistent gaze began to bother her and she glanced away. He caught her embarrassment and glanced away also, coloring.

"Have you seen your boy today?" she said.

"Not yet. I'll go up there soon. You know, I spoke to your father last night."

"You did? Why?"

"Well, to tell him I'd seen you. I know the whole story, you know. And I know his attitude. I can't say I approve of it. Of his attitude, I mean."

"I don't approve of it either."

"I even know the Blumenthals, as far as that goes. Or I know of them, rather—Mr. Blumenthal's younger brother used to play with my older brother. As kids. We all came out of the same neighborhood in Dorchester. I haven't seen any of them in years and years. But your father I know from the lodge, and from the temple, and from the store. I was in the store last year one day, and you were up on a ladder, and I could see you were obviously pregnant, so naturally I thought you were married. And it was the first time I'd seen you since you were still a kid, really. So I said to your father, 'I see your little girl is a big girl already.' And the way he answered me, I sensed by the way he answered it was out of wedlock. He just said, 'yeah, I know.' Very short, curt. And then a few months ago I saw him at a lodge supper, so I asked how you were doing. And he really let his hair down. The poor guy. I feel for him. He loves you. You're the apple of his eye. And yet it's like he bites off his nose to spite his face."

Elspeth's eyes had watered. "What did he say when you called him last night?"

"Nothing much. He wasn't rude or anything. He listened. But it wasn't like he wanted to talk, so I didn't talk too long."

Elspeth swallowed. "I've been hoping that once he understands his attitude won't make me give up Petey, he'll see it's not tenable to be on the outs forever."

"Yeah, it's not tenable," said Mr. Snyder.

The cherub brought the lunch cart. Mr. Snyder moved his chair to make room for her but showed no inclination to leave. The girl positioned the one-legged table.

Elspeth broke crackers into her soup. "My father finds it very hard to back down, once he's taken a position," she told Mr. Snyder. "He's that kind of a guy. He's got a sister in Texas he hasn't spoken to since my grandmother died. And yet, you know, he can be so nice, so warm. He's so patient with customers. They love him. He'll fix a little kid's bicycle for nothing. And he's good to people who work for him. When Homer's wife was sick Daddy paid for everything. And he used to taxi my grandmother all over the place. I mean my mother's mother. And when my mother's father was sick he'd visit him two and three times a week. And when I was nine years old I asked him for a horse, and he was really gonna buy me a horse. When I saw the horses I got nervous and changed my mind, but he was really gonna get me a horse. He'd have bought me the moon."

"A strange guy," said Mr. Snyder.

"And now he says he's glad none of the grandparents lived to see my brothers die, and me ruin my life. As if it were the same thing. It's not. I'm only nineteen. It's too soon to say my life's ruined. Okay, it would be a lot better for me and a lot better for Petey if I'd had him in a different context. And maybe it's selfish of me to want him. But right now, I think the breastfeeding does him more good than anything. If I ever find I can't provide the right home I'll give him up. And I won't have any trouble finding takers. He's such fun. The way he stretches when he wakes up, just like a little grown-up. And when I laugh, he laughs too. As if he got the joke. And when my arm was broken and sometimes I didn't pick him up right, he'd give me such a dirty look."

She wiped an eye. She resumed eating her soup.

Mr. Snyder remained there, watching her eat.

"Don't you think your son is expecting you?" Elspeth said.

"Oh," he said. "Yeah. I should go up."

"It's nice of you to visit me, but your little boy is up there waiting for you."

At last he rose, unhurriedly. "Well, take care," he said. He left.

After lunch Elspeth went to the john to pump her breasts some more. She worked at it off and on.

The second time she stepped out to let someone use it she met Harriet coming onto the ward.

"Hi. Is it visiting hours already?"

"It's just one o'clock. How are you feeling today?"

"Okay. They gave me something for my throat. Just a little tired, that's all. They keep examining me and taking blood tests. Did you see Petey? Were you upstairs?"

"Not yet. Not since yesterday. Let me sit with you and rest my feet a few minutes, and then I'll go up."

They went to Elspeth's area. Harriet had brought pajamas and slippers and a robe.

"You look sleepy," Harriet said when Elspeth was in bed. "Take a nap if you want. I'll just sit here a while and then I'll go look at the baby. Are those your flowers? Who sent you flowers?"

"Mr. Snyder. He brought them."

"Oh. He called up last night. He talked to Dad."

"I know. What's with him, Mama? He showed up this morning before visiting hours, and before he even went to see his own kid, and brought these flowers, and then he sat and stared at me."

"I guess he's taking an interest."

"But I don't get it. He doesn't know us that well. Who is he anyhow? Doesn't he work in the daytime?"

"He's partners with his brother. I think they make faucets and piping and things like that. I guess it's just a kindhearted interest, because he happened to run into us here. At least I hope it is."

"That's what I mean," said Elspeth. "He's your age. Dad's age."

"Well, he's younger than we are," said Harriet. "I'd say he's a good ten years younger, at least. I think he's younger than his sister and the other brother. But you're right. I can't believe he'd get silly or romantic about a girl your age."

"What is he, divorced?"

"His wife died a couple of years ago, and his sister looks after the children. The sister that was here with him yesterday. I know her from my literary club. I don't think he meant anything by it. What did he talk about?"

"We talked about Dad mostly."

"There, see? He'd probably bring flowers to an elderly lady too. If he were coming to see his son and he knew somebody's old mother was here. He called Dad, which was very thoughful, and then when he came today he looked in on you again. I wouldn't give it another thought. And he probably picked up the flowers at the shop downstairs. Money and gifts are nothing to him."

"Okay. A lot of guys have this tendency to stare. Old guys as much as young guys."

487

"Yes, they do. And you have too much time to think here."

"Mama! Look!"

A crib was squeaking up the aisle, pushed by an aide she hadn't seen before and escorted by the little old nurse, and Peter was in it, raised up on his hands, the little face staring wide-eyed. He caught sight of Elspeth, gave a cry and reached out, falling on his face. The crib turned and steered next to her bed.

"Petey!" said Elspeth, scrambling to lower his rail.

"Shall I change him first?" said Harriet. The nurse retreated with the aide without a word, closing the curtain.

"No! Just give him to me!"

He was still crying angrily as she gathered him in one arm and opened her pajamas with the other. The crying continued as his head reached forward, straining open-mouthed toward the breast. It stopped suddenly with a gurgle as he clamped onto it. He sucked open-eyed a moment, tears still sliding. Then he closed his eyes and nursed quietly, the tiny fingers tickling her.

"His tooth came through. Did you see it, Mama?"

"He's young for a tooth," said Harriet. "You teethed early too."

"He's not so early."

"Now's a good time to wean him. Before he bites you. Especially since they had him on the bottle upstairs."

"Mama, would you ask them if we could have some baby foods? And a spoon?"

"Who should I ask?"

"That short nurse. The older one. She's in charge."

Harriet went out. She returned in a moment with the nurse, who yanked open the curtain a few feet. "We don't have baby foods!" the nurse said irritably. "That's why you should have let him stay upstairs! Where they have all those things." She left, leaving the curtain half open.

When he stopped nursing Elspeth kissed him.

"Open your mouth," she said. "Let's show Grandma your tooth." But he didn't open his eyes. When she put her little finger to his lips he smiled but turned from it, still with closed eyes. "It's just a tiny white line," she told Harriet.

He stared up at Harriet, lying in the crib, while she changed him.

"He has a rash," Harriet said. "On his bottom."

"Naturally," said Elspeth. "They didn't change him enough up there."

The little blond doctor with the plaid jacket appeared at the opening in the curtain. He wore a drooping bowtie. He nodded to Elspeth. "How do you do. I've had the baby sent here to be with you. This is much better, I think, don't you? I couldn't see any sense in his being up there in pediatric. He's not sick. I'm having diapers sent down. And fresh sleepers and bedding. Is there anything else you need?"

"Could you get some baby food?" said Elspeth.

"Surely. No problem. I'll have it sent down. And spoons, and bowls, and bibs. Anything else you need? Juices?"

"Well, a little apple juice. Pears and apricot and tapioca are his favorite baby food."

488

"Pears, apricot, tapioca. And apple juice. I'll tell the nurse to keep it in the refrigerator. I'll see to it personally."

A young male aide appeared with a load of disposable diapers. "Baker?" the aide said. "Where do you want these?"

"In the bottom part of the night table," said Elspeth.

"In the bottom part of the night table," the doctor told the aide. "Miss Baker, if you find you need anything, just ask. We're here to serve you."

"Thanks. Thanks very much."

He nodded. The aide shut the cabinet and turned and rose to leave, and he and the doctor got into each other's way for a moment. They departed. The doctor's heels had metal that clicked on the linoleum.

"Mama, give me Petey. Let me hold him till he falls asleep."

"You should sleep too."

"I will, when he does. He'll fall asleep faster if I hold him."

Peter nestled against Elspeth. Harriet lowered the windowshade.

"That was some switch," said Elspeth. "Would you believe that was the same doctor that was so uptight about rules yesterday? He sent Petey to pediatric. He absolutely refused to let him stay with me. You couldn't talk to him."

"Really? So what changed his mind?"

"Somebody got to him. You heard him. He'd have kissed my ass if I asked him. Mr. Snyder got to somebody, obviously. He said he was going to talk to somebody, but I had no idea he had such clout. What is he? A friend of the director of the hospital or something? Or on the board of trustees?"

"Not that I know of."

"Mama, if you're gonna be here to watch, I want to leave Petey's diaper off for a while. Let the air get to his rash."

She felt herself doze. She was aware, without entirely waking, when Harriet took Peter from her.

She knew she slept long. Sometimes she wakened, sleepier than before, and let herself slide back to sleep. Once she saw Harriet reading a magazine in the changing light, and once the chair was vacant, with only Harriet's thin coat hanging upon it, and once she saw Harriet sitting and dozing.

But at last she came entirely awake.

"Well!" said Harriet. "Good morning in the afternoon. You slept over two and a half hours."

"What time is it?"

"It's after four."

"And Petey's still asleep? That's unusual. He must have gotten tired up there. He'll be awake half the evening."

"The nurse was here, and she has the baby foods and bedding and everything you want."

Elspeth went to the john. As she returned she saw that Harriet had risen and was offering a hand to Mr. Snyder. His sister was with him, and also a girl of twelve or thirteen, with long curls.

"Hello," he said, turning to Elspeth. "This is my daughter, Glory."

He turned to pull over more chairs. Elspeth got into bed. Mr. Snyder's sister sat unsmiling, at the edge of the wide separation in the curtains. Her topcoat was unbuttoned but she did not take it off.

"Glory," Mr. Snyder said, "go fill that water pitcher, and then pour a little in one of those paper cups and water those flowers."

"Mr. Snyder," said Elspeth, "thanks so much for having Petey brought back."

"Yeah. I see they brought him back. Good."

"How did you do it?"

"I put a bug in somebody's ear. I've been generous to this place over the years. So it gives me a certain entree."

"Well, you were just great. They can't do enough for me. I can't thank you enough."

"My pleasure."

"How's your son?"

"Brad? We just came from there. He's fine. Wants to go home. Maybe I'll take him tomorra. Depends what the doctor says."

Dr. Plunkett sauntered up, his thumbs in the pockets of the rounded vest, and smiled down at eveyone. "Good afternoon, folks."

"You want us to get out?" Mr. Snyder asked him.

"No need. Don't disturb yourselves. Miss Baker, we've gone over the lab studies, and I can say definitely it's just mono. Nothing else."

"Oh. That's good. Thanks."

"Now, I hope you're not one of these compulsively busy people that can't rest. Because rest is what you're going to need lots of. We'll want to keep you here another several days. And then when you go home you're going to need about six weeks of complete rest. I want you to really take it easy for a while. Do you work at a job?"

"I just got fired from one."

"Good. I don't want you to take another one for six weeks at least. I'd lay off housework, even. Try to get someone to help you with the baby if you can."

"Doctor, don't you think the breastfeeding takes a lot out of her?" Harriet asked.

"Well, I wouldn't blame it on the breastfeeding," he said. "I'm surprised the milk supply hasn't been affected, but apparently it hasn't. The baby seems healthy enough. I'd leave that up to her for now. Just get lots of liquids." He smiled at Elspeth and turned to go.

"Will the baby catch mono from her?" Harriet asked him.

"It's not as contagious as people think," he said. He turned again to go, but Mr. Snyder's young daughter returned just then with the water pitcher and he nearly bumped into her.

She ducked around him.

"I didn't know you got fired," Harriet said to Elspeth. "You mean Mrs. O'Banion fired you?"

"I'm not too clear on it, actually. I'm not sure if I resigned or if she fired me."

490

"Well, I'm glad you're out of there. I never liked you working there. And I hope you'll pay attention to what he said about rest. I know you. You'll be up running to the laundromat and scrubbing floors. I better come in every day and help you."

"No, Mama, it's a long shlep, and you can't give up everything. I'll see if I can hire somebody to help out."

"Look," Mr. Snyder said. "The baby's looking at Glory."

She had watered the flowers and now rested her arms and chin on the crib rail, looking at Peter. He had wakened and stared up at her. He smiled. She smiled. He laughed. "Isn't he darling!" she exclaimed. He chortled and kicked.

"Who can you hire?" Harriet asked.

"Maybe one of the Chinese ladies," said Elspeth. "In the building. I've got some money saved up."

"The best thing would be to go back to your parents for a while," Mr. Snyder said. "In Winslow."

"I'm afraid Daddy's not ready for that," said Elspeth.

"No," said Harriet. "It wouldn't be good."

"Why not?" said Mr. Snyder. "I can't understand that guy's attitude. How can he turn his back on a child? I'm gonna have a talk with him."

"Phil, keep out of it," his sister told him. "Don't butt in."

"Who's butting in? It's for *his* good too. He's destroying himself. If Glory here ever made a stupid mistake like that and brought home a baby out of wedlock, sure, I'd raise hell, damn right I'd raise hell, but I wouldn't turn my back on my flesh and blood!"

The girl turned crimson, and Peter's face clouded at the change in her expression.

"Phil, shut up!" his sister said. "Don't meddle in other families' affairs. They don't need you to speak for them. Nobody likes a buttinsky." She looked at her watch. "We have to be going. It's late." She rose. "Come on, Gloria. Phil, come on. We'll be in the rush hour as it is."

He rose reluctantly. "Mrs. Baker, can we drop you off? We live in the same town."

"Her name's Harriet," his sister said. "Yes, come with us."

"Well, thank you," said Harriet. "Just wait a second for me to change the baby."

Elspeth waited till their footsteps had faded away. Then she took Peter into bed with her.

She hoped Plunkett had exaggerated the need for rest. How could she buy out Chris without work? How could she even put the deal through without a certain amount of running around?

She should at least ask Harriet to get her some stationery tomorrow, and get a letter off to Chris.

I'm in the hospital, but I expect to be out in a few days. Nothing serious.
My tools are still there in my locked drawer. Also I think I left my transistor
radio on your desk. If you see it please stash it away for safekeeping.
How is Vinnie?

If you are serious about selling, don't accept any offer or option without giving me a chance to make a counter offer.

Or maybe it would be best to come straight to the point.

Dear Chris,

Are you and Vinnie interested in selling Saltmarsh Service? If so, I would like to open discussion on a basis of a firm offer of $190,000. I would put down a small binder immediately, or as soon as terms are agreed upon, passing of papers to take place within three months. I have reason to believe I can get mortgage financing.

Maybe she should even borrow stationery and a stamp from one of the patients tonight.

When the aide brought supper a jar of baby food came with it, along with a bowl and a spoon. But Elspeth nursed him before opening the baby food.

She had not nursed long when Neal McGrath appeared.

"Hi, Neal!"

"Hi. How are you feeling?" He positioned the chair and sat.

"Not bad. But it's a drag. The hives are gone but I've got mono."

"Ah," he said in sympathy. He scratched his beard. Skin eruptions were visible through it. Raveled yarn hung from the hole at his elbow. "Well, I guess things are tough all over. Corky wanted me to tell you she's sorry she hasn't been to see you yet, but she's been working like a dog. Two shifts. Somebody's been out, and she had a chance to make extra money. It really kills her feet." He rested one foot on a second chair. He still wore the big work shoes. His jeans had parted at the seam and white underwear showed. "Well, we all miss ya. Even Cicely Joyce misses ya."

"Are you getting along okay with Joyce?"

He scratched his beard on the other side. "You know how she is. If she didn't have me to kick around, she wouldn't know what to do. She's crazy. There was this girl I didn't feel like screwing, okay? This poor kid that needed shelter, but I didn't feel like screwing her, so I said I had the clap. Just a little white lie, to spare her feelings. After all, I mean, why hurt somebody's feelings? And Cicely Joyce was in the next room and she heard it. And wow, did she hit the ceiling. I didn't even know she was there. I know she's always home at a respectable hour, because the Fawcettface doesn't have a wide enough bed for all night, but I never expected her *that* early. They must have had a falling out. So there's Cicely Joyce screaming like a maniac. She throws the poor girl out, this poor, homeless waif, and then she turns on me and tells me I can't use the bathroom till I bring a letter from a doctor. She wouldn't believe me. I can't sit on the toilet seat until I bring her a letter from a bona fide physician licenced to practice medicine in the Commonwealth of Massachusetts. I said, Cicely, be reasonable. What do you want me to do? Go

492

out in the alley and shit in the barrel? I could get arrested. And she said, it's your problem. I mean, how mean can you get? So I went down the corner to the diner, and they gave me a hard time there too. The crapper's for employees only. So I said, okay. Hire me for five minutes. I won't even charge you."

"So what happened?"

"What happened? I went over to the hospital. Not this one or I'd have been up to see ya last night. The other one's nearer. At least in a hospital they don't holler if you use the shithouse. And then I went to the outpatient and this doctor gave me a letter certifying I'm clean. To whom it may concern. No VD of any kind. They're gonna send me a bill for twenty-five bucks. Try to be kind, try to spare a poor kid's feelings, and look what happens."

Peter had stopped nursing, though his eyes remained closed.

"I think he wants the other tit," said Neal.

Elspeth moved Peter to the other side. He sucked.

"I could look at your tits forever," Neal said.

"Thank you, Neal."

"I mean it. Like if you ever wanted to get married, you know to give the baby a daddy and all that crap, I'd marry you. Anytime."

"Thanks, Neal. That's sweet. I don't think between us we could support a family of three though."

"Well, there's always welfare."

"That's true. There's welfare."

"Or like if you ever want some loving. If you need some affection. I know you've been on a celibacy kick. You had this guy that gave you a kid and then split, and it was a traumatic experience. But when you feel ready to get on the horse and ride again, just give me a signal. I won't let you down. I do it with finesse. I screw like you've never been screwed. With perfect control. I use the slightest, most subtle motions. I can gently, slowly goad you to orgasm so it blows your mind. You'll cream like a flood."

"Thanks, Neal. I'll let you know."

62

ON her third morning on the ward Elspeth slept late. What surprised her was that Peter slept late also. The aide had left breakfast and one of the baby-food jars on the one-legged table without waking her.

She ate her breakfast cold, nursing him at the same time.

"That's a nice Petey. I knew you wouldn't bite me. You wouldn't get high and mighty just because you have a tooth. You wouldn't bite the tit that feeds you."

She had forgotten to get water for Mr. Snyder's daffodils. She poured some of her coffee into them.

The volunteer lady came by with the library cart. Elspeth selected a couple of books.

When she had at last wiped Peter's face she sat playing with him, leaving the books unopened on the table. She kissed the top of his head.

"Some guys think a baby around makes the atmosphere not sexy. I don't know why, Petey. I think you're very sexy."

She stroked his hair. It was longer now, and curled outward above his ears.

Mr. Snyder appeared. Somehow she had known he would stop by this morning.

"Good morning," he said. "Well, the little fella looks fine today. You look better too."

"Hi. Is your son going home today?"

"Yeah. We're taking him home. My sister's up there with him."

The three chairs were still there from the day before and he sat in one. He adjusted the crease in his trousers. His jacket had big checks of tan and creamy white, separated by lines of black. The buttons were knobs of braided leather. His tie had a big knot. His remaining hair was plastered neatly forward over the balding parts. His gaze fixed on her face so long she had to look away.

He cleared his throat. "Look," he said, his hands playing with the black chair-arm that was screwed onto tubing. "I had this idea. Well, when are they gonna discharge you? Monday? Tuesday? So why don't you come to my house, and recuperate there? It's a big house. You'll have your own private room, a big room, you and the baby, with your own private bath, and color TV, and you'll be waited on hand and foot, better than here. My sister'll take care of you. Or if she can't we'll bring in somebody. Don't get me wrong, I don't mean any monkey business. Because my sister will be there, just like a chaperone all the time. And my two kids will be there. Everything strictly on the up and up. All right, all right, I know

494

it sounds peculiar. Let me put my cards on the table completely. Let's say, just supposing, while you're recuperating there, we happen to get to like each other. Okay. My wife died going on two years ago. I'm comfortable, I'm well fixed. Financially you'd never want for a thing, and the baby I'll adopt. He's a gorgeous child, I'll be proud to be his father, and he'll inherit equally with my own children. I'm a good father, I'm the kind of a father that gets down on his hands and knees and plays horsie." He spoke more rapidly, refusing to let her answer. "All right, I'm thirty-nine years old, that seems like an old man to you. But thirty-nine isn't old. I'm very potent. And if you decide no, so okay. No harm done. You recuperate, we shake hands, you go home. No hard feelings—"

She was shaking her head desperately. "Please—" She began to cry.

"Aw," said Mr. Snyder, "now look what I did. I made you cry."

"Oh shit!" she cried out. She struck the bedding with her free hand. She rolled and turned her face from him, hugging Peter, and blubbered. Peter cried in alarm. Elspeth sat up against the pillows and stroked him. She managed to quiet her sobbing. Peter remained nervous.

Mr. Snyder rose. She thought his hand quivered as he lighted a cigarette.

"I'm sorry!" the nurse told him from the aisle. "You can't smoke here! It's bad enough you come in here before visiting time."

He dropped the cigarette to the linoleum and crushed it with his heel.

"Well, I ought to get out of here and let you alone, I guess," he said to Elspeth, "and go up and get Brad. I hate to walk away while you're crying, though."

"That's okay. I'm not crying." It had nearly subsided.

"Look, I apologize—"

"Please," Elspeth, "let's forget the whole thing."

"Do you know why you cried?"

"No."

"All right. I'll tell you why you cried." He sat again. "Because I hurt your feelings, very badly. I didn't mean to, but that's what I did. You were thinking, 'has it come to this? Have I sunk so low, that this bald-headed old gink actually has the nerve to ask me?'"

"You're more than twice my age."

"Yes, I guess that's true. Twice nineteen is thirty-eight, and I'm thirty-nine, so I'm more than twice your age."

"Mr. Snyder, I wouldn't care if you were a hundred, if I loved you. But I don't love you. I know you're a nice, good person, and you've been awful good to me, but I can't love you. I just know I couldn't. Ever. You're just not for me, and I'm not for you. It's not your fault."

"Look, as far as that goes, I knew if you married me you wouldn't love me. I understood that. But I'd be loving you."

"But I don't want that! I don't want a guy to love me when I don't love him."

Her eyes were still wet.

He sighed.

"Well," he said, "okay. Forget about marriage, loving. Like you said, it's out of the question. But move in anyway and recuperate. A month, six weeks, two months, whatever you need. That's all. Be my guest. No marriage, no sex, no nothing. No strings attached. When you're all recuperated, you move out and good-bye. Okay? What are you got to lose?" He cleared his throat.

"What's the point? What would be the point?"

"You get free room and board, that's the point. Television. Use of a car. You need a place to recuperate. That's the point."

"But I'm not gonna marry you. So what's in it for you?"

"What's in it for me? So I'm piling up good deeds in heaven, that don't hurt either, you know. It gives me pleasure. It bugs me that your old man won't let you go home."

She felt a tear slide. "Well, thanks, Mr. Snyder. I appreciate it. But I couldn't. I just couldn't."

He rose, uncertainly. His hands were buried on the pockets on his jacket.

"Well, okay," he said. "I blew it, you know? I shouldn't of mentioned about marriage. Then at least you could have accepted to move in for a few weeks."

"No. I still couldn't have. Thanks all the same."

His whole stance now was ill at ease. His eyes met hers only fleetingly. "Well, okay. Be well. So long."

"So long."

She watched him walk away. He did not look back.

She reached for a tissue.

She lay on her side, face to face with Peter. She listened to the noises of the ward. Someone was snoring. At last Peter broke into a smile.

"Would you like some juice?" the aide asked.

"Yes, please. Just leave it."

After a while she rose and changed Peter's diaper. She drank the juice with a straw. He watched from the crib, raised on his arms.

She took the hairbrush from the night table and settled back into the raised bedding. But there were footsteps, and she looked about to see Mr. Snyder's sister. "Good morning. I have to apologize for my brother. He's such a fool."

"Oh, that's okay."

Miss Snyder sat down. The hollows and lines under her eyes were deep. "I have a pretty good idea what he said to you. So ridiculous. He had a hell of a nerve, bothering you like that. Especially when you're sick in the hospital. He's not bright, you know. He was retarded as a child. I don't know if you knew that."

"No, I didn't know. But it's all right. He didn't do any harm."

"For years they didn't think he'd learn to read. I just wanted to make sure you understood. He's no use in the business. Murray runs the business. We just let Phil sit in a little office with some colored pencils, and he thinks he's working. We never should have let him get married. He drove his poor wife into the grave."

"Well, he really didn't bother me. You don't have to apologize. He meant well, and I'm afraid I kind of hurt his feelings. I tried to say something to soften it but it didn't come out right."

"I'm glad you told him off. And I assure you he'll get over it. Murray and I will send him to Grossinger's or the Concord for a couple of weeks, and he'll find girl friends his own age at the bar, and he'll take them up to his room, and he'll eat, he'll go to the sauna, he'll play a little golf. And he'll forget all about it."

63

ELSPETH had not expected to see Mr. Snyder again, and when Harriet came in the afternoon she said nothing to her about Mr. Snyder's proposal or his sister's visit. Harriet looked after Peter and allowed Elspeth to sleep.

But at the day's end, when Harriet had gone and the aide was clearing the supper dishes onto the wagon, Mr. Snyder appeared once more. He stood near the foot of the bed, unsmiling.

"I'm not gonna bother you," he said. "I just stopped for a minute on the way home from the office."

"Is your son still here?"

"No. I took him home this morning. Listen. I just want to know one thing. After we got Brad in the car Cele went into the building again for something, and I have reason to think maybe she was headed up here. Did she? Did Cele talk to you?"

"Your sister?"

"Yeah. Cele. My sister. Was she here?"

"Yes."

"I figured. All right. I just want you to know Cele's a liar. That's all. Whatever she said, don't take any stock in it. I know she always makes me out to be an imbecile. I repeated the second grade, and I had to go to summer school a few times. So what. I supervise that plant. Murray handles the sales—I run the plant. You know how much there is to know about copper tubing? Sizes, types, grades? Quality? Sources? Cost? I'd like to take you through on a guided tour. Cele doesn't know what goes on there. We tried her on the switchboard, and she didn't last two weeks. Battling with everybody. We had to get rid of her. That's why she never

497

got married. She was engaged once, and the guy broke it off. He couldn't take it. Cele ever talks to you about me, you ask her what she knows about copper tubing."

Elspeth said nothing.

"Well," he said, "okay. Be good."

He turned, and went down the aisle with a rapid gait.

Elspeth slept long and soundly through the night, even though she had napped.

Harriet knew about the proposal when she arrived the next day. Mr. Snyder had phoned Dad again.

"He told us," said Harriet. "And he said you turned him down. And he said he wasn't gonna bother you anymore. But he just wanted us to know he was sincere, and that he meant well. And that if you ever change your mind, the offer still stands."

"I didn't think it was worth mentioning when you were here yesterday. I wasn't exactly flattered."

"I know. I don't blame you. Frankly I'd rather one of the young doctors in this place would fall for you."

"Well, they've all examined me pretty thoroughly."

Harriet sighed.

"Daddy says if you have any sense you'll grab it," she said. "He wanted me to tell you that."

"You're kidding."

"Well," said Harriet, "Daddy says you probably have no idea how big A. I. Snyder and Sons is. He just wants to be sure you know what you're turning down. Mr. Snyder lives in the fanciest part of Winslow."

"Firefly Hill?"

"Yes. On Beaver Dam Road. With a magnificent view. And he's so taken with Petey. Daddy said he couldn't tell who he wants more, you or the baby. He wants to put the baby in his will, equal with his own children. But I agree with you. He's not for you. You could do worse, but it's not for you. Daddy agrees too, it would be no good if you can't love him. He just feels you should at least take the offer to recuperate in Mr. Snyder's house, and see whether you could love him. You have nothing to lose. And not just comdemn him out of hand. Oh, and you know what else? He told Dad that if you went to his house to recuperate, he'd insist that Dad visit there a lot, and stop being on the outs with you, and be a normal grandfather to the baby. And you know what Dad told him? He said in those conditions he'd be glad to. Because it would mean you're on the way to straightening out your life."

"Dad thinks marrying Mr. Snyder would be straightening out my life? It could mean messing up my life hopelessly."

"Well, not that it's Mr. Snyder. Just the idea of being married to someone substantial, who can take good care of you now. But you're right. Money can't buy happiness. That's what I told Dad."

"And what did he say?"

"You know how Dad talks. He said no, it can't, but it buys more of it than poverty does."

"Well, I'm not marrying Mr. Snyder, so let's not talk about him anymore. Okay? And as far as recuperating there, just to provide Dad with a face-saving excuse to call off the feud and meet his grandson, it wouldn't be fair to Mr. Snyder. I wouldn't do that to him. He's too nice a guy. Dad can call off the feud anytime he wants. He can come here. Or he can come to the apartment. Or I'll come home, or to the store. He just has to say the word. *He's* feuding, not me."

Harriet sighed. But she dropped the subject.

Peter wakened. Harriet changed him, and then leaned over the crib rail talking to him. He laughed. Harriet laughed. They laughed together.

When it was time to go Harriet said she would not come tomorrow. It would be Sunday and she ought to spent some time with Dad.

"And you're entitled to a rest too," said Elspeth.

"No, it's not that."

"The long ride every day's been taking a lot out of you," Elspeth said. "I can see it has. And I wish you would take a rest. I'll be okay. Or I'll tell you what. Get Dad to come and visit. Drive in together. It's enough already. I want to see him."

"He wouldn't," said Harriet.

"Tell him I said he's twice as handsome as Mr. Snyder," Elspeth said.

Harriet smiled feebly.

Monday Harriet did not come either. She telephoned, and the nurse allowed Elspeth to come to the phone at the desk just outside the ward. Harriet had shopping and errands to catch up on.

Elspeth visited sometimes about the ward. The other patients were older, but she and Peter made friends among them. Peter would gurgle and wave his arms and seem to thrust himself forward when spoken to. A patient lent Elspeth parts of Sunday's newspaper. However she could not read long without becoming drowsy.

On Tuesday afternoon, almost at the moment of Harriet's arrival, the volunteer lady came by and gave Elspeth a letter from Chris.

> Sorry you are laid up and hope you are O.K. soon. I all ready stuck your
> radio in the desk. I guess the tools are O.K. in the drawer there and you
> have the only key for the bottom so be sure and leave the key when you get
> the tools. Forget about buying our place. If you saw this morning papers
> they are talking about a access ramp to the expressway from Saltmarsh Av.
> We can't do anything till we know how that is going to come out. If they
> take our property by emmanant domaine they will probly give half of what it
> is worth and we will have to fight the state in the courts for two or three
> years but if they loop around us so we are like in the middle we will be in a
> beautiful spot with access like as good as on the high way only better and we
> will probly sell for triple to some big outfit like How. Johnson's.

Elspeth restored the letter to its envelope and put it behind the water pitcher.

"What does Mrs. O'Banion say?" Harriet asked.

"Nothing much."

"Mr. Snyder called up yesterday," said Harriet.

"Again? What's the matter with him? Doesn't he know when to quit?"

"Well, he talked a long time," said Harriet. "To me this time. Dad was in the store. He was really very nice. Sincere. He said he's sorry he hurt your feelings by proposing to you. He didn't meant to hurt your feelings and he's sorry about that."

"Oh, that's okay."

"And he said he doesn't want to be pushy, but in case you ever change your mind about recuperating in his house, he just wants you to know the offer's still open, he means it, you could go there and he wouldn't bother you."

"He's nuts. I couldn't go there."

"Well, that's what I told him. I thanked him, and I said you couldn't impose like that. So he said it's no imposition. And then he told me how it happened that he proposed to you. He said even when you were a little child, if he happened to catch a glimpse of you, like if you were with Dad and me and the boys at the temple, your face would take his breath away. Even when you were ten, or twelve, or thirteen. He never saw anybody so beautiful. You didn't know him, and he wouldn't see you for sometimes a year at a time, but then he'd go into the store and you'd happen to be there, or on Rosh Hashanah the kids would be hanging around outside the temple, and he'd see your face, and his heart would stop beating. His heart would just stop. And once he happened to drive by the store and you were out on the sidewalk, you were maybe fourteen, fifteen, and he was lucky he didn't smash into a telephone pole. And of course he was an older generation, and married already, with children, so he didn't waste time thinking about you. Even after his wife died. Only if he happened to see you, it always did that to him, and your face would be in his head for hours afterward. Even though he had sense enough not to have any intentions toward you. And then he heard that you came home from college pregnant, and he felt badly for you, but he knew you weren't a wild kid, he knew you were serious, and a good student, and so devoted to the baby. How he knew so much I don't know. But I guess everybody in Winslow knew it. And sometimes he'd be with Dad at the lodge, or the temple, or I'd see his sister at the Hadassah or the sisterhood, and I was in their house with the literary circle, but I don't think we ever talked that much. But anyway, when we met last week upstairs on the pediatrics floor, he thought it was beshairt. Do you know the word beshairt? Fated. Destined. He came down here and he saw you, how you have such trouble, and you're all alone. And all night long he thought and he thought. He knew you'd think he was old and funny-looking and bald-headed, and everybody would laugh at him, but he didn't care. He made up his mind that for once in his life he was going to listen to his heart. Regardless. All his life he listened to other people. And now just once he wanted to do what he wants in life. And if you turned him down it wouldn't be because he didn't ask. So the next morning he proposed. His first marriage was very unhappy, you know."

Elspeth's eyes watered. She said nothing.

Peter wakened. Elspeth slid out of bed to get him. "No! Let me," Harriet said. "That's what I'm here for. It's not his feeding time. You're supposed to rest."

Elspeth returned to bed. She watched Harriet cuddle Peter.

"Can I give him the water bottle?" Harriet asked.

"Sure."

Elspeth napped, but not for long. She dozed again and waked, and dozed and waked.

"I'm so sick of this hospital," she said. "Plunkett wants me to stay till Saturday. I'm gonna tell him I want to get out sooner."

"Don't rush it."

"Well, I'm going stir crazy here. And I've got to start looking for a job."

"You can't look for a job. You listen to the doctor. You have to take it easy for four to six weeks."

"Well, at least I'll be out of here. I'll be able to move around. Take Petey to the Public Garden, and the Common."

"I don't know if you can go out to the Public Garden and the Common. You better ask the doctor."

"What do you think I'm gonna do? Sit in the apartment for six weeks? That's not the way to get better, if I go out of my mind."

Corky came onto the ward. Elspeth raised both arms and cried out joyfully, so that the other patients looked her way.

Corky rushed to Elspeth, dodging around Harriet's chair, and they embraced.

"Be careful," said Harriet. "You shouldn't get so close. Mono is contagious."

"Corky won't get mono," said Elspeth. "She's too healthy."

"Forgive me for not having been around," Corky said. "It's been a whole week."

"That's okay. You were working overtime. Neal told me."

"Oh, good, he got here. One girl left, and another was out sick, and they needed me, and besides it was a chance to make some money. I couldn't get away. This is the first chance I've had. And Joyce apologizes too. She's been at the office every night till past visiting hours, and she was gonna get here on the weekend, but then she had a chance to go away. Harrington's company sent him to run a booth at a convention and she went with him. She even took yesterday off. She called in sick—she was really calling from Atlantic City but they thought she was home. But she's gonna come in and see you tonight. Or if not tonight, then tomorrow for sure."

"That's okay. I knew you'd both come when you could."

Corky pulled a chair beside Harriet's. "So how *are* you?"

"I'm okay. Bored. I sleep a lot. That's all there is to do here."

"You need the sleep," said Harriet.

"How's Neal?"

"Neal kind of disappeared," said Corky. "I guess you saw him after I did. It's nothing to worry about—he disappears every so often."

"Where does he go?"

"Who knows? He finds a friend, or he hitchhikes somewhere. He'll be back. When do you get out?"

"As soon as I can. They promised me Saturday. Corky, you were so terrific the night I came in here. The mono's nothing, but the hives were just awful. I couldn't have managed. I'd rather go through childbirth anytime than a case of hives."

"No you wouldn't."

"Seriously. I mean it, Corky. If you ever get pregnant, ask me about natural childbirth. Somebody steered me onto it and it's the best thing anybody ever did for me. Except in your case, you might have twins, and I don't know how it would be with twins. It shouldn't make that much difference, though."

It was time for Peter's feeding. Harriet gave him to Elspeth.

"Why would I have twins?" said Corky.

"Because twins run in families."

"There aren't any twins in my family."

"You and Neal."

"Me and Neal? Where'd you get that idea? He's twenty years old. I'm twenty-three."

Elspeth stroked Peter's head. She could hear his swallowing.

Elspeth told Corky how Peter had been separated from her the first morning here, and how a guy with influence in the place who knew her parents in Winslow had gotten him back. "He's an old fart with two kids, and he wants to marry me."

"Really?"

"That isn't nice," said Harriet.

"Yeah, really. A widower."

"Well, tell him to get lost," said Corky.

"I did. I hope he gets over it. There's something kind of sad about him."

"Tough," said Corky. "We can't go around marrying guys just because we feel sorry for them."

After the nursing Harriet changed Peter. "I have to go now," she said. "Corky, if you're staying maybe you can help Elspeth with the baby, because she's supposed to rest as much as possible."

"Of course. I was gonna stick around a while."

"My mother thinks I'm an invalid," said Elspeth.

"Don't knock mothers," said Corky. "You're a mother yourself."

Elspeth watched Harriet walk down the ward. Corky leaned on the crib rail, watching Peter kick.

"Corky, I've got to rap with you about this guy that wants to marry me. It bothers me. Because in a way it could make a lot of sense."

Corky looked at her.

"He's got money. And he's sort of sweet. I think he'd be nice to me. And he'd be good to Petey. Only what's so horrible is that, well, it's like smashing a girlhood dream."

Corky nodded slowly. She sat. "What's he like, actually?"

"I can't talk to my mother. If she knew I was even thinking of it a teensy bit she'd start telling me to do it. What's he like, well, he's twenty years older than me. Next year I'll be twenty and he'll be forty. Like a father-image routine. Bald like my father, only not quite as bald, and a small guy like my father, only not

502

quite as small, and he even belongs to the same temple as my father, and the same lodge I think. A shrink would have a field day with it. But my father's my father, you know. I don't need another one. I always imagined myself with a beautiful guy my own age, brilliant and terrific, who'd do anything for me, and I'd do anything for him. I don't know, Corky. I've had the thought that I'd start my own business or buy a business, with mortgage money, or a government loan if there is such a thing, and Petey and I would settle down and wait for the right guy. And meanwhile I'd go to school part-time so I'd be where the guys are. Only the reality of it can be a rat race. A constant struggle, with things going wrong every day, and the joker I'll end up marrying three years from now, or five years from now, might be no better than Phil, so what will have been the point? I can get it over with now. And let Petey have a daddy from the beginning."

"You're tired," said Corky.

"I know I'm tired. And I'm afraid in five years I might be a lot tireder. You know, living defiantly, and raising a child alone, and making a million bucks entirely on my own with nobody's help, it appeals to me only so much. There's also a certain amount of Squaresville in me. And it would be nice to be secure and cared for, and be able to do what I want, and start a business or go to school because I want to, not because I need the money and not because I'm looking for a daddy for Petey. I ask myself, if I marry Phil, what actually have I lost? If I marry a guy who's young and handsome now, in fifteen years he'll be bald and middle-aged anyhow, and I'll have forgotten what he looked like young. And anyway love turns sour. It's like the life of a mayfly. I loved Petey's father, or I thought I did, and so what. Maybe true love is just an illusion. If people are still in love after five years of marriage, or after ten years, it's a different kind of love anyhow, from having had kids together and built together. And when I'm thirty-five, and he's fifty-five, and we have seven kids, and I've made his copper company into an international conglomerate, and we've mellowed together, maybe it won't matter then that he was bald when I married him."

"How well do you know him?"

"I don't. But he wants me to move into his house while I'm recuperating, so I can get to know him. And see how I like it. Sort of see how it would be."

"What's wrong with that? Give it a try then, with your fingers crossed, and not expecting much."

"And see how I like his two kids. Because I'd be their stepmother."

"Are the kids with him or their mother?"

"With him. Their mother's dead."

"Maybe they'll resent you. Maybe the kids won't want you, and that'll decide it."

"I know. Or maybe they'll resent Petey. There's a lot of angles."

"How long will he give you for this tryout?"

"As long as I want."

"So what can you lose? Maybe it'll turn out better than you thought, and you'll stay. Or it'll be impossible, and you'll leave. It'll answer itself."

"But if I move in, it means I'm thinking about marrying him. And my parents are gonna hope I do."

"So what, Ellie. You'll stand up to your parents. You always have."

"And if I don't marry him, and move out, he's gonna be awfully hurt."

"From what you tell me, Ellie, this guy wants to get hurt. He's asking for it. So what do you care? You look out for yourself."

"Corky, tell me something, and tell me honestly. Could you ever marry a guy for his money?"

"I suppose not. I mean if it were only for money. If I couldn't stand him, or if I had no feeling for him at all. But put it this way. If I thought the chance I could love a guy was pretty slight, and he was poor, I wouldn't waste my time. But if he was rich, maybe I'd check it out more carefully, and really make sure whether I could love him or not. You kind of consider the whole picture. Ellie, once you're in his house, either he'll grow on you or he'll make you sick. You'll know. How rich is he, anyway?"

"I don't really know. I don't think he's *rich* rich. But I gather he's comfortable enough so that any worries I have won't be financial ones."

"Even if you do marry him, and it turns out after it's a mistake, you can always get divorced."

"I thought of that, but I'm not gonna marry him if I think it's gonna end in divorce. Suppose Petey gets attached to him, and then after five years we break up? I'm gonna be careful, no matter who I marry. Corky, I've lain here day and night, and I've thought and thought. For instance, he doesn't seem like what you'd call an intellectual. And I doubt if he went to college. And then I ask myself, why be a snob about that? If he looks up to me, and hangs on my every word, maybe that's better than two bright people who read all the same books and argue about them and fight about them. Maybe it's not good for people to be too equal. This guy kind of brings out the mother instinct in me in some ways, like he's vulnerable, and I want to protect him. But you're right, Corky. I risk nothing. I could go there and get well. And if it's a bad scene I pack up the valise and the crib and the changing table and good-bye. But if I don't even look, I'll never know. I've gotten kind of curious to see what his house looks like, actually."

"My advice," said Corky, "is take the free vacation. It's like when you browse in a store. You don't see anything you like, and you don't buy, and no sweat. So expect nothing. At worst it'll be good for a few laughs."

64

IN the morning Elspeth telephoned Phil Snyder. The nurse let her use the phone at the desk just outside the ward, and she sat on the desk, her feet dangling. She asked information for A. I. Snyder and Sons. A slipper fell off.

"Phil, I'd like to take you up on your offer to recuperate a while at your place, but without the marriage idea. I definitely don't want to consider getting married or engaged at this time. I don't even want to think about it. Okay? But if you've really got a spare room without inconveniencing anybody, I could use it for a week or two. Maybe a little longer."

"Sure," he said. "Why not? No problem."

"If it goes on any longer than that, I'd want to reimburse for my expenses, like laundry and stuff. And I'd want to borrow your car occasionally. I'd pay for my own gas."

"Those are details. We'll talk about it."

"You're sure I won't be in anybody's way?"

"How can you be in anyone's way? It's a big house."

"And your sister won't mind?"

"Cele? Forget about Cele. *I* own that house. The room's ready any time. I'll send ya a key, and I'll send ya directions how to find your room. Just come when you want."

"I was going to say, I'll be discharged Saturday. Could you pick us up here then and take us over?"

"All right. If I don't make it myself I'll send somebody."

"And I'd like somebody to pick up the crib and changing table and stuff from my apartment. Clothes, and the carriage and things. And some tools and stuff from where I was working. A lot of it can wait, but the crib and changing table and the hamper and the diaper pail, that I'll need immediately."

"Look, when you know just when you're gonna be discharged, you'll call and confirm. Or if I'm not here you'll tell the girl. You'll give her a list. We'll work it out."

He sounded busy.

She walked back towards her bed. She was glad he had taken it so coolly. She wandered nervously about, until the nurse told her to go to her own area and stop traipsing all over the ward.

She lifted Peter from the crib. She sat in the chair with him.

"Petey, someday you're gonna hurt, and know what it is to need what you can't have. The life without sorrow and regret, where things happen right, it just doesn't exist. It's not how the world is."

505

Harriet did not come in. Peter had become the favorite of the ward, and patients stopped by often to gush over him. So did nurses and aides. But despite the attention, and her returning of smiles, Elspeth remained lonely.

After six, when Peter had gone to sleep for the night, her cousin Bob came onto the ward.

She ran to him. "Bob!" She embraced him. "It's so good of you to come over."

"I only just heard you were sick," he said.

"But you're so busy. You didn't have to come. But I'm so glad you did."

He walked back with her, and looked over the crib rail at Peter.

"My little cousin has grown," he said. "When did I see him? It's over two months. And he looks even more like you."

"You always come when he's asleep," said Elspeth. "I wish you'd see him awake sometime."

They sat in the chrome and plastic chairs.

"I spoke to my mother," said Bob, "and she told me you were here. So I called Aunt Harriet and she filled me in. Karen sends regards. She's awfully sorry she couldn't come too. She wanted to. But she's got a term paper on deadline, and her grade for the whole course hangs on it."

"How was the New York trip? Did you meet Karen's parents?"

"Yes. They're beautiful people. I knew they would be."

"Did your car make it okay?"

"Yeah. We broke a fan belt on the way back but it only delayed us an hour. Aunt Harriet told me about this Mr. Snyder. If it's right for you, Ellie, I wish you all the best."

"Bob, I don't know what I'm gonna do about Mr. Snyder. My parents think it's a great idea. I'm gonna live there a while, like sticking my toe in the water to test the temperature. But I'll probably end up running from it."

"Aunt Harriet seems to feel there are all kinds of pros and cons."

"On balance she's for it though," said Elspeth. "She doesn't say so, but it comes through."

"I gathered that."

"Why did I have to get sick?" she said. "If I hadn't gotten sick I wouldn't have met this guy. I'd be out looking for a job. I'd have problems, but I wouldn't have this problem. You know what, Bob? Life is a dirty diaper."

"Well, I guess there are times when no one can advise you. Only you can know how much you want something."

"My teens are gone," said Elspeth. "And my life gets stupider and stupider. And someday I'm gonna die. And I guess the main problem is how to avoid compounding the mess too much more between now and then. Or at least how not to mess it up too hopelessly for those who come after, like Petey. A year ago, a year and a half ago, I thought I loved Jared. Petey's daddy. But given a free choice today, between Jared and someone like Mr. Snyder, I don't know. I don't think I'd take Jared. What's the use of looking for the right person, when we're all so alone, and so separate, that there can't ever be a right person? No matter who you marry, you

506

each still have to live with your own solitude. There's always finally a loneliness—with each person that you can feel very close to, there are always areas where you can't understand each other, where you don't share an interest, where he can't grasp what you mean, see what you see. And it can come as a shock and disillusion, after you've felt so totally unlonely with someone because of what you do share. Maybe it's wrong to think you can have that kind of total sharing with anyone."

He seemed to nod ever so slightly. His eyes were fixed on her gravely.

"Or maybe with you and Karen, it isn't so," she said. "How is it? You seem so beautiful together, so completely sharing. Is there ever that ultimate loneliness? Even for a minute? Or with you and Karen is it not there?"

"It's there. I suppose so. But if people have the same God, then I guess that doesn't matter too much."

"Do two people ever really have the same God?"

He paused before answering. "No and yes. I don't know. I guess even a father isn't the same to any two of his kids. We'll live with our separate lonelinesses, and we'll have long visits, chatting at the fence."

"When there's an infant who needs your breast," said Elspeth, "you think you're sharing. Like when two people have an orgasm together. You think you're sharing, so you're happy. But Petey will grow, and be separate too. He'll go out with girls I can't stand, and he'll move to Australia or someplace. After I've thrown my life away for him. After I've practically been a whore for him."

"Don't resent him, Ellie. Don't ever resent him for the way he's changed your life."

"You're right. If I'm gonna resent him, he'd be better off if I gave him away."

"All these material things that this Mr. Snyder would give your baby, they're important, Ellie. They're not to be sneezed at. Aunt Harriet said he's got a Steinway piano, and shelves and shelves of beautiful books. It made my mouth water. Karen and I know we're never gonna be rich. But we talk about things we'd like to own, and give our kids. We'd love to have a beautiful home. But most of the things, we'll never afford. I just hope between us we'll be able to swing a few of them. Because it's important to have things, good things. But more important than a Steinway piano is being able to play the piano. And better than owning a copy of a book is to know the contents of the book. Better than owning acres is to know all the plants you see when you walk in the woods. It's great if you can afford a season ticket to the Symphony, but what's greater is to be able to sing. I wish I could sing. Karen, and Avis, and the two kid brothers, and their mother and father, they all sing together. Around the table, you know, and it's great. And Karen and I are agreed that of all the things we want to give to our kids, the top priority is skills, and knowledge. Education. That's where we're gonna put the dollars first. There are material things that are good to have if you can, and you shouldn't belittle them. And it means a whole lot to have beautiful surroundings. But education comes way ahead. For our kids' own sake."

"I agree," said Elspeth.

"And along with education," said Bob, "moral education. Because guys with doctorates in chemistry built gas chambers, and graduate nurses led children into them. So much for education, if it's only education. Karen and I are for moral education. You can be poor and on a stringent budget. Or if you're a Mr. Snyder and the best of everything is available, so much the better. But I think either way, if those priorities are kept in order, a kid is gonna turn out okay."

Joyce walked into the ward. Elspeth waved and beckoned.

Bob rose, and put a third chair in place for Joyce.

"Hi, Joyce," said Elspeth. "This is my cousin, Bob Shoemaker. My roommate, Joyce Jencks."

Joyce sat, and crossed her legs. They were in sleek hose. "You must have gotten the mono from Neal."

"Did Neal have mono?"

"Who knows? You can catch anything you want from him. He probably used your toothbrush. He's a carrier of plagues they haven't even invented yet. Think about it, Ellie. If you were some kind of a filthy germ looking for a home, wouldn't you find a home in Neal?"

"Who's Neal?"

"Our other roommate's brother. But I could have gotten it anywhere. Maybe a customer at the gas station. I was overtired."

"Ellie, Neal goes to the john and uses other people's towels. And if there aren't any towels, he'll reach into the hamper and wipe his hands on your clothes."

The aide asked Elspeth if she'd like some juice.

"Yes. And can you bring some for my company?"

The girl took their orders.

Elspeth told Joyce she would move to Mr. Snyder's house on Saturday, and that someone would come to the apartment for her things and the baby's.

"Gee, you mean this is good-bye?"

"No. Chances are I'll be back when it doesn't work out. I'd like to keep sending you the rent every month, if it's okay with you."

"Sure. We'll hold it for you. I hope things work out the way you want, but if it doesn't you're always welcome. Corky said you were playing it kind of cautious."

"Well, I have my doubts. But sometimes I think, this is a guy who can love me an awful lot. I sense it in him. And if he loves me a whole lot, how can I not love him a little? And if one person loves a little, and the other loves a tremendous amount to make up for it, maybe that's sufficient. What do you think, Joyce? Can one love enough for both?"

"I don't know. But like you said, it's bound to stimulate some return. A little bit, anyway. Maybe it'll grow."

"And I really think he'd love me forever. I get the feeling he'd never let me down."

"How do you know?"

"It's just my instinct."

"What's against it then?"

"Just that I don't really like him much. When I think of marrying him I want to cry. I wish I could just keep him in reserve, just in case. I wish I could say, give

508

me three years to see if I can do better, and if I can't do any better I'll marry you."

They sipped their juices. The conversation turned to Joyce's weekend in Atlantic City, and thence to the ocean, and Bob's studies, and the communication systems of porpoises and whales.

Elspeth was sorry to see them go. She walked with them to the end of the ward. "Thanks so much for coming. You really cheered me up. I could kiss you both. Except my mother thinks it spreads mono."

"You're probably past the contagious stage," said Bob.

"In that case I'll kiss you." She raised herself on tiptoe. He backed off, but then bent and let himself be kissed. She kissed and hugged Joyce.

When they had gone she wandered to a window. The sun was low, and hidden by buildings. She could see a shadow lengthen slowly on the tar and gravel of a roof.

Something made her look about. Harriet and Joe were coming toward her.

"Daddy!"

She ran, her bathrobe flying, and buried her face in his neck. She wept. Their arms entwined. It was as though they fitted.

"How are you, sweetheart? How's my little girl?" She could hear the tears in his voice.

"It's so good to see you! Daddy, it's been so long. You don't know how I've missed you."

"I've missed you too, sweetheart."

She looked up and saw that Harriet's face was wet too. "Mother, wake up Petey. He's got to meet his grandpa."

They went toward the crib.

"Bob was just here," Elspeth said to Harriet.

"I know," Harriet said, wiping her eyes. "We met them coming out of the elevator. Bob and Joyce."

At the crib Joe stared down, his hands on the rail.

"I'll wake him," said Elspeth. "I want you to hold him."

"Don't wake him. I'll wait. I waited this long. Don't disturb my grandson. Let him have his beauty rest."

Peter lay on his back, his soft knees up. The gown had worked above his diaper. His face was to the side and his arms were stretched out and limp. A point of hair curled above his forehead. Joe stared fixedly. Elspeth wondered if he would remark on the resemblance to Eric.

"Isn't he beautiful?" she said.

Joe nodded, not taking his eyes from him.

"Wait till you see him awake," said Elspeth. "You'll see how alert he is."

"Of course," said Joe. "Even asleep he looks intelligent. I knew that. Could my little sweetheart have a child that would be less than perfect?"

"He looks like you, Daddy."

"Don't insult the poor kid. He doesn't look like me. He's the image of you. And your mother."

"No, wait till he's awake. One of his expressions is just like you."

At last Joe turned to her, smiling. He sat, and Harriet sat too, wiping her eyes and blowing her nose. "Sweetheart," Joe said. "It's great things I've been hearing."

"Daddy—I didn't say I'd marry him. What did he tell you? I just took his offer to convalesce there. Just a few weeks."

"Just what you said. You haven't made up your mind. That's all right. You're on the right track."

"Daddy, please. I haven't made any decision."

"I understand. You'll go there, you'll convalesce, you'll get to know each other. Phil Snyder's got character. I've known him for years. There's more to him than meets the eye. And thirty-eight, thirty-nine, that isn't so old anymore these days. So his hair's a little thin. I was balder than that when I was twenty-six. I told him to get a toupee. He'd look ten years younger. They make toupees today you'd never know the difference. You should see the room they're putting you in. I was over there. Automatic year-round temperature control, with a private bath, enormous, all ceramic tile, even a Tiffany lamp in the bathroom. And the closet's like a whole room in itself."

Elspeth sat, unsmiling.

"And he's gonna have a phone installed. You'll have your own private line, entirely separate from the family. I'm telling you, he thinks of everything. Sweetheart, what can I say? All I want is for things to come out right for you. That's all I ever wanted. As far as I'm concerned, the sun rises and sets on you. And someday Sawyer's Hardware is gonna be all yours, lock, stock and barrel, whether you need it or not, to do with as you please. You do some God damn stupid asinine things that I can't see the point of. But you're all I've got."

"That's just exactly the way I feel about you, Daddy."

IT was good to wear clothes again, instead of pajamas, gowns, robes. Phil would not let her carry her valise, but she carried Peter. His knit bonnet was tied under his chin. Phil opened the door of the Mercedes and she settled onto the leather seat, Peter on the lap of her jeans.

"Have you picked up the crib and changing table?" she asked.

"Your father went and got them. Everything's at the house."

She lowered the window. Beyond the city the road became fast, and Peter turned his face from the breeze. The forested hills were lush and green.

"I feel better already," she said.

He did not take the route through the center of Winslow but a short cut through Bobolink Acres to Firefly Hill.

It was not till they were ascending the curves of Beaver Dam Road that Phil mentioned the circumcision of Peter that had been set for the following morning.

"What!" she cried out. "Just like that? Without even asking me? The hell you are! Who do you think you are!"

"Your parents didn't tell you? I thought it was all agreeable."

"Tell me what!"

"There were two conditions. The baby gets circumcised. And you understand we only eat kosher here. My house has always been kosher."

"The kosher house is your privilege—it's your house, and your kitchen. But it's not your baby! You've got one hell of a nerve! Phil, I'm furious. Just furious."

But they had arrived. The car turned among trimmed evergreens and stopped before a door of planks, with long hinges extending half across it. The house appeared smaller and less imposing than she had expected. Behind the manicured little shrubs the bricks and stucco rose only one story, and then the black roof sloped away from her.

Phil took the valise. He unlocked the plank door. It creaked. Elspeth carried Peter silently.

She stepped onto stone tiles in a foyer that was not so much a foyer as a balcony. Before her was a railing, and from it she looked down into a vast living room. To her left a staircase curved downward from the foyer to the living-room floor, the depth of a generous entire story below her. The chandeliers out there, hanging in space, were at the level of her feet. The heavy chains that held them soared high above her and straight into the height of a beamed cathedral ceiling. At the end of the living room to her left, the wall had a big stone fireplace and chimney in its center. One corner was taken by the descending staircase, but the further corner had a door with a little window in it, to the outside, down there at the level of the living-room floor. Evidently the house was built down a slope, and she had entered at the highest story. At the end of the living room to her right, there was an archway centered in the wall, directly opposite the fireplace. Over the archway, a story higher in the same wall, was another opening, with a railing, forming a gallery with no staircase.

"Come on," he said. "Come on."

To the right the foyer-balcony led into a corridor as a wall closed it off from the living room. When the corridor turned sharply left he went no further but opened a door directly ahead.

"Your room," he said. "Make yourself comfortable. You'll find all your own stuff in the drawers. I'll be back in a little while."

"Yes. We're gonna have to have a talk."

She closed the door behind her. Peter's own crib, even with its cow-jumped-

511

over-the-moon mobile, was over there beside the ruffled four-poster. She took him into her bathroom and recognized her changing table, her diaper pail, her hamper.

She swung her shoulder bag off and took a diaper from it.

There was indeed a Tiffany lamp, a smallish one, shaped like a blossom, and green like the square tiles of the walls. The tub, the toilet and sink were of paler green.

When Peter was in his crib she stretched out on the bed, still in the jeans and flannel shirt she had worn from the hospital. She stared up at the bed's canopy.

There was a knock. "Are you decent?" said Phil's voice.

"I'm decent." She sat up, her feet to the floor, as the door opened. Cele, holding a tray, and the two children trooped in behind Phil. A spaniel followed them. "But I can't speak for the decency of anyone else."

"I don't know if you want anything or not," said Cele. "I'll just set this down here." The tray had a cup and saucer with matching teapot, creamer and sugar bowl, and a plate of little sandwiches.

"Don't get up," said Phil. "This is Brad. I think you met Glory when you were in the hospital."

"And this is Muttsy," said Gloria, indicating the floppy-eared spaniel. "Can I see Peter?" She rested her arms and chin on the crib rail and the mobile jiggled. "I love him."

"How are you feeling, Brad?" said Elspeth.

"Okay." He was dark-haired, unsmiling. He was younger than Gloria, perhaps ten or eleven.

"Have they taken your stitches out yet?"

"Nope."

"Then I guess you still have to take things easy for a while."

"Yup. Are you gonna be our new mother?"

"Don't count on it," she said.

"Nothing's decided," Phil told him. "I told you kids not to discuss that. Absolutely nothing's decided. Now you said hello, and I think everybody should go downstairs and leave Elspeth alone. She wants to rest."

"Yes, come on, children," said Cele.

Cele herded them out, but Phil remained. "I have to talk to Elspeth. I'll be down in a few minutes," he said. The two chairs had oval backs upholstered in quilted velvet and cabriole legs of polished wood. He sat. Elspeth remained sitting on the bed.

"You didn't know about the bris?" he said.

"Of course I didn't know. When I called your office and asked you if I could come here, all you said was 'no problem, no problem.' And then we talked about picking up my stuff."

"But I talked to your parents after. You don't know? I can't understand it."

"A thing like that you talk about to me. To the mother. Not to the grandparents behind my back."

"Listen, I was in a hurry when you called. And I didn't know then the baby wasn't circumcised. That was it—I didn't know. How was I supposed to know a

512

thing like that? Then later, I was talking with your parents, that evening, or that afternoon, I don't know just when, they mentioned the baby was never circumcised. So I said okay, I'll be glad to make the bris. I tried to call you. About the bris, and I also wanted to explain there's some things you can't get to eat here, we're kosher. I tried to phone, but they wouldn't put it through. You didn't have a phone and they told me they don't call a patient from the wards. Only in private rooms, if they have a phone. So I talked to your parents. I was on the phone with them two, three times a day. I thought you knew. They sounded like everything was wonderful. I invited a hundred people. I called the mohel. One mohel was busy, he found me another. I ordered the food. I brought in a case of Scotch. You haven't been in touch with your parents since you called me? I can't believe it."

"Oh, I've been in touch all right. My father and mother came in that same evening. And then my mother came in again."

"And she didn't talk about the bris?"

"Not a word."

"I don't understand it." He shook his head.

She had the feeling he was telling the truth.

"All right," he said. "You should have known. But now it's arranged. Is there anything wrong with it? You certainly don't object to the baby being circumcised. I assumed you just didn't get around to it yet, a girl all alone, your hands full—"

"It's not a matter of objecting to it. Or of being dead set against it. It's just that I never saw any need of it. I never even had my ears pierced."

He stroked his chin.

"Listen," he said, "it's something that really ought to be done. There's all kinds of health reasons. It's cleaner. It prevents cervical cancer. When a woman has a husband that's circumcised, she doesn't get cancer of the cervix."

"I think that's been disputed," said Elspeth.

"It doesn't make a boy any less virile, you know."

"I didn't say it did."

"A foreskin's no good anyway. Who needs it? He'll never miss it."

"Phil, if boys aren't supposed to have them, why are they born with them?"

He stroked his chin again. "That I don't know. I don't know. Well, what do you want to do?"

Elspeth sighed. "I don't know. It's a mess. If you don't mind, I'd like you to leave me alone for a while. I want to think."

He rose. "Okay. If you want anything holler. Or pick up the phone there. That's a separate number, in case you want to call out privately. It was just put in. So if you want to reach us downstairs just dial my number. It's on the pad there. And my phones will ring all over the house."

"Thanks."

He left, shutting the door. She lay down.

The canopy over her was not flat. It rose in a curving arch.

She didn't notice her little transistor radio until she knocked it over reaching for the beige trimline telephone. In these surroundings it looked old and grubby.

She dialed Harriet.

Harriet spoke cheerfully. "How do you like it there? Isn't it a beautiful place?"

"I've got half a mind to call a taxi and leave."

"What?"

"Mama, do you have Bob's phone number? Or can you call Aunt Frieda and get it?"

"I'll call Frieda. I don't have it. What's the matter?"

"Okay. Call Aunt Frieda and call me back. And Mama, listen. Why didn't you tell me about the bris?"

"I meant to. I guess with everything going on it slipped my mind."

Elspeth didn't answer.

"I thought you knew," Harriet said.

"No you didn't. You were afraid I wouldn't come here. Mama, it's just a little high-handed, and I don't like it."

This time Harriet said nothing.

"All right," said Elspeth. "See if you can get Bob's number." She gave her own number to Harriet.

She reached, lying on the ruffled pillows, and hung up the phone. She raised a knee and scratched the bottom of a sock.

Within five minutes by the digital clock Harriet called back.

"Frieda says it's no use trying to phone him before sundown, because it's Saturday and he won't answer the telephone. And he's probably at his girl friend's anyway, and they won't answer the phone there either. They're all very religious."

"I know. When's sundown?"

"Oh, late. Eight? Eight-thirty? The days are getting so long now."

Harriet gave her both numbers. She wrote them on the pad, below Phil's.

At last she looked through the drawers. There were clothes not only from the apartment but from home too. There were even new things for Peter she had not seen before.

She took a shower in the green tub.

She lay on the bed naked and tried some calisthenics, lifting her legs slowly to vertical. Then she dozed until Peter wakened.

At six o'clock she fed him. She was finishing when the phone rang. It was Joe.

"I just got home from the store. What's this trouble you're making about the bris? Don't you know everybody has it done? Every Cabot, every Lowell is circumcised today. Even goyim, the high-class ones. Homer is circumcised."

"Dad, you knew Phil was planning this. He's invited like a hundred people for tomorrow."

"He mentioned it, yes."

"Why didn't you tell me? Why didn't Mama tell me?"

"Why didn't I tell you? I've been running around like crazy. As soon as I closed last night I grabbed a bite and went down to Chinatown there to pick up your stuff. What's your objection? You think it'll make him less virile? Look at the Israeli army. The bravest fighting men in the world. Five countries came in to wipe them out and they beat them back. What more do you want? That proves it, doesn't it? And there's no way Phil Snyder would adopt a kid that's not circumcised. No way. He takes his religion seriously."

"Dad, I don't want to discuss it."

"We'll come over and pay you a visit."

"I'd rather you didn't. I'm tired, and I'd like to rest up."

"You're not gonna call it off?"

"I haven't decided. I have to give it some thought."

"He's invited—"

"I know."

As soon as she hung up it rang again. It was Cele, asking if she would be down for supper or if she wanted something brought up.

She put on fresh jeans, and picked up Peter. She knew there must be another way down, a backstairs, and she looked for it. She took the corridor to the right. It led across the stairless gallery, giving her another view of the living room. She found more bedrooms, a spacious master bathroom in which stood a tall physician's scale, and a laundry room. From the laundry room a spiral stair twisted down to the kitchen.

The family was already at the table. Behind nearly closed drapes she could make out the floor-to-ceiling glass and a deck beyond.

She held Peter while she ate.

"Would you like me to warm up some of the baby food?" said Cele.

"Can I feed him?" Gloria asked.

"Thanks, but I don't think he'd eat. I just now nursed him. And he'd be going to sleep for the night about now, except his nap was late."

Cele kept chattering about the bris arrangements. Phil seemed uncomfortably silent. Cele had had a fight with the accommodator. The price of whitefish had jumped. She talked of who had said they would come and who had said they wouldn't. She had never heard of this mohel they were having. The regular one was all booked up.

"I remember your bris," Gloria said to Bradley.

"You couldn't possibly," said Bradley. "You were only two years old."

After supper Elspeth returned to her room. She cuddled Peter till he fell asleep. She waited till dark to phone Bob. She tried the Kramers' number first. Avis answered.

"Ellie!" said Avis. "Hi! I've heard the news. And I hope things work out the way you want."

"Thanks. Is my cousin there, by any chance?"

"He certainly is."

Bob came to the phone.

"Bob," Elspeth said, "they're planning a bris for Petey, tomorrow morning."

"A bris? You mean he was never circumcised?"

"No, he wasn't."

"Well, I'll be there. Terrific. What time? And where?"

515

"Here at Phil's, at eleven. But that's not the point. I'm just not sure if I want it. But they've sprung it on me and I'm trying to think it through. I thought if anybody could make sense of it for me, or justify it for me, you could."

"Well, as you know, it's a commandment. The sign of the covenant between God and Israel."

"But is any explanation given? Any reason for it? Why not a sign tattooed on the chest? Why not a ring in the nose? Is there anything rational in it? Any practical reason?"

"Well, the Bible doesn't offer any, if that's what you mean. It's just a commandment. Of course all kinds of reasons have been offered since."

"Health and all that," said Elspeth. "Spock says do it to infants because in case a guy needs it when he's older it might be traumatic. But why assume he's gonna need it? Why not take out every baby's tonsils and appendix?"

"I don't know, Ellie. I don't know that much about it. Everybody seems to do it these days, whether they're Jewish or not, so it must have something going for it. Even the guys in the porno flicks are circumcised. Have you been to the movies lately? Look, I'm no doctor. But I've never heard anything against it. I've never heard a reason not to do it. Have you? Do you know a reason not to?"

"No. But I like him the way he is. I love his little cock."

"Well, the guy's not gonna cut it off, you know. He'll just make it more interesting. You'll see."

"Bob, I don't know how to say it. It's just that I want all of him."

"Maybe it won't diminish him. Maybe it'll add something. A spiritual dimension. Ellie, I'm not an expert but my feeling is that if you don't have it done you're doing him a disservice. A Jewish boy that isn't circumcised is an oddball. Look, I don't know what path he'll choose in life, or whether he'll turn his back on the whole tradition, or in what way he'll relate to it, but in some way, at some time or other, he'll have to come to terms with the fact that he came from Jews. So at least let him come from it normally, instead of as a freak. Suppose some summer he goes to a Jewish camp, and he's the only kid there who's not circumcised? He'll never forget it. Suppose he takes swimming at Harvard or MIT, and they're all in the nude. Either he'll have to pretend he's not a Jew, or else get awfully tired of being a conversation piece."

They were both silent. She heard the Kramers' stereo, and the voice of their little boy.

"Do these mohels know what they're doing?" she asked. "Should I get a surgeon?"

"The mohels are okay."

"Do they ever goof?"

"They don't goof. Who's the mohel?"

"I think his name is Castle."

"I know Castle. He's excellent. A brilliant guy. A chemist. He's a metallurgist."

"You mean he's not even a mohel full-time? When he's a mohel he's moonlighting?"

"I guess you could say that, but he's expert, Ellie. Everybody calls him. There's only about four in the whole state."

She could hear Avis's voice behind Bob, as though from across the room.

"Avis says tell you you don't have to worry about Castle," Bob said.

"I heard."

"Ellie, I'll call Castle, and maybe we'll come together in one car. And I'll introduce you to him."

Elspeth sighed. "Bob, if this guy goofs, or misses, or screws up, if he does any damage, I'll slit his throat. I promise you. I swear."

"He won't goof—"

"Do they use anesthesia?"

"No."

"No? Doesn't it hurt?"

"Well, the baby generally cries, but not all that much. Haven't you ever been to a bris?"

"Not that I remember. I don't think so."

"Well, I'd say he might cry for a minute or so. I never saw one really carry on. I'd say I've seen kids cry harder about just about anything else. I'll see you in the morning, Ellie. Karen'll be there. And Avis and Steve will try, but they don't know if they can. They have another commitment."

"Don't tell me somebody invited you. Did you know about this?"

"Of course not. But you don't need an invitation to go to a bris. It's a mitzvah."

Elspeth remained in her room for the rest of the evening. It was tiresome with nothing to do or to read. She thought of going down to browse in the living-room bookshelves. But then she would have to engage in conversation with some member of the family or other, and it was not worth it.

She reached for the remote-control switch, between the digital clock and the phone, and turned on the television. Every channel was insipid. Saturday-night fare. She shut it off. She studied the wallpaper. It was beige, and its rough surface seemed to consist of real grasses or reeds, woven together.

She recalled Dr. Goldwasser's having said to her that mohels did it better than surgeons because they specialized.

She thought of phoning Cindy Schaeffer.

She thought of phoning Corky McGrath.

But she didn't.

517

66

IN the morning Elspeth slept again after Peter's feeding. When she next awoke he was raised on his hands beside her, gurgling his repertoire of syllables.

There was a knock, and then Cele's voice. "Would you like some breakfast sent up?"

Elspeth went down to the kitchen in sweater and skirt. She had juice, coffee, rolls and cheese. The accommodator and his helper were already carrying cartons in and going back and forth to the dining room under Cele's supervision.

"He needs a highchair," Phil said, looking at Peter.

"I know, he's about ready," said Elspeth. "I'm gonna get him one."

"We've got our old one put away somewhere," said Gloria.

"No, I think we gave it to someone," Phil said.

"Am I supposed to greet the guests as they arrive?" Elspeth asked.

"No, actually you're supposed to come down with the baby and make a grand entrance. After everyone's here."

"Okay, that's good. I'd rather wait upstairs. But when my cousin Bob Shoemaker comes, send him right to my room. Okay?"

"Okay."

"Will you know him?" she asked.

"He'll introduce himself."

Her bedroom was on the front side of the house, and looked out on the shrubs and the driveway and Beaver Dam Road. But she had adjusted the blinds for privacy and avoided the window. Sometimes she heard a car, and then the door chime and the creak of the iron hinges and the arrival of guests in the balcony-foyer, not far from her room. But more often the cars she heard on the drive-way seemed to continue past. Apparently most of the guests parked down the slope at the other end of the house, and entered on the level of the living-room floor.

But at last she was certain she heard Bob and Karen in the corridor. "Come in!" she said.

The door opened. "Hi, Ellie," said Bob. "This is Joshua Castle."

"How do you do." She was surprised by the mohel's youth and sinewy good looks. He seemed in his mid-twenties, as tall as Bob or taller, and wore a well-cut suit of summery cord. There was a fringe of beard about the line of his jaw.

"Cozy little place Mr. Snyder has," said Bob.

"That living room!" said Karen, sitting on one of the oval-backed chairs. "I never saw anything like it! It's fabulous!"

"That baby's fabulous," said Castle. "He's beautiful. You didn't exaggerate."

"Mr. Castle," said Elspeth, and leaned on one of the bedposts, holding Peter, "I want to ask you some things."

"Call me Josh. Or Joshua. We're among friends."

"All right, Josh. Where did you learn to do circumcisions?"

"I was taught. By another mohel."

"Are you licensed?"

"Licensed?"

"Don't you have to have a license? Can't they arrest you for practicing medicine without a license?"

"I never heard of it. Maybe there are states where they have a license requirement. But not to my knowledge."

"How often do you do one of these?"

"It varies, naturally. Sometimes as many as three or four in a week. I have another one this afternoon, in Marblehead."

"How many have you done?"

"If you want an exact count, a hundred and sixty-four."

"Where are your instruments?"

"Downstairs. Miss Snyder's boiling water so I can sterilize them."

"What do you use? What kind of instruments?"

"Special instruments."

"Do you have children? Are you married?"

"My son is just about the age of yours. My two older ones are girls."

"And you circumcised your own son? You did it yourself?"

"Of course. On the eighth day of his life."

"You know, Petey's not eight days old. He's going on six months. He's a lot bigger."

"I know. I've done delayed cases."

"Ellie," said Bob, "if I had a child I'd trust this man with him. I've seen him operate."

"Did you ever make a mistake?" Elspeth asked Castle. "On any of those hundred and sixty-four babies?"

"No."

"Never?"

"No."

"Petey can't afford to be your first mistake."

"I understand."

"If you mess up, if your hand slips, you'll never sleep with a woman again. I'll grab a knife and fix you good."

He looked at her silently.

"So don't forget," she said. "I'm serious. I mean that. You'll be castrated on the spot."

"All right. Can I ask some questions now?"

"Like what?"

"What will your son's Hebrew name be?"

"I don't know. Does he need one?"

"We'll be giving him his name. Is he named after someone?"

"He's named after himself."

"Well, a lot of people like to keep the same initial. Although you don't have to. How about Pinchas?"

"What?"

"Pinchas. Phineas, in other words."

"You're kidding. Phineas yourself. Your father's mustache."

"Well, do you like Pesach? Peretz?"

"I like Peretz, Ellie," Karen said. "He was one of the recurring cases of the younger displacing the elder. And an ancestor of David. And hence eventually of the Messiah."

"Okay," said Elspeth.

"And Peretz was also out of wedlock," said Karen.

"Fine," said Elspeth. "It's Peretz."

"It means Breakthrough, actually," said Karen.

"And we'll need his father's Hebrew name," said Castle.

"Jared? I don't know if he has any."

"If he had a bris, or a bar mitzvah," said Bob, "they must have used a name."

"I have no idea," said Elspeth.

"Yered, that's Hebrew itself actually," said Castle, "but it probably isn't that. Nobody uses it. He's probably Yehudah. Yaakov. Yisroel. It could be anything. Yeshayahu. Yosef. Is there any way you could phone him and ask him?"

"I wouldn't phone him. And what if Phil adopts him later? Won't he get Phil's name?"

"No. He keeps the name and status of the natural father."

"I don't care, I'm not phoning him. He probably wouldn't know anyway."

"Maybe his parents would know?"

"I don't want to talk to them. Forget it."

"Okay," Castle said, "so we'll use the mother's name. Do you know your name?"

"Esther, I think. You better ask my parents."

Bob went out.

"Uncle Joe," they heard him say, apparently from the gallery. "Or Aunt Harriet. Could either of you come up for a minute?"

Elspeth recognized her father's tread on the staircase. Presently he came into the room, with Bob.

"Is my Hebrew name Esther?"

"That's right. Esther. For my mother's mother. She was a beautiful woman."

"So he's Peretz ben Esther," said Castle. "You're still gonna have to query the father's family at some point though, and find out if he's a Kohen or a Levi or not. Are you a Kohen or a Levi, Mr. Baker?"

"No."

"A firstborn has to be bought back from the priests," Karen said to Elspeth.

"Unless he's descended from priests himself. And he'll have to know for himself later anyhow."

"I know what a Kohen and a Levi are," said Elspeth. "And if Jared Blumenthal is of the tribe of the priests I'm a Chinaman."

"Okay, I think we've covered all bases," said Castle. "Maybe we should get started."

"Don't forget what I said before," Elspeth said to him.

"How could I ever forget? Wait here with Peretz, and someone will call you when we're ready."

"What did she say before?" Joe asked.

"It's personal," said Castle. "Come on. Let's go."

"I'll stay with Ellie," said Karen.

The others left.

Elspeth sat on the other chair. Peter was on her lap. The door had been left open. A steady hubbub wafted from downstairs.

"How many people are down there?" said Elspeth.

"Lots," said Karen.

"I'm nervous."

"I know."

"I don't know how I got into this. Have you been at these things before?"

"Many times," said Karen. "As far back as I can remember."

"Even when you were a kid?"

"Of course. It's a joyous occasion, Ellie."

"Maybe. If you're not the one it's being done to. How well do you know this guy?"

"Pretty well. Lots of my friends have had him."

"Did he do Avis's boy?"

"No. They lived in New York then. They came to Massachusetts just after."

Elspeth began singing to Peter quietly.

Bob called to them. Through the open door they saw him across the foyer at the head of the stairs. They rose and he went down again.

Elspeth descended slowly, holding Peter, Karen beside her. Peter stared down at the mob of faces. They were a blur to her, but she heard the hushed murmurs of approval for herself and Peter.

As she got to the bottom step a couple of Hebrew words were exclaimed loudly by several of the men and a couple of the women, more or less in unison.

She was guided through the crowd toward the archway that was directly under the other gallery. A small table, apparently a folding card table, had been set up there with a white cloth over it. Castle was in a white cotton surgeon's smock now, and a blanket-size prayer shawl of off-white wool, corner tassels and black-stripe bordering and all, was draped over the smock. The front drapings had been drawn under his arms and tied together over the back drapings, apparently to make sure they could not get in the way of his hands. A chair had been pulled nearby and Joe was sitting in it. Someone lifted Peter from Elspeth and gave him to Joe. He stared up at Joe with large-eyed concentration. Joe smiled. Castle began singing and swaying, his draped shoulders turning this way and that. Bob had a book and Bob and Karen joined in with responses, Karen rather musically, but Castle sang from memory in a strong tenor, his face raised, his eyes closed. Mostly everyone else seemed in Phil's age group, except Gloria and Bradley, who had worked their way to a front position at a side of the little table.

Elspeth insinuated herself between the pressing spectators, and took a big pointed knife from a bread tray on the huge dining table laden with food. She squeezed back to the side of the little card table, opposite Gloria and Bradley, just as someone undiapered Peter upon it. He cried. Castle's eyes moved to Elspeth. He was pulling rubber surgical gloves on. "I didn't touch him yet," he said to her.

She saw the instruments, about five pieces of gleaming steel, that lay near her on a cloth. A strange flat slotted piece, a little scissors, a bigger scissors, a scalpel, a probe.

Castle's hands opened a brandy bottle and dipped a length of thickly folded gauze bandage into it briefly. The wet strip was laid upon Peter, an end of it between his lips. Peter stopped crying and sucked. Now Castle's hands moved busily with disinfectants. Elspeth allowed the point of the knife to tilt toward Castle's groin. She moved nearer to him. Her thumb fondled the cutting edge. She saw Castle's eyes go to it.

"Ellie, put down that knife," Karen said quietly beside her. "You're making him nervous."

"She's not making me nervous," Castle muttered. "Let her be."

She saw that the slotted flat piece was a kind of clamp. Across the little table Gloria winced and grimaced, putting fingers to her face.

The glans oozed all over in a color darker than blood. Peter cried again. Elspeth felt herself quiver and her eyes filled. Castle resoaked the end of bandage and returned it to Peter's lips. Again Peter stopped crying. He sucked the cloth with eyes open, seeming to concentrate on the taste. Castle's hands moved quickly. Blood spread in cotton wads and gauze. At last Castle smiled and lifted Peter high for everyone to see. He was bandaged, and still sucked the cloth that dangled from his mouth.

Castle lowered him, pulled off the gloves and diapered him. He filled a silver goblet with wine and sang prayers, again with Karen and Bob joining. He took the brandy-soaked strip from Peter and gave him a wine-soaked one, which he seemed to enjoy as much.

"Get the baby's apple juice," Cele said to Gloria. "The little bottle with the nipple in the kitchen." Elspeth laid down the knife. She felt wilted. Castle had produced a tube of ointment from his black satchel and was telling her how to use it. Karen and Bob, on each side of her, began to sing a handclapping song in a fast rhythm, dancing with it. Cele was holding Peter, patting his back, and he seemed to take to her readily enough. She saw Phil pouring whisky. He took a yarmulka from his pocket and gave it to a man who had none. Castle joined Karen and Bob, singing, dancing, handclapping, his tenor harmonizing with Karen's soprano. Elspeth knew none of the words except mazal tov, which occurred over

522

and over. Harriet appeared and embraced her, smiling with tears. "Come and have something to eat," Harriet said.

Elspeth let herself be led into the jabbering throng around the buffet. Cheeses, black bread, white bread, whitefish, lox, carp, vegetables, egg salad, tuna salad, olives, kumquats, pastries. "Brad!" said Cele. "Don't grab!" A tall coffeemaker bubbled, and a carafe over a flame steamed with water for tea. Elspeth took an olive. Green and orange sherbet floated in red punch. She ladled a cupful. She was not hungry. She turned to look for Peter. She saw Phil sitting in the middle of one of the living-room sofas feeding Peter his apple juice, smiling as though he owned him, Joe on one side and Gloria on the other. Peter sucked the nipple, his eyes turning from Phil to Gloria and back to Phil. Joe smoked a cigar, his eyes on Peter. The spaniel lay on Gloria's feet.

"Uncle Murray!" Bradley said, over at the stairs now. "You missed the whole thing! It's all over!"

The man was coming down the staircase from the upper foyer, with a little woman. He had a full head of hair, bulging at the sides, bushy and grizzled. His glasses had heavy black rims. "Phil!" he called across. "I hear you like 'em young! Ha ha! Nice work if you can get it. Where is she? I want to look her over."

As Murray got to the bottom Bradley indicated Elspeth. Murray adjusted his glasses.

"Hey, not bad. Not bad at all. Phil, I have to hand it to ya."

He sauntered over to Elspeth. His little wife was beady-eyed, with a cynical mouth, and hair pulled tight.

"My name's Murray Snyder. Phil's brother. This is my wife, Sheila. So you're Elspeth. Well! You're really something. You know? He wasn't kidding. I have to hand it to him. I didn't know he had it in him. Isn't she a knockout, Sheila? Like a teenage kid."

"I *am* a teenage kid," said Elspeth.

"Yeah, yeah, but such a figure. A small little waistline like that? How do you do it? You had a kid after all."

"Breastfeeding does it," she said.

"Breastfeeding?" said Murray. "You mean the kid sucking up there makes like a vacuum, and pulls the stomach in down there? Naw. You're putting me on."

"I'm not putting you on. It stimulates a hormone."

"A hormone," he marveled. "It's remarkable, the things they got these days."

"Happy bris day to you—" Phil sang over on the sofa. Gloria joined in with him. "Happy bris day to you! Happy bris day dear Peter, happy bris day to you!"

67

PETER had learned to chew with his gums, though he still had only the two teeth. Gloria would sit by the highchair that Phil had bought, breaking up arrowroot crackers, and Peter would press forward and open his mouth tall for each piece. His eyes never left the plate or her fingers. Now and then while he chewed Gloria would toss a piece to the spaniel that sat up begging at her feet.

Directly after school, she would ask Elspeth if Petey was up from his nap yet, and Elspeth would let her take him out for an hour or two in the pram. She had told the neighborhood kids that Peter was her new little brother.

"Glory, you had no business telling them a thing like that," Phil told her at supper. "What did I tell you? That's terrible."

"I was only pretending."

Gloria seemed to spend every minute she could with Elspeth or Peter or both. She would diaper Peter, hold him, dance him from side to side upon her knees as she had seen Elspeth do, and sang him the same ditties she heard Elspeth sing.

> "Pickety pockety punka poo,
> Pickety pockety punka poo—"

Even if she brought her girl friend, who had braces on her teeth, their play was to change Peter's diapers, or wheel him in the pram, or take turns dancing him on their laps and making him laugh.

> "Petey got two teet,
> Petey got two teet—"

"Do you make up those songs?" the girl with braces asked.

"Elspeth makes them up," said Gloria.

"He's so darling," the girl with braces said. "The way he keeps looking you over and studying you when you're diapering him. So serious. As if he's deciding whether to give you a recommendation."

They would watch Elspeth breastfeed, silently, respectfully.

"Do you know Petey can turn himself over?" Gloria told her one day. "I had him on his back in the carriage, and he flipped himself over and got up on his hands."

524

"Are you sure?" said Elspeth. "I know he's been going from his stomach to his back by himself, but I haven't seen him go the other way."

"Positive. And he cried because then he was facing the hood, and he wanted to face front so he could see where we were going. So I turned him facing front and he was fine."

"We'll have to start using the harness," Elspeth said.

Even when Peter had gone to sleep Gloria would seek Elspeth's company. She had dropped her piano lessons a couple of years before, but if Elspeth played the big Steinway, the bulge of which extended under the staircase that rose to the balcony-foyer, Gloria would sit beside her on the bench and ask her to help her pick out tunes. Elspeth taught her On Top Of Old Smoky and Highland Laddie. They sang them and played them as duets.

"This piano could use a tuning," Elspeth said to Gloria.

Even if Elspeth took a book up to her room, Gloria would often knock and visit, sometimes cuddling a soiled and limp powder-blue elephant. She told Elspeth about her friends, about boys, about her teachers.

"I hope you marry my father," she said once.

"Why?"

"So you'll take care of me."

"Cele takes care of you."

"Aunt Cele's too crabby."

"She doesn't seem crabby to me."

"She's just nice now because *you're* here. But she's really crabby."

"Well, I don't know if I'll ever marry your father. We're a long way from any decision like that. But I'll always be your friend."

"I'll still call you Elspeth even after you marry him, because Grandma and Grandpa don't want me to call you Mom."

"Your mother's parents?"

"Yes. They say you can only have one mother. Is that okay with you?"

"That makes sense," said Elspeth.

Bradley seemed to her a reserved, quiet, unsmiling, solitary type. One evening a friend did come over, at dusk, and they occupied themselves mounting Bradley's big telescope on a tripod on the back deck. Later they sat in the living room, taking candies from the jar, and for the first time Elspeth was able to engage him in conversation at length. He spoke of having gone with his father to the Harvard Observatory, for a demonstation of how they bounce laser beams off the moon. He seemed to know a great deal more than his friend. He said he would show Elspeth the rings of Saturn and certain of the moons of Jupiter, on certain dates weeks hence, which he specified exactly, if the nights were clear. He mentioned how many times stronger his telescope was than Galileo's.

She was surprised by how little attention Phil paid to her. It was as though he ignored her for Peter. It occurred to her that it might be a deliberate strategy. If it was, she thought, it was the shrewdest one he could adopt at this point. Some nights he did not come home from the plant until nine or ten. But if he came home when Peter was still up he would at once kneel at the playpen he had bought him and talk to him and make him laugh. He brought him toys. A tiny rubber dog that squeaked whenever Peter squashed it. A music box that clamped to the playpen and had a wheel of brightly colored wooden beads. The wheel unwound slowly, tinkling Brahms's lullaby. Even at the supper table the spaniel paid more attention to Elspeth than Phil did. He would engage in silly jokes with Gloria, that Gloria thought were hilarious.

"Glory," he said, "what's the opposite of leftovers?"

"Rightunders!" Gloria said with gales of laughter. Then he asked her the present tense of Sanka.

"Do you know what you say when somebody sneezes?" he said.

"Gesundheit," Gloria said expectantly.

"And what do you say when somebody burps?"

"I don't know."

"Happy burpday."

Cele and Bradley smiled but Gloria cracked up.

His phone calls to Joe and Harriet seemed to have stopped.

"Daddy and I were thinking of dropping over," Harriet told her on her private phone, "but we didn't know if we should just barge in without an invitation. Does he have company over a lot? I know he knows lots of people."

"No. It's been pretty quiet."

"Well, maybe he think you need lots of rest. And I'm sure you do. That mob at the bris was enough excitement to last a while. And then Dad and I were thinking it might not look good if we kept barging in. Maybe he wants to feel he's more alone with you. We don't want to look like we're noodjing him."

"Mama, my guess is he'll invite you and Dad when he's ready."

"Do you think this Sunday maybe?"

"I'm sure not this Sunday. I heard him calling some guys to play golf."

After supper he would turn on the stereo softly, and if he didn't play chess with Bradley or look through the big glossy picture books with Gloria he would settle into the leather recliner in the living room, with a pipe instead of his cigarettes, and read. The spaniel would snooze in the shadow of the footrest. It was the same recliner Elspeth used at noon for breastfeeding, tilted far back, but Phil tilted it only to the middle position. He looked at the cartoons in The New Yorker without smiling. Then he picked up a fat book he had been plowing through. It was about the Medici. It was Elspeth's impression that he had not read widely, but that whatever he read he read slowly, with great concentration, and remembered it all.

Elspeth had plenty of time to wander about the house alone. When the kids were in school Cele had errands, especially marketing, and once Cele met the children at school to take them to Brookline for their dental appointment and to drop in at Phil's in-laws'.

Elspeth thought it would be a good idea to accompany Cele in the marketing, and begin to learn which stores the household liked, and which brands had the tiny kosher monograms. On Friday morning she suggested that she go along. But

Peter needed a cleaning up and Cele was in a great hurry. So Elspeth remained behind with Peter and the spaniel and the lady who came every other morning to clean her way through another few of the rooms.

It seemed to Elspeth that she would never tire of that awesome living room. In its center two sofas were back to back, and before each lay a sculptured Pakistani rug, inches thick. The cavernous stone fireplace could have burned a length of tree trunk. The banister swerved over the Steinway and rose to the foyer, where she could see Petey's carriage, parked there a story above where she stood, handy both to her room and the door to Beaver Dam Road. She thought the two chandeliers must weigh a quarter ton between them. Though they hung well above her reach they were closer to the floor than to the peaked ceiling. To her right, the door and window beside the fireplace were at her level, but before her the windows above the staircase were a whole story higher, like the windows behind her above the bookshelves. The books alone must have been worth a small fortune. Encyclopedias. Children's encyclopedias. The large-paged picture books—Mammals of the World, Indians of the Plains, El Prado—no end to them. The bookshelves ran the length of the long wall, interrupted only by a door to a screened porch.

She folded the playpen, carried it down another flight and set it up on the grass out back. The pool had not been readied for summer yet and a canvas still lay over it. Down at this level the house had still a third story. The long deck outside the sliding glass of the kitchen was actually on the roof of the bottom story. Bradley's room was down there. And a second kitchen, that she had heard they rarely used except when they entertained at the pool. A bath with a door to the patio. A room for Bradley's trains, that she heard he didn't play with much now, and his photo darkroom.

Beyond a low wall of stones at the end of the yard the forest sloped lower still, and she could hear a rivulet. But around the house the yard rose on one side in terraces and retaining walls, one of which supported a covered path between the garage and the upper of the two kitchens. At the other end of the house the rising ground had steep rock gardens, and you could climb through them on a zigzagging stairway of unpainted cedar to the paved circle outside the lower door of the living room.

The clapboard garage too was on the slope. Only the bicycles and the snowblower were in it now, because Phil had taken the Mercedes to the plant and Cele had taken the MG to the supermarket. Cele had complained about that. He was supposed to leave her the big car on shopping days but had forgotten. A driveway came downhill and widened before its broad doors. But at the back of the garage a stone foundation supported the flooring eight or nine feet above the underbrush.

She imagined her brother Mark standing here beside her in the weeds behind the garage, and she told him how she intended to remodel it. A door would be cut down here in the foundation, the dirt would be dug out, and a flooring laid down in there at this level with a stair from it up to the cars' floor. A long hole would be cut into the upper floor beneath the Mercedes and another beneath the MG, so she could stand below and work on their undersides. Won't that be great, Mark? I'll be able to drain oil, or even replace a muffler, without lying down.

527

She helped Cele put the groceries away. Yet she sensed that her presence in the kitchen was an intrusion.

She spoke to Cele of how she admired the house, the way it appeared an unpretentious single story from the street, and yet used the slope so ingeniously within and behind. But Cele said she didn't like it. It had been Phil's idea.

"Phil's idea?"

"Well, mainly. He had an architect for the technical things, but all the different rooms arranged up and down the hill like this was all Phil's mishugas. That's why he bought this land. It wasn't the architect's fault. Phil was drawing plans, and drawing plans, so the architect had to do it Phil's way naturally. It was Phil's money."

"Cele, if Phil designed this place, he's not stupid. The man has taste."

At the end of the afternoon, when the kitchen tablecloth had been laid out, Cele put plain white candles into the three-armed candelabrum, lighted them, waved her hands and covered her eyes, and moved her lips silently in the blessing. Gloria did the same with a pair of low candlesticks at the counter.

"I'm gonna ask my father to get you candlesticks, so next week you can light candles," Gloria said to Elspeth.

"Maybe Elspeth doesn't want to light candles," Cele told Gloria.

"Don't you?" Gloria asked Elspeth. "Doesn't your mother light candles?"

"My grandmother used to," said Elspeth. "My mother doesn't."

Later, at the end of supper, Elspeth said she thought she would ask her cousin Bob where she could get some kind of a basic course on Jewish stuff.

"Stuff like sabbath candles," she said, "and separating the meat utensils and dairy utensils, and why the different bread on Friday night, and all like that. Especially the theory behind it."

"Maybe there's a course at the temple," Phil said.

"There isn't," said Elspeth. "I called yesterday. Everthing's dead there now until fall, and then in the fall it's just some classes Rabbi Quint gives for the sisterhood ladies, and I've heard Quint's sermons for years and he's an ass."

"Well," Phil said, "so ask your cousin then. And something else, I wonder if you'd enjoy maybe having some sessions with a shrink. I mean, don't get me wrong. I've done it myself, and I think there's nobody that can't profit from it. What a shrink does is, they just guide you to a deeper understanding of yourself. They don't tell you what to do. But you bat your problems around, and gradually you sort out for yourself what you want in life. You're stronger. You make decisions easier. I don't say you need it. I just say if you think you'd like to give it a try, let me know. What can you lose? I went to one for years. A woman. She's terrific. She's probably all booked up, but if you wanted, I think she'd try to fit you in. As a favor to me."

It was the most Phil had spoken to her since the bris.

"Okay," she said.

"You want me to give her a call?"

"Why not."

528

"All right. I'll call her Monday." Then he turned his attention from her and began joking with Gloria.

On Saturday the man came finally to clean the swimming pool. Elspeth and Gloria sat and watched. Meanwhile a shirtless young man had come to mow and they heard his machine, first muffled in the front, then louder on the terraces and slopes. They carried the picnic table and benches out onto the patio.

"You're supposed to be resting," Gloria said.

"I feel fine," said Elspeth.

They spread one of Peter's blankets under a waterproof sheet on the grass and let him sunbathe a little while with nothing on but his hat.

"Your elephant is losing his stuffing," Elspeth said.

"I know. There's a seam I have to stitch up."

The shirtless young man came near with his mower so they moved onto the patio.

At night Elspeth phoned Bob Shoemaker. He told her the course he always recommended was given by a Rabbi Gordon who came down one evening a week from Wilmerding.

"I've heard that name before," she said. "Is he the one that got you that couple that was going to adopt Petey?"

"Yes. That's the one."

Elspeth said she had had classes at the temple when she was a kid, but she wanted something on a more mature level. "I have no idea if I'll end up permanently in this household or not, but if I do, that's just one of the many things I'll have to come to grips with. I'll be preparing a sabbath table, and Phil will be doing the bit with the wine cup, and I'll be cooking kosher, and there'll be the holidays and doing the whole house for Passover every year, and getting involved with the temple crowd, and I can't do these things like a trained monkey. If I do it at all I want to know what it means. Or at least know enough to figure out my own idea of what it means, and see if it's something I can accept. If Petey asks me someday what's the point, and I say I don't know, he'll ask me why the hell I've been doing it."

"Gordon's course would be the best for you then."

"What night is it? And where?"

"Well, it's over now. But he'll probably give it again in the fall, or something similar. I'll find out."

"I don't want to wait till fall, Bob. How about you kind of tutoring me a little in the meantime, like if you can spare an evening once in a while? Or Karen? I mean, just to give me some kind of feel of it I can make sense of. Maybe you're not this Gordon guy, but I'm sure you know more than enough for me."

The phone at her ear was silent. She thought he was going to say he'd love to but there was no way he could spare the time.

Then he said he'd try. He didn't know when. Certainly not in the next couple of weeks. He was in the midst of moving. He was going to sleep on a cot in the cellar of a Cambridge apartment building and work there as janitor, to save up some money for furniture. He and Karen hoped to get married sometime next winter

529

and move into an apartment in the building, and he would continue as janitor in lieu of rent. Besides, he had gotten a teaching fellowship and would be giving a course this summer in biochemistry, and had not much time left in which to organize it. Karen was busy too. She would be a teaching assistant at Harvard in the fall, and besides she was preparing for her generals so she could begin her dissertation.

"That's okay, Bob. I understand."

"No, I'll call. We'll find some time. You'll hear from me. Or from Karen."

On Monday Phil called the psychotherapist, whose name was Edna Le Vyne. An appointment was made for Wednesday. School ended for the summer on Tuesday, so Gloria could baby-sit, and Cele would drive her to Dr. Le Vyne. Elspeth said if she could borrow the MG she'd drive herself. But Cele said she wanted to go to Boston that day anyhow.

So Cele took Elspeth to a narrow old building in the Back Bay. She said she would shop on Newbury Street while Elspeth was with Edna, and pick her up after the hour. Elspeth rose alone in a humming elevator.

There was no receptionist. The inner door was ajar. "Come in," a voice said.

Edna sat behind a desk, her fingers working rapidly with knitting needles. She was fiftyish and quite fat, draped in a huge dress. In its tentlike folds drab purples and browns lost themselves together in a small pattern of paisley.

"I'm Elspeth Baker."

"Hello, Elspeth." Edna glanced only for an instant over the spectacles that sat low on her nose, without a smile. She kept knitting.

"Do I have to lie on the couch?"

"No, the chair will do."

Elspeth sat in her denim skirt, one leg tucked under her. Edna knitted and did not look at her.

The chair under Elspeth was of greenish imitation leather. Her shoulder bag lay over its arm. She saw Edna more from the side than from the front.

On the wall opposite the window was a large clock, simple and round. Edna said nothing. Elspeth watched her knit. She had heard that an hour with a shrink was fifty minutes, and it occurred to her that Edna might be waiting till ten past. So she waited.

But at eleven past and twelve past Edna was still knitting as though Elspeth were not there.

Maybe Edna always knitted, even when working with patients. Even so, there seemed something artificial in the studied silence. Worse than artificial. It was patronizing.

What's the gimmick? Is this supposed to shake me up and break me down? Am I supposed to blurt out my problems, and beg for her attention? And is that supposed to establish the Olympian superiority of the shrink? What does this creep want?

Why the tricks? Why not just get down to business?

The clock crept to twenty after. The knitting continued. There was no sound but the occasional tick of the clock, as the hand jumped to the next minute, and the muted traffic on the street below. Elspeth felt resentful, and then angry.

I'll be damned if I'll speak first, she promised herself. I don't care if the whole hour goes this way.

She stared at Edna. Maybe the staring would make Edna look at her. But Edna looked only at the knitting. Elspeth felt her eyes moisten. No, I'm not gonna let myself cry. That's just what she wants.

The clock was approaching half past.

It seemed a terrible waste of Phil's money though. This was costing him thirty-five dollars an hour. And here we are locked in a stubborn, childish contest, each trying to force the other to speak first. She wished now she had spoken first at the beginning of the hour, and averted this.

By now there was no comfortable way to begin. Perhaps she could start by asking Edna what she was knitting. Then Edna might ask her why she had waited so long before asking. She could say, because I didn't care what you were knitting. And Edna could say, then why do you ask now?

No. It had gone too far. To speak now would be to hand Edna too great a triumph. This whole game was just too stupid and too ridiculous to be a party to. Better to just sit here silently for the rest of the hour, watching Edna knit, and precisely at the end of the hour get up and walk out without a word. And tell Phil not to pay the bill.

Edna looked uncomfortable. The knitting slowed, speeded, slowed again. Could it be that Edna had never before encountered a patient who called her bluff? Could this possibly be the first time the gimmick hadn't worked?

Less than ten minutes left. Elspeth sensed that Edna was worried. She apparently made a mistake and undid some stitches.

Five minutes. Four. Elspeth rested in the imitation leather, eyes nearly closed, her ankles crossed before her.

When there was about a minute and a half to go she sat up and collected her shoulder bag. Edna lowered the knitting, took off the spectacles, and looked at her.

"I can see you need help—" Edna began.

"So do you," said Elspeth.

"Fortunately a patient has just finished therapy," Edna continued quickly, "so I have an opening. There's a waiting list but I'll take you because you came recommended, and because I can see you're very troubled."

Elspeth had risen but Edna was filling in an appointment card.

Edna gave Elspeth the card. Elspeth looked at it and put it in her shoulder bag. "Very good," said Edna. "I'll see you then."

Elspeth took the stairs down instead of the elevator. She found Cele in the coppery MG, double parked.

"Waiting long?" Elspeth asked, getting in.

"I just got here."

Cele moved the stick shift with a crunch and they started.

Elspeth saw no bundles. "Did you do your shopping?"

"I'm getting a jacket," said Cele. "Suede. They measured me for it. It'll take about two weeks. How did you like Edna?"

531

Elspeth shrugged.

"Are you gonna see her again?" Cele asked.

"She gave me an appointment. I don't know. I'll have to think about it."

"Phil thinks she's marvelous," said Cele. "She's full of it, if you ask me."

When they got home Elspeth found Peter in his playpen in the backyard, clean and dry, wearing his summery bonnet with air vents, and getting along well with Gloria, who kept tossing a ball for the spaniel to fetch.

Elspeth went up to her room to bathe. The showerhead made fine needles, cold and then warm.

The terrycloth mat was thick beneath her feet. The towel was as big as a toga. She draped it about her and ran the comb down through her hair, its red even darker in its clinging wetness. The green of the tiles and the Tiffany lamp and the paler green of the fixtures enriched and enhanced it.

She sauntered into the bedroom. She stretched out her arms, spreading the big towel like wings. Too bad the four-poster had a canopy. If it hadn't, she would have liked to jump on the mattress like a trampoline.

She threw the massive towel onto the bed. She stretched herself upon the terrycloth. She drew a foot to her, and with a corner of the towel on which she lay she dried between her toes.

Some mysterious sense made her pause, and focus upon the door of her closet, which hung a few inches open. She rose to her knees, clutching a great flap of the towel to cover her whole front. She reached out and threw the door open wide. Bradley sat crouching there. He blanched.

"How long have you been there?" she asked him.

His face went from white to red. His eyes averted and lowered. Otherwise he was as though frozen.

Both her arms hugged the towel. "I'm entitled to privacy, Brad. You'll have plenty of chances to see women naked when you're older. But don't ever spy on people."

"Don't tell Aunt Cele."

"Are you afraid of Aunt Cele?"

"No. But don't tell either of them. Please. I don't want them to know."

"Oh. You mean you care about your privacy. But you didn't care about mine, did you. Nobody likes to be spied on, or watched when they don't know it. I don't mean just because I'm bare. Sometimes when people are alone they make faces at themselves in the mirror, for instance, or act out an imaginary fight with somebody, or all kinds of goofy things. And then if they discover they're not alone it's very embarrassing. Understand?"

He nodded. She saw tears in his eyes.

"You wouldn't like it done to you," she said. "Would you."

He shook his head.

"Okay then. Out. And don't ever do it again."

"You mean you won't tell?"

"You ever do it again and I just might."

68

ELSPETH wakened in the nighttime stillness. She turned her face toward the night table. In the darkness a glowing yellow digit rolled downward and replaced itself almost silently. It was not quite midnight. She had slept only an hour.

She lay in the bedding, gazing out her window. She saw part of a conical fir, and beyond, half hidden by it, a streetlamp on Beaver Dam Road.

She rose and went to the crib. Her eyes were attuned to the dark. Without touching Peter she knew he was dry. When he was wet he slept on his face and his knees, his rump in the air.

For a moment she thought she heard muffled voices murmuring somewhere beyond her door. Then she did not.

She turned the knob, and the door swept over the carpet. From here the corridor to the right after a few feet became the gallery and continued beyond, while the corridor straight before her led to the balcony-foyer, and in both places dim yellow light reached up from the living room below.

"She's a bloodsucker," she heard Cele say. "She's got her fangs in your throat. And you don't know it."

Elspeth went to the right. The shadow of the railing fanned on the corridor ceiling. She looked down and saw Cele from the back, standing almost silhouetted down there in her nightgown and robe. Phil was in the recliner. The only light came from the shaded floor lamp beside him, the one with the shelf about its stem, where he kept his tobacco and pipes. Elspeth backed away from the opening.

"Beautiful eyes, and a beautiful body," Cele was saying, "and she knows what to do with them. She uses them to the hilt. She leans over that playpen in her little skirt, and you sit there looking up her ass. You think I don't notice?"

Elspeth sat in her pajamas on the carpeting, back where she could not see down, but the voice rose clearly.

"Not that I care. What gets me is the price you pay. Phil, go into Boston, and take a little walk on the sidewalks there in the Combat Zone for a couple of blocks. You'll see skirts even shorter. Sweaters even tighter. Girls even younger. And pay your twenty dollars, or your thirty dollars, and get it over with. A hundred bucks will get you all night if you want. Though what an alta kaka like you could do all night is beyond me. Oysgevorfeneh gelt, as Ma used to say. Might as well flush your money down the toilet."

"You want her to wear longer skirts?" said Phil. "If you want, I'll mention it.

Short skirts happen to be the style, that's all. But if you want her to wear longer I'm sure she'll oblige, for the sake of peace. And I've seen *your* dress go up. Every time you get out of the MG. Especially with a long-legged girdle. You think that looks so great?"

"That's not the point! I know what's going on, Phil. I know why you sit up reading so late. Well, I'm gonna stay up too, and you'll have to go in there openly. You're such a sucker. I remember a story when you were nineteen years old. A bar girl sat at your table, and started feeling you up in your pants, and while she was feeling you her other hand lifted your wallet. The whole job didn't take three minutes. And she disappeared, and you complained, and nobody knew from nothing. Nobody saw a girl at your table. Phil, you're as stupid now as you were then. I wish I could open your eyes! She's ambitious. You don't know some of the stories she told me. That gas station she worked at, she was planning to get it away from them. She had a scheme to milk the banks and set up a whole chain of gas stations. You don't believe it? She told me herself. That's why they had to get rid of her. She's as hard as steel. Ruthless. Working there not even four months and she's scheming to steal the place. I know she asked you to show her the plant. Give her a tour, she says. She wants to know everything. How tubing is made. Do you melt it with natural gas or synthetic. Profit margin. Who your customers are. Do you have your own trucks. The questions that girl asks. Phil, she'll be working there, and she'll be chairman of the board, she'll be president, you'll sign over your stock, and you'll be lucky if she lets you be night watchman. She wants to study business administration. You'll send her to college to study business administration so she can turn around and clean you out. She should have been back in those times you're reading about. In your book there. The Borgias. She'd have been everbody's mistress and slit everybody's throat. She'd have made herself Pope."

"The Medicis," he corrected her.

"The Medicis. Whatever. She'd marry Napoleon and then she'd send him to the guillotine and take France away from him."

"Cele, blow it out your ass already. Get out of here. Let me read."

"Everybody can see it but you."

"What do you mean, everybody?"

"Murray can see it. Murray sees her for what she is."

"Yeah? What did Murray say?"

"He said she's sharp."

"Of course. He meant good-looking."

"No he didn't. He said she's got a head on her shoulders."

"Of course she's got a head on her shoulders. Murray was very impressed with her."

"Because he doesn't believe you're serious. He thinks you're stringing her along. He thinks you've got a good thing going. I know how Murray thinks. Murray keeps a little shikse on the side. You think I don't know? He takes care of the rent and a monthly allowance. That's all. Murray knows how to handle those things. Not you. You're too stupid. You have to give her everything you own. And she'll take it. She'll strip you naked and nail you to the wall. You think she loves you? You think she admires this house? Don't be a fool. That's just to soft-soap you. She's got all kinds of ideas about remodeling. Even the garage. She's gonna change everything around. She doesn't love you. She's planning a marriage of pure convenience, that's all."

"Okay," he said. "I'm entitled to a marriage of convenience. You know for how many years I had a marriage of *in*convenience? I love her. I love her and I love the baby. For the first time there's light in my life. That's what you call convenience? I wish everything in the world was so convenient. Sure, I know money's part of it. I'm not the attraction. But she'll work at it. She's looking for stability. Sure, she'll study and do things. Why shouldn't she? And she wants more kids. And if she marries me it'll be to give her kid a father and have more kids. And be a mother to Glory and Brad."

"That's a laugh. Are you out of your mind? Do you know what you're saying?"

"Glory loves her."

"Gloria. What does *she* know? Show her how to give a real live baby a bath and she thinks she's a grown-up. Playing mama. In seventh heaven. Even more fun than a training bra."

"Brad likes her. You said he didn't. He told me himself. He said she's not so bad."

"Because she looks through his telescope and listens to all his stuff about the phases of Saturn and what is it—the perihelion of Mercury? She doesn't know what he's talking about but she listens. She knows how to get around anybody. Phil, she's only seven years older than Gloria. Not even seven. When Gloria's twenty she'll only be twenty-seven. Can she be a mother to Gloria, especially if anything happens to you? And she'll be a fine moral example. A baby out of wedlock."

"She's a good girl. She made one mistake. She learned her lesson."

"You don't know what she learned. She got caught, that's all. If she didn't get caught she'd still be making mistakes. You think you're gonna satisfy her? You'll be over the hill. What's she supposed to do? Sleep with the delivery boy?"

"Don't write me off. I'm good for twice a week at least. Three times. Sometimes more. Twice in a night even. Even a young kid varies, he catches cold, he's not sexy for a while."

"And in ten years? Twenty years? She'll be a young woman. And you'll be an old fart."

"Men go on forever. Don't you know that? And you know something else, if you want to know? I was reading in an article that man is not a nocturnal animal. If they did it in the daytime they'd be twice as good. It's true. You know when I feel sexiest? When I wake up in the morning. Especially right after breakfast. Don't worry about me, Cele. She'll be pregnant a lot of the time anyway. She wants a lot of kids. And I can give her all the kids she wants."

"Have you changed your will?"

"No."

"Are you going to?"

"You mean even if I don't marry her? I might. I don't know."

"And if you marry her?"

"If I marry her, then of course. What do you think."

"Of course, he says. I knew it. And if you don't die fast enough she'll have you in the divorce courts and take you for so much she'll own A. I. Snyder and Sons."

"Cele, shut up. Let me read my book, will ya? You're running off at the mouth. Now shut your mouth or I'll shut it for ya."

"All right. I'll shut up. I'll shut up. The truth is too painful, isn't it. You don't want to hear it. So you'll learn the hard way, and when it's too late don't blame me. I'm going up to bed."

Elspeth heard the footsteps on the hardwood, then silenced on the rug, then on the floor again, and finally the creak that meant the staircase. To get to her bedroom Cele would pass Elspeth's door and then across this very gallery.

Elspeth darted, her hair flying, and dove into the four-poster. She buried herself under the satin quilt. She left her door ajar lest Cele hear it close.

Then she heard Cele's voice, further away than she expected, as though Cele had stopped partway up the staircase and was talking over the banister. "Poor Phil. Poor, poor Phil. You were behind the door when the brains were passed out, that's all. A change-of-life baby, what do you expect? Ma and Pa should have quit with two children. They should have quit when they were ahead."

The footsteps started up the stairs again.

"What can I say?" Cele continued. "It's a tragedy. A fool and his money are soon parted."

ON Sunday Phil came out to the patio and told Elspeth that matinee tickets were available for Music Under the Bed, with Gwendolyn Frye and several of the original Broadway cast.

"Oh, I'd love to!" she said. "A bunch of us went down to New York from Mount Holyoke and saw her in Lady Godiva Clad. She's absolutely great."

536

"Lady Godiva Clad," said Phil. "That's the one with that song A Bent Cent?"
"That's it."
He began spontaneously to sing the line and she joined him in a brief duet.

> "A bent cent
> And a broken token.
> Nothing in my pocket but lint!"

"Okay," said Phil. "So go up and change and let's go."

They took the MG. It was a theater in the round, under a tent. Their seats were on the best side, halfway up the steep-rising tiers. Gwendolyn Frye, with her towering thighs and shaven armpits, dominated everything. Her voice could be harsh and gargly when she wished, or as clear and loud as a trumpet. Especially after the last stanza of Nu Nu Nu Whaddaya Gonna Do, she bowed and bowed, to every side, shaking her hair into place each time she came up, and had difficulty silencing the applause finally so the show could continue.

And toward the middle of the second act her rendition of It's So Sooty in the City, in which she took off her dress and washed it, brought down the house.

The tunes kept going through Elspeth's head. She sang them afterward in the MG. Phil drove to an ancient yellow clapboard farmhouse, with many wings, that had been remodeled into a restaurant. He led her into a softly lighted dining room under low ceilings supported by heavy beams. The waiter was portly and European, with drooping mustachios and a cummerbund. Phil suggested an appetizer of snails, a certain wine of the Loire, and shish kebab.

"Okay," said Elspeth.

The waiter brought the wine in a bucket of ice. In the green bottle it looked black. He showed Phil the label for his approval. Then his corkscrew tugged, squeaking. He poured.

"I thought snails weren't kosher," Elspeth said when the waiter had gone.

"They're not," said Phil. "Look, I never meant I'm a fanatic about these things. I'm proud to say I've always kept my home strictly kosher, out of respect to my parents, of blessed memory. I'm a deeply religious person. But that doesn't mean that when I go out I don't want to enjoy some of the good things of life."

The snails were brought neatly arranged in circles on metal dishes specially made to hold them, a dozen each, with special utensils. Phil showed her how to hold the spiral shell in the clamp and dig the meat out with the narrow fork. They were hot and good, though butter and garlic seemed to account for most of the flavor.

"Nice," she said. "Better than oysters."

"I think so."

The waiter brought the main course with the meat still sizzling and the vegetables steaming. He pushed them from the skewers onto the plates.

"I can almost smell the fire," said Elspeth.

It was delicious, especially with the wine. She reached for the bottle to refill her glass, but Phil did it for her.

"Tell me," he said, "has Cele been giving you a hard time at all?"

"Cele? She's been fine. Why?"

"Well, I just wondered. Sometimes she's not easy to get along with."

"She's been wonderful. Very helpful."

"Okay. That's good. With Cele you never know." He cut a piece of his meat and a piece of mushroom and put them together with some of the moist rice. "I only took her in because she doesn't like to live alone. I don't need her. The kids aren't that crazy about her, and I could have hired somebody to look after the kids, and cook and stuff. She could afford her own place. My parents left her a fair share. She just doesn't want to. She was with Murray and they couldn't take it. Sheila told him 'either *she* goes or I go.'"

Elspeth said nothing.

"You know," he said, "she thinks I'm slipping into your room at night."

"Oh?"

"She hasn't said anything to you? Snide remarks or anything?"

"No."

"Okay, good. So we'll leave it at that. But she thinks we're going at it hot and heavy."

"Where'd she get that idea?"

"No place. That's how her mind works. She never got laid in her life, so she thinks everybody's got sex on the brain."

He chewed a while, cutting his food and putting it together in various combinations.

"You're in my house to recuperate from an illness. Right? That was the deal, and I mean what I say. And suppose I might want to give you a gift once in a while, or give the baby a gift, just because it gives me pleasure. If I was sleeping with you, or even if you thought I was trying to, then we're gonna feel funny about what those gifts mean. They wouldn't be gifts. Elspeth, you're not in love with me. But we're friends. And if for instance I see an angora sweater and I want to buy it because it would look good on you, I want there to be such a thing as a gift of friendship, not with strings attached. And if you get better, and move out, okay, then the whole thing was clean and above board. And if, say, we ever did fall in love, then we'd still have plenty of time to sleep together and make up for lost time. After the abstention it would be all the sweeter. Elspeth, I like friendship. And I like sex, but I like it with love. And I'm not gonna mess up two beautiful things by mixing what doesn't go together." He took several long swallows of wine. He put down the glass. "Sex without love I can get anytime. Like last Christmas we had an office party. And I took one of the secretaries, and locked the door, and gave her a shtoop. On a pile of cushions. And the whole time she's going hee hee hee hee hee hee. I mean, what good is that? Sex without love, is like you take a beautiful meal and eat it off the floor. The way I like it, with love with it, I haven't had for a while."

"Since your wife died."

"Since before. I don't know what it was with Bertha. She was a very neurotic person. In so many ways. For one thing, she didn't know how to receive a gift, or

538

a compliment even. She couldn't handle it. I'd bring her a mink. I'd bring her jewelry. Good stuff. So she'd frown and say, 'you think I married you for your money.' That's all the thanks I'd get. I'd say, 'dearest, how can you say that? I never thought any such thing. I love you.' So she'd tell me money goes through my fingers, it's waste, I should grow up. So I'd cut down on the presents for a while. And then she'd tell people I'm cheap and I've never brought her a gift. And in bed, as soon as she had the two kids she wanted, all of a sudden I was like worse than useless. If she'd consent at all, she'd lie there with a sour face and say, 'you aren't doing it right. What's the matter with you.' And I'd try everything, and I mean everything. And no, that's not it. And I'd say, 'tell me, dearest. What do you want? I'll fix it. I'll do it.' And she'd say, 'if I have to tell you, it's no good. You have no feelings.' So I'd work harder at the foreplay, and she'd say, 'damn it, I have to get up in the morning, get on with it.' So I'd cut down on the foreplay, and she'd tell me I'm a beast, I only think of myself. But when we were first married, and before we were married, oh boy, then it was 'ooooh, Phil! Ooooh, it's heavenly! Ooooh, I can't stand it! Lover boy! Do it again!' And so help me, I was doing it exactly the same way as before."

He resumed eating, but only for a moment.

"Once I gave her this real sexy peignoir, for the bedroom. I thought we'd have some fun with it. Totally see-through. Black gauze. Ruffles, lace. She's a little fat but so what, I'm not perfect either. She wouldn't wear it. She said yeah, yeah, she'll wear it. She just forgot, tomorrow she'll wear it. And you know, one night Murray and Sheila and Cele were over, and so she mentions this great peignoir she has, and she goes upstairs and gets undressed and comes downstairs in the peignoir, nothing under it, and she models it back and forth in front of Murray and Sheila and Cele. Like she loves it, like she really appreciates how beautiful it is, and how sexy it makes her. You could see everything. It was even greater than I thought. And Murray and Sheila and Cele were saying wow. And I remember, she didn't look at me once the whole time. Like I wasn't there. And that's the only time I ever saw her in it. For me, alone, in the bedroom, she never wore it. Not even once. She gave it to the lady that comes to clean house, and the lady gave it to her daughter. Elspeth, what that woman had it in for me for, what she was mad at me for, I'll never know. Every time I'd speak, in front of company, or in front of the children, either she'd contradict me, or else in the middle of what I'm saying she'd start talking on a completely different subject. I could say, 'dear, I'm talking.' And she'd go right on. Like she didn't hear me. Once she told me there's a new hormone, she read about it, they can make a boy taller. And Brad's a little undersized, we should get him these treatments now, and when he grows up he'll be six feet tall. And I said, 'Bertha, show me that article.' So she couldn't find it. She says, 'don't you believe me?' And I said, 'Bertha, if it's something brand-new, you know, to fool around with glands can be dangerous. I'd want to check it out first with two top doctors, at least.' So she yells at me that I don't give a damn what's good for the children. So we take Brad to the pediatrician. And the pediatrician says Brad's perfectly normal, his chart says he'll be about five-feet-six, and there's no way to make him taller. Bertha misunderstood the article. They're experimenting to give female hormone to a little girl whose parents are extremely tall, so she'll reach adolescence a little younger and stop growing sooner, and end up shorter. To prevent her from shooting up over six feet like her sisters did. It makes people grow less tall. If it works. But there's no way to make anybody grow more tall. So Bertha says the pediatrician's wrong, and we take Brad to the endocrine clinic at the Children's. They're all Harvard Med professors there. And they tell us exactly what the pediatrician told us. And you know what Bertha told Brad afterward? She told him, 'the doctors could make you six feet tall, but your father won't let them, because he doesn't want you to be taller than he is."

"She said that?"

"That's what she told him. Right in front of me."

"Why did you ever marry her?"

"Well, we were just kids. We were sleeping together from before I got drafted. And the whole time I was in Korea she wrote me every day. I'd get the letters in bunches. Two weeks after I got home we got married. And Elspeth, that woman was always the great genius. She knew better than everybody about everything. That's why she died. I said, 'Bertha, for God sake, go to a doctor. Don't wait. Check it out.' But she knew better. And it's a terrible thing to say, but when they lowered her casket in the ground, I said the kaddish, and then under my breath I said 'burn in hell, shtoonk.' "

"It's sad," said Elspeth.

THEY left the restaurant without dessert, and before Phil had had his cigarette, because Elspeth wanted to be home in time to nurse Peter.

On the way home Elspeth kept singing and humming melodies from Music Under the Bed. "I'm sorry," she apologized. "I can't get those songs out of my head."

"That's okay. I enjoy hearing you."

In the driveway they found Bob Shoemaker's car parked before the oaken front door. She recognized it instantly by the fender still painted only with primer.

When they came into the foyer she saw Bob down there below on the sofa with a cup of tea. Peter was in his seat beside the playpen and Gloria sat on the rug in shorts, feeding him puree with a spoon, but Peter had turned his head and was looking up toward the foyer to see who had entered.

"Bob!" said Elspeth. "Hi!"

She came down the stairs quickly.

"Gee," she said, "I wish I'd known! We'd have been home."

"That's okay. All of a sudden I found I had time to come down, so I phoned, and Cele said you'd be back about now. I've only been here about ten minutes."

"Have you had supper?" she asked him.

"Thanks—I ate before I came."

"Can I get you a drink at least?" Phil asked.

"No thanks. Cele made me some tea."

Gloria was wiping Peter's mouth. She untied his bib. Elspeth sat back into the recliner and Gloria handed Peter up to her. He smiled.

"Did you miss me, Petey?" She danced him on her knees, and he moved his feet as though walking in the air. "Nu, nu, nu?" she sang. "Whaddaya gonna do?"

When she opened her front he tried to clamber to the breast, lips open and ready. She gave it to him.

"That little guy's more beautiful every time I see him," said Bob.

Gloria pulled over a hassock and sat on it. Elspeth saw Phil taking the Medici book from the shelf.

"I'll be done in about five minutes, Phil. If you want the recliner."

"No, no. Relax. I don't need it." He stepped into the slippers that he kept over by the bookshelves. "You don't mind if I go out and read on the porch, do you?" he said to Bob. "I assume you're here mainly to talk to Elspeth about religious observances."

"Well, I'm not as expert as she thinks I am. If she wants an expert I should have sent Karen."

"Can I stay and listen?" said Gloria.

"Sure," said Bob.

Phil picked up his pipe from the circular shelf about the floor lamp. He lighted it.

"Have you moved yet?" Elspeth asked Bob.

"Yup. I'm living in a cellar. I'm a part-time janitor."

"You mean like rooms in the cellar? Or the plain cellar?"

"The plain cellar. I've got a cot and a chair and a table, next to the furnace. Cinderblock walls. No windows."

"That's awful."

"It's not so awful, actually. It's nice and cool in summer. And it's only temporary."

Phil went out through the door that was set amid bookshelves. The screen door shut behind him.

"I figure about seven months of putting money in the bank," said Bob, "and then we move in upstairs. I know just which apartment. A guy's leaving in February and we'll sublet."

"So you're getting married in February?"

"Right. You'll get an invitation." His eyes went to Peter. He watched him nurse. He was silent, pensive.

Elspeth heard the quiet gurgle of her milk in Peter's throat. Far away she heard also the distant washer and dryer, beyond the dining room and kitchen and up the back circular stair.

Bob's eyes moved up and met hers.

"Ellie, I appreciate the excuse to come and see you, and the baby, and Phil and his family, but about your asking me to give you some kind of crash background on what you didn't learn in Sunday school, I'm not qualified. I'm only a beginner. I'm sure Phil and Cele and Gloria will tell you what you need to know to function here in the household. And if you want something more structured, take the course I mentioned in the fall. He's gonna give it again."

"You were helpful when I phoned about the bris."

"I didn't think I answered you very well. You caught me off guard."

"He's asleep," said Gloria. "Give him the other side."

Elspeth looked down at Peter. She tickled him, and he smiled shut-eyed around the nipple. She covered that breast and gave him the other one. He resumed a businesslike sucking without having opened his eyes.

"You're like me, Ellie. You like some understanding of what you're doing. Or maybe you think you have to understand first, and if you understand it, then it becomes possible to do it. But that's not how it is. Like when I first got into marine zoology, I didn't have the understanding of it I do now. Today I know a little something about the mammals of the ocean, because I've studied and worked with it the past few years. But I studied because I was drawn to it. And when I was first drawn to it, obviously I didn't yet know much. First I was drawn. Something about the whales and the ocean attracted me. And knowledge came after. And religion is like that. First I got into it. Some instinct made me feel maybe it's for me. And once I was in it, little by little I acquired some understanding of what I was into."

"You're certainly into it now."

"I'm obsessed with it. I love it. For me it's a vision of the good society. Not just abstractly. But all around me in the community I've woven myself into, the whole gang the Kramers are with in that neighborhood."

He paused, looking at Elspeth. She looked at him, stroking Peter.

"Well, okay," he said. "I guess what you probably want to ask is why all the ceremonial things, all the ritual things, that don't seem to have any connection to any moral value. Like not eating certain foods. Not putting the meat spoon in the vanilla pudding. Checking when sundown is going to be, so I can plug in timers before the sabbath and not touch the light switches. Making sure the knots in my tsitsis are correct, otherwise the tsitsis is no good and it wouldn't count to wear it.

I'm sure you wonder, okay, love thy neighbor as thyself is a good religion. But why all this other crap?"

"Okay," said Elspeth.

"Okay," he said. "A good question. I get friendly with these froomies, and I start doing like they do, doing all these millions of punctilious ritual things, and I get compulsive about them, and you ask, what the hell could God care about stuff like that? What's the point? How can a guy with scientific training buy it?"

Peter slept. His head slipped to the side. She looked down at him.

"Want me to put him to bed?" Gloria asked. "I'll change him and put him to bed."

He knit his brow, with eyes shut tight, and grasped nervously as Elspeth handed him over. Then he relaxed against Gloria. Elspeth buttoned her front.

They watched Gloria carry him up the staircase, till she disappeared across the foyer into the upper hallway.

"She's a nice little kid," said Bob.

"Yes."

"She sat here listening so politely. Not butting in."

"She was enjoying looking at you. She thinks you're handsome."

"She does?"

"That's what her eyes said. I was twelve once. Okay, so tell me. What could God care?"

"All right. All these laws that have no ethical connection, they're called chukim. The Bible states them, with no reason given, and they're irrational on their face. Sometimes people think they can see reasons for this one or that one, and maybe they're right, but the reason is after the fact, and not very obvious, and probably the same effect could have been gotten with a completely different law. And yet we've accepted them as part of the same Torah with moral things like don't murder, don't steal, don't slander. All together in one package."

He put down the empty teacup and saucer on the rug.

"Well, Ellie, now that I've been doing it a few years, let me tell you what I think it does and what it's for. A bunch of my friends are into all these practices, so I get into them, just like if half my friends were into water-skiing I'd probably try water-skiing. Something about their life-style attracts me, and I start trying it. And then, gradually, the practice of these chukim conditions you, because it's daily and constant, continually reinforced. The occasions when you have to remember not to steal and not to murder aren't usually thrown at you every day. You might even go six or seven years without being seriously tempted to assassinate the President or rob a bank, right? But the chukim hit you every day. Morning, noon and night. Every single day. I wake up, I take a crap, I wash my hands, I put phylacteries on my arm and head. I say blessings. I make sure there's no blood spots in the eggs. Day in and day out there are exercises conditioning me to feel that the Torah is real. Tangible. All around me. It makes the Torah come alive for me. Till it's as if I'd been there myself in the crowd at Sinai and heard the thunder and the trumpets. Belief is an emotional condition, Ellie. And all this daily acting out,

543

everything just so, just as if the Torah were real, every day till it gets compulsive, for two, three, four, five years, it's conditioned me to feel that it's real. And the ethical part of the law has become real and tangible too, because I've been studying that all along, week by week, with this same crowd, as part of the same package. I can't make fun of somebody, even though I can't be arrested for it, because I learned in the Talmud that it's forbidden to make fun of somebody. And if I've hurt somebody, I know I've got to set things right with him. Because somewhere along the line I've become a believer. Not in a rational way. In a Pavlovian way. If I've said 'heaven watches me' to all these little dos and don'ts, every day, till my heart believes it, I'll say 'heaven watches me' when the big test comes. When I've got to be honest to my disadvantage. Or merciful to some skunk I'd rather kick in the balls."

Elspeth nodded slowly.

"Or maybe believer isn't the word," he said. "Or maybe it is. But however you want to put it, the daily exercise has gradually programmed me to take the whole deal seriously."

His foot rattled the teacup. He reached down and moved it aside.

"I don't say reasoning isn't involved," he said. "I don't say your intellectual equipment isn't getting a workout. There's the subtlest reasoning to ensure that the application or nonapplication of chukim in all kinds of exceptional and special cases has a consistency, a poetic and logical consistency. Because if it didn't have this poetic and logical consistency you'd blow the reality of it. And enormous reasoning and scholarship in working out moral obligations. How to apply justice, and kindness, and mercy in every kind of situation. If you're serious about loving your neighbor as yourself, if it's more than just a slogan, you've got to have studied. Cases and cases, and opinions and opinions. So you can respond quickly and intelligently in a surprise situation. Real situations are complicated. You've got to know all your obligations, and their priorities, including your obligation to yourself. To know how to be fair even when you're being nice. And to know how to be sensitive, and compassionate, even when you're hurting. Even when you're troubled. You've got to have a background of learning. And studying Talmud, and the responsa and literature down to the present day is like spending a lifetime as a graduate student at the Harvard Law School. It's big, Ellie. It's as vast a study as chemistry, or physics."

Gloria came down the staircase. Bob turned and watched her. She had changed her clothes. She wore her newest dress. There was a ribbon in her hair.

She sat again on the hassock.

"Hi," Bob said to her.

"Hi."

"Did he stay asleep?" Elspeth asked her.

"Yup."

"Did you leave the door open?"

"Yup."

"Do you go to Hebrew school?" Bob asked.

544

"I go at the temple," Gloria answered. "It's over for the summer though."

"When I was your age," he said, "I didn't even know the letters of the alphabet."

"Didn't you go to Hebrew school?"

"No."

"How come?"

"I guess my parents didn't think it was important."

"Do you know Hebrew now?"

"Some."

Gloria and Bob kept looking at each other.

"Did they ever teach you," he asked, "that the Torah was created when the world was created?"

"What?"

"That's what I believe," he said. "Before the primordial proto-stuff had condensed into particles, and formed first hydrogen, and later on helium and heavier elements, and before there was such a thing as an acid or an alkali, the laws of chemistry already existed, even though there wasn't yet any chemistry. Because if atoms and molecules were to come into existence, then they'd be bound by those laws. The laws were already there waiting. And the laws of biology were there before there were any living organisms. Because if a living organism were to come into being, it would at once be bound by them. In the same way, you can say the laws of psychology preexisted consciousness. And the laws of sociology preexisted before there was society. And morality existed, right and wrong existed. Because billions of years later, when people would exist, that right and wrong would apply to them. What I mean, when I say that, is that right and wrong are real. It's part of creation. Like the laws of mathematics. It comes from God, like everything else. It's objective. It's obligatory. It's not a subjective thing or a matter of taste, for people to play with or discard."

He remained looking at Gloria. Then he looked at Elspeth.

"Ellie, the theory of law in western civilization, and the Jewish theory of law, are completely different. In western civilization law has always been perceived as created by men. By an emperor, for instance. Or a king. Or a legislature. Or the town meeting. Men made it, men can change it. Rousseau called it a social contract. In every state the legal rate of interest on credit cards is different. In some states it's lawful to turn right on red, and in some states it isn't. They can take a vote and change it tomorrow. It's not real. The preamble to the Constitution says 'We the people.' Law is set up by people. But the preamble to the Torah says 'I am the Lord your God.' Or, if you prefer, 'In the beginning God created.' That means law is real. And law applies to everything. Nothing is outside it. In western civilization, law can apply only in circumstances where it's at least theoretically possible that the cops or the feds or somebody might detect you. But in Torah that's not so. Like, suppose I avoid giving charity, in a situation where nobody can ever know if I did or I didn't. Still, God would know. And I'd know. The law applies even in my most secret solitude. Men didn't make it. God made it, and students of the law discover it. That's not to say there aren't any exceptions, or that we don't have

545

new ramifications when new conditions arise. But the exceptions too are part of the law. And so are the exceptions to the exceptions. Suppose some great rabbinical scholar says, 'in such and such a case, the dictum that we've always had won't work. Because we've got here a unique, unforeseen kind of circumstance, and we can't handle it in the old way.' He hasn't set the law aside. If the consensus of the best scholars is that his judgment was correct, and not mistaken, then it was what God wanted. And it was obligatory to make that exception. Because it was part of the law, waiting there all this time for some thinking scholar with enough background and insight to discover it. See? The exceptions and ramifications too were created long before us, when the world was created."

He paused, still looking at Elspeth. He wet his lip. He ran his hand through his hair. His potholder fell between the backs of the two sofas.

"I'll get it," said Gloria.

She squirmed on her belly under the sofa. Then she wriggled backward, and rose breathlessly, smoothing and straightening her dress. She handed him the circle of knit.

"Thanks." He refastened it on the back of his head, with its bobby pin. He looked at his watch. "Ellie, I've got to run. I've got to put out all the barrels, and then I've still got to sit up and prepare for a class."

"At your table and chair by the furnace?"

"At my table and chair by the furnace. I've got seventeen students starting biochemistry tomorrow morning." He rose. "Sorry I talked so much."

"I asked you to. I'm glad you did. I don't know if I understand religion, but at least I understand *you* a little more."

Elspeth and Gloria went up the staircase with him.

He opened the door. It creaked on its hinges. "This is a beautiful door," he said.

"Isn't it, though?" said Elspeth. It had a rounded top. Its thick planks were weathered with a grainy, uneven surface, and each of the long, tapering hinges ended in a kind of fleur-de-lis. Its little window was crisscrossed with twisted iron.

They walked to the car.

He turned. "Ellie, there's a friend of mine at Harvard Law School who told me about this big professor over there who's a brilliant legal mind, a fantastic genius. Nationally famous. A legend in his own time. And he teaches this course, with about a hundred-and-forty students in the lecture hall, and he has their names on a seating list in front of him, and sometimes he'll pick out a name and ask a question. And if he doesn't like the answer, he's got this very clever rapierlike wit, and he'll make the student into a total horse's ass. Humiliate him down to nothing. Now, if he were into Talmud, he'd know he mustn't do that. That's what law is all about."

Elspeth smiled.

He got into the car.

"How's the car?" she asked.

"Okay. When it needs a tune-up I'll call you."

They watched him drive away.

"Want to learn a song from the show I saw with your dad this afternoon?" Elspeth asked Gloria.

"Sure."

They went in.

"He's sort of highbrow," Gloria said as they descended the stairs. "Did you know what he was saying?"

"I think so."

"I never heard of that about plugging in timers. Did you ever hear of that?"

"No."

"I think he's orthodox. I can tell because he wears a yarmulka when he doesn't have to."

"Ya, he's orthodox. Once he got into it he went all the way."

They sat together on the piano bench. Elspeth began to pick out a tune, first with one finger.

"Do you have the album of Music Under the Bed?" she asked.

"No. We don't."

"I think I'll get it, for your dad. Don't tell him."

She began to play with two hands. She sang.

> "It's so sooty in the city.
> Flakes are falling everywhere.
> But the sunsets get so pretty
> When there's sulphur in the air—"

Phil came in from the porch, carrying his book. "Has your cousin gone already? So soon?"

She nodded. "He's got a lot of work. He's a biology instructor and he's a janitor."

"I'm sorry. I thought I could read a little while he talked to you, and then come in and be sociable."

He sat on a sofa. He listened to Elspeth play and sing.

"I love listening to you sing," he said.

"I'm no Gwendolyn Frye."

"That's okay. You don't have to fill a theater. You sing like you meant it. Even when you sing those little things to the baby. You sing with your heart."

"Thank you."

"The tuner's coming tomorrow, by the way."

Her hands had kept playing. She sang again. In a while Gloria began to join in.

> "I love breakfast in the city
> At a sidewalk French café,
> Though the butter's kind of gritty
> And the milk is sort of gray—"

547

In the morning Elspeth and Gloria sat at the piano again and did more of the songs. When the tuner came they moved to the sofa and sang without accompaniment, but the tuner said they were disturbing him so they went out to the pool.

They sang paddling about on the inflated mattresses. Peter rose on hands and knees and watched through the bars of the pen.

When they went in for lunch the old man was still plunking and striking his tuning forks. Gloria readied Peter for his nap while Elspeth changed for her appointment with Dr. Le Vyne.

She drove to Boston singing in the MG.

> "Nu, nu, nu?
> Whaddaya gonna do?
> Ya gotta make a living.
> But honest jobs are few—"

She had decided to speak at once to Edna at the beginning of the session, lest a second hour be wasted in that silence nonsense. But as she entered Edna spoke first.

"Good afternoon, Elspeth. Nice to see you. Please have a seat."

"Hi."

Edna was wearing the same lavender-brown paisley-pattern big dress as before. She was knitting briskly with the same pink yarn. "Why don't *you* begin," she said, looking over her spectacles for a moment and giving a little smile across the desk.

"Well," said Elspeth, "what do you want to talk about?"

"Why don't you tell me something about yourself."

"Like what?"

"Why don't you tell me what's bothering you."

"Who says anything's bothering me?"

"Of course something's bothering you. Do you mean to tell me nothing bothers you? Unless a person is quite dead, she finds some things bothersome."

"Well, that knitting bothers me. Would you mind putting it away, please?"

Edna looked up. "My knitting bothers you? Why?"

"Because you're getting thirty-five bucks for this hour and I want your full attention."

"You have my full attention. The kitting doesn't interfere."

"I find it distracting. Don't knit during my hour, please."

Edna put it away, in a drawer of the desk. She looked at Elspeth. "You don't like me. Do you, Elspeth."

Elspeth hesitated. But a frank question deserved a frank answer. "No, actually. I guess I don't."

"And why don't you like me?"

"Well, I'm not sure."

"Maybe there are a number of reasons," said Edna. "But I'm sure you can come up with something."

548

"Well, for one thing, you're fat. I find fat people kind of disturbing. Like the rabbi in my town, Rabbi Quint. He'd look a lot better if he took off about thirty pounds. A man of God should look like a man of God. God didn't create him fat. And the same with a shrink. First get your own house in order."

"Interesting," said Edna. "You have a point. And it's important for me to understand why I'm fat. But the important thing for *you* to understand is why it bothers you. Who was the first fat person you knew?"

"Santa Claus."

"Santa Claus. And what were your feelings about Santa?"

"Negative."

"Negative." Edna gave a nod. "He disappointed you, didn't he. You loved Santa. You sat on his knee. And then one day, he let you down. He was a fake. There was no Santa. Only an employee of the department store dressed up."

Elspeth tossed her head. "Look, I was kidding. I don't remember who the first fat person I met was. I just said Santa Claus to bug you. I was being facetious. I didn't think you'd take it seriously."

"Nothing a person says is without significance."

"Look, I didn't mean anything by it. I was just being funny to be a smartypants, that's all. Sarcastic. I don't connect fatness with disappointment. My baby's father disappointed me, and he's not fat. He's skinny. My brothers disappointed me. They died. And they weren't fat. And I've disappointed people. I disappointed my parents. And I disappointed people I promised to give the baby to. And I'm not fat. Anyway, don't people you love always disappoint you?"

"But Santa was at a very early age. An impressionable age."

"Look, I was never even taught to believe in Santa in the first place. So he didn't disappoint me."

"All right. But you say persons close to you have disappointed you, and you see yourself as disappointing still others. Shall we explore that? I'm sure you're not spending Phil's money just to fight with me."

71

THE organizations that Cele belonged to had no meetings in summer, so the MG was available to Elspeth more often than not. She stopped in at the hospital for a checkup, and a blood test confirmed that the mononucleosis was much improved. She saw no need to speak of it. No one had ever supposed it was the real reason for her being at Phil's and it was rarely mentioned anymore.

She took Peter to the clinic. He was given a vaccination and cried. On the way home she took him to Cabot Road for a short visit with Harriet.

"Mama, I don't know. And don't ask. Don't bug me. Phil isn't pushing me, and don't you push me either. It's all very low-key, and that's how I want it. Don't ask. Okay?"

Twice a week she drove to her appointment with Edna. She told Edna about her brothers and about her parents. It was good just to reminisce aloud, and air her thoughts about what had gone on inside the people closest to her. She talked of other relatives too. All sorts of little things came to mind, even the bathing suit Aunt Frieda had made her put on when she was twelve and quite self-conscious about herself, and before such skimpiness was altogether common. And of course she talked much about Peter. And how Phil's house seemed to be reviving her ambition to study architecture. Edna would listen quietly, sometimes with hands together and resting pursed lips on her fingertips.

Before the first of the month she sent Joyce a check, to hold her place in the apartment just in case. One evening she phoned Cindy Schaeffer and chatted for an hour and a half, lying in the canopied four-poster. Another evening she wrote to Roxie Sweetser and enclosed snaps that Phil had taken of Peter.

After Music Under the Bed and the restaurant Phil again almost ignored her at times, though his delight in Peter remained apparent. But she did not mind the laziness and the leisure and the chance to sort out her thoughts. She sent for college catalogs. She knew Phil's purpose was to give her time without pressure in which to observe him. And perhaps time to let the house grow on her, and get used to Gloria. Brad had gone away to summer camp on schedule, but Gloria elected to skip camp this summer, though her friend with the braces had been disappointed and begged her.

Phil did not even invite company. She supposed he avoided parading his friends before her because of their age. But he couldn't prevent Cele from inviting Murray and Sheila for dinner one night. Murray talked a lot and she thought him a bore.

He had a daughter in Boston somewhere, apparently some years older than herself. "She's a good kid," he said. "I'm not too keen on her life-style though."

Then one afternoon Phil came home early and asked Elspeth if she'd like to drive out to Lenox and hear the Boston Symphony under the stars. They were going to play some Stravinsky that he liked, and something by Gunther Schuller that he had heard before and wanted to hear again.

"Sure. I'd love to."

He had folded down the roof of the MG and they sped two hours on the turnpike.

He sat on the grass smoking. Elspeth saw Peter's grandfather with his bass fiddle and pointed him out to Phil.

"Oh, is that him?" Phil said. "Do you want to say hello to him after? I assume you don't."

"You assume right. I sure don't."

"I called him up, you know. Just to find out if the baby came from Kohanim or Leviim or not. That's all. He said he's not. And his son's name. His son's Hebrew name is Itchy."

"Itchy?" said Elspeth. "Itchy?"

On the way home the moon was beautiful. The night was still warm and she lay back in the breeze. The sounds of agitated strings and feverish oboes were still in her head. The turnpike banked through forested mountains. She thought he might at last pull off somewhere, and put his arms about her.

But he kept driving.

Even on the way up Beaver Dam Road it occurred to her he might go past the house and continue on up to the overlook. But he didn't. And bucket seats wouldn't have been so great for necking anyway, she said to herself as they rolled into the driveway.

His low-pressure policy continued as before. The MG was finely tuned, and Elspeth thought of picking up Mark's old timing light so she could keep it that way. She loved taking it onto the expressways and pressing the accelerator nearly to the floor, just to feel the sun, and her skirts whipping about her thighs and her hair flying about her face, even if it took a while to comb out the tangles afterward.

A couple of times, when Cele had gone for her Friday marketing and there was no one to see them but Peter in his playpen on the patio and the spaniel, Elspeth and Gloria took off their bathing suits.

"You're right," said Gloria. "It's better this way."

The dog swam too, the big wet ears floating spread and flat.

Elspeth jumped on the diving board, her breasts free. Gloria climbed up and followed her, with a tremendous splash.

They lay drying on the grass, and took off their bathing caps.

"If Aunt Cele sees me in the shower," said Gloria, "she'll know."

"Why should she see you?" said Elspeth. "Lock the door."

Once at lunch, when Cele was away, she asked Gloria to show her again which utensils were for meat and which for dairy.

"You'll catch on," Gloria assured her.

One Saturday Phil took them all to the ocean in the Mercedes. Elspeth was surprised at how well Phil swam. She stood with Gloria behind her, chest-deep in the swells, both with legs spread. Phil submerged till he wavered murkily and scarcely visible like a fish under the dark water, and glided through their legs without touching.

His head came up some distance behind them, dripping and blowing. "Stay right there," he said. "Stay in place."

The rolling sea pushed at them but they stood their ground. He dove. He slid under Gloria, but under Elspeth he rose, so that she was lifted sitting on his shoulders.

Gloria laughed. "Do it to me, Daddy!"

"Okay. Line up."

He positioned himself far in front of them. He took a breath and disappeared. Elspeth waited, legs wide, till his shadow glimmered under her. Then she looked behind her. He rose, Gloria laughing and straddling him backwards, his nose and mouth against her bikini. The spaniel ran up and down the shore meanwhile, barking at the waves and backing from them when they broke. Elspeth pushed her hair more securely under the cap and plunged. In the stillness beneath the surface she propelled herself unbreathing. He came below like a pursuing whale. In the obscurity of depth his hands grasped her, playfully and fleetingly. But she did not have his capacity to stay under.

When they came out, shivering in the wind, Cele was feeding Peter his apricots, high on the hot white sand.

His hat slid over his eyes and he cried. Cele straightened the hat and they turned their attention together again to apricots. Elspeth and Gloria wrapped themselves in big towels and sat.

Peter turned his head and the spoon hit his cheek. "He means he's had enough when he does that," Gloria told Cele.

They unwrapped the sandwiches and the hard-boiled eggs.

"Glory," said Phil, "what's the most expensive kind of tuna?"

"What," she said, munching.

"A piano tuna."

Gloria laughed. Peter laughed. Cele gave a start. "What's the baby laughing at? He doesn't understand that."

Gloria laughed and laughed and then choked. Phil gave her a swallow of lemonade. Elspeth took Peter under her towel and lowered her strap.

"He laughed because I laughed," Gloria told Cele.

At last Peter slept in the bassinet, its raised hood shading him. Phil rubbed lotion on Gloria. Then he sat behind Elspeth and put lotion on her too, his fingers massaging slowly. She half closed her eyes.

At a distance a young man stood on his head for the amusement of his party.

"My father can do that," said Gloria. "Show her, Daddy."

Phil kept massaging. But when the lotion was gone he extinguished his cigarette in the sand, walked forward and stood on his head.

Afterward Gloria asked Phil to take a walk with her and look for shells. "Want to come?" she asked Elspeth.

"I'll stay with Petey," she said. "It's Cele's turn to have some fun for a change."

She watched Cele walk away with them. Cele's suit had ruffles at the hips. Her legs began too wide and then tapered too narrowly.

Elspeth lay and stretched. Her pinky dug sand from her navel. Two boys her age plunked themselves down beside her and she opened her eyes. "Uh uh," she said. "I'm taken."

They introduced themselves.

"I don't want to know. I said I'm taken. Get lost."

They left.

Peter was still sleeping when Gloria and Phil and Cele returned with their shells. They put him into the Mercedes, bassinet and all, and drove off ahead of the traffic with the sun still high.

"Why don't we ask your folks over for supper?" Phil said as he drove. "Give them a call when we get home. When did you see them last?"

"I've stopped in on my mother a few times. I took her shopping once in the MG. And once I looked in on my dad at the store for a minute. But I'm sure they'd love to be invited."

Joe and Harriet arrived soon after Elspeth phoned them. Harriet brought a colored sack with new baby clothes.

"Mama, he's got so much stuff. Phil keeps buying him things. I don't know when he'll ever wear it all."

Joe knelt and peered through the playpen bars and talked cheerily to Peter, calling him little fella. He wound the wheel of colored beads and it rotated slowly back, tinkling Brahms.

"Dad, watch it with your cigar, will you? You're getting ashes in Phil's rug."

"Relax," said Phil. "The vacuum'll get it."

Elspeth set down an ashtray beside her father. "Even so. It's a sculptured Pakistani. It gets in deep."

"Joe, what do you drink?" said Phil.

"I'm not supposed to. I've had an ulcer problem."

Elspeth went to the kitchen with Harriet and they helped Cele prepare a cold supper.

They had it out on the deck. Peter shoved his telephone rattle off the highchair tray. Gloria put it back on the tray and he at once pushed it to the floor.

Phil was wearing a Hawaiian shirt. "I'm sorry I didn't ask you over sooner," he said. "I've been so busy at the plant, I didn't think of it. But Elspeth could have had you over. Elspeth's relatives don't have to wait for invitations here. She's free to have friends, relatives, anytime. Your nephew was here. Shoemaker. Stopped in a couple of weeks ago."

"Bob," said Joe. "That's my sister-in-law's kid. I saw him here at the bris."

"He was here again after."

"Bob's a bright kid," said Joe. "He's at MIT now, I think. But he got religion a few years ago and he kind of went off the deep end."

"That was my impression."

Peter gave a Bronx cheer.

They laughed.

He did it again and they laughed again. He did it a third time, still quite deadpan.

"He'll keep doing it as long as you laugh," said Gloria. "He does it to make you laugh."

Joe blew a little raspberry in imitation of Peter and waited for him to respond. He stared at Joe but didn't respond.

"Give him to me," said Elspeth. "Let's see if he's ready for his feeding."

Gloria lifted him from the highchair, and the way his eyes at once went to Elspeth indicated that he knew why.

He took to the breast and closed his eyes.

"It's so lovely here," said Harriet. "Out on this deck." She gazed about serenely. At the other end the long open deck became the roofed and screened porch.

"I like it," said Phil.

He took the juice pitcher, and by glances and gestures offered to refill each glass. At last he filled his own.

"There's only one thing about this place I'd do differently," he said, "if I were designing it again. I'd put another little deck up right there, over part of this one."

"Why?" said Harriet.

"Because from up there there's a fantastic view," said Elspeth. "I've had the exact same thought. You can even see Boston. Twenty-two miles."

Phil nodded. "You see those windows? That's the laundry, and Glory's room, and the big bathroom, and the picture window's my room. If I had a little deck, with a door from my bedroom, I could even sleep out there on a summer night. Or if I wake up in the middle of the night, just stroll outside. Can you picture the expanse you see up there on a moonlit night? Here and there a town twinkling in the hills? Or the shadows of hills moving across the land in the sunrise? You'd see it right from here too, if it weren't for the tops of those pines down the slope there, but I don't want to clear any more of the woods. The yard's big enough. But if I ever marry again, I'm gonna add an outside deck up there on the master bedroom. Maybe I'll add it anyway."

"It's a terrific idea, Phil," said Elspeth.

72

ON Sunday Elspeth phoned Bob at the Kramers and asked if there was a chance he could drive down and bring Karen. And the Kramers too, if they were free. He left the phone, and when he returned he surprised her by saying yes, he'd be down with Karen in the early evening.

She put Peter to bed about six. After supper Gloria left with Cele to see a movie.

Peter wakened crying while it was still daylight, and as she lifted him from the crib she saw Bob's car pass her window. In her arms he stopped crying, but a teardrop still lay on his cheek when she opened the rounded plank door to Bob and Karen. He looked at them, and then looked up to Elspeth, wrinkling his brow and pouting a quivering lower lip, threatening to cry again.

"Aw, what's the matter?" said Karen.

"I think he's teething. The first upper incisor came in today, but the one in there next to it is giving him a bad time. Or maybe he had a bad dream. Maybe he dreamed the doctor was vaccinating him again."

"Greetings," said Phil, from down in the living room. He waved.

"Why don't you go down and keep Phil company for a little while," said Elspeth. "I'll be down soon."

She returned with Peter to the bedroom.

> "Petey got twee teet.
> Petey got twee teet—"

Then she sang On Top of Old Smoky and Go Tell Aunt Rhody. At the last stanza he fell asleep.

She found Phil and Bob and Karen having gin-and-tonics on the deck. Bob sat on the rail.

"Want a gin-and-tonic?" Phil asked.

"Sure," said Elspeth. She settled into the other chaise longue. He stepped inside. A tiny green caterpillar, fallen or blown from somewhere, landed on her shorts. She tossed it under the rail into the slope of shrubs.

"It's so great here," said Karen.

"I love it," said Elspeth. "We don't even get mosquitoes. It's usually too breezy for them, because we're up so high."

She stretched an arm for the gin-and-tonic. Phil attached the foot rest to his

555

canvas chair. "Incidentally," he said to Karen and Bob, "have you ever heard of such a name as Itchy? The baby's grandfather insists his son's name is Itchy."

"Yitzchak," said Karen.

"Oh," said Phil. "Yitzchak. Isaac. You mean it's for short."

"It has to be," said Karen. "What else could it be? So Petey is Peretz ben Yitzchak."

"And he's not from Kohanim or Leviim," said Elspeth, "so are we supposed to do that firstborn thing?"

"You could have a community do it," said Karen. "Or Petey could just do it himself when he's older. It's nice. You have a party, including a friend of yours who happens to be a Kohen, and you hand him five silver dollars, and he hands you the baby. Like the Kohen represents a descendant of the ancient priests, and you're buying your firstborn back from God."

"What's he do with the money?" Elspeth asked her.

"Oh, he can give it back to you, or he can send it to your favorite charity if you want—in the old days they'd use a guy who was very poor so he could keep it."

"I think most people don't bother with it," Phil said to Elspeth. "Of course their crowd would. Karen's crowd. Bob's crowd."

"It's in the Bible," said Karen. " 'All that opens the womb is Mine.' "

"I know," said Phil. "Something like that. I read somewhere it's even older than the Bible. Before the Jews. It goes back to the Canaanites sacrificing children."

"It's possible," said Karen.

Phil swallowed from his glass, pensively. "Karen," he said, "tell me something. I hear you're a brainy girl. You're a hotshot at Radcliffe over there. So I want to ask you a question. How do you justify the separate seating of men and women in your synagogue?"

"Do I have to justify it?"

"It's segregation."

"Only in the service. Afterward we get together around the kiddush table and eat and talk and mix."

"I mean in the service. Why don't they let you sit together with your fiancé? If you're good enough to be his wife, why aren't you good enough to sit beside him in shul? Instead of like being put in the back of the bus because you're female. Don't you believe in women's lib?"

"Of course I believe in women's lib, Phil. But there's a time and a place for everything. It's very hard to pray. I mean, to really pray. And when I'm trying to pray, I don't want Bob next to me with his eyes going down my front, and I don't want a bunch of guys around me. They're gonna distract me. Real prayer is something I don't achieve often. But I try. And when I try, don't put the opposite sex in my way. No thank you."

"Well, I disagree. I can't see it. In *my* temple, people wouldn't stand for it. We're together. Men and women. We're a congregation."

"Phil," Bob said, seated on the railing with one foot up beside him and his drink on his knee, the other foot locked in the lower rail, "Karen's gonna have a fellowship in the fall that she beat out thirteen guys for. She believes in women's lib. But when it comes to the shul, I kind of agree with her. There's a social factor in mixed company. Any psychologist knows that. In mixed company you stand straighter. You pull your stomach in. Some part of you stays conscious of what you're wearing. And if your hair is right. You smile more. And not because your heart is giving its all to a confrontation with God at that moment. In mixed company the consciousness of how you look, and what sort of a figure you cut—it's never completely out of your mind. And in Karen's shul there's at least fifty or sixty women any one of which will do that to me. From age fourteen on up. Gorgeous. Married and unmarried. They're slim, they're bright, they know how to wear clothes. Karen's the best. Karen's number one. But I can't concentrate on prayer with beautiful women around me. Any more than I could concentrate on a term paper with beautiful women around me."

"You're telling me the people in your shul all have sex on the brain?"

"No, I'm not. But Phil, you belong to my Uncle Joe's temple here in Winslow, right? Would you rather listen to Steve Quint give a sermon, or would you rather gaze at an attractive woman? Come on. Tell the truth."

"The woman."

"All right. That's all I'm saying, Phil. What does an ad man put in an ad to make you look at it? A religious text? Or a pretty face? Unless the women in your temple are pretty ugly, Quint's got unfair competition. If there's one thing that attracts me more than God, it's a beautiful broad. You put a prayerbook in front of me, and a good-looking woman in front of me, and my eye's not gonna go to the prayerbook. No way. Just like if I were cramming for my doctoral examination. I'd have to say, Karen my love, do me a favor. Go out for the next few hours, and close the door. I need an A-plus on this, and I'm not gonna make it. And she'd say the same to me. And prayer's like that. When it's a serious search for God. When it's not just a phony act for social purposes."

Phil shook his head. "I still say it's segregation. There's no place for that today. You can make excuses, but you know it's not just that. The whole orthodox shtik is male-oriented."

"Well," said Bob, "let me put it to you this way. Karen's community is a total community, and the shul is just a part. And the shul is male-oriented, but the total community is not. All right, all right, you don't believe me. But listen, Phil. I accept women's lib as a whole philosophy, not as a few gimmicks. And part of the philosophy is a recognition that we need a new image of maleness. It's about time the male half of the human race learned they don't have to be hard, and belligerent, and pugnacious to prove their masculinity. We have to give boys a new kind of role model, and teach boys it's all right to be tender, and sensitive, and peace-loving. Teach boys that gentleness isn't unmasculine. That's the new idea now. And that idea is called men's lib. Right? And it's part of the idea of women's lib. The world should stop teaching girls they have to be slaves, and stop teaching boys they have to be masters."

"Right," said Phil.

557

"Okay," said Bob. "And in each culture kids are brought up with a preconceived notion of what's masculine and what's feminine. To the Eskimos, to hunt was masculine, and if a boy was too puny to make it as a hunter, then being the witch doctor was also a male option. To make clothes was feminine. Those were the two things needed for survival in the Arctic. Meat and clothes. And that's how they divided the sex roles. And every culture seems to have some kind of image like that, of what a man does to be a real he-man. Maybe there's a biological programming in the human species that compels males to identify with an idea of maleness. I don't know. Maybe it makes life sexier. But the idea of a male role model doesn't itself have to be bad. What's bad about it, is that they've got a lousy model. Practically everywhere male is defined as fighting. As domineering. Aggressive. And that's where the trouble lies. Do you agree, Phil?"

"I'd go along with that."

"Like, in Spanish culture," said Bob, "the most masculine he-man possible is the guy that goes into a bull ring with a weapon and draws blood. Kills something. Or in Japan, the idea you inherit of the ultimate in maleness is the samurai with his sword. Or the sumo wrestler, the man-mountain, who opens his act with a symbolic skull-crushing. And for the Arab kid, the male ultimate is the warrior on horseback waving his scimitar and swooping out of the desert to lop the heads off the infidels. For the French, the irresistible lover. In Italy the more a guy philanders and cheats on his wife the more masculine he is. In England, it's the ability to use your fists. Or hold your ale. Or athletic ability. The playing fields of Eton, and all that. And I've read that Russian peasant women used to expect their husbands to get soaked in vodka and give them a fat lip. If he didn't beat her up regularly she doubted his virility. And there was a time among the upper classes in Germany when you proved your manhood by contracting a venereal disease and getting a scar on your cheek in a dueling fraternity. Sure, I'm describing the extremes. Not necessarily the average shmo, or the human race would have wiped itself out before now. But that's the kind of folklore that's been the male tradition around the world. And it's made a lot of trouble. Masculinity. The longest prick. And your win-loss record as a fighter. The old Adam. And the manly art of self-defense. And all that garbage."

"So what do you do about it?" Phil asked him.

"Well, it stinks, and a lot of thinking people are fed up with it. So the cry is out now that we need to find a substitute role model. Somehow find a new definition of masculine, and sell it to people. But what most people are unaware of is that Torah has been working on just such a substitute role model. With pretty fair success. Torah believes that human nature can be changed. I remember my grandfather, when he used to come and stay with us. Remember Gramps, Ellie? Remember him davening over by the wall? And never saying a harsh word to anybody, and never knocking anybody? Phil, when I was six years old, eight years old, ten years old, I'd see my whole family involved in all kinds of horseshit. And there was Gramps in his corner, facing the wall, wrapped in his tallis, trying to shut out the horseshit. Sometimes a little kid can't be fooled. I couldn't have verbalized it. I loved my parents, and yet some part of me could sense they were full of shit. I wouldn't have known how to say it, but I'd see Gramps, and I'd know he was into something real. I knew, here was a man. With eyes in his head. You know, I never had a religious education. You and Mark and Eric had little enough, but at least Joe and Harriet sent you to a class where you learned the alphabet for a couple of years. I didn't even get that. Zilch. I knew from nothing. And the first time I ever put on tefillin, Phil, I was nineteen years old. My lab partner was a froomie, and he invited me to his parents' house for a weekend, and on Sunday morning he said, 'it's time you learned how to put on tefillin.' And he showed me. And there I was, with a big tallis around me, and my left sleeve rolled all the way up, and tefillin strapped on, and on my forehead, and facing the wall with a prayerbook in my hands, just like Gramps. And Phil, so help me. The feeling that came over me then, was a total surprise to me. It was the last thing I expected, the furthest thing from my mind. But I felt virile. In all my sinews. So help me, Phil, virile. I wasn't looking for that, and I would never have thought to predict it in a million years. But it like knocked me over. Tremendous. Overwhelming. Crazy. I can't describe it. It was like hair on my chest. All of a sudden I was a man, a mensch, ten feet tall. I don't mean when I put it on today—it's a one-time feeling I can't recapture. But I haven't forgotten it. I was totally unprepared for the way it got me. Nothing was ever like that. Not the first time I jerked off when I was a kid. Not even the first time I got laid. My sister started getting laid when she was fourteen, and she was two years older than me, and I got laid for the first time when I was sixteen, and I knew I'd never catch up with her. Was that thunder?"

"I think so," said Karen.

There had been a rumbling in the distance. In the west, where the sky should have been golden, it had turned purple and dark, though overhead it was clear and blue.

"Phil," said Bob, "you go into the home of a suburban Jewish family, where they don't know Talmud from third base, but they know all the batting averages in both leagues. And there hanging on the wall in the entry you see this cornball painting. The old bearded guy in a black yarmulka, sitting at a table, studying an open book. Sometimes in a tallis and tefillin. A real sentimental piece of nonart. Junk. Whatever they paid for it they were robbed. But why do they put it there? Because somewhere in their bones they've got this dim memory. That old guy is an ideal. His beard is white. But he's not embarrassed by the fact that he's too old to get it up anymore. He doesn't know an uppercut from a karate chop. But he knows that to be virile is to be with a book. He knows that to be virile is to pray three times a day, asking God to help him be decent, and soft-spoken. He knows that to be super-masculine is to spend a lifetime studying the science of gentleness. And Phil, over the centuries it's had an effect. Do you realize that Jews have the lowest homicide rate of any people on earth? That's a fact. You can say, so what. But think about it. It has to mean something." He took a long swallow, and when he lowered the glass it held only the wedge of lime. "How often do you hear of rape, or wife-beating, or child-abuse in a Jewish community? Seriously? I keep

559

reading in the papers, all these cases of child-abuse. The baby cries too much, so the mother's boyfriend throws the baby out the window. Newspaper stories that make you sick. Two-year-olds with welts, and cigarette burns. And I haven't yet in one of these stories seen a Jewish name. I hope I never do. But so far I haven't. Not once. And why? Don't tell me it has nothing to do with it. For centuries we persuaded boys that the shul was a boy thing. Kid, you want to be masculine, like the men? Go to shul. Daven. You don't have to bloody anybody's nose. You want to feel masculine? Like your uncles? Open the books and study the technique of loving your neighbor as yourself. That's what puts hair on your chest. In the whole world, there's no people and no culture less turned on by bullfighting. Or cockfighting. Or hunting. Killing for sport. Shooting at a flock of migrating ducks for the pleasure of seeing them drop out of the sky. Or shooting at squirrels with a BB gun. Isn't that true? They don't know from such stuff. The Arabs haven't even accused the Israelis of rape. What army, the Americans, the Russians, anybody, did you ever hear of that never got accused of rape? And the Arabs have accused Israel of every crime under the sun. And they've distorted history fifty ways. But they completely forgot to accuse Israeli soldiers of raping Arab girls. How come? How could the PLO omit to say such a thing? Unless the idea was so ridiculous, so remote from everything they know about Jews, that it just never crossed their minds?"

In the darkest corner of the sky lightning shot out crooked branches. Again there was distant thunder.

"Phil," Bob went on, "when Nasser got mad and cut off the water to punish his own troops, the Israelis airlifted water to the enemy. I'm telling you, they don't know how to hate. Maybe that's why they're in trouble. They learn to fight, because in the Middle East if you can't fight you're dead. But to them it's like paying taxes, or shlepping the garbage, or washing a corpse, the kind of rotten necessity they'd give anything to be rid of. Like when four countries mobilized and swore to wipe Israel off the map, and promised a massacre worse than the Mongols with blood flowing like rivers, and then the Israelis pushed them all back beyond the starting line in six days, in spite of being outmanned and outweaponed three to one, the world stood up and cheered. But the Israelis didn't even have a victory parade. It didn't occur to them. They were just glad they were alive. And what's more remarkable, is that nobody else even remarked on their failure to have a victory parade. Nobody mentioned it. The idea of Jews having a military parade was so unlikely, and so remote from anything Jews get their kicks from, that no Jew thought of it, and no goy thought of it. Why do you think the Israeli army has this reputation for dressing like slobs, and calling their officers by their first names? You think it's just that they're so democratic? It's not just that. It's because military spit and polish doesn't turn them on. It makes them puke. In the War of Independence, in forty-eight, the girls carried rifles just like the boys. It never occurred to them that fighting was a boy thing. And the Arabs got highly insulted."

"You exaggerate a lot," Phil said.

"No, I don't think I exaggerate. I think you can say that a boy who's being raised the way Karen's little nephew is being raised is not gonna get his kicks from violence.

From the macho stuff. Ed Gordon even says circumcision could tie in with it."

"Really?" Karen asked. "How did he mean?"

"Well," Bob said, "it was just a thought we tossed around once in Rabbi Ed's class. Circumcision says listen, buster, don't get too carried away with your masculinity. Don't worship Priapus, the great god of the prick, and don't think he's the source of your strength. Because he's been knocked over by One greater. Phil, I wish someone would make a comparison of movies, for instance. Israeli films as compared to American. Or the Yiddish-language films they used to make in Warsaw. I haven't seen that many, but I bet that when a movie is made for a specifically Jewish audience, it doesn't have the punches in the guts, and the chair smashing the window, and the car tumbling down the cliff in flames. All the staple socko-whack-bif-bam. I don't know if a study's been made. But it would be interesting. For Jews, violence is dumb. They just don't dig it. Loving children, and educating children, that's what they dig. Are you gonna tell me Torah study hasn't transformed a people? Why do you suppose Jews became the world's diamond dealers? Because if a diamond ring needed repair, people knew they could hand it to a Jew, and not have to worry that he'd swipe it or take a chip off the bottom. Why did Jews become the first bankers? Because in the Middle Ages, when people looked for somebody to entrust their gold to, they knew that Jews were honest. In spite of all the rotten things they were saying about them."

"In Israel they have a whole different theory of law," Elspeth said to Phil. "Law was made by God, when the world was created. It's not something made by people."

"Ellie, I guess you misunderstood me on that," Bob said. "I'm sorry. It was my fault. I didn't mean it in that context. Israel is a parliamentary democracy. The parliament votes the laws, like anyplace else. How else can you run a country today? Even the orthodox are divided six ways. There are those who believe Torah is relevant to every century, including the twentieth, and there are those that are afraid to come into the twentieth century and find out. But I meant there are people who try to live by God's law. In Israel, and here. And I hope there'll be more."

"Bob," said Phil, "you're a good talker. You should have been a lawyer. You missed your calling."

The darkened sky was nearer. Lightning cracked it.

"I only tell it like it is," said Bob.

"No you don't. And you don't convince me. I asked Karen a simple question, and you took over. I asked Karen about segregation in shul, and you tell me about the Six-Day War. Now shut up, Bob. I want to hear from Karen. How about it, Karen? Don't the women have a right to study how to love their neighbor?"

"Sure," said Karen. "And they do. But they don't have to study as hard. They aren't as rotten to begin with. They don't have the Y chromosome."

"All right. All right," Phil said to her. "I'm talking about the shul. I assume you attend your shul pretty regularly?"

"Saturday mornings, usually. And holidays."

"And all your life you've been segregated."

"Not all my life. The little girls can run around in the men's section, and the little boys run around in the women's section. They go back and forth. It's only when they get old enough to be interesting to each other that they're separated."

"Okay, so since puberty then. It doesn't make you feel like a second-class citizen?"

"No. I don't need that to make me first-class. I don't need a boy's job in shul anymore than I need a beard. Men need it to make them first-class. I'm first-class already."

"Karen, listen, week after week you sit there, you stand up and sit down with the ladies and say your prayers, and you see the men run the whole show. That doesn't bother you? Maybe you have more talent than they do."

"Well, I'm beginning to understand what you mean," she said. "In suburbia, I guess they tend to consider a service as like a talent show. And sure, if I thought it was a show, I'd want my right to perform and strut and do my thing. But in the neighborhood where I was brought up, we didn't understand a religious service as a show. We understood it as an obligation. And the obligation fell on the boys. My mother drags the blankets off my father at six o'clock on a weekday morning, and she says 'get up and go to shul, sleepyhead, they're waiting for you.' And there's no way he can say 'oh yeah, how about you.' She lies there and grabs all the blankets. And if it's winter, he says, 'it's still dark.' And my mother says, 'by the time you get out of shul the sun will be up. Go on, move, get cracking, before I get up and pour ice water on your face. I promised them you'd be there.' And my father pulls on his overshoes and goes out in the snow, and my mother goes back to sleep. And after shul he grabs a quick coffee and catches the train to work. It's part of the price he has to pay for the tough luck of being a boy. I went to the same school as my brothers, but the guys had to be there forty-five minutes earlier to daven shachris, or they'd get a detention. And we could skip it and do our French."

Phil shook his head. He took several swallows, draining his glass. "Well," he said, "you kids are so locked in on an idea that it's hard to talk to you."

The sky rolled like smoke. A thunderclap exploded around them, together with a flash that blinked and wavered in its instant like a bad connection yet with a universal brightness. All the echoes came banging in unison.

"Is there a lightning rod on this house?" said Karen.

"Above the television antenna," said Phil. "Let's go in. I felt some drops."

"Let's go up to the master bedroom and watch from the big window," said Elspeth. "I've got to see how it looks from there in a storm. Whenever it flashes we'll see whole areas illuminated," she said to Bob and Karen, "under the lightning. In different places. Miles apart. It's got to be a magnificent sight."

73

EDNA LE VYNE said that Bob's notions about masculinity pointed to a disturbed personality. "I don't know your relatives," she said, her chin against her fingertips, "except through the eyes of you, the patient. But from what you've told me, I'd say your cousin perceives his mother and his older sister as very threatening female figures. His problems with them are not resolved. And he sees his father as a weakling."

At the next session Elspeth spoke of Bob again, and this time Edna replied that she had checked with a rabbi of her acquaintance.

"He found your cousin's notions quite bizarre. And he said he never learned anything like that in the rabbinical college. So, you see, your cousin was rationalizing. There can be little doubt that basically your cousin Robert was impelled by a need to reject his father. But the classic means of rejecting a father had already been pre-empted by his sister. Marrying outside one's ancestral faith invariably on the subconscious level represents a rejection of one's father. Even if the father was not himself religious. And even if the child on the conscious level denies that intent. Marriage outside of one's color, or one's group, or one's social class, whatever the merits of it, also has that significance. I'm speaking of the subconscious, of course. But Robert's older sister had also had a need to reject their father and had used precisely that means, which ruled it out as an option for Robert. His antagonism toward his older sister, and his fear of domination by her, were much too great to allow him to endorse his sister's position by aping her behavior. So poor Robert's only option was to reject his father by precisely the opposite method. By insisting upon the ancestral faith ad nauseam, to the point of absurdity, fanaticism, travesty even. And thus using it as a reproach to his father. Turning the tables, playing the holier-than-thou role and becoming his father's father, so to speak, so he can reprimand his father. Making his father appear as the defector, the backslider. And thus Robert enables himself to see the rejected sister and the rejected father as really allied to one another, whereas in fact they are not. Now, for Robert's fiancée, it's a very different matter. It may appear to you that Robert and his fiancée stand united, of one mind. But their motivations have nothing in common. The fiancée grew up in a very old-fashioned religious household. And religious systems of that type all make use of a very powerful, cruel sanction to keep their members in line. Namely the fear of being cut off from their closest ties, shut out, excommunicated. So at a very early age she internalized the dread of being rejected and shunned by

563

her parents and her siblings, teachers, schoolmates, her whole neighborhood and world, as the terrible punishment reserved for those who dare to deviate."

"I don't know," said Elspeth. "You make it all so—I don't know. As if they had nothing to do with it. Bob and Karen are pretty smart people."

"Of course they are," said Edna.

"Bob's a very sincere guy. Even like when he was a kid, when he was interested in animals, and taking care of an injured bird or something, he'd always kind of think everything out. I mean, isn't it possible he just digs it? Like he says?"

"Of course he digs it. Rationalizations are necessary. And frequently they're valid. But a trained person also looks beneath the surfaces."

"Well, I wish you wouldn't. It kind of spoils everything."

"Of course there's more to it. There are many, many factors, and motivations are infinitely complex. For example, Robert's attraction to the tightly-knit orthodox community, the froomies as you call them, is part of his search for a surrogate family. Robert and his sister each compensated for the family breakup in a different way. The sister through intimacy with lovers, and Robert through a closed inward-looking community with strong inner loyalties."

"There's a flaw, though," said Elspeth. "Bob was already froom before Diana got married."

"No matter. He knew which way she'd go. I'm sure it was obvious to everyone around her."

"I guess it was."

"Of course it was," said Edna.

"And another thing. You say families like Karen's kids are afraid to deviate. But Karen and her sister and her brothers are even froomer than their parents. So how do you account for that?"

"It's very common. Young people typically have a passion for consistency. They want to see things as all black or all white. Older people are more inclined to be pragmatic. And in any case children of that type know their parents will approve. Because the fanatic can't help but admire the super-fanatic."

Elspeth sometimes drove to Cambridge now after her sessions with Edna and met Karen for a late lunch. She did not tell Karen much about the sessions usually, but she did mention that she had told Edna what Bob had said, and that Edna had told a rabbi, and the rabbi had called it bizarre.

"Who was the rabbi?" Karen asked.

"I don't know."

"Well, maybe she didn't explain it to him right," said Karen. "There's nothing bizarre about it. Or maybe the rabbi was a shmuck. You know, a shmuck can go to five colleges and get six degrees, and he's still a shmuck."

Elspeth began lunching with Karen after almost every session. Edna's office was within a block of the river, opposite Cambridge, and from there the MG could get to Karen's area in ten or fifteen minutes. Karen had showed her an easy place to park, down by the trolley yards, and they would meet at a vegetarian place that offered black bread, good soup, and unlimited refills at the salad bar.

564

Elspeth urged Karen to come to Winslow and use the pool, and to bring Avis's family. However Karen had little free time. And Avis was hopelessly busy, on too many committees.

Karen found a free afternoon when the first half of the summer school ended. She brought her bathing suit, met Elspeth for lunch as usual, and afterward they walked in the shimmering heat to the unpaved lot where the MG was parked. They had arranged that Bob would come to Winslow later for supper if he could and take Karen back, and that Elspeth would take her home if he couldn't.

The top was down and the ride was breezy. Elspeth talked as she drove about getting married and then going back to school. She said she'd like to make a lot of money on her own. Even if she didn't need it. For kicks. Maybe as a builder and developer, acting as her own architect. Anyway she would include some architecture and some business administration in her studies. Her father was talking of taking her into the store as a partner, and he was going to give it to her someday anyway. Maybe she could use it as a springboard to something bigger.

"Do you plan to have more children?" Karen asked.

"Lots. If Petey's a fair sample of what comes out of me, I'd as soon have six or eight like that. A dozen."

"A dozen's a lot."

"Well, I don't know how many. I'll have them one at a time, I guess, as they come. Until I get tired of it."

They played in the pool, Karen in her sleek maillot and Elspeth in her bikini. The spaniel plunged in with them.

They lay on the lawn chairs. When Peter wakened, Gloria brought him down and placed him naked in a little circular pool that Phil had bought. It had a few inches of water and inflated balloon sides. He sat splashing. He fell on his face. He raised himself on his arms, eyes shut, snorting and blowing, but didn't seem to mind.

He sat in a hooded terrycloth on Gloria's lap while she dried him, and stared at Karen.

"Sometimes he looks so wise," said Karen. "As if he's older than any of us."

"I know," said Elspeth.

When Gloria had diapered him he amused himself in the playpen. Elspeth brought cold drinks from the lower kitchen and settled into the lawn chair once more.

"He's pulling all the stuffing out of your elephant," she said to Gloria.

"That's okay. It only cost seven cents. I got it at a yard sale."

Elspeth sipped her drink. "Shall I put something on the stereo?" she asked. "Or shall we just listen to the crickets?"

"The crickets," said Gloria.

Elspeth said that in addition to whatever college she enrolled in she wanted to try the weekly evening classes given by Rabbi Ed that Bob had spoken of. If they weren't too advanced.

"I don't think they're too advanced," said Karen. "He talks in a very down-to-earth way."

"What does he talk about?"

"Well, some of the things you've heard Bob talk about. It varies. He might take something like, say, monotheism, and spend several classes on it. How Western civilization has always had a polytheistic psychology, and still does. How monotheism and polytheism represent totally different ways of seeing the universe. It's not just an arithmetic difference, about how many gods there are."

"How so?"

"Well, for example, the idea of a binding law that ultimately covers every contingency. You can only feel like that if you presuppose monotheism. Without monotheism, you can't really have law. Because one god's right is another god's wrong. The Greeks saw many forces, or essences, or principles at work in the world. And the gods were these different essences or principles, seen as real forces. For instance, the different ways of living as a woman, or even different aspects of the same woman, were seen as different principles, or different goddesses. Hera is wife and mother. And Athena is woman as careerist. Woman as executive, strategist. And Aphrodite is the centerfold of Penthouse, or Playboy, or whatever, the girl in the nudie bar. As if domesticity and brains and sexiness were separate distinct entities in conflict with one another. Hera and Athena and Aphrodite couldn't stand each other. And you know what happened, Ellie. They hated one another's guts. And along came Discord, and threw in a golden apple marked 'for the fairest', and Hera and Athena and Aphrodite all claimed it. So Paris, the prince of Troy, was asked to be the judge. I guess because they all thought he was a pretty cute kid. He appealed to Hera's protective instinct, and Athena admired his intellect, and Aphrodite admired the bulge in his pants. So who does he award the prize to? Being male, and a goy, naturally he opts for the centerfold. And Hera and Athena were mad as hell. And the result was the Trojan War. Troy was destroyed because its prince was caught up in a situation where he had to choose between the gods. And that's how it was for the Greeks. What you did to placate one god might offend another god. So you lived in a kind of risky tension. A few Greeks would become priests of one god or another, and rely on that god for protection, and stick pretty close to the temple, to that god's turf, so another god couldn't zap him. For instance, a priestess of Vesta had to be a virgin. But a priestess of Aphrodite had to be a whore. And both within the same culture. But the average Greek or Roman wasn't a priest, naturally, and so he had to try to placate every god a little bit, and hope to stay out of trouble. Try to be on fairly good terms with all the gods, and yet not suck up to one a little too much because you might make another god jealous. And that's why Aristotle recommended the half-assed golden mean. Each god was like an extreme, a pure essence, undiluted in its abstract perfection. And this earthly life of mortals was just a bunch of compromises. A bunch of imperfections that you tried to balance carefully against each other. And it's still like that, Ellie. For instance, in the advice column in the newspaper it says 'send fifty cents and a stamped envelope for a booklet on What's Prudish, What's Okay, How Far Should I Go.' And what does that mean, actually? It means this dumb society we live in is still looking for the Aristotelian golden mean between the undiluted pure essences.

566

On one side there's the god of uninhibited sexual freedom, and on the other side there's the god of respectability and propriety and Victorianism. And each hates the other one's guts. But you still have to give a little bit of homage to each. If you fail to give enough homage to the sex god, you're gonna end up frigid, with all kinds of hang-ups, and frustrated, and lonely. And if you fail to give enough homage to the respectability god, then the whole town's gonna be talking about you, and you'll be a laughingstock and the boys will write your phone number on the shithouse wall. Offend either one of these two gods that hate each other, and you can end up on the psychiatrist's couch. So you don't dare give either god as much as he demands. You try to steer a middle course. You're not supposed to jump into bed with every nice guy that takes you out, but you're supposed to kiss him just as warmly as if you meant to. And I bet if you send in the fifty cents for the booklet, it'll be just a lot of stuff about the Aristotelian mean. No kind of solid road map. I bet it's just vagueness like 'honeybunch, you mustn't be too uptight for warm relationships, you mustn't hold the boys at arm's length, and on the other hand you mustn't go overboard either.' You're dumb if you do, and you're dumber if you don't. You can't win. So the poor kid feels kind of guilty because she lets the guy go as far as she does, and at the same time she feels kind of guilty because she doesn't let him go any further. It's like a bunch of kids from the Sunday-school class in a making-out party—they live part of the time by one standard and part of the time by another. And aware that what they do is right by one standard and at the same time wrong by another. And aware of being ruled by both. And that's just how it was for the ancient Greeks. Except for the very few who become complete devotees of one extreme at the cost of total alienation from the other, life for the great majority is a half-assed diluted mixture."

Karen scratched her ankle. Elspeth drew her feet up close to her on the lawn chair and sipped her drink thoughtfully. Gloria had turned her attention to Peter, as though she found the discussion over her head. The elephant was sadly limp and the playpen was littered with stuffing. Gloria took some from Peter's mouth.

Karen refilled her glass from the pitcher. She gave her short hair a toss and drank.

The sun was somewhat lower now, piercing around the tops of the highest pines.

"But if you're into Torah," Karen said, "it's a whole different ball game. Things aren't fragmented. When a froomie comes home from shul to supper on Friday and sings the Woman of Valor to his wife, he's praising her as Hera-Athena-Aphrodite, homogenized. The complete woman. Manager and everything else. He's got one God, who tells him there's a time to get laid and a time to abstain, all calculated according to his wife's periods, so that his horniest time is forced into phase with her horniest time. But you look around you at Western civilization, or goyish civilization, or whatever you want to call it, and everywhere you see dichotomy. Split. Schizophrenia. Like take marriage and divorce. To get married they go to clergymen in a church. And to get divorced they go to lawyers in a court. Just as if marriage and divorce were two different gods, with two different priesthoods. And when they stand before the clergyman in the church, they say 'till death do us

567

part,' just as if there's no such thing as divorce. And when they sit with the lawyers in the divorce court it's all bickering and counter-accusation, as if there'd never been a shred of love. The lawyers warn them not to say anything good about each other because it might screw up the divorce. Either way, you don't dare to bring one god's incense into the other god's temple. But in Torah, the marriage contract you sign at the wedding states within it what's to be done in case of divorce. And to get divorced you go to a court of rabbis. You get married and divorced in the same world. Not in two different worlds."

"But Christianity is monotheistic," Elspeth said.

"Well, it tries," said Karen. "What happened was that the Greeks and Romans got fed up with the tensions of polytheism, so they decided to switch to the Jewish God and monotheism. But the habits of polytheistic thinking were so ingrained, and so deep in their entire worldview, that they didn't realize they were only borrowing the forms of monotheism, and continuing to think in a polytheistic frame of reference. They took the veneer, and the terminology, but they hadn't changed their way of seeing the world. They didn't grasp that God is the God of everything, and I mean everything. Everything. They thought He was the God of religion. Of church. Of goodness. And if He was the extreme essence of goodness, then there had to be some other extreme essence in opposition. So they identified Him with Jupiter mostly, the Sky-Father, and hunks of some of the other gods, and certain other gods they threw out. For instance, they knew the Jews took a pretty dim view of the cult of Astarte. And Astarte was the same as Aphrodite. And to the Greek mind, Aphrodite was the word for sex. In Hebrew a word is dever—a thing. It's not a god. But in Greek a word is logos. A principle, an essence, a god. They couldn't distinguish between rejecting the god and rejecting sex. So they thought they were supposed to have a religion without sex. So they had a virgin birth, and celibate nuns, and celibate monks, and hung these drapery-type robes on the clergy to make them look like some kind of sexless creatures. But their sex drives were still there. And that was a problem. If sex wasn't God's stuff, then there must be some other essence. They had to cook up a Devil. Antichrist. And if sex is fun, and if sex is outside God's turf, then they figured God must be against fun. So all their pictures of God showed him as a sourpuss. And the monks and the nuns went in for mortification of the flesh, and tried to feel as miserable as they could. If you look at Renaissance art, for instance, they never showed God or saints or angels as smiling. Or laughing. Never. Always either unhappy or deadpan. And if sex was the Devil's turf, then pleasure must be his turf, and if fun is his turf, then laughter must be his turf. So the folklore of Western civilization pictures the Devil as always grinning. And the imps as grinning. And the old witches as cackling. And the Devil and the imps all have pitchforks, and horns, and pointed tails, in other words busting out all over with organs of penetration. And the angels all wear these dumb draperies that make it impossible to tell a male from a female. So they built all these cathedrals, with sexless saints, but the more they tried to suppress sex the more it asserted itself. Until by the late Middle Ages the guys were wearing the tightest possible tights, with these brightly-colored codpieces to draw attention to their private parts. Like today, you have a church with a steeple, and just down the block there's the X-rated movie house. In the same town. In the same culture. And the minister doesn't go to the dirty movies, and the guy that makes the dirty movies probably doesn't show his face in the church, but the average citizen samples a little of each. And keeps them strictly compartmentalized. He wouldn't mention the dirty movie when he's in church. He wouldn't even tell funny stories in church. He still sees the world as a bunch of separate essences, like the Greeks."

"It's a lot to think about," said Elspeth. "You mean if I take this guy's classes this fall he'll cover all this?"

"I don't know. If he's done it recently he'll probably do other topics."

Gloria pulled Peter up onto her lap. "He gets tired of the playpen," she said.

"You mean," Elspeth said to Karen, "if they'd understood monotheism, or if they hadn't busted it up to fit their previous kind of logic, then Western civilization wouldn't have had to struggle with these sex hang-ups?"

"Well," said Karen, "there was a certain pope, Innocent the Third I think, who wrote that celibacy is best because when a husband and wife have carnal relations the Divine Presence leaves the room in shame. And meanwhile the rabbis were writing just the opposite, that when a husband and wife really make it the Divine Presence gets turned on."

"Will you keep entertaining Petey while Karen and I go up and change?" Elspeth said to Gloria. "And then you can change while I feed him. We're gonna have to make our own supper. Cele went to the music tent with a theater party," she said to Karen, "and she won't be back till later."

They changed in Elspeth's room. Elspeth returned to the patio to nurse Peter in the lawn chair. A patch of tiny ripples came and went on the stillness of the pool. A few inches above it a dragonfly moved. It stopped, like a hummingbird, then darted almost sideways.

"I hear what you're saying," she said when Karen joined her. "Like if you're pregnant, they tell you it's unsexy. And if you're holding a baby, that's supposed to mean you're putting guys off. As if Hera and Aphrodite are mutually exclusive."

"And if you're too intelligent," Karen added, "*that's* supposed to be unsexy. Or if you're too capable, or too successful. Not only unsexy, it's also supposed to be incompatible with raising a family properly. Athena is mutually exclusive of both of them."

"It's such a disjunctive way of seeing things," said Elspeth.

"It's polytheistic," said Karen. They heard the Mercedes descend toward the garage and shut off. Then there was the sound of another car.

Presently Phil appeared on the deck above them. "Hi," he said. Bob Shoemaker was behind him.

"What happened?" said Elspeth. "Did you arrive together?"

"I guess he followed me up the road," said Phil. "So I told him to bring the car down behind me and save a flight of stairs."

"Come on down," said Elspeth. "We thought we'd eat at the picnic table."

"I can't really stay," said Bob. "I just came to get Karen."

"That's okay. Karen's having supper with us and we're gonna take care of it right away. You can eat and run."

The lower kitchen was under the deck. Its floor was of big glazed ceramic tiles. Gloria brought dishes out to the patio. Elspeth and Karen prepared a supper of cold fish, and a salad with many things in it, spinach, red onion, black olives, avocado.

For dessert Elspeth scooped vanilla ice cream into five little bowls of cut crystal. As a sauce she poured a Swiss liqueur that blended the flavors of cherry and chocolate.

"So what did you girls do this afternoon?" said Phil. "Swim in the pool?"

"We swam," said Elspeth. "And we talked. About Western civilization and polytheism."

"Western civilization and polytheism? So what's the latest scoop on Western civilization and polytheism?"

"Well," said Elspeth, "polytheism leads to a world that doesn't make any sense. Because what one god stands for another god contradicts."

"That's right," said Bob. "It's like you're the child of divorced parents. You're always in trouble. If you please one you offend the other."

"Right," said Karen. "And in Western civilization the tendency has always been to define concepts in terms of the pure essences. In other words, the extremes always form the points of reference. And because of that it's essentially unstable, without consistency. And that's why the history of Western civilization has always been a history of dialectic. Thesis and antithesis. And no sooner a synthesis than some new thesis and antithesis. Like a swinging pendulum. Constantly pulling in different directions. Instability. Crisis, always crisis. Correction, and overcorrection, and overcorrection of the overcorrection. Fads, and newer fads. Running to whatever's the latest, from one side of the boat to the other. Cromwell, Restoration. Hemlines go up practically to the bellybutton, and wait a couple of years and it'll be on the floor and we'll trip over it. One decade the wisdom is the open classroom, and ungraded courses and unlimited electives, and the next decade it's back to the basics. One decade it's cold war, and the next decade it's all out for détente. Cars get bigger and bigger, and then littler and littler. A decade of gray flannel suits, then a decade of blue jeans."

"And so have you got all the answers somewhere?" said Phil. "I think you kids have a lot to learn. Don't knock Western civilization so cavalierly."

"I'm not condemning it generally, Phil," Karen said. "I'm just talking about a certain aspect of it. Like for instance, in the value system of Western civilization, what's considered the highest form of sainthood?"

"How do you mean?"

"What does it regard as the highest degree of sainthood? Sacrificing yourself for others. Ultimately giving your life for the benefit of someone else. Father Damien dying for the lepers. Sydney Carton in A Tale of Two Cities. Jesus on the Cross. And turning the other cheek, forgiving everything, and the rottener they treat you the more glorious your forgiveness. And at the same time, in the same culture, there's contempt for people who let themselves be pushed around. Keep your powder dry. Millions for defense but not one cent for tribute. Speak softly and carry a big stick. And warriors are heroes. Completely contradictory. In one breath they accuse us of going to the gas chambers like sheep, as if unprepared civilians could have resisted more than they did. And in the next breath, if we retaliate against the PLO, or straighten our defense lines, they say naughty, naughty, mustn't do that, to fight back is to stoop to the level of those who attack you. Western civilization walks around with one eye on the kingdom of heaven and the other eye on the buck, and shits on the weak, and preaches to you while they sell you."

"She's right, Phil," said Bob. "Paleface speak with forked tongue."

"All right, let me tell you about Western civilization," said Phil. "As it happens, I've been reading a book about Florence under the Medici family. Do you have any idea of the accomplishments of the Italian Renaissance?"

"Karen's field is the history of the Renaissance," said Bob.

"All right, but have you been over there? Have you seen the art? The most magnificent treasures in the world. The museums of Florence. Venice. Rome. In Italy alone, before I even mention Paris, or Madrid. I've seen it. I hope you kids will. You've got an experience in store."

"Phil's got a point," said Elspeth. "And what about the music? Italian opera? There's nothing like it. The Italian language just sings, all by itself. Opera rises right out of it."

"And the architecture," said Phil. "The cathedrals. Don't talk about architecture till you've seen Europe. I want to go again as soon as I can, and soak up more. If I get married again I'll certainly take my bride on the grand tour."

"You're absolutely right, Phil," Bob said. "And as a scientist, nobody owes more to Western civilization than I do. All those names around the frieze at MIT— Lavoisier, Faraday, Darwin, Newton—all the sciences, the whole scientific method— all a product of Western civilization. Where would we be without physics. Chemistry. The calculus."

"And political democracy," Karen added. "Free government. Parliamentarianism. Also a creation of the West. Sure, Phil, every culture outside of Western civilization is in debt to it. No culture has given so much to all the others. Even the Eskimos prefer a Sears Roebuck outboard to a sealskin kayak. But that doesn't mean that Western civilization has nothing to learn from any of the others. And religion is one area where I think it's still primitive. And I also think I'm into a religious outlook that will someday do for religion what the Italians did for art."

"Well," said Phil, "who's to say all religions aren't primitive. I'm a religious man, and I'm a reverent man. But I'm also a thinking man. And I doubt if you kids have all the answers. You say there's an outlook around that's contradictory, and doesn't make any sense. I say the trouble isn't in the outlook. It's in the world itself. The world itself doesn't make any sense. Consider the monstrous evils that have taken place. Even in our own century. And if you can say truthfully, deep in your heart, you really believe in God after that—kid, when you say your prayers, you tell Him I've got a million complaints. A perfectionist He isn't. And if He

571

created the world, you tell Him I said His taste is abominable."

"Phil," Bob said, "God who creates good is also God who creates evil. Even Isaiah says so. God isn't Santa Claus. That may be hard to take, but it's reality. Who are we to presume that God is morally bound to run the universe in a way that's convenient for *us*? How self-centered can we get? I don't see human beings running it in a way that's convenient for any other species. Humans couldn't care less how many baby whales they leave motherless. Or how many species we poison to extinction. But let humans get kicked in the ass in the same way, and we're outraged, we scream that God should be impeached. You'd think we pay God's salary. You'd think it was us that brought the universe into being. If God were to exterminate the whole human species, believe me, all the other species on the face of this earth would praise Him for His justice. I don't say that's why there's evil. I only mention it to show how narrow our frame of reference is. I don't know why there's evil. I've been into the sciences since I was a kid, and I don't even know why there's a universe at all. I've studied how primordial particles, elementary nothings full of energy, balanced each other off to become what we call atoms of hydrogen. And how some then fused to become helium. And coagulation into stars, exploding, shrinking, and eventually the nucleosynthesis of heavier elements in hundreds of millions of degrees of heat. And I try to keep abreast of the research on how organic compounds might have come into being. Amino acids. Proteinoid droplets, stumbling into existence. I can lecture on it. I can put reactions on a blackboard, various alternative possibilities. If I focus on a small enough step, yes, sometimes I understand the step. And the more we labor and accumulate little answers, the bigger the question gets. And the more elusive. The more I learn, the less I know. I can't grasp why there was even anything in the first place. Why? How did it get there? How did space get there? How did time get there? I can't grasp why things ever began to perk at all. Why there was a bang of energy twenty billion years ago, if there was, expanding without end, or what preceded it. And I can't grasp how infinitesimal charges spinning in orbit have the capacity to become you and me. Even taking it a step at a time, I can't grasp that infinitesimal charges spinning in orbit are somehow the subjective awareness that studies the infinitesimal charges spinning in orbit. I can't grasp how a trillion orbiting non-things, if arranged just so, are a little boy with a brain, sucking Ellie's tit. And if I can't grasp the universe, my grasp of its Creator is even less. I know as much about it as a clam under the beach knows about the politics of the thirteen Colonies. We know zilch about God. We know zilch about what His considerations are. So let's not pretend we do. All He's given us to know is what He expects of us. He's given us a law, and the means to study our shoulds and our oughts, and change our personalities for the better. He's revealed nothing except our own assignment. Phil, maybe we have to create God. Look at it that way. If I behave in a way that's consistent and decent, it gets a little easier for people around me to believe there's a God. And if enough of us are committed to learning to put justice and love into everything we do, systematically and practically, then we might make a world in which it's even possible to believe in God. But if we go around slaughtering the innocent, then naturally we make a world where it's no longer possible to believe. It's human behavior that brings God into the world, or shuts Him out. If what we do to each other, what we do with our freedom, makes no sense, then the world can't make sense. Not for us. For sea otters or penguins maybe. At least until humans intrude on their world and wreck it. But not for us."

"When you tell me we have to create God," said Phil, "you're in effect admitting to me you're not a believer."

"On the contrary," said Karen. "When a guy says we have to create God, and means it, he already believes."

"Dad," said Gloria, "when you take Elspeth to Europe, can I go?"

"Hey, take it easy," he said to her. "First things first. Let's take things as they come, okay? I think you're high on the liqueur."

"I just mean if. If you two do get married."

"We'll see. Maybe not the first trip. But at some point."

"I'll help you clear the table and then I guess we have to run," said Bob. "Thanks for supper, Ellie. A delicious supper."

"I'm glad you came down."

"I'm glad I did too. In my cellar I'd have had a sandwich and a pickle. And no company. Except a spider. A very nice spider though."

They brought the dishes into the kitchen.

Phil led the way up to the other kitchen and out to the driveway. The left front fender still had primer but no enamel.

"I want to ask you a question," Phil said. "Suppose it was the sabbath and you were sick. You needed a doctor. Or Karen was sick. Would you pick up the phone?"

"Oh, Phil," said Elspeth, "don't bug them. Let them do their thing."

"I'm not bugging them. I just want an answer."

"I'd phone for a doctor. Or an ambulance. Yes."

"Okay, and now suppose nobody's sick. And the phone rings. You'd just let it ring and ring?"

"On shabat? I'd ignore it. I'd let it ring, yes."

"You just let it ring till it stops? You don't care who it is? How can you live like that? Maybe it's an important call."

"Phil, when my phone rings on shabat, it's got to be either my mother calling up to yell at me about something, or a student selling a laundry service, or a wrong number that rings when I'm in the bathroom with my pants down. The people I want to hear from don't call me on shabat."

"How do you know it's not Elspeth? Or me?"

"Obviously it wouldn't be you."

"Why wouldn't it? It could be. I use the phone."

"But you wouldn't use it to call *me*. Because you know I don't answer. So you'd wait until sundown. One day a week, Phil, my telephone doesn't own me. One day a week I'm not the running slave of a ringing telephone."

Karen had gone to the other side of the car. They got in and shut the doors.

"Bob, one of these days you're gonna have to paint that fender," Elspeth said. "Or come over and I'll paint it."

"It's not important."

"Karen might refuse to ride with you."

"Why?" he said. "Do you think she loves me for my fenders?"

"Yeah," said Karen. "I'm not marrying him for his fenders. I'm marrying him for the whole car."

Bob blew Elspeth a kiss. The car backed up the slope. It angled before the house, and headed out past the cone-shaped evergreens to Beaver Dam Road.

"They sure are a pair," said Phil. "A couple of dillies. They were made for each other."

"ELSPETH," said Edna, "why did you have the baby?"

"Why?" Elspeth repeated.

"Yes, why. Don't answer too quickly. I want you to think about that."

"Well, because his life made sense. And mine didn't."

Edna looked puzzled. "Your life doesn't make sense? But the baby's does?"

"Well, maybe it won't by the time he's my age. But when he's too little to have had time to mess it up yet, it does."

Edna scribbled something in her notebook.

"Except," Elspeth added, "if I turned him into a pile of garbage in some gynecologist's wastebasket, then it wouldn't."

Edna put down her notebook. "All right. Now let's talk seriously. Certainly the decision to have a child took place over a long period. I wonder if you can recall considerations that weighed on you at one time or another."

"Well, for one thing, there'd been so much death around."

"Yes, there had been, hadn't there. You're referring to your brothers, of course."

"Yes."

"Very good. But let's go back even before the question of whether or not to abort. There had to be a conception."

"Which was an accident."

"There are no accidents."

"That's what Jared said, and it's not true. There are too accidents. They happen all the time. Do you think I'd do a dumb thing like that on purpose?"

"You mean you wouldn't do it consciously. And I quite agree. Jared was right, Elspeth. But not for the reason he supposed. Of course you knew a baby wouldn't bind Jared to you. You knew from the first he'd leave you shortly. Baby or no baby. No, Elspeth, the reason for having a baby had little to do with Jared. And it was a reason that precluded your giving him up for adoption, even after Jared was out of the picture."

"What are you driving at?"

"Elspeth, a moment ago you pointed out that there had been a lot of death around, as you put it. And let me ask you something else. Who is the most important man in your life?"

"You mean my father?"

Edna nodded.

"You mean I had Petey on account of my father?" said Elspeth. "Because he lost two sons? You've got to be kidding. My father went through the roof! He was exploding! He was ready to wring my neck! You think I thought he'd like it? I had the baby in spite of my father, over his dead body practically."

Edna was unperturbed. "Ah. But you were shrewder than you give yourself credit for. You obtained his full, undivided attention, did you not? Even after you left, you knew you were on his mind twenty-four hours a day, seven days a week. And now you've engineered a reconciliation, as you had known you would."

Elspeth opened her mouth to speak, but Edna lifted a hand to silence her.

"Elspeth, I know you're aware of the Electra complex, and perhaps you don't take it seriously. No one wants to believe that one has desires that the culture considers abnormal, or forbidden. It's natural to avoid looking too deeply into oneself, for fear of what one may find. Still, there's overwhelming evidence that rivalry with the parent of the same sex is virtually universal. Look, Elspeth. Your mother bore your father two sons. But they died, with your mother already approaching the menopause. So your mother had failed him. Your mother did not give him sons who survived. And you saw that, at least subconsciously, as your opportunity for a masterstroke. What more dramatic way for you to supplant your mother, than by presenting your father with a male heir?"

"What's so great about a male heir? My father preferred female heirs. He thinks girls are the greatest."

"If so, why did you spend your childhood years trying to be a boy? Tinkering with cars. Learning to be a plumber, and electrician. Carpentry."

"I wasn't trying to be a boy. I was interested, that's all."

"In masculine activities?"

"Who says they're masculine? They don't have to be. Listen, I was the favorite in my family. They all adored me. I'd bust something, and my father would jump on my brothers and blame them, and my brothers wouldn't even tell on me. And I'd confess so they wouldn't get blamed, and my father would quiet right down."

"Because you were the baby, perhaps. The youngest. Not because you were a girl."

"Listen, when my mother was pregnant with me, my father and mother were both hoping for a girl. And my brothers were hoping for a little sister."

"Because you were the third child, and there were already two boys. Rest assured that if you were the first child, your father and mother would each have felt a twinge of disappointment that you weren't a boy."

"Who says?"

"Everyone prefers the first child to be a boy, Elspeth. It's not normal not to."

"Not in my family."

"In every family, Elspeth. Whether or not they admit it. It's part of the whole culture."

"What whole culture?"

"The general culture. Everybody."

"You mean Western civ? Western civ doesn't have all the answers, you know."

"Elspeth, if it weren't so, why were you so anxious that your own child be a son?"

"I wasn't."

"But you were. You fantasized constantly about the son you'd have. What do you think those fantasies meant? Your son, running for Congress. Your son, managing the hardware store."

"I said daughter, not son. You must have gotten me mixed up with some other patient."

"I don't mix up patients. It's in my notes." Edna picked up the notebook. She lifted page after page over the spiral binding, slowly. "Aha. Right here. I even made a note of the name of your fantasy child. Jon. For Jonathan."

"Are you sure it isn't Jen, for Jennifer?"

Edna stared at the page. She reddened somewhat.

"If I fantasized Jonathan," said Elspeth, "then why didn't I name him Jonathan when he was born? Why did I name him Peter?"

"For someone in your family, perhaps?"

"No. I just liked it."

Edna put the notebook away. "Well, the hour's over. We'll have to pursue this further. I'm afraid I may have overestimated how ready you are for certain insights. Though I do feel that on the whole you're making excellent progress. You've certainly arrived at many insights. For example, the resemblance of Phil to your father, which you were able to verbalize last time."

"That's no insight. It was obvious from the beginning. Two little bald-headed guys. How could anybody miss it? And there are a lot of differences. Their personalities are completely different. Phil's a lot more stable, for one thing."

"That's true, there are differences," said Edna.

Phil never asked her about her sessions with Edna. And that's another difference, she thought as she drove. If Daddy were paying those bills, he'd be asking her if the sessions were doing any good.

The differences between Daddy and Phil were far deeper than the few superficial resemblances. Take just about anything. Daddy was the usual automatic-transmission type, but Phil could appreciate a tachometer in the dash and a standard shift that you pushed manually through four forward speeds.

Phil had been taking her to movies and to concerts more often. Sometimes they took Gloria with them to a movie or a restaurant, and Bradley too after his return from camp. If Cele clearly had nothing else to do Phil would ask perfunctorily if she wanted to join them, and occasionally she did.

Still he managed to take Elspeth out alone more frequently. At the movies, or on walks up Beaver Dam Road to the lookout, he would take her hand.

There was a studied casualness about his affection, as though he did not want to force decisions upon her yet, but wanted to be able to retreat if necessary without losing face. If his hand rested on her shoulder, or on her waist, or on her hip, it did so almost neutrally, as though neither of them noticed.

At the lookout the spark of Phil's cigarette moved in the darkness. She watched the clouds slide over the moon. The highest towers of Boston projected above a tiny segment of the horizon, their lights flickering and blue. They talked easily, as though reliving their lives from a comfortable vantage point, and told each other the stories that came to mind. She raised her skirts to climb onto the rail at the lookout's edge.

His fingers touched her thigh weightlessly, rose to carry the cigarette to his lips, and alighted on her leg again airily. He assured her that he liked Bob and Karen.

"That's good," she said. "Because I'd like them to be our friends." She realized only as the word slipped from her that it was the first time she had said our, as though she meant to remain with him.

"You have to take them with a grain of salt though," he said. "They're entitled to their opinions, and their theories, but they color things. Like that stuff about Western civilization is polytheistic because it had ideas like Devil and Antichrist. That's bunk. That doesn't make it polytheistic. The Jews had Satan too."

"I know they did," said Elspeth. "And I asked Karen about that, and it's not the same. In Jewish folklore Satan was only an angel who has the job of reporting on us when we backslide. So from our point of view he's a bad guy, the way Internal Revenue auditors are bad guys. Because they don't suit our convenience, and we wish they weren't so conscientious. But from God's point of view, he's not a bad guy at all. He's just doing his job. He's working for God. When we sin against God, he reports to God and presses charges, and we can't bribe him to keep his damn trap shut. That's what the word means—Satan means Accuser, like a district attorney. But in the Christian view Satan is something completely different. He's against God. Like a separate force."

"Your cousin told you that?"

"Karen."

Elspeth told Karen the next day how she had inadvertently said our to Phil.

"It just slipped out, so I let it pass. I haven't really decided, though."

"Are you happy?" Karen asked her.

"I don't know about happy actually, but I feel content, sort of. Maybe that's a good sign. Or maybe it's lethargy. The aftereffects of the mono."

Peter had new tricks every day. In the highchair he could pick up peas from the tray, one at a time, delicately between thumb and forefinger, his pinky aloft. He had learned to crawl, and liked the tunnel the two sofas formed between their backs. Sometimes he crawled into a cul-de-sac, behind the boots in the closet, or between Gloria's night table and the corner of the room, and cried there because he hadn't yet learned how to back up.

The mattress in his crib had been lowered to the bottom notch, and his plastic seat had been tilted up to the highest notch.

Bradley was neither friendly nor unfriendly. Usually he spoke little. Often he took off on his bicycle, or a friend called for him and they bicycled away together. Sometimes in the living room he chose his seat so as to be able to see up Gloria's skirt, and Elspeth would signal to Gloria to close her legs.

He set up his telescope again on the deck. He let Elspeth peer through it, and directed her attention to a small, faint elongated smudge in the midst of the stars. He said it was the Andromeda galaxy. It was scarcely visible.

"Do you think there's anyone there, looking back this way?" she asked.

"Well," said Brad, "Andromeda is billions of suns. I can't believe that not one of those suns has a planet that supports life."

"Will we ever communicate with them?"

"Nope."

"Why?"

"Because if we sent a signal, do you know how many years it would take for the signal to get there?"

"How many?"

"About three million."

Gloria insisted that they try baking bread one afternoon when Cele was out. They ate it hot. It was good, even the blackened crust on the bottom.

"Let's clean up the kitchen now," Elspeth said, "before your aunt gets back."

"I wish we had a real stone oven," said Gloria. "They say bread is best when it's baked on stone. How about asking my father to put in a stone oven."

"Me? I can't ask him that. Ask him yourself."

"He wouldn't listen to me. He thinks I'm a child."

"It seems to me he listens to you."

"But he'd think I'd use it just once, like a new toy, and then forget about it."

"Why don't you get Cele to ask him then."

"Are you kidding? He wouldn't do anything Aunt Cele asked him."

"But he would if I asked him?"

"Of course. Don't you know that?"

"Well, even so, I can't ask him to spend money and put fixtures into the house. Not yet, anyway."

Phil went out of town for a few days. Elspeth took him to the airport in the MG. She put a quarter in the meter and walked all the way into the terminal with him, and kissed him at the embarking ramp.

She sped homeward under the burning sun, the folds of the lowered roof flapping behind her, long strands of her hair swinging across her mouth, her cheeks, a chill gale filling her skirts.

She left the expressway at the Winslow exit but did not head directly home. There was something about being behind the wheel of a car that had always seemed relaxing, cleansing.

In the flat section where Winslow merged into Dowling there were attached townhouses under construction. They looked like a barracks. She remembered the cornfields that used to be here. She drove beyond, winding into the wooded hills.

Why didn't they think of putting their attached townhouses up and down these hills, like steps, overlooking one another, at every angle? Why can't they accept what's beautiful, and build upon it?

Even after supper, and nursing Peter and putting him to bed, she remained somehow unrelaxed. She phoned Karen and suggested a movie. But Karen was going with Bob to see a dance troupe from Ghana that was performing in Cambridge. She asked Elspeth to come along.

So she did. The dances were varied. In one the full company threw their bodies into a symphony of rhythms against a syncopation of tom-toms, their faces as frozen as their limbs and torsos were expressive.

Afterward Elspeth strolled with Karen and Bob down the busy sidewalk. "They were so deadpan," said Elspeth.

"The deadpan dance represented the idea of cool," said Bob. "Total mastery of the emotions. A guy from Gambia explained it to me. It's a whole philosophy."

They found an ice-cream parlor. In the conversation over sodas she somehow told them how a bank had paid a week's interest on a million dollars of imaginary money.

Karen laughed.

"Run through that again?" Bob asked.

She explained it again.

"How much did you make on it?" he asked.

"Oh, it's about a thousand by now, with the interest on the interest. I may have to pay a little income tax on it. I only hope that if the bank catches me and I have to make restitution, it won't be a hassle to get my tax payment back."

Karen laughed again.

"Look," said Elspeth, "obviously there's something wrong with it ethically. But my question is, have I committed a crime in Massachusetts law, or Federal law or whatever, or haven't I?"

"I don't know," said Bob. "Maybe you should ask a lawyer."

"I bet if she asked two lawyers she'd get two opinions," said Karen.

"There was no forgery," said Elspeth.

"And it wasn't theft," said Karen. "You didn't take anything. And you didn't sneak in and fool around with the computers."

"What about using the mails to defraud?" said Bob.

"Gee," said Elspeth. "I never thought of that."

"And that'd be a Federal offense," said Bob. "The big time."

"But fraud implies lying," said Karen. "Did she tell a lie? Does a check constitute a statement that the money actually exists? I don't think it does. Like sometimes they date checks ahead. Or they make a deposit Monday morning to cover checks they gave out Friday afternoon. I'd say all a check implies is that it'll be backed by the time it gets back to its own bank. And Ellie's checks were. They backed each other."

"But isn't there such a thing as a certified check?" said Bob. "And that means the money's there."

"That only proves my point, Bob," Karen said. "Don't you see? Yes, a certified check says the money is there and earmarked and waiting. So if a certified check says that, it means other checks don't say that. Ergo, Ellie's checks did not say the money was there. Ergo, she did not lie. Ergo, no fraud."

"Why don't you become a lawyer?" Elspeth asked her.

"It doesn't interest me."

"Ellie," said Bob, "if Karen were any smarter her head would hurt."

"Well," said Elspeth, "you kids would probably say it's still not right, or that I put a stumbling block before the blind or something. But I screwed the system, and you're not gonna deprive me of that. I'm gonna just let it lie where it is until after the statute of limitations. And then maybe I'll think about it. Maybe I'll give it to the poor. But not till then."

They walked to the MG. Bob bent himself into the space behind the bucket seats. They directed Elspeth to the building where Bob lived.

It was several stories high.

"Want to come in and see his dungeon?" said Karen.

Elspeth followed them past galvanized barrels, and down cement steps, where he paused to unlock a door.

Then he led down a windowless corridor of cinderblock, under pipes wrapped in insulation, lighted at far intervals by yellow bulbs. A turn past coin-operated washing and drying machines, and at last a wider space, where two bulging furnaces gave many arms up into the piping. There was a cot with a blanket that bore the insignia of the United States Army, and a wooden table and chair. Books, notebooks and papers were stacked on the floor. A wall phone was affixed to a board next to the fuse boxes. The one bulb in the area spread strong shadows.

"Bob, I feel so guilty," said Elspeth. "I'm living in the lap of luxury, and you're down here without a window."

"See what he'll do to save money, just so he can marry me?" said Karen. "He's out of his mind."

"Look, I'm not here that much. And it's cool and comfortable down here, on the hottest nights." He had sat on the cot.

"You don't even have a faucet," said Elspeth.

"There's a john down there. And there's a sink in the broom closet."

Suddenly in Bob's eyes Elspeth saw a roundness quite like Peter's, a resemblance she had not noticed before.

Karen bent and kissed him lightly. "Pleasant dreams, sweetie. Call me tomorrow, okay?"

Elspeth returned with Karen to the MG.

They sped over the broad, lamplit bridge, and turned toward Karen's neighborhood.

"Where did Phil go?" Karen asked her.

"New Jersey. There's a plant there that buys metal scrap and reclaims it, but they haven't been doing too well and A. I. Snyder and Sons is gonna take it over. And would you believe I haven't even seen the main plant yet? The Boston plant? He's suggested it a few times, but I've kind of put it off."

"Why?"

"Well, mainly because it would give Cele something to talk about. She thinks I'm on the make. There's time. I'll get there."

She halted for the signal at a large intersection, where straight avenues fanned in several directions.

"You know what? I'm gonna marry the man, Karen. I'm gonna tell him as soon as he gets back. It makes as much sense now as it's ever going to."

"Gee, Ellie. If you think it's right, I'm sure it is. I mean, you're pretty sensible. I wish you every happiness. I really do."

"I know you do. But you know, there's about twenty reasons to marry this guy and not one reason not to. And I think maybe that's better than a grand passion with gongs sounding and rockets exploding. You look at him one way, and he's not much. But he's a guy you can always depend on to do things right. And that's not a trivial thing. Even a detail like designing the house so the laundry is on the same floor as the bedrooms. But never mind reasons. The main thing is, he's a guy who's been hurt. He's suffered, and it's made him understanding. Compassionate. I put him on a plane to New Jersey today, and I already miss him. He's just sweet to have around."

75

PHIL returned late in an evening, by airport limousine and taxi, without phoning ahead. He had presents for everyone. For Gloria there was a closed box, decorated all over with a mosaic of various woods. But when you knew the secret some of the pieces could be slid about to reveal a hidden compartment from which a key dropped, and sliding another polished square uncovered a keyhole. For Bradley there was a huge glossy book of the best photographs from the world's largest telescopes, and for Cele a set of white teacups decorated with Chinese calligraphy. For Peter a fuzzy reclining lion, larger than himself. For Elspeth, a smoky topaz on a delicate golden chain. She lifted her hair and he fastened it about her neck. She touched her lips gently to his, though Cele and Gloria and Brad were there. But he was tired, and there was no opportunity to talk to him alone.

In the morning he went off to the plant in the MG, so that Cele could take Brad for his allergy shot and both children to their grandparents.

Elspeth found the day long. She took the Wall Street Journal out to the lawn chairs. The spaniel followed Peter as he crawled among the bushes. If there were only a car around she could drive to Boston, surprise Phil for lunch, and accept his proposal.

When Peter took his midday nap she angled the blinds and lay in the four-poster. She reached for her phone and dialed Phil.

"What's the matter?" he said when he heard her voice.

"Nothing's the matter. Phil, is your offer to marry me still open?"

"Of course. Why shouldn't it be?"

"Well, I've decided. Yes."

"What?"

"Yes."

"You'll marry me, you mean?"

"Yes."

"Jesus. I'll come right home. My God, I can't believe it."

"No, don't wreck your work day. Just come home at your usual time, and we'll go out. Okay?"

"I can't believe it. I love you, Elspeth. I've got to come home. Do you realize what you've said to me? This is a holiday. I can't work."

"Sweetie, we'll have lots of holidays. It's your first day back and I know you've got piles of stuff you have to do, and I didn't mean to break up your day. Just the opposite. I just called to forewarn you, so you can play it cool later. We can drive somewhere for supper tonight. Okay? And now you put me out of your mind and get back to your work. Because I really shouldn't interrupt you in the middle of the day like this."

"Well, I'll try. I'll try. I'll try."

Then she lay back on the quilting. She stretched her arms, her legs. She felt good.

Peter wakened in about half an hour. That was good. A short nap like that meant he would go to sleep for the night quite early.

He was dry. She danced him on her lap.

"Oombedoah hooga hum,
Oombedoah hooga hum—"

When at last he needed changing she took him to the table in her bathroom.

"Shall I diaper you up again, Petey? Or shall we take a bath. What'll it be? A bath, okay?"

The spout poured noisily. She adjusted the handle to tepid. She dropped her clothes where she stood.

She turned it off. She tested the temperature with a toe. She unstrapped Peter and lifted him to her. She heard the MG. He had come home after all. Its sound descended on the kitchen side and stopped.

Elspeth slung the big towel about her and went to her door, holding Peter. She went out to the gallery.

"Phil?" she called down. "Phil?"

"Hi," his voice said. He had come in by the kitchen and was not in sight.

"Petey and I were just gonna take a bath. Want to watch?"

There was no reply.

She ran back to the tub. She settled into the water. Peter sat between her ankles, holding his fingers above the moving surface, and smiled up at Elspeth with his four teeth. She lifted water onto her arms, her shoulders, her front, and it dripped down. Reflections played all around the green porcelain, and the water lapped it. The doors were ajar.

Her moist hair clung in strands.

She did not know if Phil would use the back spiral stairs or the big staircase that curved over the Steinway, and she made no special effort to listen for his footsteps. But she heard them cross the tile of the upper foyer before the carpeting silenced them again.

He stood at her bathroom threshold and his form in the doorway made a change in the light. She looked up. His Adam's apple moved. She could see the veins of his temples. She loved the expression on his face.

"Hi," she said.

"Hi," said Phil.

Peter was busily slapping the water with both hands.

Phil squashed out his cigarette on the sink without a glance at it. He sat on the toilet cover. He wore a white summery shirt of a clinging weave with short sleeves and open collar, and dark slacks. Then he came closer and sat on the mat beside the tub, adjusting the knees of his trousers to preserve the crease, but did not take his gaze from her. His lips were parted.

"Sweetie," said Elspeth, "is that how your face looked when you were looking at stuff in those museums in Florence?"

"I doubt it."

She followed his eyes.

"That color," he said. "That marvelous color. You know, sometimes I'd think about it, and I'd try to picture it, and I'd wonder if it could really match the hair on your head."

"You should have told me. I'd have showed you."

"It really matches."

"Of course."

"So beautiful," he said. "So beautiful."

"I like me too," said Elspeth. "I like my whole body. It's nice to live in. I like my body, and I like your house."

Phil was quiet. Peter was still occupied in splashing.

"I not only love that body," Phil said, "I love what's living inside."

"That's a lovely thing to say."

"You're a great young girl, and someday when you're old, you're gonna be a wonderful old lady. You're just superb."

She moved a foot to give Peter more room, placing her further arm on the top of the tub. The adjustment made a little splash. Her flesh rubbed the porcelain with a squeak and her breasts vibrated.

Phil leaned closer. He put a hand to the back of her head. It moved down the wet tresses slowly, to her vertebrae.

"I've never seen your eyes so green."

"It's the tile."

"I know. It's as if I made this room for you. As if I was guided."

His other hand lifted a breast, and let it quiver back. He traced its outline. He traced the outline of the other one, then held it, testing its softness. His fingers were gentle. She turned her face to meet the approach of his parted lips. Their mouths fitted.

She closed her eyes. The kiss continued, tongues playing, and her toes caressed Peter about the waist and ribs meanwhile, checking his position.

She heard the Mercedes. Phil broke from her. "Christ," he said. "Cele's back!" He scrambled to his knees and up.

"So what. Lock the door."

"Naw, naw. The kids are with her. Another time."

584

76

ELSPETH telephoned Harriet from the restaurant.

"What did they say?" Phil asked her when she came back to the table.

"My mother started crying," Elspeth told him. "But they say they're very happy. Go talk to them. They're still on the phone."

Later, when she had flopped into the four-poster, her trimline phone rang on the night table. She reached for it.

"Where were you so late?" Harriet asked her.

"No place. After dinner we rode around, and then we went for ice cream."

"Well, you know, now that you're engaged, you really ought to come home. And live with me and Daddy now. Until the wedding."

"What for? Move the crib and changing table and everything to Cabot Road, and then in six weeks have to bring it all back here again? What's the point?"

"It would just look a lot better."

"Why? If it was okay to live under his roof when we weren't even engaged it should be more okay now, not less."

"Well," said Harriet, "you're right, but you're also not right. Before he was just doing a good deed. He was just giving you a place to recuperate, that's all, and Cele and the kids were still in the house. Officially he wasn't interested in you."

"Of *course* he was interested in me. That was the whole point. We all knew that. And Cele and the kids are *still* in the house."

"I know, but officially he wasn't. But now that you're engaged, if you're living there everybody will assume there's hanky-panky going on. Even with Cele and the kids there."

"Mama, it's dumb. It's cockeyed. And suppose there *was* hanky-panky. Whose business is it?"

"I know, darling. But appearances are important. Especially under the circumstances, it's good to make things look ultra respectable and don't give people anything to talk about. It's only a few weeks. I'm sure you can wait. Phil wants a big wedding, so let the celebration really stand for something. And he's got a million arrangements to make, with his lawyer, and the adoption, and the will, and helping Cele find an apartment and furnish it, and you'll be shopping for your trousseau, and you'll all be in each other's hair. And especially with the holidays coming up right now, everybody will be as busy as a one-armed paperhanger. It's good to be apart for a few weeks now, so you can get all the things done you have to. Then at the wedding you can start fresh. And it'll give you time to see a doctor and get a new diaphragm. One that works."

Apparently Harriet telephoned Phil the next day at his office, because at supper Harriet and Joe showed up with the van. Phil seemed to have expected them, and to have already accepted Harriet's idea as entirely reasonable.

So after supper Elspeth folded the changing table and helped Joe and Phil unscrew the parts of the crib, while Peter slept on Harriet's lap. They loaded everything into the van.

The crib was reassembled in her old bedroom, over by the varnished table, and Peter was placed in it without having wakened.

Elspeth lay on the upper bunk. The crib and the mobile figures cut shadows in the moonlight on the braided ovals of the rug. Mark's high school diploma still hung near her on the wall. It was less than a year since she had last lain here, but it seemed much longer. She heard the tick tock and bong of the grandfather clock out there at the top of the stairs.

Peter took the change of surroundings in stride the next morning. Elspeth sat him on her lap at the vanity, and he looked gravely at the three Peters and three Elspeths in the mirrors. He looked about and up at Elspeth, and then at the mirrors again. At last he caught her eye in one of them and they laughed. He crawled rapidly about the living room and dining room and kitchen as though he had always lived there. He lifted a cup of clear plastic in order to look at Harriet through it and laugh. He sat in the paneled basement examining a toy and listening to Elspeth play the upright piano. But the half-hour bong of the grandfather clock always made him pause suddenly with a serious expression. And when it bonged a number of hours he would point solemnly to the ceiling with an index finger, till the last reverberation died away. But the ting of the gold-cased mantelpiece clock with the painted china face only made him halt in his crawling a moment to glance up, and only if he was nearby.

Joe brought a jump seat for Peter home from the store and attached it to the rear of Elspeth's bicycle. And on Sunday morning Joe crawled with Peter on all fours. They followed each other about. Peter had begun vocalizing a lot, and would say ba ba ba, or bumm, or ayayayayayaya, and Joe said he was having conversations with him. Whenever Joe picked him up or held him on his lap Peter would make a grab for the lighted end of the cigar, so Joe had to get rid of it. Then Peter would explore with his fingers in Joe's nostrils or eyes.

When Peter sat in the highchair Joe made clicks, and kisses, that Peter imitated with careful precision. He tried to teach Peter to clap hands, but Peter could not get the hang of it. One of his hands would clasp the other and he would study them in confusion.

In the afternoon Joe took Peter for a stroll in the pram. Peter needed a harness in the pram now. He would get up on his hands and knees in it, or rock in it, or put his head over the edge of it, or fling the rubber bird out of it, or put teeth marks in the plastic trim.

Elspeth reminded Harriet to save bottles and cans and paper bags for recycling.

"Were you always bothering Cele about that too?" Harriet asked.

"I was a big enough problem for Cele without that. But in the new regime we'll recycle. The world is running out of resources."

She was sorry that Joe and Harriet had let the vegetable garden go to pot. "I can't take all that bending down anymore," Harriet told her. "And mostly I just wasn't in the mood to plant anything. Last spring. The way things were."

"Well, that's okay," said Elspeth. "We're gonna grow vegetables at Phil's house next year. Gloria and I have it all planned out, just where it's gonna be and what we're gonna plant. Brad even wants to help. He kind of surprised me."

She found herself quite busy. She shopped for clothing. At first she would take the Dart, but then Phil brought the MG over to Cabot Road and insisted that it be left there for her use. Cele had bought herself a Volkswagen. Elspeth stopped seeing Edna. She selected patterns for china and cutlery, as Cele was going to take most of Phil's stuff. She strapped a harness to the MG's bucket seat for Peter. She worked with Harriet on an invitation list. Harriet decided that Harry Shoemaker and his wife shouldn't be invited. It would only offend Frieda, and he was only an ex-uncle by marriage anyway. There was an uncle in Minneapolis and an aunt in Texas that Harriet was unsure whether to invite.

"Who are you going to have for maid of honor?" Harriet asked.

"Well, I'd like to have Karen, if Cindy's feelings wouldn't be too hurt. Cindy's my oldest friend sort of, but we don't see that much of each other these days."

"Old friends are best," said Harriet.

"Or maybe it would be a good idea to ask Cele to be maid of honor," Elspeth added. "She kind of feels rejected, as if I'm throwing her out, so it might be good to have her feel included."

"That's a good idea," said Harriet.

Elspeth did not herself list very many. Karen and Bob. Avis and husband. Cindy and mother and sister. Corky and brother. Joyce and boyfriend. Roxie Sweetser.

"What about Diana and her husband?" said Harriet.

"Okay. I assumed you were putting them down."

Harriet's list of relatives was many times longer. Cousins and cousins and cousins, Joe's, Harriet's. And apparently Phil's list was going to be two or three times as big as Harriet's. Phil had insisted on footing the bill for the wedding. Joe had protested. But Phil said he had piles of cousins, and second cousins, and friends, and people from the temple, and the lodge, and business acquaintances, and he could buy and sell Joe ten times over so why should Joe pay for it, and besides the whole situation was fairly unorthodox anyhow so there was no sense in standing on ceremony.

He also insisted on a diamond. Elspeth said she didn't need one and that the smoky topaz on the neck chain was enough. But he made her come to Boston and they sat with a jeweler at a little triangular table. She chose one of the smaller stones, but he made her take a bigger one.

Phil's idea of a honeymoon was three weeks in London and Paris. Elspeth preferred a weekend in a Boston hotel and taking Peter along. So they compromised, and plans were made to spend a night in Boston and fly the next morning to the Caribbean for a week. Peter would stay behind with Harriet. He was ready for weaning anyhow. Though she still gave him the breast two or three times a day he was already taking juices from a cup.

Sometimes Elspeth and Phil were both so busy that she did not see him for days on end. Cele was taking curtains and lamps and linens she said were hers, and the selection of replacements was left to Elspeth. Cele's bedroom was to become Peter's nursery. Elspeth spent time helping Cele too, moving articles to the condominium Cele was to have beyond the shopping mall, and looking at wallpaper samples with her.

When she and Phil did have time to go out for an evening they preferred the Mercedes to the MG. But when the necking grew steamy and her skirt rose he managed to check himself. "What's the use of making it in a car," he said. "It won't be that long and we'll do it right. In the biggest bed in the Ritz-Carlton."

He undid her bra while they looked at the moon. And later, in the front hall, he caressed her underpants while they kissed goodnight.

When they did not see each other he still telephoned at least once a day, even from New Jersey when he made another trip to the new property, and always he stated exactly how many weeks and days were left until the wedding. Sometimes he sent flowers, or a wood carving, or a record album, or a little leather-bound volume.

Elspeth told Cele she wanted to come over and cook a dinner.

"You know I don't like anybody fooling around my kitchen," said Cele. "Why can't you wait till I'm out of here."

"Well, there are two kitchens. Suppose I just use the downstairs one."

"Why can't you wait," Cele said again. "Because you want to show Phil you can cook, right? You don't have to. He's already convinced you can do anything. He thinks everything you do is wonderful. Lamaze childbirth and everything else."

"I just thought it would be nice. I've never made a meal for him."

"So why don't you cook him a meal at *your* house, if you're so anxious to prove something."

Elspeth looked through the cookbooks. She wanted something unusual, far out. If it were exotic enough, he would know that Harriet had not helped her.

She settled on veal kidney sauteed in almond oil, sprinkled with sunflower seeds. A dry white wine. An appetizer of avocado mashed with egg, impregnated with lemon juice, a dash of garlic, and thin slices of raw mushroom, all on a leaf of lettuce with some rings of red onion.

She considered whether to invite the children too. If she did she would have to invite Cele also, or it would be an affront. And that meant cooking for seven people, including her parents. Cele might beg off, but would resent her cooking for the children even more than her cooking for Phil. It was too much to do to Cele all at once. Better let Gloria and Bradley wait till after the wedding.

She experimented with the kidneys. They turned out best with lots of oil, cooked for a long time over a low flame to a greasy crispness.

She stood a pair of tall candles in Harriet's best candlesticks, on Harriet's heaviest linen.

She showed Phil where to sit, and sat opposite him, looking at him between the candle flames. She had seated Harriet opposite Joe. The appetizer was fantastic. Phil had a second helping, and then the scrapings of the bowl.

She would not even let Harriet clear the dishes. "Sit still, Mama. This is my show."

She poured the wine.

"The kidneys are from Cele's butcher," she told Phil. "I guess it's not really kosher because my mother's stove and plates and stuff aren't kosher, but when I'm in your house I won't have that problem."

"Don't call it my house," he said. "It's our house."

There was a dessert of ices. Afterward she shepherded Phil and Joe and Harriet to the living room and opened a new bottle of amaretto.

She said she was going upstairs to check on Peter, but when she came down she brought items of her trousseau. She laid them on the end of the sofa.

"Want to see some of my stuff?" she said to Phil.

She pushed off her shoes and stepped into a pair of ankle boots. She stamped a foot.

Then with both hands she held up a wisp of panties. They were a lustrous white, with a ribbon working in and out around the low upper edge. At the sides their depth was scarcely more than the ribbon. Joe sucked his cigar. Phil sipped his amaretto. Elspeth smoothed the panties before her on the tweedy fabric of her skirt. She turned a knee and angled a hip.

"She was always a charmer," said Joe. "She'll have you twisted around her finger. You wait."

"She has me twisted around her finger now," said Phil.

"When she was two years old," said Joe, "she already knew just how to hunch up her shoulders and sashay around. Two years old. So help me. She'd find some hats, and tilt them down over one eye, you know, and stand in front of the mirror, and turn this way and that way. Smile at herself. Hand on her little hip."

She tossed the panties back to the pile. She slipped into a long coat of canvas, pale beige, with large flat buttons of the same precise shade. It had deep cuffs. She held it open, showing the black furry lining.

"Like it, sweetie?"

"I love it," said Phil.

She buttoned it and spun about. She belted it. She raised the hood, which had lain as a folded triangle on her back. It spread amply about her face. It extended far forward, almost like a visor.

"I love it when she calls me sweetie," Phil said to Joe and Harriet. "Bertha never called me anything like that. Usually she didn't call me anything. She'd just talk. Like I was mister no-name. If she had to, she'd say, hey! Or, Philip! If she couldn't avoid it. That was the best she could do. But anything like honey, dear, darling?

Forget it. It wasn't in her vocabulary. The only way she ever called me dear was the expression ich hob dir."

"What's that mean?" said Elspeth.

"It's not very complimentary," said Harriet.

JOE and Harriet went again on their annual visit to the graves of Mark and Eric, but Elspeth told them she had already been. She had found herself near the cemetery one day in the MG. She had unstrapped Peter from his harness and sat on the grass, letting him crawl about. He had taken hold of one of the little headstones and pulled himself to standing.

On the eve of Rosh Hashanah Phil called for her in the Mercedes, with Cele and Gloria and Bradley already in the car, and they went to the temple. Joe and Harriet went only on the first morning, but Elspeth went both mornings and sat with Phil. Harriet reminded her to put on her ring. She did not usually wear the diamond unless she were going to see Phil.

Except for the eerie trumpet calls on the ram's horn, blown by the same red-faced man who did it every year, she found the services a drag. The voice of Cantor Burns was tedious and unvaried. In the entrance hall people who knew Phil crowded around him and Elspeth after each service, and he delighted in their congratulations. She could feel his pride. Some of the faces were familiar, from years past or from the bris. He kept introducing her to more. Occasionally she caught the eye of parents of kids she had grown up with, but they tended to back away shyly.

Yom Kippur was even more of a drag. In early afternoon the service was recessed for a while and they went to Phil's. Elspeth played chess with Brad in the living room. Phil lay in the recliner with eyes closed. He said fasting always gave him a headache.

Brad checkmated Elspeth in remarkably few moves. They set up the board once more and Elspeth studied her moves with extra care, though Brad made his with little hesitation. He quickly confronted her with a choice of losing a bishop or a knight.

"It's not fair," said Gloria. "You're fasting and he's not, so it puts you at a disadvantage."

"No, I'm okay," said Elspeth. "He's just very good."

In another few days it was Sukkot, and Elspeth thought Phil would be going to the temple again, but he didn't. "I do when the holidays come out on weekends," he said, "but when they all fall in the middle of the week like this, it's just too many at this time of year. Every week, more holidays. I can't stay away from the plant that much. I take both days of Rosh Hashanah, and I take Yom Kippur, and that's it."

So Elspeth didn't go either. Harriet took a box down from a closet shelf and showed Elspeth her old wedding dress. "I used to dream you'd wear this someday. But I suppose it wouldn't look right under the circumstances, I don't know. What do you think? Maybe we could go to the library and look in Amy Vanderbilt."

Elspeth shook her head. "You were right the first time. It would be a bit much. I'll wear a suit, Mama. Don't worry. Someday it'll get worn. Maybe my stepdaughter will wear it. Gloria. Or I'll have daughters of my own. Or Petey's bride will wear it."

Harriet brushed away a tear.

On the second day of the holiday it occurred to Elspeth to drive in toward the city, to the neighborhood where Karen lived, and see the synagogue that Karen and Bob attended. She studied her map to check the location of the street.

She found the building. It was a simple rectangle of gray brick, above which a low clerestory of glass and steel seemed to run around the entire circumference. She drove on past and parked the MG further down the block.

She entered a carpeted lobby, past coat racks and bulletin boards, and heard devotional voices from the sets of doors beyond, some rising above others. On one side the lobby rose four steps. Elspeth guessed that the women would be on the higher level. She went up and pushed open a pair of doors, and found herself in the front of the women's section, which rose in tiers along a whole side. She looked up, scanning the crowded rows for Karen. Then she saw her nearby, in the lowest front row before her, leaning out and grinning and beckoning.

She squeezed her way toward Karen. Girls made way for her.

"Hi," Karen said. She gave Elspeth her prayerbook, open to the page, and found another.

Before them was a low barrier of polished wood and beyond that the floor was lower and flat, with the men's pews around two sides, the sloping reading table in the middle of the room and the curtained ark at the further end.

People around Elspeth began to rise to their feet, not all together, and when Karen rose Elspeth did too. The men below her were wrapped in enormous prayer-shawls, each bigger even than the bath towels in Phil's house. They hung in classic drapes, down the men's backs to their knees and further.

The lanky red-bearded young man who led the service was reciting the ancient language with rapid fluency, his eyes squinting toward the ceiling. The draped folds that hung about him swung this way and that as his body twisted. Many of the men were reaching under their pews and coming up with the bundles of long thin palm leaf prescribed for Sukkot, even while shouting jumbled responses to parts of the leader's prayer.

The leader paused, still rocking before his lectern, and then seemed to begin something new and more melodious. Someone had given him a palm bundle too, three or four feet long and tightly bound, with sprigs of willow and myrtle spreading at its bottom where his hands held it, together with the yellow citron. Elspeth knew they called the tied sheaf lulav and the lemony fruit esrog, but she had never seen more than one at a time. There were so many. More than half the men had them. The voice of the red-bearded leader died away, and the voices of the congregants flooded in from all directions, Karen and the women about her, and the men down there before her, but not as a chorus. Some cried out the lines and some mumbled, some sang, some with rapid excitement, others with slow savoring. The men particularly never seemed to stand still. Some nodded, some turned, some swayed, each in his own style, their white woolen drapes and tall spears of palm leaf swinging with them.

When the last of the congregational voices faded the leader resurged, strongly. This time, when the congregation came in it was as a chorus. The melody had tremendous range. Voices soared and plunged. It made Elspeth think of mountains with reflections mirrored deep below them. The red-bearded soloist would sing a phrase and the chorus would repeat it, harmonizing, higher still, or deeper. Some phrases rose and fell, as though rounding peaks, but the low ones probed ever downward as though settling on the bottom.

"Wow!" Elspeth said at its conclusion. "What was that?"

"The Hundred-and-fourteenth Psalm," Karen told her. "Isn't it gorgeous?"

The leader gave the edge of his prayershawl a hoist as its folds had slid from his shoulder. The congregation's unity had ended with the melody. Phrases were exclaimed, murmured, or even chanted with flourishes, from here and from there, ahead of the leader, or lagging some words behind him. Among the women and among the men it seemed to Elspeth that most were young, in their twenties or thirties, but there were older ones too, and teenagers. There must have been two hundred or three hundred people. Behind them was the same gray brick she had seen from the outside, and a band of clear glass admitting daylight just below the ceiling. Her eyes looked for Bob. She saw Josh Castle, the metallurgist and circumciser. He bobbed rhythmically and weaved, eyes upward and nearly shut, his lips moving as though reciting from memory, the citron and palm clutched before him. At last she saw Steve Kramer and next to him her cousin Bob, over by the far wall, his big prayershawl pulled up nearly over his head, so that it framed his face like a cowl.

The first bars of clear melody again brought the congregation together in precise harmony. Karen sang with the others. Elspeth listened.

"I love your cantor," Elspeth said to Karen, when the next helter-skelter portion came.

"You mean Yossi? He's not a cantor. We don't have a cantor."

"What is he?"

"He's in the cement business."

"You're kidding. Does he always lead the service?"

"No. I guess it was his turn."

Nearby there was a brief electronic signal, sharp and high-pitched. Further down the pew a young woman rose and pressed toward the aisle. Elspeth turned her knees to let her pass.

"Is she wearing a beeper?" Elspeth asked Karen.

"Ya, Penny's beeper beeped. She's a doctor."

Yossi sang another melody, nearly solo, almost everyone listening.

Then he began to shake his long bundle of palm with each word, both hands gripping it at its base together with the citron. He stabbed the air with it, up toward the ceiling. And slanting to the right for the next word. The stiff leaves rattled. Back over his shoulder. Every which way. To the left. Forward. Down. When he ceased everyone sang the phrases in repetition, the men who held palm bundles stabbing the air and rustling them as Yossi had done. They went through several bars like that, first Yossi, then the repetition in chorus.

Avis came in and squeezed her way along the pew, smiling, till she was next to Elspeth. She embraced Elspeth. Then she slipped out of her cape and took up a prayerbook.

Elspeth's book was open to the same page from which Karen sang, but she noticed that Avis turned to a different page, far back toward the beginning. Avis stood moving her lips silently, as though oblivious to the ceremonies before her. Karen leaned over the barrier. "Hey, Ronnie," she called in a subdued voice to one of the men and put a hand out for his palm leaves. He handed them up with the citron and Karen gave them to Elspeth.

She showed Elspeth how to hold them. She angled the citron differently. Elspeth repeated the blessing after her, a word at a time. Then, with Karen guiding her hands, she rattled the stiff leaves in each direction. They came near to Avis's face when they tilted that way but Avis seemed lost in a world of her own. Karen made Elspeth give them a few thrusts back over her shoulder and Elspeth glanced behind her to make sure she did not poke anyone in the eye. The girls behind her smiled.

Karen lowered the palm and citron to its owner. Other people who had them had put them away, sliding them into plastic sheaths and stashing them under pews. Some people had sat down, but now everyone stood again. Somebody pulled a cord to draw open the velvet curtains of the ark. Some were singing along with Yossi. But Avis still stood as if in her private service, her lips moving. Sometimes she bowed briefly or bent her knees. Elspeth nudged Karen and pointed to Avis discreetly and questioningly.

The scrolls were brought out, and one was spread on the reading table. A different man now replaced Yossi. He intoned aloud from the parchment, keeping his place with a silver pointer the way the cantor in Winslow did.

593

"Who's this guy?" Elspeth asked Karen. "He's not a cantor either?"

"Billy? He's a surgeon. An orthopedic surgeon."

She liked his style of intoning from the scroll. It was better than the Winslow cantor's. It was faster, and despite the characteristic intonation it seemed to have a conversational naturalness that convinced her he understood all he said, though she knew not a word.

At the breaks in the readings there were murmurings of conversation about her, and there seemed to be an easy familiarity around the reading desk. A man who stood to the side would consult with whichever man had just stood beside Billy and then seemed to improvise a sentence of prayer in Hebrew. A couple of times what he said made people laugh.

Then, at one of these times, the congregation suddenly began singing and hand-clapping, Karen too. Everybody was grinning and almost dancing about with the rhythmic handclapping. Only Avis stood silently, lost again in her prayerbook. There was something familiar in the rapid song, which had the air of a ditty. Then Elspeth realized it was the same that Karen and Bob and Josh Castle had sung with handclapping after Peter was circumcised. A chair was brought over, the guy who had last stood beside Billy was pushed back into it, and four guys, each holding a leg of the chair, lifted him high over their heads chair and all, while the singing and handclapping grew louder amid laughter. The man borne aloft held tight to the chair.

"What's this about?" said Elspeth. Karen seemed carried away with merriment and Elspeth had to ask her again.

"His wife gave birth to a girl yesterday," Karen told her.

The chair was put down finally and the man allowed off. Billy resumed intoning, his silver pointer moving along the lines of brushwork.

But at the next break the same song and the handclapping burst forth again, and another man was pushed onto the chair and lifted overhead. The chair tilted suddenly and he gave a start, but it was steadied.

"Don't tell me this guy's wife just had a baby too," said Elspeth.

"A girl," said Karen, dancing and handclapping. "Sunday night. Isn't it wonderful?"

"Is his wife here?"

"She's still home with the baby. Taking it easy. If she were here we'd lift her up on a chair too."

Afterward it was quiet again and Billy continued. He had changed to another scroll. When his last reading was finished and the scroll had been bound up and covered another man intoned aloud for a while from a book, all alone at the reading table, but people paid less attention to him than they had to Billy. Avis had apparently caught up. She sat, took another book and followed the reading.

Still another man took charge. He and a colleague carried the wrapped scrolls and everyone rose, sometimes singing along or coming in for refrains. The new leader was lean and smooth-faced and looked like a college kid. He had the best voice yet.

"Who's this one?" Elspeth asked. "I love his voice."

"We call him Shloym. It's really Stewart."

"And what is he? Another orthopedist? Or in the cement business? Don't tell me he's actually a professional singer."

"He's on some aerospace project. At Harvard."

When the scrolls had been shut away in the ark everyone stood praying a while earnestly, in silence or near silence. They sat down each at a different time, apparently whenever they finished. Karen sat before Avis did. Elspeth looked at Avis, and at Karen, and sat.

All at once Shloym began to pray aloud, his voice caressing the words in a sweet solo. Everyone stood. For a while their refrains all but drowned him out. But then the others sat, and Shloym again sang alone, standing at his lectern, facing the wall alongside the ark. Some people shouted amen, as though at ends of paragraphs, and some turned and chatted quietly with neighbors, and here and there some got up and slipped out together at the door.

"Why are those guys going out?" Elspeth asked.

"They're priests," Karen told her. "And the Levites. They go out to the kitchen, and the priests line up at the sink and the Levites pour water over their hands."

The priests returned while Shloym was still praying solo. They gathered not far from him, before the steps of the ark, about a dozen or fifteen of them, pushing off their shoes. A few were teenaged kids, and one freckled-faced boy could not have been more than thirteen or fourteen. The congregation rose. The priests pulled their prayershawls till the woolen hung like canopies draped completely over each head and a pair of forward extended arms. They stood swaying, each in his own way, their faces completely hidden, only hands sticking out from under the wool, with fingers spread toward the congregation strangely—two fingers together and two fingers together with a space between. Only Shloym remained as before, rocking at his lectern, looking at the wall, his back to the priests. He sang a word toward the wall, very quietly yet audibly, and the priests said it after him loudly. The priests and their extended hands somehow remained in continuous motion, though with feet planted. Their voices came more or less in unison, young voices and older voices from heads invisible as though buried under tentlike hoods. Elspeth noticed that many of the congregation turned to the side or looked at the floor, or shielded their eyes with a lifted corner of prayershawl. Karen had raised her book before her face, and Avis stood with head bowed and a hand like a protecting visor, as though she feared radiation or a bright light. The priests paused and sang a wordless melody together. Then they resumed shouting words, again one word at a time, always waiting for Shloym to give them first his soft-voiced cue.

At last the priests emerged from their prayershawls, human again, stepping into their shoes, returning amid handshakes to their places in the congregation while men again reached under pews, unsheathing their palm leaves and taking citrons from their boxes.

"How does a priest know he's a priest?" Elspeth asked. "I mean, he knows his father was a priest and his grandfather was a priest so he's a priest, but how do they know somebody's great-great-great-great-grandfather didn't move to a different village a couple of hundred years ago and fake it? I mean, how do they know?"

"They don't," said Avis.

The long slim bundles of palm were carried in a crowded procession around the reading table, amid singing. Then a teenager took over from Shloym and led a few pieces rapidly. A boy who could scarcely have been eleven or twelve took over from the teenager and led one song, and the service ended. Avis picked up her cape. Men stood folding their big prayershawls like bedsheets.

The lobby was crowded. Young girls were shepherding small children noisily up from a basement. Mothers and fathers were unfolding strollers.

"Just stay put," Avis said. "The kids and the guys will find us."

They were near a wall. Elspeth turned and read the bulletin board. Papers and flyers were pinned all over it. There were cards with phone numbers asking for baby sitters and cards asking for roommates. There were posters for fundraisers, auctions, bazaars, performances, and the Red Cross Bloodmobile. There was a listing of housecleaning committees and dates. There was a list of courses apparently given weekly here at the synagogue by members of the congregation, with days, hours, and instructors. There were three different Talmud courses, naming strange-sounding tractates. And there were courses entitled Modern Hebrew Poetry, Political Realities in the Middle East, The Book of Job, Continental Cuisine, Physical Fitness. There was a course by a Heather Miriam Pinkovitz Ph.D. entitled Twenty Ann Landers Columns Analyzed In the Light of Halakhah.

A tall girl with bangs put her hand on Elspeth's arm and smiled down at her. "Hi. Would you like to come to our house for lunch?" she asked. There was a guy with her, apparently her husband.

"She's with me," Karen told them. "We're going to my sister's. Ellie Baker. Bob's cousin."

"Oh. Hi."

Avis's son Mickey came running through the crowd with a shout. A girl of about eleven was carrying Jeannine, who had grown to toddler size, and handed her to Avis. In the same moment Steve and Bob came to them, Steve with a folded stroller. There was a boy with them, curly-haired, gangling, dark-eyed, serious.

"Ellie, this is Alan, my brother," Karen said.

"Oh, sure," said Elspeth. "Hi." She remembered having seen him near Steve and Bob in the service without having known who he was.

On the street Jeannine rode in the stroller, with Steve pushing, his palm bundle propped erect in the back of it, and a pacifier in her face. Families strolling homeward had spread all over the street, and a car came toward them, creeping as it picked its way among pedestrians.

"We're interfering with traffic," Elspeth said.

There were strollers, and parents calling to young children. Avis introduced Elspeth to a couple named Eugene and Linda. There was a girl of about nine with them and another of about six or seven. They fell into step with the Kramers and Bob, and Elspeth realized they were coming to lunch.

"I didn't mean to impose for lunch," Elspeth said quietly, walking behind with Karen and Alan.

"Ellie, please. You're not imposing. Say no more."

"But Avis has a full house. She's got invited company, and there's you, and Bob, and your brother. I can't come barging in like this."

"Ellie, if you don't, Avis will be crushed. Disappointed. Devastated. It's a holiday. Some people back there in shul even invited you, didn't they? And I refused for you. I said you're coming to us."

"Yeah, why did they do that? They didn't even know me."

"Because you were an unfamiliar face. They wanted to be sure you wouldn't have to eat alone."

"Do they always do that?"

"Of course. I would too. What's a holiday without guests? You're doing us a favor, Ellie."

Bob walked past the parked MG, polished and gleaming in the sun, without a comment or a glance, as though he hadn't seen it, and so did Karen, though they had been in it often enough. Because it's a holy day, Elspeth thought.

"Did you come up from New York for the holiday?" she asked Karen's brother. He hadn't spoken at all in their walk.

"No, I'm in school here now."

"He's at Harvard," said Karen.

"Oh," said Elspeth. "How do you like it?"

"I don't know. Okay, I guess."

"He's still homesick," said Karen. "Freshmanitis. It'll take some getting used to."

At the Kramer's building they all went up to the apartment, and took turns at the bathroom, and then came down the three flights of stairs again to the sukkah out back. Elspeth carried the bowl of coleslaw.

The sukkah was a makeshift of unpainted lumber, mostly plywood panels and two-by-threes, that made three walls, the brick of the building forming a fourth. It was spacious. The long redwood picnic table and benches were large enough for twelve.

"You have your own private sukkah?" said Elspeth.

"We put it up together with two other families in the building," Karen said. "We share it. But they're both invited to other people today."

"To other people's sukkahs," her little nephew Mickey said.

Overhead it was semiopen. Slats lay loose on the two-by-threes, and on the slats lay cut boughs of pine and dry cornstalks, that made speckled shade and sunlight on the tablecloth that Elspeth spread with Linda, and on the paper plates she laid out with Linda and the nine-year-old. Fruits and vegetables hung from the pine boughs on strings.

There was the libation of wine around the redwood table, and then a handwashing at a pitcher and basin on a card table that stood in a corner. They returned to the long table of redwood and climbed into place. Jeannine was boosted on telephone directories. Steve slid his knife like a sword this way and that across a shiny braided loaf and tossed everyone a hunk of bread.

"Did you ever see such great sukkah weather?" said Linda.

"Perfect," said Avis. "Indian summer."

"Last year we ate in our coats," said Linda.

"I see a papaya," said Elspeth, looking above her. "It's too bad Renoir never saw a sukkah. You know, the sun and the shade. And I see a red pepper. I see a big crooked yam. What's that one? A ginger root?"

"And I see a caterpillar in your salad," Bob said. "A woolly bear."

"Poor woolly bear," said Elspeth. She picked it from her food and tossed it out to the yard. "Now he's sticky with vinegar. I bet he doesn't like it."

"When he's a butterfly he won't have to fall in the salad anymore," Mickey said. "Because then he can fly."

"Pine needles in the food I expect in a sukkah," said Eugene. He was a big man with a broad forehead. "Caterpillars we don't need."

"Dig in," said Steve.

There was a large bowl of meaty stew.

"Do you live around here?" Eugene asked Elspeth.

"In Winslow."

"Mickey," said Steve, "how many sukkahs did you see yesterday?"

"Fourteen."

"And he ate in all of them, too," said Avis. "We called it quits after we did the block. He was ready to go to every backyard in town. Chocolate chip cookies. Brownies. Strudel. Jelly roll. Orange cake."

"Is it his fault your friends are good cooks?" said Steve.

"Mints," Avis went on. "Nuts. You name it. It's a wonder he's not sick."

"Remember Gramps's sukkah?" Bob asked Elspeth.

"I don't think so. It must have been before my time."

"Well, I guess he wasn't up to it the last few years. But he used to knock one together out of a few old doors he had. He'd drag them out of the cellar every year. And he'd take his supper out to it and eat all alone, poor guy. Some years in his scarf and overcoat."

"How did you like our shul?" Eugene asked Elspeth.

"I liked it. Frankly, I felt like an Indian visiting the reservation for the first time."

"Yeah, I know what you mean," Eugene said. "But this morning was nothing. Stick around. We get *really* crazy. There's a morning next week where we all get down and whack willow twigs against the floor. And there's a night in summer when we sit on the floor with our shoes off and the lights out and read the Book of Lamentations, holding candles."

"Some hold flashlights," said Linda.

"Flashlights or candles," said Eugene. "Your choice. And every month a bunch of us go out on the grass together on a clear night and bless the new moon. So far the neighbors haven't called the police. Knock on wood."

"It's a far cry from Winslow," said Elspeth. "In the Winslow temple everybody sits there prim and proper, and middle-aged, in their best outfits, with pancake makeup, and the rabbi and the cantor do the whole show. And Rabbi Quint throws a hand signal and they all stand up, and he throws another hand signal and they all sit down. And if Rabbi Quint didn't throw hand signals nobody would know when they're supposed to stand up or sit down."

"Deadly," said Eugene. "You mean they don't do anything? They're just dumb like an audience?"

"Well, sometimes Rabbi Quint says 'let us pray together, on page such and such.' And then they all read one of the translations out loud."

" 'Let us pray together' is Anglo-Saxon Protestant shtik," Eugene said.

"Well, sure, in your place everybody kind of does his own thing," said Elspeth, "but in Winslow it's a different ball game. It's more decorous in unison, I guess."

"There's no such thing as praying in unison," Karen said to her. "How can you pray in unison? Sure, it's easier to pray when everybody's trying to pray, but you're still on your own. How can your heart mean the words when it's not your tempo, when your whole concentration is taken up with trying to keep every syllable in step with somebody else's drumbeat?"

Elspeth nodded. "I'll buy that." She refilled her glass from the pitcher. "Do you have a rabbi? I noticed there was no sermon this morning."

"No, we don't have one," Avis told her. "We're looking for one. We did have a terrific one, but he got hired away. To Montreal."

"Some of the congregants have rabbinical degrees," said Steve. "Along with their doctorates."

"But they don't work as rabbis," said Bob. "A couple of physicists. An engineer."

"We should have had a sermon, though," said Eugene. "Somebody should have prepared one."

"We had a sermon yesterday," said Linda.

"Who gave it?" said Elspeth.

"I did," said Eugene.

"Jeannine is picking her nose," said Mickey.

78

PHIL had gone to the New Jersey plant again. When he phoned, Elspeth lay on her parents' bed and told him on Harriet's pink telephone about the Kramers' sukkah, and how after lunch Karen and Bob had taken her sukkah-hopping through the neighborhood. Everybody built them there, every year for the holiday, in their own backyards, not like in Winslow where there was only the one behind the temple. And they actually used them, had their meals in them. Some were decorated with greeting cards, and some with strings of popcorn and strings of cranberries, and some had children's drawings thumbtacked to the walls.

And in some of the sukkahs they had found the people still sitting around over dessert and singing Hebrew in these haunting melodies, double harmony and triple harmony in fantastic ways, lines from the Bible actually, like, how good it is when brethren dwell together.

And she told Phil they were going to get a bunch of bird feeders as a wedding gift from Karen and Bob. They would be suspended from wires strung from the back of the house to the pines, in full view of the sliding glass panels of the kitchen. Each feeder would be designed for different birds, and all together they would attract at least twenty species. There would be a feeder shaped like Saturn and its rings, that Brad ought to like, specially for chickadees and titmice. And a little one with a tubular reservoir for hummingbirds.

And Karen was becoming a veggie and was going to give her all her old cookbooks. "Well, I haven't given you any chance to talk," she said finally, "and it's your nickel."

"That's okay," said Phil. "I love to listen to you."

"How's the new plant?"

"The plant's fine," he said. "Twelve more days, and thirteen-and-a-half more hours, and we'll be husband and wife."

The maple outside her window had turned yellow. The morning light inside the house was suffused with its tint. The oak by the back fence was red. She buckled Peter into the seat on the back of the bicycle and pedaled and coasted through the breeze, looking at the foliage. On Peacemaker Avenue there were arching trees.

In the center she stopped before Sawyer's, a foot on the sidewalk, and waved. Joe stopped in the midst of waiting on someone and made all the customers come out to admire his grandson. Peter stared at them sternly from under the turned-down brim of his hat. There was an elastic under his chin.

"Dad, you left the cash register open," said Elspeth.

She continued across town, pumping in her shorts. A bunch of guys rode past in a car with open windows and screamed.

She panted up the long curve of Beaver Dam Road, standing on the pedals. At Phil's house no one was home. Cele must have been on errands, because the Volks was not in the garage, and the kids were in school.

Elspeth had not brought her key. She changed Peter's diaper on the grass. Then they biked up to the lookout.

She leaned on the lookout rail, still on the bike.

"Look, Petey," she said. "Look. What do you think of that?"

The astonishing expanse of hills lay below them, miles and miles of hue undulating after hue toward uttermost horizons, gold blazing again beyond brilliant reds and darker reds, even bursts of pink and bursts of lavender, and pine streaking green up ridges amid the rust. Here and there in the valleys a tiny white steeple pierced up through the color.

They stayed gazing, till Peter grew restless. Then she turned back to the road, swerved, leaned, then faster downward into the wind. It lifted her hair. She knew her hair swept back and forth over Peter's face, and she knew he didn't mind.

Peter had many new tricks, and when she came home from a day of shopping she would find Harriet fatigued. He had learned to pull himself to standing in the playpen, and would then cry because he didn't know how to let himself down. Harriet would help him down, but he would immediately pull himself to standing and cry to be shown the way down once more.

If Harriet took him for a stroll in the pram he delighted in flinging all his toys to the sidewalk, and the pillow and the diaper box and his hat as well. Harriet would brush them off and put them back into the pram, but he would promptly throw them out again, every which way. If Harriet stashed them into the deep shopping bag that hung from the pram handle he cried and gave her ferocious looks.

Harriet would feed him in the highchair, opening her own mouth wide each time she offered the spoon. But now he no longer turned his cheek when he had had enough. Instead he batted the spoon from Harriet's hand across the kitchen.

Harriet was not sure if he was actually beginning to speak words or not. She said she didn't know if his ga meant Grandma, but Elspeth saw that much of the time it clearly did. Certainly he understood his own name, and the word no, and words for half the objects in the house. If Elspeth asked where's the little clock, he would pause in his crawling and point to the mantel. If she asked where's the big clock he would crawl rapidly to the foyer and point up the stairs.

Elspeth meant to drive to Karen's synagogue again to see the congregants get down among the pews and whack willow twigs against the floor. It was to happen on a certain morning in the daily service, at seven, before people went to work. But she didn't make it. Peter happened to oversleep, and so did she.

But a couple of days later it was Simchat Torah, the Rejoicing, which would be the last of the holidays for a while. She left Peter with Harriet and drove up. This time she parked the MG even farther from the synagogue and around a corner.

When she pushed open the double doors the place seemed in turmoil. Some of the pews that would have been nearest her had been pushed or carried to the further side, leaving a clear area in which women now danced in a circle, clapping their hands high over their heads, swinging feet, and skipping up and down the tiers of the flooring. Other girls sat on the barrier rail. In the flat area below, the men were dancing too, many of them holding little girls or boys on their shoulders or on their heads.

Karen, whom she hadn't noticed, seized her by the arm and pulled her into another group of girls, higher on the tiers, who danced like flickering fires, their hands and arms quivering lightly upward as if their bodies were weightless. Elspeth kicked off her shoes and tried to fall in with their steps and gestures and the light motions of their bodies.

The dancing stopped. From the men's section a stately singing arose. The men walked solemnly in a single-file procession, those in front carrying wrapped scrolls. The women joined their singing, and together they made an imposing chorus. The children who had ridden on the men's shoulders and heads were on the floor now, standing or walking about, some of them tots that must have been still in diapers.

A somewhat older child ran out and tied a pull-toy by a string to the prayershawl of one of the men. It was a yellow plastic duck and as it rolled after the slow line of marchers it quacked.

The tempo of the singing grew faster, and then faster still. The marchers began kicking and bouncing gaily and the procession fell apart into dancing. The men who carried the heavy scrolls lifted them erect and high, holding their poles at the bottom, and dancing backwards away from one another, and then forward till they met, then backwards and away and forward again and together. Other men formed a big dancing circle about them, arms locked over one another's shoulders. The singing was loud.

It seemed to Elspeth that the dancing of the women up here in the tiers was more orderly. The men in the circle did not kick in step and others seemed to improvise, each dancing in his own way. She saw Bob with a laughing little girl on his head. His hands held her ankles. She was in a checkered pinafore, holding a flag in one hand and grasping Bob's hair with the other, her locks bouncing with his dance. But up here the women moved in unison as though they knew folk dances. There were graceful ones, and leaping ones that kept throwing the hair of an energetic fourteen or fifteen-year-old about her face and her miniskirt above her underpants.

Down among the men a guy danced in the Russian style, arms folded before him and his feet kicking out in rapid alternation while his whole body gradually sank lower and lower toward the floor. Elspeth was amazed at the speed of his tireless feet. Sweat ran down his red face. Everyone had stopped to watch, and clapped to his rhythm.

But in a few moments the whole mood changed. A procession began as before.

A hymn arose loftily. People reached out to touch the scrolls as they were carried slowly past, and kissed their fingertips.

Elspeth was sweaty now from having danced, but she felt good. A young woman asked her if she had an invitation for lunch.

"Probably," said Elspeth. "I'm with Avis Kramer. And Karen Slater."

"Oh. Okay."

Again the majesty of the procession did not last long. The singing speeded into exuberant rhythms and soon everyone was dancing about. Occasionally she was with Karen or Avis, but at other times Karen dropped out to rest, or Elspeth joined a new group to learn their step, or stood and watched, or sat and watched. Women taught each other dances. The youngest teenagers practiced together in a corner, alternating flexed knees with stiff-legged kicks, like a kind of discreet cancan.

Each time a procession began, with new guys carrying the scrolls, there was renewed solemnity, but now it scarcely lasted half a minute. A second girl asked Elspeth if she had plans for lunch, and Elspeth said she thought she'd be expected at the Kramers'.

"Oh, you're Bob Shoemaker's cousin!" the girl said. "That's right. I remember. But I think they're going to Uri and Priscilla's house though. Aren't they?"

"Gee, I don't know."

"I think they are. I'll check."

The girls dragged their pews back into place and sat. The dancing was apparently over. A scroll was unwrapped on the reading table and a guy read from it with fluency as Billy had the week before. He had longish hair and sideburns and a smooth young face. At last all the children came to the reading table, and four guys held a big prayershawl aloft high over as many of them as possible, stretching it at the corners. The kids squeezed under it, bigger kids pulling the littlest ones in closer. The reader read some more. A boy who couldn't have been more than a year and a half fell on his rump and picked himself up.

Afterward one of the older members took charge, a short fiftyish man with spectacles down on his nose and a grizzled beard. The scrolls were carried to the ark and put away. Little Mickey had come into the women's section, and while the congregation stood rocking silently over their prayerbooks he held to Avis's skirt. Avis slipped an arm about him while she prayed. Elspeth had taken up a prayerbook and turned a page whenever Karen did.

People sat one by one as they finished, as she had seen them do the week before. They rose when the man with the grizzled beard began to sing prayers aloud. They sang some responses with him. Then they sat and he continued solo at his lectern, facing the wall. She thought she saw a guy in the congregation pour from a brown bottle for another guy.

"Is that whiskey?" she asked.

Then she saw a bottle of apricot brandy passed among the women in her own pew with a stack of little paper cups.

"Want some apricot?" Karen asked.

Elspeth held a cup and Karen poured. The liquor was sweet and hot.

She heard some snickering around her. Then she saw a boy crawling stealthily toward the grizzle-bearded man who chanted the service. He carefully pulled the man's shoelaces undone, and then knotted the two shoes together, but the man continued the service without interruption, as though he hadn't noticed.

A young man sauntered over to him, holding something behind his back. Suddenly he clapped a plumed and visored shako on the bearded man backwards. There was laughter. The hat was hard and shiny, cylindrical and tall, with spangled letters that said TULANE. But the man continued unfazed, chanting rapidly, rocking over his lectern. Another guy turned the hat around frontwards and pushed the visor down over the bearded man's eyes. There was more laughter. But the bearded man continued without pause, apparently reciting the service from memory.

A third guy threw a lei around the bearded man's neck.

Then two of the young guys grasped him by the legs and hoisted him off the floor, upright between them. His prayers went on without a break. They carried him about. He took off the marching-band shako and placed it on one of the men who carried him, and adjusted his eyeglasses down on the tip of his nose, praying all the while. He put the shako on again, and closed his prayerbook, still praying clearly and rapidly. The two guys had lifted him higher still. He whacked one of them on the head with his prayerbook, quite hard, making him wince. Elspeth heard the smack. The congregation was laughing more than ever. The bearded man passed the prayerbook to the other hand and walloped the other guy with it, just as hard, still chanting his prayer at the same fast clip. They let him down to the floor and rubbed their heads. He kicked off his knotted shoes, apparently without skipping a syllable, and returned with his prayerbook to the lectern, still wearing the lei and his big prayershawl and the shako.

When he finished some children took over to lead the closing prayers. The bearded man walked about meanwhile, receiving handshakes. Kids tried on the shako and men stood folding their prayershawls. "Priscilla's having us to lunch," Avis said to Elspeth. "You're invited too. I accepted for you. Okay?"

In the lobby she was introduced to Priscilla and Uri and their four children. The youngest was in a stroller. Their party spread out into the street, Steve and Uri pushing squeaky strollers side by side.

Elspeth walked behind with Bob and Karen and Alan.

"You people do a lot of inviting back and forth," she said.

"We're a community," Karen said to her.

"I see that. You know everybody. And you know when anybody has a baby."

"Community is a biological need," said Bob. "It's programmed into the species. That's why the primal ape-man ran in packs. They did, you know. Like baboons. And that's why people used to live in villages. And why people join communes, and street gangs, and communities like this one."

"Well," said Elspeth, "I like your world."

79

ELSPETH told Phil she hadn't been to a movie in a while. So they picked up Karen in the Mercedes, and then Bob, and saw a black-and-white double feature near Harvard Square, a revival of a couple of classic thrillers. Phil insisted on paying for all their tickets.

Afterward they found a table for four in an ice-cream parlor.

At a table across the room a bearded young man and a blond woman in glasses and braids rose to leave, and Elspeth saw that the woman wore a corduroy contraption that held a sleeping infant against her front. "Hey, look at that," said Elspeth. "It's the third one I've seen. They're catching on. And the principle is exactly right. I wish they'd been around when Petey was a newborn. It's so obvious. I would have designed it and marketed it myself if I'd had the time."

The couple paid their bill at the register. A ruddy-faced girl came to the table with her pencil and order pad, but Elspeth still watched the woman with the infant on her front. Her husband opened the glass door.

"If Western civ is finally starting to realize that newborns should be upright," Elspeth said, "and next to a warm body so they can hear a heartbeat, well, I guess there's actually hope for it."

Karen ordered a pistachio sundae with nuts and whipped cream but Elspeth asked for a dish of plain vanilla.

"She likes ice cream to taste like ice cream," Phil said. "Just like she always takes coffee black, so the coffee should taste like coffee. See, I know all her shtik already. Maybe you should have caramel sauce and marshmallow sauce on it, because you like goo to be gooey."

"No," said Elspeth, "just ice cream. The simple life."

The place was warm. Bob hung his jacket on the back of the chair, crossed his legs and teetered.

When the girl brought their orders she put down four checks. Phil picked them up. His ice cream was maple walnut. He spooned it slowly. Sometimes he took a sip of the seltzer he had asked for in place of plain water.

"Bob," he said, "look at that pair of hairdos over at the register there. The Afros." With a slight gesture of his spoon he indicated a boy and a girl receiving change from the cashier. They wore leather jackets. "Tell me, did you ever stop to think that when they go around with their hair bushed out like that, and you go around with tsitsis hanging out, and a yarmulka on your head, it's really the same kind of thing? Did you ever think of that?"

605

"Very definitely," said Bob.

"You did?" said Phil. "You thought of that?" His tongue emptied the hollow of his spoon. "Well, it's exactly the same thing."

"There are certainly points in common," said Bob. "I don't know if I'm prepared to say they're identical in every particular. Just for instance, I could chuck these outward signs and blend into the landscape. The black can't. He's visibly black, whether he wears an Afro or not."

"So why don't you want to blend with the landscape?" Phil asked.

"Why should I want to do that?"

"Well, because it's divisive," Phil said. "In the old days, when I was your age, not so long ago, you could say we had an ideal of unity. Many different strands, but one American people. Of course the black can't change his color, and everybody is entitled to his own religion according to his conscience, but there was an outward effort to conform. A guy didn't go around in public with tsitsis hanging out, and you wore a yarmulka in the temple, not on the street. Unless you were some kind of a nut."

"But I *am* some kind of a nut. I thought that was pretty obvious."

"Look, I didn't mean it that way. With all due respect. I know, these days it's different. It's like a fad now—you're not the only one. These days anything goes. But what I mean is, in those days, in my time, nobody would. Not even a nut would. You didn't see students walking around Harvard and MIT with yarmulkas on. Everybody felt a responsibility for unity. One nation, indivisible. Sure, the blacks couldn't change their color. But at least a black lady could go into a beauty parlor and get her hair straightened. And they did."

"Why should they?"

"Why should they? Because I think these trends today are wrong, that's all. All the emphasis is on disunity, differences. 'Black is beautiful.' "

"Well, white can be pretty ugly."

"Next thing you know the Chinese kids will start wearing pigtails," Phil answered him. "Yellow is beautiful. It's destroying a nation, that's all. Look, I know you're into this, but I wouldn't do it. I wouldn't wear tsitsis, and I wouldn't make a spectacle of myself wearing a yarmulka on my head in a public place where there's no call for it. Flaunting it. It's not my philosophy. I believe your own thing is for in private. Within your own four walls. And in public the emphasis has got to be how alike we all are, not how different we are. The unity of all races and creeds, in a harmonious American nation. That's what the strength of this country is based on. Unity is strength. That's what the public school system is for. They mix. They learn tolerance. They learn to get along with all kinds. It built this country. And I understand you kids don't even believe in the public school. What's the matter? You want to divide this country, the way Canada is divided?"

"I don't see that it divides, Phil. My closest buddy at MIT and at the Oceanographic Institute is a guy I guess you'd say is an atheist, a couple of generations removed from the Episcopalians on his father's side and the Unitarians on his mother's. A Wasp type. He's into the way that whales communicate—he's done brilliant work.

And Karen and I have gotten very close to him and his wife. We go out together. We visit back and forth. We've gone camping together, and sailing together, all over the Cape and the islands. And the fact that we're different doesn't get in the way. I don't try to convert him and he doesn't try to convert me. But we worked together, and kind of liked each other's sense of humor, and we kind of took to each other."

"That's because you've got so much else in common," said Phil. "That's okay. I've got friends of different religions too."

"Of course."

"But when you go down the street among strangers, and in your getup, that's a different thing. That to me is like looking for disharmony."

"I don't see it that way," said Bob. "On the contrary. When I walk down the street I know how it feels to be different, and to look different. And it makes me tolerant. Because when I see somebody else who's peculiar and different in some other way, I know how he feels. When I love my difference, I understand how you love yours."

"That's right," said Karen. "Like when I read about the Chinese in San Francisco struggling to keep their schools going, or the Catalans in Barcelona not being allowed to use their language, I feel their hurt. I know the beauty of vive la différence, and I know that they know. It's not people who are different who can't stand differences. It's people who want everybody to be the same who can't stand differences. The unification people are the intolerant ones. Assimilationists, universalists, they're the most intolerant people in the world. Teach a kid that everybody should blend into one homogenized unified unification, and then you show him the Amish, or somebody else who won't go along, and he doesn't understand. He thinks they're unenlightened. But if I see a Hopi do a dance holding a snake in his mouth, it doesn't faze me. And I don't feel like I'm a tourist looking at a savage. Because on my calendar there's a day to get down between the pews and whack bunches of willow on the floor. And one's as far out as the other. I look at the Hopi and I think, brother, lantsman, you know what it's like to be a human being. You've got a calendar too."

Bob was nodding his head. He licked his spoon. "Those are my sentiments," he said.

The lights blinked off and came on again. Besides the four of them at the table there was no one there but the boy in white mopping the linoleum and the ruddy-faced girl at the register.

"I think they're trying to tell us something," Elspeth said.

Phil put down a tip. They went with him to the register and he paid the checks. The cashier unlocked the glass door and let them out.

They walked to the Mercedes.

Karen and Bob sat in back. Elspeth fiddled with the radio dial and found a folk singer.

"Phil," Bob said from the back seat, "it just doesn't turn me on to be an antiseptic, civilized modern man, with all the color bleached out. A human being that's for real should be a subject for anthropology. Not just a smartass that reads about it."

It took scarcely five minutes to drive to Bob's building. Then it took another ten to take Karen home. In the back seat Karen sang with the radio.

"Thanks for everything," she said when she got out.

"My pleasure," said Phil.

"See you at the wedding."

For a while Phil and Elspeth rode toward Winslow without conversation. The radio played.

Phil took the expressway, and sped in the night.

"They're fanatics," Phil said suddenly. "You can't talk to them. Forget it. Whatever argument you give them they'll always take what you say and stand it on its head."

He pressed the lighter into the dash. He took a cigarette.

"I always think of the right thing to say to them afterward," he said when he had lighted it. "After they've gone it comes to me. Not when I'm talking to them. They're too glib. They don't give you time to think. And they gang up on ya. The two of them."

"What did you think of afterward?"

"It doesn't matter. You can't win with them anyway. But if you look at it, they as much as admitted that all this orthodox and shmorthodox is just another one of these counter-culture gimmicks. Another excuse to make a nuisance of yourself. I don't like the Afro haircuts either. And I don't like vegetarians. And I don't like pot, and drugs, and I don't like T-shirts with wiseguy remarks printed on, and tie-dye shirts, and macrobiotics, and communes, and sandals, and the whole shmear. And I don't like shredded shorts. Nobody wants to be normal anymore. Everybody wants to be something different. What's wrong with just being plain ordinary regular people? Is it out of style?"

He was silent again, and tense. When he had finished the cigarette he took another. It seemed gradually to calm him. He drove more slowly.

He swung down the ramp, through black woods, and through the underpass.

"You just want to be dropped off right away, or should we go up to the lookout first?"

"The lookout's okay," said Elspeth.

He wound through the short cut under low branches. The headlights showed dead leaves on the bumpy road. At last they climbed Firefly Hill, past his own house without stopping.

They parked at the lookout, facing the rail. He put out the cigarette.

The Big Dipper was strung out before them, its edge pointing at the up-ended Little Dipper.

The landscape below was blacker than the sky. The lights of villages were like huddled constellations, far from one another. The radio was low and fuzzy. Phil clicked it off.

"You know what his trouble is?" he said. "He was brought up with no religion, and he came to it all at once, and he gets carried away. There's a lot of kids like that now. There's this rabbi up there with whiskers and a big fur hat, and he pulls in the college kids like the Pied Piper. He sings them songs, and he tells them stories, and the girls meet the boys there and the boys meet the girls there and the food's good, and they learn a couple of words of Yiddish and they get all excited. Because they never had it before. You take a guy like me, I was brought up in a religious home. I've always had it. So I have a sense of proportion, I don't have to go crazy. Even my parents were getting away from a lot of it. I'm a sincere guy. I'm one of the steadiest supporters that temple has. And I still keep a kosher home. And I fast on Yom Kippur, and there aren't that many that can say that. But these college kids up there, they go for a weekend with the rabbi with the big fur hat, and it's all new to them. So they don't know when to stop. They think they have to be orthodox and shmorthodox. They think they discovered it. They think it's authentic."

"Bob doesn't even like the guy with the big fur hat. He goes to the other place, down the other end. With the intellectual crowd."

"Oh, so they're divided into twenty-eight different factions already? That's typical. Oh well. Enough of that."

He reached and slipped a cassette into place. He turned a knob.

The music was soft, soothing.

Elspeth put her head to his shoulder. He cupped his hand upon her, and her woolly knit moved with his fingers on the slippery underthings.

He undid her top button.

"Sweetie," she said, "after we're married I'd like us to join the Audubon Society. Okay? A family membership."

"Of course, precious. Your wish is my command."

He undid the next button.

"Another thing, sweetie," said Elspeth. "Karen was telling me about the mikveh. And I thought I'd like to dunk in it before the wedding. And maybe give it a try after, if you didn't mind too much."

"Mikveh? Are you serious? You can't be serious. Do you know what a mikveh is?"

"Of course I know."

"It's the most moth-eaten superstition there is. That doesn't exist today. Nobody does that."

"Avis does. She goes to the mikveh every month."

"Where the hell does she find one?"

"There's a community mikveh up there, and there's a mikveh lady that lives upstairs and takes care of it. They say it's beautiful. All tile and modern, with showers and hair dryers, and they're even gonna put in a sauna if they ever get the money. And they have a manicurist and a pedicurist that'll come in if you want."

"Listen, precious. Your friend Karen is a nut. I thought we agreed on that. She's a good kid but she's a nut, and her sister's another nut. Mikvehs were for Europe. In Russia, where they lived in mud huts with a dirt floor and they never saw a bathtub."

"No, it's something beautiful, sweetie. It's not for a bath. They have to take a shower before they even get in it. It's like a cool spring. It's rainwater. They've got these big cisterns on the roof that collect rain for it. And two weeks after the start of her period Avis goes down these stone steps into the rainwater, and immerses completely. Over her head. The rain gets to every part of her."

"Look, precious. There's nothing dirty about menstruation. There's nothing that requires rainwater."

"I know there isn't. I didn't say there was. That's not the point. It makes a sex cycle. It's good for marriage. It kind of pulls the man into the woman's cycle. You know how it is with most couples in this dumb civilization. They screw when the man is horny. And sex after marriage is considered like yesterday's fish warmed over anyway. But not in the mikveh system. Because it keeps them hot for each other. Sex is kept garden-fresh, like a perpetual honeymoon. For two weeks Steve can't touch her. Not even a kiss. Nothing. For two weeks. And then just when Avis is ovulating she immerses in the rainwater, and she comes out like a water nymph, like a love nymph, and fixes her hair different, and when she comes home from the mikveh Steve has such a tremendous hard-on he practically pole-vaults into the bed. And then they go at it hot and heavy for the next two weeks. Every chance they get. For two weeks they're like a couple of rabbits, till they're all worn out. And by the time her next period starts, Steve's balls are empty. And then for two weeks his balls are slowly filling up again, just like the rain filling those cisterns, and he's getting hotter for her and hotter for her. And then one afternoon she walks in fresh from the mikveh, and wow! Bang! He's got a hard on like a zucchini. Ten inches."

Phil sounded a sigh of frustration. In the darkness she saw him gesture. "Precious," he said, "I don't know what you're going through, but I don't want to see you get hooked on this stuff."

"You don't think you could go for it? Why? Because you don't want to be restricted? But discipline makes art, doesn't it?"

"I'd feel like a jackass."

"Well, I thought about it, sweetie. I'd like it, I think, but I decided, okay, if you don't want it, we'll skip it then. I'll just go the one time before the wedding."

"What for? Why do you have to go to the mikveh before the wedding? Tell me. Who the hell needs it? Did your mother ever go?"

"No."

"I'll bet you never even heard of a mikveh until these kids got to you. When did you first hear of it?"

"About a week ago."

"About a week ago. All your life you never knew it existed. And now all of a sudden you have to go dunk before the wedding."

"So it'll enhance the wedding. It'll add to it."

"How does it add to it?"

"I'll feel like a bride. I'll be clean."

"That's what gets me! You *are* clean!"

"I mean spiritually clean."

"You *are* spiritually clean!"

"Okay, okay, but look, when I have a period a human cell is expelled. It didn't get fertilized, so it's lost and dies. It's like as if symbolically there's been a contact with death. But then in two weeks my ovaries have made a new cell, and I'm like in the fetal position surrounded by rainwater, like I'm born again. It makes you sensitive to what your body's doing. You're more attuned. More alive. I mean, if there are gonna be sex laws, why not beautiful sex laws, instead of just a bunch of don'ts?"

"Damn those kids! Are you actually hooked on all this garbage?"

"I don't know. It depends what you mean by hooked. But I said I won't insist on the mikveh system if you don't like it. I understand. I can see that it sort of seems like a bit much. But why should you mind if I just go the one time before the wedding?"

"It bothers me that you want to. I just hope you're not gonna turn into one of these nuts. It's contagious, this crap."

The cassette still played, somewhat plaintive, with a sound of recorders and lutes.

"Phil," said Elspeth, "I'm so agnostic I don't even know if I'm an agnostic. Maybe we have beliefs in our hearts we don't even know we have. Look, I don't know if there's anything there. You can't prove it by me. I don't even know if Bob and Karen really believe, or if they're just psyching themselves up to think they believe. But we still have to live. And place our bets and make our choices. You can choose to live as though it's real, or you can choose to live as though it's a bunch of bullshit. Just like you're in a boat, with no compass, and no stars to navigate by, and you don't know where anything is—you're an agnostic. You still have to pick a direction and sail."

She heard him sigh through his nostrils.

"I don't know if faith is the word," she said. "Maybe trust is the word. Like people don't really have faith in the bank, or in the government, or the police force. But as a pragmatic thing they end up choosing to trust them most of the time. I guess because the alternative is to sock your money in the mattress and bolt the doors and go out of your mind."

Phil sighed again. "Well, I see they've really gotten to you, haven't they. I don't blame Karen so much. I know you and Karen are a regular mutual admiration society, but she's not the one I blame. You know who I blame? Your guru. Your cousin, Bob Shoemaker. Every word that comes out of his mouth, you think it's haylik lokshen."

"It's what?"

"Holy noodles."

"Holy noodles?"

"It's an expression, haylik lokshen, holy noodles. You think that guy is Jesus H. Christ on roller skates. Sure, he's your cousin, he's family, you're loyal. And he's a nice guy, and he loves animals and birds and porpoises and stuff. And I like to see a young guy turning to religion. Only there's such a thing as too much of a good thing. He overdoes it. And that's why his own mother and father can't stand him. He's still a kid, he's wet behind the ears, and he doesn't have the judgment.

He goes overboard. If he eats a piece of cake, there's a special blessing to say for cake. He takes a shot of whiskey, and there's a blessing for whiskey."

"Not out loud."

"To himself. I've seen him. If he takes an apple from the fruit bowl, there's the blessing to say for fruit. I bet when he goes to the bathroom he says a blessing for that."

"He does," said Elspeth.

"He does what?"

"What you said. When he goes to the bathroom he says a blessing. At least the first time in the morning."

"Are you serious? I was exaggerating. There's no blessing for going to the bathroom."

"There is," said Elspeth. "It's in the book. He showed me. And he said when his Uncle Sid had the colostomy, and he saw him there in the hospital, and the surgeons had to outfit him with a rubber shit bag, that's when he really began to understand what that blessing meant, and why it's there. And the other guy, the guy that shared the semiprivate with his uncle, he had prostate trouble and he saw him lying there in the hospital with a catheter in him. It's something to be thankful for that your plumbing is healthy, and all your wonderful complexity is coordinating, the way nature intended. You should appreciate it. And appreciate that you haven't got some malfunctioning duct that's doing you in."

In the darkness she saw Phil shake his head. "He actually says a prayer when he goes to the bathroom? I never heard of such a thing."

"It's a this-worldly religion," she told him. "It's even concerned with the secretions in your eyelids when you wake up in the morning. It even covers what you should do if you're standing wrapped in your tallis, with your tefillin bound on your head and your arm, and you're saying your daily prayers, and all of a sudden right in the middle of the most important prayer you feel a big fart coming on."

"So what do you do?"

"You stop praying, and you take six steps backward, and fart, and then there's something you say admitting you're an asshole, and then you take six steps forward, and resume the prayer where you left off."

"Bob does that?"

"He said that's what you do *if*. He didn't mean that situation ever happened to him. It probably never did. You try to avoid it. If you think you're gonna fart you postpone the prayers. You don't put tefillin on."

Phil shook his head again.

"What's the matter, Phil?" said Elspeth. "If a religion is real, it's big enough for every possible contingency. If it couldn't even cope with a fart, then a fart could break the whole illusion. It would wreck the mood."

"How ridiculous can they get. That does it. They're loony. They're even loonier than I thought."

"Phil, do you think religion is about some never-never-land in the sky, where nobody ever has to go to the bathroom? Don't you understand monotheism? We thank God for food, don't we? So why shouldn't we thank Him that we can shit?"

80

PHIL and Elspeth went together to the Town Clerk's office to file for the marriage license. Then they drove to Phil's internist in Boston for their blood tests.

In late afternoon they had a conference with Rabbi Quint at the temple, and spoke of the caterer and the florist. Rabbi Quint showed her the temple's little bridal chamber, where she would be able to primp at a dressing table and change her clothes.

Then he surprised her by siding with her when Phil told him about her wanting to dunk in a mikveh. "I don't see any reason to feel uptight about it," Quint said, "if it's just a one-time thing before the wedding. True, it's pretty much of a bygone age, and frankly I doubt if it's really making much of a comeback. But the young are always incurably romantic. And if it gives her a nice feeling of preparing for the wedding in some age-old way, certainly it's a harmless indulgence. I think it's a rather charming idea, actually."

The next day Harriet became upset with her on learning that she intended that Peter be present at the wedding. Harriet had meant to engage a high-school girl as a sitter.

"No," said Elspeth. "No sitter. We're not leaving him at home. The wedding's this Sunday. There's no time to break in a new sitter and get him used to her before then. You and I and Cele and Gloria are the only ones he knows."

"So I'll hire the girl for every afternoon between now and then, if you insist. And they'll have Wednesday Thursday Friday and Saturday, four days to get used to each other."

"Mama, it's not necessary. It's silly. How long is the ceremony, twenty minutes? And then we'll give him his noon meal in that little bridal room in the temple there, and his last taste of the breast, and he'll go right to sleep. You'll have the bassinet on the floor by your table, and he'll sleep through the whole dinner and music and everything. He always conks right out after the noon feeding and he's usually good for two hours at least. Probably more."

"You don't bring babies to a wedding! What if he cries in the ceremony?"

"If he does you could take him outside, or Cele or Gloria could take him out, but he won't. You'll have a little juice bottle just in case."

"I think it looks perfectly terrible. On that day of all days, the baby isn't something you brag about."

"You think I should hide him? Everybody knows he exists."

"I don't think Phil will stand for it. He'll put his foot down."

"He already knows. You ask him when he picks me up tonight. We're going out for supper."

When Joe came home from the store Phil had not yet arrived. Joe agreed with Harriet.

"Are you planning to carry the baby down the aisle?"

"Of course not! He'll be with Mama. Do you think I'm crazy?"

"With you ya never know. Are you gonna take the baby along on the honeymoon?"

"No. He'll be here with you and Mama. And Gloria or Cele will help out sometimes. He's being weaned. But the wedding's different. There's no sitter he's used to that won't be there."

When Phil arrived he confirmed that he and Elspeth had discussed it.

"It's her wedding," he said. "Let her have it like she wants. If she wants the baby there, so okay. I'm not gonna argue. Look, it's my baby too. I love him. I'm adopting him. Besides, when Elspeth makes up her mind to something, she's as tough as nails."

"You can say *that* again," said Joe.

Phil and Elspeth had supper in a dark steak house that had several crackling fireplaces and a salad bar that extended on and on. The waitresses were young and wore tight red showgirl outfits. The beams and the tables were full of crooked grooves.

Elspeth lifted her schooner of ale and looked over the top of it at Phil. "Cheers," she said.

The glass was heavy. They sipped.

"Phil, I've had a terrific idea. About the wedding. Let's have Bob marry us, instead of Quint."

"What?"

"We can ask Bob to do it. I mean in the temple and everything. Everything just like we planned, only Bob will marry us. He's gonna be there anyhow. So let's have somebody we like do it. Somebody that means something to us."

"What kind of business is this? Bob can't marry us! He's not a rabbi! You don't just get your cousin, or a friend! He's a rabbi now by you? Jesus! Where do you get these ideas? Certain people are qualified to perform marriages. An ordained rabbi who's got a certificate, a diploma. Or a justice of the peace. A recognized minister. A priest. Somebody bona fide. There's laws about these things."

"No, honest, Phil. It was a surprise to me too, but Karen said we don't need a rabbi. She said she bets if we ask Quint about it he'll even say she's right."

"God! Karen again. I might have known. She doesn't know what she's talking about. I'd think your own common sense would tell you. There's laws in this Commonwealth. And in every state. And if we don't get married according to the law, we're just a couple of hippies doing their thing, that's all. Living together. Is that what you want?"

"Sweetie, all I'm saying is, let's just ask Quint if Karen's right. And if he says no, then fine. We'll go by what Quint says, completely, because we've got no choice. I don't want to rock the boat. But how do we know he won't say okay?"

"Of course he won't say okay."

"Maybe he won't. But it can't hurt to ask him, can it? Karen said anybody can officiate at a wedding. You don't even need to have anybody officiating. You're even allowed to just do it yourselves with nobody officiating. It's right in the Talmud. Like if a guy gives you some object of recognized value, like a ring, or even a coin, like a nickel or a dime, or even a cent, and the guy says to you, by this object you're set apart for me, you're made special for me according to our laws, and you accept the object without any protest, then that's it. You're married. You do it yourself. And if you have some guy officiating, whether he's a rabbi or not, all he can do is tell you to do it yourself. He's really superfluous. Except to be a prompter, so you don't get nervous and flub something or forget the words."

"The rabbi has to bless you. Solemnize it."

"No. Karen said he doesn't."

"Well, I never heard of it. Never. And I must have been to weddings in fifty different temples in my time. And nobody else ever heard of it either. Except Karen. You and Karen. Why the hell does Karen keep interfering? Whose wedding is it, anyhow? Can't she let you alone?"

"She wasn't interfering. We were just talking. And I got this idea."

"I'd feel like an idiot calling Rabbi Quint and asking him to check out a stupid thing like that. Besides it's an insult to him. He's been hired already. And now we come talking like we don't want him."

"Sweetie, we'll pay his fee. Let me call him. I'll go to the phone booth while we're waiting for dinner, and I'll just ask if we can have an appointment to talk about something. Okay? I'll do it in a way that won't hurt his feelings."

"Why can't we just get married in the ordinary way? Like we were gonna?"

"We can. And if Quint says there's no other option we will. On the other hand, if he's happy to put everything at our disposal and let us do it our way and no sweat, why not? Clergymen do innovations all the time. They're glad to help a couple make it more meaningful."

Phil sighed. His hand wiped his forehead.

"Okay," he said. "I'll call him. I'll see if he's got time for an appointment in the next couple of days." He shoved his chair back.

The phone booth was in a far corner. Elspeth could see him when he shut himself into it. She sipped her ale.

The baby-faced waitress returned, and warned that the plates were hot. The sizzling fat smelled of charcoal. With the steaks there were mushrooms and steaming baked potatoes. She wore black stockings. A big red bow on the top of her head matched her brief suit.

Elspeth saw Phil mop his brow with a handkerchief.

When he emerged from the booth and found his way among the tables she thought he looked downcast.

"What did he say?" she asked as he took his chair.

"He said come on over. To his house. I said we'll come over after dinner."

"What time?"

"Any time. When we finish eating. So we'll see what he says. But if you say the officiating person doesn't really do anything essential anyway, then I don't see why the rabbi is any less meaningful than your cousin. That's all. If he's really unessential, your cousin would be unessential too. You shouldn't care who it is."

"It's just that our wedding is too beautiful a thing to entrust to Quint. I don't like him. If we have to face Rabbi Quint when we stand there, it's that much harder to feel spiritual. Eat your steak."

At the rabbi's house Mrs. Quint let them in. She was smiling and dumpy, with faded hair piled high. She took the light coats they wore, and then she led through the living room to a small den outfitted as a study, with books from floor to ceiling. Rabbi Quint rose, smiling, shook their hands and offered chairs. Before he sat he also offered a jar of hard candies. Phil took one.

Rabbi Quint listened to Elspeth and lolled behind his desk, a hard candy making a lump in his cheek. Now and then he lifted a hand from his stomach to stroke the squarish goatee with an attentive nod.

"Essentially, what your friend told you is correct," he said at last. "For practical purposes. I won't go into the technical concepts, which don't translate exactly. And of course much has been added. There's the marriage contract, to protect the rights of the woman. There's the custom of the canopy. And the wine. The blessings. Breaking the glass. These things have become universal, dear to us. And it's become established to have a rabbi officiate. To make sure there's no bar to the marriage, and no flaws. Because a wedding is an important step. Just as if you bought a house, you'd have an expert attorney check over the deed. But yes. Phil's placing the ring on your finger, while he recites the prescribed formula, and your acquiescence in that, is what effectuates the legal tie. And it does that in and of itself. Even if there's no wine, no rabbi."

"Then we can have my cousin!"

He raised a cautioning hand. "Just a moment. But there's also the Commonwealth of Massachusetts. We have to satisfy its requirements too. And that mandates either a justice of the peace, or a pastor who actually holds a congregational pulpit in a recognized denomination. One or the other. That's state law. A pastor of a congregation, or a justice of the peace. And I take it your cousin is neither."

She saw Phil nod. "That's right," said Phil. "He's neither. An MIT kid. A biologist. A student."

"However," Quint said, tilting back, lowering his whiskered chin and pouting his lip. "Let me suggest a possibility. Suppose I stand off to the side, almost like a spectator, playing no role, and your cousin stands before you and plays the role of rabbi as I normally would. I think as long as my signature is on the document the state will be satisfied. How would that suit you? Your cousin will officiate and marry you, conduct the ceremony. And I'll sign the state's papers."

"Oh, wonderful! Great! That's lovely! That's just what I want!"

"Is that legal?" Phil asked him.

"Why not?" he said to Phil. "If I sign, then I've officiated so far as the state is concerned, and I've certified that a wedding was duly performed according to our faith. And it will have been. The state doesn't care about nice points of Talmud, and it doesn't want descriptions of the ceremony. As far as the state is concerned you can get married naked, or standing on your head. All it wants to know is that the pastor in charge was a recognized one and that the ceremony was kosher in the eyes of his church."

"Rabbi," Elspeth said, "I could kiss you. That's beautiful."

"I'm happy I could be of help. Now, I just hope your cousin has background enough. I suggest you bring him down Saturday night for our rehearsal. So we can run through it together a few times, till he's got it down pat. So Sunday morning I can stand aside and not say a word, and not have to intrude myself with corrections." He rose. "Suppose we adjourn to the dining room now for some tea and butterscotch squares. They're my wife's. Delicious."

"I'd rather just get to the phone," said Elspeth. "And make sure Bob can make it Saturday night."

"Have some tea first," said Quint.

"He'll make it, don't worry," said Phil. "He'll drop everything."

They sat at the dining room table, and smiling Mrs. Quint served mint-and-chocolate squares as well as the butterscotch. "Well, is everything all set for Sunday?" she asked them.

"I think so," said the rabbi. "Elspeth is a girl with a mind of her own. But where there's a will there's a way."

"The rabbi's been awfully helpful," Elspeth said to her.

She thanked him again when he saw them to the door.

She walked with Phil cross the columned porch and down the walk. He unlocked the Mercedes. He went to the other side glumly, got in beside her, and turned the key in the dash. He shifted and they rolled.

"Well, the rabbi's certainly been in your corner. All the way. On everything."

"I know," she said. "He's not as much of a stuffed shirt as I thought."

"You see? So do you like him a little better now?"

"Yeah, I guess I've misjudged him."

"But you still don't want him to do it?"

"No. When we're standing up there Sunday before all those people, and you say to me that according to the law of Moses I'm now your wife, I want to believe it's all real. I want it to feel real. So I'd rather we didn't have to be looking at a man of God that can't even control his calorie intake."

They paused for a stop sign. Phil heaved a sigh. They turned onto the avenue.

"Well," he said, "what's gonna be the next brainstorm? What idea are you gonna spring on me tomorrow?"

"That's all. No more ideas."

81

FRIDAY morning Elspeth picked up Karen in the MG, its convertible roof in place and latched, and they went to the mikveh. Karen had made their appointment early in the forenoon because Fridays were busy there later in the day. It was in a large frame house that had been remodeled, not far from Karen's neighborhood. The mikveh lady came down from the upstairs apartment holding a paring knife that smelled of onions. She was short and middle-aged and wore a kerchief. She took a key from her apron and unlocked the door. "All right, you said you'd go in with her. It's good you're early. You're the first ones here. All right. I'm too busy now. So you know what to do. You been with your sister. Just don't forget when you go out you lock up the door."

Karen led Elspeth through a parlor to a dressing room. It had pink wallpaper with a pattern of vines. There was a dressing table. A hair dryer was angled on a pole and stand. Beyond there was a shower with a door of stippled glass.

"Okay," said Karen, "first you shower, and clean your fingernails and toenails, and you have to comb all the tangles out of your hair. And then the pool's through that other door."

"The rainwater?"

"Yes. The rainwater's in the pool."

She sat on a table, watching Elspeth undress, and swung her legs in her jeans.

"You have a super body, you know it?" said Karen.

"Thank you."

"Hey, no bathing cap," Karen said. "You can't have it in the pool so there's no sense in wearing it in the shower. And besides it'll give you tangles."

Elspeth took off the cap. She stepped onto the tile and shut herself in. She adjusted the shower, first to hot, then to cold.

"Great," she said. "Needles."

Through the stippled glass she saw Karen spread a terrycloth towel on a chair.

When she came out Karen hung another big towel on her shoulders and then draped a sheet about her wetness.

"Okay, I'll help you comb," said Karen. "Hey, you have to take off the pendant. The topaz."

Elspeth bent her head and allowed Karen to unfasten the chain.

She sat. In the mirror her clinging hair shone. Together they combed it.

She took a file, drew a foot to the chair and checked her toes.

"Okay?" Karen said. "Come on."

Elspeth rose in the towel and the sheet. Karen shepherded her through the further door.

The room she came into was windowless, with fluorescent lighting. It was of stone and brick and tile. It contained nothing but the clear pool, about five feet square, the steps down into it and their silvery rail, and the strip of flagstone floor on which they stood.

Elspeth let the sheet and the towel fall. She started down slowly into the water and curving ripples spread out from her.

"Hey!" said Karen. "Have you got your engagement ring on? I told you, you have to go into that rainwater naked as a jaybird. Like when you were born."

"I can't even wear the ring? I was like wearing it for Phil. He loves this diamond."

"No! Nothing. Not even lipstick. That ring could keep the water from getting to some teensy speck of skin, and it has to get to all of you." She put out her hand.

Elspeth paused on a slab of stair, the water ringing her thighs. She twisted the diamond and its band, and pulled it from her finger. She handed it to Karen, turned from her, and descended, the coolness rising to envelop her.

The brick bottom under her feet was flat. The water reached to her neck. She lifted her feet, allowed the water to bear her arms weightlessly, and let herself half float. Her breasts rose. Her hair drifted and spread.

"How is it?" Karen asked.

"Lovely. I feel purer already."

"Go under. Take a breath and go under."

Elspeth inhaled, shut her mouth and went down. In the green dimness the stairs and tiles had changed their dimensions. Over her the surface was a quivering mirror with upside-down stairs above it. She knew Karen was saying something but she could neither see her nor make out a syllable. She came up. Hair hung down her face, running water.

"The top of your head didn't get completely under," Karen told her. "Try it again. Get way way down. Empty your lungs."

Elspeth immersed. Her ears heard the stillness. She exhaled a mass of silent bubbles and saw them rise before her.

She put her head out of the water and her feet to the bottom. "How was that?"

"Good. Fine. Now put this on your head while you say the blessing." Karen stooped and handed down a white hand towel.

Elspeth draped the folded towel over her head sideways.

"Now you say what I say."

Karen said the Hebrew carefully with pauses, one word at a time. Elspeth repeated each, her hands at the sides of her head to hold the towel in place.

Karen crouched at the edge and reached for the towel. Elspeth handed it back up.

"Okay. Now dunk again. All the way under. All your head and all your hair has to get under."

Elspeth submerged. She blew bubbles till she couldn't anymore, and pulled the squirming hair down about her face.

When she could stay down no longer she came up. She caught her breath.

"That was good," said Karen.

"Is this where baptism came from?"

"You guessed it. Now get your breath, and a complete immersion a third time, and you're all done."

She tried to stay down even longer. She touched the brick bottom with her hands. She came up and gasped for air. She blinked.

"It's such a magnificent temperature," she said. She lay back and paddled. "I think I'll stay here. I like it. Will I get purer the longer I stay?"

"No. You're as pure as you're gonna get. No extra brownie points. Come on, Ellie. I've got things to do. Come out and put on the sheet."

Elspeth mounted the stairs dripping, her hand on the rail.

"What's so magnificent about the temperature?" Karen asked. She squatted at the edge in her jeans and splashed her hands about.

"It was perfect," said Elspeth, putting the sheet about her. "Like half a degree cooler than my skin. Haven't you ever tried it?"

"No. I've been mikveh lady for Avis but I haven't been in. You don't usually, till before your wedding. Hey, you're right. It's nice." Karen had pushed up her sleeves and immersed her arms to the elbows.

Elspeth stepped quickly behind her, crouched to slip hands under Karen and gave a sudden lift. Karen tumbled head first with a great showering splash. Waves shot up the tile walls and shipped onto the flagstones.

For an instant Elspeth was alarmed by Karen's slowness in coming to the surface. Then Karen came up, snorting, squinting, blowing, spitting, her short hair hugging her head.

"You little shit, you," Karen said.

"I didn't mean for you to really go in. I just meant to like startle you, for fun. Scare you. I thought you'd catch your balance. Honest. I'm sorry."

"Oh sure."

"I am. I'm awful sorry."

"Why are you laughing then?"

"Because it's funny. But I didn't mean it."

Karen climbed out on the steps, grasping the rail, her jeans and her shirt clinging and draining.

"I think some dye came out," said Elspeth.

Karen looked around. "You're right. Just wait till the mikveh lady sees that. She'll have you drawn and quartered. How'm I gonna get dry? I'm sopping to the skin."

"We'll aim the hair dryer on you. My hair can wait."

They came into the dressing room and Elspeth wiped herself with the big terrycloth. Karen took off her flannel shirt and wrung it over the sink. She draped it over the mirror. Then she stepped out of the jeans and hung them over the back of the chair. Elspeth began to dress, watching her. Karen pulled the dryer, on its heavy base and casters, and focused the hood down toward the jeans. She switched it on. Its fan hummed.

"It's not gonna be enough," said Karen. "I'll get the one from the other dressing room." She went out, the wet panties on her behind like skin laced with white wrinkles.

The jeans dripped a puddle on the linoleum and another on the chair. The flannel shirt on the mirror was already soaked again at its bottom edge and drops fell to the table. Karen returned, pushing another dryer with its pole and base. The heavy black wire dragged behind.

She positioned the second dryer opposite the first, aiming it at the jeans also, and turned on the switch. Elspeth got down and plugged the wire into an outlet. "I hope we don't blow a fuse."

Karen took off her bra and hung it on a corner of the chair's back, toward one of the dryers. Then she hung the panties toward the other dryer.

"I don't dare blow heat on the shirt," she said. "It could shrink."

"I feel awful about it," Elspeth said. She snapped her jeans and began buttoning her sweater. "I really just meant for you to just get scared and catch yourself. Not fall in. But it was a real dumb childish thing even so. I just sort of got carried away."

"Okay, you're forgiven already. If these things don't dry I'll have to give you my key so you can go to my house and get me some things."

"Honestly, Karen, I hope you believe me. You can slap my wrist, or I'll bend over and you can kick my ass, or throw me in the mikveh if you want, with all my clothes on."

"Forget it, I believe you. I said you're forgiven."

Elspeth tied her sneakers. She put her hands to her neck, under the damp hair, and fastened the pendant. "Have you got my diamond?" she asked.

"Oh. It's in the mikveh. On the floor there."

"It must be in your jeans. Didn't you put it in your pocket?"

"These jeans don't have pockets. I put it on the floor."

They opened the door and went back to the mikveh together, Elspeth dressed now and Karen nude.

"There it is," said Elspeth. The ring was on the flagstones above the pool's edge, over toward the further wall.

She went toward it, but as she bent to it a hard shove knocked her hip forward and sideways. She stepped wide and put out her free hand to regain her balance but she was too near the water. She tumbled and plunged.

She sank bubbling. She struggled to right herself and her feet found the bottom. When she put her head out Karen was laughing gleefully.

"You stinker," said Elspeth, pushing her hair from her face. "I thought you said I was forgiven."

"Of course you're forgiven! What makes you think you're not forgiven? Have you got the ring?"

Elspeth displayed it between thumb and forefinger.

"Okay," said Karen. "Let's go. We've really got a problem now. There aren't enough dryers."

Elspeth climbed the stairs drenched and Karen gave her a hand. Her clothes rained onto the flagstones. Her sneakers made oozing and sucking noises.

"I'm sorry, Ellie," said Karen. "I couldn't resist."

"Okay, okay, I had it coming. And I'm sorry I called you a stinker."

"That's okay. I think I called *you* something at the time."

In the dressing room Elspeth took off her clothes. She dropped her sweater in the sink.

"Too bad there's no dry-heat room," said Karen. "A sauna."

"You know what?" said Elspeth. "Let's tilt the dryers back and throw the clothes right in them like baskets. And keep tumbling them with our hands. I'll do our jeans in one and you do our underwear in the other."

They pushed back the dryer hoods as far as they went, but it was not far enough to hold anything.

"Well, we'll do the best we can," said Elspeth. "Hold everything up close to the heat."

They worked hard. They had to hold their loads as well as turn them over and over beneath the hoods. The dryers made their steady whispering drone.

"You've got the hard load," said Karen. "The jeans are heavier than the underwear. I'll trade and take turns."

"No, that's okay."

"It's working," said Karen. "I think the panties are getting a little drier."

"When the underwear's dry," said Elspeth, "we can put one pair of jeans under each dryer, and they'll dry faster."

"And when the jeans are dry, we can dry our hair."

"How are we gonna get your shirt and my sweater dry without shrinking? We'll have to turn the dials to low, I guess, and hope for the best."

"Maybe we can put them on and run around," said Karen.

Elspeth began to sing Go Tell Aunt Rhody. Karen joined her, harmonizing. Their hands kept turning clothing under the hot windy hoods.

"This is gonna kill our hands," said Karen. "I'm gonna put some lotion on."

They dropped the crumpled clothing on the linoleum and rubbed hand lotion.

They returned to the dryers. "Hey, why didn't I think of it before," said Elspeth. "Let's lay these things down on the floor, and then we can drop the clothes right in." She pulled at it. The pole and the base were of heavy steel, but she brought the whole assembly to a tilt. Then she lowered it with care, till it was horizontal on the linoleum, the dryer hood exhaling upward.

Karen began to do the same to the other.

"Away from the puddle," said Elspeth. "Let's not take any chances with an electric shock."

They sat on the linoleum, still both naked, with legs tucked under them, and tumbled clothes lightly in the rising heat. "This is lots easier," said Karen.

"Actually we couldn't have done it this way at the start," said Elspeth. "Not when stuff was really sopping. If it dripped in on the coils it could short."

The door burst open and they stopped tossing. The mikveh lady stared at them wide-eyed, a spreading scowl bulging her cheeks against the kerchief. Her color grew florid. "What's this! What's this! What you doing there!"

"We fell in, Mrs. Zindle," said Karen quietly. "We have to dry our clothes." She did not rise and neither did Elspeth.

"You can't do that! That's for the hair! You'll break the dryers! Get dressed! What you doing! Go out from here! Go way!"

"In wet clothes, Mrs. Zindle?" said Karen. "We'd catch our death. We wouldn't make *you* go out in wet clothes and catch pneumonia if *you* fell in, Mrs. Zindle."

"What you mean you fell in! With your clothes? You went in there the two with your clothes? It's one to the mikveh and one to watch! You don't go in there two people with your clothes! Nobody falls in! Who told you to fall in?"

"It was an accident, Mrs. Zindle," said Karen.

"I'm sorry, I don't let this! It's Friday. You have to go out from here. Any minute there's women coming. We need the dressing room, the dryers. Geh! Darf zein meshuggeh."

"Let us come to your kitchen and dry off then, Mrs. Zindle. You have a clothes dryer in your kitchen."

"All right, all right! Put on the sheets. I'll take you up the backstairs."

They followed her in sheets, carrying their clothes as she puffed between the walls of the narrow staircase.

In the kitchen she adjusted the square enameled dryer, and helped them throw their things into it. She hung the sweater and the flannel shirt on hangers from the curtain rod of an open window, exposed to the sun, and spread a folded towel to catch the drippings. She brought tea to Karen and Elspeth at the table. She put out a jar of honey. Elspeth saw that her forearm had death-camp numbers.

"Mrs. Zindle, this is my friend Ellie Baker. Ellie, this is Mrs. Zindle. Ellie's getting married Sunday."

"Oh, that's nice! I'm so glad. But tell me, Karen darling, you're such an intelligent girl. How could it happen? I never heard such a thing, to fall in a mikveh."

"Well, I was giving Ellie a guided tour, to show her the mikveh, and she had a dizzy spell. She gets these spells. She's subject to them. And I tried to catch her, but we both lost our balance."

"Oy!" Mrs. Zindle put a hand above her bosom. "Dizzy spell? It happens a lot? They can't do anything for that?"

"Not a thing. The doctors had her all apart and put her back together and there's not a thing they can do. She's brain-damaged."

"Oy oy oy oy. My poor child. Karen darling, you shouldn't leave her alone."

"We don't. Somebody always has to watch her."

A doorbell buzzed on the wall.

"See? Already they're coming, appointments. I have to go down. Karen darling, make more tea, you shouldn't catch cold the two of you. And Karen darling, look, when you take her downstairs, make sure she holds on tight by the banistairs. And hold onto her."

"I will, Mrs. Zindle."

"With both hands."

623

"Yes, Mrs. Zindle."

"Don't forget."

"I won't, Mrs. Zindle."

The dryer by the wall kept churning and clunking. They had a second cup of tea, and a third, and found lemon juice in the refrigerator. From time to time they wrung the bottom edges of the shirt and sweater, and tested the clothes in the dryer.

At last they dressed, but the shirt and sweater were still damp.

"I don't know about you," said Karen, "but I'd as soon let it dry *on* me at this point. I have to teach a class at eleven."

"Okay."

They went down to the MG and settled into its bucket seats. Elspeth turned on the heater.

"Shall I take you home first or shall I take you straight to Cambridge?"

"I guess I better go straight to Cambridge."

When the chance came Elspeth cut into the traffic.

"I'm sorry about everything."

"That's okay."

"Does Mrs. Zindle own the mikveh?"

"No, she works for us. It's a nonprofit organization."

"Will I see you tomorrow night? At the rehearsal? Will you come down with Bob?"

"Of course."

But early Saturday evening Karen phoned to say she couldn't come after all. Avis and Steve had Symphony tickets and the sitter's mother had just called to say that the sitter had the flu.

"I'm really sorry. It would have been fun. But Bob's the only one you actually need for the rehearsal. And all of us'll be there tomorrow. Good luck, Ellie."

Things were hectic. Aunt Ada and Uncle Normie from New Jersey stopped in at the house on the way to their motel. So did Uncle Ira from Minneapolis, whom she scarcely knew, and gave her a sloppy kiss.

Then Bob phoned that he didn't have his car, and asked if Elspeth could pick him up. The Coffeys had borrowed his car to look at a ski lodge in New Hampshire they might take with two other couples, and they had been delayed. So Elspeth drove to Cambridge and got him.

When she brought him to the temple in Winslow it was a quarter to nine. Joe and Phil and Rabbi Quint were waiting for them up on the raised area down front. Phil was smoking a cigarette and Joe and the rabbi smoked cigars.

"Didn't Mama come?"

"How could Mama come?" Joe said to her. "She's with the baby."

"He could have slept in the bassinet from the carriage."

"Well, there was no sense in disturbing him."

Bob introduced himself to the rabbi.

"Glad to know you," said Quint. "I've heard lots about you. Okay. It's late, so we'll get started. For now we'll rehearse without the canopy. The janitor will set it up tomorrow early. I told him eight, so it'll be already up in place when the florist gets here. Now remember we have to meet in my office at ten-thirty sharp, for the signing of the ketubah. You too, Bob. You and I will be the witnesses. And then we'll have the ceremony here at eleven. I'll be over to the side here with Joe and Harriet, and the baby will be with Phil's daughter down in the audience, and Phil's sister-in-law will help her. Okay. And Phil's brother and sister will stand on that side, and you'll stand right here. In the middle. Like you're the rabbi. And Phil will come down the aisle, and stand before you, facing you. And then when the organ plays Here Comes the Bride Elspeth comes down. Got that, Elspeth? You want to rehearse that part? The organist's not here but we can hum it."

"That's okay," she said.

"Okay," said Quint to Bob, "now I see you brought your own siddur. You want to wear my robe? It might be a little short for you."

"No, I'll just wear a suit, with a tallis over it. I'll bring my own."

"Okay, whatever you want. Now let's hear you read. Do you know the order of the service? Phil, Elspeth, you stand before him, like he's marrying you. Okay, Bob, let's hear you."

Bob opened his book. He read a few lines of rhythmic Hebrew in a fluent singsong.

"Good," said Quint. "Excellent. You must have had a good background."

"Me? I'm a Johnny-come-lately."

"Well, you've learned it somewhere. And you've picked up the style. Now what comes next?"

"The wine," said Bob. "The first cup."

"Right. And the bottle's right over on this table, with the glass and the tray, right where it'll be tomorrow. I'll pour and hand it to you. Or better, let Joe do it, so I can keep a low profile. Let's run through that. Joe?"

"Can you put out your cigars?" said Elspeth. "It's getting smoky."

The rabbi squashed out his cigar on the wine tray and Joe did also. Joe filled the glass and gave it to Bob. Bob held it, singing the blessings.

Quint nodded. "Very good," he said. "Now the bride and groom each take a drink. You're gonna need it."

Bob gave the glass first to Phil and then to Elspeth. When she had sipped he gave it back to Joe.

"Next?" said Quint.

"The ring," said Bob.

"Right. We won't go through that now, because if we did they'd be married, and the guests would come tomorrow for nothing. But Phil's brother will be best man. And Phil, when Bob tells you to place the ring on the bride's finger, you'll give your brother the nod, and get the ring from him and put it on her finger. The index finger, remember—she can switch it to the fourth finger after the ceremony."

"I know," said Phil.

"And Bob, you say 'repeat after me,' and then you'll say the words for Phil slowly and clearly, one at a time, and wait for him to repeat each word. While he puts the ring on her finger. The ring's on her finger while he says the words, with his fingers still on it, and he doesn't let go till after the last word. Okay. Have we got that?"

Everyone nodded.

"Now, some people like me to give a sermon at this point," Quint said. "Would you like to give a sermon, Bob?"

"We don't need a sermon," said Elspeth.

"All right. In that case we could have the reading of the ketubah at this point. Can you read it, Bob? It's in Aramaic. It's not easy."

"I've been practicing on my fiancée's sister's," said Bob. "I've had it at my bedside for the past three days."

"All right. Let's give it a try. Joe, hand him that rolled document from behind the wine tray there."

It rattled stiffly when Bob unrolled it. He held it before him with two hands.

Bob read with a fairly steady pace. Quint kept nodding. Only once did Bob slow down, as though a phrase were unfamiliar.

"Fine," Quint said at last. "Of course tomorrow the names will have been filled in. I think we can skip the English side for now, but tomorrow you can turn it over at this point and read the English off the back. Okay. Now roll it up again and give it back to your uncle. And he can give it to Elspeth after the ceremony. Maybe we can tie it with a nice ribbon. Now, Bob, what's the next step?"

"Wine. With seven blessings."

Quint nodded approval. "Joe? The wine."

With the glass in one hand and his book in the other Bob read the Hebrew liltingly, with rising and falling inflections, sometimes prolonging a final syllable musically. At last he gave a drink to Phil and to Elspeth.

"And now?" said Quint.

"I put the glass on the floor, and Phil smashes it with his foot."

"Exactly. We can leave that till tomorrow. It's less to clean up. And then the organist plays the recessional, and Phil and Elspeth march back up the aisle, smiling, arm in arm. You can both go to the bridal chamber this time. And change your clothes if you want. Well, then. I'm satisfied. I don't think we have to run through it again. So remember, everybody. At my office, ten-thirty sharp, a half hour before the ceremony."

"Thanks, rabbi," said Elspeth.

"My pleasure. And I think being married by a relative, a member of the family, is a beautiful idea. A lovely idea. I see no problems tomorrow. It's going to go off very smoothly. And now how would all of you like to come over to my house for a snack?"

"Thanks, rabbi," she said, "but I've got to take Bob home, and it's a big day tomorrow. I want all the sleep I can get."

"Well, I think you're wise," he said to her.

She walked out to the parking lot with Bob silently and they got into the MG. Bob settled deep into the bucket seat and closed his eyes.

They said nothing till she drove up the ramp to the expressway. "Are you awake?" she asked.

Bob's eyes opened.

"I've been having thoughts about real estate lately," she said. "I've been running around, looking at vacant land. Over in Dowling, stuff the builders don't look at seriously because it's too hilly. They like level tracts. Or areas they can make level. But I think I can build condominiums even where it's steep, like attached townhouses running right up and down the hills. Each unit different, some in dark brick, some in light brick, some in gray brick, each at a different height, but attached at the side to the one next door, and each with different gables and design. And some can support an upper story that would be a whole separate house facing back the other way, at a street level where the road swings back at a high level behind. Up and down the hills. And cobbled roads for better traction. I mean it, Bob. I've zeroed in on four different tracts, as possibilities. The steep land in those hills is valued at about a tenth of the flat areas. Those jerks think they're not buildable. And I've looked up the deeds, and I've looked up the zoning. It'll look like a fairy-tale village. I'm serious. As soon as I'm settled down in Phil's house I'm gonna start approaching the owners of those tracts."

"Have you talked to Phil about this?"

"A while ago. I showed him some plans and drawings I sketched out."

"Won't your roads be kind of hard to get up in winter?"

"No. If each leg of each hairpin is long enough, they won't be steep, no matter how steep the hillsides actually are. And especially with cobblestones."

When they approached the city they grew quiet. Bob again closed his eyes.

In Cambridge she parked on the left, before his building. He got out, walked around to the sidewalk, and smiled down at her through the lowered window.

She looked up at him.

"You look a little sad," he said. "Or wistful."

She looked at the steering wheel. "I wish I loved Phil more."

"I thought you did."

"Yeah, I love him. I just wish I loved him more."

She looked up at him.

"Bob, will you marry me?"

"Of course," he said. "Just like we went through it tonight. You heard Quint. It's completely valid. I'll do the whole thing."

"I don't mean that. I mean, will you marry me?"

For an instant that seemed longer his face was unchanged. Then color crept in and he swallowed. She looked down at the wheel again, downcast and angry with herself for having embarrassed him.

"Get a good night's sleep," he said gently.

82

WHEN the two windows of the corner bedroom showed the first gray hint of dawn Peter sat up in the blackness and had a discussion with himself. He had a way now of stringing together an endless flow of varied syllables so that it sounded like a language.

Elspeth lay on the bunk bed, her eyes aching.

Then she rose and lifted him from the crib. She kissed him, carried him to the bathroom and buckled him onto the changing table. Harriet came to the door in a dressing gown. She looked tired.

"Well, today's the big day," said Harriet.

Elspeth busied herself cleaning Peter.

"I know you didn't sleep," said Harriet. "I heard you walking around. I'll bring you some coffee."

"I slept," said Elspeth. "I was up a lot, but in between I slept."

"Well, it's the excitement," said Harriet. "I couldn't sleep either. I heard the clock every time. What's Petey going to wear? I tried the little gray suit on him and it's adorable. It just fits now. And the booties. If he doesn't wear them now he'll never get to."

Elspeth began fastening a fresh diaper.

"Are you crying?" Harriet said suddenly.

"No, my eyes just keep watering. I think it's an allergy or something."

Joe appeared at the bathroom door in trousers and an undershirt. "Who's crying?" he said. "What's the matter with her?"

"I think all brides cry a little," said Harriet. "It's sentiment."

"The hell it is," said Joe.

"I'm not crying! Look, I'm not like sobbing or anything, am I?"

"There's tears running down your face."

"So my eyes are running, that's all. Like a runny nose."

"She says it's an allergy," Harriet told him.

"Yeah? When did it start?"

"A while ago," said Elspeth.

"I'll give her some eye drops," said Harriet. "She didn't sleep."

"Well, you'd better give her something," said Joe. "It'll look like hell if she goes down the aisle like that."

Downstairs there was the thud of the Sunday newspaper against the door. Joe turned and went down.

"Put the coffee on," Harriet said after him. "I'll be down in a few minutes."

Elspeth wiped her eyes with a tissue. She blew her nose. She took Peter back to her bedroom. Harriet followed her.

She sat Peter in his crib and studied her eyes in the mirrors. They were reddish. "They're not watering as much," she said. She allowed Harriet to apply some eye drops.

Peter watched as she unbuttoned her pajamas and when a breast was bared he extended his hands. She sat on the bunk bed. He sucked shut-eyed. Milk gurgled in his throat.

"You really think you should still be nursing him so much? It's going to be very abrupt for him."

"I know, I haven't worked at the weaning as much as I should. Especially in the mornings, my breasts are brim full. He'll be okay, though. He's used to the bottles too."

Harriet sat by the varnished table and watched her.

"Mama, do me a favor. Call up Phil and ask him to come over right away. I have to see him."

"Now? This morning? It's bad luck. You're not supposed to see each other before, on the wedding day. Don't you know that?"

"Mama, listen. It's important. Phil and I have to call it off, or postpone it, and I owe it to him to see him face to face, and explain. It's too bad we didn't know before, but better late than never. It's best for both of us. And he'll need every minute. To see if any of the expense can still be saved, and just to get his bearings, and figure what we should say to people. Mama! Pull yourself together! Let me tell you how it is—"

Harriet's eyes were moist and she shook her head, her mouth opening and closing and opening. "You can't do that—"

"Mama, he's a strong guy inside. He can handle it. And he'll understand, I know he will. And you'll understand too, when I explain. Maybe in six months or a year, if he's still not married, and I haven't found a guy, maybe we'll still get together. But I doubt it. It's not right. Anyhow to go ahead and marry him is too precipitous right now. I'm changing too much, and we need more time. Mama, just call him while I finish feeding Petey, okay?" He was making noises and squirming. She moved him to the other breast. "And don't say anything to Dad. If you won't call I'll call. We need every minute that's left. To work out how we can cancel jointly, with a little dignity. Maybe we'll say we both decided to think it over a while."

"You're crazy! You're gonna throw him away? What do you mean, if you haven't found a guy in a year! You expect him to wait? Who are you gonna find that's better? A movie star? Don't you know when you're well off? Who's gonna marry you, with an illegitimate child?"

"I'm gonna take an apartment with Petey up in Karen's neighborhood, and find me a froomie."

"You mean those religious kids? Bob's friends? They're not for you! They'd drive you out of your mind! And they're very strict! They're not gonna be interested in somebody with an illegitimate child! That's a big sin with them!"

"Mama, they're very marriage-minded. And baby-minded. They like to marry young, and all their guys are looking to get married, and they're all born matchmakers. They'll introduce me to all their guys, and if none of them want me they'll start importing their brothers and friends and cousins from New York. They won't rest till they've married me off. And as far as my having Petey is concerned, they have this rule that if somebody goofs and messes up, and then tries to make it good, you never remind them how they blew it before. You never throw people's past mistakes at them. That's their rule. It's very important. And anyway they'll feel that Petey is theirs. They'll go all out for him—he'll have a ball. They've got this rule that all Israel is responsible one for another, and if I can't afford Petey's tuition at the day school then they'll send him for free. And when he's older he'll be sleeping over in pajama parties with *their* kids. And even if I weren't married he'd have lots of male role models. Because it's a very tight community."

Harriet had been gaping haggardly. She came forward and felt Elspeth's forehead. "Do you feel all right?"

"I feel all right." But her mother's hand kept testing her forehead. She brushed it away.

"Maybe the excitement has gotten to you," said Harriet. "Maybe I better call Dr. Morrison."

"I'm not sick. Anyway Morrison doesn't make house calls, remember? That's why we took Eric to the Lapham."

"He'll see you in his office."

"I'm not sick, Mama!"

"You've been under a strain. Elspeth! I know those kids have been nice to you, but that's because you're Bob's cousin. They're not your type, and you're not *their* type. Bob's different, he's that kind of a meshugganer. But what are you gonna do when you find you can't put up with them?"

"I don't know what type I am. But I know if I'm gonna die someday, like my grandparents, and like my brothers, and if Petey's gonna die someday, then I've got to live my life confronting ultimate questions. It's bad enough to bring forth a child into a senseless universe. What can I do? Be happy in a three-story house on Firefly Hill? That's okay as far as it goes. But I can't just drug myself with consumer goods, even if they're advertised in the New Yorker, and with the latest theorist's bullshit according to the Sunday Times, and what's in and what's out. Trying to forget that at bottom it makes no sense anyway. There's got to be more. I don't know if I'm a believer, or if I'll ever be a believer, but I want to be around believers. Mama, it's not that I think the froomies will give me answers. I don't think any of them have them. I think most of them know they don't. That's the whole idea. They're just refusing to duck the question. Like they have this prayer where they all croak and flop into their chairs and collapse with their head on their arm and ask God why we're getting the shaft."

Harriet was moist-eyed. "Darling, you're under a strain." Her voice was breaking.

"You're not talking right. I'm calling Dr. Morrison."

"Not Dr. Morrison. Call Phil! Will you call him or do *I* call him?" Peter's mouth pinched the nipple sporadically. His eyes were closed.

"I'll call him," Harriet said miserably, hurrying out. "I just hope he'll know what to do."

Elspeth carried Peter to the bathroom and changed him once more.

Then she sat him in the crib with some toys. These days he liked to put things into things. He had plastic blocks, each a different color, and would drop them one by one into a wide-mouthed square bottle of semitransparent plastic. Then he would pour them out before him and do it again.

She recognized her father's sharp knock. "Sweetheart?" he said.

"Come in."

He came only a few feet into the room and stood looking at her with a tired scowl. He was still in his undershirt.

"Mama says you're under a strain. What is it, sweetheart? Are you sick? Delirious? Or just out of your mind? Because what Mama said to me is so crazy I don't even believe it."

Elspeth said nothing.

"She said you told her you decided all of a sudden to go look for a religious kid. Move in an apartment, and push the baby up and down the street in a stroller every day there where that orthodox bunch is, and hope one of those cross-eyed shnooks with his nose in the Talmud notices you and decides to save your soul and marry you. Sweetheart, I never heard anything so ridiculous."

She still said nothing.

"Never mind that it's the stupidest idea I ever heard. Never mind how illogical it is. I just don't see you as one of these religious freaks. It isn't like you. It's not your style. There's something gone haywire. Delirious is right."

"Did Mama call Phil?"

"She's calling him. And I suppose he'll come over and try to talk some sense into you. Lots of luck to him. If he has any sense he'll come over with a straitjacket. Jesus! It was too good to be true, I guess. You had me fooled there for a few months. I was congratulating myself. I was saying, thank God, she's straightened out. Thank God, she's straightened out. I should have known better. So what do we do now? Have your head examined? Have the doctors put you in a machine and measure brain waves? They can examine you from now until doomsday and it won't do any good. Something about you enjoys trouble. That mind of yours is always working, to think up what kind of a big mess you can make, and kill everybody, and make everybody miserable. It gives you an orgasm."

"Dad, I want to get dressed. Would you leave me for a few minutes? Phil will be here any second."

He turned to go, drearily, heavily. Then he turned to her again. "I'm supposed to tell you go down for breakfast. Mama has breakfast for you. Still kowtowing to you. She ought to throw it in your face."

"I'll have breakfast after. It won't take Phil that long to get here."

631

This time he went out. "I should break your neck," he muttered. "Only I don't have the strength anymore. You've got me half in the grave." He left the door ajar.

She closed it. She got into her jeans. She buttoned her sweater. Then she sat at the dressing table, brushing her hair. The diamond caught her eye. She slipped it onto her finger, and resumed brushing. It was too bad Karen's brothers were too young for her. The oldest was only a freshman. No use waiting for them to grow up.

Behind her a plastic block hit the floor. In the dresser's mirror she saw Peter drop the blocks one at a time through the bars, carefully, his pinky aloft. Then he sat looking at her. She saw him studying the three images of her in the mirrors.

She heard footsteps on the stairs. It was her father's tread, not Phil's. She brushed more slowly.

He didn't come in. In a few minutes he went down. Then she heard her mother come up.

Harriet came in and Elspeth caught her eye in the mirror. "Don't you want any breakfast?" said Harriet. "All right, you're probably too nervous for breakfast."

"Why is Phil taking so long?"

Harriet began to sit on the bunk bed but then took the desk chair instead. "I can never sit on that bed. It's too low. He's not coming. He said to get Dr. Le Vyne. He gave me the number."

Elspeth swung around. "You didn't call her, did you?" Harriet was half hidden by the back of the crib.

"Yes, I called her. She's coming right away. Phil said to call her."

"Dr. Le Vyne?" The hairbrush fell at her feet. "Edna? That creep? I don't want to talk to *her*! I want to talk to Phil! There's not much time! I have to see him *now*! If we don't use this little time it's gonna be awful!"

"Darling, try to relax. Phil thought it was best for the psychologist to see you. Maybe she can help you. I know it's very natural for a bride to be frightened before the wedding. Lots of girls have last-minute doubts. And they go down the aisle wondering if they're doing the right thing. It's such a big decision. Where are you going?"

"I'm gonna call Phil."

She went quickly past the stair landing to her parents' bedroom, with Harriet following. She looked across the pink quilting of the unmade bed to the night table.

"Where's the phone?"

"Daddy unplugged it."

"So I wouldn't call Phil? And if I go down to the kitchen phone I suppose Dad'll put his hand on the hook. And if I try to drive over there he probably won't let me out the door. Well, would you tell Phil he's the one I want? Not any Dr. Le Vyne. I'm not talking to her. And call Dr. Le Vyne back and tell her to cancel it." She started back toward her room.

Harriet followed. "She's probably on her way."

"What did she say?"

"Well, she asked what was happening, and I told her. And she said she was dressed and she was leaving immediately. So she's probably left."

"Oh, Jesus," Elspeth sighed. She sat down low on the bunk bed, her knees apart, her wrists on them limply. Peter pulled himself to standing and looked at her while he bit the rail.

"I couldn't help it," said Harriet. "I told Phil what you said, you wanted to see him, but he kept asking what's the matter. So I had to tell him, he kept asking. So he said it's better if he doesn't come and Dr. Le Vyne sees you. Look, she's coming, so talk to her. And see what she says. She'll help you understand what's bothering you."

"I *know* what's bothering me. I'm doing an awful dirty trick to a real nice guy, but if I married him it would be a dirtier trick. He doesn't deserve *me* and I don't deserve *him*."

"What do you mean, you don't deserve him? He thinks you're wonderful. He thinks there's nothing you don't deserve."

"Mama, his first wife was bad news. And for his second he deserves something more than a kid who's using him."

"Elspeth," Harriet said, lowering herself into the desk chair, which she turned away from the varnished table and toward Elspeth, and trying to smile, "do you have guilt feelings? Because you don't have to. And that's just what a psychologist is for, to help you not have guilt feelings."

"Mama, to the extent that I'm guilty, I'm entitled to guilt feelings."

"But you're not just using him. I know you're not. You have feeling for him. You told me yourself. You said when you got to know him you liked him more and more. You said every day you liked him a little better."

"Yes, I did. But it kind of peaked. He's a sweet guy, and I respect him, and in a way I love him. But he's entitled to a girl that wants him. And he'll find one, because he's a very appealing person. That's what I have to tell him. If any guy on this earth ever deserved to have a girl that really wants him, Phil does. And I'm not gonna see him done out of that. He'll understand, Mama. He'll understand, but he'll thank me. Now will you call him again please? Dad took the phone and I'm like incommunicado here. I'm not gonna talk to Edna. I'm not letting her in here. I can't waste time on her. I've got to talk to Phil, without any more delay. Now he's got a right to know what I said. Will you tell him, please?"

Harriet rose with tears in her eyes. "All right, I'll tell him."

Elspeth did not watch her go out. Her own eyes moistened in sympathy with her mother's. Peter gave a cry.

"What do you want?" she asked him. "You want to be on the floor?"

She lifted him over the rail. She sat him on the braided rug. She gave him his ball. He pushed it from him, with both hands. It rolled. He crawled after it.

Elspeth wandered to the back window, between the bunk bed and the varnished table. The maple had lost half its leaves. A few more circled down as she watched.

She sat on the bunk bed. "Petey, what are we gonna do?" Whenever he retrieved the ball, he pushed it away. He followed it from one part of the room to another. It lodged in a corner. She placed it behind him. But he had tired of it. She lifted him to her lap at the dressing table and positioned the mirrors so that he saw three of himself.

Harriet returned with a tray. "Try to eat something, like a good girl," Harriet said. "You'll feel a hundred percent better."

"Okay. Put it on the desk."

She gave Peter to Harriet. The coffee was hot.

"Did you call Phil again?"

"Yes, I told him what you said, and he says wait and let's see what Dr. Le Vyne can do first. And I tried to call Dr. Le Vyne again too, just to tell her what you said, but there was no answer. So I guess she's on the way."

"And if she left right away she'll be here soon. On Sunday morning you can do it in half an hour easy." Elspeth sighed. "She's just gonna be in the way. Well, it wasn't *your* fault."

She blew on the coffee.

Harriet was on the dressing-table bench and Peter squirmed on her lap.

"I guess you better put him on the floor, Mama. He wants to crawl."

Harriet put him down. "Elspeth, what's bothering you? His age? Because men stay youthful longer than women, you know."

"It's not his age."

"It isn't? What then? His children? You don't like the word stepmother? I thought you got on so well with them. And in a few years his kids will be off to college and out of your way anyway."

"Mama, his kids have nothing to do with it."

"So what's the matter then?"

"Two things."

"What two things?"

"Me, and him."

"Elspeth, don't you realize how he adores you? That man would try so hard to make you happy."

"That's just the trouble, Mama. He'd try *too* hard, and it wouldn't be good for either of us. He's trying too hard already. When people are right for each other they don't have to try hard. Mama, I should have seen it sooner. Both of us should have, and there'd have been less hurt. I guess I would have seen it sooner, if he weren't so awfully nice. And I guess he liked me so much he was kind of refusing to see it. I bet it worries him, though. I bet he has to struggle like crazy not to see it."

Again Harriet's eyes filled. "You're just impossible." Her voice cracked. "I can't talk to you. Phil's right. You need a trained psychologist to talk to you. I can't make you see what a mistake you're making. Well, I'm gonna go down and have some breakfast myself."

Elspeth opened her mouth, but there was nothing comforting she could say. Harriet left, shutting the door.

Peter had crawled under Elspeth's chair and through her legs, and sat now under the varnished table that she called a desk. She drank her coffee.

Peter crawled out, and pulled himself to standing, holding the edge of her chair. Elspeth broke a small piece from her toast. His mouth opened as she offered it.

She fed him another and another. His big round eyes never left her fingers.

She thought she heard a car pull up. She listened. But for what seemed a long wait she heard nothing more. Then the doorbell chimed. She lifted Peter into the crib and went out to the head of the stairs. "If that's Dr. Le Vyne," she called down, "just tell her to get Phil."

In the lower hall her parents were going toward the door. Joe had a shirt now. Harriet was still in her housecoat. Joe pulled open the door. "Dr. Le Vyne?"

Edna's hat was a small turban of felt. Joe was helping her out of a massive coat. She looked up at Elspeth. "How are you, Elspeth?"

"As good as can be expected. Edna, just call Phil, will you? I have to see him."

"Let's have a chat first."

"Edna, the time's short, so cut it, will you?"

"Not till we've had a chat."

"An hour of bullshit at a time like this? Edna, please—"

Edna started up the stairs, bending in her voluminous brown dress, gripping the banister.

"Damn it," said Elspeth, "do I have to block the stairs? Don't I make myself clear?" She put her arms around the grandfather clock, her hands tugging the sides of it from behind, and tried to drag it toward her to the center of the landing. It was heavy, with its front edge dug into its spot on the carpet runner and the back on hardwood. The tick stopped and the pendulum shivered against the case. With rapid efforts she pulled in hard little zigzags. This side swung forward a bit, then that side, then the first side. It tottered. She fought to steady it but at once it leaned with an overwhelming weight and flew from her, stinging her fingers.

She saw it plunge, seemingly within an inch of Edna, who had backed sideways, pressing her bulk and her arms to the banister. Harriet screamed, her fingertips clutching her cheeks. It crashed head down on the stairs with a discord of metals and glass, the bong reverberating after the rest. Its length slid another stair or two and stopped. Edna's eyes were bulging, with whites above the pupils. Her face was gray. Her chest was heaving and she gasped. Her knees sagged and she almost hung, her spread arms and her hands clinging to the slant of the rail behind her. "My God," Edna croaked breathlessly. "She tried to kill me. Call the police."

Joe was hurrying upstairs fiercely, though in the narrow space between the clock and the wall he had to put one foot directly before the other and nearly stumbled, putting down a hand on the long panel of mahogany, which had cracked unevenly, showing a rough edge of clean pine. Elspeth ran to her room and slammed the door shut. She heard the doorknob on the other side fall off.

She dragged the high bureau across the door, but stopped to pull out the knob on her own side with its attached rod. She heard her father pound and the door before her face vibrated.

"Open up! Elspeth! What the hell's the matter with you?"

She lay down on the floor, bracing her feet against the bureau and her shoulders and head against a sturdy post of the bunk bed.

"Hey! Open the door!"

In the crib Peter laughed.

"Hey! Can you hear me? Are you all right?"

"I can hear you. But I won't open the door."

He banged again.

Peter laughed again.

"Listen, you're in trouble. She's talking about the Psychopathic. Are you opening that door?"

"No."

"You want me to take it off the hinges?"

"You can't. The hinges are on *my* side."

He seemed to sigh. She heard him go to the landing and down a few steps, and a scrape and creak of wood as he tried to move the clock. Apparently he gave up. She heard him pick his way around it.

She sat up, breathing deeply, her feet still against the bureau and the bureau against the door.

She turned her head and looked at Peter. He was standing in the crib, holding the rail. He laughed.

"It's not funny, you little bastard."

Peter sobered.

She sat there, waiting. She looked at Peter again. He had sat, and was looking at her from under his brows, seriously now. Downstairs she could hear the voices, her mother's tearful, but she could not make out what they said. Then she couldn't hear them at all. The minutes seemed to pass slowly.

In time she heard Joe's feet finding their way up around the clock again.

There was a knock. "Elspeth! You still there?"

"Of course I'm still here. Did you think I went out the window and down the tree?"

"Now listen," he said through the closed door. "We talked to Phil."

"Is he coming?"

"No he isn't. But he's trying to help you. Listen. The doctor wants to put you in the Boston Psychopathic for ten days of observation, but Phil talked her out of it. It would wreck the honeymoon. You've got reservations. So she's agreeable now that if you'll go along like a nice girl to the temple and get married like you said you would, she'll lay off for now and not wreck the honeymoon, provided Phil takes responsibility and you check into the Psychopathic as soon as you get back. Okay? And who knows? Maybe by the time you get back she'll have cooled down and she'll forget about the Psychopathic. The Massachusetts Mental Health, whatever they call it now. It used to be the Psychopathic. But if you're not going with Phil, then she wants you looked over now. Today. She wants you in the Psychopathic for ten days. And she means it. She says to make sure you get there she's going straight to the police and she'll charge you with assault. And believe me, Elspeth, if you ditch Phil now, I don't blame her. I'll go along with her. So which is it gonna be? Huh? Do you hear me? The temple? Or the Psychopathic? Which?"

"The Psychopathic."

"What's the matter with you? Are you crazy?"

"Yes."

"No you're not. You're just a stubborn mule. I'm telling you, sweetheart, don't fool around, because I don't think that lady's kidding. She says you're dangerous. And she's a shrink, with credentials."

Elspeth didn't answer.

He rapped the door. Then it sounded as though he pressed his hands against it. "You know, sweetheart, ten days in the Psychopathic doesn't guarantee you get out in ten days. Depending on what they decide, they can ship you from there to a long-term place. She said you're a disturbed personality. Psychotic undercurrents. That's what she called it. For God sake, sweetheart. You're in trouble. How can you be so blasé?"

She still didn't answer. Her eyes overflowed. He gave up. She heard him pick his way down around the clock.

She went to the bureau and found a handkerchief. She soaked it, and then soaked another one, before the tears stopped. She thought she heard a door downstairs, but she wasn't sure. Maybe it was the back door. She blew her nose. There were murmurs of conversation but she could not even identify voices. What were they up to?

She pushed the bureau back a few inches and stood with her ear against the door. The sounds were no clearer. She looked at Peter. He sat watching her.

There were footsteps on the stairs. She knew when they slowed around the clock. She pulled the bureau to its barrier position and lay down with feet braced against it.

"Sweetheart, listen," said her father's voice. "Bob's here. Will you talk to Bob at least? Will you open the door and talk to him?"

"Don't give me that. Bob's not here."

"She doesn't believe me. Bob, talk to her."

"Yes, it's me, Ellie." It was Bob's voice.

"How come, Bob? Did they call you?"

"Nobody called me. But I'd like a chance to talk to you."

"Who's with you?"

"Nobody. Just Uncle Joe."

"If I open the door will my father grab me or anything? No tricks?"

"Uncle Joe?" she heard Bob ask him.

"No, no, no," her father said. "Bob, talk to her."

"Okay, wait a second," Elspeth said. She gave the bureau a shove, leaning on it, and it scraped back to its proper place. She inserted the knob into the door and opened it.

Bob was lean and tall in a dark suit with a matching vest. He wore a tie and a white shirt, as though prepared for the formality of conducting a wedding.

"All right, Bob, see what you can do," Joe said. "She won't listen to us—maybe she'll listen to you. She respects you. Straighten her out. Don't let her lose this chance. She needs a normal existence, not that religious stuff. It's different for you. With all due respect, you went and studied with rabbis—I admire that. Somebody has to keep it going. But it's not for her. You've got to be practical, for the kid's sake at least. This guy loves her, he loves the kid! He'll adopt her! Adopt the kid, I mean! He'll give them everything!"

"Wait downstairs, Uncle Joe. Okay?"

Joe took a step toward the stairs. He stopped and turned. "Bob, how did you know to come? I mean, how did you know things weren't right? It's like you had a sixth sense."

"It was something she said last night."

"Oh. Well, you know, she's contrary, that's the trouble. Tell her black, she says white. Tell her up, she says down. Like when she jumped off the table that time! Never grew up! I spoiled her! I did! And God, do I regret it! Whatever people tell her, she's got to do the opposite, whether it makes sense or not, just to show she's the great Queen! The Empress! The Almighty! Not taking any orders from anybody! If a doctor told her to eat, she'd starve herself to death! Just to show who's boss! We should have told her, don't marry that guy! If you marry Phil Snyder I'll break your neck! Stay single! That's what we should've said! I don't know why I didn't think of it! Then she'd marry him!"

"Uncle Joe, please. Go downstairs. Stay with Dr. Le Vyne. Okay? Let me talk to her." He put a hand gently to Joe's shoulder as though turning him toward the stairs.

At last Joe went down. Bob came into the bedroom, shutting the door carefully behind him. As it latched the knob slid half out on its rod. He put it in place and turned to Elspeth.

He was close to her. He put his hands to her arms, and looked down at her. "Ellie, I don't believe this. What the hell did you push the clock down on her for? You could hurt somebody."

"I didn't push it. I was just trying to block the landing."

"She says you tried to kill her. You want to kill your mother and sleep with your father, but you can't kill your mother, so you transferred it to her. Because she's a mother image."

"What!"

"That's what she said. She said she never saw a more classic case."

"Edna's a mother image? That tub of grease? She's nothing like my mother! She flatters herself!"

"All right, never mind that. Ellie, listen, and let's keep our voices down. I've been up all night, trying to figure this out. It has to be a clean break. Just run off to a state where there's no waiting and get it done, without prolonging everybody's agony. It's easier that way on everybody. Karen, Phil, everybody. When it's done it's done, and they can't fight it and they'll adjust faster and bounce back faster. We'll come back and I'll grab the first vacancy in the building—there's gonna be at least one in December. And I'll get free rent as janitor. And meanwhile there's a tenant that's away for the semester and they said I could use their place. Friends of mine. I said I wouldn't need it. But we'll move in. I'm sure it's okay."

"What are you talking about?"

"You proposed to me, didn't you? You meant it. I know you meant it. Ellie, I've loved you all my life."

"You love Karen!"

"Sure, I love Karen. But not like I love you."

"You're nuts, Bob! You're my cousin!"

"Yeah, I'm your cousin, and that's why I was always afraid to do anything, show anything. I was in love with you before you had breasts, for Christ sake. Only you were off limits. I just assumed it was impossible. If I ever tried to ask you for a date or something, can you imagine how your mother and my mother would have talked? And the whole damn family? Can you imagine it? Ha ha ha, Bobby wants to take Elspeth to the movies and buy her an ice cream, ha ha ha, he likes her, isn't that funny. And you'd be embarrassed and you'd never look at me again. I didn't dare, for God sake. And then last night, you kind of blurted it, and I thought, my God! It's possible! All night I was walking around thinking, it's possible! It's possible! She feels it too! Maybe it was the desperation, the last closing of the door that brought it out, but it's there! It's real. Only it has to be now. Another few hours, and it's gone. She'll marry this guy, and they'll have more kids and be bound together, and I'll be married to Karen, and everything's tangled up forever. Ellie! Don't stand there with your mouth open. Get the baby. We have to move."

She sank to the floor and sat, her knees up. His hands, which had rested high on her arms, slid the length of them. He stood looking down at her. He was holding her hands.

"Are you okay?"

"Bob, you're crazy!"

"Yeah, I'm crazy. Do you love me?"

"Yeah."

"Well, come on. Get up. We have to play this cool. We have to talk our way out of here."

"What'll I do?"

"Get Petey and a box of diapers, and let's go. I'll handle it."

"Where are we going?"

"Pretty far. I'll tell you on the way."

Elspeth got to her feet.

"Meanwhile we'll tell them we're going out to talk," he said. "And let's hope it works. That doctor wants your scalp. She's practically hysterical."

"She's feeling rejected, that's all. Should I pack? I'll just stash a change of underwear with the diapers. If I pack they'll know."

"Yeah, don't pack. Have you got any cash? I brought my checkbook, but I don't have a lot of cash."

"I've got a Master Charge."

"Take it."

Peter was dry. She fitted him into a sweater. She tied his hat, the knit one with the pom. She rolled his hooded pullover and some sleepers and put them with the diapers in the shoulder bag. Bob stepped this way and that, nervously.

She put her white canvas coat over the sweater and jeans. She put on the shoulder bag and picked up Peter.

"Okay," she said.

He opened the door.

She followed him carefully down the stairs. At one end of the clock the space between it and the wall was so narrow that one foot had to be placed directly before the other. Broken glass was scattered all the way down to the entrance hall. Joe and Harriet came through the living-room arch and stared at Bob and Elspeth.

"Ellie's coming with me," Bob told them.

"Oh, thank God!" said Harriet.

Joe was still staring. "How'd you get her to?"

"I asked her."

"Bob, you're a godsend. We couldn't do a thing with her."

"Wait! Wait!" said Harriet. "She has got to get dressed first!"

"Aunt Harriet, please. Just let us go."

"Yes, for God sake, Harriet," Joe said. "Don't interfere with a delicate situation. Use your head. Let him do it his way. We'll bring the clothes to the temple."

Through the arch Elspeth saw Edna seated on the sofa, looking at her. Her feet were spread and her arms were limp. She still breathed heavily.

"Excuse me, Uncle Joe," Bob said, reaching for the door handle.

"The whole thing's against my better judgment," said Edna, her voice cracked and hoarse. "Phil has to be warned what he's getting into."

"He knows, he knows!" Joe told her.

"Well, perhaps to some extent he does," said Edna. She kept pausing for breath. "And ten days after the honeymoon he'll have their findings at Mass Mental Health, and that protects him. If there's ground for annulment, he can decide then. She's a morass of unresolved conflicts. Even her desire to be a male. That kind of gross violence is very uncharacteristic of females."

"But Phil's very understanding," Harriet wept. "He's very forgiving."

"Uncle Joe, please," said Bob. "You're blocking the door."

"Oh. Sorry."

"Joe, get the bassinet! Get them the bassinet!" Harriet said. "Out of the carriage!"

"Let them go already! Don't complicate it. We'll bring the bassinet later."

"No, they need it! What if the baby falls asleep?"

Elspeth went with Bob down the walk. They passed between the yews and descended the brick steps. Bob opened the car and she settled in with Peter. Bob went to the other side. Joe came running down the walk holding the canvas bassinet before him. Bob paused. Then he tilted the driver's seat far forward and went to meet Joe at the foot of the brick steps.

"Thanks, Uncle Joe."

"Thanks, Dad," said Elspeth.

Bob and Joe went around the car and Bob slid the bassinet into the back.

"Wait!" Harriet was running down the walk in slippers, the green housecoat billowing over the pink slip. She was carrying the suit aloft on a hanger in one hand and the valise in the other.

She came down the brick stairs a step at a time like a child, half sideways, panting and red-faced. Bob took the suit from her and Joe took the round blue valise.

"Is there a place to hang it?" said Joe.

Bob hung the suit from a shoulder-harness fitting. He put the valise on the floor.

"The hat's in the valise," Harriet said breathlessly. "And the pantyhose. And the shoes, in the elastic pocket. And I put in some makeup. And the eyedrops. Have you got your diamond? I couldn't find the diamond."

Elspeth showed the ring.

"Oh. Have you got enough diapers? We'll be over as soon as we're dressed. I'll bring a bottle for the baby. And what kind of baby food? The pears? Or the plums? Oh! And his little suit and the bootees!"

"Don't rush, Aunt Harriet." He was seated behind the wheel. "I need all the headway I can get. There's a lot of ground to cover."

"Yes, leave them alone," Joe told her. "Give him a chance. If we're there at ten-thirty it's time enough."

Bob started the engine. Elspeth had fastened her seat belt and was clutching Peter.

"You know, they could leave the baby here meanwhile," said Harriet. "We'll bring him. I'll dress the baby."

"Aunt Harriet, don't slow me down."

"Yeah, Harriet, for Christ sake already!" Joe said. "Leave well enough alone! She's going, she's going, don't keep holding her up! Let him get started! He needs time to talk to her!" Then he smiled tiredly at Bob. "Bob, you saved the day."

"Don't count on it," said Bob. "The day's not over yet. I don't promise you a thing. All I can say is, there's a prayer in my heart."

Elspeth saw Joe make a gesture of success to Bob, still smiling, thumb and forefinger in a circle. She saw Harriet drying her eyes. Peter waved bye-bye to Joe and Harriet.

83

THEY paused at the stop sign, and swung left onto Peacemaker Avenue, away from Winslow Center and toward Winslow-in-the-Meadow and the expressway beyond.

"Is this for real, Bob? We're getting married? Like now?"

"You want to?"

"Yes," she said.

"You sure?"

She nodded. His eye was on her.

"Then that's it." The car accelerated.

"But what about Karen? You're supposed to marry her in February."

"Well, we're on our way to talk to Karen now. We have to break it to her, and hold her hand a while. There's just no other way. And then Virginia or North Carolina. Like I said to your parents, we've got a lot of ground to cover."

"Virginia or North Carolina?"

"North Carolina's probably the best. According to what information I could get. I mean, who can you call on a Sunday morning? I waited till seven-thirty, and I called up Yudi. He's at Harvard Law. And I woke him up. And I said, what's the nearest state where you can get married with no waiting period? And he said, how the hell do *I* know. And I said, well, find out. I explained I had to know now, immediately, I'm desperate. So he said, there's no libraries open, what do you want me to do? Put my head in a noose, call up my professor at this hour on a Sunday? And I said, yes. So he did. He cussed me out, but he did. Ellie, Virginia has no waiting except for a blood test, and I don't know what's involved there, if you have to hang around a couple of days while it goes to a lab or what. But North Carolina's the next state down, and in some counties there's no nothing. Just walk in. So it might be quicker to just keep going till we're in North Carolina. I hope the car gets us there. I was supposed to call you for a tune-up but I never did."

"It sounds okay."

"The fan belt's fairly new," he said. "We better take a good look at the tires though, first chance we get."

The traffic light at Plymouth Road was only a green blinker on Sunday mornings. They sped.

"Bob, I don't know how we're gonna face Karen. I don't know how you can do this. She doesn't deserve it, no way. I think Phil was kind of like with his fingers

642

crossed from the beginning. Like worried, sort of not quite believing it. But for Karen it's out of the blue. You love her. You acted like you did. She thought you did."

"I do love her. I love both of you. What could I do, Ellie? I had to choose. What do you think I was doing all night? Do you think I slept? I don't think I even sat down. But first, I love you more. And second, I know she's gonna be okay. It's gonna hit her hard, and the suddeness is rough. But she's gonna bounce back, and fast. What's going for her is that she's highly desirable, and she's not gonna be lonesome. There are guys up there that've got more than I have in every department, and they're all gonna be hot for her. She just wasn't noticing them because I'd become a habit. But she's gonna come out way ahead."

On the expressway the steadiness of the hum made Peter doze.

"Are you sure they let cousins marry?" said Elspeth. "Maybe they've got laws or something about that."

"I don't know. I had in mind to ask Yudi that, but then I forgot until he called back, and then I couldn't make the poor guy bother his professor a second time."

"So what do we do?"

"Well, maybe they won't ask. And if they don't ask, we're not gonna bring it up. I asked Yudi if he was asked that when he went for his marriage license. And he said he didn't remember, but he didn't think so."

"What state was it?"

"I don't know. Massachusetts, I guess. Maybe New York. Look, I don't care. In Jewish law it's permitted. You can marry your first cousin. And if it's okay with God it's okay with me. The state thing is just a gimmick for our protection, that's all. So Phil and Uncle Joe and that shrink lady and everybody will understand we're not just shacking up. Look, we've taken the step and we're not gonna stop now. We go to the nearest state where they give a license immediately and let you get married the same day. And we'll take our chances. We've got no choice. If it turns out they're gonna give us a hard time about cousins, then we'll look for a place where they won't."

"I'm with you," she said. She stroked Peter, who slept against her front. "Will there be any problem about our genes?"

"You mean, like an increased risk of defective kids or something?"

"Yes."

"I don't think so. We don't have any freaky relatives I've ever heard of. So I don't see any reason why we shouldn't have as many babies as we can handle."

"That's good," she said.

"I don't even know of a relative with poor eyesight," he added. "And I'm not a Tay-Sachs carrier. Karen and I were checked out."

His hand found the knee of her jeans. She held Peter with one hand, and entwined her fingers with Bob's. Traffic was light. The needle hovered between five and ten miles above speed limit. The sky was a radiant blue. Marshes lay in sun. Then rising hills of pine made shadows.

"Bob, I'm just thinking out loud. Suppose nobody in North Carolina thinks to ask if we're cousins, just because it hardly ever happens. And we get married there, and afterward it turns out they had a law against it all the time. Could somebody take us to court and get it annulled?"

"I don't know. Gee. Maybe they could. I don't know the answer to that."

"Or what if there's no law against it in North Carolina but there's a law against it in Massachusetts," she said. "What happens when we come home? Will it be valid here?"

"I don't know, Ellie. At this point I'm in favor of doing it first and asking a lawyer second."

"That's fine with me."

"Would Phil blow the whistle on us? I don't think he would."

"He wouldn't," said Elspeth. "Our families might, though. My father."

"Yeah."

"It depends how he reacts. I know he'll think of it. And he'll say it. And even odds he'll call Mr. Rosenbaum."

"But would he be that stupid? The main thing is, he wants to get you married. So once we're married, why should he rock the boat? I think at that point he'll leave well enough alone. Because we'd live together anyhow."

Elspeth nodded.

"As soon as we have a marriage certificate," said Bob, "phone him."

"I intend to."

"And another thing, Ellie. Once you let me put a ring on your finger and say the formula in front of witnesses, a rabbi can't marry you to anyone else anyway, even if Uncle Joe goes to court and gets us annulled. Not without a religious divorce. And if I don't give you one, then we've got all the rabbis over a barrel. You're stuck with me."

"Good. Beautiful. When my father hears that he'll let us alone."

"And what about that shrink? She'll calm down after a stiff drink and a night's sleep, won't she?"

"Edna? I hope so."

"I don't see what she could do by herself anyway, if Uncle Joe and Phil aren't with her. I've got lawyer friends too. And we'd come into court with a marriage certificate and Petey, and plead marriage and motherhood, and she'd look pretty silly. The clock didn't actually hit her, did it? My impression was she was mostly scared."

"She was scared. And insulted. I mean, she couldn't miss the point that she'd been scorned."

"Maybe it can't be annulled anyhow," he said. "We're only guessing. For all we know we could come home with a certificate that's airtight. So let's not worry."

When they came off the expressway Peter wakened, his eyes wide. He looked about.

"I didn't know you'd been seeing a shrink," Bob said.

"Karen knew. We talked about it."

"Was she helping you any?"

"Not really. I'd stopped, actually. She was somebody that helped Phil a lot in the past."

"I had some sessions with a shrink a few years ago," Bob said. "My mother and Diana talked me into it."

"Did he do you any good?"

"Well, he probably wasn't the right one for me. He kept thinking my hanging out with froomies was some kind of a quest for the comfort of certainty. Which confidentially was a bunch of crap, between you and me. I haven't got an ounce of certainty. I never did. I don't understand God any more than Job did. Like I told you, I don't even comprehend the orbiting particles that make up the physical universe. Let alone God, or what His purposes are. It seemed to me the shrink was the one that was on a certainty trip. He was certain he knew what made everybody tick. And completely comfortable in that certainty. Sitting behind his desk there, the mighty oracle. If you disagreed with him it only proved you were sick."

Near a stone church of many spires there were Sunday crowds. A policeman with a whistle in his mouth directed traffic.

Then signal lights slowed them. They came nearer to Karen's neighborhood.

"Well, we just have to tell her," Bob said. "This isn't gonna be easy. But we can't just pull a sneak act like we did on your parents. And we didn't tell Phil. We should've."

"I tried."

"I know you did. Actually I didn't want to do that to your parents either. All the way down, I was rehearsing in my head how to say it to them. How I was gonna explain it, and how they shouldn't worry about first cousins, because I'm a biologist and I've studied these things, and how we're gonna go out of state and do it right away to show how sincere we are, and how it's my fault, I should've seen it sooner, and I've loved you all my life, and it's all for the best, and all that. And then I walked in there and I lost my nerve. There was this shrink wanting to call the cops and put you in the Psychopathic. Attempted murder. Attempted mayhem. And Uncle Joe isn't the most stable guy in the world either."

"He's been through a lot."

"I know. But they were all too hysterical. I was afraid marrying your first cousin might just be the last straw."

They came onto Karen's block.

"Stop the car," Elspeth said quietly. "Bob, we just can't do this."

The car rolled to the curb. He looked at her. The engine was still running.

"It's too rotten. I can't do this to her. She's my best friend."

"And what's the alternative? What can I do, Ellie? Marry Karen when I know I love you better? Should I do *that* to Karen?"

Elspeth didn't answer.

"It's not as if this was a passing thing," said Bob. "You're in my bones. You always have been and you always will be. It's Karen's good luck as well as mine that I realized it in time."

Elspeth hugged Peter, her head lowered. "Bob, she loves you. Like I love you. What's she supposed to do? Just go find somebody new to be in love with, like going down to the lot and picking out a used car?"

"Okay, I know. It takes time. But in her case I think the prognosis happens to be for a very speedy recovery. I know especially of a least a couple of guys that are gonna give her a lot of attention, as soon as word gets around. And there are probably a lot more. There's this tall thin beautiful guy, he can't take his eyes off her. Whenever he sees that I've caught him staring at her he looks away fast, you know. He had the highest grade in the country in some math exam. Actually number one in the whole United States, two years in a row. He won all the prizes at Princeton and now he's on some project at the Harvard-Smithsonian. And he ran in the Marathon last spring."

"Did he win?"

"He didn't win, but he finished. Twenty-six miles. Ellie, you won't believe this guy. I remember once he was giving a class at the shul one Sunday morning on the Moreh N'vuchim of Maimonides, with the Hebrew text and the Arabic text both open in front of him, and Aquinas in Latin just to point out a couple of parallels, and all of a sudden he gets an emergency call, and the Government pulled him out of the class and flew him to Cape Canaveral. And besides he can sing. He writes his own music. She loves guys who can sing. And I can't. And the brother of the guy I called yesterday about marriage laws likes her too. A medical student. He's into karate just to keep in shape. Second year medical school and a brown belt."

"Obviously she preferred you."

"Only because I got to her first. I met her when she was new in town, before her sister was even in the area. And she's very loyal, and warm, and outgoing, with this great capacity to appreciate people and make a strong friendship."

Elspeth sighed.

"You'll see," he said. "And she can marry into a better family than mine, that's for sure. You'll meet some of these guys and you'll see what I mean. They marry young. And they know what they want. And Karen is what they want. And when they see what they want they don't sit around."

"At least give her the option of throwing *you* over, instead of you throwing *her* over. I'll go and hide somewhere for a few months. And give her time to break off with you. And then when she's got a new guy and she's happy I'll marry you then. It'll keep."

He rested his arms on the wheel. "Ellie, if you insist I'll offer her that. But she won't go for it. You know she won't. She doesn't go for charades." He sat up. "Come on. We have to talk to her. We can't just sit here."

The car rolled slowly down the street.

"Petey and I will wait down here in the car," Elspeth said, "and you go up and tell her."

He parked in front of Karen's building.

"No, Ellie. I was thinking, you and Petey go to the back seat, and I'll go up and bring Karen down. And we'll all go for a little ride around, and we'll break it to her together."

"Why, Bob? What's the sense in that? I'll wait for you here, and you go up and tell her in the apartment. Then if she faints or something she's got her sister right there to give her smelling salts."

"That's just it, Ellie. When I tell Karen, I don't want Avis to be there. Avis's fury is something I don't want to face."

84

BOB and Karen came out of the building and toward the car. Elspeth had moved with Peter to the back seat. Karen was in jeans. She hurried ahead of Bob, her eyes on Elspeth anxiously. "God, Ellie, what's up? What happened?"

Elspeth opened her mouth but found no words. Her eyes misted. She looked at Bob. He went around the car and got in, looking at no one. "Come on, let's take a ride," he said. "And we'll talk."

Karen slipped in beside Bob and Bob started the car. Karen turned, and extended an arm over the back of the seat. Her hand touched Elspeth's knee and rested there.

Karen smiled gently. "Okay. I know you're leaving Phil. I know you're not going through with it. You don't have to tell me. And Ellie, anything I can do to help— Ellie, it's yours. A shoulder to cry on. Or if you want a place to stay a while, and sort things out. I know Avis won't mind, and we're set up for babies. We're your friends."

Elspeth's eyes watered.

Karen's hand patted her. "What are friends for, Ellie? I promise you you'll feel a lot better tomorrow than you do today. I promise."

Elspeth felt a tear roll on her cheek. She looked at Bob. Even the back of his neck had blushed. He drove hunched low over the wheel.

Elspeth lowered her eyes, and Karen responded by turning her gaze from her.

Bob drove fast. Peter slept again. They went up a hill and down, then slowly along the curving road by the reservoir. The sunny ripples on the blue surface showed the direction of the wind.

The car rolled to a stop beside the grass. In the distance an elderly couple was strolling along the sandy path that followed the iron fence circling the reservoir. A brown leaf spiraled onto the car's hood.

Bob sighed, looking at the steering wheel. "Karen, it's more complicated than just Ellie running out on Phil. I really don't know how to say it. How to begin. Except to plunge in and begin."

Karen was looking at him. She seemed puzzled, listening with full attention, her forehead somewhat wrinkled.

Bob still didn't look at her. "Karen—" He took a breath. "Ellie and I are gonna get married. We're gonna run away and get married. I love her. What can I say? I love you too. I love both of you. Honest, I love both of you. But I've loved her longer."

He looked at her. Karen swallowed. It seemed to Elspeth as though time stopped.

"Is this a joke? Some kind of a gag?" Karen's voice was faint.

"It's not a gag. We were loving each other and just didn't know. All of a sudden, after the rehearsal, we knew. What can I do, Karen? This hit me—I was up all night with it. There's a rightness in it. You know how it is, when every bone in you tells you it's right?"

She looked dumbfounded at him. She turned to Elspeth. Elspeth nodded slightly, with lips parted.

For a moment Karen stared. Then her face crinkled and she turned away and burst into tears. She pushed open the door and ran from the car.

Bob ran around to follow her, but she had a head start. Elspeth got out too, holding Peter against her canvas coat, and stood watching.

Near the iron fence Karen turned suddenly. "Get away from me!" she screamed. "Don't touch me!"

Bob stopped short, a few feet from her. Peter let out a wail. Elspeth caressed him.

Karen shifted her gaze past Bob to Elspeth. "You scum! You slimy thing! And I thought you were sincere! When you were always asking me questions, like you wanted to learn all about being a froomie and everything. I thought you were really interested. I didn't know you were just trying to get Bob away from me." Her voice broke. "I never suspected."

Peter kept crying, tears running on his face. "I *was* sincere," Elspeth pleaded.

"How could I be so dense?" said Karen. "It never crossed my mind! Were you two making it together?"

"Karen—" Bob began.

"I might as well hear it all," Karen said in her broken voice. "I should get some kind of prize for dumbness. I never suspected! Right under my nose! I didn't suspect a thing!"

"Karen," Bob said, "it wasn't like that. That's what I'm telling you. We didn't suspect either. Believe me—"

"How can I believe *anything*?"

"I haven't even touched her. There hasn't been time. We didn't even know till now. We didn't know. You think we'd do this to you if we knew? All of a sudden when she dropped me off last night she said something, let it slip—I wasn't even sure she meant it—but I haven't slept. I just banged my head all night long. And when the sun came up I knew I had to go down there and grab her. If she hadn't changed her mind. Karen, I wish I could have it both ways. I do. I wish I could marry both of you. I fell for you honestly, like Ellie was just my sister or something. I could have gone on like that for the rest of my life. And married you, and been happy. Except last night, it's like the skies opened up and the voice of heaven spoke to me and said, Shoemaker, you shmuck! She's not your sister! Karen, I almost wish it hadn't happened. But what can we do, you and me? How can we get married? Now that I know how I feel about Ellie?"

Karen's chin quivered. The wet-eyed, open-mouthed stare gave way and her face puckered again. "Why does this have to happen to me? Why? What did I do wrong?"

Bob put out his hands to her but she recoiled. She turned from him and walked down the path, shaking with sobs.

"Karen—"

"Shut up!" she yelled, turning. Then she ran from him faster. In Elspeth's arms Peter cried again.

Bob followed Karen uncertainly. "Can I take you home or someplace? Karen, please."

"Can't you shut up? Let me alone!"

Bob stopped. Elspeth sat on the end of the car's rear seat, her feet out on the grass. She stroked Peter.

Karen had slowed to a walk but continued further from them, down the path that bordered the fence, without looking back.

Bob moved nearer to the car. "What do we do?" he said to Elspeth. "I have to take her home. I can't just dump her and leave her here."

Elspeth said nothing. They watched Karen. She walked further away but more slowly. They saw her stop and draw a long stem of tufted grass from its sheath. She studied it absently. She chewed it pensively. Then she threw it away nervously.

She came slowly back toward them, looking at the ground and frowning. She was not crying now, though the tear stains were still on her face.

"I feel like dirt," Bob said to her when she came near.

"Good." She walked past him, still looking at the ground.

She got back into the front of the car and pulled the door shut.

"Listen," she said, still not looking at them. "I've got an idea. Get in. You too, Ellie. This is for you too."

Bob got in behind the steering wheel and closed the door. Elspeth pulled her feet in and closed her door too. She held Peter close and waited for Karen to speak.

Karen was looking down at the dashboard. "Okay," she said. "You said you wish you could marry both of us. So okay then. Marry both of us."

Bob stared. She looked at him.

"What do you mean?" he said.

"You'll have two wives," said Karen. "Like in Bible days. What's wrong with that? We'll get along fine. Ellie and I are good friends." She turned to Elspeth. "What do you say, Ellie? Are you willing to share?"

"You're not serious," Bob said.

"Why not?" said Karen. "Basically it's permitted. And it was certainly never more justified."

"It's not permitted," he said. "You know perfectly well it's not. Once upon a time, but not today."

"It isn't, but it is," said Karen. "Sure, along comes the takanah of Rav Gershom in Europe nine hundred years ago, and says we don't take more than one wife anymore. Okay. But you go ahead anyway, and give another one the contract and ring and everything, just like the Talmud says, exactly like you did with the first wife, and okay, you're a bum, you're a fink, you violated the takanah of Rav Gershom. But the fact remains you've still got yourself two wives. That's the law, Bob."

"Except the first contract with the first girl always has a clause that forbids marrying any extra ones."

"So you violate the contract," she told him. "or you leave that clause out in the first place. The fact that they put in a clause making you promise you won't only proves that they know you could. If you couldn't, then they wouldn't have to make you promise not to."

"Karen, if I married two girls, in two ceremonies, with two contracts, and two rings, and all that, you know what would happen? Any rabbi would tell me to give one or the other of you a divorce. Every rabbi you know, and every rabbi your parents know, they'd all tell me I have to give one of the wives a divorce. Forthwith. Immediately."

"So what? Don't listen. Refuse. Hang up the phone on them. Sure they'd tell you. And why? Because they admit that both marriages are real and valid. If they weren't valid marriages, they wouldn't need a divorce."

He sighed. He gestured. "There's also secular laws. State laws. It's bigamy. They put people in jail for that. Even in Israel they don't allow it. Except for Moslems."

"As a matter of fact they do allow it. If you're a Jew from a Moslem country the takanah doesn't apply. And if they already had the extra wives before they came to Israel they can come in with their wives and keep them. So you know what we do? We stop over first in Morocco. Casablanca. And we stay like a week there, and we get married there. The three of us. And then we go on to Israel."

"Karen, for Christ sake. I know you're shook up. But try to be rational. We can't go to Morocco."

"Why not? Why?"

"It takes time. You need visas. Passports."

"So we get the visas and passports."

"And my teaching fellowship? I take a fellowship at MIT and just chuck it? And yours? You beat out fourteen candidates for that appointment."

"What's more important?"

"And anyway it goes by country of origin. We're not Moroccans. We're Americans, so the takanah would apply. As soon as we landed in Israel we'd be yanked before a rabbinical court and I'd be ordered to divorce whichever wife I married second."

"If you refuse they can't make you."

"They could throw me in jail, and say rot there until you hand over a divorce."

"No they couldn't, because they can't separate us. A guy has to satisfy his wife. He's required to. All his wives. It's right there in the Bible. 'Her conjugal rights he shall not diminish.' "

"Karen, it'd be a mess. An uproar. We'd be a cause célèbre. Every Israeli would have an opinion. You know how Israelis are. Every taxi driver would argue the Shoemaker case. The country would be torn apart. Debates in parliament. A cabinet crisis."

"Until they get tired of us, and then they'll go on to the next cause célèbre."

He shook his head. He looked distraught. Elspeth was wet-eyed. She kissed the top of Peter's head. He was sitting on her lap, looking at Bob and Karen.

"Hey!" said Karen. "I've got the answer! It just came to me. Look. It's simple. We don't even have to go to Israel. We become naturalized citizens of Morocco, the three of us, and then we get married there. And come back here as Moroccan citizens."

"We can't do a crazy thing like that. Ellie's a refugee from the Psychopathic already."

"What's crazy about it? Rabbinically the bottom line's the same. We got married in violation of a nine-hundred-year-old rule, but that doesn't invalidate the marriages. And as far as the United States is concerned, every state will recognize it, because we're Moroccan citizens and the marriages were performed in Morocco under Moroccan law. There are treaties about those things. Reciprocal credence. Just like every state in the Union has to recognize a Mexican divorce."

"Bullshit."

"What do you mean, bullshit. When the king of Saudi Arabia had surgery at the Mass General they let him come to Boston with twenty-six wives."

"The king of Saudi Arabia has clout. I don't. Karen, this has hit you hard, and it's not fair, and the suddenness is terrible. But you're gonna have a guy of your own. It won't take long. Things are gonna look a lot better than the way they look right now. You don't want a ménage à trois."

Bob and Karen continued looking at one another. Then her eyes filled. Her lip quivered. She turned forward and wept quietly. Bob tried awkwardly to pat her shoulder. She neither avoided his hand nor responded.

Elspeth took some tissues from her shoulder bag and handed them forward. Karen took them without turning.

Bob started the car. They drove slowly.

"When are you leaving?" Karen said.

"Right away, I guess," said Bob. "It's such a mess, I figure the sooner it's over with the better."

651

"Where will you go?"

"Out of state."

"Where out of state?"

"Karen, do us a favor, don't tell anybody where. Okay? Chances are when Ellie and I don't show at the temple, somebody will get the idea to phone and see if we're at *your* house. And I'd rather you didn't give them any clues. Just in case Ellie's father takes a notion to call the police. Just tell them not Ontario. Or something like that. Okay? And we'll call you when we get back. If you'll talk to us."

"No, Bob," said Elspeth. "If it were the other way around, I wouldn't want to hear from us. Not that soon. If ever. We're a couple of finks, Bob."

Karen blew her nose, sniffled, and continued weeping quietly.

"Karen," Bob said, "listen to me. It may be hard to believe now, but you're gonna be glad. Because you'll come out ahead. You can do better than me. And you're going to. You can do lots better than me."

"That's what my parents keep telling me."

"What?" He glanced at her, but she looked only at the tissues.

"That's what my parents keep telling me."

"Well, I mean it," he said. "Guys are gonna be lined up down the block. I know at least two guys that can't take their eyes off you."

"Shloym and Milt," Karen said.

"You know it?"

"Of course I know it."

He swallowed. "Well, I mean it. You got used to me before those guys came to town, or I wouldn't have had a chance. Shloym especially. He's the catch of the community. He's got me beat ten ways."

"That's what Avis says."

Bob looked at her. He drove more slowly. "I thought your family liked me."

"They liked you. I mean, you were acceptable. It's just that they think their little girl should have the best, that's all."

She didn't look at him. She softly blew her nose. No one said anything more.

When they got to her building Bob turned to her but she left the car quickly, without looking back, and ran to her door. Peter waved bye-bye.

652

85

MURMURINGS and whisperings were already throughout the pews before Murray quickly mounted the few stairs up front. He stumbled over a basket of flowers and bent to straighten it. In front of the marriage canopy he turned, with his back to it, and raised both hands. He cleared his throat.

He waited for quiet. Light from the chandeliers glinted on his black-framed glasses.

"All right, folks. You've been hearing rumors. Well, we've got word now. The bride won't be here. I'm not gonna tell you she's sick, or anything like that. You wouldn't believe me anyhow. It seems she changed her mind. She's got other plans."

Before the hubbub could rise Phil leaped onto a pew far in the rear, near the double doors. "Hey!" he called out over all the turning heads, and gestured with hands spread wide. "Please, everybody, don't go yet! The caterer's here with a mountain of food. Tons of food. It's paid for. What am I gonna do with it? Please! Help me eat! Help me get drunk! If I ever needed you I need you now. There's waitresses out there with trays of hot hors d'oeuvres—that stuff doesn't freeze. There's a frosted cake out there a mile high. An artistic wonder. Don't make me throw it in the garbage. It'd break my heart. Please! I need people around me! Don't leave me here alone."

Once more the talking rose everywhere. Husbands were helping wives with coats. Phil climbed down from the pew.

"Phil, I admire your spirit," a man said to him. "You're a strong guy."

"Look, I've taken a lot," Phil answered. "I'm used to it. I'm not a kid. You'll stay?"

"I'll stay."

"The condemned man ate a hearty meal," someone muttered in the crush at the door.

Gloria ran to Phil and clasped him, burying her tearful face against his chest. He clasped her too, with one arm. "Marge!" he called to someone. "Irwin! You can't leave! It's lunch time! Ya got to eat! What are you gonna do, go out and grab a hamburger somewheres?"

He stationed himself in the wide entrance hall, still holding Gloria to him, and continued to call to guests by name. Some went to the coatroom anyhow, avoiding him, but others others went across to the social hall.

"Any table," he said. "Never mind the numbers. Murray! Tell them to start the music. Go in, folks. There's three bartenders, tell them what you want. Jack! Stick around. Good."

"I warned him," Cele was saying near him to a man and a woman. "I warned him. He wouldn't listen."

"He's probably well out of it," said the man.

"It could be a blessing in disguise," said the woman.

"Jerome," said Phil. "Ruthie. Come on, keep me company. It'll cheer me up. There's thirty kinds of dessert, the Viennese smorgasbord." He seized someone by the sleeve. "You're staying, Maxwell?"

"We'll stay. We won't let you down."

"Good. Keep me company."

He walked to the swinging doors of the social hall with Gloria, arms about one another. Near the doors Bradley stood with hands in the pockets of his dark suit, coolly talking to another kid. Inside the music started.

Phil went in with Cele and Sheila. Gloria was still clinging to him. The bar was just inside the door.

"What'll it be, Phil?" Murray asked him.

"Vodka and tonic."

"Get me a brandy," said Sheila.

"Cele?" Murray asked.

"Oh, the sparkling stuff. Cold duck, whatever they call it."

They took a table near the corner. Perhaps half the tables had been taken, none of them fully occupied, but there were people at the bar. Far at the other end the five musicians in coats of dazzling blue sat before the curtained stage, the fingers of the clarinetist fluttering and the drummer striking out this way and that. The leader rose to his feet and sang, the hand microphone too close to his mouth. The caterer's girls were teenagers in plain white uniforms, the hems high. They carried trays among the tables.

With Phil sitting between Cele and Sheila, and Gloria standing and leaning with her arm about his shoulder, they scarcely took up half their round table. A few middle-aged couples were dancing to the music.

"Nobody from her side stayed," said Sheila.

"Can you blame them?" said Cele. "They're mortified. They even had cousins that came in from the West somewhere. Motel expense and everything. Just no consideration. And what do you expect? She's a kid. She acts like a kid."

"Glory, don't cry," Phil said. "Go over to the kids' table. Try the punch. There's sherbet in it."

"I want to stay with you."

"I know, you want to comfort me. Glory, as long as I have you, I'll be okay. I mean that. But you know what you can do for me now? Help me entertain guests. There's your cousin Maddie over there by the punchbowl. She came all this way. Introduce her to the other kids."

Gloria set out across the floor, her head down.

"What am I gonna do with the condominium now?" Cele said. "Phil's gonna need me in the house."

"Rent it furnished," said Sheila. "A condominium's a good investment."

"Hey! What have you got there?" Phil said to a waitress.

The girl lowered her tray.

"Hot stuffed mushrooms," said Phil. "They're delicious. Sheila, try these." He speared two with toothpicks. "Have you got the cocktail franks?" he asked the girl. "You know what I mean? Wrapped in pastrami?"

"They'll be out," the girl said.

Phil watched her go to the next table. She bent again with her tray and the hemline rose.

"You know," Phil said to Sheila and Cele, "I'd like sometime to have just all kinds of hors d'oeuvres, and all kinds of desserts. No main course. I asked the caterer but he wouldn't do it. Rock Cornish game hen, peas, potatoes, who needs it? Just fills you up, so you can't enjoy the good stuff."

A gravel-voiced gray-haired man with a big stomach and a protruding lip put a hand on Phil's shoulder. "Chin up, Phil," he said. "You know the old saying. A woman's only a woman, but a good cigar is a smoke." He was holding a drink.

"Yeah, yeah," Phil said drearily, " a rag a bone and a hank of hair."

Murray arrived with four drinks. The man nodded to him and moved on. Murray set the drinks down. He pulled out a chair and sat. He lifted his glass. "Cheers, Phil," he said.

They all sipped, Sheila her cordial glass, Cele her champagne glass, Phil his vodka and tonic.

"How about one of these waitresses, Phil?" Murray said. "They young enough for you?"

Phil swallowed slowly, saying nothing.

"Cheer up, Phil," said Murray. "You had the best of her. They sour after marriage. You know that. Even the best. It's inevitable."

"If you ask me he got out of it easy," Cele said. "He got out of it cheap. Do you know what she'd have cost him if she married him and hung around a year or two and then ditched him? He 's lucky she didn't have the patience."

"I heard she wasn't stable," said Sheila.

"Of course she's unstable," said Cele. "If she had her wits about her she'd have married him and divorced him and taken him to the cleaners. That's why I say he's lucky. Edna wanted to put her in the Boston Psychopathic."

"Just for ten days of observation," Phil said.

"They should put *you* in for ten days of observation too," Cele told him. "They'd never let you out. Her they'd let out. She's the smart one. Not you."

Another white-clad girl offered a tray.

"Ah, chicken wings Hawaiian," said Phil. "I love this." He dipped the morsel into the sauce at the tray's center, and took it on a napkin.

"So it just cost him the diamond," said Cele. "That diamond is bigger than his brain, I think. And the MG. He gave her the MG."

"You did?" said Murray.

"No," said Phil. "I gave it to her to use. There was no reason to change the title. It's in my name."

"That's good," said Sheila.

"So it just cost him the ring, the diamond," Murray said.

"And the topaz," said Cele.

"The topaz is bopkes," said Murray. "That girl was first quality, you know. That was taste, Phil. She had something. Never mind Cele, what does Cele know. You knew what you were doing. A broad like that. You could spend your money on two-hundred-dollar-a-night call girls and you'd never see stuff like that. Class isn't the word for it. That was one in a million. She had zing. Exquisite. I'm telling you, Phil, I envy you. How long did you have her? Four months? Four and a half months? What's that, about twenty weeks? What's that come to? Say a hundred and forty nights, give or take? For that lousy diamond? My God, cheap at the price! Dirt cheap. That's not even a hundred dollars a night! For goods like that? Just the way her tits keep giving that smallest little shake when she walks across a room. She just has to take a step, and they start doing their thing. That little delicate shake. Like a shiver. Just barely enough to pick it up on the seismograph. And when she walks down that big staircase there, in your house, Jesus. If a guy had a weak heart it could be dangerous. Why do you think I was here practically an hour ahead of time? I was the first one here. I wanted to make sure I had an aisle seat, to see her come walking down the aisle. Unobstructed view. You think I came to see *you*?"

"Phil wasn't sleeping with her," said Cele. "At least he says he wasn't."

"You're kidding," said Murray.

"It was on the up and up," Phil said. "We were gonna do our best to make a marriage, that's all. We were gonna try. And we saved it for the honeymoon, for the setting it deserved. Just like a diamond deserves a setting. Give it the bridal suite at the Ritz. Look, I wasn't buying her. I loved her. And she needed a home and a father for the kid. We knew that. And I knew she loved her cousin, but I didn't know *she* knew it. I couldn't help but know it, the first time I met the guy. It was in her eyes. He could do no wrong. If he sneezed, to her it was music. If he scratched himself, to her it was the ballet. But I didn't know she actually knew it, I thought she didn't see herself, and I didn't know *he* knew it. He had a girl friend."

"Wait a minute," said Murray slowly. "You're telling me you weren't banging her? You had her there in the house, in the palm of your hand, and you didn't know what to do with it?"

Phil and Murray looked at each other in silence. The orchestra leader was announcing his next number, the hand-mike close to his lips. Inside the heavy black frames Murray's eyes were magnified. Cele sat tiredly, dark pockets under her solemn eyes. Sheila sipped brandy with her mouth in a slight twist. Her little eyes above the glass were beady.

Murray's voice was low, almost quavering. "You're telling me that? You know how my mouth watered? How I was proud of you? And you tell me you had that, and you weren't doing anything? Phil, you have any idea how I ate my heart out, wishing I was in your shoes? I'd have ripped the clothes off her and chased her up and down those stairs naked! The front stairs, the back stairs! I'd have bent her over that picnic table and reamed her up the ass! Aw, Phil! I could cry. What's the matter with you? No wonder you lost her. She probably figured you couldn't get it up."

"She didn't think that," said Phil.

"Don't you know the way to a woman's heart is between her legs?" said Murray. "When you were a kid yet, didn't I teach you the way to a woman's heart is between her legs? Didn't I teach you that? If I told you once I told you a hundred times."

"Murray, all you can see is tits and an ass. I saw a soul. When she'd hold the boychik, there, in her lap, and sing to him, in that voice, it was so beautiful. I can't tell you how beautiful."

There was a catch in Murray's voice. "Listen to him. Phil, I'm ashamed of you. I'm embarrassed for you. Phil, Phil, what am I gonna do with you? You break my heart. There's no excuse. What the hell were you afraid of?"

ELSPETH moved with Peter quickly to the front seat. Even before she had quite pulled the door shut Bob started the car. A quick gesture wiped sweat from his brow.

At the end of the block he turned the corner, sped another two blocks, and stopped suddenly at the curb. With the engine still running Bob threw himself on Elspeth and kissed her hard and long on the lips. She responded to the kiss, one arm about him, and her other arm about Peter who was pressed on her white canvas coat between them.

Peter gave a muffled cry and Bob drew back. Peter was crying red-faced, his mouth wide, his eyes shut, and the knit bonnet askew with its pom.

"Sorry, fella," Bob apologized to him. "I didn't mean to squash you."

Elspeth nuzzled Peter and straightened his hat. Bob put the car in gear and they drove off. Peter stole an angry, resentful glance at Bob, lower lip pouting and quivering. Then he cried again, burying his face against Elspeth.

"He didn't mean it," Elspeth said. "He's your new daddy. He's gonna be your daddy."

They stopped at a crossing. She saw Bob watch the traffic light edgily, creeping forward an inch at a time. The instant the light changed they plunged ahead.

"Bob," Elspeth said, still stroking Peter, "I still hate myself about Karen. I hope the Shloym thing is true. But even if it is, I didn't know that. She loves you. It's plain that she loves you. We just about drove her out of her mind. When she was talking about marrying both of us I thought she'd really gone off her rocker."

"She had me worried there for a while."

"I was just about ready to change my mind and forget the whole thing. And leave you to her. Except we'd already wrecked it for her. Even if I'd pulled out it could never be the same between you again."

"No, it couldn't. Ellie, stop blaming yourself. We did what we had to."

"I was sitting there thinking, it's like what Jared did to *me*."

"It's not the same. Jared made you pregnant. Karen's a virgin."

"But Jared hadn't ever promised to marry me. He hadn't. And Janice wasn't somebody that got to be my friend and then stabbed me in the back. She didn't even know me hardly."

"Ellie, you have to stop lacerating yourself. It wasn't a betrayal. It was a correction. I feel we were meant for each other. Don't you feel that?"

She sighed. "But I've lost a friend. I've gained you, but I've lost a friend. I love Karen."

"She loves you too."

"Not anymore."

"She does. Or she wouldn't have come up with that ménage à trois idea. Even if she didn't mean it."

"Bob, she thinks I was scheming from the beginning. She thinks my whole friendship was just a pretense. She even thinks everything I asked her about being a froomie was just a pretense."

They circled up the ramp to the expressway.

"She doesn't, Ellie. She said it, but she was in shock. She was striking out in anger. But Ellie, for everybody that becomes religious, their coming to God is in the first instance through another person. Through somebody you love and admire, who's a believer, and for whom it seems to work. That's what ticks it off. And without that kind of relationship with somebody in your life, who was religious before you, it doesn't happen. We perceive God through another person. For Karen it was her parents. For me it was Gramps. And for you it was Karen. Or maybe Karen and me together. Maybe mainly Karen. And she knows that. She does, Ellie. And because of it, you and she are gonna love each other forever. Ellie, even though everyone's relationship to God is very private and individual, and different, and even though you pray on your own, with your own heart, still your coming to God in the first place is always through someone else. Everyone who believes, is a believer because of someone he knew. That's how it happens. Not intellectually. Belief is an emotional state, and you get it through another person."

Her eyes moistened. The car hummed on the broad straight highway. She took a tissue from the shoulder bag. Bob drove looking straight ahead, but he put a hand to her knee. They held hands.

"And I'll tell you something else, Ellie. We never see God in ourselves. We see God in each other. Each one thinks, my friends think I'm for real, but I know what a phony I am inside. But wow, that one over there is such a saint, it brings me nearer to God. They make God real for me. They bring tears of joy to my heart. Their good deeds, their kindness, they charge my batteries. Even though each one thinks, what, me charge anybody's batteries? You're kidding. Me, I'm a fake, I'm the black sheep in this bunch. I bet even Gramps felt like that. He thought he'd blown it. He thought he was the last of the line. He never knew what effect he had on me."

Peter had begun squirming and whining, with an occasional yammer. Elspeth unbuttoned her sweater. The bra unfastened in front.

He nursed resting on her arm, his eyes closed. "I was supposed to get him all weaned by today," she said. "But I'm glad I didn't. The breast is easiest for travel."

Somewhere in Rhode Island Bob left the expressway.

"I want to stay away from the more obvious routes, and toll booths and stuff," he said. "Even if it takes us a little longer. Just in case Uncle Joe takes a notion to come after us with a butterfly net."

But the road was still straight and fairly wide. They sped over yellow concrete, the tires bumping at intervals over lines of tar.

"When we phone my parents are you gonna call yours too?"

"Nah. Why waste a call? Aunt Harriet will call my mother."

"How do you think your parents will take it?"

He shrugged. "They've written me off as a crackpot anyhow."

Again Peter became fussy, though her breasts were empty now. She clicked on the radio but got only a rush of static.

"I have to get someone to fix it," said Bob.

She twirled the dial but the static was uniform everywhere. She turned it off. She played peekaboo with Peter.

Then she sang to him with vigor, making him jump and jump on her lap.

> "Wulla hoo hoo, wulla hoo hoo!
> Biggledy boggledy buggledy boo!"

He thought this new song hilarious. He laughed as though he would split, through encore after encore.

But at last the laughter dissolved into whimpering.

"Can we find a store and get some baby food?" Elspeth said. "He's used to a supplement now after the feeding."

At a crossroad they came upon a shabby grocery in a clapboard building with a gasoline pump in front. The road was edged with gravel and weeds. A big sign hung over the door, with Coca Cola in swirling calligraphy.

An elderly lady was in charge. There were no other customers. Elspeth found jars of baby food on a shelf, and a package of plastic spoons on a hook. Bob opened the refrigerated cabinets and took cartons of yogurt. "Is there a diner around, where we can get some coffee?" he asked.

"You can get coffee right here," the lady said.

They saw the coffeemaker next to the register and a tray of sticky doughnuts and a stack of paper cups.

Bob pressed the spigot and dribbled steaming coffee. The lady allowed Elspeth to sit Peter on the wooden counter and tie his bib. He leaned into each approach of the spoon, never taking his eyes from it. Bob stood watching, and blew on his coffee between sips.

"I'll take him to the car and change him if you want," Bob said after a while, "and give you a chance to have some coffee."

The lady let her use the bathroom. Afterward she chose a few apples and pears. She took a bunch of celery and a couple of carrots.

She came to the car with her bundle under an arm and a coffee in each hand. She found Bob sharing a yogurt with Peter.

"How did you manage with the diaper?" she asked.

"Okay."

"He must have been soaked."

"Par for the course, I guess."

"Any b.m.?"

"Nope."

"I see you found the plastic thing for the diaper." It was on the floor.

They sat in the parked car eating yogurts, and took turns giving Peter an occasional sample. Bob had more coffee.

"Is Petey named after anybody?"

"No. It's just his name."

"How come you didn't name him after Mark or Eric? Or Gramps, even?"

"I don't know. I could have. I thought of it. Except I didn't know if it's considered an insult to somebody to name a bastard after them, and if the family would take it wrong, or what. And meanwhile I just kind of started calling him Petey." With a tissue she wiped yogurt from his chin. "And then later when my father was refusing to see him, and trying to get him taken away by the courts and everything, I thought of changing it to name him for my father's father. Your know, to bring him around."

"Why didn't you?"

"Well, I didn't know if it would help any. And it was sort of too late. He was already Petey to me."

"He's not a bastard, you know. Not in Jewish law."

"He's not? How come?"

"Didn't you know that? If he were a child of incest, like if his parents were brother and sister, then he'd be a bastard. Or say if you were married, and you cheated on your husband and had a child by another guy, then the child would be a bastard. But a child of an unmarried woman isn't a bastard."

"Well, now, what do you know!" She laughed. "Hear that, Petey? You're one up on William the Conqueror!" She undid the string of his knit hat and cleaned yogurt from his neck. "You want to give him a middle name after somebody?" she asked Bob. "Like after Gramps?"

"You want to?"

"If you want to. It's fine with me."

"Okay," he said. "Gramps was Asher. It means happy. What name do you like that starts with A?"

"Andrew," said Elspeth.

"Okay," said Bob. "Do you like that, Petey? Peter Andrew Shoemaker. Or would you rather be Peter Piper Picklemaker?"

But Peter sat asleep, limp against Elspeth's front, his cheeks puffed in the bonnet.

"Ready to go?" said Bob. He dropped his empty coffee cup to the floor, leaned and kissed Elspeth gently. Peter moved an arm nervously but did not waken. Elspeth lifted her face into the kiss and slid an arm around Bob. His mouth seemed clean, firm. She liked the whole fit of his face.

When they separated he started the car. She moved closer to him.

As they rode she leaned on his arm. Her eyes would not stay open.

She rose and fell through levels of sleep and half sleep. Sometimes she wakened without opening her eyes, and adjusted her position against his shoulder, and her grip on Peter, and knew from the sounds of traffic and the changes of speed whether they were in a town or a stretch of country. Sometimes she felt light and shade pass across her face. Sometimes her eyes blinked open and she looked up at Bob's profile.

At a gas station he got out, and she sat up.

"Want my Master Charge?" she asked through the window.

"I've still got some cash left."

"Don't spend it all. We may need the cash for groceries."

But he was already paying for the gas.

"Want me to drive for a while? Aren't you tired?"

"No, I'm okay."

"You sure? You didn't sleep all night."

"Neither did you."

"I did a little. And I've had a nap."

"I'm okay."

The hood rose and hid him when he checked the oil. Peter still slept.

Bob got in and started the car. She was sinking again into drowsiness. She rested on his arm and shoulder, and her cheek nestled deeper and deeper into the fabric. We fit perfectly, she thought.

She must have slept soundly. She did not know how long. Her eyes opened squinting into the sun. It was dazzling and oppressively brilliant, surrounded by

661

high industrial chimneys against a sky still blue and clear. On her lap Peter still slept.

"What time is it?" she asked.

"About three."

"Where are we?"

"Bridgeport."

She shifted position to ease a stiff muscle.

She sat up, and talked a while. She said someday she wanted to build a house for them, with her own hands. He said he'd help. She'd be in charge, and he'd be her assistant.

And she said that meanwhile, when they got back to Cambridge, she'd help with his janitor job. She knew all about heating systems and plumbing and electric systems. Maybe they'd talk to the owners, and she could supervise more buildings.

"Are you still gonna build that townhouse project in Dowling? Like a village up and down the steep hills?"

"I'd like to. I'm gonna try. Why? What do you think of it?"

"I think it's great."

"I've got a folder full of sketches."

"Where'll you get the financing?"

"Well, if I can get an option on somebody's seemingly useless hillside real cheap, that would be the first step. The idea's sound. And then it's a matter of persuading a backer that it is. If I'm lucky, you'll be a graduate student with a rich wife. And if I'm not, I guess we'll find a way for me to study to be an architect."

"I could see Steve Kramer's Uncle Lennie taking a flyer on a project like that. He's always got an eye for a smart investment. Except they'll be mad at us now."

"Sure. And my father. And Phil, and his brother and sister. They've all got their reasons for being mad at me. And Marvin Gilbert. But I wouldn't hold that against them. I wouldn't deny any of them a piece of the action on that account. And maybe I'll see my banker at the Eggleston-Uphams about a loan. Who owns our building in Cambridge? Do you think they'd like a crack at a few shares?"

"Two brothers. Armenian guys. They just might. We'll talk to them."

"We'll prepare a prospectus," she said.

And anyway she'd begin to take courses. Maybe at MIT at night, when Bob was home with Petey.

She settled against his sleeve. She slept again.

Peter wakened and she woke. They seemed to ride on cobblestones and potholes, and sunshine and shadow now slid over them rapidly in slanting stripes. An elevated train clattered loudly overhead, its shadow galloping over storefronts. Peter raised both index fingers high.

"Are we in New York?" she asked.

"Yeah. Ever been here before?"

"A bunch of us came down from Mount Holyoke one weekend."

"We're in the Bronx," he said.

She looked at Bob. He drove doggedly between riveted girders.

"Let's find a hotel and get some sleep," she said. "Enough's enough. We'll go to North Carolina tomorrow. Or at midnight, whenever we wake up. Your eyes look like pee holes in the snow."

"Okay."

They slowed further. A taxi darted around them, the driver shouting something angrily.

"I see a hotel," said Elspeth.

He was steering to the right of the girders, along a line of parked cars.

He double-parked. A canopy extended out over the sidewalk. "It doesn't look exactly first class," said Bob.

"That's okay. As long as it has a bed. Why don't you go in and see if there's a vacancy, and then we'll look for a place to park."

Bob left. Peter stood at the car window and watched him till he disappeared. A train thundered above like an earthquake, this time in the other direction. Peter fell back onto Elspeth's lap and looked about in amazement. He pointed his index fingers upward.

Most of the stores here seemed to be open. Across the street, in front of what appeared to be a smallish supermarket, she saw a car preparing to pull out of a parking space. She sat Peter beside her and turned the starter key. Edging cautiously, with her head half out the window and her signal light blinking, she awaited her chance and then swung rapidly through the girders in a U-turn. Peter tumbled over sideways on the seat without hurting himself.

Elspeth backed into the space. Then she watched for Bob, holding Peter at the window. When he came out of the hotel and looked about she honked.

"How is it?" she called as he approached.

"I don't know. I signed us in, but we don't get a key until we bring in the suitcases. It's twenty bucks and for five bucks more they'll set up a crib."

"Okay," she said. "There's a store here. Let's collect some supplies first, in case we get up in the night and want to push on."

They steered Peter through the store aisles in a shopping cart. They picked out canned goods, packaged cheeses, powdered milk, instant coffee, plastic ware, paper plates, a melon, tomatoes, oranges, an aluminum pot, a small salami, cans of soda, a package of rolls, a box of cookies, disposable diapers, paper towels and napkins, a couple of serrated knives, a can opener, and a coiled electric device that was supposed to boil water if placed in a pot.

"Is there a place open where I can buy stationery?" Elspeth asked at the checkout.

"Next door," the gruff man at the register said.

"Can we borrow the shopping cart?" Bob asked him.

"Where are you going with it?"

"The hotel across the street. I'll bring it right back."

"No."

"Then would you put all the light things together in one bag, please? We've got three big bags and the baby."

"Come on, come on, move it. Don't hold me up."

Elspeth lifted Peter from the shopping cart. "It's okay, Bob. I can take one."

They came out to the sidewalk as another train roared. Peter buried his face in Elspeth's neck and spotty light and shadow sped over him. "What do you want stationery for?" Bob asked her.

"To write a letter to Phil."

"Well, let's lock the groceries in the car then. And after we're settled I'll get our stuff."

He put his bundles on the pavement and unlocked the car.

"Let's take the cookies, though, if you can find them," Elspeth said.

It was not so much a stationery store as a kind of variety store. It was quite cramped, with a soda fountain and stools taking up a side. A huge man behind the counter conversed with an unshaven man in a squashed fedora hat and leather windbreaker who sat on one of the stools. The other wall had racks of magazines, books, newspapers, toys, tobacco. There were glass cases full of candy. A pimply boy of fourteen or fifteen with bushy dark hair stood looking through a magazine at the rack. In the back two pinball machines stood idle.

"Want a milkshake?" Bob asked.

"Just a glass of milk," said Elspeth.

Bob sat on a stool, holding Peter. "Two milks," he told the big man. Elspeth stood studying the stationery assortment.

The man placed conical cups in metal containers and poured the milks. He was tall and burly, with an apron over a massive stomach. His nose was flat, and his jowls were wider than the top of his head. Bob gave Peter a sip of milk.

"Tyew," Peter chirped. "Tyew." He sipped again.

"Hear that?" said Elspeth. "He's saying juice. It means anything he drinks from a cup."

She compared boxes of stationery. Most were too cutesy.

"Ellie, see if any of those rings will fit you," Bob said, "and I'll use it to marry you. I thought I was gonna have to devise one from a piece of copper wire I brought, but those will do fine."

The display of children's rings was near her, several to a hook. They had monograms.

"They all fit," she said. They were of soft metal and opened to adjust.

She brought a box of blue stationery and a ring to the marbled counter. She climbed onto a stool and took a swallow of milk. She was still in her jeans. Bob was in the three-piece dark suit he had worn to the house in the morning. It had become wrinkled in the car. Peter picked up the ring. He examined it, with both hands. He put it to his mouth. Bob took it and looked at him through it with one eye.

"That reminds me," said Elspeth. "I have to send Phil his ring. I'll have to find a little box."

"Hey, Frankie!" the burly man called to the pimply boy. "How many magazines you gonna read and not buy nothing? Fifty thousand?" He spoke slowly, enunciating every consonant with a kind of lisp. His tongue seemed too wide for his mouth.

The boy turned a page.

"Hey, Frankie!" the man said. "Does you father know you look at that garbage?"

"It's not garbage," said the man in the squashed fedora. "It's girls. What's the matter, girls is garbage by you?"

"Naked broads," said the big man behind the counter, his tongue filling his mouth. "I wouldn't lower myself to look at that stuff."

"Would you happen to have a little box?" Elspeth asked him.

"Just file card boxes," he said. "For recipes. Over by where you found the box of letter paper."

She slipped off the stool.

"Do you have condoms?" Bob asked him."

"Lubricated or regular?" he said slowly. Each consonant seemed exaggerated in its own distinct way.

"Regular," said Bob.

"A dozen?"

"Fine."

"If it's garbage by you," said the man in the squashed hat, "how come you sell it in your store?"

"Because the customer is always right. Just like the man here asks for condoms, rubbers. I got to sell him condoms." He turned away. Elspeth returned and put a hand lightly on Bob's shoulder. "I meant to tell you," she said quietly. "I'm newly equipped."

"Oh. Good. That's preferable, actually."

The big man turned. "What?"

"Nothing," Bob said to him.

The man slapped the little white box onto the counter.

Elspeth put a gray plastic box for three-by-five cards onto the counter and climbed onto the stool.

"Isn't that big to send a ring in?" said Bob.

"It's perfect," she said. "I'll stuff it with paper. If it were too small they'd lose it."

She put the file box on top of the stationery box, and the box of condoms on top of that. She put the toy ring on the condoms.

"I just wanted you to know I'm at your service," Bob told her softly.

"Will that be all?" said the man.

"Ellie, let's get married," Bob said. He gave Peter to her. "If these gentlemen will be kind enough to be our witnesses. Would you guys mind witnessing a wedding?" He took a folded sheet of lined paper from the inside pocket of his jacket. "I'm gonna give her that ring, and read her this document, and you just have to witness that it took place, that's all. It'll just take a couple of minutes."

"When?" said the man in the squashed hat.

"Now." He unfolded the paper. Elspeth saw that he had lettered it all over, line after line, vowel-points and all. He had even turned the page upside down to put the red margin on the right, because the curly alphabet ran from right to left.

"You mean now?" said squashed-hat. "Right here? Like you're getting married?"

"Sure. It just takes a minute."

"You copied all that out yourself?" said Elspeth. "When did you get time to do that?"

"Well, I've had Avis's at my place all week, you know. I was practicing from it. Which reminds me, we've got to get it back to her. And I had it all written out here too to practice from, because a lot of the real ones don't have the vowels. Gentlemen, will you accommodate us?"

"What's this, a fraternity stunt?" said squashed-hat. The boy was looking at them over his magazine.

"You need a rabbi to get married," said the big man.

"All I need," said Bob, "is a woman and a ring. And preferably a marriage contract."

"What do we have to do?" said squashed-hat.

"Just watch. The witnesses don't sign it. I'll write your names on here as witnesses, and if anyone ever asks you if you saw these proceedings, you say what you saw. But nobody will ever ask you."

"Not me," said the man behind the counter. "Leave me out. I don't get involved."

"Come on," squashed-hat urged him. "Go with the gag."

"No. Look, you never know. I get all kinds in here. This morning some black guy comes in and tells me he's the Emperor of the Universe. I told him, in *this* store, *I'm* the Emperor."

"Give it to me, kid," squashed-hat said. "I'll be your witness."

"Don't get involved," the big man told him darkly.

"What's to get involved?" he countered. "It's only in Jewish anyways. It don't mean nothing."

Bob had wheeled around on the stool, pen in hand. "What's your Hebrew name?" he asked squashed-hat.

"Moish."

Bob drew three letters, from right to left. "And your father's name?"

"Velvel."

"There's no such name," said the big man.

"Don't tell me there's no such name! That's his name! Take it or leave it."

Bob was writing. "And can I have your English name, and address and phone? Just in case we ever have to get in touch?"

"See?" said the big man. "What did I tell ya? Now you're getting involved."

Squashed-hat said a name, and spelled it as Bob wrote. He gave an address and a phone number.

"We need one more witness," said Bob finally. "Frankie, are you Jewish?"

"Of course he's Jewish," said squashed-hat. "What the hell do you think he is?"

"What's your Hebrew name?" Bob asked.

"Him?" said squashed-hat. "His name is Pisher."

The boy gave a double name, followed by a multiple patronymic and a designation of hereditary priesthood. He repeated it all a second time slowly, a name at a time, and Bob carefully wrote it down, from right to left.

"Is that spelled with a tet or a tav?" Bob asked at one point. The boy told him.

At last Bob asked for his English name and address.

"Don't tell him," said the big man.

"Don't listen to Butch," said squashed-hat. "Butch is afraid of everybody. As big as he is. He's probably even afraid of you."

The boy gave a name and address, and then a phone.

"Ain't that baby the image of his father, though?" said squashed-hat. "He looks just *like* you, kid. The spitting image. Except the hair. He's got her hair."

Bob closed the pen and restored it to his pocket, leaving the document unfolded on the counter. He rotated on the stool toward Elspeth. "What happened to the ring?"

She had been amusing Peter by putting the ring about one of his tiny fingers after another. She gave it to Bob. She held Peter on her lap with one arm, and raised her index finger before Bob.

She watched him place the ring carefully on her finger. Then his eyes fixed on hers. There was a glow in his face. He had not let go of her finger, or the ring on it. His eyes seemed to look into her deeply. She felt his enclosing hand lightly caress her finger and the ring, and he recited the Hebrew formula, slowly, precisely. Then, without releasing the finger and ring, he repeated it in English. "Take notice, with this ring you become sacred for me, as per the code of Moses and Israel."

He dropped his hand. With the hand that held Peter she tightened the ring.

"Okay, Ellie," Bob said quietly. "Now you own me. Not according to the state, which was made yesterday, but according to God, who created the sky, the earth, the sea and all that is in them."

"That don't count," said the big man.

"What do you mean it don't count," said squashed-hat. "You sold him rubbers. You didn't ask if they're married or not. I'm with *you*, kid. Rabbis don't know nothing."

Bob had taken up the paper from the counter. He held it in both hands. "We have to read the contract," he said.

He carefully read the Aramaic, line after line, sometimes glancing up at her, and once or twice losing his place and stumbling. Not a word was intelligible to her, except for her name and his. But he was beautiful. Even the little hesitations and the self-consciousness were beautiful. She knew that Peter was fascinated by him too.

He folded the paper. He gave it to her. She put it into the shoulder bag.

"Now you two guys are really involved," the big man enunciated slowly, his tongue filling his mouth. "Supposing she's found murdered? And they investigate the corpse, and they find that paper in the bag there, with your name on it?"

Elspeth put the stationery and the plastic box and the box of condoms into the shoulder bag too.

"There's just one more thing I'd like you guys to do," Bob said. "And that's witness that I took her into that hotel there across the street. You don't have to come across the street. But watch through the window here, till we're out of sight. That's part of the wedding too. Actually the formality is that the two of us went into a room alone together. You know, even for a couple of minutes. But if you see me take her into a hotel, especially after you saw me buy rubbers, I'm sure that more than covers it."

"Pay for your stuff before you go anywhere," the big man said.

"What do we owe you?"

"Let me add it." He wrote with a pencil, wrinkling his brow. "Two milks, twenty-five each. Ring, twenty-five and tax. Letter paper, one-ninety-five and tax. Rubbers, two-seventy-five and tax."

"File box," said Elspeth.

"Oh, yeah. Eighty-nine and tax."

They waited while he puzzled and calculated.

Bob paid him and received some change. Then he took a five-dollar bill from his wallet and extended it to squashed-hat. "My friend, I want you and Frankie to split this. Buy yourselves a cigar or whatever."

"Aw, you don't have to do that. It was our pleasure."

"Please," said Bob. "You've been to a wedding. You should celebrate. I'm sorry we can't do more."

He scratched his head under the squashed fedora, looking at the bill in Bob's hand and shrugging sheepishly. He looked at the boy. "Well, what do you say, Frankie? They want us to celebrate. So we'll watch through the window till they go in the hotel there, and then we'll have Butch fix us each an egg cream, and he'll give us our change, and you'll buy yourself a magazine. And hide it so your parents don't find it." He took the money.

"What's an egg cream?" said Elspeth.

"You don't know what an egg cream is?" said squashed-hat. "Where do you come from?"

"Boston," she said. "Near Boston."

"Boston," said squashed-hat. "Bahston. I should've realized. You've got the accent all right."

87

HER eyes opened as a train hammered past the window. The glass rattled with it loudly in its wooden frame, as it had with every train through the night. The whole building shook. Even through the mattress she felt it throb. Even the brass pipes of the bed frame vibrated in harmony with it, giving out a tone that grew louder and then dropped an octave. Above her, in the murky dawn, the ceiling fixture swung wildly on its chain, the beads of its pull-cord striking its glass blossom. The train pounded and pounded. How many cars could it have? Fifteen? Twenty? But at last it had sped away. The building no longer shuddered, and overhead the dusty blossom swung in a diminishing arc. Now she could hear the windblown beat of the rain on the window and the sounds of early morning traffic below. Beside her Bob slept. She gazed at the landscape of his body, the variety of its hairs and textures, and the shadows it cast upon itself in the somber blue-gray half-light. She thought of reaching out to fondle him. But she hesitated to wake him.

The blankets had slid to the floor. But the room was hot. The radiators were ticking. In the darkest corner stood the chipped iron crib, and she could see Peter sleeping with his rump raised.

The bathroom door was so caked with paint that she could not pull it completely shut. The flushing was a copious roar under high pressure.

She stepped into the tub and turned on the shower. It was scalding. She adjusted it. Then she turned the shower head to an angle to avoid drenching her hair.

When she had dried herself she did calisthenics, swinging her fingers to her toes.

The mirror had a film of moisture that clouded up again when she wiped it, and she could not see to brush her hair. She returned to the bedroom.

Bob's head turned to her, his eyes open.

"Hey, look at you," said Elspeth. "Isn't that thing tired yet? It just goes on and on?"

His face seemed luminous. "Ellie, if you walked through a cemetery, the skeletons would have erections. God outdid Himself when He created you. I don't know which part of you to look at first."

"But all night long? Nonstop? I didn't know you were such a sex fiend." She put the hairbrush on the rickety bureau. She sat on the mattress near where he lay and it sagged beneath her. She slid her fingers on him affectionately. "And that was after no sleep the night before. How do you do it?"

"You inspired me."

"And sometimes it just didn't end. I'd have a climax, and you'd still be there inside me, and I'd have another, and another, and another, and another, all in one screw. I'd come, and I'd think you must have come, and you hadn't. You'd still be there. You'd wait, and slowly the crescendo starts again."

"Well, if you noticed, toward morning they got shorter. The prolonging is easier when you're full."

"And sometimes in those long ones," she said, "a train came by, and the whole hotel would shake, and the bed would shake, and you'd shake inside me, like some kind of a vibrator or something."

He laughed.

"And once when you were inside me—I don't know what time it was, but I was on top, like sitting up on it—and two trains came by at the same time, in opposite directions. Remember that? I thought I'd explode! I started crying."

"I thought I'd hurt you."

"You didn't hurt me. It was just more than I could handle. Bobby honey, let's come back here every year for our anniversary, and screw by the trains."

"Okay." He tugged easily at her arm to incline her down toward him. "Now how about one for the road? You're quite a lay yourself, you know. Your vagina clutches me. It breathes."

"That's not all it can do. Petey came out of it."

"So I understand. Come on. A quickie. You call the position."

She escaped from his hand and remained sitting. "Don't overdo it. You won't have any left for tomorrow. See, look, it did get tired."

"You just wait a while, and stay here next to me, and it'll come up again."

"Why don't you get up out of bed and say your morning prayers?"

"I'm exempt from prayers this week."

"You are? How come?"

"Because I'm a new bridegroom. I'm supposed to give you my undivided attention."

"Heck. I want to see how you'd look saying your prayers naked. A yarmulka on your head, and a big tallis draping down your back, and tefillin strapped on, and nothing else on, not a stitch else. And while you're praying I'll sneak up and tangle the strings around your prick."

Peter uttered garbled syllables. He got to his hands and knees, and grinned at them through the bars.

"Good morning, Peter Andrew Shoemaker," said Bob without stirring. Elspeth still sat beside him and he lay with his hand on her thigh.

Peter pulled himself up and stood holding the rail, still grinning. The diaper dropped to his feet.

"I guess I didn't do such a great job with the diaper last time," said Bob.

"I guess you didn't."

"Okay, I'll change him," he said. "I see I need the practice."

He got up. He lifted Peter over the rail and carried him to the bathroom.

Elspeth got up too. She found fresh panties in the shoulder bag and pulled them on. She could hear Bob talking to Peter. She brushed her hair at the bureau mirror.

In a while Bob returned holding Peter. "When that toilet flushes in there, it's like a cataract," he said.

"I know. Isn't it wonderful? It's like taking a crap into Niagara Falls. Why don't we get dressed, so we can start on our way."

"Don't you want to give Petey his breakfast first?"

"I thought we'd go out for breakfast," she said, "and give him some solid food. And save the breast for later, in case we need it in the car."

Bob began to lower him in the crib, but he hollered.

"Where'll I put him?" Bob said. "The carpet looks kind of dirty."

"Maybe he'd like to sit in the open suitcase there on the floor."

Bob sat Peter in the suitcase. He seemed happy there. He began picking up articles of clothing, some in one hand and some in the other, and throwing them out. A train shook the place but Peter gave it no notice.

Bob took Elspeth in his arms. He stood pressing her to him. She let her arms fold about him too, still holding the hairbrush. She rested her cheek against his shoulder and neck. He hugged her tighter. She heard him breathe.

"Ellie, for me to have you, it was worth the fifteen or twenty billion years it took for the universe to be created, and evolve, and come to this point. It was. It was worth it for this."

His hands moved, on her shoulder blades, her vertebrae, the small of her back. They warmed her skin. They stretched the waistband, and coasted slowly down inside the panties.

"Such an exquisite ass," he said. "The most graceful curve."

"My father said that. When I was a little girl he used to tell me I had the most beautiful toshy in the world and it was too bad I couldn't see it."

"He was right."

"So I used to look at it in the mirror."

His embrace rose higher upon her back and they stood clasped together, swaying slightly. She saw Peter glance up at her. She gave Bob a little kiss, and put her hands to his chest to edge herself from him. "Come on, pussycat," she said softly, "we're in a hurry to get to North Carolina. So get dressed. Stop dawdling."

"Who, me? You're not dressed either."

"I've at least got underpants on," she said. "You haven't got a thing on. I've made more progress than you have."

Bob collected his clothing that Peter had thrown about. The rain still beat on the window.

"I don't have another change of underwear for tomorrow," said Elspeth. "We'll have to stop on the way somewhere so I can get some clothes. You're lucky. You were able to pack and hide your stuff in the car."

"No, you're lucky. You get to buy new stuff."

He put on frayed khaki trousers this time, and a dark shaggy sweater.

The three-piece suit he has worn yesterday hung now on a hanger. "I'm gonna try to fold this into the suitcase for now," he said. "So it doesn't get soaked crossing the street."

"Swipe the hotel's hanger."

"No, it can go together on the one your wedding suit is on in the car."

"Don't forget the diaper box. I think you left it in the john."

In the dim hallway they rang for the elevator. Each time they pressed the button they heard a clattering bell down in the shaft. But nothing happened. Bob pushed open the emergency door at the end of the hallway, and they descended the metal staircase.

As they entered the lobby the rumbling of a train made the dust in the carpet jump. A vibrating letter opener on the clerk's desk changed direction. But the white-haired clerk slept, his chin on his chest.

Bob put down his suitcase. He slammed the bell. The clerk woke with a start. They paid with the credit card.

They hurried up the block, close to the buildings for shelter from the driving downpour. The grumble of trucks and the slosh of tires under the elevated was constant. At the corner a blind man with a scarf about his face and a visored cloth cap pulled over his ears hawked newspapers, feeling coins and bills with quick efficiency and making change, while rain ran down the sheeting that protected his booth. Bob pulled open the door of a dairy restaurant called Citron's and Elspeth ducked inside clutching Peter.

They found a small table near the wall. The place was busy and noisy and smelled of raincoats. The broad glass was filmed with steam, blurring the scene outside.

A smiling waddling old lady who must have been less than five feet tall waited on them. "You want I should bring for the baby a highchair?"

"Oh, that would be wonderful," said Elspeth. "Thanks very much."

There was already a plate of sliced black bread on the table, along with the napkin dispenser and the salt and pepper. Elspeth broke little pieces and fed them to Peter.

At a neighboring table a young woman with jewelry dangling from her ears stared toward Peter and sipped coffee. "You have a beautiful child," she said. She pronounced it beautyful choyld.

"Thank you," Bob smiled. "I think so too."

A stocky bald waiter with a cummerbund but no jacket set up the highchair noisily and unsmiling. The waddling little lady brought their cereal and grapefruits and steaming coffees. Elspeth took Peter's bib from the shoulder bag.

He ate dry cereal, taking bits between thumb and forefinger one at a time. His admirer at the next table kept watching. Bob gave her another little smile.

Then he set his watch by the clock on the wall. "It's seven-forty," he said to Elspeth. "About eight-thirty I want to make a couple of long-distance calls. I have to let them know at MIT I'm not meeting my classes for a couple of days. And my friends have to know about us so they can start setting up shiva brochos."

"Start setting up what?"

"Shiva brochos. It's parties people make for a bride and groom after the wedding. You have seven dinner parties in seven nights, each one in a different house."

"I never heard of that."

"I never heard of it either, until I got involved with the froomies. We'll have missed two, last night and tonight. But if Uncle Joe sounds okay when we call from Carolina, and the coast is clear to come home, we can be home by tomorrow night and we'll still get five."

"Will they do that for us? They're all Karen's friends too. And Avis's friends."

"Oh, I'm sure they will. I can't imagine them not doing it."

"After what we did to Karen?"

"Look, in the first place they'll understand. And besides they see it as an obligation. A good time, but an obligation. Just like you have an obligation to bring mourners their meals, and comfort them. And like you have an obligation to visit the sick. You're obligated to help a bride and groom rejoice."

"What kind of a party is it?"

"Well, after dessert you're all sitting around the table, and they say seven blessings. That's what it means—shiva brochos is seven blessings. Each one is said by a different person. We point to people, and each one says a blessing. Blessings about creation, and reproduction, and the bride and groom having fun together, and wine, stuff like that. And then they all drink the wine, and lots and lots of singing. And maybe the girls will lift you up high on a chair, if the ceiling's high enough, and carry you around on it, and the guys will lift me on another chair, and all the dancing and the handclapping and that kind of stuff. And the next night they do it in another house, maybe with some new people. It goes on for a week."

"When do they go on a honeymoon trip?"

"Who needs a honeymoon trip?" he said. "It's instead of a honeymoon trip."

Elspeth ran her tongue pensively along the hollow of her spoon. "Actually," she said, "it's the exact opposite of a honeymoon trip. Instead of a trip you stay home."

"You stay where your friends are," he said, "or you can go to different friends in different towns, provided you get from one to the next in a day's time. I mean, why run away when you're happy? Joy was meant to be shared. You know how honeymoons started? In the ancient world nobody went on honeymoons."

She gave a little shrug, looking at him.

"Well," he said, "you know Western civ got fouled up with this very schizophrenic and unmonotheistic hang-up about sex. Aphrodite was sex. So when the pagans became Christianized, they remembered sex as one of the pagan gods, so they thought sex was for pagans, and the Devil and the bad guys. So screwing didn't fit in with the church's sanctimonious scheme of things. And since it didn't, it got to be a matter of embarrassment and jokes and stuff. And that's why the bride and groom would run away after the wedding to some other town where nobody knew them. So they wouldn't have to hang around and blush and listen to their friends' wedding-night jokes."

Elspeth nodded, still spooning cereal. "You really think we'll come home to a round of parties?"

"I'm sure of it."

673

"You just have to let your friends know we're married, and they'll go to work on it? Just like that?"

"That's how they operate. We're a community. If somebody gets married they don't just sit there."

"Well, I hope so," said Elspeth. "It'll be a chance for them to get to know me, and vice versa. And it'll help me forget to feel rotten for a while about what we did to a couple of other people. Because I know one member of the community that'll be conspicuous by her absence."

"Of course," he said. "Obviously Karen won't show, under the circumstances. And Avis and Steve won't. And maybe her closest buddies will feel uncomfortable and stay away."

"Avis is probably burning us in effigy. On principle. Even if she does prefer Shloym. You really think it's gonna be okay?"

"I'm sure of it. Even without Shloym. That crowd won't let her be lonesome. And when she gets married you and I will host one of the shiva brochos parties. Okay? We'll insist on it."

He fed Peter a bit of grapefruit.

"That floored me," he said. "I mean that Avis was working on her to dump me."

"Do you think she would have?"

"I don't know. She might have, eventually. That family's awfully close." He shook his head. "You just never know about people."

"I thought they were such a community of saints."

"Well, we try. I can't blame her for taking a last look around before the closing of the gates."

She watched him feed Peter more grapefruit. Peter seemed fascinated by the sourness. With each morsel the little face puckered anew with a bright expression of amusement and surprise. His admirer at the next table had gone.

"He has such a wonderful face," said Bob.

"Yup," said Elspeth. "And you do too."

She took the box of blue stationery from the shoulder bag. She cleaned an area of the table with a crumpled napkin. She opened a pen.

"Writing to Phil?" Bob asked.

"Ya. I want to get it into the mail as soon as possible."

Without putting down a word she thought through phrase after phrase, rejecting them, searching for the right tone. With each try, the more impossible it seemed to become. The kinder the words, somehow the more they smacked of insincerity. And Phil was perceptive enough to distinguish between real and fake.

"You know what I'm gonna do after Petey learns to walk?" Bob said. "I'm gonna walk him on my feet, like Gramps used to do to me, when I was little. You know what I mean? He'd stand me on his shoes, facing him, and he'd hold my hands, and I'd walk around the kitchen riding on Gramps's feet."

"He did that to me too," she smiled. "And my brothers. All the kids."

"Ellie, what do you say we celebrate this rainy morning with a multi-course breakfast? We didn't eat much yesterday, and we've got a long trip ahead. It'll give you more time to do that letter before we get out of here too."

"Okay."

"How does kippers and eggs grab you?"

"Motion seconded. And a soft-boiled egg for Petey."

He stacked their cereal and grapefruit bowls, and looked about for the old lady. Elspeth smiled at him. "Are we really married?"

He turned again to her. "Well, I think so. According to the oldest legal code still in use we're married. You know it, and I know it. I mean, how married can we get? The only thing I'd like to have been more solid is those witnesses. But even so, with or without the witnesses, if we tell our story, Rabbi Quint is still gonna tell Uncle Joe there's enough presumption of marriage so that you can't marry anybody else until we consent to a religious divorce. So we've still got him over a barrel."

"What's wrong with our witnesses?"

"It's just that it's better to have unimpeachable witnesses. I'm sure we couldn't prove by those guys that I said the words right. Hey, you know what we can do though? We can do it again one night at the shiva brochos. They'll love it. And we'll bust the glass, and all the stuff we left out. And they'll spread out a tallis over us by the four corners. And we'll have the contract redone by a fancy calligrapher, suitable for framing. And we'll have a decent ring."

"I like this ring."

"That's a kid's toy. We can do better than that. I'll hock my watch." The old lady waddled over. Bob spoke to her.

Elspeth studied the blank sheet of blue paper. Phil, I kind of came to the realization that I can't make you as happy as I want you to be. No. Nauseating. Contrived.

Dear Phil. I've hurt you, and if there's anybody in the world that doesn't deserve to be hurt, it's you. I hurt people, and you don't. I hope someday I'll learn to be as nice as you. Yukh. What sticky slop.

Phil, someday when I can, you've got to let me reimburse you for what the caterer cost. No. Transparently phony. He'd never let me. And he knows that I know he wouldn't.

With elbows on the table, she rested her mouth on a wrist. Then she rested her chin on a palm. She gazed across tables to the foggy glass speckled all over with rain, and the scurrying forms beyond it. She pressed a thumbnail to her lower teeth. She looked again at the little blue sheet. She wrote.

Dearest Phil,

The gasoline cards are enclosed. I'll send the diamond separately by registered mail with tons of insurance. I will take care of it when I mail this,
which I hope will be very shortly, when the P.O. opens.

It was an honest try on both our parts, and the try is not to be regretted. I
know that if I could have sorted things out enough to tell you what was in
my heart, you'd have advised me to do what I did.

675

Phil, darling, you were there when I needed you. I admire you much. If anybody ever tells you I didn't, tell them to go take a flying leap. Your house is the greatest, and you are greater than your house.

She read what she had written. It was right to make no mention of the topaz. There would have been a coldness in returning absolutely everything. Maybe sometime in the future she would find a tactful way to give back the topaz. Or maybe she would retain it. Or maybe it could be a very special gift for Gloria in a year or two, when she graduates from junior high.

88

THEY did not avoid toll booths anymore. The caution of the day before now seemed excessive. "If we're being looked for, an unpainted fender on an out-of-state car is gonna stick out like a sore thumb on the slower roads too," Elspeth said. "And we don't even know if my father called the cops. Maybe he didn't. Maybe he has more sense than we give him credit for, at least after a night's sleep. What would the cops care anyhow? It's not a stolen car. We're not children. We've got a right to be here."

Gradually the rain diminished. They crossed the high span over the Delaware River in fog.

South of Washington the sky cleared. Toward one o'clock they left the expressway and stopped at a shopping plaza, where a branch of a Fredericksburg bank advanced Eldpeth a hundred dollars on her credit card. She kept fifty and gave Bob fifty. Then she used the card again in the discount place next door, shopping quickly for socks, underpants, a cheap flannel shirt, and for Peter a creeper outfit, a couple of undershirts and nightgowns, and another bib.

When she returned to the car Bob was sitting in it with Peter. She walked around the car once, judging the pressure of each tire by its appearance. When she got in Bob was amusing Peter with a handclapping game. "You're a good daddy," she said.

She took Peter and gave him a breast. He fell asleep on it at once. Elspeth jiggled him, tickled his nose, gave a tug at his earlobe. Bob cut pieces of cheese meanwhile and fed them to her. But Peter gave no response.

"Maybe having solid food for breakfast made him think it was lunch," she said. "His schedule is all discombooberated."

"Maybe he didn't sleep as much in the night as we thought," said Bob.

They returned to the expressway with Elspeth driving. Bob fell asleep too. She glanced at him from time to time. On taking the wheel she had moved the seat far forward and one of his feet was raised awkwardly on the transmission. His body sank in the shoulder harness against the locked door, but his arm held Peter securely against his front. His head would droop and spring up again, with no sign of waking.

The highway was straight. The car sped with a monotonous hum. She ignored speed limits, so long as there were speeders in sight ahead of her and behind her to assure her that no police were about. Her breasts felt full. The trees here were only beginning to turn.

In North Carolina she turned off onto a slower road. She stopped in a town and ran down the window to ask a policeman for advice and directions, but Bob and Peter still slept.

She drove on, watching for signs to point her way. Not even the ringing of a bell and the rolling of freight cars at a crossing wakened them.

In time she leaned across Bob and Peter and rolled down their window to talk to another policeman. It was the middle of a village. Bob wakened dimly and squinted. The policeman came to the car. At first she did not understand his accent.

"I'm sorry, I didn't quite hear you."

"I said, the police chief's a jay pee. But he's gone down to his mother-in-law's wake in Scotland Neck. I don't expect he'll be back before midnight."

Bob dozed off, his head falling with a bounce.

"Oh. Isn't there anyone else?"

"There's the church right yonder. Waldo Stubbs is the pastor. He lives in the yellow house just alongside."

She saw the wooden church, and the sun fading behind the steeple and the pines.

"I mean a regular justice of the peace. Not a pastor."

"Well, they say Yancey Butler's still a justice of the peace. You go look for Yancey Butler. Right on the way you're headed, about a mile give or take, you'll see a kind of purple-color house off to your right, right smack before you get to a gas station."

"Thank you, my friend. Much obliged."

They left the policeman behind and she turned on the parking lights. She released a hand from the wheel and squeezed Bob's knee.

"Hey, Bobby boy, time to wake up," she said. "We're on our way to wedding number two, just yonder down the road a stretch. And when we get home and get your gang together we'll have wedding number three."

He was sitting erect, as though determined to remain awake, not yet speaking. Both his arms held Peter.

"You had a long, long sleep," she said.

At the purple house she parked on an area of bare earth beside a red pickup. She saw someone move a curtain to peek at them from the bay window. Her dungarees were sticky from sitting.

The white-haired lady opened the door for them before they got to it.

"Is Mr. Yancey Butler here?" said Elspeth. "The justice of the peace?"

"I'll call him. Why don't you come in."

They stepped into a musty living room. Peter slept on Bob's shoulder.

"Just make yourselves comfortable. He won't be but a minute."

"Is there someplace we can wash up meanwhile?" Bob asked.

"At the top of the stairs."

Even in the bathroom Peter slept.

"Still dry," said Elspeth. "I can't believe it."

Bob put a hand to the knit circle pinned to his head. "I better put this in my pocket. If they don't know what it is they'll think it's disrespectful."

"Leave it," said Elspeth. "It's so far back they won't even see it."

Yancey Butler was waiting at the bottom of the stairs, watching them descend. He was tall and big-framed, as white-haired as the lady, and wore pillow-striped overalls with bronze clasps fastening the straps. Flabby cheeks hung about the corners of his mouth. Elspeth carried Peter now.

"You looking for me, son?" the man asked solemnly.

"Are you a justice of the peace?" said Bob. "Do you marry people?"

"Right this way." His hand made a gracious sweep.

They went with him into a little column-flanked alcove opposite the living room. The lady was already there. Elspeth saw the electric organ first, then a metal desk, a chair with cushions tied to the back and the seat, a floor lamp with a fringed shade, and an iron sewing machine of pedal-pump vintage. The only picture was a flat-chested Maxfield Parrish nude, high on a swing above clouds and castles. On a small oriental rug a cat rolled about with a tiny cushion of catnip.

Yancey Butler had seated himself behind the desk. "You fill this out, son. And the young lady fills one out too, separate." Elspeth reached into the shoulder bag for a pen.

"I'll hold him for you," said the lady, and took Peter. His eyes popped open. He looked at the strange face, then looked about frantically till he saw Elspeth. His forehead wrinkled in alarm and his lip projected in a pout. He twisted, extending his arms to Elspeth, and wailed.

She took him, patting him. She smiled at Mrs. Butler. "It's okay."

She stood over the desk beside Bob, holding Peter with her left arm and writing with her right. There were no troublesome questions. Age. Residence. Names of previous spouses, if any, and how the marriages were terminated and where and when.

Yancey Butler studied the two forms side by side. He had put on small reading glasses which were only half circles, with frames below but none above.

"Favors his mother now, don't he," said Mrs. Butler. "Specially round the eyes."

"You think so?" Bob asked her. "A guy in New York yesterday thought he looked exactly like me. Except the hair, of course."

"Well, yes, now you mention it. He favors both."

Yancey Butler looked up over the reading glasses. "You all have some identification?"

They handed over driving licenses. He studied the two laminated rectangles, one in each hand.

He glanced at his wife. "Massachusetts, Mother." He looked at Bob and Elspeth. "We used to get them from all over. Nowadays lots of folks don't bother to get married." He handed back the rectangles. "You children are doing the right thing. For the child's sake."

"Never too late, my Granny Huckens used to say," said Mrs. Butler.

"That'll be eight dollars for the license. That goes in to the state. And I get nineteen dollars for the ceremony. That's twenty-seven dollars all told. Had to raise my price. Everything's going up. Of course that includes Mrs. Butler at the organ. No checks, please."

"Is it cheaper without the organ?" Elspeth asked him.

"No, same price. Organ comes with it. Just a few bars at the little old organ. Background music. Gives it a little style."

"Do you accept Master Charge?" she asked.

"Why, no, I can't do that. Why, to do that, I'd have to go out and unlock the filling station. And get it all mixed up with the filling-station receipts."

Bob gave him three tens. He rose and counted out change from his pocket. A one, and quarters, dimes, nickels.

From the drawer of the desk he took a book. Then he came out and stood tall before Elspeth, Peter and Bob, opening the book. Mrs. Butler had seated herself at the organ. She pulled and pushed some stops.

"Ready, Daddy?" she asked.

He glanced down at her. "Ready, Mother."

Her hands pressed the keys. A chord beeped, electronically nasal. Peter gave a wail. Then he vomited onto Elspeth's shoulder. The cat ran from the room.

"Oh, Petey." She pulled a disposable diaper from the shoulder bag.

Mrs. Butler went to the window. She parted the curtains, raised the shade, and flung up the sash. Its weights clunked inside the wall. A chill breeze stirred Peter's hair.

Elspeth wiped the vomit from his mouth, his chin, and all the creases of his neck. "Young man, you are a stinkypoo." She took another disposable and wiped his little pullover.

Yancey Butler stood with the open book, sighing. He tapped a foot. Bob was helping her. He pulled more disposables and rubbed the shaggy hairs of Elspeth's sweater.

"We got to move right along, people," said Yancey Butler. "I put my sign on the filling station. 'Back in ten minutes.'"

Bob did not glance at him. He worked at the sweater. At last he put all the soiled disposables together as a ball and rolled them into a fresh disposable. Elspeth stuffed the whole wad into the shoulder bag.

Bob stood beside her. Yancey Butler adjusted the reading glasses and cleared his throat.

Mrs. Butler looked up across the organ. "Ready, Daddy?"

"Ready, Mother."

Her hands wafted over the keyboard, drawing forth strains of the Lohengrin march. Boop, beep, badeep. Boop, beep, badeep. Again Peter wailed.

Quickly Elspeth undid her buttons and opened the front clasp of the bra. Peter and the pale breast seemed to leap to one another. He clamped and sucked, eyes closed, his fingers caressing the fullness.

Yancey Butler looked down over his glasses slack-jawed, the cheeks aquiver. Elspeth smiled up at him.

"Proceed," she said.